# Garrett
# on the Case

# Garrett on the Case

## Angry Lead Skies
## Whispering Nickel Idols

## Glen Cook

**FANTASY**

# Garrett on the Case

# Contents

# Angry Lead Skies

# 1

Mom was too embarrassed to tell the truth. She never said a word. But I'm not entirely stupid. I figured it out on my own.

I was born under an evil star. Maybe an evil galaxy. With zigging mad lights quarreling all over angry lead skies.

The planets had to've been so cruelly misaligned that no equally malignant conjunction will be possible for another hundred lifetimes.

I have a feeling, though, that my partner will be there to gloat when those celestial maladroits again foregather to conspire.

Grumbling, head aching, empty mug in shaky hand, I stomped toward the front door. Some soon-to-be sporting an iron hook for a hand pest refused to stop bruising the oak with his knuckles.

The air shivered with amusement that only rendered me more glum.

Anything my partner found entertaining was bound to be unpleasant for me.

In the small front room the Goddamn Parrot harangued himself in his sleep, his language fit to pinken the cheeks of amazons.

I had to preserve the woodwork personally because Dean was out visiting his gaggle of homely nieces. And the Dead Man won't get off his can and answer no matter what the circumstances might be. He's had a severe attitude problem for about four hundred years. He figures just because somebody stuck a knife in him back then he doesn't have to do anything for himself anymore.

I peeked through the peephole.

I cussed some. Which always makes me feel better when that

old devil sixth sense tells me that things are about to stop going
my way.

Nowhere in sight, for as far as my eagle eye could see, was
there even one tasty morsel of femininity.

I was so disappointed I grumbled, "But it always starts with a
girl." My seventh and eighth senses started perking. They couldn't
find a girl, either.

Then my natural optimism kicked in. There wasn't a girl
around! There wasn't a girl around! There wasn't anybody out
there but my old pal Playmate and a skinny gink who had to be a
foreigner because there was no way a Karentine of his type could
have survived the war in the Cantard.

No girl meant no trouble. No girl meant nothing starting. No
girl meant not having to go to work. All was right with the world
after all. I could deal with this in about ten minutes, then draw a
beer and get back to plotting my revenge on Morley Dotes for
having stuck me with the Goddamn Parrot.

Another ghost of amusement tinkled through the stale air. It
reminded me that the impossible is only barely less likely than the
normal around here.

It was time to air the place out.

Then I made my big mistake.

I opened the door.

# 2

Playmate isn't really nine feet tall. He just seems to fill up that much space. Though he did stoop getting through the doorway. And his shoulders were almost too wide to make it. And there wasn't an ounce of fat on the not really nine feet of him.

Playmate owns a stable. He does the work himself, including all the blacksmithery and most of the pitchfork management. He looks scary but he's a sweetheart. His great dream is to get into the ministry racket. His great sorrow is the fact that TunFaire is a city already hagridden by a backbreaking oversupply of priests and religions.

"Hey, Garrett," he said. Repartee isn't his main talent. But he does have a sharp eye.

That's me. Garrett. Six feet and change inches of the handsomest, most endearing former Marine you'd ever hope to meet. The super kind of fellow who can dance and drink the night away and still retain the skill and coordination to open a door and let a friend in at barely the crack of noon the next day. "That's not your usual homily, buddy." I've had a listen or two on occasions when I wasn't fast enough or sly enough to produce a convincing excuse for missing one of his ministerial guest appearances or amateur night sermons at some decrepit storefront church.

Playmate favored me with a sneer. He's got a talent for that which exceeds mine with the one raised eyebrow. The right side of his upper lip rises up and twists and begins to shimmy and quiver like a belly dancer's fanny. "I save the good sermons for people whose characters would appear to offer some teeny little hint of a possibility that there's still hope for their salvation."

Over in the small front room the Goddamn Parrot cackled like he was trying to lay a porcupine egg. And that amusement stuff was polluting the psychic atmosphere again.

The dark planets were shagging their heinies into line.

Playmate preempted my opportunity to deploy one of my belated but brilliantly lethal rejoinders. "This is my friend Cypres Prose, Garrett." Cypres Prose was a whisper more than five feet tall. He had wild blond hair, crazy blue eyes, a million freckles, and a permanent case of the fidgets. He scratched. He twitched. His head kept twisting on his neck. "He invents things. After what happened this morning I promised you'd help him."

"Why, thank you, Playmate. And I'm glad you came over because I promised the Metropolitan that you'd swing by the Dream Quarter to help put up decorations for the Feast of the Immaculate Deception."

Playmate glowered. He has serious problems with the Orthodox Rite. I gave him a look at my own second-team sneer. It don't dance. "*You* promised him? For me? That's what friends are for, eh?"

"Uh, all right. Maybe I overstepped." His tone said he didn't think that for a second. "Sorry."

"You're sorry? Oh. That's good. That makes everything all right, then. You're not presuming on my friendship the way Morley Dotes or Winger or Saucerhead Tharpe might." I would never presume on *them*. Not me. No way.

The scrawny little dink behind Playmate kept trying to peek around him. He never stopped talking. He strengthened his case constantly with remarks like, "Is that him, Play? He ain't much. From the way you talked I thought he was gonna be ten feet tall."

I said, "I am, kid. But I'm not on duty right now." Cypres Prose had a nasal edge on a cracking soprano voice that I found extremely irritating. I wanted to clout him upside the head and tell him to speak Karentine like a man.

Oh, boy! After closer appraisal I saw that Prose wasn't as old as I'd thought.

Now I knew how he'd survived the Cantard. By being too young to have gone.

Playmate put on a big-eyed, pleading face. "He's as bright as the sun, Garrett, but not real long on social skills."

The boy managed to wriggle past Playmate's brown bulk. Ah, this child was definitely the sort who got himself pounded regularly because he just couldn't get his brilliance wrapped around the notion of keeping his mouth shut. He just naturally had to tell large, slow-witted, overmuscled, swift-tempered types that they were wrong. About whatever it was they were wrong about. What would not matter.

I observed, "And the truth shall bring you great pain."

"You understand." Playmate sighed.

"But don't hardly sympathize." I grabbed the kid as he tried to weasel his million freckles into the small front room. "Not with somebody who just can't make the connection between cause and effect where people are concerned." I shifted my grip, brought the kid's right arm up behind his back. Eventually he recognized a connection between pain and not holding still.

The Goddamn Parrot decided this was the ideal moment to begin preaching, "I know a girl who lives in a shack . . ."

Playmate's friend turned red.

I said, "Why don't we go into my office?" My office is a custodian's closet with delusions of grandeur. Playmate is big enough to clog the doorway all by himself. We could manage the kid in there. If I dragged him inside first.

In passing I noted that my partner had no obvious, immediate interest in participating—beyond being amused at my expense. Same old story. Everybody takes advantage of Mama Garrett's favorite boy.

"In there, Kip!" Playmate is a paragon of patience. This kid, though, was taking him to his limit. He laid a huge hand on the boy's shoulder, pinched. That would smart. Playmate can squeeze chunks of granite into gravel. I turned loose, went and got behind my desk. I like to think I look good back there.

Playmate set Cypres Prose in the client's chair. He stood behind the kid, one hand always on the boy's shoulder, as though the kid might get away if he wasn't restrained every second. For the time being, though, the boy was focused. Totally.

He had discovered Eleanor.

She's the central figure in the painting that hangs behind my desk. That portrays a terrified woman fleeing from a looming, shadowy manor house that has a lamp burning in one high window. The surrounding darkness reeks of evil menace. The painting has a lot of dark magic in it. Once upon a time it had a whole lot more. It helped nail Eleanor's killer.

At one time, if you were evil enough, you might see your own face portrayed in the shadowy margins.

Eleanor had poleaxed my young visitor. She startles everyone at first glimpse but this reaction was exceptional.

"I take it he has a touch of paranormal talent."

Playmate nodded, showed me an acre of white teeth, mouthed the words, "There might be a wizard in the woodpile somewhere."

I raised an eyebrow now.

Playmate mouthed, "Father unknown."

"Ah." Our lords from the Hill do get around. Often playing no more fairly than the randier gods in some of the less upright pantheons. Offspring produced without benefit of wedlock are not entirely uncommon. Not infrequently those reveal signs of having received the parental gift.

I asked, "Am I going to grow a beard before I find out what's on your mind?" I heard a thump from upstairs. Katie must be awake. She would boggle the boy, too.

"All right. Like I told you, this's Cypres Prose. Kip for short. I've known him since he was this high. He's always hung around the stable. He adores horses. Lately he's been inventing things."

Another black mark behind the kid's name. Horses are the angels of darkness. And they're clever enough to fool almost everybody else into thinking that they're good for something.

"And this matters to me because?"

That air of amused presence became more noticeable. Kip definitely felt it. His eyes got big. He lost interest in Eleanor. He peered around nervously. He told Playmate, "I think they're here! I feel . . . something." He frowned. "But this's different. This's something old and earthy, like a troll."

"Ha!" I chuckled. "More like a troll's ugly, illegitimate uncle." Nobody had compared the Dead Man to a troll before—except possibly in reference to his social attitudes.

I felt him starting to steam up.

The boy getting the Dead Man's goat should've told me something but instead left me a tad open-minded at a time when my finances didn't at all require me looking at work. Money had been accumulating faster than I could waste it. "I'll give you five minutes, Playmate. Talk to me."

# 3

Playmate said, "It would be better if Kip explained."

"But can he pay attention long enough to do it? Somebody *please* tell me something." Patience is not one of my virtues when I've got a sneaking suspicion that somebody wants me to work.

Kip opened and closed his mouth several times. He was trying but he'd become distracted again.

I sighed. Playmate did, too. "He lives in his own reality, Garrett."

"So it would seem. You know him. Long time know him, yes yes. You tell me, Horsepooperscoopinman. He invents things, yes yes? You're here, yes yes. Why?"

"Somebody—and I have a feeling it might actually be more than one somebody—has been following him around. He claims they've been trying to dig around inside his head. Then this morning somebody tried to kidnap him."

I looked at Kip. I looked at Playmate. I looked at Kip again. Heroic me, I managed to keep a straight face. But only because I deal with these problems myself on a regular basis. Particularly threats of mental vandalism and larceny.

Another cascade of remote amusement. Kip jerked in his chair.

I suggested, "Tell me why anybody would bother."

Playmate shrugged. He seemed a little embarrassed, no longer sure seeing me was the best idea. "Because he invents things? That's what he thinks."

"So what's he invent?"

"Ideas, mostly. Lots of ideas for devices and mechanisms that look like they'd work just fine if we could get the right tools and the proper materials to build them. We've been trying to put a couple of the simpler ones together. In practical terms he's mainly made little things of not much value. Like a writing stick that doesn't crumble in your fingers like charcoal can but that doesn't have to be dipped in an inkwell or water every few seconds. Eliminates the problems you have with wet ink. And there was a marvellous tool sharpener. And a new style bit that isn't nearly as hard on a horse's mouth. I'm already using that one and it's been selling pretty well. And he has all sorts of ideas for complicated engines, most of which I just don't understand."

Kip's head bobbed a little, agreeing with Playmate but about what I have no idea.

"What about family?"

Playmate winced. That wasn't a question with which he was comfortable. Not in front of the kid, anyway. "Kip is the youngest of three. He has a sister and a brother. His sister Cassie is the oldest. She has four years on his brother Rhafi, who has a couple on Kip. His mother is . . . unusual." He tapped his temple. "Their father is missing." He held up two, then three fingers to indicate that multiple fathers had to be considered. Possibly Cypres wasn't aware. In such matters, sometimes, mothers can be less than forthcoming.

"The war?"

Playmate shook his head. He rested both of his hands solidly on Kip's shoulders. It was impossible for that kid to sit still. He had begun rifling through the stuff on my desk, reading snippets. He could read. That was not common amongst youngsters. I was willing to bet his literacy was Playmate's fault.

I pulled my inkwell out of harm's way while thinking that eliminating wet ink might be an amazingly wonderful trick. When I get going I get the stuff all over the place.

The boy said, "There are more of them all the time, you know. They're looking for Lastyr and Noodiss. They've hired a man named Bic Gonlit to help them."

"Garrett?" Playmate demanded. "What?"

"I know Bic Gonlit. Know of him, anyway."

"And? You look puzzled."

"Only because I am. Bic Gonlit is a bounty hunter. He specializes in bringing them back alive. Why would he be interested in Kip?"

Kip's tone told me he wondered why everyone else in this

world had to be so thick. "He's not looking for me. They don't care about me. They want Lastyr and Noodiss. They're only bothering with me because they think I know where those two are."

"And do you?" Lastyr and Noodiss?

"No." Not entirely convincingly, I thought.

Those names didn't fit any recognizable slot. Not quite elvish. Maybe upcountry dwarfish. Possibly ogreish, if they represented nicknames. Noodiss sounded like something scatological in ogre dialect.

"Who are they?"

Kip said, "You can't tell them from real people. They make you think you're looking at real people. Unless you look at their eyes. They can't disguise their eyes."

Who can't? "What the hell is he talking about, Play?"

"I'm not sure, Garrett. I can't get any more sense out of him than that. That's why I brought him to you."

"Thanks. Your confidence makes me feel warm and fuzzy all over."

Playmate ignored my sarcasm. He knew me too well. "I thought he was mental, too, at first. This's been going on for a while. And I never saw anything to convince me that he wasn't making up another one of his stories. But then somebody broke into his flat. While some of his family were there. Which is weird, because the Proses don't have a pot to pee in. Then, next day, this morning, they came to the stable. Three of them. Three strange, shiny women. I've been letting Kip use a corner of the smithy for a workshop. He does his projects there. They tried to drag him off."

"You didn't let them?"

"Of course I didn't let them." He was offended because I'd even asked. "Though it wasn't all me. They seemed extremely distracted by the horses. Afraid of them, even."

"That just sounds like basic common sense to me."

"You shouldn't joke that way, Garrett." Playmate just will not believe the truth about horses.

"These guys know horses mean trouble and they've got a beef with this kid and those things are somehow a surprise to you?"

Some people view the world through a whole different set of spectacles.

Playmate chose not to pursue the debate. "Their eyes *were* weird, Garrett. Almost like holes. Or like there were little patches of fog right there hiding them when they looked straight at you."

I tried to imagine the encounter. Playmate abhors violence,

yet, for a nonviolent idealist, he can be totally convincing in any argument that steps on a banana peel and slides off the intellectual plane. Playmate has sense enough to understand that not everyone shares his views. There are some people that need hammering and others that just plain need killing. There are people out there even a mother couldn't love.

"These visitors some new kind of breed?" All the races infesting TunFaire seem capable of interbreeding. Often the mechanics aren't easy to visualize but the results are out there on the street. At times nature takes a very strange turn. And some of the strangest are among my friends.

Kip shook his head. Playmate told me, "Give me a sheet of paper. I'll draw you a picture." He produced a small, polished cherrywood box with silver fittings. When opened it revealed a battery of artist's tools. He took out a couple of sticks I decided had to be Kip's inventions.

"Another unsuspected talent." I pushed over a torn sheet of paper. I'd only just started using its back side.

I recalled seeing charcoal drawings around Playmate's place but I never wondered enough about them to make a direct connection.

This detecting business requires great curiosity and attention to the tiniest details.

I was amazed once Playmate got started. "You're in the wrong racket, Play."

"Not much call for this kind of thing, Garrett." His hand moved swiftly and confidently. "Maybe in a carnival." He was a lefty, of course. They always are. The guy who did Eleanor probably had two left hands.

The portrait took shape rapidly.

"The original must've been one ugly critter." It had a head like a bottom-up pear. It had a mouth so small it was fit to eat nothing but soup. No ears were evident but Playmate was still drawing.

His hand moved slower and slower. A frown creased his forehead. Pinhead sweat beads appeared. He strained mightily to get his hand to do something it didn't want to do.

He gasped, "Less call than there is for new preachers."

"What's wrong?"

"This won't come out like what I saw. I wanted to draw the woman in charge. A small woman, average-looking with ginger hair. Cut off straight above her eyes and straight all the way around the rest, two inches down from where her ears should've been."

The thing he had drawn owned no ears.

He was drawing something that wasn't human. Its head was shaped something like an inverted pear. Its eyes were oversize, bulgy, teardrops shaped, evidently without pupils. He did not put in a nose. Instead, there were slits, unconnected, forming an inverted Y.

I observed, "There isn't any nose. And what about ears?"

"I thought they were hidden under her hair. I guess . . . not. There're these dark, bruise-looking patches down here, practically on the neck. Maybe they do the same job."

That *was* weird. I couldn't think of a race that didn't have ears of some kind. In fact, most races have ears that make our human ones look like afterthoughts. Great hairy, pointy, or dangly things all covered with scales and warts.

"Old Bones, you've got to help us out here. Why can't Play draw what he really saw?"

Grumpy atmospherics. Kip squeaked. The Dead Man observed, *Mr. Playmate appears to be reproducing what was actually in front of him rather than what he believes he saw. It is possible he was gulled by some illusion. The illustration does resemble the boy's recollections of his elven acquaintances.*

"Wonderful. Play, I'll bet Colonel Block wishes he had somebody who could draw pictures like this of the villains he wants to catch."

"The Guard can go on wishing. You know I'm a simple man, Garrett. Not greedy at all. But I do have to point out that a second-rate stable operator like myself still makes a better living than the best-paid honest policeman."

"Most everything pays better than being honest. You want to work for Block and Relway, you'd better have a bone-deep law and order calling. Now what?"

Kip was making noises. He wasn't as impressed with the sketch as I was. "The eyes aren't right, Play."

"They wouldn't be, would they?" Playmate growled. "Since whenever they look straight at you they go all smoky. And they aren't eyes like ours, anyway. They don't have any eyelids."

"It's not that. It's their shape. They're bulgier. . . ."

*Garrett!*

The kid jumped, squealed, went paper pale in an instant, scattered the documents on my desk. He moaned, "They're here! They're trying to get into my head again!" He tried to jump past Playmate.

"Hang on to him!" I said. "That's just old Chuckles deciding to pick on me for a minute."

Old Chuckles demurred. He sent, *The young man is entirely correct, Garrett. There is an unknown creature in the alleyway out back trying to look into the house. I am confusing it and blocking it but that is extremely difficult. The work requires most of the attention of most of my minds.*

The Dead Man belongs to a rare species known as Loghyr. They have that knack. Of having multiple minds capable of parallel and independent function. I've heard that some develop multiple personalities. I can't imagine. Old Bones is a complete horror show being just one of himself.

Simultaneous shrieks sounded upstairs and in the small front room. I don't know what Katie's problem was but it was audibly obvious that the Goddamn Parrot had decided to focus his powers of persuasion on convincing the world that he was about as sane as a drunken butterfly.

*The creature is now confused by what I have done. Which is to connect it to a couple of marginally sensitive but completely empty minds. Perhaps it will become equally lost.*

"That's no way to talk about my girlfriend."

The Dead Man was able to make the air sneer. And I suppose he had a point. Nature endowed Katie with countless delicious attributes. At first glance excessive intellect doesn't appear to be one of those. But, actually, bimbo is a survival strategy that she has let get out of control.

The kid began babbling soft nonsense not unlike that of yon inebriated megamouth. It sounded suspiciously like some of the nonsense Katie whispered when she was about half-asleep and purring. I asked Playmate, "Kip have a history with booze or drugs?" The kid was now not speaking any form of Karentine I recognized. My place isn't the neighborhood ranting ground for any of those cults that specialize in speaking in tongues.

Even so, soon every fourth word out of Kip's mouth sounded vaguely familiar. They may even have been real words—completely out of context.

"No. Never. He doesn't have that kind of imagination. But this's exactly the way he got when those elves came looking for him."

"Elves? What elves? Are we suddenly starting to get somewhere?"

"No. I just feel more comfortable calling them elves. Say they were elf-sized but they weren't like any elves that we know. They were female. You ever see a female elf who didn't look like the devil's disciple?"

Not my choice of descriptives but I knew what he meant. Even the ugly elf girls are pretty enough and wicked enough to melt your spine with a wink and a smile and a wiggle if the fancy takes them. "No. Never have."

"These girls . . . weren't. They were almost asexual."

"How did you know?"

*Garrett! I do not enjoy such an oversufficiency of mindspace that I can waste any following your digressions. Save that for later. The creature is in the alley. It is confused. It can be captured. Will you please see to that and cease this passing the time of day with Mr. Playmate?*

"Play, my sedentary sidekick tells me one of your elves is skulking around in the alley out back. Why don't we go invite him to the party? We can smack him around a little to break his concentration. Old Bones can ransack his mind while he's distracted. Which means I'll be able to find out what this's all about and you'll find out if there's any real reason for you to worry."

Damn! That wasn't the best word to use. Playmate worries. All the time. And his worry-to-success equation is an inverse proportion. He only gives up worrying and fussing when things get truly awful.

*Garrett!*

"All right!" He's so damned lazy he can't be bothered to die but he expects me to scurry like bees getting ready for winter. And sees no inconsistency. "All right. Here's the official plan, Play."

# 4

Playmate's job was to come into the alley from its Wizard's Reach
end. Being younger and more athletic I took the longer way
around so I could close in from the other direction. I trotted west
on Macunado, then ducked into a narrow, fetid breezeway, where
I kicked up a covey of pixies who were living under an overturned
basket. Poor, new immigrants, obviously. I knew before I saw
their ragged country costumes. "You folks better find yourselves
someplace where you won't have to fight off the cats and dogs and
rats." Though TunFaire's dogs and cats do, mostly, know better
than to bother little people. But rats, while cunning, aren't always
real bright. And as for the others, hunger has a way of overwhelming even the most pointed of past lessons.

These little folk thanked me for my concern by swarming
around me, cursing in tiny voices while threatening to stick me
with teensy poisoned rapiers.

When I entered the breezeway the Goddamned Parrot was a
passenger on my shoulder. He was behaving. But once I started
leaping and swatting at those damned mosquitoes he flapped toward a perch high above, whence he spouted gratuitous advice. To
the pixies: "Stay to his left! He doesn't see as well on that
side. . . . Awk!"

The racket had attracted the interest of one of those leather-
winged flying lizards that sometimes nap up on the rooftops between pigeon snacks. They aren't common anymore, mostly
because they have trouble outthinking large rocks. They make rats
and pigeons look like shining intellectuals. They are very slow
learners.

This one looked particularly shopworn. The trailing edges of its wings were tattered. It had patches of mold on its chest.

When it looked at the Goddamn Parrot it saw the answer to all its prayers.

It was the scruffiest flying lizard I'd ever seen but it still looked like the answer to a prayer or two of my own. Life would be so much simpler if I got rid of the chicken in the clown suit—as long as I could manage it in some way that wouldn't aggravate the Dead Man or Morley Dotes. Morley had gifted me with the jabbering vulture, accompanied by a strong suggestion that no harm should come to the monster, at my hand or through my negligence.

The pixies lost interest in me the moment the lizard started trying to get into the breezeway. They knew a real threat when they smelled one. A chorus of squeals preceded a general surge of the flock toward the scrofulous flyer.

The Goddamn Parrot dropped back down to my shoulder. He was shaking. For once in his sorry existence he was fresh out of smart-ass remarks.

As I got out of there the pixies proved that they'd been playing with me all along. As I left the breezeway a matron zipped over to ask which cuts interested me. "They's good eatin' on them things, Big'un. The giblets is real tasty when they's grilled."

"You people keep the whole thing. I brought my lunch." I jerked a thumb at my shoulder ornament.

"Ooh. . . . Pretty," one small voiced piped.

Another wanted to know, "Kin we have some of the feathers?"

I sensed a once-in-a-lifetime opportunity.

Something came over me. My jaw locked up. I couldn't mouth the offer I make almost every day, as many as a dozen times. I wanted to shriek.

I couldn't turn loose of the dodo in the clown suit!

The air seemed to tinkle and sparkle with invisible chuckles.

So! Old Bones wasn't quite as preoccupied elsewhere as he wanted me to think. I should've gotten suspicious when the painted jungle buzzard demonstrated such exceptional manners.

Interesting. The Dead Man hadn't ever before touched me directly this far from the house. Maybe he *was* distracted. Maybe distracted so much that he couldn't be as careful keeping the full range of his abilities concealed. Or maybe he just liked the Goddamn Parrot too much to let him go.

Wish I had time to experiment.

After our initial divergence of viewpoint the pixies and I went our ways on friendly terms. Meaning they were too busy harvesting everything but the flyer's squeak to waste time tormenting a Big'un. Though a couple of youngsters did follow me, mainly to get out of doing chores.

I headed east, down the alley, afraid my delays might have allowed my quarry to give me the slip. Though if I'd thought I would've realized that my foul-beaked companion would've been barking like the wolf at the end of the world if the Dead Man had suffered a moment's disappointment.

Something buzzed behind my ear. Not the family birdbrain, who was on patrol now, or, more likely, hitting on some nitwitted pigeon. I started to swat the sound, held up just in time. A pixie girl, definitely a little inexperienced, unwittingly drifted forward far enough to be seen from the corner of my eye.

One key to success in my racket is making friends. Lots of friends. In as broad a range of stations, races, and professions as is possible. A pixie ally would be a huge resource.

I started sweet-talking.

No telling what I might have accomplished if Fate hadn't decided to roll my bones.

The pixies let out startled shrieks at the same moment that the Goddamn Parrot barked my name.

# 5

I got about a tenth of second's glimpse of a man who fit his name perfectly. Unusual. He was all rounds. He had a round head with dwindling thickets of hair sagging to the south, leaving a blinding shine behind. He had a round mouth with puffy, round lips, round eyes, and a nose that was almost round as a hog's snoot. He had a round body, too. I didn't get a good look at his feet.

The whole globular package didn't stand but maybe five inches over five feet tall.

This was Bic Gonlit. Bounty hunter. A man you'd peg as an apple-cheeked little baker addicted to his own products. Or a guy who cracked feeble jokes in place of real entertainment in some dive harboring upwardly mobile aspirations toward the lower lower class. He was a man who had to wear elevator boots to get up enough altitude to cork a big, handsome boy like me.

Had to be the boots. He was known for the boots. Legend said he had had them specially made by a dwarfish cobbler in a sleazy little shop off Bleak on the southern edge of the Tenderloin. So rumor would have it, because the boots had been made into Gonlit's signature inside the TunFaire underworld.

Or maybe he'd brought a ladder, since ordinarily he was way shorter than me. The boots only made him two inches taller.

I didn't get a real gander at the infamous boots. I didn't see any ladder, either. I did get a vague glimpse of what looked like an overweight donkey behind my assailant, then an outstanding look at an upwardly rushing alley surface after Gonlit leaped up and whacked me across the back of my skull. The one tap turned my bones to jelly. I sagged into the muck like a candle left out in the summer sun. The Goddamn Parrot and the pixie girl cheered me on. Or jeered me. Or something. They made a lot of noise. I think the donkey started laughing.

Playmate was fanning me when I opened my eyes, hoping for some blond angel of mercy. Good friend that he is, he had dragged me into the shade and propped me against a wall, all before anyone found me and explored my pockets for hidden treasure. I made a crippled kitten sort of sound to express my appreciation and ask when the angel would arrive.

Playmate said, "I wouldn't move around, was I you."

"I am me. And I don't plan to even breathe hard. My head! And I didn't drink a drop." This morning. "I've got to get ahold of a war-surplus helmet. One of the kind with that big-ass spike on top."

"You'd still have to remember to wear it. What happened?"

"I was going to ask you."

"I don't know. I heard your bird screaming. Made me suspect that you'd found yourself on the short end again. You've got a talent for that. I charged up here. Behold! You really were in trouble. A roly-poly little bald guy who looked a lot like Bic Gonlit was strutting around you measuring you for a hearty whack with the great hairy club he was packing."

"It was Bic Gonlit. I caught a glimpse before the lights went out. He must've been wearing his extra special tall boots, though."

"This isn't his normal style, Garrett."

"You know him?" I for sure wanted to know him better than I did now. What little I did know was hearsay. He was a bounty hunter who brought them in alive. He had quirks and unusual personal habits and magic boots. I'd seen him just often enough to recognize him. "You failed to mention that when the name came up before."

"I didn't need to mention it. Kip told you all you needed. Then. I only know his reputation, anyway. Which doesn't include murder. He grew up in my part of town. He'd be a little older than me. He's supposed to have a big taste for fine food and good wine. Including the TunFaire Gold when he can get it. But if that really was him he's sure gone downhill since the last time I saw him."

"That was him. Or his evil twin. Maybe he's been eating so high he's had to expand his repertoire."

"He wouldn't just bushwhack a guy."

"Why the hell not?" Could Playmate be that naive? Even I

would bushwhack a guy fifteen inches taller and fifteen years younger than me, not to mention fifteen stone lighter. Assuming that I was adequately motivated.

The quality and the nature of the motivation is what's worth debating.

On reflection Playmate decided he had no ready answer.

I asked, "Where is he now?"

"He took off when he saw me coming. Jumped on a burro not much bigger than him and rode off, covering his face."

"Think he recognized you?"

"I expect that's why he bothered to hide his face. I mean, how many people of my size and coloring are there? And how many of those are likely to be caught hanging around with you?"

If Bic Gonlit knew who we were he was about to become scarcer than lizard hair. "Good points. I wonder. Did he know whose head he was bopping before he tried to brain me?" I have a reputation, partly for lacking humor about things like headbashing when it's my melon involved, partly for having acquired a number of close friends whose responses would be unpredictable if something unpleasant happened to me that wasn't my own fault. Some might start sharpening their teeth.

It's hard to imagine it being my own fault, but, in the laws of obligatory revenge there *are* exit codicils about "He asked for it," and "He needed it."

Playmate might be one of those friends. My partner is, definitely. I like to believe that Saucerhead Tharpe and Morley Dotes are others, along with several powerful, wealthy family chieftains I've helped in my time. Those include the beermaking Weiders, the shoemaking Tates, and the we-don't-talk-about-what-we-do Contagues.

The Contagues would be the real worry for any villain, though the least likely avengers. The Contagues captain the Outfit, the Syndicate, the Commission, the central committee of the city's organized crime. Their strength and reach and savagery when roused are legendary. Even our wizardly overlords on the Hill concern themselves about needlessly rousing the ire of Chodo Contague and his daughter Belinda. Chodo and Belinda do not allow themselves to be constrained by traditional legal customs or the normal rules of evidence. They hurt people. And they kill people. They're supposed to be my friends and they scare the whiskers off me.

At the time it did not occur to me that Bic Gonlit might have wanted to collect a bounty on me.

"What do you want to do?" Playmate asked.

"Besides find Bic Gonlit and whip fifty pounds of lard off his broad butt? Go home and get cleaned up." TunFaire's alleyways aren't paved. Neither are they kept clean. Where they exist at all they're little more than broad, shallow trenches where refuse can accumulate in anticipation of eventual rains heavy enough to carry some of the waste down into one of the storm channels that drain into the river.

It takes a conscientious sort, willing to make an extra effort, to take advantage of the travel opportunities offered by TunFaire's alleys. The King's good and lazy subjects employ them when they're too shy to dispose of something in the street out front. So by the grace of Bic Gonlit I made the intimate acquaintance of some of my neighbors' greatest embarrassments—most of which, of course, would seem trivial to a disinterested witness.

Often the secret vice that concerns you most is of no interest whatsoever to anyone whose opinion you dread. The main problem exists inside your own head.

That's one of those things most of us learn too late. A life-skills version of the destroyer comeback that pops up wearing a big, goofy grin three hours after some boor qualifies for a sound verbal caning.

"Thanks," I told Playmate. "Your timing was perfect."

"We aim to please."

"Where's the other one?"

"Who?"

"The guy we came out here to watch. The weird elf."

Playmate shrugged. "If he was still here he had a knack for the invisible. Maybe the Dead Man was able to keep track."

Probably wouldn't admit it if he did. "Let's say I'm cynical about his ability." There was no sign of the Goddamn Parrot, either. Nor any of pixies. Did some small-size skulls get cracked, too? Might be worth the headache if somebody capped that dodo. "Did you notice what happened to Mr. Big? My bird?"

Playmate shook his head.

"Never mind." I wouldn't bet two dead flies on tripping over the amount of good luck necessary to get me shut of that magpie cleanly. "Let's get out of here."

Playmate grunted. He was uncomfortable there. He was a preacher, not an adventurer. And unwanted adventures seemed to bubble up around me. Maybe it's my diet. Though if complained at I'd point out that he'd brought this one on himself.

We abandoned the alley, brokenhearted over our failure.

Folks on Wizard's Reach raised eyebrows, pinched their noses, and turned away. But nothing helped me. It didn't matter which way I turned my head or how tightly I pinched my nose, I could still smell me. And I was way past ripe.

Maybe a sudden thunderstorm would come up and wash me down to the river.

Maybe they ought to put all the unemployed ex-soldiers to work cleaning the city.

Never happen. Makes too much sense. And it would cost public monies that can be put to better use lining somebody's pockets.

The neighbors lost interest in me when somebody hollered, "There goes one!" and everything came to a halt while the entire population stared at the sky. I was a couple beats late. I saw nothing. "What the hell is that all about?"

Playmate looked at me like he'd just flipped a boulder and discovered a new species of fool. "*Where* have you been? There've been strange lights in the sky and weird things hurtling around overhead for weeks. Longer than that, if you believe some people. I thought everybody in TunFaire knew about them and was watching for them."

"Well, not me. Tell me."

Playmate shook his head. "You have to get out of the house more, Garrett. Even when you're not working. You need to know what's going on around you."

I couldn't argue with that.

# 6

"What the hell?" My front door stood wide open.

"Maybe Kip ran away." From the vantage of his superior altitude Playmate surveyed Macunado Street, uphill and down. "Which would be stupid. He can't find his own way home."

I gave him a raised eyebrow look. "Where do you find them?" He's worse than Dean is. Dean being the antediluvian artifact who serves as my live-in cook and housekeeper. Who has several huge personality flaws. Those include acting like my mom and my dad and having a soft heart bigger than my often somnolent sidekick. But Dean does confine his overweening charity to kittens and strange young women. Playmate will take in anything, including birds with broken wings and nearly grown boys who need a guide to get around their own hometown.

Playmate was too concerned to talk. He charged up my front steps and into the house. I followed at a more dignified pace. I wasn't used to all that exercise.

"Hey, Garrett! He's right where we left him."

Absolutely. Kip was nailed to the client's chair, wearing an expression like he'd just enjoyed a divine visitation. The Dead Man was holding him there. But that couldn't account for the goofy expression.

"Then who left the door open?"

*Your lady friend became distressed when she could find no one willing to make her breakfast. When the boy just stared at her and drooled she stormed out.* That sparkling sense of amusement hung in the air once more, rich and mellow, with well-defined edges.

"But you had plenty of brainpower left over to hold and manage this nimrod."

Being dead had corrupted somebody's sense of relative values. The streets are swamped with goofballs. But Katie is unique. Katie is like a religious epiphany. "And what happened to the talking buzzard?" He would know. The Goddamn Parrot was almost a third arm and extra mouth for him anymore. He's going to weep great tears when that vulture bites the dust. Though Morley is fond of reminding me that parrots can live about a million years. If something doesn't wring their scrawny necks.

I'll weep myself when he's gone. Tears of joy.

*Mr. Big is tracking the creature you failed to capture because you were unable keep your attention on the matter at hand.*

"You mean Bic Gonlit, the guy who made his escape on a galloping donkey? Because nobody bothered to warn me that it was him hanging around in the alley, leaving me unprepared?"

*Apparently an oversight on my part. I detected no second presence out there. Which is no longer of any consequence, now, anyway. But I would be remiss if I failed to point out that you should have been better prepared, knowing there could be difficulty.*

"No consequence? Difficulty? You aren't the one the little pork-ball whapped upside the head."

*Spare us your unconvincing histrionics, Garrett.*

Unconvincing? I was convinced. I took a deep breath. I'd never gotten in the last word yet but like an old-timer married fifty years I'm an eternal optimist. It could happen. There might come a day. It might be today.

Actually, it'll probably come when I'm on my deathbed and the Reaper snatches me before Old Bones can come back at me. Except that Chuckles might decide to come after me. He's already got a head start.

Death. Now there's a guy who knows how to have the last word.

*Mr. Big is following the creature I sensed in the alley, Garrett. Not any sad little manhunter named Gonlit. I had thought you would understand that. A most unusual creature this is, too. Nothing like it has entered my ken before. Most notably, it seems capable of rendering itself invisible by fogging the minds of those around it. It is amazing.*

"And you keep telling me there's nothing new under the sun."

Playmate's scrawny young buddy finally collected himself

enough to notice us. "What happened to you guys? You smell awful."

My good and true friend Playmate announced, "What you smell is Garrett. I myself am redolent of roses, lilacs, and other sweet herbal delights."

I glared at Playmate. "We ran into Bic Gonlit." I turned my glower on the boy. He did not leap at the opportunity to have a chuckle at my expense. Maybe he wasn't a total social disaster at all times. Maybe he retained some rudimentary, skewed sense of self-preservation.

That's Mama Garrett's big boy. He can find a silver lining inside the ugliest sow's ear.

Maybe he didn't have any sense of humor at all.

Kip looked to Playmate for confirmation. Playmate told him, "It was Gonlit." Then he told me, "Do something about your sweet self. I have a strong feeling we're about to get out amongst the people. I wouldn't want you to embarrass yourself."

Yet again the stardust of amusement twinkled in the air.

*I would propose that Mr. Playmate has offered excellent advice, Garrett.*

I smelled doom. I smelled it like I'd smelled leaf mold in the jungle every time it'd rained while I was in the islands. It was in the air, sneezing thick. I did not have to sniff to catch a whiff.

I was about to be cursed. Squirm as I might I was about to have to go to work. All because I had been dim enough to open my door and let trouble walk in.

I whined, "Where on the gods' green earth is the beautiful girl?" It'd never failed before. I'd always gotten some wonderful eye-candy out of . . . "Yike!"

Old Dean, who pretends to be the chief cook and housekeeper around here, but who is really the wicked stepmother, had stuck his bitter, persimmon-sucking face into the office. "Mr. Garrett? Why is it that I return home to find the front door standing wide open?"

"It was an experiment. I was trying to learn if crabby old people will kick a door shut *before* they start complaining about it having been left open. Of particular interest are crabby old men who live in a household where their status more closely approximates that of a guest than something more eternal. So you tell me. Do you have any idea? Where's the girl?"

Dean doesn't have much of a sense of humor. He offered me

the full benefit of his hard, gray-eyed stare. As always, he was rock-confident he could demonstrate to the world that my second greatest flaw is my frivolous, incautious nature.

He believes my greatest failing to be my persistent bachelor-hood. That from a character who never got within rock-flinging range of matrimony himself. I put up with him because he *is* a wonderful cook and housekeeper. When the mood takes him. And because he's cranky enough to hold his own with the Dead Man— though when he has his druthers he has nothing to do with Old Bones at all.

"Let's not fuss," I told him. "I have a client here."

Bad word choice. That brightened Dean right up. Little pleases him more than knowing that I'm working.

I ground my teeth a bit, then continued, "So let's get this sorted out quickly. I've got to catch up with Katie." Before she developed an attitude toward me that I was sure to regret.

Dean scowled as he headed toward the kitchen. Katie isn't one of his favorites. He doesn't approve of Katie. He hasn't been able to charm her the way he did my few other, occasional female friends.

*I fear Miss Shaver will have to wait, Garrett.*

"No. Not hardly. Right now there's nothing more important than Miss Shaver."

Playmate and Kip appeared startled. Old Bones hadn't included them in his message. Though Kip did look baffled and kept rubbing his head and looking around like he knew something was going on.

*I have exceeded myself somewhat, ethically, in reviewing the boy's memories. There being so many questions accompanied by so few answers it seemed possible that the best course was to see if he might not know something without being aware that he knew it.*

Plausible, if prolix. I had used that argument on him a time or three, trying to prod him into becoming a little more aggressive in mining the thoughts of visitors and suspects. "And what did you discover?" You have to give him his line or he won't communicate.

*Very little, to tell the truth. This boy has no more than two toes anchored inside our reality. His head is occupied by a totally eclectic jumble of fantasic nonsense and it is amidst that that he lives most of the time. He is always the hero in his own tale.*

Well, aren't we all?

*Some of his fantasies recall well-known epics and sagas. Some have their genesis in common storytellers' tales. Some are mutant versions of historical events. And even a few things might possibly have some basis in truth—behind the fantasy stuff he has built on top of genuine events. Inside his head it is impossible to discern the real from the imagined.*

"If most of it concerns girls it sounds like the inside of a normal boy's head."

*You would think that way. And you would be incorrect. While it does concern girls, some of it, it does so principally in the clever and daring methods by which he rescues the enchanted princess or other damsel in distress. While there are several of them I have yet to discover any of his fantasy women less than chastely clad or treated.*

I gave Kip a quick glance consisting of about eighty percent worry and twenty percent accolade. Though I suspected that respect for women was not a real part of the equation. Naïveté would be the real culprit.

The Dead Man continued, *He* is *acquainted with creatures he knows as Lastyr and Noodiss. They are not human but the boy has not cared enough about the answer to find out what they really are. The images in his mind are not familiar to me.*

The image that appeared in my mind, then, was unfamiliar to me as well. "Inbreeding? Or interbreeding?" You need only stroll around TunFaire a few hours to see the incredible range of Nature's artistry and her bottomless capacity for the cruel practical joke.

*Perhaps. And, perhaps, they are something never before seen. In this world.*

"Let's not turn alarmist!" I growled. Alarmed. Once upon a time not long ago I got into a head-butting contest with something never before seen at that time: very nasty, never-brush-their-teeth and talk-back-to-their-mamas foul, elder gods who thought that the god racket would be a lot softer if they could bust out of the dark place where they were confined and could come set up shop in our world.

*There was nothing supernatural about the watcher in the alley, Garrett. Quite the opposite, I think. There was no magic in it at all. It seemed as though it stood entirely outside the realms of the magical, the metaphysical, and the supernatural.*

I gobbled a couple pints of air while I tried to make sense of that, trying to sort through the countless implications. A world without magic! A place of order and predictability, with all evil fled!

Darker possibilities occurred to me as well.

Playmate began to poke and prod me with a singletree forefinger. "Garrett, I know it's a big, empty wasteland without many landmarks but how about you don't get lost inside your own head right now?"

I shook the gourd in question. The waste space was anything but empty right now. Most of that speculation seemed to be leaking over from the Dead Man's secondary minds. Suggesting that the puzzle had him sufficiently intrigued that he had become incautious where his thoughts strayed.

"Sorry. Chuckles got me going for a minute."

" 'Twould seem that he's gotten Kip going, too."

The boy was as rigid as a fence post. All the color had drained from behind his freckles. His eyelids were closed. When I lifted one I found his eyeball rolled up so that he seemed to have no pupil.

"What did you do here, Smiley?"

The Dead Man launched a long-winded paean of self-exoneration. I sensed its complete lack of substance right away and focused on Playmate. "So cut the bull and tell me what you want from me."

"I suppose what I really want is for you to look out for him. Kip's a royal pain sometimes, Garrett, but that's mostly because nobody ever taught him how to get along with people. He befriended a couple of strays. Lost souls in the physical sense. He took care of them. They were grateful. That made him feel important. Same as I feel when I take care of him and the horses. He shouldn't get hurt for that."

Playmate was right. The world needed more helpful and considerate people. But I was looking at something else. Some very complex things seemed to be going on inside Playmate right now. He was taking this more personally than he should.

"You wouldn't be the missing father here, would you?"

That stunned Playmate. He chomped air a couple of times, in a way that left me wondering if I hadn't somehow struck nearer the mark than I'd thought possible. One glance and even the most cynical student of human folly would understand that Cypres Prose was no kin to Playmate.

"Don't try to provoke me, Garrett."

"Huh?" Provocation isn't my style. Not with my friends. Not very often, anyway. Not the ones that're three feet taller than me and strong enough to hold a horse under one arm while using the off hand to change the monster's shoes.

"I'm sorry. I apologize. This mess is keeping me on edge."

"Why is that?" By now I had resigned myself to not being able to make peace with Katie anytime soon. "Why don't you just lay this whole thing out so we don't have to pick you guys apart just so we can assemble enough information for me to start?"

I've found that clients never want to tell the whole story. Never. Another given is that they're going to lie to you about half of what they tell you. They want results without having to reveal anything embarrassing. They lie about almost everything. The worst offenders are those who have fallen victim to their own greed or stupidity. They expect results, too.

Playmate was not a bad client. His fib quotient was pretty low, probably, as much because he knew about my partner as because he's naturally a good guy. He talked a good deal but failed to tell me much more than I had gotten already. Kip had become friendly with a pair of oddballs named Lastyr and Noodiss, no other names given. He had helped them learn their way around. After a while other oddballs turned up looking for the first two. Inasmuch as they never explained their interest, that was not taken to be benign. Especially considering recent events at the stable and Kip's home. Not all of the oddballs were necessarily the same kind of oddball.

Lastyr and Noodiss had been around for most of a year. Those hunting them had shown up only recently. All the elves seemed very determined.

Kip nodded a lot and didn't add anything. I trusted the Dead Man would collect anything that reached the surface of the boy's thoughts.

Playmate told me, "It may be coincidence. Kip's always made up fantastic stories. But it was right after those first two characters showed up that he started inventing things. I mean, things that worked or looked like maybe you could make them work."

*The boy's head is bursting with the images of the most amazing mechanisms, Garrett.*

He seemed completely thrilled.

I asked, "What would you suggest I do?"

"Just stick with us for a while," Playmate said.

*Investigate.*

"Investigate what?"

*Let your experience be your guide.* And, *Whatever else you do, do try to catch one of those creatures and bring it here to see me.*

"I'm the miracle worker of TunFaire, aren't I?"

Aren't I?

# 7

There was no sign of Katie when we stepped out the front door, me freshly bathed and cleanly dressed in hand-me-down apparel that approached the respectable. My sweetie had an hour head start now. And would be boiling like an overheated teapot.

Katie was going to require some cautious cooling down. I definitely didn't want her getting too cold.

I did spot Dean. Headed home. Where the hell had he been? He wasn't carrying anything.

He dropped a coin—a coin that belonged to me because he'd never give away a chipped copper of his own—onto the tattered blanket of a streetside fortune-teller. That caught her completely by surprise. Nevertheless, she gave him a toothless blessing.

There was an idea. I ought to hang out a shingle proclaiming myself a great psychic. Old Bones could rummage around inside their heads and feed me the items I would use to impress them enough to make them turn loose of their money.

*An open mouth precludes open ears.*

"What the hell does that mean?" I hadn't said anything. "I hate it when you talk that ancient wisdom stuff. The butterfly is silent when the eagle walks upon the sand."

I patted myself down. I was equipped with an arsenal of—mostly—nonlethal tools of mayhem. "Lead on, Play."

Playmate descended the steps and turned left. I followed, keeping Kip between us.

Dean met us at the foot of the steps. "Where you been?" I asked.

"Running a couple of errands."

"Ah." I said no more. No point letting him know he gave himself away whenever he was sneaking around doing something on the Dead Man's orders. "Let us continue, friend Playmate." I studied the street as we resumed moving. I saw nothing out of place.

Macunado Street is a busy thoroughfare, day or night. A ferocious downpour or bitter winter weather are about all that will clear it. The street was particularly busy today. But it was conventionally busy. Not one known villain, nor a potential riot, was anywhere in sight.

"Who was that?" Playmate asked after I waved to a neighbor.

"Mrs. Cardonlos. The police spy. Sometimes tormenting her is the only fun to be had."

"There're occasions when I despair of you, Garrett. There're times when you appear to be your own worst enemy. Why on earth would you want to taunt someone who has the power to tell lies about you to people who'd just as soon feed you to the rats?"

"Because Relway's bunch would be more suspicious if I didn't." Deal Relway is the master of TunFaire's unacknowledged secret police force. I know him because I was there when that particular terrorbird hatched. Its existence has become an open secret, anyway.

I do get nervous sometimes, knowing what I do know about some key individuals. Relway wouldn't hesitate to bend or break the law in his determination to maintain law and order. He might not hesitate to bend or break me.

Playmate's livery establishment was less than an hour away. We reached it without running into trouble. Once we did I borrowed his kitchen to brew myself a fresh mug of headache medicine.

# 8

Kip's little workshop didn't tell me much. It was evident the kid knew his tools, though. He had a hell of a collection, half of which I didn't know what they were. He had a hundred unidentifiable projects going. As soon as we walked in he grabbed a file and went to work on notches in a round metal plate about eight inches in diameter. It took him only a few seconds to become totally focused.

"What the hell?" I asked.

Playmate shrugged. "I don't know. Part of one of his machines. I can show you the picture he had me draw."

"I meant, how come he suddenly goes from being something you have to keep on a leash to being somebody who's blind to the whole damned world?"

Another expressive shrug. Playmate showed me into his forge area, which had expanded considerably since my last visit and which was an amazing clutter of junk and what looked like things half-built. I wondered how he got any shoeing done.

From some niche Playmate produced a leather folder filled with dozens of sheets of good linen paper. He shuffled through unsuspectedly good bits of artwork until he located the piece he wanted. I glimpsed my own likeness in passing. "Now that was a good-looking young man."

Playmate grunted. I think that was meant to be neutral but failed to sound like it when he observed, "The operative word being 'was.'"

There were more portrait sketches. They were all good. I recognized several people.

How many hidden talents did Playmate have? He surprised me every few months.

The portfolio contained more sketches of devices than of people. Some were really complicated, highly unlikely mechanisms. And a few didn't seem complicated at all. One of those was a little two-wheeler cart with a pair of long shafts sticking out in front. A man had been sketched in as pulling it, conveying another seated in the cart.

Something like that, without the shafts, sat about ten feet from where I stood. "You're trying to build some of these things?"

"Unh? Oh. Yeah. All of them, eventually. But there're problems. With that thing I'm having trouble finding long enough poles that're still light. But we did test it. It'll work."

"Why?"

"Because we have an extremely lazy complement of wealthy people in this town. And a lot of unemployed young men who need something to keep them out of trouble. My notion is to build a fleet of those things and rent them out at nominal fees so some of those young men have a way to make a living. Which will keep them out of trouble at the same time."

Having a way to make a living didn't keep me out of trouble.

That was Playmate, though. Finding a way to get rich doing good deeds. Except that then he would end up giving away any wealth he acquired.

Next to the cart stood a second mechanism. I could not figure it out. It had three wheels. Two were about a foot in diameter and were mounted at the ends of a wooden axle. The other was about two and a half feet in diameter, turning on a hardwood pin which passed through the ends of a two-tined wooden fork. That rose through the upper end of an arc of hardwood that curved down to the two-wheel axle. A curved crossbar above the hardwood arc allowed the larger wheel to be turned right and left.

I did not see a sketch of that in Playmate's folio. "What is that?"

"We just call it a three-wheel. Let me finish showing you this. Then I'll let you see how it works. Here. Check this. It's a two-wheel. It's a more complicated cousin of that." He extracted a drawing.

This mechanism had two wheels of equal size, fore and aft, with a rider perched amidships, as though astride a horse. "I'm not sure I get this."

"Oh, I don't, either. Kip explains these things when he has me draw them but I seldom understand. However, everything he finishes putting together does what he says it will do. And sometimes it seems so obvious afterward that I wonder why nobody ever thought of it before. So I take him on faith. This engine—and that one there—gets around on power provided by the rider's legs. If you want to know much more than that you'll have to ask Kip. He'll turn human after a while. Come here." He led me to the three-wheel.

"Climb up here and sit down."

The wooden arc part of the mechanism boasted a sort of saddle barely big enough for a mouse. When I sat on it my butt ached immediately. "So what is it? Some kind of walker with wheels?" If so, my legs were too long. "I've seen lots better wheelchairs." Chodo Contague has one that is so luxurious it comes with a crew of four footmen and has its own heating system.

"Put your feet up on these things." He used the toe of a boot to indicate an L-shaped bar that protruded from the hub of the big wheel up front. "The one on the other side, too. Good. Now push. With your right foot. Your other right foot."

The three-wheel moved. I zipped around in a tight circle. "Hey! This's neat." My foot slipped off. The end of the iron L clipped my anklebone. I iterated several words that would have turned Mom red. I reiterated them with considerable gusto.

"We're working on that. That can't be much fun. We're going to drill a hole down the center of a flat piece of hardwood . . ."

I got the hang of the three-wheel quickly. But there wasn't enough room to enjoy it properly in there. "How about I take it out in the street?"

"I'd really rather you didn't. I'm sure that's why we've had the trouble we've had. Kip took it out there, racing around, and before he got back he had several people try to take it away from him. And right afterward the strange people started coming around."

I scooted around the stable for a few minutes more, then gave up because I couldn't enjoy the machine's full potential under such constrained circumstances. "Are you planning to make three-wheels, too? Because if you are, I want one. If I can afford it."

Playmate's eyes lighted up as he saw the possibility of paying my fees without having to part with any actual money. "I might. But honesty compels me to admit that we're having problems with it. Especially with getting the wheels and the steering bar to move freely. Lard doesn't seem to be the ideal lubricant."

"And it draws flies." Plenty of those were around. But the place was a stable, after all.

"That, too. And the kinds of hardwoods we need to make the parts aren't common. Not to mention that we'd have to come up with whole teams of woodworking craftsmen if we were to build even a fraction of the number of them we think we'd need to satisfy the demand there'd be once people started seeing them in the streets."

"Hire some of those out-of-work veterans to make them."

"How many of them, you figure, are likely to be skilled joiners and cabinetmakers?"

"Uhn. Not to mention wheelwrights." I walked around the three-wheel. "That geekoid kid over there actually thought this up?"

"This thing and a whole lot more, Garrett. It'll be a mechanical revolution if we ever figure out how to build all of the things he can imagine."

I slid down off the three-wheeler. "What do you call this?"

"Like I told you. Just three-wheel."

There had to be something that sounded more dramatic. "Here's a notion. You could train your veterans just to do what it takes to manufacture three-wheels. That wouldn't be like them having to learn all about making cabinets and furniture."

"And then I'd have guild trouble."

I stared at the three-wheel, sighed, told Playmate, "I guarantee you, somebody's going to get rich off this thing." My knack for prophecy is limited but that was a prediction I made with complete conviction. I had no trouble picturing the streets of the better neighborhoods overrun with three-wheels.

"Someone with fewer ethical disadvantages than I have, you mean?"

"That wasn't what I was getting at, but it's a fact. As soon as you get some of those things out there you're going to have people trying to build knockoffs." I had a thought. Lest it get lonely I sent it out into the world. "You said Kip took this one out and somebody tried to take it away from him?"

Playmate nodded.

"Could it be that Kip's having problems because somebody wants to steal his ideas?" I'm sure that I'm not the only royal subject bright enough to see the potential of Kip's inventions.

Playmate nodded. "That could be going on, too. But there's definitely something to the trouble with the weird elves. And right now I'm more worried about them. Stay here and keep an eye on Kip while I make us all a pot of tea."

Ever civilized, my friend Playmate. In the midst of chaos he'll take time for amenities, all with the appropriate service.

# 9

Kip tired of filing his metal wheel. He put it aside and started fiddling with something wooden. I watched from the corner of one eye while I thumbed through Playmate's drawings and sketches. The man really was good. More so than with portraits, he had a talent for translating Kip's ideas into visual images. There was a lot of written information on some of the sheets, inscribed in a hand that was not Playmate's.

"How do you come up with this stuff?" I asked Kip. I didn't expect an answer. If he heard it at all the question was sure to irritate him. Creative people get it all the time. They get tired of questions that imply that the artist couldn't possibly produce something out of the whole cloth of the mind. It was a question I wouldn't have asked a painter or poet.

Kip surprised me by responding, "I don't know, Mr. Garrett. They just come to me. Sometimes in my dreams. I've always had ideas and a head full of stories. But lately those have been getting better than they ever were before." He did not look up from the piece of wood he was shaping.

He had become a different person now that he was settled in the sanctuary of his workshop. He was calm and he was confident.

I wondered how much puberty had to do with his problems and creativity.

Tucked into the back of Playmate's folio, folded so I nearly overlooked them, were four smaller sketches of strange "elves."

"Would these be some of the people who're giving you a hard time?"

The boy looked up from his work. "Those two are Noodiss

and Lastyr. Left and right. They're the good ones. I don't know the other two. They may be some of the ones Play ran off."

Playmate arrived with the tea. "They are."

"I told you your talent would be a wonderful tool in the war against evil. See? We have two villains identified already."

"Do we, then?"

No, we doedn't, doed we? We had sketches of a couple of likely baddies about whom we knew nothing whatsoever. I wasn't even sure they were the same kind of elves as the other two. They didn't look like the same breed in the sketches.

I changed the subject. "I have an idea, too."

Man and boy looked at me skeptically.

"It can happen!" I insisted. "Look. You see how much work it was making the steering handles for your three-wheel? You could use ox horns instead. You could get them from the slaughter-houses." Though the two of them began to look aghast I warmed to greater possibilities. "You could get them to save you the whole skull with the horns still attached. You could produce a special death's-head model three-wheel for customers from the Hill."

Playmate shook his head. "Drink your tea, Garrett. And plan to go to bed early tonight. You need the rest."

I offered him a hard glower.

Guess I need to practice up. He wasn't impressed. He just smiled and told me, "You're starting to hallucinate."

"And I should leave that to the experts. All right. Why don't I do some work? What can you tell me about these maybe elves that you haven't told me already?"

"They eat a lot of ugly soup," Playmate told me. "My drawings don't do them justice."

None of them appeared particularly repulsive to me. And I said so. Those homely boys didn't know it but I was looking out for them.

"Call it an inner glow kind of thing. You'll see what I mean when you meet one." He sounded confident that I'd do so.

"Kip? Anything you can say to help out here? It's really your ass that's on the line."

Playmate advised, "Despite earlier events Kip still isn't quite convinced that he's in any trouble himself."

Most people are that way. They just can't believe that all this crap is raining down on them. Not even when somebody is using a hammer to beat them over the head. And they particularly can't believe that it's *because* of them.

We talked while we enjoyed our tea. I asked more questions. Lots of questions, most of them not too pointed. I didn't get many useful answers. Kip never said so, of course, but now that he was where he felt safe himself his main concern was his friends with the absurd names. He had decided that not telling me anything was the best way to shield them.

"It's not me you need to protect them from," I grumbled. "It's not me that's looking for them." He might not know exactly where they were hiding but I was willing to bet he had a good idea where to start looking.

Playmate offered nothing but a shrug when I sent him a mute look of appeal. So he was going to be no help.

Playmate is a firm believer in letting our young people learn from their mistakes. He had enlisted me in this thing because he wanted to keep Kip's educational process from turning lethal. Now he was going to step back and let events unfold instructionally.

"You do know that I'm not real fond of bodyguard work?" I told Playmate.

"I do know you're not fond of any kind of work that doesn't include the consumption of beer as the main responsibility of the job."

"Possibly. But asking me to bodyguard is like asking an opera diva to sing on the corner with a hurdy-gurdy man. I have more talent than that. If you just want the kid kept safe you should round up Saucerhead Tharpe." Tharpe is so big you can't hurt him by whacking him with a wagon tongue and so dumb he won't back off from a job as long as he's still awake and breathing.

"It was your remarkable talents that brought me to your door," Playmate responded, his pinky wagging in the wind as he plied his teacup. "Saucerhead Tharpe resembles a force of nature. Powerful but unthinking. Rather like a falling boulder. Unlikely to change course if the moment requires a flexible response. Unlikely to become proactive when innovation could be the best course."

I think that was supposed to be complimentary. "You're blowing smoke, aren't you? You can't afford Saucerhead." I'd begun roaming through the junk and unfinished inventions, growing ever more amazed. "He'd want to get paid up front. Just in case your faith in him was misplaced."

"Well, there is that, too."

The rat. He'd counted on the Dead Man's curiosity to keep me involved with this nonsense, whether or not I got paid.

Don't you hate it when friends take advantage of you?

I picked up the most unusual crossbow I'd ever seen. "I used to be pretty good with one of these things. What's this one for? Shooting through castle walls?" Instead of the usual lever this crossbow was quipped with a pair of hand cranks and a whole array of gears. Cranking like mad barely drew the string back. Which was a misnomer. That was a cable that looked tough enough for towing canal boats.

"We're trying to develop a range of nonlethal weaponry, too," Playmate told me. "That's meant for knocking down a man in heavy armor without doing any permanent injury."

I didn't ask why you'd want to do that. Didn't mention that, sooner or later, the guy was going to get back up and get after you with renewed enthusiasm. I just hefted the crossbow. "Supposed to be a man-portable ballista, eh?" It had some heft to it.

"The bolts are there in that thing that looks like a pipe rack."

"Huh?" I wouldn't have recognized them otherwise. They looked more like miniature, deformed juggler's clubs. Two had padded ends. Again I refrained from telling Playmate what I thought.

I believe I understood what Morley feels each time I shy off what I consider gratuitous throat-cutting. Playmate's boundary of acceptable violence was as much gentler than mine as mine was gentler than friend Morley's.

I loaded one of the quarrels, looked around for a target, shrugged when Playmate grumbled, "Not inside, Garrett," exactly as he no doubt had at Kip a few hundred times.

"All right," I said. "Kip. You never did tell me why these elves want to catch your friends with the strange names."

"I don't know." He didn't look at me. He was a lousy liar. It was obvious that he had some idea.

I looked at Playmate. He gave me a little shrug and a little headshake. He wasn't ready to push it.

I asked, "So where do we go from here?"

Playmate shrugged again. "I was looking at doing the trapdoor spider thing."

"That'll work."

The trapdoor spider hunkers down in a hole, under a door she makes, and waits for somebody edible to come prancing by. Then she jumps out and has lunch. Playmate's reference, though, was to an ambush tactic used by both sides in the recent war in the Cantard, employing the same principle. He meant he was going to sit down and wait for something to happen.

# 10

Without going headlong I kept after Kip about his strange friends. He frustrated me with his determined loyalty. He could not fully grasp the notion that I was there to help.

I needed more time with the Dead Man. I needed to figure out what Old Bones knew as well as how to insert myself into the fantasy worlds where Cypres Prose lived. Apparently his fantasy life was so rich that it influenced his whole attitude toward real life.

After a half hour of mostly polite tea conversation during which my main discovery was that Cypres Prose could avoid a subject almost as slickly as my partner, I was getting frustrated. I was prowling like a cat, poking at half-finished engines and mysterious mechanisms again.

"Garrett!" Playmate exploded. He pointed. His eyes had grown huge.

A small hole had appeared in the stable wall. It glowed scarlet. A harsh beam of red light pushed through. It swung left and right, slicing through the heavy wooden planks. Hardwood smoke flooded the stable, overcoming the sweet rotted-grass odor of fresh horse manure. It made me think both of smokehouses and of campfires in the wild.

Campfires do not have a place in any happy memories of mine. Campfires in my past all had a very nasty war going on somewhere nearby. They always attracted horrible, bloodsucking bugs and starving vertebrates with teeth as long as my fingers. Hardwood smoke gets my battle juices going lots more often than it makes my mouth water.

I picked up the overweight crossbow and inserted the quarrel that had no padding.

The wall cutout collapsed inward. Sunlight blazed through. An oddly shaped being stood silhouetted against the bright.

I shot my bolt.

I used to be pretty good with a crossbow. Somebody found out that I still was. I got him right in the breadbasket. With plenty of *oomph!*, because the recoil was enough to throw me back a step and spin me halfway around.

The villain folded up around the blunt quarrel, out of action. Unfortunately, he was not alone. His friends did not give me time to crank the crossbow back up to full tension. A shortcoming of the instrument that I would have to mention to Playmate. Its cycle time was much too long.

I snatched up a smith's hammer. It seemed the most convincing tool I was likely to lay hands on. The things I had hidden about my person wouldn't have nearly as much impact.

Two shimmering forms came through the hole in the wall, unremarkable street people who flashed silver each few seconds. The one I had shot lay folded up like a hairpin outside, entirely silver now. Another silvery figure ministered to it, briefly flashing into the form of a bum every ten seconds. Only the fallen one didn't shimmer like I was seeing it through a lot of hot air. My bolt must have disrupted a serious compound illusion sorcery.

Playmate stepped up and tried to talk to them. In Playmate's universe reason should be able to solve anything.

I've got to admire his courage and convictions. My own response to those critters was the only behavior I could imagine.

One invader had something shiny in his right hand. He extended it toward Playmate. The big man folded into himself as though every muscle in his body had turned to flab.

I let the hammer fly.

Ever since I was a kid I've had a fascination with the hammer as a missile weapon. I used to enjoy playing at throwing hammers, when I could get my hands on one without anyone knowing that I was risking damage to something so valuable. I knew that in olden times the hammer had been a warrior's weapon and the little bit of Cypres Prose resident within me had woven mighty legends around Garrett the Hammer.

Garrett the Hammer was dead on with his throw. But his target saw it coming and shifted its weight slightly, just in time, so that the speeding hammer brushed its shimmer only obliquely, ricocheted off, and continued on in a rainbow arc that brought the metal end into contact with the back of the head of the silvery figure trying to resurrect the villain I'd knocked down earlier.

That blow should've busted a hole in the thing's skull. No such luck, though. The impact just caused it to fling forward and sprawl across the creature that was down already.

These were Playmate's elves, it was obvious, but equally obvious was the truth of his contention that his sketches did not capture their real nature.

The one who had downed Playmate closed in on me. The other one chased Kip. Kip demonstrated the sort of character I expected. He had great faith in the patron saint of every man for himself. He made a valiant effort to get the hell out of there.

Kip's pursuer extended something shiny in his direction. The kid followed Playmate's example. He demonstrated substantially less style in his collapse.

I avoided the same fate for seconds on end by staying light on my feet and putting great enthusiasm into an effort to saturate the air with flying tools. But, too soon, I began feeling like I had been drinking a whole lot of something more potent than beer. I slowed down.

The dizziness didn't last long.

# 11

I do not recall the darkness coming. My next clear memory is of Morley Dotes with his pretty little nose only inches from mine. He's reminding me that to stay alive one *must* remember to breathe. From the corner of my eye I see Saucerhead Tharpe trying to sell the same idea to Playmate while the ratgirl Pular Singe scuttles around nervously, sniffing and whining.

The disorientation faded faster than the effects of alcohol ever do. Without leaving much hangover. But none of those clowns were willing to believe that high-potency libations hadn't been involved in my destruction. When people go on a nag they aren't the least bit interested in evidence that might contradict their prejudices.

Pular Singe, ratgirl genius, was my principal advocate.

What can you do? "You two are a couple of frigid old ladies," I told Morley and Saucerhead. "Thank you for your faith, Singe. Oh, my head!" I didn't have a hangover from this but I did have one from last night. The latest headache powder wasn't helping.

"And you'd like us to believe that you don't have a hangover," Morley sneered. Weakly. One side of his face wasn't working so good.

Not a lot of time had passed since the advent of the silvery people. Smoke still wisped off the cut ends of some of the wall planks. I suppose it was a near miracle that no fire had gotten going. Perhaps, less miraculously, that was due to the sudden appearance of Dotes, Tharpe, and Pular.

"Singe!" I barked at the ratgirl. "Where did you guys come from?" She was likely to give me a straight answer. "Why're you here?" Bellows that Morley and Saucerhead would accept indifferently could rattle Singe deeply. Ratfolk are timid by nature and Singe was trying to make her own way outside her native society. Ratfolk males don't yell and threaten and promise massive bloodshed unless they intend to deliver. They don't banter.

When Singe is around I usually tread on larks' eggs because I don't want to upset her. It's like working with your mom wearing a rat suit.

She didn't get a chance to answer. Morley cracked, "This one's all right. He woke up cranking."

"What're you guys doing here, Morley?"

"Thank you, Mr. Dotes, for scaring off the baddies."

"Thank you, Mr. Dotes, for scaring off the baddies."

"See? You can learn if you put your mind to it."

"I was doing pretty good there on my own." The side of his face that wasn't working well had a sizable young bruise developing. "That's gonna be a brute when it grows up. What happened?" Morley's stylish clothing was torn and filthy, too. Which would hurt him more than mere physical damage could.

"I had a special request from the Dead Man. Round up Singe and a squad of heavyweights, come over here and keep an eye on you. You're a major trouble magnet, my friend. We're not even in place yet and we find the excitement already happening. What were those things?"

With more help from Singe than from Morley I made it to a standing position. "Where's the kid?"

"There was a kid? Maybe that's who your silvery friends were hauling away. Who were they, Garrett?"

"I don't know. You didn't stop them?"

"Let me see. No. I was too busy being bounced off walls and rolled through horse excrement. You couldn't hurt those guys." He looked as sour as he could manage with only half a face cooperating. "I broke my swordcane on one of them."

I couldn't resist a snicker. Morley is a lethally handsome halfbreed, partly human but mostly dark elf. He's the guy fathers of young women wake up screaming about in the wee hours of the night. His vanity is substantial. His dress is always impeccable and at the forefront of fashion. He considers disarray a horror and dirt of any sort an abomination.

Dirt seems to feel the same way about him. It avoids him religiously.

I snickered again.

"It must be the concussion," Morley grumped. "I know my good friend Garrett would never mock me in my misfortune."

"Mockery." I couldn't resist another snicker. "Heh-heh. Misfortune." I glanced around. "Damn! Where'd he go? I only looked away for a second. Too bad. You're stuck with his evil twin instead of a friend."

"I hate it when that happens."

Singe had seen us in action often enough to discount most of what she heard but she still couldn't quite grasp what was going on. She watched us now, long fingers entwined so she could keep her hands from flying around. Her myopic eyes squinted. Her snout twitched. Her whiskers waggled. She drew more information from the world through her sense of smell than with any other.

She tended to be emotional and excitable but now remained collected. If she had learned anything from me it was better self-control. I felt it to be a cruel miscarriage of propriety that my companionship hadn't had a similar impact on the rest of my friends.

She took advantage of a lull to inquire, "What is this situation, Garrett? I did not understand the message I received from the Dead Man."

And yet she had come out of hiding. Because she had a chance to help me.

Morley smirked. I would hear about that as soon as Singe wasn't around to get her feelings hurt. She had an adolescent crush on me. And Morley, known to have broken the bones of persons having thrown ethnic slurs his way, thought it was great fun to torment me about being mooned over by a ratgirl.

He could commit every crime of prejudice he hated when they were directed toward him, yet would never, ever, recognize any inconsistency. Because ratpeople were a created race, products of the malificent sorcerous investigations of some of our lords of the Hill during the heyday of the last century, most people don't even consider them people. Morley Dotes included.

I told her, "Anything you heard from His Nibs makes you better informed than I am, Singe." Her particular line of ratpeople place their personal names second. Just to confuse things, other lines do the opposite, in imitation of local humans. "He didn't tell me anything. Not that he was interested in what's happening here nor even that he was planning to make you a part of things."

"What *is* happening here?" Morley asked.

"Can you handle that one, Playmate?" Saucerhead had the big stablekeeper up on his hind legs now.

"I don' t'ink," Playmate mumbled.

I tried to tell everybody what I knew, not holding back anything, the way my partner would. Well, some little details, maybe, like about how good the Dead Man was at sneaking peeks into unprepared minds. Nobody needs to know that but me.

"You sure you ain't been jobbed?" Saucerhead wanted to know. "That sure ain't much. Play, you runnin' a game on my man Garrett?"

I waved him off. "It's not that." Chances were good the Dead Man would've clued me in if that were the case. My concern was more that Kip and Playmate were being manipulated. "But I do wonder if someone isn't running a game on Kip. Play, you ever met Lastyr or Noodiss?"

"Not formally. Not to talk to. I've seen them a few times. Not so much recently, though. They used to come around here a lot. When they thought Kip would be here alone."

I grunted, irritated. Atop all the aches and pains it looked like the only way I was going to learn anything of substance would be to catch me a silver elf and squeeze him.

Which was a conclusion my partner must have reached before I left the house. Else how to explain Singe's presence?

Besides being my only friend from TunFaire's lowest lower class, Pular Singe is the finest tracker amongst a species known for individuals able to follow a trail through the insane stew of foul odors that complement the soul of this mad city.

"Singe? You find a scent yet?" I knew she was sniffing. She couldn't help herself. And she was clever enough to understand why she had been invited to the party.

She tried to shrug, then to shake her head. Ratfolk find both human gestures difficult. Singe wants to be human so bad. Each time I see it I hurt for her. I get embarrassed. Because most of the time we aren't worthy of imitation.

Failing, she spoke: "No. Not the elves. Though there is a unique odor where the two fell. But that exists only there. It does not go anywhere. And it does not smell like any odor from a living thing."

"Wow." Her human speech had improved dramatically since last I had seen her. It was almost free of accent—except when she tried a contraction. Her improvement was miraculous considering the voice box she had to use. No other rat in my experience had come close to matching her. Yet she was said to suffer from a hearing deficiency. According to the rat thug Reliance, who first brought her to my attention. "You've even mastered the sibilants."

Determination can take you a long way.

Her sibilants still had a strong serpentine quality. But Singe needs a lot of encouragement to keep going. She gets almost none of that from her own people.

"So what do we do now?" Morley asked. He wasn't interested, really. Not much. He was trying to work out how he could get back to The Palms and get cleaned up and changed before anyone noticed his disreputable condition. I had a feeling that, any minute now, I would find my best pal missing.

Singe said, "I cannot follow the strange elves. But Garrett taught me to follow the horses when I cannot follow a target who becomes a passenger in a vehicle that horses are pulling."

What a talent, that Garrett guy. After a moment, I confessed, "The student lost even the teacher on that one, Singe."

She looked at me like she knew I was just saying that so she'd feel good, getting to explain. "The elves took the boy. Him I can track. So I will follow him. Wherever he stops moving, there will we find your elves."

"The girl is a genius," I said. "Let's all go raid Playmate's pantry before we go on the road."

That idea was acclaimed enthusiastically by everyone not named Playmate. Or Morley. Playmate because his charity is limited when its wannabe beneficiaries are solvent. Morley because the weasel wasn't around to vote.

Ah, well. My elven friend would be out there somewhere, a desperate fugitive fleeing the wrath of the good-grooming gods.

# 12

Saucerhead's impatient pacing took him across the narrow street and back three times as he tried to establish a safe passage around a particularly irritable camel. No owner of the beast was in evidence. I was surprised to see it. Camels are rare this far south. Possibly no one would have this one. Possibly it had been abandoned. It was a beast as foul as the Goddamn Parrot. It voided its bowels, then nipped at Saucerhead. I muttered, "That's what I feel like right now."

"Which end?" Singe asked, testing her theory of humor. She giggled. So bold, this ratgirl who came out in the daytime, then dared to make jokes in front of human beings.

"Take your pick. You know what that thing really is? A horse without its disguise on."

Even Singe thought that was absurd. And she has less love for the four-legged terrors than I do. You could say a state of war, of low intensity, exists between her species and theirs. Horses dislike ratpeople more than most humans do.

Playmate said, "One day I fully expect to find you on the steps of the Chancery, between Barking Dog Amato and Woodie Granger, foaming at the mouth as you rant at the King and the whole royal family because they're pawns of the great equine conspiracy, Garrett."

The Chancery is a principal government building where, traditionally, anyone with a grievance can voice it publicly on the outside steps. Inevitably, the Chancery steps have acquired a bevy of professional complainers and outright lunatics. Most people consider them cheap entertainment.

I said, "You shouldn't talk about it! They're going to get you now." Singe started looking worried, frowning. "All right. Maybe I exaggerate a little. But they're still vicious, nasty critters. They'll turn on you in a second."

The resident nasty critter spit at Saucerhead. Saucerhead responded with a jab to the camel's nose. It was a calm, professional blow of the sort that earned him his living. But he put his weight and muscle behind it. The camel rocked back. Its eyes wobbled. Its front knees buckled.

Tharpe said, "Come on." Once we were past the camel, he added, "Sometimes polite ain't enough. You just gotta show'em who's boss."

We walked another hundred feet. And stopped. The street didn't go anywhere. It ended at a wall. Which was improbable.

"What the hell?" Saucerhead demanded. "When did we start blocking off streets?"

He had a point. TunFaire has thousands of dead-end alleys and breezeways but something that happened in antiquity made our rulers issue regulations against blocking thoroughfares. Possibly because they'd wanted to be able to make a run for it in either direction. And while what we were following wasn't much of a street, it was a street officially. Complete with symbols painted on walls at intersections to indicate that its name was something like Stonebone. Exactly what was impossible to tell. The paint hadn't been renewed in my lifetime.

The wall ahead was old gray limestone. Exactly like the wall to our left. Needing the attention of a mason just as badly. But something about it made all four of us nervous.

"It sure don't look like something somebody threw up over the weekend," I said. Believe it or not, some Karentine subjects are wicked enough to ignore established regulations and will construct something illegal while the city functionaries are off duty.

Nobody stepped up to the wall. Until Singe snorted the way only a woman can do when she's exasperated with men being men. She shuffled right up till her pointy big nose was half an inch from the limestone. "The track of the boy goes straight on, Garrett. And this wall smells almost the same as the odor I found where the two elves fell on one another."

Playmate took a few steps backward, found a bit of broken brick that hadn't yet been scrounged by the street children. (They sell brick chips and chunks back to the brickyards, where they're powdered and added to the clay of new bricks.) He started to wind up, but paused and said, "Garrett, have you bothered to look up?"

I hadn't. Why would I?

None of the others had, either.

We all looked now.

That wall wasn't part of anything. It might not even be stone. It just went up a ways, then turned fuzzy and wiggly and lizard's belly white. Then it turned misty. Then it turned into nothing.

"It's an illusion."

Playmate chucked his brickbat.

The missile proceeded to proceed despite the presence of a wall that appeared completely solid, if improbably cold and damp when I extended a cautious finger to test it. Saucerhead Tharpe isn't nearly as careful as Mama Garrett's only surviving son. He reached out to thump that wall. And his fist went right on through.

We all stepped back. We exchanged troubled looks. I said, "That's an illusion of the highest order."

Singe said, "I hear someone calling from the other side."

Playmate observed, "An illusion that persists, that can be used as camouflage, requires the efforts of a master wizard."

I grunted. In this town that meant somebody off the Hill. It meant one of six dozen or so people who are the real masters in Karenta.

Singe said, "There is somebody over there. Yelling at you, Garrett."

I asked Playmate, "What do you think?" I admit to being intimidated by Hill people. But I've never backed down just because they stuck a finger in somewhere. I wouldn't back down now. Kip's kidnapping had me irked and interested. Of everyone I asked, "Anybody want to walk away?"

Nobody volunteered to leave, though Saucerhead gulped a pail of air, Playmate seemed to go a little green and Singe started shaking like she was naked in a blizzard and didn't have a clue which way to the warm. She made some kind of chalk sign on a real wall, maybe to ward off evil.

"You're the Marine," Playmate said. "Show us your stuff."

Saucerhead pasted on a huge grin. He was ex-army, too. And he had heard my opinions concerning the relative merits of the services more often than had Playmate. He refused to see the light. It's a debate that seems doomed to persist forever because army types are too dim to recognize the truth when it kicks them in the teeth.

Saucerhead's whole face threatened to open up. I thought the top half of his head was going to tip over backward onto his shoulders. He gasped out, "Yeah, Garrett. Let's see some of that old Marine Corps 'Hey diddle diddle, straight up the middle.' "

Ominously, Singe said, "There is no yelling anymore."

"I'm thinking about giving *you* some of that good old, big boy." I took a deep breath and squared off with the illusory wall.

Saucerhead chuckled. He knows I'd never come straight at him if I did think I had to get after him. Business led us to butt heads briefly once upon a time, long ago. The results had been far from satisfactory from my point of view.

I whooped like I was going in, back in my island warfare days, straight up the middle indeed. Something that we did not actually do very often, as I recall. Us and the Venageti both very much preferred sneaking around, stabbing in the back, to any straightforward and personally risky charging.

That wall was more than just an illusion. It resisted me. Hitting it felt a little like belly flopping, though with more stretch and give to the surface. Which popped after a moment. And which felt as cold as a god's heart until it did.

My efforts evidently weakened the wall considerably because the big army types followed me through as though there wasn't any resistance at all. And the civilian followed them. But I wasn't really keeping track.

We'd overtaken our quarry where they'd holed up temporarily, either so they could interrogate Kip or so their injured buddies could recuperate. There was another imaginary wall beyond them. That one had a bricklike look even though it was semitransparent. From my point of view.

My heart jumped. Our approach had to have been noticed.

In that instant I sensed movement. The corner of the eye kind of movement you get when your imagination is running wild. Only what I wasn't imagining was happening right in front of me and I couldn't get a solid look at it. Then, for a moment, I saw silver elves and Kip with something clamped over his mouth and I realized that Singe's sharp ears must've caught his cries for help back when she'd kept talking and nobody had bothered to listen.

A shimmering silver elf extended a hand toward me.

I dodged.

I didn't move soon enough.

Once again I didn't feel the darkness arrive.

# 13

Morley Dotes was right there in my face again when I woke up. "Some kind of party you must throw, Garrett. Blitzed into extinction again. And the sun still hasn't gone down." He looked around as I tried to sit up. My head pounded worse than before. "But in an alley? Even if it is a pretty clean one for this burg?"

"Gods! My head! I don't know what they did to me but it's enough to make me consider giving up liquor."

"You give up your beer? Don't try to kid a kidder, kid."

"I said liquor, nimrod. Beer is a holy elixir. One shuns beer only at the risk of one's immortal soul. I see you're all freshly prettied up. How'd you find us?"

Two of Morley's henchmen had accompanied him. I didn't know them. They were clad in the outfits waiters at The Palms usually wear but they were much younger than Sarge and Puddle and Morley's other traditional associates. Maybe the old guys were getting too old.

"Your girlfriend left us a trail to follow. Standard rat chalk symbols. You didn't notice? A trained detective like you?"

Pride made me consider fibbing. "No. I didn't. Not really." Ten years ago I couldn't have admitted any failing. Which, at times, had left me looking just a whole lot stupider than a simple confession would've done.

People are strange. And sometimes I think I might be the strangest people I know.

Morley's boys didn't lift a finger to help anybody. Dotes himself didn't do anything but talk. Which told me he thought none of us had been hurt badly. "What happened to the illusion?"

"What illusion?"

I explained. Morley wanted to disbelieve but dared not in the face of Saucerhead's confirmation. Tharpe doesn't have the imagination to dress himself up with excuses as complex as this.

"So you scared them into running when they're not really up to it. They have two casualties and a prisoner to manage."

"We don't know that any of them were hurt."

"Yes, we do, Garrett. Use that brain the Dead Man thinks you have. If they don't have someone injured they don't have any reason not to just drag the kid straight off to wherever it is they want to take him. Let's get back on the trail. They can't have gone far."

Maybe he was right. Maybe the villains were just around the corner. But I didn't have any way to track them. Right now.

Singe was still out, stone cold.

"I wonder if they understand how we found them." I was afraid the elves might've given Singe an extra dose of darkness because of her nose.

"Me, I'm wondering why they didn't hurt you a lot more than they did," Morley countered. His cure for most ills is to exterminate everybody involved. "For some reason they've slapped you down twice without doing any permanent harm." He has difficulty comprehending that kind of thinking.

He emphasized "permanent" because my expression revealed the depth and breadth of the temporary harm I was suffering.

"You all right, Saucerhead?"

"Got a miserable headache." Tharpe's voice was gravelly. His temper would be extremely short. Best not to disturb him at all.

"How 'bout you, Play?"

"What he said. And don't yell. Makes it hurt even more."

He didn't need to yell back.

Maybe I was lucky. All the practice I've had dealing with hangovers. I turned to Singe. "Seems a shame to disturb her." She did look rather peaceful.

"Kiss her and let's get on with it," Morley grumped. Without having been blessed by the elves.

"What?"

He opened his mouth to crack wise about the sleeping beauty, thought better of it, beckoned me. I followed him for as far as he felt was far enough to keep his remarks from being overhead by sharp rat ears. "She isn't really out, Garrett. She's giving you a chance to show some special concern."

The fact that he didn't make mock let me know that he was serious, that he was concerned about bruising Singe's tender ego. Though the motives behind his concern were, probably, wholly selfish.

"Understood," I told him, though that wasn't entirely true.

I don't like the responsibility that piles onto me when Singe gives way to these juvenile urges to manipulate me. That smacks of emotional blackmail. In fact, it *is* emotional blackmail. She just doesn't understand that it is. And I'm not all that well equipped to deal with it. More than one lady of my acquaintance would suggest that I'm not far enough away from adolescence myself.

I went to the ratgirl, dropped to my knees beside her. "Singe?"

She didn't respond. I thought her breathing was too rapid for someone who was supposed to be unconscious, though.

How do you tell someone that their relationship fantasies can never become anything more than that? Everything I could possibly say to Singe would be true but would sound so stupidly cliché if said that I could do no good talking to her. She was important to me, personally and professionally. She had become one of the half dozen closest friends I had. I enjoyed teaching her how to cope in a world where she was less than welcome. But she could never be anything but a friend, a business associate, and a student. And I have no idea how to make her understand that without causing her pain.

When she first broke away from the dominance of her own people, where females have fewer rights than do horses amongst humans, I considered letting her move into my place. I thought of making her part of the team. I still think well of that idea. But the Dead Man did assure me that, in her desperation to be wanted and liked and loved, Pular Singe would give the offer far more weight than I intended.

I touched her throat. Her pulse was rapid. I glanced around. There was no immediate salvation apparent. Morley was grinning, exposing about a thousand bright white needle teeth in a silent taunt.

"You want I should carry her, Garrett?" Saucerhead asked. There went Tharpe, being thoughtful despite his pain. Like most human beings, he can be a mess of contradictions.

"That might be good. Any of you guys know anything about doctoring ratfolk? If we can't fix her up ourselves we'll have to take her back to Reliance."

That ought to be the perfect medicine. The very philosopher's stone.

Reliance is a sort of ratman godfather, a highly respected and greatly feared leader of that community who's involved in a lot of questionable and some outright illegal activities. Reliance believes that Pular Singe belongs to him. There's a chance he's right within the rules of rat society. There is some sort of indenture involved. But rat society isn't paramount in TunFaire. And that guy Garrett don't much care about anybody's customs or rules when he makes up his mind what's right and what's wrong.

"She wouldn't be real happy about the boss rat getting his paws on her again, Garrett," Tharpe assured me. With a wink, showing he'd gotten it. "He tried to hire me once to bring her back." He grinned a grin filled with bad teeth.

Well. Maybe I was going to get some help with this after all, from the least likely source.

Saucerhead really can be a sensitive kind of guy.

And Singe, wonder of wonders, was stirring suddenly.

"So why didn't you take the job?"

"Old Reliance, he's too damned cheap for one thing. He just can't get it through his head that it ain't just a matter of rounding up one dumb female and dropping her off where he wants her delivered. He can't get it through his skull that she can actually think for herself and that she can have made friends who'd be willing to look out for her. He just figures you're trying to hold him up on your fee when you try to explain it to him."

"You'd think he'd have figured it all out from direct experience. Whoops! Look here. It's alive. Hi, sleepyhead. You're the last one awake."

Singe mumbled something.

"We're just waiting on you."

Singe smiled a weak rat smile. She probably thought she heard relief in my voice. Possibly she did. I was relieved that her problem wasn't real.

Pular Singe's recovery was dramatically swift once she decided that she needed to get healthy. Reliance's name made a great whip.

Morley told one of his waiters to make a bread and cheese run while the rest of us sat around staking claims on being in worse shape than the other guy. Food was a great idea, I thought, but when the man came back with a basket filled with chow I didn't feel much like eating.

A similar lack of appetite afflicted Saucerhead, Playmate, and Singe. And none of those three liked it even a little, either. They loved their food. Singe, in particular, always ate like a starved alley cat or one of her feral cousins. Everything in sight, steadily, gobbling so fast that the bugs never got a share.

I grumbled, "I think we've got us an invention right here. A new weight loss program for the lords and ladies." Nobody else in this burg ever gets fat.

Soon enough, heads still aching and stomachs still empty, we proceeded as Singe picked up Kip's trail. Though it had begun to get dark she had no trouble finding the way. Sight was never her master sense. Though it did become more important after nightfall. She could see in the dark better than Morley. And Morley has eyes like an owl.

This time the chase didn't last twenty minutes.

This time the camouflage didn't catch us unaware, either, though it existed as an addition to a building rather than as something thrown across a street. From the viewpoint of the silver elves the trouble was that the building they'd scabbed onto was one that Saucerhead and I knew. And had we not known it ourselves there were at least twenty local Tenderloin folk hanging around in the gloaming trying to figure out what was going on. That addition hadn't been there half an hour earlier.

Playmate observed, "These people aren't very good at what they're doing, are they?"

"I get the feeling that this isn't anything they've had to do before. What do you say we just charge in there and grab the kid back?" I wasn't eager to get myself another bout of sleep because of my habit of waking up afterward with a ferocious hangover. I didn't need another one of those. I was working on a couple already.

Still, they had the boy. Obnoxious though he was. Which didn't incline them to throw him back out, apparently. They wanted him pretty bad.

I suppose a throbbing headache can impair your judgement. And a friend like Morley Dotes can have a similar effect. Once he had winkled out the complete details of our last encounter he was ready to go. "They aren't going to kill anybody, Garrett. There are six of us." Singe bristled, knowing she hadn't been included in the count. "They can't get all of us."

# 14

They got all of us, most of the bystanders, quite a few passersby, and even a handful of people inside neighboring buildings who didn't know what was going on and never knew what hit them.

I came out of it faster than before, my head pounding worse than last time. The first thing I saw was my eager beaver buddy Morley Dotes. Yet again. Only this time he had his temples grasped tightly and looked like he was working real hard on trying not to scream. Or was, possibly, contemplating the delights of suicide.

I grumbled, "Now we know why they didn't ask you to be a general during the recent scuffle with Venageta." Though considering the performances of some of the generals we'd had, who'd earned their bells by picking the right venue as a place of birth, Morley might've fit right in.

Dotes whined something irrelevant about the whole thing having been my idea and registered a plea for a lot less vocal volume.

"Pussy. I wake up feeling like this three or four times a week. And I function. What the hell are those people roaring about?" Neighbors not struck down were rushing into the street. In normal times their voices would have been considered restrained. Not so now.

They all stared at the sky.

I looked up just in time to see something large and shiny and shaped like a discus disappear behind nearby rooftops, heading north. "What the hell was that?" I glanced at Morley. "Never mind. Don't tell me. Your cousins just got away in one of those flying lights that people keep seeing."

"Cousins? Those things weren't elves, Garrett. Not elves of any kind. Their mouths and eyes were all wrong. They didn't have elven teeth. Maybe they're some kind of foreign, deformed humans. You might look into that. But they're definitely not elves."

Playmate came around. Between groans he asked, "Did we get him back?"

"Kip? We didn't even get a wink this time. Let's see what we did get. Maybe that whore Fate has a heart of gold after all."

We managed to collect a few scraps of silvery cloth and nearly a dozen other items of wildly varying shape and no obvious utility. Those included several small, torn bags made of a silvery, somewhat paperlike material. The rest resembled smooth gray rocks with a very unrocklike feel that came in varying regular shapes. Most had markings in green and red and yellow that looked like writing but which were in no familiar alphabet.

One of Morley's men came up with a bag that hadn't been opened. Its contents turned out to be two thick biscuits the texture of oatmeal cakes. They had a sorghum molasses odor.

"Food," Playmate said. "We broke up a meal."

"I could use something to eat," Saucerhead said by way of announcing his recovery. "We still got that cheese basket?" He rubbed his forehead as he looked around. He has an amazingly high threshhold of pain but now he had begun to respond to it. "What happened?" He reached out and helped himself to the elven oatmeal cakes. He wolfed them down before anybody could remind him of the legends about fairy food.

Nobody answered his question. Because nobody had an answer.

"Lookit there!" somebody shrieked. In a second half the crowd were pointing skyward again.

The silver disk was back. And it was in a big hurry. It left a thunderclap behind as it streaked off southward.

"Hey! There's another one!"

One turned into three in a matter of seconds. Only these weren't disks. They looked like giant glowing gas balls. On a smaller scale I'd seen something similar in the will-o'-the-wisps of the swamps on the islands I'd visited during the war.

The glowing globes chased the silvery disk.

Morley murmured, "I've been hearing about these things for weeks but I'd about made up my mind that they were pure popular hysteria."

I looked around for an easily accessible high place. I wanted a clear line of sight to the west, toward the heart of town. Toward the Hill. To discover if those lights ended up there. Because this looked like the sort of thing those people would pull. Squabbling amongst themselves using experimental sorceries while the folk of the city got run over.

Morley asked, "You think your friends the unemployed gods might be back, Garrett?"

That hadn't occurred to me. "I doubt it. They were more reserved. They didn't show themselves unless they wanted to be seen. Mainly because they couldn't be seen by nonbelievers unless they made a huge effort."

"I don't think that these people would attract attention if they were given an option. Something intense is going on with them, sufficient to make being noticed the lesser concern."

"Probably." I did think he was right. Logically, if you were a foreigner running around in an alien town you wouldn't let yourself be noticed unless it was unavoidable. "You think Saucerhead is going to croak on us?"

Tharpe had turned several indescribable colors, near as I could tell by torchlight. Torches and lanterns were turning up now that the curious felt safe enough to come out of their homes. Just as well that they hadn't before, too. We'd have awakened to find ourselves plucked of everything but our toenails.

"I think he might want to die," Morley said. "I think we ought to discover ourselves in another location sometime soon. This much activity is bound to attract lawmen."

And he wouldn't want the notice, however much he protests his innocence of the illegal of late.

Maybe old habits die hard.

These days, with the postwar economic depression becoming entrenched, the new secret police are very interested in any center of excitement. A minor bit no more scary than a street party can turn into a riot at the bump of a belly between an unemployed human and almost any nonhuman he might suspect of having moved into a human's job while human soldiers were away risking their lives on behalf of the kingdom.

These are social problems that aren't going to go away anytime soon.

I said, "We do have everything we need for a blowup."

Morley nodded. He understood. He shared my concern.

He has become very sensitive in these changing times. He doesn't like the way things are headed. Though it isn't the conflict that bothers him. That can be exploited to produce big profits.

What he abhors is the growing power of the Crown and its determined interference in our everyday lives.

An elven trait, to believe that that government governs best
which doesn't govern at all. Chaos is more fun. Anarchy is the
ideal. And only the strong survive.

Morley would admit that a sustained harsh dose of genuine
anarchy most likely would result in the extinction or expulsion of
every species of elf currently calling TunFaire home.

I told Morley, "That was an absolutely marvelous suggestion,
old friend. Can I assume that it'll be you carrying Pular
Singe . . . ? What?"

Singe was still unconscious. But I wasn't concerned about her.
"Morley. I just saw Bic Gonlit. He was watching us from across
the street."

"So let's get Singe put back together and see if she can get on
his trail. He just might know where to look for Playmate's kid."

"You don't think she can track Kip from here?"

"Not if he got carried away inside a giant flying wheel, I
don't."

An excellent point. Not one I'd wanted to look at close up yet,
though. You hope you can catch an occasional break.

Singe was getting her feet under her now, with a little help
from Playmate.

"Let's see about traveling on, then," I told Morley. "I just spotted another familiar face. This one I recollect seeing in the vicin-
ity of Colonel Block and Deal Relway in a none too distant past."
I made a big effort to remember such faces so I can exercise some
sort of exit strategy when I see one again. "I'll help with Singe."

# 15

The secret police evidently didn't have an interest strong enough to pursue us. At the moment. But I was willing to bet that I'd hear from Westman Block if anyone in the Tenderloin had recognized me.

Colonel Westman Block, erstwhile acquaintance of that handsome Marine named Garrett, oversaw all police forces and functions in TunFaire. That included the secret police. Theoretically. On paper.

We gathered in a dark place, half a mile from the excitement, and considered, "What now?"

Singe said, "I cannot possibly follow a man who flew away through the air, inside a flying boat made out of metal." She then wondered aloud, "Why are you looking at me like that?"

"Because Morley said almost exactly the same thing just before you woke up. We decided to chase Bic Gonlit instead." She knew the name from discussions of what was happening, back when we were tracking Kip. "As soon as we were sure we'd shaken the police."

"You must tell me more about this Bic Gonlit."

Playmate and I both tried to explain Bic Gonlit and his place in what was happening. A challenging task, of course, since we had almost no idea ourselves. I added, "Only, I'm not sure if he's actually part of what happened this afternoon."

"You people like to think you are so much smarter than us but sometimes you are really dumb, Garrett. You start talking before you think. How do you expect me to follow someone who is just another face in a crowd?"

"She's got you there," Morley said, content to leave all the blame with me. "I could use a little more information myself. Bic Gonlit is only a name to me."

"He's this little round fat guy who wears funny boots—"

"There was a little round fat man with hugely thick-soled boots I saw several times on the way down here. I thought he might be doing something for you because your parrot was right there near him."

"I didn't see him," Playmate said. "Not the bird, either."

"Nor did I," I confessed. My parrot. Following me around. And I never noticed.

It might be time to consider alternative careers.

"I noticed the bird," Singe said. "I saw the fat man, too. But I did not know Mr. Big was following him. I thought he was following you, Garrett. He is still around. I saw him just a minute ago. Yes. Over there. Where we came from. Up on that cornice thing where the pigeons are sleeping."

"I've made up my mind. I'm going to see Weider and tell him I'm taking the security job at the brewery." I felt completely blind and useless. It was so dark I couldn't find the end of my arm.

"There is a short little fat man over there watching us, too," Singe told me. "He is hiding behind those steps right under the parrot."

Like anybody could see all that if they just looked. Grrr! The only thing I could see was a glow in the distance, about where we'd lost track of Kip.

I really was inclined to tell Max Weider I was ready to come on board. Truly. At that moment. But, before I hung it up, I had to try another stunt or two. "I have a thought. We're all tired. Why don't we head for my place? If Gonlit really is following us, we can lead him to the Dead Man."

I was past ready to go home. I was desperate for something to take the edge off my headache. And I was hungry. And I was tired. Getting knocked unconscious regularly takes the vinegar out of you fast, even if you're not going out by getting bopped on the head.

My plan, as proposed, didn't stir a word of protest. Much to my amazement. Morley is naturally contentious. He'll get involved in arguments just to entertain himself. But all he said was, "I'm worn-out, too. And The Palms is headed into its busiest time. And I left Puddle in charge."

"I got a thing going myself," Saucerhead said. "I need to get back, too, unless something starts happening."

Even Playmate was willing to shut it down for the night. And to desert me when he did. "Nobody's been at the stable all day. I need to get back there before the animals get so upset they . . ." He stopped. I think he was about to let slip something terrible about the conspiracy amongst horses but realized that me finding out might turn out to be bad luck for him. He changed the subject. "And somebody's going to have to tell Kip's family what's happened."

A while later, after a period of silence, Playmate asked, "You wouldn't consider taking care of that for me, would you, Garrett?"

"Not likely, old buddy. Not likely. After today's adventures you're not real high on my 'please, God, let me do him a favor' list."

The tiniest flicker of a smirk crossed Playmate's features before he settled on an expression of stolid resignation. I had the feeling that I'd just gotten jobbed but couldn't figure out how.

# 16

I never saw the Goddamn Parrot before he dropped onto my shoulder in Wizard's Reach, two blocks from home. Or one block through the alley to my back fence. By then the only companions I had were the bird and Pular Singe. None of us were inclined to lose any sleep looking for Cypres Prose anymore.

Maybe I was just telling myself what I wanted to hear when I reasoned that Kip was in no physical danger because the silver elves had shown no inclination to do anyone any permanent harm.

So far.

Kip's personality might trigger the extra effort.

The bird said nothing. His presence was the message. The Dead Man knew we were coming. And he knew that Bic Gonlit was on our trail.

Now we would see how well the little fat man had done his homework.

If he knew much about the Dead Man he wouldn't get too close to the house. Not as close as he'd gotten in the alley. Though how close is really too close is something even I don't know.

The Goddamn Parrot whispered, "He has stopped, Garrett. He has positioned himself behind the Bailnoc stoop. From there he can see the front of our house while he stays far enough removed that I cannot read much more than his moods."

He didn't seem to mind Singe finding out that he could chat with me through the ugly rooster. I didn't think he was dumb enough to believe that she was too dim to catch on. So he trusted her completely.

Handy to know just how trustworthy your associates are.

I looked back. I couldn't see a thing. I wondered how Gonlit could be watching me. I wondered about his connections. He'd have to have some potent ones helping right now. Otherwise, he wouldn't be able to follow me around unnoticed.

That takes some advanced magic.

I think I'm pretty good at this stuff I do. I don't normally get tailed without noticing unless the tail comes armed with some pretty potent sorcerous tools.

As Singe and I climbed the stoop a sleepy-angry tittering broke out somewhere up under the eaves. Something as fast as a hummingbird dropped down and circled us several times too swiftly to be seen clearly.

My front door opened. Dean must've been alerted by the Dead Man. He stood there in his nightshirt, scowling, holding a lamp above his head, disapproving of birth, death, and most everything in between.

"Early night?" I asked. The nightshirt was for commentary only. It wasn't yet time for him to retire. He doesn't change until he's ready to slide into bed. Unless he wants to make some point that will remain obscure to everyone but him.

He grunted and rewarded me with an even blacker scowl.

"What's with the gang of pixies up there?" I expected their presence would keep us arguing like pixies for weeks.

"Ask the thing. He's the one who decided to adopt them."

Ah. Live and learn. And discover the real root of Dean's bad temper. The Dead Man had done something to offend his sense of rectitude.

Dean was aggrieved further because I'd been all set to blame him. Because that's the kind of thing he's likely to do. Every time I turn around he's trying to take in another stray.

This might require some untangling.

"I'll talk to him," I promised. I wasn't really happy, either.

Living near pixies is like setting up housekeeping inside a colony of sparrows. The squabbling never stops. And this bunch was making themselves at home right above my bedroom window.

None of that would bother Old Bones. He's dead. He doesn't have to listen to the racket.

Darkly, I added, "Failing him seeing reason, I know where I can come up with a nest of bumblebees." Bumblebees and the smallest of the little people were feuding before the appearance of the first men. If you credit the legends of the wee folk.

Dean growled something about, "Then how do we get rid of the bumblebees?"

He grows ever more pessimistic as he ages.

"One step at a time, brother. One step at a time. Right now we've got trouble on a grander scale. I lost the boy who came here looking for help today. In circumstances surpassing strange. Make some tea, slap together some sandwiches, bring everything in with His Nibs, and I'll fill you in."

The old man headed for the kitchen. I'd triggered his concern for the lost and the hopeless. Earlier he'd been ready to stuff Kip into a gunnysack with a couple boulders so the boy could have a close-up look at the lost treasures on the bottom of the river somewhere off the Landing.

Singe watched while I took the Goddamn Parrot to his perch in the small front room. The Dead Man had withdrawn his control and inhibiting influence. The feathered weasel was returning to normal. He muttered like a stevedore but his big interest at the moment was food, not obnoxious chatter meant to get his owner crucified. He let Singe stroke his feathers as long as she didn't interfere with his dining.

Singe was pleased. Normally that jungle buzzard is less kind to her than he is to me. She looked up at me and tried to smile.

"Wish you wouldn't do that."

"Am I doing it wrong?"

"No. But you're not people. Be content to be the brightest and best ratwoman who ever lived. Be true to yourself." I felt like somebody's dad, spouting clichés. Then, of course, I felt really awful because I was old enough to understand what the clichés were all about. Embarrassment followed that as I remembered the cocksure boys we'd been when we were getting showered with the stupid stuff that turned out to be Joe Everyman's way of trying to pass along his accumulated wisdom.

*She is young, Garrett. And she has only just escaped a state closely approximating slavery. She will need time and numerous opportunities to shore up her belief in herself.*

Old Bones has a soft spot for Singe, too. Though he'd never admit that if it were suggested aloud. He'd never confess to any form of emotional vulnerability or sentimental weakness.

I kept thinking about old men and clichés. And I kept trying to avoid considering how often the Dean Man threw those things my way. Because I resented his advice almost as much as I'd resented advice from men of my father's generation when I was fifteen. I guess neither the old men nor the young men ever learn, but they keep on trying.

Dean nearly beat us to the Dead Man's room with the refreshments. I got a lamp going. Singe dragged in a special chair I'd had made that let her sit without having to worry about her troublesome tail. In moments she and I were hard at work. On the tea and sandwiches.

"Damn!" I woofed around a glob of bread and ham. "I didn't realize how hungry I was. The effects of that knockout spell must be all the way worn off now."

Singe grunted. She didn't have time for anything else. Once she gulped down everything Dean didn't nibble and I didn't devour, she looked around like she hoped there was still a whole roast pig she'd overlooked. I knew a reinforced battalion of young women who'd gladly kill, and who'd certainly hate Singe, for her ability to eat and eat and never gain an inappropriate ounce.

There are no fat ratpeople.

The Dead Man had me tell my story first.

I have a knack for accurate recollection. I provided the details I believed were necessary for an understanding of events while the Dead Man observed those events as memories drifting across the surface of my mind. He asked only a handful of questions, waiting until I was finished talking to go to the first. He seemed particularly interested in even the most minute details of the silver elves' sorceries.

*At first blush I would have to agree with Mr. Dotes' assessment that those people are not elves, Garrett. Perhaps they belong to a single family of unusual breeding. A mixture of human and kef sidhe sounds plausible, considering their descriptions. Though their apparel seems most unusual. Let us examine the materials you managed to recover at your last contact site. All three of you, please. So that I may have the benefit of three divergent viewpoints and minds and sets of eyes.*

Once scattered atop the little table that is one of the few pieces of furniture in the Dead Man's room my plunder did not appear especially exciting. Because he was able to see the inside of my head, anyway, I admitted, "It seems to be mostly trash."

Having contemplated the take through our several viewpoints, Old Bones responded, *You are correct, Garrett. The silver people did abandon what they considered to be waste.*

How did he know?

*Through exactly the same process you used to come to that identical conclusion, supplemented by experience and unlimited intellect. It is a pity, however, that neither of you can recall the exact circumstances of the kidnappers' final escape.*

"A huge pity," I grumped. My headache remained on duty, totally devoted. Singe, though smitten harder at the time, had recovered completely already.

The Dead Man must've been more interested in events than he let on. When I started feeling sorry for myself and lusting after a beer he interfered with nature. He reached inside my head and did something that made the pain fade away. Some. Enough. Though a reminder remained in the background, eager to come back.

*What can we tell from the kidnappers' trash?* the Dead Man asked.

I couldn't tell a thing other than that they were no more fastidious than any other Karentine subject.

Singe sniffed each item yet again before carefully showing us her best imitation human shrug. From its look she'd practiced a lot. Ratpeople don't move like that normally.

She said, "This all smells very cold. Very sterile. There is no soul in it. There is no magic."

That was an interesting observation, considering what we'd seen and suffered. But I kept my thoughts to myself. Singe needed her confidence. And for all I really knew, she was right on the mark.

*She might be indeed, Garrett.*

I scowled his way. He was not supposed to eavesdrop on the inside of my head when I wasn't reporting.

*I am not prying into your mind. I just know how you think. I believe that it is now time to interview Mr. Bic Gonlit. His place in all this appears to be anomalous. Though I do have several hypotheses about what could be transpiring. His testimony should tell me which of those I can reasonably discard.*

"Why do I get the feeling that I'm going to do all the work, inviting him in?"

*Perhaps because you are irrationally pessimistic. Your part will require very little work, Garrett. I will be the one forced to stretch himself to his limits after you have invested just a few minutes in rounding him up and bringing him here. Be sure you take your convincing stick.*

"Never leave home without one." That's my partner. Like some kind of priest or professor, his vegetating is hard and honorable work. All my sweat and agony is barely worth a mention because what I do involves occasionally engaging a muscle.

# 17

Bic Gonlit had no intention of cooperating. Bic Gonlit could pick his dogs up and put them down when he was scared. Who'd have thought a little round guy with chubby, stubby legs could lead me on such a long chase?

Not me. Not before I lived it.

After several blocks I was glad the Dead Man had insisted on sending the Goddamn Parrot out to scout for me. By then it was obvious that Bic Gonlit could see in the dark. And I could not, which wasn't a major news flash. And the people of my neighborhood aren't rich enough to maintain adequate streetlamps.

The multicolored chicken did his part. He kept up a running lot of howling and cursing, some evidently adapted from the cant of old-time formal hunts. Highbrow and embarrassing. And, likely, everybody he woke up would assume that it was all my fault.

There'd be complaints. There'd be angry presentations. There'd be intemperate talk about chasing me out of the neighborhood. That would be followed by calmer heads appealing for reason. The older residents all know I share my place with a cranky dead Loghyr. An *irritated* cranky dead Loghyr can make life a lot more unpleasant for a lot of people for a long time. Why go looking for trouble?

I needed to stop playing around. I needed to put on a burst of speed that would nail the fat man.

I should've planned for this phase before I let everybody go home.

Just off the Arsenal High Street, a little my way from the

brewery district, is a small remnant of old-time imperial TunFaire that wasn't consumed in the Great Fire. It's known as Prune Tastity for reasons nobody recalls anymore. Prune Tastity is a sort of museum of ancient times, all cramped-together buildings and covered alleyways barely wide enough to let the air circulate. Following the fire wider alleys and streets were mandated by law.

There is less disease in areas where the buildings are farther apart, too.

The wonder buzzard's shrieks told me my quarry was going to try to lose us both by ducking into Prune Tastity's tangle of covered alleyways.

I've been in there a few times. The place is a maze, at times rising five stories high. What Gonlit apparently didn't realize was that I was familiar enough with Prune Tastity to know that there're only a handful of entrances to the maze. He'd gone in the far side hoping I'd follow and get lost. If he meant to leave without running into me again he'd have to come out not far from where I stood listening to the Goddamn Parrot's progress report.

I got myself into position with minutes to spare. I used every second to get more wind back into my lungs. I needed my breathing under control if Gonlit wasn't going to hear me puffing for a block before he arrived.

I needn't have worried. Bic was puffing so hard himself that he couldn't have heard the ringing of the bell that's supposed to announce the end of the world. His head was down, his arms and legs were pumping, and he wasn't even making a fast walk anymore. But he was still moving. He sounded like he was going to expire if he didn't take a break and concentrate on his breathing.

I timed my move, caught his collar as he shuffled past. He made one feeble attempt to get away, then gave up. And I mean gave up completely. He just folded up on the street and refused to do anything but gasp for air.

Ten minutes later he was still curled up like a pillbug, daring me to make him do anything he didn't want to do. He seemed confident he knew enough about me to be sure I wouldn't kill him for being uncooperative.

Morley is right. I need to become less predictable. And I need to develop a more savage reputation.

Because of the Dead Man's reminder I had not left the house without my convincing stick, eighteen inches of oak with a pound of lead in its active end. It proved useful on this unfriendly night.

I tapped my new friend just below the kneecap on each leg,

not hard enough to break anything. Just hard enough to turn his legs to water temporarily. I didn't want him able to put up much of a fight when I took his precious boots.

He understood before I got the first boot off. He started yelping. He called for help. He begged for mercy. The Goddamn Parrot came down and chimed in, carrying on loudly in several obviously nonhuman voices. Not that any witnesses were likely to drop their street sense in order to jump in and rescue any of us. That was not the way of the city.

"You sonofabitch, you want to keep your pretty boots, you'd better get real cooperative real sudden." I thumped Mr. Gonlit once atop each shoulder, briskly, not far from the sides of his neck.

Instantly, Bic began to have trouble lifting his arms.

The little man was tough in his way. He never stopped struggling—until I dragged the second boot off him. Then he went limp again. Without volunteering to make my life any easier.

"Bic, I'm gonna take your shoes home with me. Maybe give me a good shine." It had been my intention to drag him along with me, too, but I'd just heard a troubling sound, one I'd honestly never expected to hear. But rumors had been circulating for weeks so I recognized it in plenty of time.

The sound was a whistle. Rather like the shrill of a boatswain's pipe. Somebody from the guard's foot patrol wasn't far away and he'd heard that there was trouble. He was summoning assistance.

Changing times. Relway and Block just have way too many ideas for advancing the case of law and order. Not that I mind too much when they interfere in someone else's business. But my business is mine.

I said, "My friend and I have to run. I'll take good care of your boots. You know where to find them. When the mood hits you, drop by the house. You can pick them up."

I was drawing to an inside straight, betting his boots were that important to him. I would've talked more but now whistles from several sources were sounding closer and closer.

I headed for home. I was halfway there before I realized that the Goddamn Parrot wasn't with me. When I got home I went straight to the Dead Man to find out why.

*The manner in which you dealt with the exigencies of your situation seems well chosen. However, it did leave considerable leeway in the hands of Mr. Gonlit. It seemed prudent to keep watching eyes and a nagging voice somewhere near him. Lest he surrender to a fit of common sense and just abandon his boots.*

*You do have those still? Excellent. Would you summon Miss Pular? She is in the kitchen helping herself to a snack. Dean has retired for the night.*

*We will try to discover why the boots mean so much to our rotund nemesis.*

*Did you, by the by, discover how it was that he was able to see in the dark?*

" 'Fraid not. The question went right out of my head when I heard those whistles."

Old Bones was wide-awake and in rare form, nothing escaping the notice of his several minds. I wasn't going to be allowed anything less than wide-awake myself until he sucked up all the outside information he wanted.

# 18

Singe sniffed Gonlit's boots. That wasn't a task I envied her. Their fragrance had been less than appealing while I was toting them, even carried at the ends of their strings. But ratpeople don't seem to be repelled by odors the same way we humans are. Nor are they offended by the same scents.

Hard to credit in some cases but I've been around Singe long enough to know that it's true.

The famous Gonlit boots had soles layered more than two inches thick. They had fake glass emeralds and rubies and little brass rivet heads all over them. I thought they looked pretty shabby these days. Maybe old Bic was farther down on his luck than rumor suggested. He wasn't so big-time that popular interest tracked his every step.

At one time the boots had been white. At one time, so the story went, Bic Gonlit had dressed all in white, even unto the extremity of an all-white, wide-brimmed version of the Unorthodox missionary's hat.

That would have been years ago, though, when Bic would have been more prosperous because he was less well known. That would have been during the days before he learned that having a signature look was no advantage in the bounty-hunting business. Your quarry would see you coming.

The boots themselves, by reputation, were enchanted. How so remained an open question. They hadn't added anything to his getaway speed. But, on the other hand, he'd been able to see in the dark.

Maybe we'd winkle out all the facts when Bic came to reclaim his treasures.

The Dead Man and Singe communed about those boots.

I jumped suddenly. My eyes had fallen shut. I don't know for how long. Long enough for the lamp to have gone out. Now just a single candle burned on the top shelf of the Dead Man's memorabilia case. He and Singe weren't troubled by the shortage of light.

*Garrett.*

I heard a racket up front.

One of the two nuisances had awakened me.

The Dead Man wasn't going anywhere. I got up and stalked to the front door. The racket there persisted. I began thinking that maybe Mr. Gonlit needed a whipping, just to remind him of his manners.

I used the peephole for its dedicated purpose.

Surprise. That wasn't Bic Gonlit trying to make my neighbors dislike me even more. That was three or four guys who had no manners to be reminded of. The loudest was none other than our beloved chief of the city Guards, Colonel Westman Block himself.

It'd been a while since we two had crossed paths. He seemed to have grown in that time, both in stature and in confidence.

I turned away on the theory that he could use a little deflation.

*Allow the colonel to enter, Garrett. That will serve us better in the long run.*

"Took you long—" Block snarled as I swung the door inward. "Damn! Garrett!" he barked when I swung it right back shut, bruising his nose.

*Garrett!*

"Just a little courtesy lesson." I opened the door again.

Colonel Block appeared more flustered than angry. And his goons—three gorillas damned near as big as Saucerhead Tharpe—wore dazed looks, as though they were asleep on their feet, with their eyes open.

"Good evening, Colonel. How can I help you?"

Evidently the shock had been enough to startle Block into a case of the courtesies. That or some light touch from the Dead Man. "Yes. We've had reports of some unusual events, Garrett."

"This's TunFaire. We have wizards and priests enough here to supply the world with weird."

I led Block into the Dead Man's room while we talked. His goons remained outside, still as memorial pillars. He replied,

"But in this instance there's reason to believe that you might be involved."

"What? Me? How come I get blamed for everything?"

"Because someone fitting your description, accompanied by persons fitting the descriptions of known associates of yours, including a cursing parrot, was seen near the sites of several unusual incidents. I'm disinclined to accept the explanation that your evil twin was out there trying to scuttle your reputation. You don't have one."

*Go ahead and tell him the truth, Garrett.*

I've cooperated with the authorities on most occasions. It rankles but, to be honest, it's never been that huge an inconvenience.

So I told him the whole story. Sort of. Almost. In the young peoples' abridged form.

Then he told me a story. His was a lot shorter.

"Coming up here we ran into a crowd of ratpeople. Twenty or thirty of them, trying to work up their nerve for some villainy. When they recognized us they scattered like roaches. A couple of my guys mentioned seeing a little fat man running with them. Either one of you want to say something about that?"

"I would if I could, boss. But I don't have any idea."

The Dead Man had no comment at all.

Block asked, "Any ideas about these lights in the sky, these flying helmets and whatnot? People keep seeing them and getting upset about them so other people keep telling me that I have to do something about them. Nobody has any suggestions about what the hell that might be and I don't have any brilliant ideas of my own."

"You've started to regress. You had your language so cleaned up you could've fit in at court."

"That's what's causing it. Polite society. Those folks have more demands, and can make bigger pains in the ass of themselves, than any three normal human beings."

"Who's telling you to do something about those things? Do they really think you'd interfere in wizards' experiments?"

"Get real. It's wizards doing the demanding, Garrett. They can't figure out what's going on. So they expect Colonel Westman Block of His Majesty's Royal TunFairen Civil Guards to unravel the mystery for them. Meantime, Wes Block can't keep his own feet untangled. But they don't need to know that. How much does the Prose kid know?"

I'd been afraid we'd get to that as soon as he'd mentioned the failed investigations of our lords of the Hill. "I don't know. Not much more than squat, but he'd like everybody to think he's in on the secrets of the universe. He's a loon. Eighty percent of what he says is complete 'I-want-you-to-think-I'm-special' hooey."

"Does he know where to find those stray elves he picked up?"

"My guess is, he can get in touch somehow if it's critical. But we don't know where he is."

"Yes. That's right, isn't it? That other bunch snatched the boy up. So you say." He gave me a look filled with suspicion. He was succumbing to Relway's Disease. Trusting no civilian.

Sometimes I think Deal Relway divides the population into three categories. The smaller two consist of known criminals and of policemen, with a very fuzzy boundary in between. The other, largest category includes all the rest of us. And we're all just crooks who haven't been found out yet. And we should be treated accordingly.

Block eyed the Dead Man. "Is he asleep again?" Old Chuckles had shown no sign of sentience since the colonel's arrival.

"An excellent question. Lately I'm getting random moments of nonsense but nothing consistent. I'm worried. He may be on that last level ground before he hits the slippery slope down."

Block scowled, still suspicious. He had heard this one before.

I said, "Indulge my curiosity. How come you're out prowling the streets yourself? I thought you guys had a division of labor where the colonel stays back at the Al-Khar snoozing and harassing prisoners while the rest of the guys do all the real work."

Block didn't respond right away. He glanced at the Dead Man again, definitely wondering if he could get away with telling me less than the whole truth. "When your name came up I knew it was bound to get exciting. It made sense to get close to the center of the action right at the beginning."

I didn't need the Dead Man to tell me that Block was dealing me a steaming hot load. The Hill might not be behind the flying lights and pots but somebody up there wanted to be involved. And when the Hill wants something even its biggest detractors put on a show of flashing heels and flying elbows. Not many people relish the notion of spending the rest of their lives dead and being tortured.

Which is no contradiction where the top-ranked sorcerers are involved.

You might, by a stretch, be able to say that Colonel Block and I are friends. Not thick and thin, hell and high water, blood brother friends but guys who like and respect one another, who are willing to lend a helping hand to one another, where it's possible to do so.

It was conceivable that Block was doing so at the moment, so that I wouldn't walk into something entirely blind. And so that, in return, he could tap me for a little information that would keep him in good odor with the people prodding him from behind.

I can do that for him. It's worked out for us in the past. The tricky part is keeping outsiders from forming the idea that we can get along.

Block observed, "You really are a big old barrel of nothing, aren't you . . . ? What the hell is that?"

The pixies out front had declared war. Possibly on themselves, they were so raucous.

They'd been silent since my return. So much so that I'd begun to suspect an evil influence at work.

"Pixies," I told Block. "I seem to have adopted a mob. Against my will. I'd better see what's got them excited." Inasmuch as the Dead Man didn't seem inclined to inform me.

I heaved out of my chair and headed up front. In the small front room the Goddamn Parrot was asleep already, muttering in his diabolical dreams. No doubt he had protested his recent utilization by making a mess Dean would nag me about for weeks.

Block followed me. Through the peephole I watched one of his escorts fling something upward. I said, "Your boys are tormenting my pixies."

"I'd better get them out of here before it gets out of hand, then. Don't hesitate to let me know if you learn anything useful."

"You wouldn't accidentally let slip which sorcerer types are interested in my problem, would you?"

"Not hardly. Not even if I knew. But I think you can safely assume that just about anybody up there would be interested in gaining the secrets of flight." He opened the door, went out growling. "What the devil do you men think you're doing?"

"They started it. They were throwing . . ."

*Chunk!* The door cut it off.

# 19

I returned to the Dead Man's room. "So how come we needed to chase Block and his pals away? And how the hell did the God-damn Parrot get back in the house?"

*Mr. Bic Gonlit is out there awaiting an opportunity to reclaim his magical boots. Colonel Block was unable to add anything more to our meager knowledge.*

*Miss Pular opened the door for Mister Big while you were napping.*

"*Did* Block add anything to our meager knowledge?" I didn't like that business about Singe opening the door with nobody to back her up. Old Bones isn't always attentive to detail.

*Only internal confirmation of most of what he told you. The people on the Hill have become exceptionally interested in un-usual celestial events of late. In Block's mind they're convinced the flying objects represent a threat from foreign sorcerers. Al-though a minority believe that a rogue cabal of Karentine wizards are behind what has been happening, hoping to elbow the rest out of the inner circles of power. Whatever the truth, the root concern is those people's fear for their positions.*

"Oh, they wouldn't like to lose their power, would they? Do I need to go out and catch Bic Gonlit?" Because I was bone-tired. I was ready to hit the sack, skipping the evening's last five or six mugs of beer.

*Judging by your stunning success in that direction before, per-haps your ideal course would be to wait for him to come to you. He does seem to be extremely superstitious about his boots. They are a controlling factor in his life.*

Singe came in from the kitchen carrying a tray. She'd hidden out there while Block was in the house. And she hadn't wasted her time. She'd made more sandwiches. And had drawn me a mug off the keg in the cold well.

I gave her a look at my raised eyebrow trick as I went to work on a sandwich. Her whiskers twitched and pulled back in the ratkind equivalent of turning pink.

"It's all right, Singe. You're welcome. Old Bones. I'm not going to be able to keep my eyes open much longer. If I get him in here can you handle the interview?"

His exasperation with mortal weakness became palpable. *Get him in here. That is the key first step. Then you two can run off to bed whilst I labor. . . .*

Singe squeaked. Her whiskers went back so far it looked like they were about to pop out.

"He doesn't mean *that,* Singe. He just means sleep. You take the guest room on the third floor." She was familiar with it. She'd used it before. "I'll see if Block's gone."

*He is. Though an observer remained behind and is seated on Mrs. Cardonlos' stoop, pretending to be drunk. He is about to fall asleep at his post.*

I went to the front door certain that any sleepiness being experienced by Colonel Block's man had an artificial origin. Unlike my own.

Singe followed me. She carried a lamp. Its light silhouetted me when I opened the door.

Bic Gonlit arrived five minutes later. He was about as hangdog as it's possible for a man to look.

"Bic, old buddy," I said, "why'd you want to go and bring a bunch of ratpeople around to my place?"

"You still got my boots?"

"They're in a place of honor. But I'm going to burn them and scatter their ashes on the river if I don't hear some explanations."

"You don't have a reputation for being that hard, Garrett."

"You've got a rep as a bring them in alive kind of bounty hunter, Bic. So besides the answer to my ratpeople question— which I want to hear real soon now—I'd sure like to know why you're hanging around me. But where are my manners? Come on in. We don't want to do business out here. The Guard keeps a watch on me."

Gonlit jumped. He looked back nervously. He sure was a worried little man. And barefoot, too.

He slipped past me, taking one final troubled look back as he did so.

"Tell me about the rats, Bic."

He stared at Pular Singe. "Because there's a huge reward out for her. Reliance wants her bad. I thought I'd get my boots back during the confusion when Reliance's gang were grabbing her."

"Plus you'd've made a few marks," I said. "I appreciate your honesty. So I'm not going to hold a very big grudge. All you need to do is explain why you were hanging around in the alley out back and just had to slug me. We're going in here." I held the door to the Dead Man's room. Bic's boots were in there, sitting on the table next to Singe's sandwiches. But I had a feeling it would be a while before they enjoyed a loving reunion with Bic's feet. "Take a seat, brother."

"I just want my boots, Garrett."

"We all have dreams, Bic. Sometimes we have to give a little something to attain them. What about the alley?"

"What alley?"

"Now we're going to play tough?" Exasperated, I snapped, "The goddamn alley behind my house. Where you bushwhacked me and pounded me over the head with a sap."

Gonlit looked at me like I'd just sprouted antlers.

*Garrett.*

I jumped. So did Bic and Singe.

"Yeah?"

*Bizarre as it may seem, the man really does have no idea what you are talking about. I now find myself examining the hypothesis that the Bic Gonlit you encountered in the alley was not the man who is here with us now. Either this man has a twin or what you ran into was the creature I sensed and set you to collect, somehow projecting an illusion based upon the expectations of Cypres Prose.*

*I now agree that it is time you went to bed. Have the man sit down.* Bic hadn't yet accepted my invitation. *Then go. I will see that he dozes off, too.*

Pular Singe made an offer that was difficult to refuse because she was so fragile emotionally. "Not tonight, Singe. I'm so tired I'd fall asleep in the middle of things. And you'd get your feelings hurt. While you kept telling me that it was all your fault." She was getting used to hearing me yell at her about embracing blame for what other people did.

That wasn't as honest as I should've been. But it did buy me time to think about an answer that would leave Singe with her tender dignity intact, feeling good about herself.

The more I considered it the more I suspected that I'd need the Dead Man's help to work this one out. Singe was at an age and stage where she wasn't going to hear much from me that she didn't want to hear.

Though I must say my "not tonight, another time" response certainly seemed to ease her anxieties for the moment.

Maybe she wouldn't find the nerve to bring it up again.

# 20

Those damned pixies woke me up twice during the night. And both times I got a touch from the Dead Man indicating that we had a prowler outside. He didn't trouble himself enough to report what kind of prowler. And I was too groggy to care.

The pixies made good watchdogs. Yet if that was what I wanted I'd just as soon get something big but quiet that would eat the prowlers without waking me up or disturbing my neighbors.

It was near the crack of noon when I stumbled downstairs and found a sullen Dean sharing his kitchen with Pular Singe. Singe was at the table eating. She had dragged her custom chair in from the Dead Man's room.

Dean was doing dishes and wrestling with his prejudices. Not many folks have much use for ratpeople. I've always belonged to the majority myself. But I do try my best to contain my dislike. That's been a lot easier since Singe came along.

I mumbled, "You're going to get fatter than the Dead Man, Singe." I flopped into my own chair. "My head still hurts." Though a lot less than it had.

Dean said, "I've warned you and warned you to ease up on the beer, Garrett."

"It wasn't beer this time."

Dean rattled some dishes and snorted, not believing me.

"It's not. Singe can tell you. I got knocked out by some kind of wizardry a few times yesterday. And every time I woke up I had a worse headache than before."

"Then explain why I had to send out for a new keg this morning. It hasn't been ten days since you finished the last one."

"New keg? But the old one shouldn't be . . ."

Singe had developed a fierce interest in a fly doing acrobatics from the ceiling.

"And you don't have a bit of a hangover from all that, either. Do you, girl?"

She shook her head, tried one of her want-to-be human smiles.

"Gah! This's the cruelest of all cruel worlds." I would've teased her about selling her back to Reliance or something but she'd probably have taken me seriously.

Dean took his hands out of the water long enough to pour a mug of tea and set a breakfast platter in front of me. That was mostly seasonal fruit, accompanied by small chunks of cold ham.

A typical meal, really. Which left me wondering how Dean managed to produce so many dirty dishes, pots, and pans.

I downed a long slug of tea. There was something in that cup besides plain tea. It left a bitter taste underneath the honey. So Dean had counted on me showing up with a headache. Since he doesn't coddle my hangovers he must've been forewarned. So his fuss was all for form.

So the Dead Man was good for something after all.

Though he wouldn't have coddled a hangover, either.

Singe tried to fuss over me. Dean looked disgusted. I showed him my evil eye. Of all the females to pass through my kitchen the one he'd pick to dislike actively would be the only one who was willing to treat me special.

He was plenty willing to climb all over me when it came to me not treating every girl as if she was uniquely special.

I tossed back some more tea while thinking my house was turning into a nest of cranky old bachelors.

The pixies started acting up out front. Dean ignored them. He had his cutting board out and was getting ready to mutilate vegetables.

"You going to check that out?" I asked.

"No. Happens every fifteen minutes. If it means anything the thing in the other room will let us know."

If he wasn't asleep. The Dead Man has a habit of falling asleep, sometimes for months, usually at the most inconvenient times, businesswise.

I finished feeding. The medication in the tea had begun its work. The world seemed a less dark and cruel place already. "Singe, let's go see old Chuckles." Got to keep that premature optimism under control. And he was just the boy to rein it in.

"Hey, Old Bones. What's on the table today? Bic Gonlit. How you doing this morning, man? Dean get you something to eat?"

Whatever Dean put into the tea, maybe he used a little too much.

I got no response from the Dead Man. Gonlit did respond with a big scowl. "I want my boots, Garrett."

"I'm sure you do. They say you've got your whole personality tied up in those things. So why do you want to get them all filthy, romping around in the alley behind my house?"

Bic rolled his eyes. "Not again!"

*I have exhausted that line of inquiry, Garrett. Mr. Gonlit sincerely believes that he has never been in that alley. There is no shaking his conviction on that count. Therefore, I am inclined to believe him. However, he cannot account for his whereabouts at the time of the alley event. He is more troubled about that than we are.*

I wasn't troubled at all. "Maybe it was him being used by one of the silver guys the way you use the Goddamn Parrot."

*That possibility occurred to me. There is no residue in Mr. Gonlit's mind of the sort I would expect to find if he had been manipulated. What is there consists of hints that he may have been asleep. Inasmuch as he does not recall sleeping, we might reasonably suspect that the sleep was induced. Perhaps by the same means as were used on you yesterday.*

"All right. And?"

*The boy, Cyprus Prose, brought Mr. Gonlit's name into play first.*

I'd just been thinking that. Had Kip set us up somehow? Could the Dead Man have missed that while the kid was here?

*No.*

"Bic, did anybody hire you to hunt down a couple elves name of—"

"Lastyr and Noodiss. I'm tired of that one, too. Give me my damned boots."

*He believes he never heard those names before he came in here last night.*

I growled. The excitement and optimism were beginning to fade. "Then how come he was following me and you were following him with the Goddamn Parrot?"

*Are you genuinely certain you want Mr. Gonlit to hear more about my abilities than you have given away already?*

"All right. I wasn't thinking."

*Not a first, I might note.*

"You might. You might also answer me."

*He was following Miss Pular, Garrett. Mr. Big was following you. Insofar as I have been able to determine, their appearance of being together was caused by the proximities of yourself and Miss Pular.*

"There've been too damned many coincidences already, Old Bones. You know I believe in them but I don't like them. Next thing you're going to tell me is that good buddy Bic just happened to stumble over Singe as she and Saucerhead were coming to help me out. And being the ingenious fellow that he is, Bic just latched right on. Seizing the day, as it were."

*That is quite close to the truth. As Mr. Gonlit knows it. Except for the fact that he was hunting Miss Pular long before we became involved in events. He had traced her to the area where we had her hidden. My call for assistance, unfortunately, brought her out just in time to be spotted.*

I generated harrumphing old man noises. I didn't like the way things were going.

*You never do. But you have a knack for blundering around, knocking things over, until everything works out.*

I harrumphed some more. Practicing. I have plans for an extremely extended old age.

*I was profoundly embarrassed by the fact that it took me so long to discover Mr. Gonlit's presence on your backtrail.*

"Oh-oh." The Dead Man seldom admits lacks, flaws, or shortcomings. He is, after all, the most perfect of that perfect race, the Loghyr. Just ask him.

When he messes up it's always someone else's fault.

Behold! *Then I began to understand. The description I had was entirely inadequate.*

"So you didn't figure it was unusual for a guy to be turning up everywhere Singe and I did?" It really is pointless to indicate the holes in his excuse-making. At best he just ignores you.

*I should like to engage in a much deeper look into your encounter with the false Bic Gonlit of the alleyway. It is entirely possible that you may have noticed something we passed over as trivial when we were confident that we knew who your conqueror was.*

The real Bic Gonlit had grown very restless. "Let me give the man his soles back so he can go on his way." Charged up with uncertain ideas about his place in the grander scheme, his head a nest of confused, false memories.

*Turn the bird loose once Mr. Gonlit is a block down the street.*

"Of course. There's always hope he'll run into a parrot-eating eagle. Bic, here're your boots. Get going. Stay away from me and stay away from Pular Singe. I guarantee you, Reliance's reward isn't worth it. Belinda Contague used to be my girlfriend."

Bic went pale. He'd heard that rumor. I was still alive. So maybe I could conjure the helpmate of death.

*Foolish, Garrett.*

He was right. That was a stupid threat. If word got back to Belinda I could end up on crutches. If she happened to be in a generous mood.

I waved bye-bye from the stoop. Then I flung our lowlife, low-profile spy into the air. Then I rejoined Singe and the Dead Man.

# 21

Returning to life after having the Dead Man dig around in the muck in the cellars of my mind was less painful than getting whomped unconscious by a silver elf's spell but it did leave me feeling just as lousy emotionally. It left me wanting nothing more than to go back to bed, where I could curl up in a ball and suck my thumb.

That kind of invasion doesn't happen often. And never happens without my permission. But each time it does I swear I'll never let it happen again, no matter how desperate the crisis. But when the time comes I always go ahead, trusting him and knowing I'll get through it. And maybe it's even good for me in the long run. That dark, unhappy memories always seem to settle a little deeper and a little more comfortably, like a bucket full of gravel when you shake and beat it.

I took some cleansing breaths. Some of that martial arts stuff of Morley's really does work if you let yourself believe in it. I found a place removed from my center by just a few miles. "Did we learn anything that makes it worth all my misery?"

*I believe we did. Though it is indeed a small thing at first glimpse.*

He didn't go on. He wanted me to ask him to show off his brilliance. I wasn't feeling patient enough to get involved in the usual games. "And that was?"

*The Bic Gonlit in our alleyway was not wearing the signature boots. You had mentioned missing seeing them earlier but at that time I overlooked the chance that you had not seen them because they were not there. At that time there was no reason to look be-*

*yond the obvious. Also, the Gonlit you met out back was several inches taller than this specimen, even without the leather lifts.*

"So where does that leave us?"

*Essentially still lost but now forearmed with the knowledge that the opposition might appear to us in the guise of someone we know. But not in the form of a perfect replica.*

Grumble. "Don't tell me it's shapeshifters again."

*I promise. There are no shapeshifters here. There does seem to be some remarkable illusory sorcery, however.*

"You said there wasn't any sorcery in the alley."

*I did. I do not believe there was. It is a conundrum, is it not?*

"Great. So good old Bic is innocent of everything more sinister than trying to score the bounty on Singe. Stipulating that, I want to know how come Kip knew the name and thought Gonlit was after his strange friends. And I'd like to know how that elf got to know Bic well enough to masquerade as him without Bic knowing there was anything going on."

*All excellent questions, Garrett. You are learning to think. Unfortunately, Mr. Gonlit does not have any of the answers. We will have to flush those out somewhere else. Inasmuch as we have no hope of uncovering a direct trail to the boy I suspect a visit to the mother has some chance of being productive.*

"You think she might know . . . ? I see. Anything she can give us could be a thread to pull or a pointer to a path that might lead to somebody who does have an idea where to look for the boy."

*Indeed. Which is why I suggest the mother. She may even have an idea where to find the mysterious Noodiss and his associate.*

A possibility that, no doubt, must've occurred to the people already in that hunt.

"I get the feeling these others are real amateurs." How much less gentle would have been the hunt had the Outfit been seeking the missing elves?

*True. Miss Pular should remain here. It is a certainty that Reliance has people watching the house.*

"Relway, too, probably."

*Just so.*

"Then maybe I shouldn't go out there, either." A career in the home-based beer-tasting industry sounded good at the moment.

*You are too concerned about your reputation. I will ensure that any spies remain ignorant of your departure.*

Once again, a hint that he had greater abilities than those to which he admitted. Though this was a trick he had used before, several times. I've never been sure how it works. It might blind everyone in the neighborhood to my movements.

Which would be handy if I had to raise some cash real fast.

I had been considering a career change. Why not become an invisible pickpocket?

The air seemed to crackle. Like the sharp whispering of river ice just starting to break up. My partner didn't approve of my thoughts. Not even with those being entirely in jest.

When this day was done I was going to get away from all these people. Maybe I'd get me off to one of the taverns where old Marines gather to slough off the dust of lesser mortals. Or possibly somewhere where I might glimpse a shapely ankle.

*Garrett, there will be no diversions, neither of the heart nor of the mind nor of the flesh, if you do not get out and try to find some threads that I can unravel while you are reviving your reputation as a rogue, a rake, and a wastrel.*

He did have a point.

# 22

I went to Playmate's stable first. He'd have to show me where to find Kip's family.

"I don't know if that'll do any good," Playmate said when I explained what I wanted. "I guarantee you his mother doesn't know anything useful. If she did she'd already have been out there wherever yanking those elves' ears till they talked."

"Thought they didn't have ears."

"Maybe they ran into Kayne Prose already."

"Hardcase, eh?"

"A very determined mom. You don't mess with her kids. Otherwise, she's just a hardworking widow looking for enough work to get by."

There're a lot of those in TunFaire, though in the final few, most desperate years of the war the Crown tried taking younger conscripts so there wouldn't be as many widows created.

"Uh . . ." I said. "I must be confused. You didn't say anything about her being a widow yesterday."

Playmate looked at me like he wondered if I was really that dumb. Widow is a euphemism as old as mothers without husbands. "She wouldn't brag about having three out-of-wedlock children by three different fathers, one of them maybe off the Hill. Though two of the fathers really are dead. And the maybe wizard probably is. He hasn't been seen since the supply boat he was aboard left the TunFaire waterfront. When Kip was still a bun in the oven. The *Leitmark* never made it to Full Harbor."

"Pirates?"

Playmate shrugged. "At this date it doesn't matter. Kayne has bad luck with men. They die on her. Or they go away. But she's an unswerving optimist. She keeps on trying. After Kip came along I finally managed to convince her she should invest in avoiding any more pregnancies. She owed that to the kids she already had."

"You sound like you might have a little emotion invested in the Prose family yourself."

"I like the kids. They turned out pretty good, considering. And Kayne is a good woman who doesn't really deserve everything she's suffered. But she does bring it on herself."

"Self-destructive, eh?" I might know a little about that myself.

"Definitely. But mainly in the area of men. She keeps rejecting everybody who might be good for her and welcoming the villains who're sure to treat her badly."

There might've been a slight hint of disappointment there. If so, it was so faint that I didn't think it was worth pursuing.

Time would tell me about Playmate and Kayne Prose. I was about to see how they acted around each other.

# 23

Leaving Playmate's stable, we walked about a mile toward the river, skirting Prune Tastity, to reach the southwestern-most fringe of the garment district. Which actually takes up less land area than Prune Tastity. It was on the fringe that we found Kip's mom.

Kayne Prose was doing seamstress work in a small co-op operated round the clock by teams of women whose situations were all much the same. They were all dirt-poor, with children, without husbands, without other salable skills, and most with too many miles on them to compete as prostitutes or taxi dancers. I found the atmosphere inside that place oppressive. The walls had become impregnated with despair.

But every woman there had an air of grim determination. They were survivors, those women, doing what they had to do. Same as me, back when it was crocodiles on the one hand, Venageti rangers on the other, and poisonous bugs, snakes, spiders, and bats everywhere else. Neither we, then, nor these women, now, would let the despair work its seduction. These ladies would battle on until doom sounded its final bell.

Give them the supreme compliment. They would've made good Marines.

There were eight women sewing when we arrived. I picked Kayne Prose out immediately. There was a lot of her in Kip. Only . . .

"Damn, Play. She's a looker. You sure . . . ? That woman's got three kids, one of them nineteen years old?" No doubt the weak light did her a favor but she didn't look much older than me. If that old. She *could* have competed in the flesh markets. And would've done pretty well, I'd guess.

Maybe it was the long blond hair that shone like that of a girl half her age. Maybe it was her skin, which seemed far too smooth for a woman of mature years. Maybe it was her face, which the hardships of poverty hadn't etched nearly as deeply as I would've expected. Maybe it was some sort of inner fire. There are those one-in-a-thousand people who just never seem to get old.

I guess I stood there stunned, maybe dribbling from the corner of my mouth, for a while, because I heard this whisper: "That's exactly how everyone reacts when they meet her for the first time."

Everyone male, I figured.

Kayne Prose's sparkling baby blues met mine. The twinkle there told me she could read my mind as surely as the Dead Man could. A tiny smile told me she didn't mind my sort of thinking, either.

Oh, the gods had been generous when they'd shaped Kayne Prose. And some real artists had gone in on the architecture. Nor had childbearing been unkind. There would be plenty of women ten, even fifteen years younger who'd just plain hate Kayne Prose for existing.

Seven of that sort were planted right there in that room.

"Hello, Play," she said. And, oh my, her voice was as deep and husky and sensual as Katie's. It turned my spine to water. And I was there on business. Feeling guilty because I'd let her son get spirited away. And she was fully aware of the effect she was having. It was an effect she'd been having on men for twenty-five years, probably.

I was willing to bet there was elven blood in her, no further than a grandparent away.

She said, "I can't get up. I fell behind yesterday. Who's your friend?" She looked me over like she was checking out vegetables at the market, yet from her it was flattering rather than offensive.

And the same from me right back.

She definitely liked being looked at. Which was probably a symptom of her problem.

Playmate's expression soured. Proof that there was substance to my earlier suspicion. I tried to rein in my boyish charm.

Playmate said, "Kayne, this's Garrett. The man who was going to help Kip. Now he's going to help us find Kip."

For a moment Kayne Prose turned entirely into a worried mother. She turned up a look I remembered from childhood. Which

left me nose to nose with the scary speculation that my mother
might have been capable of that other, nonmotherly behavior, too.

No. Never. She was Mom.

"Whatever I can do to contribute, I will, Mr. Garrett," she said.
All business now, I'm afraid. Well, almost all business. Kayne
Prose was incapable of stifling her sensual side.

Man.

I said, "I'm here because I don't know where else to start. Can
you talk while you work?" The place wasn't a sweatshop, it was a
co-op, but none of the women were pleased to have Playmate and
me upsetting their routine. Though a couple of them eyed Playmate like they were measuring him for a wedding suit.

It being a co-op there wouldn't be killer piecework quotas but,
still, for the women to make much income they'd have to put in
fourteen-hour days. They'd have some formula for a fair division
of the co-op's income.

"Talk away. But there ain't much I can tell you. If I knew anything I probably wouldn't've lost my kid. Those two goofballs
don't mean anything to me."

"Noodiss and Lastyr?"

"We know any other goofballs in this mess?"

"The four who weren't those two, that took your son. And the
three who tried and failed earlier." I didn't think the two crews
were the same. But I hadn't seen Playmate's female elves. Then,
inspired, I said, "Tell me about Bic Gonlit." If Kip knew the guy,
then so might she.

Pay dirt.

Her needle slowed for a moment, possibly snagging somehow.
She studied her last stitch for half a second. Then she glanced up
at Playmate. Her stitching fell back into rhythm. "What do you
want to know?"

"Everything." There was something here. Maybe nothing I'd
find useful but definitely a connection.

Again she glanced at Playmate. So I did the same, only to
have him shrug in response, then ask, "Will you be more comfortable if I go outside, Kayne?"

Kayne Prose winced.

I doubted that the woman was long on sensitivity. Life
wouldn't have afforded her the luxury. But she had something on
her mind. She thought Playmate would be disappointed or hurt.
She cherished his good opinion. Or maybe needed it as an emotional foundation stone. Whatever, she could see some value in a

man who was too good to become an active accomplice in her game of self-destruction.

Playmate is one of those guys who is just too damned nice for his own good. And everyone in the place recognized that Playmate felt that his good could be the woman who looked like she had made a pact with the agents of darkness. Except for Kayne Prose herself, of course.

Kayne Prose told Playmate, "You don't need to go, Play. If I'm embarrassed by something I tell Mr. Garrett, then I deserve the full impact. Mr. Garrett, I enjoyed—for want of a more appropriate description—a brief relationship with Bic Gonlit not long ago." Her fingers flew, sewing a sleeve onto something for a child maybe six years old. Something for a little girl who would never suffer the miseries and indignities so intimately known to the woman who had assembled her dress. "I don't believe he saw it in the same light as I did, though." With an intonation implying that they never do.

"Interesting." The Dead Man hadn't mentioned this tantalizing tidbit. Did he want me to find out for myself? Or wasn't there anything interesting there? Or maybe Bic hadn't remembered because it wasn't important to him. "Was this anytime recently?"

Kayne nodded. "I ended it three days ago. When I realized he was using me." Damn! The woman made the act of breathing a sensual promise. No wonder old Bic took her wrong.

The rest of the women adjusted their positions as Kayne finished, each commenting without saying a word. Possibly unfairly. I didn't get the feeling that Kayne Prose made herself a public utility, only that she really enjoyed men but always conspired with her own inner devils to make sure she picked the ones who would be bad for her.

"I see. This was a good idea, Play. I've learned more in the last three minutes than I did up till then. Kayne, did it get physical? Did he ever take his boots off?" Rumor suggested that Bic might not.

Kayne Prose turned bright red, something her co-op pals probably found amazing. I wondered if that would have happened had Playmate not been with me.

"He . . . He had a problem. He said . . . What do you mean about boots?"

"Bic Gonlit's big legend revolves around his custom-made, hugely ugly, possibly magical boots. They're boots a ratman wouldn't steal. They're white with fake gems all over them. They

have thick elevator soles. You're probably a good four inches
taller than Bic in his bare feet."

"He's as tall as me. And I never noticed any special boots. Or
shoes. Or anything else."

I exchanged glances with Playmate.

"What?" Kayne demanded.

I told her, "That wasn't the real Bic Gonlit, then. That was one
of the elves who're looking for Kip's friends. He uses some kind
of sorcery to make people think they're seeing Bic Gonlit. But the
illusion doesn't include the boots. Or enough of the short."

"You know, you're right. I never thought about it before. When
we were kids Bic always had a thing about his shoes."

"You've known him a long time?"

"Not well. But since I was Kip's age. We grew up on the same
street. I saw him around sometimes. We said 'Hi.' I never paid him
much attention. And he never paid me any. I thought that was because he might be a little . . . fey. Like maybe he didn't know what
he wanted to be. And he was always kind of a jerk. But a month ago
he started coming around and acting like he was really interested.
He'd gotten a case of the manners and he could talk a pretty good
game. But he never did nothing else. Sooner or later, and mostly
sooner, the conversation got around to Kip and his friends. He was
always asking questions. A man who never does nothing but talk
about your kids don't stay real interesting and ain't much fun."

You hear that, Play? I thought. This one has a "me" streak.
And it's what keeps causing her problems. Clever men would play
to it. And would think less of her because they were able to.

"I stand cautioned. But I do have to bring the brats up some in
order to get my job done."

One of the women groaned dramatically.

Playmate blessed the lot with a righteous glower. He drew
himself up stiffly erect, like he was about to go on a rant about
hellfire and sin and chucking first rocks.

I asked, "Kip did know this Bic, too?"

"Better than I did. He figured out right away that Bic just
wanted to get next to the two spooky critters."

"Lastyr and Noodiss."

"Still the ones, buddy." The furnace wasn't burning nearly as
hot as it had.

I'd managed to work myself down off the A list.

"You have any idea how I could find this Bic Gonlit? Could
you get ahold of him somehow if you wanted?"

She thought about her answer for a while. I'd begun to suspect that her lights didn't burn too bright and that the woman was something of a flake besides. More factors contributing to her string of failed relationships.

The substance behind the beauty and the intense sensuality was thin. Which I wouldn't find all that big a handicap most of the time. But, businesswise, it makes for endless problems.

From the corners of my eyes I noted the other women watching to see how long it would take me to catch on—and if it would matter. Maybe with a touch more malice toward me than toward Kayne Prose. In some ways they might live vicariously through Kayne. Kayne wasn't afraid to indulge herself.

She let me look and think for a while, probably so I could reflect on what I was talking myself out of, before she said, "Yeah. Play, take Mr. Garrett over to my place. Rhafi can show you guys where Bic used to hole up. And if the creep is still there, break a couple limbs for me. All of them if he don't give Kip back."

I was about to explain that it wasn't likely the false Bic Gonlit had the boy. Playmate nudged me. That was irrelevant. It was time to go.

Good idea, too. Because, atop everything else, Kayne Prose had a kind of narcotic quality to her. I could see myself sliding into addiction. Just like my dusky pal.

I kept thinking that, if she hadn't had so many incompatible personality quirks, she could've set herself up for life by getting into the mistress racket. In a prime position.

That she was where she was, looking as good as she did, never having done better, was one more warning flag about the woman inside that marvellously attractive shell.

A long time ago, almost a whole day now, Playmate had told me that Cypres Prose's mom was different and had pointed to his temple. Based on information gleaned, I'd say the man was right. But that didn't stop me from wanting to turn right around and go back and try to score some points for the future.

# 24

Playmate asked, "What did you think of Kayne?"

"Honest answer, Play? I never saw her before in my life. But I wanted to trip her and beat her to the floor. And ten seconds after that I just wanted to beat her. And ten seconds after that I was completely confused about what I wanted. And right now the animal side of my soul is screaming at me not to walk away from this wonderful chance. There's a perverse, self-destructive urge in there somewhere that she just shrieks out to."

He wasn't offended. "That's how a lot of men react. You a little faster than most, but that's just you being you. And after years of studying Kayne Prose I think it's all because of what's going on inside her. She doesn't just hurt herself in these doomed relationships. And the harder it is on the guys, the harder they try to make it work."

We were strolling. Playmate needed to air out some thoughts. It was clear that he was a Kayne Prose addict and willing to risk destruction. And maybe Kayne Prose thought too much of Playmate to give him a hit of poison.

People are the strangest creatures.

"What's it all mean?" I asked, just to keep open the windows of his mental house.

"I think it means that Kayne has a low-grade form of what the Dead Man has. The mind thing." Which could mean *another* wizard in the woodpile, a generation further back. "Just enough to read you faintly and to touch you just as weakly. Without knowing it on a conscious level. But using it all the time when men are around. In such a way that whatever is going on inside her will be reflected right back at her from outside. And maybe it'll feed on it-self if it starts running into something dark."

I considered. "You could be right." I started trying to compare, in my head, Kayne Prose's impact with the jolt my friend Katie could deliver. Katie can reduce this man to jelly with just a look. When Katie gets interested there are no distractions. Katie is the closest I've ever come to having had a religious epiphany.

I'd just considered that to be a matter of focus. But maybe it was something more. Maybe there was a weak, crude mental con-nection involved.

Playmate said, "It's just a hypothesis." With a tone so defen-sive that an apology was implied.

"A damned good hypothesis, I'd say. You ought to get com-pletely alone with her sometime, no distractions whatsoever, and test it out."

He sputtered.

"Play? You're embarrassed?"

"I'm not that kind of guy, Garrett."

"Maybe you ought to be. Tell me about Kayne's other kids. Are they problem folks like their mother and brother?"

"Not like their mother and brother. But problems enough. You'll like Cassie."

He didn't tell me much more. But he was right about Cassie. Cassie was a very likeable child indeed.

# 25

Cassie Doap was nineteen. Physically, Cassie was her mother a decade and a half younger, with the overpowering sensuality less controlled. Cassie Doap would break hearts just by going out where men could see her and understand that they would live out their years never having gotten any closer than they were at the moment when first they spotted her. Cassie Doap filled up a room with her presence but didn't spark the confusion that came with being around her mother.

Cassie Doap was smarter than Kayne, too. She understood the impact she had on men but had no intention of letting that define who and what she was. If Kayne Prose had done one useful thing for her daughter it was to set an example of how not to live her life.

All that I understood before Cassie Doap and I exchanged a word. Because Cassie Doap was an easy read. She wanted it that way.

I wondered what hidden, horrible flaw had a poor woman as gorgeous as this still living with her mother at her age. A hyperactive sense of self-worth?

Playmate performed the introductions. I managed to shake hands while avoiding stepping on my tongue, distracting myself by concentrating on business. I'm able to do that occasionally, though there're some who would have the world believe otherwise. It's just that the Kaynes and Cassies of the world make it so hard.

With Cassie there I almost overlooked her brother Rhafi. He wasn't the sort to attract much attention.

I told Cassie, "We're trying to find Kip. We think . . ."

"If Play hadn't guaranteed it was the real thing I would've bet the little twerp staged the whole damned thing."

"Why would you think that?" I noted that, unlike her mother, Cassie did nothing to make sure I understood just how much woman she was.

"Because that's the way his evil little pea brain works." Brother Rhafi nodded his head vigorously. "He lives inside his own imagination. Everything in there is high drama. Perilous chases, deadly duels, narrow escapes, beautiful princesses, and monstrous villains."

Playmate chuckled. "Sounds like your life, Garrett," he quipped.

"Except for a severe shortage of princesses, beautiful or otherwise. You wouldn't be a long-lost princess, left in a basket on your mother's doorstep, would you, Cassie?"

"Long-lost, anyway. If that was intended to be a compliment you get points for being a little more subtle than the usual, 'Gods, you're beautiful. Lie down because I think I love you.' "

"Must've been army type guys. Marines are all smooth and crafty." Had we just gotten a hint of why Cassie Doap hadn't wriggled her way into the sweet life? Everybody knows that's a girl's easiest way out of the poor side of town. Or was she in a constant rage because Fate had decreed she should be so beautiful that everybody wanted her? I don't recall ever having run into a woman who resented her own appeal, only women who hated their sisters for having more of it than they did. But I could understand the notion, in principle. In someone who could, genuinely, separate self from body.

Possibly Kayne's past behavior had loaded Cassie up with outside expectations as well. Perhaps the whole neighborhood figured like mother, like daughter. That's the sort of ignorant thinking you can expect from human type beings. And the sort that would park a big old chip on somebody's shoulder.

Playmate said, "Kayne told us you could show us where Bic Gonlit stayed when he was coming around here." His tone was strained, neutral. And Cassie heard that. And she understood.

"I can't. I stayed away from that creep. He was always trying to get me to go somewhere with him when Kayne wasn't around."

But Kayne had told us that Bic hadn't shown any physical interest in her. If he hadn't gone for the mom why would he take a run at the daughter?

Make the assumption he wasn't a good, red-blooded Karentine boy and you might think he could want something else.
Maybe he'd had a notion that snatching Cassie would give him a
lever he could use to get Kip to tell him what he wanted to know.

Hard to imagine just wanting Cassie as a hostage. She was the
kind of girl you have to keep away from the old men. Or you'll
have them dropping like flies from strokes and heart attacks. Hell,
I was having palpitations myself and I was just there looking for
her nimrod brother.

I had trouble seeing anything else. Especially not brother
Rhafi, who vanished in Cassie's glare. That poor kid didn't even
have Kip's unpleasant character traits. He was just there, a gangly
six-footer with unkempt dark hair, brown eyes, a ghost of a mustache, the beginnings of a set of bad teeth, and no meat on his
bones. I got the impression that he'd rather be somewhere else.
That, like his brother, he had a preference for the habitués of
worlds of his own devising.

Physically, it was obvious that Rhafi did not share a father
with Kip. Cassie . . . She might pass as Kip's full sister if anybody
wanted to pretend. But she did have that different last name.

No matter. As pleasant a task as it was staring at Cassie and
drooling, I was in the business of rescuing obnoxious teenagers.
"Rhafi, I'm Garrett." Like maybe he'd forgotten. But I'd decided
to deal with him the way I dealt with Singe. Carefully. He seemed
of an age to be volatile. "I specialize in finding things that get
lost." Or about anything else that needs doing, that clients don't
want to do for themselves, and that I don't think is wrong.

"Like Bic Gonlit."

"Well, sure. Though the reason I want to find him is because
he may know where to find your brother."

Petulantly, "I mean, Bic Gonlit finds things that're missing.
He said so."

"The real Bic Gonlit specializes in finding people for other
people. People who're willing to pay well to have them found."

Playmate told me, "Let's don't complicate things, Garrett.
Rhafi, please show us where Bic Gonlit stayed."

"He tried to get me up there, too, you know. Like he did
Cassie."

"And you found out where he stayed. Good job." Playmate's
approach was the same as mine but the boy responded better.
Probably because he knew and trusted Playmate.

Playmate does exude trustworthiness. I've seen total strangers entrust him with everything but their souls.

Playmate kept talking. And Rhafi responded.

The boy did not enjoy Kip's one redeeming quality. He wasn't bright. And he was spoiled. As much as a near-destitute child can be spoiled.

I stepped back and let the master work.

"Shall we?" I asked Cassie, offering her my arm and a glimpse of my raised eyebrow. The trick that kills them dead.

"I think I'll just stay here."

Whimpering, every bone crushed, I dragged my battered carcass out of the Prose flat, following Playmate and Rhafi.

# 26

Playmate said, "I told you you'd like Cassie."

"Hell, I love her. But I'm not so hot for the thing that's inside of her, wearing her like a suit."

Rhafi started laughing. I mean, he got one of those cases of the giggles where you just can't shut it off, no matter how hard you try.

"I didn't think it was that funny," I said.

Playmate agreed. "It wasn't funny at all."

Rhafi gasped, "But you don't know Cassie. You don't have to live with her. You don't have to suffer through it when she tries on different personalities like some rich bitch trying on different clothes." He hacked and gasped all the way through that. "I know it isn't that funny. But it was just so perfect for the bitch that she's trying to be this week."

"She's always been an actress," Playmate said, demonstratively not using the word in its pejorative form, which means whore. "That's her way of coping."

"Ever get the idea that the dysfunctional folks outnumber those who aren't? Every damned day I'm more of the opinion that everybody's knot is tied too loose or too tight. And some just cover it up better than others. It's only a matter of time. Except for me and thee, of course."

"And sometimes we wonder about thee, Garrett. I'm sorry you feel that way. You might consider surrounding yourself with different people. Excluding myself, naturally. Or you might find a different line of work. One less likely to turn you cynical."

"Me? Cynical? That's impossible. I am one with the universe.

I have the perfect life. Except for the fact that I do have to work once in a while."

"You should've picked a mother who lived on the Hill."

"That was a little shortsighted of me, wasn't it?"

Rhafi, in a moment when the giggles were under control, observed, "You guys must be getting older than you look." Outside of the Prose flat, out of the shadow of his intimidating sister, he developed some substance.

"Yeah? How come do you say that?" That was a bitter draught, even from a kid as strange as he.

"You both think too much."

The little philosopher. "Damn!" I said. "There's an accusation that hasn't been flung in my face for a long time."

"Possibly never," Playmate opined. "I recall the opposite fault getting mentioned with some frequency, however . . . Hello. What do we have here?"

Clumps of people occupied the street ahead, staring down a cross lane and pointing at the sky.

"I have an uncomfortable feeling. Rhafi, how far to Bic Gonlit's place?"

"Next block. I bet they're looking at one of those . . . Oh, yeah!"

The crowd all made awed noises. Everyone pointed, reminding me of crowd scenes in paintings of the imperial circus, the people saluting as the emperor arrived.

A silvery discus, that I guessed to be pretty high up in the air, had appeared from behind a tile rooftop. It drifted our way for a few seconds, then moved back out of sight again. Some of the watchers complained bitterly because it hadn't come closer. I supposed similar groups of gawkers could be found all over town.

I overheard several people claiming to have had contact with creatures who lived inside the silver disk. One insisted that he had been a captive of creatures who lived inside the balls of light I had seen last night. That turned into a contest: who could concoct the tallest tale about the outrages done them by the silver elves.

The human imagination is very fertile. And exceedingly grotesque.

"Did I say something about them outnumbering us?" I asked. "Play, you heard of those silver things coming out in the daytime before?" Sightings had been going on for at least a month but I hadn't paid much attention. There's always something weird going on in TunFaire. Like most of His Majesty's subjects, if the something weird ain't happening to me I don't worry about it.

"Oh, sure. Just as often as at night. As I recollect, all of the earliest sightings, over a year ago now, came during the daytime."

"I do remember. It was one of those one-day wonders. Nothing happened so I forgot about it. These people are getting a little thick here," I grumbled. I eased into Playmate's wake. He had little trouble pushing through the crowd. Many of them probably recognized him. He was always out here doing the charitable side of the ministry thing.

Always something weird happening. These flying things. The silver elves. People catching on fire and burning up, up on the north side. The other day news that another juvenile male mammoth had wandered in through an unwatched gate and was creating havoc, also on the north side. If one of Block's people was supposed to have been on duty there he'd better be prepared to eat the mammoth. Dereliction of duty was close to a capital crime in the eyes of Colonel Westman Block and Deal Relway.

It might behoove me to keep better track since so much of the weird stuff pulls me in eventually.

"Is something the matter, Mr. Garrett?" Rhafi asked from behind me. "You jumped."

I'd thought about voluntarily creating work for myself, that was what was the matter. No need to share that with the kid, though. "Aren't we there yet?"

"The yellow brick dump."

And dump it was. The tenement in question, easily more than a hundred years old, was a hideous four-story memorial to the disdain lavished on housing for the poor during the last century. When they actually still built tenements with the idea that poor people needed housing. I knew the inside perfectly before we ever passed through the doorless entry, stepping over and around squatters, trying not to inhale too deeply. The nearest public baths would be miles away.

Cooking smells, heavy on rancid grease, did help suppress the body odors somewhat.

Every room in the structure would be overcrowded. Entire extended families would occupy a space at most ten feet by eight, some members possibly sleeping standing up, leaning on a rope. Certainly sleeping in shifts, the majority always on the street trying to score an honest or dishonest copper. When you're that poor that distinction is too fine to notice.

It's the way of much of the world. And once you've looked into a place like that tenement you tend to appreciate your own better fortune a good deal more.

That tenement made Kayne Prose's situation appear considerably less awful.

I asked Rhafi, "You know where he stayed here?"

The boy shrugged. "Upstairs. I think he said the top floor."

"Oh, my aching knees."

"Not exactly the digs you'd expect of the Bic Gonlit who enjoys gourmet dining and fine wines," Playmate observed.

"Definitely not. You think Bic maybe used this place as a safe house?" I stepped over and past several big-eyed ragamuffins, the eldest possibly four, all huddling on the bottom steps of the stairs.

I knew the answer to my question. The Bic Gonlit who had come to see me in search of magical boots knew nothing about the other Bic. The Dead Man would have winkled that out right away.

The opposite, of course, could not be true.

Possibly the real Bic had a relationship of some sort with the artificial Bic and didn't know it. Puffing, I asked Playmate, "Bic have any brothers or cousins?"

"Only child of an only child, far as I know. Top floor. How come you're having so much trouble breathing? Which room, Rhafi?"

Rhafi didn't know. Rhafi wasn't bright but Rhafi was cunning enough not to let himself be lured into something by someone weird. Unless that someone happened to be flashing coin.

There were eight doorways on that fourth floor. The one farthest back on the right had an actual door in its frame. Several others had rag curtains hung up. A couple had nothing. And the doorway on the right, next forward from the one with a real door, had been boarded up. So well that no entrepreneur had been able to pry the boards off and return them to the local economy.

I said, "Has to be the one with the door, Play."

Curious faces poked out of neighboring doorways, most of them low to the floor and dirty. Only a couple of older people had the nerve to be nosy.

In TunFaire nosiness can be a deadly disease.

Playmate said, "Look at that. A key lock." He knocked. There was no response. "Looks like the one you have over at your place."

"That's because it was made by the same crooked locksmith." After having suffered Dean to spend a young fortune to buy and install a lock I'd learned that the machine could be picked easily. I knew how myself, having had to develop the skill because, once he got the lock installed, Dean used it. Without regard to my location in relation to my front door, or whether I'd remembered to take my key when I went out.

I knocked, too. There was no response to my magic knuckles, either.

I felt the door. Like maybe that would clue me in to what was going on behind it. It wasn't hot or cold or wet so the weather was fine. The door did rattle in its frame, which was no surprise in that dump. It was a replacement door, likely to vanish as soon as some entrepreneur could get on the other side and reach its hinges.

I tried the knob.

It turned. "What the hell?"

The door wasn't locked. It wasn't barred or chained on the inside. It creaked inward at the slightest shove.

With our backs to the wall either side of the doorway, Playmate and I exchanged looks of surprise. There were whispers down the hall, tenants kicking themselves for not having noticed and seized the day.

If you want to live alone in a place this low you'd better have a pet thunder lizard or be able to leave some really nasty booby traps behind when you go out.

Nothing with lots of teeth and bad breath came to see who was calling.

I produced my oaken headknocker. I used it to push the door open a little wider.

The room behind it appeared clean and neat, almost sterile. Its plaster was in perfect repair and had been painted gray. The wooden floor had been sanded and polished. Overall, the place appeared to be in better shape than it had been the day it first accepted a tenant.

There were rugs on the floor. The furniture included a small table and two wooden chairs. One of those sat in front of a fine cherrywood writing desk cluttered with paper and both quill and metal-tipped pens. There was an overstuffed chair that faced the one small window. That window had real, clear glass in it. A little table beside the chair supported a top-quality brass-and-glass oil lamp.

I whispered, "Looks like our man does a lot of reading." There were shelves beside the cherrywood desk. Those held at least thirty books, a veritable fortune. The bindings on the bound volumes suggested old and expensive and rare, which almost certainly meant stolen.

Playmate grunted. "This fellow isn't poor."

"Makes you wonder, don't it?"

"Be careful going in there."

"What's this, army telling Marines how to play the game? Here's an idea. Why don't I just toss Rhafi in? We can wander on in after the smoke clears away." I was beginning to suspect sorcery. I couldn't think of any other reason for anybody to have so many books.

"Do that and you'll ruin your chances forever with Kayne and Cassie both."

"Right now I'm not sure that'd bother me a whole lot, Play. I must be getting old. I'm taking Morley seriously. I'm losing my taste for women who're crazier than me." I dropped down, reached inside with my stick, felt around. Slowly and carefully. The setters of traps like to put their triplines down where you're less likely to notice them. I didn't find the threads I expected. Which is what I'd have used if I was rigging a setup like this. "I can't find anything here, Play. But it still don't smell right."

This time army didn't have any advice. This time army awaited Marine Corps' professional assessment.

The Marine chose to use his magic wand some more. There was a very small throw rug lying right inside the doorway. I started to push it away, to see what was underneath it.

I heard the sound of water falling into a vat of boiling grease. Then came a blinding flash of light accompanied by a baby thunderclap. I flung myself sideways, dragged me upward until I was sitting with my back against the wall.

When my vision cleared and my hearing returned I saw Rhafi swatting at a smoking patch of wall across the narrow hallway. A couple of tenants were yelling for water. The precursors of a human stampede were taking shape.

I smelled the stench of burnt hair.

Playmate told me, "My man, you're going to have to wear a hat for a while."

I felt the top of my head. I spoke a few syllables that my mom wouldn't have approved even on this occasion. "I'll just have Dean give me a haircut. I'm sure he thinks I'm overdue, anyway." I got back down on my belly and poked that little rug again.

Crackle. Flash. Clap. But all much less energetic than before.

I slithered into Bic's place, disturbing that little rug as I went. The booby trap barely popped. And that was the end of that.

# 27

"This guy had a whole lot of time on his hands," I said. We'd been over the place three times. We hadn't found anything to help us trace Kip. But we knew this Bic Gonlit liked to read books about TunFaire and Karenta, modern and past, and we knew he must enjoy rehabilitating run-down property because he'd completely redone this room and the sealed-up place next door, which he reached through a doorway he'd cut through the separating wall.

"Not to mention having enough spare change to afford several expensive hobbies." Those had to include paying someone to steal all those innocuous texts."

"We need to interview the neighbors."

"They aren't going to say anything. None of their business."

"You just have to know how to ask, Play. They'll sing like a herd of canaries if you happen to have some change in your hand while you're talking."

"Don't look at me."

"All right. Tell me something, then. Who's the client in this case? I didn't come to you and Kip. Am I getting my head shaved by some kind of lightning just for the exercise? I don't like exercise. Am I short the most focused and talented girlfriend I've had in a while because I'd rather be out rolling around in the slums with the lowest of the lowlifes, spending my own money so that they'll maybe give me a clue how to find a kid who probably should've been sewn into a sack with some bricks and thrown in the river ten years ago?"

"Don't go getting cranky on me, Garrett. I need some time. I honestly didn't think it was going to get this complicated."

"You didn't think. You're an idealist, Play. And like every damned idealist I've ever met you really think that things should happen, and will happen, because they're the right things to happen. Never mind the fact that people are involved and people are the most perverse and blackheartedly uncooperative creatures the gods ever invented."

"Garrett! That's enough logs on the fire."

"I'm just getting going."

"Never mind. You've made your point."

"So we'll start talking to people out in the hall. You will." I didn't want anyone else getting into our quarry's rooms. There'd be too much temptation to make off with inexplicable trinkets.

There were unknown items everywhere that resembled the little oblongs and soap bar-size boxes that had been left behind when Kip was snatched. They had foreign writing on them. Which in itself is a big so what in TunFaire, where almost everyone speaks several languages and maybe one in ten people can even read one or more. They had little colored arrows and dots. I assumed they were some sort of sorcerer's tools and left them alone.

There wasn't much else to see in the first room. The second was used as a bedroom and was set up pretty much like my own, with the wall where the hallway door used to be concealed behind a curtain, which made a closet. That contained clothing in a broader range of styles than you'd find anywhere else, and a rack of sixteen wigs. The diversity amongst those told me our boy enjoyed going out in disguise. But nothing I uncovered ever moved us one step closer to finding Cypres Prose.

I gave Playmate what coins I had. After a careful count. "Don't be generous. These people won't expect it."

"What should I tell them when they ask me why we want to know?"

"Don't tell them anything. We're collecting information, not passing it out. Just let them see the money. If somebody tells you something interesting, give him a little extra. If he sounds like he's making it up to impress you, kick his ass and talk to somebody else. I'll listen in from back here."

Rhafi wanted to know, "How come you want Play to do all the asking?"

"On account of he looks more like a guy they can trust." It was that preacher man look he cultivates. "I look like a guy who'd send for the Guard if I heard anything interesting. If I'm not underground Guard myself."

The simple existence of Deal Relway's secret police gang was making life more difficult already. People were paranoid about those in authority. No doubt with good reason in most cases.

I continued to potter around the place while Playmate and Rhafi held court in the hallway. I invested a fair amount of time examining the door lock.

It exhibited no scratches to indicate that it had been picked. There was no damage to show that the door had been jimmied. There was nothing else to make me think anything but that our man had gone out without locking his door.

I found that hard to credit. This is TunFaire. Despite having heard a thousand times from country folk how they never had to lock their doors at home, I couldn't believe that anyone would do it here. But there was no evidence whatsoever to indicate otherwise. Unless the man who lived here *wanted* somebody to walk in. And maybe get blasted.

I called Rhafi in from the hallway. "Is there any way you know of that Bic Gonlit could've been warned that we were coming?"

"Huh? How could anybody know that?"

How indeed?

# 28

I'd caught a whiff of a red herring. And in less time than it takes to yell, "I'm a dope!" I sold myself a duffel bag full of wrong ideas.

Lucky for me somebody came along before I invested a whole lot of time and anger in trying to figure out how Kayne or Cassie or somebody had gotten word over in time for a trap to be set.

First hint came when the fourth floor hallway suffered a case of illuminated roaches effect. In less than a minute, without explanation to anyone whatsoever, the entire population of the ugly yellow tenement took cover in their home rooms.

I beckoned Rhafi and Playmate into Bic's room. "Go hide out in the bedroom. And stay quiet." I pushed the door shut behind them, locked it, then recalled that it hadn't been locked and undid that. Then I nudged the little throw rug into place just behind the door.

We waited.

I wasn't yet sure what for. When a whole crowd of people suddenly do something all together, like a flock of birds turning, and you don't get it, you'd better lie low and keep your eyes open.

That was my master plan for the moment.

The door handle jiggled as a key probed the lock. I tensed. The tenant was home? Was that why everybody had scattered? Playmate's interviews hadn't achieved much but to reveal that the denizens of the tenement were scared of him. Though nobody had produced a concrete reason.

How would he respond to finding his door unlocked?

Probably with extreme caution. Unless he'd left it unlocked.

I continued to nurse a paranoid streak on that matter.

The door opened. Nobody came in right away. I held my

breath. I was thinking that only a blind man could've overlooked the scorching on the wall across the hallway. Only a man with no sense of smell would miss the stink of burnt hair.

But then somebody did a little hop forward, over the throw rug. I shoved the door shut. "Play."

Playmate popped out of the other room before the man finished turning toward me. He considered his options and elected to do nothing immediately. He was trapped in a confined space, between two men much bigger than he.

He was just a little scrub, maybe five-foot-seven, and skinny. He was much too well dressed for the neighborhood.

I asked Playmate, "You know this guy?"

Playmate shook his head.

"Rhafi? How about you?"

"I seen him around. I don't know him."

"Sit, friend," I directed. "Hands on top of the table." Playmate moved the chair for the elf, then positioned himself behind it. Mindful of what we'd found in the other room, I said, "Pull his hair."

His hair came off. And when it did bits of flesh began to peel back along the former boundary between hair and naked skin. The part of the head that had been covered by the wig was hairless and pale gray.

I tugged at the peeling edges of the face. It came off. What lay beneath was a ringer for one of Playmate's elf sketches. The gray face betrayed no more emotion than had the motionless human mask when that had been in place.

"Holy shit!" Rhafi burst out. "It really is one of them things Kip was always talking about. I never believed him, even when he got Mom to say she'd seen them, too. He was always making up stories."

"I've seen them, too," Playmate said. "So has Mr. Garrett. But never quite this close."

"Which one is this?" I knew it wasn't any of the ones I'd seen before. It had more meat on it.

"I don't know. Not one of Kip's friends, though. It might be the first one who came looking for them."

I considered the elf. So-called because we didn't know what he really was. The Dead Man's suggestion of kef sidhe half-breeding didn't seem more likely than true elven origins. Maybe it hailed from the far north or from the heart of the Cantard. Some strange beings have been coming out of that desert since the end of the war with Venageta.

The elf seemed calm. Even relaxed. Without a concern.

I said a little something to Playmate in the pidgin dwarfish I could manage. Playmate nodded. He thought the elf was too confident, too.

I told the critter, "I owe you one for bopping me in that alley, guy. But I'm going to try not to remember that while we're talking."

My words had no effect. In fact, I got the distinct impression that the elf felt that he was in control of the situation, that he was playing along just to see how much he could find out.

I said, "Rhafi, go into the other room and see if you can find something we can use for a bag. A pillowcase, for instance. Anything will do."

Rhafi was back in seconds with an actual bag. It was made of that silvery stuff we had found right after Kip was taken.

I said, "Just start throwing in all the little odds and ends and knicknacks. Keep your back to us when you do. And stay between whatever you're bagging and our friend." I wasn't quite sure why I was giving him those instructions but it sure seemed like the right thing to do. And Rhafi was a good boy who did exactly what he was told.

I told Playmate, "Kayne maybe did her best job with this one."

"Don't be fooled," he whispered. "You're on him at a good time. He can be more trouble than the other two put together."

I jerked my head toward our captive. "Does this guy talk?"

"I expect so. He's been getting by by pretending to be human. Can't manage that without saying something sometime."

A touch of tension seemed to have developed in the elf. He wasn't pleased with Rhafi's activities.

"Good job, Rhafi," I said. "When that bag is full I want you to take it downstairs and leave it in the street." It shouldn't take more than a few minutes for the contents to disappear forever, whether or not anyone could figure out any use for the trinkets.

I watched the elf closely. So did Playmate. This would be the time when he would try something. If he was going to do so.

The gray elf's strange Y-shaped nostril opened wide. Air whistled inside. The nostril closed. The elf's skinny little mouth began to work, though no sounds came forth.

The elf exhaled, then drew a second deep breath. I got the notion he'd tried something he hadn't expected to work and had been disappointed by the results.

The elf spoke. "Mr. Garrett. Mr. Wheeler."

Who the hell was Mr. Wheeler?

Oh. I'd never known Playmate by any other name, except once upon a time when I'd told everybody his name was Sweetheart, just to confuse things if they decided to go looking for him.

Playmate shook his head and pointed at Rhafi. Three different fathers. Well. I hadn't thought about the kid's patronymic. Or even that Kayne might have used it if she wasn't married to the man. But she had been, hadn't she? As I recalled Playmate explaining it.

Meantime, my new pseudoelven buddy was going on, "I believe that we may be able to help one another." His Karentine was flawless, upper-class, but more like a loud, metallic whisper than a normal voice. It took me a moment to realize that that was because he wasn't really using a voice.

More legs on the millipedal mystery. Every intelligent creature I've ever met had a voice. Even the Dead Man did, back when he was still alive.

"Who are you?" I asked. "What are you?"

"Policeman? One who tracks and captures evildoers and delivers them to the justiciars? Do you have that concept?"

"Sure. Only in these parts it's track and catch lawbreakers, not evildoers. Big difference, here in TunFaire. Where are you from?"

He ignored my question, more or less. "The distinction, perhaps, is not always observed in my country, either, though there are those of us who refuse to bend in the wind."

Damn! I got me a gray-skinned Relway?

He continued, "Be that as it may, I have come to your country in search of two criminals. They have proven extremely elusive. And lately my search has been complicated by the arrival of other hunters, newly alerted to approximately where these two now can be found."

Damn. Wouldn't it be great to have the Dead Man listening in here? The guy's story was good, so far, though hard to follow because it was delivered in six- or eight-word puffs separated by long inhalations.

I was inclined to suspect that the creature normally communicated mind to mind, like the Dead Man.

I asked, "How can we help each other?"

"You wish to recover the boy, Cypres Prose, who has been taken captive by the recently arrived Masker elements. I wish to capture the two villains I was sent to apprehend. My superiors are growing impatient. I believe I may be able to locate the boy by locating the criminals holding him. I do not have the power to wrest him from the hands of his captors alone, however. Join me in doing that. Then get the boy to tell us where my criminals are hidden. Once I have them in hand I'll go away. Life here can return to normal."

"That's just about good enough to gobble up. Even if life here is never any normaler than it is right now. What do you think, Play? Are Lastyr and Noodiss desperate criminals?"

"I don't think they're any danger to Chodo Contague, based on the little I saw, but they never really acted like innocent men. Sounds like a workable swap. What are those two wanted for?"

"They are Brotherhood of Light. Their exact crimes are unknown to me. I do not need to know those to do my job."

I said, "If we're going to be partners we're going to have to call you something besides, 'Hey, You!' You got a name of your own?"

He had to think about it. "As If, Unum Ydnik, Waterborn. Which I cannot explain so that you would understand. Call me Casey. I heard that name recently. I like the sound. And it will be easier for you."

In words my friend Winger might have used had she been around, this old boy was slicker than greased owl shit. He always had a good answer ready to go. Though I got no sense of insincerity from him. I was almost certainly less sincere than he was.

All the time we were talking Rhafi kept maneuvering back and forth, trying to reach the door with his sack of plunder. While trying to keep facing away from Casey and keeping me or Playmate in between.

I told him, "You can forget what I said, Rhafi. I think we're all going to work the same side."

The boy stayed behind Playmate while he said, "Kip won't give those guys up."

"Then maybe we'll just toss him back to the bad guys." I hadn't fallen in love with Cypres Prose during my brief exposure to the kid. I kept wondering what I was doing, not just dropping the whole thing. Doing a favor for a friend? I did owe for all those times when Playmate had done really big favors for me.

"Just leave the bag on the table, please," Casey told Rhafi. "I will return everything to its proper place. Mr. Garrett, when would you like to pursue this matter?"

"I'm going to take it as stipulated that you're the expert on the people holding Kip. How dangerous is that situation?" There was a time when I did a lot of work related to kidnappings and hostage holdings. Unless the villains belong to one of just a handful of professional gangs the victim's chances are slim. And they deteriorate with time.

"By the standards of your city those scoundrels are a waste of flesh. You people are more casually cruel to your own families and friends, without thought, than Maskers can be under full force of malice. The dangers enveloping Cypres Prose are almost entirely emotional and spiritual, perils of the soul your people almost entirely discount as irrelevant at best."

I could buy that. I didn't know what the hell he was talking about. Which was, probably, his point. "They aren't breaking his teeth or shoving hot needles under his nails?"

Casey managed to project an aura of horror so strong that it got me thinking about some of the other feelings I'd experienced since he'd shown up. "No. Nothing like that."

"Then, if he's in no immediate physical danger, I'm going home and getting something to eat. And maybe I'll take a nap." And then maybe I could dash over to Katie's and see what I could do to patch things up. Hoping her father wasn't home. Katie's father doesn't realize that she isn't twelve years old anymore. "And I'm sure Playmate is worried sick about his stable." Down deep Playmate has to know what monsters he's harboring.

Casey shuddered. He projected quietly controlled terror. He knew the truth.

I might like this guy after all. Even if I didn't trust him farther than I could throw the proverbial bull mammoth.

I suggested, "Why don't we all wrap up all our other business, then meet at my place in the morning. We can go find Kip from there."

"Your morning or real morning?" Playmate asked. "We need to get that established." He couldn't conceal his sneer.

In addition to his completely self-delusory regard for the equine race Playmate is a devoted adherent of that perverse doctrine which suggests that it's a *good* thing to be up and working ere ever the sun peeps over the horizon. Which goes to show just how broad-minded a guy I am. I still consider him a friend.

"Solar morning. But no before the crack of dawn stuff. Moderation in all things, that's my motto."

"Even in telling us what your motto is, evidently," Playmate cracked. "Because I've never been there to hear you state it. Before now."

"After sunrise," I grumped. "Rhafi, we're leaving now. You go out first. Playmate, you follow. Casey, I know you're a stranger here. But you've been here a while and those books tell me you've been trying to learn your way around. Here's a tip. Don't ever leave your door unlocked again. I guarantee you, next time you do these people here, your neighbors, will steal everything but your middle name before you get down the stairs to the street."

I backed out of the room myself. I retreated cautiously until I reached the head of the stairs. Needlessly. Casey never stuck his head out of his room.

# 29

"That was clever, Garrett," Playmate said after we hit the street.

"I thought so myself. But, knowing my luck, the Dead Man will be sound asleep when Casey shows up tomorrow."

Playmate chuckled.

I stopped the parade half a block from the yellow tenement. "Rhafi. What did you take?"

"Take? What do you mean? I didn't take . . ."

I had been fishing because it seemed in character. His response betrayed him. "I saw you. I want it. Right now. And no holding back."

"Aw . . ."

Playmate explained, "Look, if you make Casey mad he might not help us get Kip back."

There followed an exchange during which Playmate almost lost his temper because he couldn't make the kid understand how Casey could guess that *he* had taken anything that turned up missing.

Rhafi hadn't gotten the brains or the looks.

Rhafi began to look like he wanted to cry. But he held it in. He produced three small gray objects, two dark and one light, in varying shapes and sizes, though none had a major dimension exceeding four inches. Except for colored markings on their surfaces all three items looked like they had been cast from some material that resembled ivory or bone when it hardened. All three items had slightly roughened surfaces.

We stood in a triangle, facing inward, examining Rhafi's loot. I handled everything with extreme care. There was almost certainly some kind of sorcery involved with those things and I had no desire to wake it up. I concealed them about my person carefully. "Good. Now I have a job assignment for you, Rhafi. I want you to stay right here and watch that yellow brick tenement. See if anybody who might be our friend Casey ever leaves. Keeping in mind that he'll be wearing some kind of disguise. You saw the clothes and stuff he had."

"You want me to see where he goes?" As I'd hoped, he was all excited.

"No. No. Don't do that. I don't want you to end up like Kip. You just stay here till a man named Saucerhead Tharpe shows up. You'll know him by how big he is and because he has bad teeth. If Casey does leave, make sure you can give Saucerhead a good description of his disguise. Whatever, once Saucerhead shows up, you go home. I want you to tell your mom that we don't think Kip is in any physical danger, that we're on the trail, and that it looks like we might get them back as early as tomorrow. Got all that?"

"Sure, Mr. Garrett."

"Excellent. You make a good operative."

As soon as we were out of earshot, Playmate asked, "Do you believe that? That Kip's not in any real danger?"

"I think our new pal Casey believes that. I'm not sure how come but I could tell what he was feeling. Maybe it's because of all the time I spend around the Dead Man. Then I get close to somebody who probably communicates the same way and I just kind of cue in. I'll ask His Nibs."

"Uhm. Darn. I've got to find somebody to watch the stable. I can't keep walking away like this. The horses need attention. Somebody has to be there to deal with customers."

"Not to mention thieves."

"That's not a problem in my neighborhood." He stated that with complete conviction. I hoped his optimism wasn't misplaced.

"You ought to get yourself a wife."

"I'm reminded of an old saw about talking pots and black kettles."

He would be. "I'm doing something with *my* bachelorhood. I'm laying in memories for those long, cool years down the road. Look, I've got to send Saucerhead down to relieve Rhafi. Saucerhead will know where to find Winger. I can have him tell her to come over and cover for you."

Playmate made growlie noises. He grumbled. He whined. Winger has a million faults but her country origins qualified her to baby-sit a stable. And she'd probably do a decent job as long as she was getting paid. Assuming Playmate had sense enough not to leave any valuables lying around. Winger has a real hard time resisting temptation.

It was the getting paid part that had been giving my large friend problems throughout this mess. He'd made commitments without first considering the fact that somebody would have to part with some money to see them met.

Winger would expect to be paid. Saucerhead would expect to be paid. Garrett the professional snoop might be gouged for a favor or two but you couldn't expect him to pay his own expenses. And he was out of pocket already for help from several people, including Mr. Tharpe, Pular Singe the tracker, and the generous assistance of the Morley Dotes glee club and bone-breaking society.

Hell, even my partner, who didn't have much else to do and didn't require much upkeep, might insist on some sort of compensation, just so the forms of commerce were observed.

He can be a stickler for form and propriety.

Sometimes I suspect he isn't aging all that well.

Playmate said, "There isn't any money in this, Garrett! You saw Kayne and her kids."

"We could always auction off a few horses. They're begging for them down at Kansas and Love's, way I hear."

Playmate was so aghast he couldn't even sputter. From his point of view my simple mention of a slaughterhouse was so far beyond the pale that he found it impossible to believe that such words could have issued from a human mouth.

And I just couldn't resist needling him. "Which is hard to understand, what with all the surplus horses there ought to be these days."

"Garrett!" he gasped. "Don't. Enough. Not funny, man."

"All right. All right. You'll wake up someday. And I'll sing a thirty-seven-verse serenade of 'I Told You So,' outside your window."

He just shook his head.

"I'll get Winger headed your way. Maybe we can work out a deal where we'll all take a percentage of the profits from Kip's inventions."

That actually began to sound like a good idea once it got away. I might talk to the Dead Man. And to Max Weider at the Weider brewery, where I'm on retainer, next time I ran a surprise check on floor losses for him. Max Weider has a good eye for what people might want to buy and plenty of practical knowledge about how to get them together with your product so they have an opportunity to realize just how much they can't live without it.

Moments after Playmate and I parted my head was awash in grand schemes that would make me one of TunFaire's great commercial magnates.

# 30

The Dead Man was still awake. And still intrigued. Which left me vaguely uncomfortable. Usually a major part of the work I do consists of getting him to wake up, then getting him interested enough to participate, then keeping him awake until we finish. Any prolonged period of self-stimulated interest and cooperation generally constitutes a harbinger of an equally prolonged period where neither cataclysm nor calamity will stir him.

I described my day and refused to rise to the bait when he chided me for having knocked off work so early.

*It might be interesting to interview the mother and sister. Arrange to bring them around. . . . You are incorrigible, sir.*

"So don't incorrige me."

*A weakness for punning is one of the onset signatures of senility, Garrett. I would suggest that a hands-off approach might be the safest policy with these women, if indeed your characterization captures the reality.*

"I probably can't argue with you there. But, oh, are they scrumdidlyicious to look at."

*A status you appear to accord almost any female you encounter if she is able to stand up on her hind legs.*

"Unless she's related to Dean. It's a marvel how many homely women that family can pull together in one place."

*The Casey creature. You did indeed feel that he was honest?*

"Yeah. Well, he thought he was. We need to talk more about how I was sensing him. If that was for real, and I think it was, I want to be able to use it. As long as I have a good feel for what he's thinking I can keep him from putting one over on us primitives."

*Primitives?* He knew what I was getting at but wanted me to articulate it better so I'd be clearer about it in my own mind.

"Possibly 'primitive' is the wrong word. He had an aura of superiority about him. It had a strong moral edge to it. A self-righteousness. Like Dean, only much more carefully concealed."

Dean doesn't hide much. He isn't concerned about getting along with anybody. He knows he's right. When you're right other people have to worry about getting along with you.

We reviewed my day again, me underscoring events that had attracted my attention. "You see how I came to that conclusion? Even the criminals are too civilized to hurt somebody. If they're actually criminals."

*Intriguing. It might be interesting to explore a system of thought that is, indeed, that alien.*

"I set it up so we'll all get together here in the morning."

*He will not come.*

I didn't think he would, either. But I could hope.

"Where's the Goddamn Parrot?"

*In transit here as we converse. The watch on the genuine Bic Gonlit has not been particularly productive. However, Mr. Gonlit did meet with Reliance's people. He has not given up on collecting the bounty on Miss Pular. He did have a prolonged argument with the ratmen concerning his fee. He took the not unreasonable position that he ought to be paid because what he had been hired to do was to find her. Which he did. But now they insist that he has to get her out of this house, away from you, and deliver her to them. Mr. Gonlit then argued that they were destroying their own credibility by changing the terms of a contract while that contract was in force and that that could not help but come back to haunt them. They would not listen. They seem to have an exaggerated and irrational fear of your prowess as a street fighter. I suppose it is possible that they have confused you with someone else.*

"That must be it. I sure never worried anybody before. Now what's going on?" The pixies out front were acting up.

*Mr. Big has arrived. But take your time letting him in. There are watchers. They do not need to know that we are aware of the bird when it is out of our sight.*

"Watchers? Reliance's people or Relway's?"

*Both of those and possibly more.*

"More? Who?"

*I believe Colonel Block mentioned a strong interest on the Hill.*

He had, hadn't he?

Singe suddenly bustled in with a tray of food and drinks suitable for a party of ten. She offered me one of her forced smiles. "Dean is teaching me how to prepare meals."

"Tell him he has to let up on the spices a little when he's working with you. You have a delicate and precious nose."

"And hello to you, too, Mr. Garrett. How was your day?"

"Evidently sarcasm is on the training schedule, too. My day was pretty much like every working day. I walked a couple thousand miles. I interviewed a lot of people who were either crazy or born-again liars. Tomorrow I'll round up some of them and go check out something that might sort out the liars from the loons."

"I will go with you."

I barely got my mouth open.

*She will go with you.*

"Well, that's nice of you. I hope Reliance isn't in too black a mood when he catches us."

"I do not fear Reliance. Reliance fears me." Singe spoke around a mouthful of roll. The already-depleted state of the tray she'd brought warned me that I'd better grab fast if I wanted my share.

What she said was at least half-true. Getting Pular Singe back must, by now, be as much a fear of consequences matter as it was a bruised ego thing for Reliance. Strongmen, and even strongrats, have to keep on demonstrating their strength. The moment they show a hint of weakness some younger, hungrier strongarm is going to reach up and pull them down.

I glanced at Singe—she waved a fried chicken wing and nodded to let me know it was some good eating—then at the Dead Man. Old Bones wasn't sending it out but I could sense that he was entertained. He knew I was eager to run off and find Katie. I'd been rehearsing my most abject excuses and humble apologies all day long. I wanted to get cleaned up and get going, to take my personal life back.

I wondered how much Singe knew. I wondered if Dean's sudden interest in Singe might not be anything but another triumph of the old man's basic decency. He didn't approve of Katie, though you'd never guess it from overhearing one of their conversations. Katie was too much like me. And I've mentioned his attitude toward my approach to life.

Ain't none of us going to get out of it alive so we might as well get all the enjoyment out of it we can while we've got it.

I said, "I need to get cleaned up."

*First you need to let Mr. Big into the house. He is becoming impatient. I believe he is hungry. In any event, he is about to denounce your taste for—*

"I'm on my way." That damned wonder buzzard was invincible.

Somebody, once upon a time, said you surround yourself with the friends that you deserve. I need to take some time to lean back and think about that.

# 31

Katie's dad wouldn't let me in. Katie was home but he refused to tell her I wanted to see her. He didn't like anyone male, liked anyone interested in his daughter even less, and me least of all. I've never been real good on any musical instrument so I couldn't get her attention with a serenade. Grumping, I stood around in the street wondering, "What now?" I could wander over to the Tate compound and see if Tinnie was talking to me this week. I could try a couple of other young and incredibly attractive women of my acquaintance, though it was getting late of a workday evening to be turning up on anybody's doorstep. Or I could go somewhere and hang out with other guys like me—dateless and not wanting to stay home—and pay five times retail price per mug of Weider beer not bought at home by the keg.

Laziness and a long lack of the companionship of men who remembered drew me toward Grubb Gruber's Leatherneck Heaven. Which is as fat a misnomer as the one that used to hang on Morley's place back when he called it The Joy House. Grubb's joint isn't exactly a pit of despair where lost souls go to drink in solitude, perhaps in search of oblivion, certainly nurturing a sad pretense that camaraderie might break out at any moment. But you don't hear a whole lot of laughter in there. As the evening progresses the reminiscing turns inward, private, and maudlin, to memories that as individuals we cannot easily share. And I'm always surprised when there isn't any of the whimpering and screaming that had so often come around in the darkest hours of the night, down in the killing zone.

When those memories come, and somebody in Gruber's place

starts wrestling with them, somebody else will hoist a mug and summon a ghost. "Banner-sergeant Hamond Barbidon, the meanest mortarforker what ever . . ."

And the cups will rise up. And ten thousand ghosts will rise with them.

"Corporal Savlind Knaab."

"Lance Fanta Pantaza."

"Andro Pat."

"Jellybelly Ibles."

"Mags Cooper."

And each name will remind somebody of another. "Cooper Away, the best damned platoon sergeant in the Corps."

Plenty of men would be prepared to dispute that because everybody remembered a particular sergeant who brought him along. The sergeants are the backbone of the Corps. And if you lived very long out there you grew up to become one.

Chances are you never heard of any of the toastees because they'd fallen in different places and different times. But they were Corps, so you honored them. You remembered them and you wanted to weep because those people out there in the street didn't know, didn't have any idea, and already, just months after the long war's end, were beginning not to care.

Sometimes it isn't that difficult to understand why the really ugly, militant, racist veterans' organizations have so much appeal for men who survived the Cantard.

Nobody who wasn't down there will ever really understand. Not even those who shook our hands when we left. Not even those who welcomed us back with mighty hugs and no conception whatsoever what it was like to sit there watching the life bleed out of a man whose throat you'd cut so you could go on, undetected, to murder some other poor boy whose bad luck had placed him in your path at the wrongest time possible in the entire history of the human species. So that someday, somewhere far away, some woman would cry because she no longer had a son.

I decided that what I wanted was to spend an evening at Grubb Gruber's place. But, apparently, I never arrived.

# 32

Eventually a moment came when I was rational enough to realize where it was that I was regaining consciousness. Guess who was looking down at me with an unhappy glint in his eye? I croaked, "We godda sta dis romance, Morley. Wha da my doin' here?"

"I've been hoping you could explain that to me, friend. The evening is just getting started. I've got some swanks from the high ground down here slumming, carpeting the floors with silver. Then you burst in, obviously not part of the entertainment. You're all torn up. You have blood all over you. You have a snarling rat-man hanging on your back. You crash through three tables before you collapse. Five minutes later I'm standing here watching you leak all over a Molnar rug because all my customers have abandoned me and I don't have anything else to do."

I tried to get up. My body wouldn't respond. I'd used up my reserves talking, evidently.

Morley looked up as his man Puddle entered my field of vision. Puddle was about eighty pounds overweight and appeared to be about as out of shape as a man could be and still stay upright. He had a lot of miles on him, too. But looks are deceiving. He was strong. He was hard and he was tough and he had a lot more stamina than was credible for a man his size. He was dressed as a cook. He needed a shave.

"Need to shave, Puddle," I crooned.

I thought about going back to sleep. But I thought I probably ought to hear what Puddle had to say first.

Morley asked, "What did you find?"

"A long trail, a broken ratman and puddles a blood, boss. Da skink was a reglur one-man army."

"Corps," I said, not loud enough to be heard.

"And the ones who were after him when he staggered in here?"

"Split. Hauled ass out'n here da second we come out a da door."

"Reliance's gang, you think?"

"Not sure, boss. But dis's his part a rat city." TunFaire can be considered as many cities which occupy the same site. In some cases this fact is acknowledged publicly but in most the pretense is strongly in the other direction.

"No matter. We'll get the real story when Sleeping Beauty over there wakes up."

I managed to roll my head a short way. A ratman in worse shape than I found myself was sort of strewn around the floor ten feet closer to the front door, being stepped over and around by people cleaning up the mess.

Morley said, "Sarge, come give Puddle a hand. Get Garrett sitting up in a chair. Then we'll find out what happened."

Good. Good. Because I really wanted to know.

A second very large man, who could've passed as Puddle's tattooed big brother, appeared beside Puddle. Straining for breath, both men bent toward me. Each grabbed a hand. Up I floated. I tried to say something. What crawled out of my mouth didn't make sense even to me.

They dropped me into a comfortable chair. At least, it was comfortable under the circumstances. I wasn't yet quite certain what the circumstances were.

I had the uncomfortable feeling that I'd been on the losing side in a major brawl.

Morley said, "Somebody bring the medical box." The existence of which I noted. A fact that would weigh in on the other side the next time my good friend insisted he was completely out of his former underworld life. Which he might want me to believe because he thought I was thick with Colonel Block and Deal Relway. "Sarge, start checking him out."

Sarge is Sarge for the obvious and traditional reason. And, some think, for his tattoos, which let the whole world know that here's a man who made something of himself in the army. Here's a man who was tough enough and ferocious enough to have survived years of leading men in the witch's cauldron that was in the Cantard.

What that name and tattoos don't tell is what kind of soldier Sarge was.

Not many know, Sarge never brags. He doesn't look the type. But if he wanted he could stay drunk the rest of his life on drinks bought for him by other guys who'd been to and come back from the land beyond the far walls of Hell.

Sarge was a field medic down there. Which means he spent more time with his neck under the blade than did most of us. *And* during most of that time he couldn't have enjoyed the luxury of fighting back against the Venageti trying to kill him because he was too damned busy trying to do something to salvage something from amongst an overabundance of freshly mutilated bodies.

I tried to tell Sarge he was all right for a groundpounder. Almost an honorary Marine. Maybe he understood some of what I was trying to say because a sudden, horrible pain shot from my neck down my spine, through my hips and into my legs, all the way to my toenails. I believe I squealed in protest.

"He's been worked over real good," Sarge said. "But not by nobody who was able ta do whatever he wanted. What he's got is da kin' a wounds and bruises ya see when a whole bunch a clumsy guys gang up on somebody what's fightin' back."

So I put up a fight. Good for me.

If I'd been worked over like a plowed field, then how come I didn't ache in places I didn't even know I had?

"Anything broken?" Morley asked.

"Nah. He'll heal."

"Damn!" Puddle observed. "An' here I was tinking we could finally grab us a break, assuming we could a caught dis ole boy. . . . Oh, my stars! Da man his own self is awake."

Puddle is full of it. I consider him a friend even though he's always saying things like that. Because he doesn't just say them about me. You could get the idea that he wants to drown Morley and Sarge. In fact, he's always rooting for everybody to get out of his life and leave it a whole lot less complicated.

Morley leaned closer. "So what was it, Garrett? To what do I owe the pleasure of your presence this time?"

I croaked, "I don' know. Can' remember. Goin' to Katie's."

Morley gave me a dark, unforgiving look. He'll never forgive me for having found Katie first. Her impact on him is just as ferocious as it is on me. Which is hard to believe, considering how I start drooling and stammering whenever she comes around me and how much more practiced and slick Morley is when dealing with the obstinate sex.

"Maybe you got there."

Puddle got it and laughed his goofy laugh. Sarge asked, "Den how come dem ratmen was all over him when—" Puddle nudged him with an elbow, hard enough to loosen a lever or two somewhere inside his bean-size brain. "Oh. He caught da wildcat. Dat's pretty funny, boss."

"And maybe he didn't. That cat would've scared those mice away. So what's your game with the ratpeople, Garrett?"

I couldn't remember. But if ratmen did this to me there could be only one answer. "Singe. I guess."

"Reliance. The old boy does seem to be getting a little fixated on that particular subject. Don't you think?"

"I do t'ink." I had a strong feeling that Singe was becoming a major issue inside the world of ratfolk organized crime. Reliance was ancient for one of his kind. The up-and-coming youngsters must be getting impatient.

I tried explaining that to Morley. I faded in and out a few times before he got it.

"Bet you're right, Garrett. It isn't about Singe at all. Not really. And I think I know how to settle the whole mess. And turn Reliance into your best buddy while we're at it. Sarge, the rat's breathing just picked up. He'll be ready to sing in a few minutes."

"What're you gonna do?" With stalwart assistance from Puddle I was having considerable success at staying in my chair. My speech was clearing up some, too.

"I'll just remind Belinda that a broken-down ex-Marine named Garrett, with help from his ratgirl honey and a certain suave and incredibly handsome restaurateur, saved her sweet slim behind not all that long ago. I'll include some suggested topics for discussion with Reliance and his troops. Like the troops should leave the general alone. And the general should remember that he's indebted to you now, not the other way around."

"I don' like it."

"Of course you don't. You're Garrett. You have to do everything the hard way. Marshall. Curry. Help Mr. Garrett to a seat at the table in the back corner. And whichever one of you heathens has a little brandy squirreled away, I'd like to see a dram turn up in front of my friend."

Guys started looking for the apocryphal friend. The usual un-

complimentary remarks passed between Puddle and Sarge. I
didn't think I liked the guy they were talking about very much myself. We needed to track him down and spank him.

Marshall and Curry turned out to be the young thugs Morley
had brought along for the Cypres Prose chase.

Somehow, while Morley was away consulting his two weight-
iest henchmen, a beer stein brimming with spirits appeared before
me. The smirk on the mug of the cook who delivered it told me it
had been donated involuntarily from someone else's stash. Probably that of *faux* cooks Sarge and Puddle.

I am amused by the fact that none of Morley's guys share his
tastes for vegetarianism and teetotaling. They respected him
enough not to bring their slabs of dead cow to work with them, but
a few can't, or don't want to, get by without a little nip of firewa-
ter now and again.

A few sips got my brain clanking along. Just well enough to
make me wonder why I wasn't hurting as much as I ought to be.
Those ratmen must've tried to get some kind of drug into me. And
they must've had some success.

I didn't feel well but I didn't feel nearly as badly as I knew I
would when whatever it was wore off.

Morley dropped into the chair opposite me, showing a lot of
pointy teeth. His place was ready for business again. And, naturally, customers began to drift in.

Dotes said, "Bring me up to date on your adventures."

I could talk in fits and starts now, almost clearly, so I did. But
I still couldn't tell him anything about what'd happened in the last
few hours.

I noted that my cohort in delivering disaster, the ratman, had
indeed been swept up and taken away. Some of Morley's less
skilled waitstaff and kitchen help were not in evidence, either.

I'd say it wasn't a good evening to be a ratman foot soldier.

Of course, so far, it wasn't that great an evening to be me, either.

# 33

I wasn't seeing double from drugs or concussion anymore. I was doing that from the bite of a pretty good brandy. Suddenly, I spotted a couple of Katie Shavers coming in the front door, dressed to stop the hearts of celibate clerics and to start those of guys who'd taken up layabout duty in the morgue.

I gawked. And muttered, "One for each of us."

Morley said, "Excuse me?"

"What's she doing here?"

"Well . . . I believe she received a message explaining that you'd been badly mugged on your way over to her place. So make like you've got one foot over the line and she's the only thing holding you back."

"Not to worry. She ain't the only thing but as long as she's here on this side, I'm staying, too. Hello, darling."

Katie just kind of smiled and ate me alive with her eyes. Which is part of what Katie does so well. She doesn't say much, most of the time, but she's great to be with when she does. She has red hair, an all-time crop of freckles, and eyes that are a sort of gray-blue slate instead of the green you might expect. Nor is the red hair that brilliant shade that always comes with a difficult nature.

Conversations stopped while Katie walked the length of The Palms. Women punched or gouged their men. Yet for all that, Katie is not a great beauty—though not even a madman would try to make the claim that she's the least little bit unattractive.

What she has most is tremendous presence and animal intensity. Every minute with Katie is like a minute spent in a cage with a restless panther.

"You are in bad shape," she told me, like she was surprised to encounter the truth. Her voice husked, of course, yet managed to sound like she was going to bust out laughing any second.

I tried to tell her she ought to see the other guys. My mouth wouldn't form the words. The effects of the drug kept coming back.

Katie scooted a chair around beside me, sat down next to me, took my hand, and leaned against me. "Cure for most anything," I croaked in Morley's direction. And all was right with the world.

Morley nodded and drifted away.

After a long time purring I managed to get out words to the effect, "I tried to see you to apologize for getting tied up with my work but your dad wouldn't even tell you I was there."

"That's all right. I tried to see you, too. But Dean said you were out and he wouldn't let me in to wait."

And never mentioned the fact that she'd come around, either. "What time was that?"

"Midmorning."

Ah. I *was* out. But she wouldn't believe that if I told her because she knows my habits. If I defended Dean at all she'd decide that I must've been with somebody else. Sometimes her mind works in nonsequential directions, disdaining cause and effect. "We need to get those two together."

"Who?"

"Dean and your father."

"That's probably not a good idea. The only thing they'd agree about is that they should keep us away from each other."

"You're right."

"I'm always right, darling. You need to remember that."

"You're right." They all are. All the time. Which means that there're really tens of thousands of realities all around us, happening all at the same time. Has to be, on the face of the evidence.

Which brings to mind a joke first told me by Winger, of all people, and by just about everyone else I know since. If a man speaks in the heart of a forest and no woman is there to hear him, is he still wrong?

Katie asked, "Have you been drinking?"

"Yes I have. A little bit. Medicinal brandy. But the reason I'm goofy is because the ratmen tried to drug me."

Morley returned now, accompanied by Marshall and Curry. The whole gang dragged me upstairs and put me away in a guest room, where Katie did her best to keep me awake while I was suffering a threat of concussion.

# 34

The Palms by daylight is a different world. As a soft light will flatter some women, so night and candlelight do wonders for Morley's nightclub. By day the cheap wall coverings and decorations that had upgraded the place from its former status as The Joy House revealed their shabbiness.

The Joy House hadn't been what it sounds like. It used to be the same thing it was now, just patronized by a different clientele. Lowlifes. Grifters and pickpockets and low-level professional criminals. Ticks on the underbelly of society. The Palms, on the other hand, caters to parasites able to afford new clothes. But the upscale appurtenances have begun to show wear.

I sat at that same back corner table sucking down herbal tea and trying to figure out if my head hurt because of the ratmen's drug, the brandy I'd consumed, or because various blunt instruments had thumped my skull in passing. It was a valuable exercise, in theory. If I could figure it out I could shun the causes in future. All I'd have to do is give up drinking or get a real job.

Morley bent down to look me in the eye. He couldn't restrain a smirk.

I grumped, "This place is starting to look tacky, buddy. Maybe you ought to start setting yourself up for another format change. Try selling granite wine to dwarves and trolls for a while, maybe."

"Those kinds of people are much too hard on the furniture. The overhead would be too high. You started to remember anything about what happened?"

He knew blows to the head sometimes work that way. Chunks of memory from right before the trauma disappear.

"Some. I was headed for Grubb Gruber's place. Katie's dad had just told me to get lost. I hadn't seen the guys down there since before that business with The Call. It seemed like a good time to drop in."

Morley offered me a thinly veiled look of despair. He asked, "Why would you want to hang around with that tribe of has-beens?"

Because what they has been is what I has been, I didn't say. Morley would never understand. Guys down at Gruber's know what everybody else went through. Not many others do. And less than anyone those who stayed home to comfort the lonely soldiers' wives. Some of us don't need to go in there as often as others. "Because I learn more from them about what's going on around town than I can anywhere else. None of those guys feels like he's got anything to hide or anything to hold back."

"Ouch! How the bee doth sting."

I asked, "Did you perchance send word out about what happened? I was supposed to meet some people this morning."

"I informed your partner. At his request I passed the word along to Playmate, too." Morley grinned. "He had a huge row with Winger. About whether or not she ought to get paid. Until he decided he had to relay the news to someone else."

Morley seemed more curious than I found comfortable. Naturally suspicious, I examined that from a couple of angles while also wondering if it wasn't natural to want to know what was going on when you were involved. Hell, I wanted to know what was going on myself.

Some of Morley's guys were sweeping, mopping, otherwise halfheartedly getting ready for the coming evening's business. Of a sudden, with no perceptible change in attitude or speed, they all headed for the kitchen. In moments the place was empty except for myself and the owner. And the owner no longer looked happy.

I muttered, "Maybe I should head for the kitchen, too." Because I had a feeling I wasn't going to like what was about to happen.

Imminence became actuality.

The approaching coach, the rattle of which had cued the troops to vanish, wasn't approaching anymore. It had arrived.

Morley said, "I do wish she'd take a little less of a personal interest in her business. It's your fault, you know. Nobody ever sees her till your name comes up."

Two thugs pushed into The Palms. Once they stepped out of the bright sunlight they looked like miniature trolls, ugly and hard as jasper. I don't know where they find them. Maybe there's a mine where they dig them up. One held the door for Belinda Contague.

Despite being who and what she is, Belinda persists in dressing herself as the Slut of Doom, the Vampire Whore in Black. She wore black today but with the light behind her not much of her shape remained a mystery.

That ended when the door closed. Her dress was black and unusual but not particularly revealing without the backlighting.

She said something to her henchmen. Both nodded. One went back outside. The other assumed a relaxed stance watching Morley and me.

Belinda approached, perfectly aware of the impact she had because she worked hard at creating it. She was tall, with a shape well-favored by nature. She had a particularly attractive face, which, unfortunately, she insisted on covering with makeup as pale as paper. Her lips were painted bright red and slightly exaggerated by the color.

We have been lovers. We might be again if she really insists.

Very few things frighten me. Belinda Contague is one of them.

Belinda isn't sane. But she has her madness under control and uses it as a weapon. She is deadlier and scarier than her father ever was because she's so much more unpredictable.

She bent and kissed me on the cheek, lingering in case I cared to turn for something with a little more bite. I had to fight it.

Belinda has her positive attributes.

She sensed my temptation and was satisfied. She dropped into the seat beside me. The one Katie had occupied just last night. Luckily, Katie had gone home.

Sometimes it's a curse being a red-blooded Karentine boy. Especially when the red-blooded Karentine girls won't leave you alone.

I asked, "How'd you get here so fast?" I did know that Morley had sent her a message about the Reliance situation.

"I was in town already. There was a matter I had to see to personally. I'm making arrangements for my father's birthday. This one is the big six-zero. I want to give him a party. I'll want you guys to be there. I wouldn't be around if it wasn't for you."

Morley and I exchanged the looks of men suddenly and unexpectedly condemned.

Belinda said, "Tell me about your problem with Reliance."

I did so.

"Why's this Pular Singe so important to you?"

"She's my friend."

"Do you make her squeal?"

"She's *just* a friend, Belinda."

"I'm *just* a friend but you've made me squeal a few times."

"It isn't like that, Belinda. I've also helped you out a few times because you're a friend."

She showed me some teeth and a flash of tongue. She was pleased with herself. "I owe you for Crask and Sadler. So I'll send out word, the way you suggested. That'll set you up. And it'll close out my debt to him for his part in saving me from those two."

"You all over that now? You all right?" She'd been tortured and brutalized during the incident she'd mentioned.

"Back to my old self. Able to best a Marine two falls out of three. Know where I could find a Marine who wants to wrestle?"

"You're turning into a forward little sweetmeat."

Morley made a face but kept his groan to himself.

"Sometimes you've got to be direct. When all anyone does is worry about whether you're planning to cut their throat. I'm no black widow, Garrett."

So she said. I had no trouble picturing her with a scarlet hourglass on the front of that dress, accentuating her already-enticing shape. She had no reputation for that sort of thing but there was ample precedent in her own father's treatment of her mother.

"I don't think you are. What I wish you weren't is somebody who twists my head into knots every time I see you because that really gets in the way when I try to do business with you."

She leaned against me. "Poor baby."

Morley sat there in absolute silence, showing no inclination to draw attention to himself. He had no personal relationship with Belinda to help shield him from her unpredictable wrath. He preferred by far to do business at a grand remove.

Belinda told me, "Tell me a little more about this case you're working." So I did. I could see no way that it would hurt. And there was always a chance she'd get a wild hair and do something that would help.

"How does that tie in with your rat girlfriend?"

"It doesn't, far as I can see."

"I'll look around."

In TunFaire it's far harder to hide from the Outfit than it is to hide from me or Colonel Block. The Outfit commands far vaster resources.

"This have anything to do with all those flying lights everybody's been seeing?" she asked.

"It might," I conceded, grudgingly, not really having considered the possibility before. There was no evidence to suggest it.

Belinda popped up, in a bright good mood suddenly. Her mercurial mood swings are another thing that makes her a scary thing. She's much more changeable than most women.

She planted another kiss, this time at the corner of my mouth. "Give my best to Tinnie."

"We're on the outs. This week."

"Alyx, then."

"Nothing going on there, either."

"There's hope for me yet. I'll definitely want you to come to Daddy's party." Out the door she went, bouncing like she'd shed a decade of life and a century of conscience.

Morley exhaled like he'd been holding his breath the whole time. "You know what that means?"

"Belinda having a party for the kingpin?"

"Yes. He's not going to be sixty. Not yet. And I think his birthday really isn't for a couple of months yet, either."

"It means she's confident enough of her hold on the Outfit to roll Chodo out and let everybody see what his condition really is."

The purported overlord of organized crime in TunFaire is a stroke victim, alive still but a complete vegetable. Belinda has been hiding that fact and ruling in his name for some time now. Questions have arisen but the combination of Chodo's past propensity for bizarre behavior, a little truth, and Belinda's utterly ferocious, ruthless suppression of challengers have kept the kingpin position safely a Contague prerogative.

Morley said, "There're some old underbosses who'll revolt. They won't take orders from a woman, no matter who she is."

I sighed, too.

Chances were good Belinda knew that better than we did. Chances were good that Belinda was ready to retire those old boys, and might do it at this marvellous party.

I could figure that but they couldn't because they didn't know what I knew about Chodo.

"How many times have you saved her life?" Morley asked. "Several, right?"

"Uhm." He'd been there a few times.

"I think she's gotten superstitious about you. I think she's decided you're her guardian angel. That no matter how bad it gets, if she's in trouble good old Garrett will bail her out."

"That's not true."

"But she believes it. Which means you don't really have anything to fear from her."

"Except for her expectations."

A sly look flicked across Morley's features. "You think she bought your story about Singe?"

It took me a moment to get it. "You butthead."

# 35

I said, "I was afraid of something like this."

Another woman had just stamped into The Palms. She headed toward me and Morley, elbowing Morley's men aside.

Winger definitely survives more by luck than by any good sense.

"Winger." Morley's greeting was less than enthusiastic. I suspect he'd had a bad personal experience there, once upon a time. Which would teach him to pay attention to his own rule about not getting involved with women who're crazier than he is.

"The very one," she retorted.

Winger is a big old gal, more than six feet tall, and solidly built, though she's actually quite attractive when she bothers to clean herself up. If she was a foot shorter and knew how to simper she'd be breaking hearts wholesale just by looking the wrong way.

"Hey, Garrett," she roared. "What the hell are you doing sitting on your ass in this nancy dump? You was supposed to—"

"You don't listen too well, do you? Word went out that I got the snot beat out of me last night. To you, too. The man who told you is standing right over there. Meantime, I've got bruises on my bruises. I'm stiff all over."

"Yeah? How 'bout where it counts? Didn't think so. You're another one that's just all talk." She glared at Morley. "Get up and walk it off."

Winger is something like a thunderstorm and something like a female Saucerhead. Except with better teeth. And she's a lot more stubborn than Tharpe. It may take Saucerhead a while to work something out but he'll change his mind. Winger has never been

wrong in her life. Unless it was that time she thought she was
wrong but it turned out that she wasn't.

Big, blond, meaty, goofy, completely dangerous where your
valuables are concerned, she's likely to be part of or taken in by
the most outrageous scams imaginable. And yet she's one of my
friends. One of the inner circle. One of those who'd take steps if
something happened to me. And I've never figured out why we
like each other.

"Come on, Garrett. Get up off that fat ass. Don't you figure
you done left Saucerhead twisting in the wind about long
enough?"

I did think that. But Saucerhead was getting paid. And he, too,
had been told of my misfortune.

I asked, "Where's Playmate? You're supposed to be covering
for Playmate."

"Oh, he went off somewhere this morning, before your messenger came. When I got bored I decided . . ."

I sighed. Morley shook his head.

"What?"

I said, "I'm sure you've heard the word 'responsibility' a few
times. You have any idea what it means?"

Chances were she did but just didn't care.

"What?" Winger demanded again.

"If you came over here because you're bored, who's minding
Playmate's stable so the other crooks don't walk off with everything in sight?" It was really stupid of us to have left all of Kip's
inventions unguarded. But the gods of fools had been with us.
Word had come that Playmate hadn't suffered any losses. He had
wonderful neighbors. "Who's getting paid to make sure that
doesn't happen?"

"Other crooks? What do you mean, other crooks? Wiseass.
Look, I'm actually here because I'm kind of worried about Play. I
thought he was going off to meet you. I figured he'd come back
when he heard you wimped out on account of you got a couple of
bruises and a scrape."

I said, "Well, I've had all the fun here that I can take. I'm going home."

It took me nearly a minute to get out of my chair. Then I
couldn't stand up straight. "Guess I'll have to look on the bright
side." I looked left. I looked right. "So where the hell is it?

"Winger, for heaven's sake, go take care of that damned stable." I had visions of footpads absconding with my own personal

three-wheel. "And don't give me any of that crap about I'm picking on you because you're a woman. I'm picking on you because somebody hired you to do a job and you're just letting it slide. Again."

"Gods. Somebody get this man a drink. He's gone totally cranky."

# 36

Singe and Dean both awaited me on the stoop. The old man came down the steps to help me make the climb.

Winger had been right. A little exercise had loosened me up. But hardly enough. I still moved like somebody twice my age, suffering from rheumatism. I'd begun to worry that the ratmen might have done me some internal damage.

Once I'd eaten and downed a quart of Dean's medicinal tea, though, I no longer felt like we needed to send for a witch doctor.

With Singe's help Dean moved a padded chair from the small front room into the Dead Man's room. I occupied it, prepared to discuss business. Instead, I went to sleep. I stayed that way a long time. When I awakened Dean was there with more food and fresh tea. Singe fluttered about nervously.

*We find ourselves facing a disquieting development. Mr. Playmate has disappeared.*

"No. I didn't want to hear that." I don't like losing a client. That means I have to work three times as hard. Usually for no pay.

*Miss Winger sent word to the effect that he has not yet surfaced. I took the liberty of sending Dean to Mr. Dotes with an appeal that he send a few men to support Miss Winger. This would seem an opportune time for raiders to try scooping up Cypres Prose's inventions.*

"It would, wouldn't it? And it's Mrs. Winger. She's got a husband and a couple of kids she abandoned, somewhere out in the country."

*The good news is, an hour ago a messenger delivered a letter from Reliance. It was a bit formal, stiff, and strained, but he re-nounced all further interest in Miss Pular.*

"Hear that, Singe? You can go outside without worrying about the bad guys. . . ."

*Reliance cannot, and does not, guarantee the good behavior of all ratmen, Garrett. Call it a weasel clause if you like, but he did advise us that he is not able to control the actions of some of the younger ratmen. He denounced a certain John Stretch in particular.*

"To be expected, I guess. We're still better off than we were. I can't imagine too many of those youngsters being crazy enough to want to get the Outfit after their tails."

*The young often cannot connect cause and effect, Garrett. You see stupid behavior on the street every day. It will take only one fool who believes he can outwit Reliance and the Outfit to ruin Miss Pular's prospects.*

"I'm pretty sure Miss Pular is bright enough to outwit any of her kind who might be stupid enough to come after her."

*Indeed.*

Singe preened.

*But she will have to remain alert and ready for trouble for some time to come. Until the rat tribes acclimate themselves to the new situation. Reliance's letter is there before you. I asked Dean to leave it when he finished reading it to me.*

His mention of the letter was a hint that I should read it. I did so, wondering who had written it. I'd never heard of a ratman who could read or write.

"I'd say this is less than a total victory for Singe."

*That is correct.*

Singe asked, "What is wrong?"

"The way Reliance states this, he isn't just giving up his claims on you, he's telling us you don't have any more claims on the community of the ratpeople. He won't let you."

Singe thought for a while. Then, "Please explain more. In case I do not understand correctly."

"He's exiled you from your people. You know exile?" She nod-ded. "He's basically saying that since you won't play by his rules he isn't going to let you have anything to do with your own people. I guess you'll have to decide if that's a price you're willing to pay."

"I have decided already."

"Are you . . . ?"

"Reliance does not have much longer. And while he does last

he cannot be everywhere, keeping me from making contacts I might want. He is too old and too slow. And an enforced exile will compel me to learn my way around the rest of the city more quickly."

"Wow!" I said.

*Yes. Perhaps you should marry her after all. In five years you might be a king.*

Old Bones let Singe in on the part where he showed that he was impressed. The rest he sent only to me. One of his poor excuses for a joke.

*Garrett. Miss Pular. You will have to pick up Mr. Playmate's trail at his stable. Track him to wherever his hidden demons have taken him. You might search the boy's workshop. It is conceivable that Mr. Playmate found something there that led him to believe he could find the boy on his own.*

Actually a notion that had occurred to me when first I'd heard that he was still missing.

I said, "Excellent thinking, Old Bones. I see only one problem with the scheme. I'm so beat-up I can hardly move. At my best speed today I can grow a foot-long beard faster than I can make it to the river."

*A difficulty anticipated and overcome. In my communications with Mr. Dotes I arranged for you to be transported wherever Miss Pular's nose leads her.*

"Who's going to pay for all of this? We've got Saucerhead out there somewhere getting gray. We've got Singe and Winger working. We've got who knows how many of Morley's gang backing up Winger. Where's the money coming from? Kayne Prose don't have a pot to pee in. Her kids don't seem to be producing. Playmate isn't much better off than Kayne. Anytime he gets two extra coppers to rub together he gives one of them away."

*You are going to pay for it. As an advance cut out of your share of that lake of gold you see yourself tapping in the future.*

"What? Are you digging around in my head again?" There was entirely too much of that stuff going on around here lately.

The outbreak of warfare amongst the pixies prevented me from going off on a rant.

The Goddamn Parrot wanted a part of this action. He started hooting and hollering and cursing the pixies.

*I believe your help has arrived.*

# 37

Somebody knocked on the door with a battering ram. Plaster dust fell all over the house. The pounding didn't stop. Dean came roaring out of the kitchen armed with a cleaver, ready to offer somebody some advanced training in etiquette. He beat me to the door. He was in such an evil temper that he opened the door without first using the peephole.

"Gah!"

Who would've thought a man that old could jump that far? And backward at that, while inscribing sagas on the air with the edge of his lightning cleaver.

I caught him "Hey! Maybe you want to settle down. Before you damage the woodwork. It can't be all that bad."

"I'm all right," Dean insisted right away. "They just caught me by surprise."

An odor wafted in through the open doorway, like the southern extremity of a northbound skunk or, more likely, the last thing you smell when you meet up with one of the big flesh-eating thunder lizards out in the woods. It was bad breath on an epic scale. I hadn't encountered it in a long time but I knew it of old. Its provenance was just coming back to me when I got up to the door and leaned out just in time to get the full benefit of the exhalations of a pair of humongous creatures who'd bent down to peer into my house.

These boys both fell out of the ugly tree at a young age, hitting every damned branch on the way down. Then their mommas whupped them with an ugly stick and fed them ugly soup every day of their lives. They were *Uh-glee,* with a couple of capital double-ugs.

"Doris. Marsha. How're you fellas doing?"

Doris and Marsha Rose were two of three brothers who insisted they were triplets born of different mothers. Doris and Marsha have a greenish cast and stand twenty feet tall. They have teeth that stick out all which way. One is cross-eyed and one is walleyed but I can't keep that straight. Sometimes they trade off. They're grolls, a seldom-seen result of what can happen when giants and trolls fall in love. Doris and Marsha aren't very bright. But they don't have to be. They're so big hardly anything else matters.

"We're all doing marvellously, actually," a small voice piped. Of course. The grolls seldom went anywhere without the third triplet, Dojango, who, being a half-wit, was the brains of the family.

Dojango Rose isn't much over five feet tall. Well, taller than Bic Gonlit, so maybe he's five and a half. He's indistinguishable from a thousand other weasel-eyed, furtive little grifters on the streets of TunFaire. He'd have no trouble passing for human if he wanted, though he can't be more than one-eighth human in reality. In some fashion he's distantly related to Morley Dotes. Morley tosses snippets of work his way when finesse and a low profile aren't critical components in the grand scheme.

I descended the front steps amidst booming greetings from the larger brethren and the worst carrying-on by the pixies since their own arrival. I barely noticed. Already their hell-raising was becoming a commonplace, part of the background noise of the city. Seldom is TunFaire completely quiet.

Dojango Rose had himself in harness between the shafts of Kip Prose's two-wheeler man-hauling cart. He grinned. "Bet this's something you never thought you'd see, actually."

"Actually. You really think you can haul that thing around town with somebody in it?" Dojango seemed to have gone a few rounds with consumption since last I'd seen him. He looked lucky to be able to shift himself.

Based on prior experience chances were good he had his brothers carrying him most of the time.

"I am kind of counting on my brothers to help, actually," Rose admitted. "But there's more to me than you think, actually."

"Actually." Dojango Rose had some annoying verbal tics. "There just about has to be. Hey! Knock it off! Let her go."

Doris unpinched thumb and forefinger. A pixie buzzed away in dazed, staggering flight.

Amazing. Some people will respond automatically to any loud, commanding voice.

"Ah, Garrett, I was just—"

"I know what you was just." I climbed into the cart, every muscle arguing back. "Save it for the villains. We're liable to run into some. Godsdammit!"

There I was in the street about a thousand steps downhill from my front door and I hadn't brought anything out with me. . . . Dean and Singe materialized, each with arms filled. They clattered down the steps. Singe dumped her load into my lap. That consisted of enough instruments of mayhem for me to start up my own small army.

Singe and Dean stayed busy around the back of the cart for a while, with trips into the house and outside again. Then the old man headed back up the steps. Eventually, Singe came up beside me. "We are ready to travel." She tossed Dean a cheerful wave. Dean returned the gesture.

She had outstubborned him and overcome his prejudice by force of personality. Singe was, indeed, a wonder girl.

"What were you doing back there?"

"Storing provisions. You do not plan your travels properly. Especially in the area of food. So Dean and I fixed us something to take along."

While I was digesting that Dojango suddenly called out, "Where to, boss?"

# 38

There were subtle signs that some parts of Playmate's place had been searched. I asked Winger, "Has anybody been in here since you took over? Since Playmate wandered off?"

"No."

"You're sure?"

"Absolutely." She was irked. I was daring to question her faithfulness to her commission.

"I didn't think so. So *you* have to quit going through Playmate's stuff." While she sputtered I took a lamp into Kip's workshop. At first glance the only change there was the absence of the cart I'd ridden over here. Behind one or another of the grolls, mostly. As I'd anticipated.

Three blocks from my house Dojango was already trying to mooch a ride.

With Doris or Marsha pulling the cart, though, there were problems. Problems which sprang from their size. Neither could fit between the cart's long shafts. So whichever one was on the job dragged the cart along one-handed. The ride became a series of wild jerks as the groll swung his arms.

Then there was the problem of height. The grolls' hands were eight feet off the ground when they stood up straight. When they pulled the cart I ended up lying on my back.

But we had arrived at Playmate's stable. Marsha had volunteered to carry me around in his arms when he saw how much trouble I had levering my stiff old bones out of the cart. "I'd take you up on it, too," I told him. "Except for the fact that you're too tall to go anywhere inside here."

That was one big problem with being those two guys. Hardly any structure in Tun-Faire was tall enough to accommodate them.

So I limped a lot and leaned on things. I was crabby. I snarled at people for no good reason. And I didn't find a single clue as to where Playmate had gone. But I did have Singe. She'd located Playmate's newest track and was ready to move out on it long before I finished my rounds of Playmate's digs. I swore there had to be something incriminating somewhere. Something to tie him into the evil equine empire.

I kept returning to Kip's workshop, convinced that there was something I was overlooking. There was nothing missing and nothing wrong there but something deep inside me kept telling me to watch out for something.

I never did figure out what it was. But I trusted my hunch. I told Morley's associates to keep a close eye on Kip's junk. "Something here has something to do with what's going on. I don't know what it is yet. So I don't want you to let anybody in. Don't let anybody touch anything. And in particular, don't let Winger touch anything. But otherwise, consider her to be in charge."

I gave Winger a big grin and a glimpse of the old raised eyebrow trick.

Winger gave me the finger.

"Promises, promises."

That earned me a matched set of flying fingers.

# 39

Singe was having trouble concentrating. Dojango kept distracting her. He wouldn't shut up. Which was a habit of his that I'd forgotten. Kind of the way you forget how much a broken bone hurts until the next time you bust one.

I explained, on three separate occasions, how difficult it was for Singe to follow a trace as old as Playmate's, to explain that she had to concentrate all her attention on the task at hand.

"Oh, yeah. Oh, yeah. I understand, Garrett, actually." And thirty seconds later it would be, "This's just like the time me and Doris and Marsha was running the bag for Eddie the Gimp, actually. If we wasn't right on top of what we was doing every second . . ."

I sent a look of appeal up toward Doris, whose turn it was to walk beside the cart. But it was too dark out for him to notice. So I asked, "Doris. How the hell do I get your little brother to shut up?"

"Huh?"

I got ready to groan.

"I don't know. I just shut him out. Is he running off at the mouth again?"

"Still. I can't get him to stay quiet for twenty seconds straight. He's driving me crazy and he's making it impossible for Singe to keep her mind on her work." I suffered a moment of inspiration. "If we don't pull this thing off, if we don't find this guy, we blow the job. Which means that none of us will get paid."

"Dojango, shut the fuck up. You even cough, I'm gonna slug you." Doris waved a fist about the size of a bull's head in his brother's face. "Where we gonna put him when I do, Garrett? 'Cause I'm guaranteed gonna gotta do it on account of he can't even keep his mouth shut when he's asleep."

"He managed to shut up when he had to that time we all went to the Cantard."

"Yeah. But like they say, long ago and far away. And times change."

They do indeed. I'd just gotten more words out of one of the grolls than I'd heard before in all the years I'd known them.

Dojango couldn't help observing, "Actually, it ain't really polite to be talking about somebody like they ain't even there when you—"

*Bop!*

Doris's blow was almost casual. Dojango rocked and wilted. His brother scooped him up and carried him like a baby.

I asked, "Wasn't that a little harsh?"

"He ought to be getting used to it, Garrett. Actually." Doris grinned broadly. Moonlight glistened off his snaggle teeth. "This ain't the first time his mouth has caused us some trouble."

"Amen, brother," Marsha said from up front. "We gotta love the guy on account of he's family, but sometimes . . . If it wasn't for his connection with Cousin Morley . . ."

"Guys, we all have relatives like that. I've got a great-uncle Medford that somebody should've poisoned a hundred years ago."

Singe stopped. "You are quite right about Medford Shale, Garrett." Great-uncle Medford had figured prominently in the case where I'd first made Singe's acquaintance. "Just as you were right about me needing no distractions if I am to follow this trail. Perhaps I can have Doris knock you out, then have Marsha knock Doris out, then pray that a building collapses on Marsha."

"Or we could all take a hint and save the chatter till later."

"You could do that. But I am willing to bet that none of you are able."

Was it Mama Garrett's boy who'd said that this ratgirl desperately needed some self-confidence? She sure didn't lack for it in this crowd.

Ten minutes later, I called, "Singe, I know where we're going." We were headed for the Prose homestead. Maybe Playmate's luck had changed. Or, from his point of view, maybe he had given in to temptation. "We're headed for the boy's mother's flat."

"All right. If you think so. If you want to go there and wait for me, go ahead. I would prefer to stick to the trail. That will reveal if there were other stops he made along the way."

A gentle admonition from the expert. I decided to heed it. The girl had a point. Suppose Playmate was headed for Kayne Prose's place but never made it there?

# 40

He did make it. But he'd gone away again. Singe explained that to me before I ever went upstairs and found a very frightened Cassie Doap holed up behind a barricaded door, refusing to open up for anybody.

"Cassie, come on. This's Garrett. The man Playmate hired to find your brother Kip. Now Playmate's disappeared and I'm trying to track him down, too." I hoped he turned up soon. My body was doing a lot of aching. "He came here about . . ." I looked at Singe, whispered, "How long ago?"

"This morning."

"He came here this morning. Why was that? Where did he go from here?"

Cassie kept telling us to go away. She was terrified. But Singe could detect no odors that would justify such a strong response. And none of the neighbors showed any curiosity, which suggested that great dramas by Cassie Doap were not at all uncommon.

I recalled Rhafi telling me that Cassie was an actress. She put on characters like clothing. Maybe she was overacting now.

I wished I had one of my human lady friends along. Particularly Tinnie Tate of the shoemaking Tates. That professional redhead would know how to manage a mere blonde. Tinnie was an accomplished actress herself. At least where the manipulation of guys named Garrett was concerned.

Singe did make a few calming remarks, loudly enough to be heard through the door, while I tried to talk Cassie out of her hysteria. Singe's comments were kind of childish but they had their

effect. At some point Cassie decided to open the door a crack to
see who was out there in the hallway with me.

I don't know why my having a ratgirl along should've been reassuring, but it was enough so that Cassie decided she'd talk to us.
She asked, "What do you want to know, Mr. Garrett?"

My heart broke. That delectable young woman had called me
"mister." I was nothing but a "mister." I wasn't on her list of
prospects.

It's a cruel world indeed.

Probably just as well, though. Cassie was the kind of woman
Mom warned me against. One goofier than me.

"Where's Playmate, Cassie?"

"I don't know. He went to find my mom."

All right. That made sense. Maybe. To her.

She was definitely afraid, for real. She had referred to her
mother as Mom. She'd always called her Kayne before. "And why
did he do that, Cassie? Was she in trouble?"

"I don't know. She went to find Rhafi when he didn't come
home. Then she didn't come home. So I went and got Playmate.
And he decided to go looking for both of them. . . ."

Without bothering to inform me. Or even Winger. Who hadn't
mentioned Cassie. Which probably meant that Winger wasn't paying attention to what she was supposed to be doing.

"Just as an aside, did you see a tall blond woman at Playmate's
stable?"

"No. Is that important?"

"Probably not. All right. Let's go back. Rhafi disappeared?
What's the story on that?"

"That man you had watching Bic Gonlit. Rhafi was hanging
around with him. Covering for him when he had to go off. Like
that. Then Rhafi just disappeared. While that man was away getting them something to eat. He told us when Kayne and me went
to find Rhafi on account of Rhafi was supposed to start a new job
today. It's getting really hard to find somebody who'll give him a
chance anymore. Kayne really didn't want him to screw it up this
time."

Now that she'd decided to trust me Cassie gushed, getting rid
of the fear and the tension through a flood of words. She didn't really have much to say except that Rhafi had disappeared, then
Kayne had gone looking for him while sending her to tell Playmate. Then Playmate had gone after Kayne. And *he* hadn't been

seen since. And now Cassie was firmly convinced that the forces of darkness would come for her soon.

"You get back inside and barricade your door again. I'll take care of it." I hoped. I'd done somewhat less than take care of things on several occasions lately.

# 41

"You still have a trail?" I asked Singe.

"Yes. Getting better than it was."

I grunted. I didn't try to shortcut this time, though I expected the track to lead us straight to Saucerhead.

Which it did. More or less. Though Tharpe wasn't at his post.

I didn't even ask. I just left Singe to work her wonders.

"It is not entirely clear but it seems that Mr. Tharpe accompanied Mr. Playmate. Or he followed him within a very short time."

"And they went over to that ugly yellow building, right?"

"They were headed in that direction when they left here."

That was Singe. Making no assumptions.

"Can you detect any other odors here? That you might've noticed in that place we just visited?"

"That blond woman was here earlier today. And maybe others who left traces in that building. The odors are very faint."

"But there's nothing to contradict the story Cassie told us?"

"You do not trust her?"

"I've found that it's best to trust no one completely when I'm working a case. Nobody is ever completely honest with me."

"Truly?"

"Truly. Nobody wants to admit that they're desperate. But they are. Or they wouldn't come to me in the first place. They almost never do until things are out of hand. But that's human nature. You don't want people to know you can't manage your life. You're afraid to look weak."

We walked while Singe and I talked. I was moving more freely now but I still hurt. Doris and Marsha were doing a wonderful job of keeping their mouths shut. Dojango was still napping. He was in the cart.

I had everybody wait in front of the ugly yellow structure while I gave it a careful once-over from outside. The grolls attracted attention wherever they went, of course, but they knew how to discourage gawkers. A growl and a wave of the club each carried, more as decoration than as armament, were enough to discourage most people. For a while.

I wondered if they would use their clubs if pressed. They'd employed them during our visit to the Cantard but they hadn't really wanted to. They were actually gentle people, the Rose triplets. Though the two big ones did get a kick out of panicking people once in a while.

It seemed to me that it might be useful to know what was happening inside Casey's place before I went storming upstairs. "Doris. I need you to hoist me up so I can peek through a window."

Only there wasn't any window.

I stared at the blank brick, tried to visualize the inside of the tenement to see if I'd gotten turned around. I hadn't. So how had I misplaced a window made of glass?

I had Doris put me down. Then I worked my way around the ugly structure. It did have a few unglazed windows, but very few, indicating that it had been erected during the last attempt at establishing a window tax, with the minimum legal number of openings. None of the existing windows were on the fourth floor.

What the hell?

Which was what the place had to be in summer.

"How high can you count?" I asked Doris.

"Garrett, I don't think questions like that are polite."

"You're probably right. But I suspect that I don't much care. Here's what I want. Six minutes after I go in the front door you take your club and knock a hole through the bricks right up there where I was feeling the wall. Don't be shy about it. Haul off and pound a hole right through."

"And then what? When they come to arrest me. Go down fighting? I don't think so."

"Hey . . . !"

"You're a big-time bullshitter, Garrett, but you ain't big-time enough to bullshit me out of knocking somebody's building down."

"All right. All right." The recent outbreak of law and order was getting to be a real pain. "So don't bust a hole through the wall.

Just thump on it hard enough to distract whoever's on the other side. Better give me eight minutes to get up there, though. That's a lot of stairs."

Doris grunted, shuffled over to his brother. They muttered at one another, not pleased because whatever happened here would do so in front of witnesses.

The grolls were beginning to attract gawkers who wouldn't run from a growl and a brandished club. Mostly they were youngsters who should've been asleep, but adults would gather, too, if it became obvious that the grolls would have some entertainment value.

"Singe, you come with me." I headed for the entrance to the tenement. That was filled with spectators who wanted to know what was going on. "We're hunting for Kagyars," I told them, which dumbfounded everyone.

The people of TunFaire and Karenta aren't much interested in their own history.

My remark would've melted their spines half a millennium earlier. The Empire was still in place then but was suffering a swift decline because it was being choked to death by fanatic members of the Orthodox Rite. The Kagyars had been members of a gentle, nonviolent heretical cult whose beliefs must've terrified the hierarchy of the established religion. They invested all their energies and all the treasure of the state in a hundred-year campaign to exterminate the Kagyar heresy.

All that horror and cruelty and evil and today not one Karentine in a thousand can tell you what a Kagyar was. Possibly not even one in ten thousand.

# 42

"What will you do?" Singe asked.

"Knock on the door and see if anybody answers. Whack them over the head if they do." I brandished my headknocker. There was no peephole in Casey's door so he would have to open up in order to respond.

I knocked. Singe looked around nervously. And sniffed. She said, "It's hard to tell but I think they may have gone back downstairs again."

I knocked some more. "Playmate, Rhafi and I did come up and go down before."

Still no answer to my knock.

The building shuddered. Doris was on the job.

Something fell behind the door.

I did a fast picklock job between club strokes. "Get back against the wall," I told Singe. "Squeeze your eyes tight shut." I pushed the door inward, knelt, tripped the rug booby trap. I got the same crackle, pop, and flash. I avoided problems with my hair this time but did get the fuzz crisped off the outside of my forearm. Casey must've adjusted the aim of his sorcerous implement.

A glance across the hallway assured me that was true. The wall was smoking at a site two feet removed from the previous. And the crisped area was significantly larger.

I began to suspect that Casey might not plan to honor our new alliance. And I began to reflect on the fact that this particular silver elf wasn't as reluctant as the others to resort to violence.

"Don't expose yourself yet," I told Singe. "This thing's going to pop a couple more times."

Second try wasn't a charm. As before, the fury of the sorcery was considerably lessened. But its aim had shifted since the first flash. I lost most of my stick and got a mild case of roasted knuckles. The lead from the end of my stick was still liquid when I peeked.

We were collecting witnesses now, the older ones probably thinking about launching a raid as soon as the dangerous people got out of the way.

Doris kept whapping the outside wall. That was sure to attract attention out there. Police attention, eventually.

I told Singe, "We probably won't have much more time." But haste could be painful. Or even lethal.

I got down on the floor and slid my arm in to trip the third flash. It was more feeble than the last time I'd done this, though plenty bright enough to have me seeing spots.

Then I recalled Casey having just hopped over the trigger carpet.

Better safe than sorry.

I hopped.

There were no changes in the room behind the door. Casey had returned his possessions to their appointed places. Every item in the place looked precisely positioned.

I had a suspicion that Deal Relway's place would be very much like this.

I looked at the window that wasn't there on the outside of the building. The view it presented was impossible. What it should have shown was the wall of the building next door. Instead, I found myself looking down into the street out front.

Interesting.

Something thumped behind the closed curtain of Casey's bedroom.

"Come in and close the door," I told Singe. "Keep an eye on this window. Look for anybody who might belong to the Guard. Or who just gives you the feeling that they might be trouble." I yanked the curtain aside. And said, "Well, hello."

I'd found some of my missing people. Rhafi and his mother. Kayne was unconscious. So was Rhafi, but he was restless. Neither had a stitch on. Rhafi's clothing lay on the floor, as though discarded by someone undressing in a hurry. Nowhere could I find anything that looked like it might have come off Kayne.

I tried not to get distracted by the still life.

"Hey, Singe. You think you could track somebody's clothes if somebody else was wearing them?"

She stepped over where she could see what I saw. "My." She kept looking back and forth between the window and the naked people. "Well." And, "Can you wake them up?"

I was trying to do that already. I wasn't having any luck. I tried to avoid any expression as Singe took her opportunity to inform herself of the nature of human bodies.

"Would you consider the female attractive?" she asked.

With any other woman I know I'd have to consider that a trick or loaded question. Singe, I guessed, actually wanted to know. "Yes, she is. Especially considering her age and the fact that she's borne three children."

Singe becomes horrified whenever she contemplates the size of human babies. Her people have babies in litters of up to eight, the aggregate weight usually being less than that of one human newborn.

"And the male? Is he attractive?"

"Not to me. But that's partly because I know him. He could be attractive to some women." Nature appeared to have blessed Rhafi in one respect. I returned to my question. "Could you track the woman's clothing? I think our villain might've used it to disguise himself."

Singe eyed Rhafi dubiously, looked at me in mild alarm, then shifted her attention to the window. She thought. I kept trying to waken Kayne and her son.

It became obvious that they were under some kind of enchantment that I couldn't penetrate.

After several minutes of silence, Singe told me, "I can follow the horses again."

"Meaning?"

"Following the clothing would be extremely difficult. But I will have no trouble following Mr. Playmate and Mr. Tharpe. Who would have been with or who would have been following what they believed to be this woman." She eyed Rhafi again, growing more uneasy with what she saw.

I opened my mouth to ask a question, then realized that I'd been outreasoned by a ratgirl. A ratgirl who had other things on her mind.

Rhafi was getting more of her eye time than that window was. Casey had spun the tables on me.

He needed help to get to Kip. He'd told me so. But he didn't want to be anybody's partner. So he became Kayne Prose and lured Playmate and Saucerhead into going where he wanted, where they would, doubtless, fight like lions to defend the lovely Kayne from the villainous silver elves.

"Garrett! Something's happening!"

Dopey me, I glanced at Rhafi first, figuring maybe he was having a happy dream. But nothing to startle Singe was happening there.

"What?"

"The window. It keeps showing different things."

I stepped over.

She was right. It kept alternating between four different live scenes. "Did you touch it? Did you do anything?"

"No! I was over here, looking at . . . I never thought they were so big. . . . I *was* picking at the colored spots on this strange gray stone." She shoved a paw at me. Her whiskers were way back. But she just had to take another look at Rhafi.

I took the "stone." A number of not dissimilar items were scattered around the room. But not nearly so many as there had been during my previous visit. Which suggested that Casey might have taken some with him.

Those elves we'd chased, who'd knocked me out over and over, had used some small fetish or amulet or whatnot to do so. Maybe all those things were different magical devices.

Which got me thinking. We had a small collection back at the house, from that last place where Kip's kidnappers knocked us down, plus those I'd taken away from Rhafi. Should they stay there, dangerously near my partner, when we didn't know their capabilities? Might it not be more useful to surrender them to Colonel Block? That might earn me some obligation points. And might even be a service to the Crown. If these silver elves actually were a sorcerous threat from foreign lands.

Singe made a squealing sound that might have been surprise, fright, dismay, or all three together. I glanced into the other room.

I asked Singe the same question. "Did you touch it? Did you do anything?"

Singe backed out of the room but couldn't stop staring until I closed the curtain. I chuckled but didn't pursue the subject. I did suspect that in future she'd be less inclined toward romantic experimentation.

I thought it might be a good idea to gather up everything of potential interest to the people Block represented because minutes after Singe and I left it, Casey's place was going to get picked clean.

"Garrett?"

"Uhm?"

"You said tell you if I saw anything interesting?"

"You found Rhafi interesting, did you?"

"Not that." Her tone put me in my place for my having my mind in the gutter. "In the window."

I saw what she meant when the view of the street out front came up.

Three silver elves had taken station across the way. They weren't out in traffic but, even so, you'd think people dressed that weird would attract some notice. That they attracted none whatsoever told me that some sort of enchantment concealed them from passersby but couldn't fool the window's eye.

A hint of a flicker of afterimage indicated that they were pretending to be women. Women who didn't know their ways around. One stared at something in her hand as she swung her partially extended arm right and left.

"We did something to attract Casey's enemies," I said. "And they got here fast. But they still don't quite know where to find him. We'd better get out of here while we can." I squinted at the window when the street view came back up. Did those elves really have waists and breasts? That was a fine crop of nubbins, to be sure, but damned if it didn't look like *something* was there, putting a little appeal into those elegant silver lines.

# 43

The silver elves weren't visible anywhere when Singe and I reached the street. I felt them vaguely, though, in the back of my mind.

"Can you smell anything?"

"Something cold. . . . Like what I smelled when we were tracking that boy. But not quite the same."

"I think that's because this's a different bunch of elves. We have some kind of pyramid here. There's one guy, Casey, who's hunting two guys, Lastyr and Noodiss, because they're wanted for unspecified crimes. Then we have these three elves, evidently all female. In times past they raided Playmate's stable and the Prose flat, trying to lay hands on Kip. Then we have the four who actually did capture Kip. Unless Casey was lying—and his lips weren't moving at the time, on account of he doesn't have any—these people are all involved in criminal enterprises of some sort."

We were moving away from the ugly yellow structure, Singe picking the way, me limping along in her wake lugging a sack filled with trinkets rescued from Casey's digs. I nodded to Doris and Marsha as I passed. I felt the invisible elves start moving behind me.

Singe observed, "Reliance is involved in criminal enterprises. But a lot of his activities don't appear to be morally questionable."

Though she hadn't stated it perfectly I was proud that Singe could reason to that level. "True. The law isn't always about what's right. Or wrong. A lot of times it's about somebody being guaranteed an advantage over somebody else. And that's human nature. That's the nature of any sentient species, I think. Damn!

Those invisible people really are moving back there. I get the feeling that they're crossing to Casey's place."

I hoped that was what they were doing, rather than falling in behind us.

They were sure to walk in on some excitement if they went upstairs. I hoped they'd find Casey's place crawling with scavengers and voyeurs.

I said, "I think it might be a good idea if we checked back to see how Rhafi and Kayne are doing, later." Those two could end up in deep trouble if that sleep spell didn't wear off.

"Shush. I need to concentrate."

So now it was me who was the distraction. The triplets weren't because they were keeping their distance, pretending they weren't with me. Good on whichever one of them thought of that. But I needed to toss my swag bag into the cart with Dojango. I wasn't about to carry it forever.

My aches and pains had receded somewhat but they continued to hamper me. I limped and gimped and had no sense of humor at all. I couldn't even work myself into a state of amusement over Singe's recent discombobulation. And that was pretty damned funny. It could become a classic after a few retellings polished it up.

When our path took us around a corner, thus taking us out of sight of any eyes tagging along behind, I halted. I didn't move until Doris and Marsha appeared.

I tossed my swag bag into Dojango's lap. The results were satisfactory. Rose's enthusiastic barking demonstrated that he had been faking unconsciousness.

I left him to his brothers. Singe and I traveled on into the night, me limping and groaning and demonstrating grand vigor in protesting my determination to find a new way to make a living.

"Where in hell are we going?" I muttered. We'd been walking for hours. It was the middle of the night. I felt every step in every muscle and every joint. We were way up north, passing through neighborhoods where real elves roamed. Singe and I drew stares from folks curious about whether we were a couple. I could've told them that we were a couple of idiots.

This was dangerous country. But if we stuck to the main thoroughfare, the Grand Avenue, we should be all right, partly because it was customarily safe ground, partly because Doris and Marsha were ambling along with us, their clubs dragging the cobblestones and their knuckles threatening to get down there soon.

"I am following the trail, Garrett. I am not creating it." Singe was getting cranky, too. Probably needed to get some food in her.

"This is why I hate working. Once you get started you can't just knock off when you feel like it and have a couple of beers. You've got to keep going until you drop. Why don't you eat one of your sandwiches?"

Singe immediately went to the back of the cart and dug out several. "If it makes you feel better knowing, we are much closer than we were. Their scent is almost fresh. They are less than three hours ahead."

Every silver lining has a cloud.

"That's the godsdamned gate up there!" I grumbled, glaring at an island of light in the far distance. "Please don't tell me they left town."

"All right." Singe sounded troubled. And she should. For rat-people TunFaire's outer wall constitutes the edge of the world. Go past it and you fall off into the misty void.

The situation wasn't much better for me. I don't like not-city. I don't go outside often. When I do I prefer to visit some rich man's estate, where I can be comfortable while I take care of business. I get back to town as fast as I can.

If we kept going this general direction for a few hours we could drop in on the Contague estate.

Although I know better intellectually, emotionally I feel like the deadly wilderness is clamoring at the city gate, all carnivorous or poisonous plants and animals, most of them bigger and faster than me, while the air is so full of man-eating bugs that you don't dare breathe deep. In reality, most of the countryside near Tun-Faire is well tamed. If it wasn't it wouldn't be able to feed the city. The exceptions are some bits unsuited for exploitation or which the wealthy and powerful have set aside as hunting reserves or whatnot. The rare incursions of thunder lizards, mammoths, or even bears or giant ground sloths, are just that: rare. But they sure do get talked about plenty.

Marsha said, "We maybe need to take a sleep break first if we're really going to go out there, Garrett."

He had a point. A good point. Or, at least, a damned good excuse for us not to go wandering around the wilderness in the dark. Even if we were only a few hours behind our friends.

# 44

Wilderness is relative. Before sunrise we were in wild country compared to where I live. But we were in a carefully tamed and only mildly unkempt park compared to the places where I fought my share of the war.

Of course, this was the worst nightmare wilderness Singe had ever seen. She couldn't take ten steps without stopping to sniff the morning air for the warning stench of approaching monsters. I kept after her to move faster. "The quicker we get there the quicker we get it over with and the quicker we get back to town. You don't want to spend the night out here, do you?" But instinct is hard to overcome. I prove that every time I get too close to Belinda Contague. "Besides, the grolls can handle anything we're likely to meet."

Dojango had been yakking all morning, inconsequentialities. Typical of him, actually. So much so that nobody paid him the least attention. Though Doris did drag him out of the cart and have him pull it as one way of slowing his jaw down.

"Wait a minute," I said. "What was that?"

Because Dojango's mouth runs with no real connection to his brain he just chomped air for a minute. What might he have said that could interest me? He hadn't been listening. Then he went into mild shock because somebody *was* interested in something that he'd said. "Uh, I don't remember, actually."

"About the thing you saw in the sky."

"Oh. That happened while you were all asleep, actually."

When the time had come we'd all just planted ourselves at

streetside, grolls on the flanks, and started snoring. We hadn't been bothered.

Size *does* matter.

Dojango continued, "I decided I'd stand watch on account of all of the rest of you were out like the dead."

He was fibbing. He hadn't been able to sleep because he'd spent all that time snoozing in the cart. It's easy to tell when Dojango is revising history. He forgets to use his favorite word.

"And?"

"And a ball of light came in out of the east, from beyond the river. It went somewhere south of us. It stopped for a while. I could see the glow. Then it came north, slowly, drifting back and forth over Grand Avenue. I had a feeling it was looking for something, actually."

"And it came to a stop up above us?"

"Yeah. After a while it shined a really bright light down on us. And that's all I remember." He shuddered, though. So there was something more.

"What else?"

He didn't want to talk about it but Dojango Rose is incapable of resisting an invitation to speak. "Just a really bad dream where the light lifted me up and took me inside the glow, into a weird, lead-gray place. They did really awful things to me, these weird, shiny little women. This one wouldn't leave my thing alone."

"I see." He'd healed wondrous fast if he'd been tortured. "Something to keep in mind." I did some thinking. Some consideration of the circumstances. I came up with some ideas.

The first time we approached a sizable woodlot which boasted enough tangled undergrowth to suggest that it wasn't used much I had Doris and Marsha carry the cart and its cargo deep inside and camouflage it with branches.

Dojango cried like a baby.

"I guarantee you I don't have a whole lot of sympathy, buddy. Why don't you use your sore feet to make the rest of you mad enough to smack some of those elves around when we catch up with them?"

That bought me a respite. Dojango Rose is a lover, not a fighter. He probably heard his mother calling but couldn't run away as long as his brothers stuck it out.

We passed gated estates. The grolls attracted considerable attention. Most of the guards were friendlier than they might have been had I tried to engage them in conversation on my own. Doris and Marsha make a convincing argument just standing around, leaning on their clubs.

Some of those guards had seen Saucerhead and Playmate go by. But not a one had seen Kayne Prose. Or any other willowy blonde. Tharpe and Playmate had been bickering, according to several witnesses. They were, also, not making very good time. We were still only a few hours behind them despite our pause to enjoy a stone mattress.

"We keep on with this and we're going to find ourselves out in the real country pretty soon," I observed. We were past the truck gardens and wheatfields and starting up the slope into wine country. Ahead the hills started growing up. Fast.

We popped over a ridgeline, me cursing the day Kayne met Kip's pop and, even more bloodily, the day I let myself get into debt to Playmate. "Whoa! There it is. That's perfect."

"There what is?" Dojango asked. I'd stopped. He'd sat down. He had one boot off already.

"That bowl of land down there. Filled with trees. It has a pond in there. You can see the water. Runs down off all these hills. Looks like a great hiding place. Bet you that's where—"

Some sort of flash happened under the trees. A dark brown smoke ring rolled up through the foliage. There was a rumble like a very large troll clearing his throat.

"That was different," Dojango said. He levered his other boot off.

"My guess is, our friends just found the elven sorcerers."

Nobody rushed off to help. Dojango massaged his blisters and distinctly looked like he'd rather head some other direction. Any other direction.

Singe had the sensibilities of a soldier. "If we can see what is happening down there, then whoever is down there can see what is happening up here."

"Absolutely." I responded by dropping into the shade of a split rail fence. The Rose boys didn't need the whole speech, either. The big ones made themselves as scarce as possible on an open road that ran downhill through a vineyard where the plants were seldom more than hip high. To me. Dojango rolled into a ditch.

A look around showed me a countryside not made for sneaking. The wooded bowl was entirely surrounded by vineyards. I could cover some ground on hands and knees amongst the vines but there wasn't a whole lot of cover for guys twenty feet tall.

And there were people out working the vineyards. Some not

that far from us, eyeing us askance because of our odd behavior. Before long most of the workers began to amble downhill to see what was going on.

"There's our cue, people. Look like you've got grape skins between your toes."

Dojango began to whine in earnest. Once out of his boots his feet had swollen. He couldn't get them back on.

It was real. We'd have to leave him behind. Which was just as well, actually. Dojango has a talent for screwing things up by getting underfoot when times begin to get exciting.

I told him, "We'll pick you up on the way back."

He didn't act like his feelings were hurt.

# 45

Most of the vineyard workers reached the wood well before we did. Which was fine by me. Because something unpleasant was going on in amongst the trees. Something flashy, noisy, then smoky. Another doughnut of brown smoke rolled up out of the trees.

The vineyard people decided they wanted no part of that. They went scooting right back up the hills. Not a one was interested in wasting valuable running time gawking at my odd company.

At a guess I'd say people in the area had had bad experiences down there before.

Once you penetrated the dozen yards of dense brush and brambles on the outer perimeter of the wood you found yourself in a perfectly groomed, parklike grove. Without undergrowth. With grass almost like a lawn. With a pond an acre in size, somewhat off center to the west. And with a big silver discus thing smack in the middle, standing eight feet above the grass on spindly metal legs. A flimsy ladder rose from the grass to an opening in the disk's belly. A silver elf lay at the foot of that, unconscious or dead. Likewise, one Saucerhead Tharpe, right hand gripping the elf's ankle, whose scattered attitude suggested that he'd been dragged back out of the discus.

I saw nothing to explain the brown smoke rings, nor all the racket we'd heard while we were coming down the hill.

The wood was perfectly still now. Not a bird had a word to say. Not a bug sang one bar to his ladylove. A few leaves did stir in the breeze but they kept their voices down. The only sounds to be heard were the distant, excited voices of vineyard workers who had decided they were far enough away to slow down and gossip.

When I stopped and counted them up in my head I doubted that there'd been more than a dozen workers, total.

We four froze with the moment, some listening, some sniffing. I turned slowly, trying to get a direction for the sense of presence I'd begun to feel.

I whispered to Singe, "The Casey creature is here in the grove somewhere. Can you scent him?"

"The odors here are very strange, Garrett. I am confused. I do scent something that might be Casey but I cannot locate him."

A breeze stirred the leaves and branches. My eye kept going to an oddity of shadow that didn't stir with everything else. I examined it from the corners of my eyes. I squinted, right and left and direct. I moved several times so I could try everything from a variety of angles. Several times the dance of bright sunlight and deep leaf shadow made me think that I had glimpsed something that might have been Kayne Prose crumpled up beside a stump, trapped inside something like a heat shimmer. When I concentrated I discovered a shadow being cast onto the ground by something not apparent to the naked eye.

I looked left and right. Nothing told me why the vineyard hands had run for it. Nothing told me where Playmate might be now. Nothing indicated the current whereabouts of the three silver elves not sprawled underneath their silvery discus. Nothing told me much of anything.

I drifted toward the shadow that shouldn't have been, beckoning Marsha to follow, laying a finger to my lips. I got a few more glimpses of Kayne Prose. She didn't appear to be awake. The invisibility spell keeping her unseen was sputtering and maybe needed a little punching up from somebody who'd had enough schooling to know what they were doing.

The spell did a whole lot of nothing to fool my sense of touch.

I got Marsha down on his knees, guided his hands. "That's his head. You hang on in case he wakes up. If he does, let him know who's in control. Without killing him, if possible."

"Gotcha."

I began the task of frisking and disrobing a body I couldn't see. The stripping part didn't go well at all.

A totally bedraggled imitation Kayne Prose materialized suddenly. In the same moment Singe said, "Gleep! Where did Garrett go?"

Inasmuch as I had not gone anywhere I gazed with suspicion at the small gray fetish I'd just taken off Casey. "Singe. Come over here." When she arrived I put the device into her paw. She vanished. I assume I reappeared. "Now you're invisible. Hang on to that. It might come in handy."

"Nobody can see me? Whoo! Ha-ha! What I could do with this!"

"What couldn't we all do? Why don't you sneak over there and see if Saucerhead is still breathing?" I had a recollection of having turned up horizontal myself a few times after running into these elves. Only they hadn't knocked themselves out, too, those times.

I couldn't see Singe but she did still cast some shadow when she stepped into the light. She said, "Mr. Playmate must have climbed up the ladder."

"Singe! Don't go in there!"

My last two words even I couldn't hear over the *Crump!* as a sudden ring of brown smoke blew down off the bottom of the discus. The smoke hit the ground, ricocheted back upward, into the sky. It seemed much less substantial than had the earlier clouds.

"Singe? You all right?"

A ratlike squeak resolved itself into, "Garrett? Can you hear me? I cannot hear right now. But otherwise I am all right. I am going to finish climbing the ladder now."

"You damned fool! That's what just—"

"I found Mr. Playmate. He is right inside here. Out cold. Lying on a metal floor with two more elves. One has a broken arm. At least it is bent the wrong way."

Meanwhile, on the ground, I was continuing to make sure that Casey and the other unconscious elf wouldn't be able to go anywhere when they woke up. "Let's see if we can't get this costume off this one." I'd given up trying to strip Casey. And to Singe, "That's a good job, Singe. Don't go wandering around in there. Singe?"

She didn't respond.

The girl was getting a little *too* sure of herself. "Would one of you guys reach up in there and drag Playmate out?"

Doris had taken over trying to get Casey's silver suit off him so Marsha crawled under the discus. It was a tight fit. He ended up twisting himself around so he was seated on the grass, his head and shoulders inside the opening. "Gosh, Garrett, it's weird in here." A moment later he dropped an elf.

"Hey! You damned near hit me with that." I was having no luck stripping the elf who had fallen with Saucerhead. The new arrival didn't look like he'd be any easier.

"Here comes the one with the broken arm. You might want to take him so he don't get hurt any worse."

I jumped up just in time to grab the body Marsha handed down. The elf weighed hardly anything at all.

"Hey, Garrett! Look at this."

I turned. Doris was standing up, his top half up in the foliage. He seemed to be looking back up the hill that we had descended to get to this adventure. I shed my burden, skipped a dozen yards to a point where I could see the hillside myself.

I thought the vineyard workers would be up to something. But they were just making tracks.

Instead, Dojango was in deep sludge. But he hadn't noticed yet.

# 46

It was kind of funny, actually, because he didn't see it coming until after Doris and I began watching. He was, probably, just sitting there throwing pebbles at grasshoppers and congratulating himself on having gotten out of all the work when he spotted the glowing balls. By that time they'd bracketed him and were descending.

Doris said, "Maybe he didn't make up all that shit about them pulling him inside and doing something to him. They sure didn't have no trouble finding him again, did they? Even after we ditched that cart and all that magical stuff."

"An excellent observation, brother." I watched Dojango jump up, try to run in several directions, all of which turned out to be blocked as soon as he chose them. He never stopped trying though, like a squirrel in a box trap. While prancing on stones because his tender feet were bare.

I noted that the vineyard workers were trying to make themselves seem scarce while they watched, too.

Once the balls of light were on the ground they faded to become three eggs of lead-gray metal with little in the way of exterior features.

I said, "We can probably expect their company in a few minutes. We'd better roll up our sleeves and get ready." Playmate came flopping down out of the discus. Marsha started dragging him away. I said, "Hide all these people in the woods. Under the brush, maybe. Then get yourselves out of sight. Where is that girl?" I hopped over the foot of the ladder. "Singe!"

Singe didn't respond.

I said, "On second thought, leave Saucerhead and Playmate

lying out in the open. This guy, too." I used a toe to nudge the silver elf lying nearest the ladder. "That'll give them something to focus on. So they'll maybe overlook the rest of us. You guys hide. Take whatever steps seem appropriate."

Gritting my teeth, I reached out and touched the metal ladder. Quick and cautious, using just the tip of one finger.

Nothing happened.

Not even a hint of brown smoke.

# 47

The ladder took me up into a small metal room that was maybe
ten feet across. Its ceiling was five feet high. I had to move in a
stoop that started my back aching in moments. At its extremities
the room's floor conformed to the external curve of the discus.
The room itself seemed suitable only for storage.

"Singe?"

My voice sounded strange in that place.

Singe didn't answer me.

"Don't be playing games just because you're invisible."

Still no answer.

The back side of the ladder went on up to another level. I
swung around there, looked up.

There did seem to be an opening—which was closed. Mostly
closed. A bit of fabric had gotten caught in a gap where the closure abutted the head of the ladder. The lighting was poor but the
fabric resembled that of Singe's shirt.

I pushed. Nothing gave but the muscles in my back. I tried
again, twisting. The closure slid sideways an inch. I thought I had
it now. I pushed and twisted some more. The crack widened a few
more inches, then wouldn't respond to any effort I made.

I tried to look through the crack. I couldn't see anything but
nothing. I followed up by snaking a cautious hand in to feel
around. Nobody stomped on my fingers. It's a wonderful life
when the highlight of your working day is that nobody stomped
on your fingers.

I felt around some more. It seemed that the main reason the
entry wouldn't open any farther was that Singe was lying on it.

Getting her off proved to be a challenge. But I was up to it. I was a trained, veteran Royal Marine.

Eventually I slithered through the gap. Singe was lying in plain sight, mostly on another metal floor like the one below. This room was perfectly round, with another ceiling that had to be uncomfortably low even for the elves who used it. One of those was slumped in one of four chairs gracing the room. The chairs were all fixed to the floor.

The wonders of that round room were too numerous to recount. I think I was too numb to recognize a lot of them as anything special. There seemed to be thousands of little glowing lights, for example. Some were green or red, or yellow or purple or even white. Some kept flashing on and off. Most seemed content just to be there, showing themselves.

I've seen some wild sorcery in my day, including the kind that melts mountains. Yet I was more impressed with this vision than I'd been with anything I'd seen before. The numbers were what did it.

Then there were windows something like the one at Casey's, most of them more nearly horizontal than vertical. But the really eye-popping thing, the overwhelming thing, was the outer wall, all the way around the room.

It was like that was missing, not there at all until you touched it. The woods were visible there pretty much as I would've seen them had I been standing on a fifteen-foot-high platform. I was seeing the world from the altitude that Doris and Marsha saw it.

I couldn't hear anything, though.

I checked Singe's pulse. She'd be all right. I checked the elf. Somebody had slugged this one from behind. I'd bet on an invisible ratgirl. I couldn't find a pulse in any of the usual places but he was twitching already. I got him plucked of his possessions and tied up with odds and ends. Just in time.

And just in time for the arrival of the three glowing balls. Those touched down carefully after a wary approach.

When he saw that happening, my captive elf began to kick and struggle. He wasn't pleased. I felt an inarticulate mental pressure but he never said an actual word.

I shut the door in the floor and parked both Singe and the elf atop it. When he tried to move I admonished him gently with a toe. He learned faster than a pup.

I looked outward again.

The three glowing objects gradually stopped doing that. They turned out to be dull gray lopsided metal eggs not more than ten feet tall, the fat half of each egg downward. Each stood on three metal legs as skinny as broom handles.

Nothing happened for a while. Then, as an opening began to appear in the side of one of the gray eggs, Doris came bounding out of the woods and dealt that very egg a mighty overhand smack with his club. The blow left a sizable dent.

Then there was a flash. And Doris staggered away, not knocked down but not real sure where he was anymore. A vaguely feminine silver elf dropped a ladder from the assaulted egg and scrambled down to the ground. She seemed to be seeing the fact but didn't want to believe that Doris hadn't been destroyed by the flash.

I got all that from feelings within me and from elven body language that probably meant nothing of the sort because the creature wasn't human.

It hit the ground running toward Doris, in a truly foul mood. The groll himself had gotten lost in the woods. He was blundering around in confusion.

The other two silver elves left their eggs. They showed hints of femininity, too. From the remove at which I watched I couldn't be completely sure, however. Though there did seem to be minor physical differences from the other elves, nothing was absolutely convincing. Maybe if you were a silver elf you could tell. Kind of the way slugs can tell the boys from the girls.

Plainly, they didn't label themselves the way humans do, sexually or by pinpointing weirdness, physical disparity, or attractiveness.

Never mind. I don't need to get my ulcers burning about human nature. I'm all growed up now, Maw. I know we ain't gonna get nowhere wishin' an' hopin'. People are too damned stubborn.

Speaking of stubborn. Here came Marsha, half the size of a house, crawling on his belly, sneaking up on the lead egg only abandoned a moment earlier by a silver elf with cute little crabapple breasts. Marsha had learned something while watching his brother's precipitate attack.

When he was close enough Marsha reached out and, with a sideways swipe of his club, swatted one of the egg's legs out from under it.

Which didn't turn out to be quite as clever as I'd thought before he did it.

When the egg fell it tipped straight toward him. He had to scramble to get out of the way. And even then he wasn't safe.

The elves decided to chase him.

The violence of the egg's fall shook the discus. For a second I was afraid I was going down, too.

The fallen egg began to glow in a patch on its bottom. Then it started sliding around drunkenly, darting and stopping like a water bug, spinning, tearing up trees. It knocked over the only uninjured egg, struck the discus a ferocious glancing blow, and panicked the new arrivals. They didn't know which way to run. Finally, the egg blistered off in a straight line, ripped through the pond and the woods beyond, then plowed a deep furrow through a vineyard almost all the way to the top of the slope before it came to rest. At that point it seemed both to melt and to sink slowly into the earth.

Marsha had to be amazed by what he'd accomplished.

The silver elves were amazed, too. And distraught in the extreme.

I was now reasonably confident that they did communicate the way the Dead Man does. I couldn't pick out any words but the atmosphere was pregnant with emotion. There was a lot of blaming and finger-pointing going on, driven by a terror of being marooned. That fear became a notch more intense when the three examined their surviving egg and discovered that Doris's ill-advised attack had crippled it somehow.

"Uh-oh."

The three all stared at the disk like it might be their salvation. After a brief commune they all produced a variety of gray fetishes and began poking at them with long, skinny, nailless fingers. One of the little girls came forward, toward me, passing out of view beneath my feet. Two minutes later there was a whining noise from the area where Singe and the captive elf lay sprawled.

I scooted over there. The door in the floor was trying to move. The weight piled on it kept it from doing so. I sensed a considerable frustration down below. That was one—maybe—lady who didn't think things ought to be going this way. A—maybe—woman whose day had been on the brink of triumph, but which had turned to shit in her hands in a matter of minutes.

"Been there, sweetheart," I muttered. I began to look around, seeking something identifiable as a nonlethal weapon. I didn't want to hurt anybody if I really was dealing with women. Possibly the most bizarre aspect of this business so far was the fact that no one had gotten killed. We had one elf with a broken arm and we had me with a bumper crop of aches and bruises—acquired from ratpeople not directly involved in the case—but otherwise the whole thing was almost civilized. And no silver elf had yet done anyone a direct physical injury.

I didn't find anything that could be used as a weapon. Maybe I could rip an arm off the elf I did have and use it to harvest the new crop. I did retain plenty of pieces of steel in a variety of shapes and sizes, all with very sharp edges, should the situation grow hair, though.

Even so, these weird people didn't seem to be impressed by weapons. Which left me wondering just how bright they could be.

The elf downstairs tried to get the floor door open again. I sat down nearby, ready to crack her knuckles with the butt of a knife if she stuck a hand through the way I had. I'm not always a perfect gentleman.

Some of the little flashy lights expired suddenly. Outside, the most voluptuous elf began to jump up and down. Evidently she'd solved some puzzle and was totally excited. She didn't jiggle much, though.

The other elf looked over her shoulder. Clearly, she disapproved of her sidekick's demonstration but was pleased with their results. Her daddy longlegs fingers began to prance across another of those gray fetish things.

More lights went out. There was a declining whine, fading fast, never noticed until it went.

"I don't think that's a good sign," I told myself.

Still more lights went out.

"Definitely not a good sign."

Up on the see-through wall—which I just now noticed had a curved shape in the vertical dimension that allowed it to show a lot more than a flat window would—I saw a large piece of deadwood come arcing out of the woods, spinning end for end horizontally. It was a log I would've had trouble lifting.

It got both silver elves.

I felt their rush of pain inside my head.

# 48

The elf downstairs made a run for it. She dropped out the bottom of the disk and headed up the path already blazed by the self-immolating egg. Marsha didn't have any luck catching her. I didn't let it worry me. She was completely weird and doubtless had no clue how to get by in the country, without help from her strange, sorcerous toys. She should not be hard to track. Just follow the commotion she caused.

Maybe Colonel Block could get me a big fat medal for having saved Karenta from the foreign sorcerers and sorceresses. Maybe the flying pigs would start evicting the pigeons from their traditional roosts. Which sure would leave a mess around all those dead and incompetent generals posing outside the Chancery.

The common wisdom among former grunts is that *competent* generals wouldn't have screwed up so bad they got themselves killed and therefore there wouldn't have been any need for a memorial.

Soldiers are a cynical bunch.

In the process of exploring the interior of the discus I discovered Cypres Prose installed in a padded box behind a door that locked from the outside. The little horizontal closet was soundproof. It was on a floor above the one with the marvelous lights and the wonderful view.

The upper level seemed to constitute crew quarters and such, if you went over it just guessing.

My years in the Corps, with its ancient and traditional naval associations, clicked in at last. This thing had to be some kind of aerial ship or boat. With a crew. With decks and bulkheads and hatches instead of floors and walls and doors. With heads instead of toilets and galleys instead of kitchens—and all that special navy talk us Marines always resented.

The silver elves must have been trying to teach Kip something, stashing him in a padded box. But they hadn't been harsh enough. Their rewards and punishments must have been too subtle. The boy began to complain the second the door opened, never once going for a "Good to see you again," or, "Thanks for coming to find me, Garrett." That being the case I shut him back in while I went on to explore the rest of the aerial ship.

After a while I reopened the hatch confining Kip. "Where can I find Lastyr and Noodiss?"

Bitch, bitch, piss, and moan.

"All right. Your call." I shut the hatch.

I went back outside "Hey, Marsha, did you happen to look for Dojango? I'm pretty sure they dragged him into one of those lead eggs."

In the excitement we'd forgotten the little brother.

Marsha went over to the fallen egg and yelled in the doorway. He didn't get a response. For a moment he and I both stared up the hill along the path taken by the berserk egg. Then Marsha went and yelled into the dented egg. That didn't do any good either.

"I'd better look," I said. "Chances are they wouldn't have left him in any condition where he could do some mischief." These silver elves were highly weird but I doubted that they were highly stupid.

I was right. I found Dojango in the dented ship, as unconscious as Singe and Playmate and Saucerhead Tharpe. "This is not good," I kept muttering to myself. Until my superior intellect finally seized the day.

I went up into the vineyards and asked around until I found a somberly clad, gloomily serious young man willing to abandon his post for a fee. I gave him messages to deliver to the Dead Man, to Morley Dotes, and to Colonel Block. In that order. I gave him half of his handsome messenger's stipend before he departed, giving him to understand that receipt of the balance was contingent upon his getting the job done right. He nodded a lot. All his mates seemed to think his going to the city was a huge joke.

Then I just felt like I could lie back and take it easy until reinforcements arrived. Taking a few minutes every hour to go see if Kip had started to catch on yet.

That boy was slow. After a while he mentioned hunger. "That

right there's you one more motive for turning cooperative, I'd say. Whew! It's really starting to get ripe in there, too. Guess those good old silver boys let you out when you had to go." He refused to understand that right away, too.

Back outside, I asked, "How is Doris looking, Marsha?" I'd been rooting for a swift recovery. Making small talk with the healthy brother had worn thin in a hurry. Once we'd used up business and gossip all Marsha could talk about was the shortage of suitable females within his size range.

"An' you can stuff them ideas right there, Garrett. On account of I've already heard all the jokes about mastodons and blue oxen."

"Then I shan't belabor the obvious. Actually, I was going to suggest that you jog up and get our cart back. Singe packed us a load of sandwiches." She'd also eaten a load of sandwiches along the way but I hoped a few might have survived. And if not, I'd at least get a respite from the mighty lover's whining.

Marsha thought that was about the best idea he'd heard all week. He took off right away, tossing back, "Keep an eye on Doris, will you?"

"I will indeed." On account of I didn't want to be in the wrong place when the big goof tripped over his own feet and came tumbling down.

I made my rounds of prisoners and patients. They were all being incredibly stubborn about recovering, though I now saw some signs that they were coming back. Singe had begun babbling in her sleep, thankfully mostly in ratfolk cant. My grasp of the dialect is feeble. I was embarrassed only about half the time.

Doris was coming along fine. He made sense about seventy percent of the time. He stayed fine as long as he didn't get up and try to walk around. His sense of balance was out of whack. When he did try to walk he drifted sideways. Then he fell over.

Twenty minutes after Marsha left we had a visitor. Some sort of vineyard manager or overseer or supervisor, name of Boroba Thring. Boroba was a fat little brown guy on a skinny little brown donkey. He believed devoutly in his right to claim everyone and everything in sight in the name of his employer, evicting me in the meantime. Evidently he seldom dealt with anyone who told him "No." He'd come visiting alone and didn't see that as a disadvantage. He was one of those particularly irritating characters who couldn't conceive of anyone thwarting him, let alone ignoring him. Which is what I did for a while when first he spouted his nonsense. Once I became sufficiently sick of his voice, I said, "Hey, Doris. You can have this one to play with."

Thring didn't last long. I had Doris dump him in with the other prisoners. After that I passed the time amusing myself by figuring out how to strip silver elves.

The material they wore was tough but I discovered that it wouldn't stand up to a really sharp piece of steel.

Marsha arrived with the cart. "You're probably gonna want to keep those people in the shade, Garrett. I've seen albinos with more color to them."

"They definitely don't get out much." My, oh, my, the cargo area on the back of the cart still contained sandwiches that Singe hadn't eaten. And some beer in stoneware bottles. That was a nice surprise. I shared the sandwiches with the grolls. I shared the beer with me. I reserved the last sandwich and went to see Kip.

# 49

"This is the way it goes, kid." I waved the sandwich, took a small bite. "You can talk to me, the nice guy who's here to help you. Or you can talk to the Guard when they get here and take over. I know. You're a tough guy. You've been getting yourself ready for this in your daydreams for the last fifteen years. And so far it hasn't hurt much more than an ordinary dream. But when the Guards get here they'll have someone from the Hill with them. And you know those people won't think any more of stepping on you than they would of stomping a roach."

I looked into Kip's eyes and tried to imagine what he was seeing as he looked at me. Definitely not what I thought I was. Probably just a minor villain, laughing and rubbing his hands together while cackling about having ways to make him talk.

Time was getting to be a problem.

What I had to get around was Kip's absolute vision of himself as the hero of his own story. Which at this point meant crushing him in a major way because I couldn't come up with a means by which he could see an honorable escape route he could use without believing his escape was some sort of wicked betrayal.

I did some estimating of how much time I might yet have before those I'd summoned arrived. Seemed like it should be quite a while yet if things ran their usual course in officialdom.

I did some soul-searching, too. Because I wanted to know why some part of me was so convinced that it was important for me to get to Lastyr and Noodiss.

When I start thinking, and wondering about my own motives,

life really starts to slow down. I can see why Morley gets impatient with me.

Marsha built us a fire. Doris had recovered enough to help without falling in. I gathered some of my favorite people in the circle of warmth. Singe. Playmate. Saucerhead. Casey and a member each from the other crews. They didn't look like much naked. The males were like shriveled up old prunes. Like mummies. One of the two females wasn't much more promising. The other got barely passing marks from me because I possess a prejudiced eye.

I hoped somebody would thaw out and tell me something interesting.

Neither Doris nor Marsha had any trouble leaving brother Dojango a subject in the realm of silence. Dojango never said anything interesting. Dojango just said.

Saucerhead recovered first. He was in a predictably foul temper. He insisted he was starving.

"Save yourself some agony," I told him. "I've been where you're at now, three times. If you try to eat anything it'll come right back up."

"Let me learn the hard way." His stomach growled agreement.

"Your choice. But the only edibles in the area are those grapes up yonder. And if those were ripe they would've been picked already."

Saucerhead wasn't interested in common sense or rationality but he could handle them when they happened. "Then I'm going back to sleep." Presumably a trick he'd learned in the army. Doze as much as you can until flying misfortune makes you get up and go to work.

"Don't get into it too deep. I sent for the Guard. I can't see you wanting to be lying around here napping when they show."

"Which won't be for a while. And I can count on my good friend Garrett to kick me in the slats and wake me up as soon as he sees them coming over yonder ridge. Go on and get away from me. My head is pounding and I ain't in no mood."

I did get a smile out of Playmate before he turned nasty on me. Somehow, while he was unconscious, all his pain and misery had become my fault. Ignoring the incredibly stupid thing he'd done, chasing after a Kayne Prose who wasn't even the real deal, a dozen miles into the countryside.

Singe tried harder to be nice when she came around, but she did find it difficult to be understanding about the food shortage.

Seems I spend my whole life listening to people complain.

Maybe I should get into the priest racket. But I'm either too cynical or not cynical enough.

I told Singe, "If hunger becomes a bad enough problem we'll eat our pal Casey over there."

Casey didn't respond even though he was awake.

None of the elves seemed able to communicate without their clothes on.

# 50

I took a nap myself. It lasted through most of the night. I awakened to find my accomplices feeling better physically but no less testy. They all complained of hunger. The prisoners were all awake now, too, but were unable, or unwilling, to communicate. When I gave Casey his suit back, in hopes that that would help, but he just stared at the ruins and shook his head. Evidently my knifework had deprived him of his sorcery permanently.

I said, "I've had a thought."

Saucerhead grumbled, "Don't go spraining your brain."

"This one just popped right up, no work at all."

"Like a toadstool, probably. Growing on a cow pie.'

"Somebody from town should be showing up pretty soon. But they don't need to find the rest of you here. They don't know about you so there's no need for you to deal with their crap."

Playmate said, "They'll just hunt us down later."

"Not if I don't tell them. None of these elves can talk."

"There's that grapestomper."

"He's only seen the big guys. I can make him a deal that'll guarantee his silence."

Playmate gave up arguing. He enjoyed official scrutiny as little as the next man. "What about Kip? We haven't found Kip. Kip is what this mess is all about. It's all a waste of time, money, and pain if we don't get the kid back."

"I'll keep looking. He's got to be here somewhere."

"I have to take him back, Garrett."

"I know." Overly moral me, I'd decided that I couldn't let a kid fall into Colonel Block's hands. Not even that kid. Block is a decent enough guy—for a royal functionary—but there are a lot of people, way nastier than me, that he's obliged to keep happy. And Kip meant nothing to him personally. There were ten thousand Kips in town.

Maybe I get him together with Kayne Prose. Make Kip mean something long enough for the Hill folk to lose interest.

I strolled over to the discus. I climbed inside. The bulk of a sandwich awaited me beside the hatch to Kip's compartment. I was tempted to enjoy it myself. But I was concerned, too. That sandwich had drawn no flies. When I reflected on the matter I realized that I had yet to see any insect inside the aerial ship.

Now there was a sorcery worth stealing.

"Hello, Kip. This could be your lucky day. I have something for you to eat *and* a chance for you to get out of here before Baron Dreadlore and the Civil Guards arrive." Dreadlore was a fabrication but somebody with a name very much like that would turn up soon. Maybe several of them, considering how much damage a sorcerer could imagine himself doing if he owned the secret magery of flight.

"Water."

"Dang me, Kip." I hadn't even thought about water. I should have. I must be getting senile. "There's a whole big pond of the stuff right outside. And a nice cold spring. You still want to be stubborn?"

Yes, he did.

I told him, "They got hold of your mother and Rhafi, you know."

He croaked, "That was Casey."

"How would you know? How would you know that name?"

"The Drople and the Graple both told me. They have ways of observing things that are happening in the city." He didn't explain who the Drople and the Graple were. Two of his captors, presumably.

"They talked to you?"

"They hoped to convert me to their cause. They didn't get the job done." It was nice to see the kid too weak to be a smart-ass. "I couldn't understand what they were talking about. Lastyr and Noodiss are the only ones of them that I ever actually do get. They just want to go home."

"How'd they get here in the first place?"

"In a sky vessel. Like this one. But they didn't know how to work it well enough. They crashed it."

"I don't recall the incident."

"They crashed in the river. Whatever's left of their ship is underwater."

At last I was starting to dig something out. Not that it made a lick of sense.

"That being the case, why not let Casey take them home?"

"Because Casey isn't here to take them home. Casey is here to take them to prison."

"They're escaped convicts?"

Kip was losing patience with me and my questions. "No. They have the wrong politics. Although politics isn't exactly what it is. Not like what we mean when we say politics here. It's all politics and philosophy and science and law and research with all three groups. And even though I've talked and talked about it with Lastyr and Noodiss I still don't understand much better than you do without ever having heard them explain anything. It seems like there's a war going on between people who've got different ideas about how knowledge should be handled. The party Lastyr and Noodiss belong to, the Brotherhood of Light, believe that knowledge is the birthright of all intelligent life-forms. That it should be freely shared with anybody able to understand it. That's why they came here. So they could teach us."

I believe I've mentioned my tendency toward the cynical reaction. I sneered at the charity of Kip's friends.

I said, "The way you're hacking and croaking, I'll bet you're ready for a long, cool drink of springwater."

Kip grunted.

"So point the way for me."

In complete exasperation, the boy told me, "I don't know where they are!"

"You know how to contact them. Let's go, Kip. It isn't a game anymore. It isn't an adventure. People are coming for you who'll pull pieces off you like you're a bug. The stakes are probably a lot bigger than either of us can imagine."

He gave me a look that belittled my imagination. I kept plugging. "We need to do whatever we can to get ourselves out of their way."

The kid looked at the stale sandwich but didn't fold. I had to admire him even if, from my point of view, he was being stubborn for all the wrong reasons.

"You win, kid. Eat hearty." Time to change over to Plan Q.

# 51

"I found him," I told Playmate. "They had him stashed in some kind of locker. Marsha! Get everybody ready to hit the road. We're gonna move as soon as we can get the kid cleaned up. Playmate, take him to the pond."

My instructions inspired a hundred questions. I ignored them all, located my local buddy Mr. Thring. He had value under the new plan. He glared daggers once I removed his blindfold but he'd begun to understand that bluster and attitude weren't his best tools here. "Mr. Thring. Good morning. I've been talking with my associates about what we should do with you. Most of them think we should take you over to the pond and hold you under until you can't remember names or faces anymore."

Surprise and fear lit up the dusky round face of the estate manager.

"But it seems to me that you might be more use to us healthy. If you'll help us with a little something and can leave us comfortably assured that you wouldn't discuss your adventures with anyone later on."

Thring was eager to provide assurances. He couldn't by virtue of having been bound and gagged.

"What I'm looking for is a little-known path or road we can use to slip away from here." Inside I was kicking myself for not having pulled this together last night, when we'd had a lot bigger lead on the folks who'd be headed our way now.

That messenger was going to end up having to whistle for the second half of his stipend.

"You do know this country well enough to help us with that,

don't you? Probably grew up around here? Came right back after you did your five? Right?"

The man nodded his head.

"Good. I'm going to take your gag off now. And we'll get started on making you one of the crew."

I scanned the group. This wasn't a promising crowd for making a running retreat. Kip was in no shape to travel. Neither was Mr. Thring. Dojango would whine a lot but he could walk. Limping. He'd soaked his feet. Playmate and Saucerhead would manage what they had to manage. Doris and Marsha would end up doing more than their reasonable share, as usual, probably by having to carry somebody. And I would want to take an elf or two along.

The females seemed the most promising hostages. They were lighter and from what little I could sense of what was going on inside them, they seemed more cooperative, more likely to talk about things none of the several crews wanted known.

Playmate, Saucerhead, and I could take turns pulling our prisoner cart.

Saucerhead approached. "What's up, Garrett?"

"I've decided not to wait for Colonel Block. Mr. Thring here has been generous enough to offer to guide us out of here by back ways so we can get out and go home without having to deal with those special people who're likely to show up here with the Guard."

"I gotcha. Good idea. You suppose he could guide us somewhere where we could get something to eat?"

"I'll talk to him about that."

A little hunger probably wouldn't hurt us nearly as much as leaving a clear backtrail. Once we put some miles between ourselves and the wrecked skyships, though . . .

I was ready for a snack myself.

# 52

I was so agitated. All my paranoia went to waste.

When I reached home, after an epic death march that brought the survivors and me into town through the west gate, I learned that the Dead Man hadn't received my message at all. Neither had Morley, because Morley would've contacted His Nibs if he had.

What that meant was, there was still a gang of elves out there, tied up and maybe dying of thirst and exposure.

I headed for the al-Khar immediately. There wasn't much of me left when I got there. I need to work on my strength and endurance.

I had no trouble getting in to see Colonel Block. He really was interested in what I was doing.

I related a comprehensive version of my story. It ran light on the sorcery side and came up short on names but was solid enough to let the colonel know that here was a matter genuinely in need of his attention.

Block asked, "Did you happen to catch the name of this weirdly dressed fellow who was supposed to bring me your message?"

"Yeah. Earp. Eritytie Earp."

"Was he Michorite? That sounds Michorite."

"Possibly. Maybe one of those cults, now that you mention it. He dressed the part."

"And I'll bet all the other hands yucked it up when he volunteered to take the job. Am I right?"

"There was some amusement. But nobody else volunteered."

"You know what? Your boy is going to wake up in the Tenderloin stone-cold broke, without even his farmboy brogans, undoubtedly so wrecked that he can't remember his own name, let

alone those of people he was supposed to give messages. Those
ascetic cultists don't deal with temptation well when they come up
against it without all their sour fart buddies watching over their
shoulders, holding them back."

"Hell, that could be me. But at least I've been there enough
times that I know what I'm missing."

Block gave me a concerned look. "You may end up with some
legal problems if any of those elves die. Can you produce trustworthy witnesses to back you up when you say they kidnapped
this kid?"

"Hell, Wes, you had a guy there when it happened."

"Not exactly. Oh, I do believe you. More or less."

"So why don't I just stipulate that you've got me over a barrel?
Get somebody out there. Those creatures can't do you any good
dead. If you *really* need me, you know where I live."

"I thought you'd go along. Be right there handy when questions start popping up."

"You thought wrong. I'm going home. I'm going to eat and
sleep and not do anything else for about nine days. I'm allergic to
the country. It takes me a long time to get over it. I'm just trying to
do my civic duty here, anyway."

"You always were a bullshitter, Garrett. I'll let you know how
it comes out."

I'd heard that before. He'd forget about me the second I left.
The only reason he'd mentioned taking me along was to make me
more eager to get out of there. He wanted to grab the benefits of
this for Westman Block.

Damn, that was smart of me, being stupid enough to hire a
messenger who'd get lost in the red-light district before he
thought of doing anything else.

From the little I've heard about the Michonites and related
cults, that's a rite of passage. They—the men—get one chance to
sneak away and wallow in sin and depravity. Then they spend the
rest of their lives keeping an eye on each other, every miserable
man making sure nobody else has any fun ever again.

"In your hands," I said. "I hope you get more out of it than I did."

"Go on. Before I change my mind."

He might, just to show me that he could, so I got.


The house was crowded, what with Singe, Kip, and the captive
silver elves staying over. Singe offered to ease the crowding by
moving into my room with me.

I begged off again. Kip and the elves ended up sleeping on the floor in the Dead Man's room, where he'd have the least trouble keeping them under control.

I'd really hoped that Singe's encounter with Rhafi unclothed would scare her off. It seemed to have whetted her curiosity instead.

The situation amused His Nibs immensely. He wasn't going to help me get out of it, either. I fell asleep in a household drenched in the miasma of his amusement.

# 53

Dean never gave the bitching a minute's rest but he did cook up breakfast enough for the whole wretched crowd.

The elf women joined in timidly. Dean tried them on everything in his arsenal. Tea they found acceptable. Honey seemed to be all right, in tea or straight from the pot. One nibbled a biscuit, also with honey aboard. Bacon revolted the two of them. The more obviously feminine member of the pair—the one who looked like she'd actually made it a few weeks into puberty—attacked the mustard once she discovered it. Dean scowled and muttered to himself. A lot of work goes into grinding seed and preparing the condiment. There's always a pot on the table, mainly because I don't much like mustard.

The other elf woman, the elder and senior woman—judging by wrinkles—seemed terrified, though no one even spoke to her. I got the feeling she'd never seen the inner workings of a Karentine household.

Fear or no, she did appear to me immensely curious about everything.

Kip was a shuddering zombie, controlled by an increasingly exasperated Dead Man. Kip never stopped fighting him. Something was missing in that boy's makeup. I couldn't understand how he'd managed to stay alive this long.

Singe and I removed to the Dead Man's room as soon as I'd had enough to eat. She brought a platter along with her, loaded with seconds or thirds. Having no better idea what to do with herself, the slimmer elf woman tagged along. She wouldn't sit when I offered her my chair because that would leave me standing between her and the door. The other one stayed with Dean, exploring the wonders of the kitchen.

"So where do we stand, Old Bones? Have we learned anything?"

*Perhaps. At the first instance, probably that we should not have allowed emotion to sweep us away and get us involved in this. As I see it now, we have stormed into the middle of something that was none of our business. We have done nothing but trail chaos and dismay wherever we have gone.*

"What do you mean, 'we,' Big Daddy Homely? You can't really talk about someone else in the royal plural, can you?"

*Do not become tedious. I am struggling to translate what little recognizable material I find in the thin creature's mind. This is truly an alien intelligence, Garrett. I have encountered nothing like it in all my years. Nor have I ever heard of such creatures . . . Unless . . . There may have been similar folk here when I was a child. Visitors, they were called then. They were all murdered for their secrets. Inasmuch as they did not reveal anything they were soon forgotten.*

*I am having difficulty communicating not just because of what you would call a language barrier but also because of her fear. She is awash in fear, not just of us, here, whom she finds terrifying enough, but of being cut off from her own people. She is completely unmanned by the possibility that she may never be able to return home. And least of all, but still there in the mix, is a fear of the consequences of the failure of her mission.*

"And that would be?"

*I do not know. That is in a sealed part of her mind.*

"What about the other one?"

*She is frightened, too. And her mind is more closed. But behind her fear there is a hint of her seeing this personal disaster as a potential opportunity for . . . I do not know what. Something compulsive. Possibly obsessive. Possibly something wicked. Worms of temptation have begun to awaken way down in the black, mucky deeps. . . .*

I hate it when he meanders off on a free association, poetic ramble. I guess because I can't ever figure out what the hell he's babbling about. "What about Kip? Did you get anything new out of him?"

*Yes. Once I became aware that there was something that should be there. But it is not much. And I do not know if we can justify hunting down Lastyr and Noodiss.*

"Of course we can." But I couldn't think of any reasonable argument in favor of that. "Is there any chance some of those elves might've put a compulsion into my head somewhere along the way? Like one of those times when I was knocked out?"

*At the moment I am unable to investigate. All of my mental capacity is occupied by the boy and these foreign women.*

"They definitely are both women, then."

*By birth. You unclothed them. You saw.*

"I didn't see much." But what I had seen had been curiously interesting. "The one in the kitchen at least raised a crop of lemons."

*Many human women are not as voluptuous as those in the range you usually find interesting. This one's primary sexual characteristics are somewhat atrophied. I would expect that to be true of the others, as well.*

"I did notice that." In the women it all added up to a sort of virginal innocence that was attractive in its own fashion.

Singe hissed at me. I think it was supposed to be laughter.

*I suspect that this is not an individual aberration. I suspect that we would find the males even more atrophied.*

"Weird." I shuddered. "The ones I stripped down out there definitely weren't built to boogie. Maybe I ought to introduce this old gal to Morley."

The pixies out front launched one of their racket shows, which wakened the Goddamned Parrot.

*She may be beyond seduction, Garrett. They may have tried to breed the sexual impulse out of themselves. The same madness has been tried by countless cults in our part of the world in a shortsighted effort to shove all those distractions aside.*

"How the hell do they get little elves, then?"

*Exactly. No such cult lasts more than a generation. Perhaps the silver elves have found a way around that limitation. Possibly they have a separate breeder caste. I do not know. I do know that no living creature I have ever encountered, save the rare mutant, has lacked desire, however distorted the core impulse might have become because of stresses upon the individual. I would suspect them to be present in these elves. But buried deep.*

"So have you gotten anything out of the kid concerning his two weird pals?"

*Truly, he does not know how or where to find them. He does not have a reliable means of attracting their attention. His method worked only two times in five tries. The rest of the time they just*

*turned up at their own discretion, almost always when he was
alone. It has not occurred to Kip to wonder but they almost certainly knew that he was alone before they visited.*

Dean stuck his head in. "That racket out front is because the
wee folk have spotted Bic Gonlit."

Dean was talking to the pixies now? Times change. I gave him
the fish-eye, on general principles. He wouldn't be feeding them,
too, would he?

"Now why would Bic . . . ?"

*I have him. Go bring him in, Garrett.* He flashed me a
pixie's-eye view of the spot from which Bic was watching the
house. I noted that it was farther away than the Dead Man had
shown he could reach before when trying to manipulate a human
being. *After that, take Kip home to his mother. He is nothing but a
distraction here.*

"This is the real Bic Gonlit?"

*The genuine article. Evidently determined to be foolish. Help
me find out why. He will not run this time. He will not see you
leave the house.*

# 54

Though he was mad as hell Bic couldn't get his body to move. He couldn't do anything but flinch when my hand settled on his shoulder. "Bic, my man, here you are again. Lurking. Let's go for a walk."

Gonlit stood up and zombie-walked over to the house with me. I talked to him all the way, mainly in an admonitory tone. There was no need to get any other watchers overly excited.

I did blow Mrs. Cardonlos a kiss. She was out on her porch, keeping her eyes open. She needed her reward.

*Mr. Gonlit is after Miss Pular again. Now on behalf of a rat-man who calls himself John Stretch.*

"You get the joke, Singe? John Stretch?"

"No. Why would the name John Stretch be a joke?" The notion seemed to irritate her.

"John Stretch is what they used to call the hangman, before we got civilized and started lopping off heads instead."

"Is that true? I wonder who he could be." Singe had almost no accent left, despite her vastly different throat and voice box. Scary how talented the girl was. But her tone was so controlled even I knew she was dancing around something. I was surprised the Dead Man didn't get after her. Although, sometimes, he just doesn't pay attention to anything but himself.

*Mr. Gonlit does not know who John Stretch is. He does not care. One of the hard-nosed youngsters with ambitions toward Reliance's throne, if you care to call it that. A somewhat naive youngster willing to pay part of Mr. Gonlit's fee up front.*

*Mr. Gonlit enjoyed a wonderful gourmet dinner last night. He followed it with a bottle of TunFaire Gold and a deep pipe filled with the finest imported broadleaf tobacco. Probably a Poster-saldt. Now Mr. Gonlit finds himself in a position where he has to deliver something that will please John Stretch.*

"Hey, Bic. You know we warned you to back away from us."

Gonlit shrugged. "People warn *you* off, pal. I don't recollect you ever running away."

That stuff is pretty obnoxious when somebody else is throwing it into *your* face.

"Must be the boots talking, Bic. Making you braver than you ought to be."

"What're you gonna do, pal? Send me to the Cantard?"

Bic tried hard not to betray his interest in the silver elf woman. Her interest in Bic, however, was both frank, blatant, and troubled. The manly posturing thing seemed both to excite and repel her. She was eager to see what happened next.

"There's an original question, Bic. Well, I have work to do. Errands to run. I hope you took that John Stretch for a potful of gold. By the time I get back home you'll probably be unemployed. Kip! Where the hell are you? Get your sorry ass ready. I'm taking you home." With a side trip to The Palms along the way, of course.

I needed to see my old buddy, my pal, Morley the celery stalker and carrot killer.

# 55

I passed the word to Morley. "The number one boy out to scrub Reliance is a rat who calls himself John Stretch."

"That's cute. What've you been up to?"

"I thought Reliance might be interested. What do you think? How do you mean, up to? Why do you want to know?"

"We've had some unusual people turn up here the last couple of nights. They're the sort who dress up in black and manage to suck all the joy out of a room just by entering it."

"Why would they come here?"

"I thought you might be able to tell me."

"Not a clue here." And I really didn't have one.

"That the kid you were looking for?"

"The very one. Am I good, or what?"

"So you got him back."

"Damn me with faint praise if you want. I'm taking him home to his mother now."

"You think he's smart enough to make it there, then?" Kip had just done something to test Sarge's patience.

"I have hopes. I'm counting on his ego. And once I'm shut of him I'll be the happiest boy in town. I'd go on a toot if I didn't have work to do."

"Ooh! You have another job lined up already?"

"Nope. Just studying the excesses of the rest of you. I'm considering entrepreneur stuff. Because I'm going into business for myself."

Morley looked at me for a while. "All right. This ought to be entertaining."

"What? You don't think I can be a serious businessman?"

"No. Because a serious businessman has to stay sober most of the time. A serious businessman has to make his decisions untouched by emotion. And, most of all, a serious businessman has to *work*. All day, every day, enduring longer hours than the most dedicated character on his payroll."

I took a deep, cleansing breath, sighed. "O ye of little faith."

"Exactly. Tell me everything you've left out about your adventures, Garrett."

When I got to the part about the Michonite messenger Morley began to laugh. He said, "I guess that explains the kid who turned up here a few hours ago."

"What?"

"He was a dark-haired boy of draft age, as handsome as they come, some mother's son, wearing nothing but a loincloth. But he stank like an alley in the drought season."

"How long did you fiddle with the words to put that together?"

"Then till now. Sounded good, didn't it? He couldn't remember why he was supposed to see me. The boys in the kitchen gave him some leftovers and sent him on his way."

I grunted sourly. "Hey, Sarge, no need to hold back on my account. The kid asks for it, smack him. Probably won't do any good. But he's got to learn somehow, someday."

Though I was just about convinced that Kip never would.

Only seconds later, *Smack!*

Kip bounced off Sarge's fist, slammed into a wall, folded up into a very surprised pile of dirty laundry.

Morley said, "Sarge wasn't just a medic. He did one tour training recruits."

I asked, "How'd you teach that kind when you were in the army, Sarge?"

"Ain't dat hard, Garrett. But foist ya do got ta get dere attenshun."

Excellent, in theory. But we were dealing with Cyprus Prose who, I feared, could not be reached by mortal man.

The kid got up, still looking surprised as he shook his head. He started to say something.

Sarge popped him again. Harder.

And, moments later, again, harder still.

And that was all it took. Kip looked right at Sarge, as though really seeing him for the first time.

"Dere. Dat's better. Let's you an' me talk, boy."

Then a miracle occurred.

Kip paid attention.

Morley opined, "I believe it has to do with Sarge having no emotional investment. Everyone else who ever tried to teach the boy manners didn't want to hurt him. Down deep he always knew they'd pull their punches. And they'd give up after they'd failed a few times. So he learned to outlast them. Sarge doesn't have an investment. He doesn't care if the kid lives or dies. He'll just keep on hitting, harder and harder, until he gets results. People sense that. They give him their direction. The way the boy has. *Ouch!*"

Sarge had smacked Kip again, this time turning him ass over appetite.

"A smart mouth always calls for a little reminder. Let the master work a while. You'll be glad you did."

So I did. I kept one ear turned Sarge's direction while Morley and I tried to figure out what the hell I'd gotten myself into this time. Sarge talked to Kip softly, gently, probing his core knowledge of courtesy and the social graces. Kip knew the forms. What he lacked was any understanding. Sarge managed to pound a few insights into his thick, young-adult skull.

I told Morley, "That sonofabitch just went up about ten notches on my approval board. He had me fooled. You think he could do anything with a blasphemous parrot?"

"Where is the lovable Mr. Big?"

"I'm sure he's out there somewhere, spying on me."

Morley chuckled, but said only, "There's more to almost anyone once you get to know them, Garrett. But you knew that already. It's the kind of thing you're always throwing at me when I've decided it's time to break some totally deserving jerk's arm."

Most of the time he goes for the neck, actually. "That's different."

"Oh, absolutely. Garrett, at the risk of causing you a seizure because of my departure from the norm, you're full of shit."

Morley gets a kick out of arguing morals and ethics with anybody who'll sit still for it.

I said, "I need to get going. I only wanted to get the word to Reliance."

"You're beginning to pile up a real debt."

"I don't think so. You do still recollect who it was who didn't bother to tell his buddy that he was lugging a coffin full of vampire to a certain meeting with the gentleman who was the kingpin before our current, lovable Chodo Contague? What was that villain's name?"

Dotes rolled his eyes, looked to heaven and to hell. "I'm never going to hear the end of that, am I? I'm *never* going to hear the end of that."

"Nope. At least not while I have a parrot on staff. Hey, Kip. It's time to take you home."

# 56

Naturally, Kip had to find out if it was possible to resurrect the old order. I told him, "I learned something today, too. Bottom line, what it adds up to is, I don't put up with any more attitude from you. You give me any crap, I pop you. You don't behave like a human being, I hit you even harder than Sarge did. Sarge is a good man but he never was a Marine."

I led Kip to Kayne Prose's co-op. Kayne was pleased. Kayne squealed in delight, like a girl younger than her daughter. She hugged and kissed her baby. She hugged and kissed her baby's rescuer. She refused to turn the latter loose until he promised her an opportunity to demonstrate her gratitude more fully.

But when the smoke cleared away and the emotions settled out, Kayne still had sewing to do. She asked me to take Kip home. Where I found his sister Cassie trying on a new personality. This one was much more appealing. This one was very friendly indeed. I account it a miracle that I was able to escape still wearing my trousers, trailing a "Maybe later" that started me drooling every time I thought even a little bit about Cassie Doap.

What a life.

Rhafi did get the job.

# 57

One of the good things to happen in my life has been the unshakable friendship I've formed with Max Weider, the brewery magnate. I've done several jobs for Max. They didn't all work out the way we hoped but we did become friends of the sort who trust one another absolutely.

Where money and women are not concerned.

Max has a very lovely daughter named Alyx. Alyx is a bit of an adventuress, in her own mind. Alyx could complicate things without even trying.

A new man answered the door at the Weider mansion. Max doesn't go out much anymore. Like the old *majordomo,* this character's pointy nose spent most of its time higher in the air than did that of any member of the Weider family. That nose wrinkled when he saw me. I told him, "Go tell Gilbey that Garrett is here. It's business."

I cooled my heels outside until I began to suspect that the *majordomo* hadn't bothered to deliver my message. Manvil Gilbey, Max Weider's lifelong sidekick, wasn't as keen on me as everyone would be in a perfect world, but he was certain to let new help know. . . . How do you get a job like that? If you're the employer, how do you find somebody to do it?

The door opened. This time Manvil Gilbey himself stood on the other side. Behind him lurked a disappointed doorman. "I'm sorry, Garrett. Rogers only started yesterday. In all the confusion I forgot to let him know that you're one of the people we always want to see. Is there something going on at the brewery?"

"Could be. But this don't have anything to do with it." I told the doorman, "Thanks for nothing, Bubba. Hey, Gilbey, how do you go about finding and hiring a guy who can be snooty about opening doors?"

"Max is in the study. Napping when last I checked. Let's go up. Maybe if you needle *him* a little he'll show some interest in life. Are you involved in anything? I believe it would be useful if we had you work your magic at a few of the smaller breweries we've acquired the past couple of years. Two or three of them keep showing some screwed-up numbers."

"You kept the original workforces, right?"

"Top to bottom." Max always did, till individuals proved themselves not worth keeping. Weider wasn't sentimental about deadwood or crooks. "We only put in a handful of our takeover guys. To study their processes. We try not to change the final product. Unless it's really awful. But we do look for ways to increase profitability. You'd be amazed how many inefficiencies persist in this industry simply because things have always been done a certain way."

From the day they launched their first brewing operation Weider and Gilbey had produced a quality product the most efficient way possible. Today they control seventy percent of the human-directed brewing in the city. And they have shares in many of the nonhuman breweries. Even ogres understand enhanced profit margins and good beer.

Gilbey pushed through the second floor door to Max's study, held it for me. I passed through into the heat.

Max always has a bonfire going in the fireplace there, these days.

I missed a step. Max had aged a decade in the weeks since last I'd seen him. He used to be a little round-faced, red-cheeked, bald on top, smiling, twinkling-eye sort of guy. Not now. He looked terrible. He had suffered a severe decline in a very short time. Which wasn't that huge a surprise. Life had been exceedingly cruel to Max of late. He'd had two children murdered and his wife pass away, all on one horrible day.

Max wasn't napping after all. "Garrett. I see that you're not here to brighten my day. And that your wardrobe has begun to decline already."

"I guess I'm just a natural-born slob."

"Do we have trouble on the floor again?"

"Not that I'm aware of. Manvil did ask me to check out a couple of the new satellite breweries. And I'll get to that right away.

Before the end of the week. But what I came for this time is to beg the borrow of some business expertise."

Weider steepled his spidery, blue-veined fingers in front of his nose. The rheum went out of his eyes. His now nearly gaunt face showed a bit of light. I'd managed to pique his interest.

Gilbey, who had moved to a post beside his employer's chair, shot me a look that told me to get on with it while there was a chance of getting Max interested and engaged.

I could do this. I know how to keep a corpse awake and interested. Sometimes.

Manvil Gilbey isn't just Max Weider's number one lieutenant, he's his oldest and closest friend. They go back to their war years together. Which makes for a hell of a bond.

"What it is," I said, "is that I've stumbled across this kid who invents things. All kinds of things. Some are completely weird. Some are completely useless. And some are really neat. What I want is for somebody with a lot more commercial sense than I've got to eyeball the inventions and tell me if I'm fooling myself when I think somebody could get rich making some of them."

"Ah," Max said. "Another business opportunity. First time this week we've been offered the chance to get in on the ground floor, isn't it, Manvil?"

I pretended to miss his sarcasm. "I'm not looking for anybody to go in on it with me. I have that part worked out. If I could just have Manvil give me his honest opinion of the stuff in the kid's workshop, and if it matches mine, I'll see if the Tates want to manufacture them. Now that the war's over there isn't much demand for the army boots and leather whatnots they've been making for the last sixty years."

Max asked, "What's your take, Manvil?" He was well aware of my precarious relationship with one of the Tate girls. And he thought I was a raving romantic instead of a tough, lone, honest man battling to scourge evil from the mean streets, which is what I know that I really am. As long as I don't have to get up before noon to work the flails.

"I think friend Garrett might be even less devious than we've always thought. You weren't going to cut us in, Garrett?"

"Huh? Why should I? You guys already got more money than God and more work than—"

Max stilled me with a wave. "See what he's got, Manvil. Garrett, Willard Tate is a good choice. He's an excellent manager. And he does have that gorgeous redheaded niece besides." He knows about Tinnie because Tinnie and his daughter Alyx are friends. "I like your thinking there." Maybe because a Garrett involved with a Tinnie Tate again meant a Garrett not involved with any Weider daughters.

We may be friends but he's also a father.

Max leaned his head back and closed his eyes. End of consultation. For now.

Manvil actually smiled. I'd managed to get his buddy interested in something, at least for a little while.

## 58

"Sounds like a riot," I said. Gilbey and I, in the Weider coach, were nearing Playmate's stable.

Possibly it was a neighborhood war. A lot of sturdy subject types, armed with knives and cudgels, were trying to adjust the larcenous attitudes of the biggest daytime mob of ratmen I'd ever seen. There were dozens of them. And things weren't going their way. The street was littered with ratmen already down. The survivors were trying to retreat, burdened with booty. And just as Manvil and I arrived the Domains of Chaos spewed another ingredient into the cauldron.

At least twenty more ratmen appeared. They attacked the smash-and-grab guys with a ferocity I hadn't seen since the islands. They were determined to leave bodies behind. And they got as good as they gave.

I leaned out the coach door and told our driver, "Just stay real still and try to think invisible thoughts till this blows over."

"What's happening?" Gilbey asked. There was no color left in his face. He didn't get out on the town much.

"We seem to have strayed into the middle of a factional skirmish amongst members of the ratman underworld. What it was before it turned into that I won't know until I get a chance to look around." But I had a feeling it boded no good for me and my industrial schemes.

"Your life is never dull, is it?"

"A little dull wouldn't hurt, some days. I've thought about calling my autobiography *Trouble Follows Me*. The problem with that is, the troubles in my life are usually waiting when I get there."

The battle outside turned tricornered. Playmate's sturdy subject type neighbors couldn't tell one ratman from another. And most of them just plain welcomed a chance to whack on a thieving ratman anyway.

Whistles sounded in the distance. The Guards were gathering. I expected that, like the Watch before them, they would move in only after they were confident that they had nobody to deal with but people who couldn't crawl away.

I slipped down out of the coach. "Better stay in here for now, Manvil."

"No problem. I used up my adventurous side a long time ago."

One thing that's never in short supply around Playmate's stable is the rough hemp twine his hay-and-straw man uses to bundle his products before he brings them into town. Playmate saves the twine and gives it back.

I gathered a load and started tying rats. Neighbors thought that was a marvelous idea and joined right in.

"Not that one," I told one of the sturdy subjects. "The ones wearing the green armbands are the good guys. Sort of. We can fail to see them getting away if they're able to go."

That earned me some dark looks but no real arguments. Emotions were surprisingly cool, considering.

I tied fourteen ratmen personally before the Guard arrived. There were more still unbound. Almost all of the neighbors had started to carry Playmate's possessions back into the stable. They ignored instructions not to disturb the evidence. Most of that, I noted, was stuff that had been looted from Kip's workshop.

I returned to the Weider coach. "Come on. Let's see if they left anything I can show you."

To my delight, the three-wheel, *my* three-wheel, hadn't been disturbed. "This's the main thing I want to make. The biggest thing. Right here. Watch this." I climbed aboard, zoomed around as best I could in the confined space. "I can see every rich family in town wanting one of these for a toy. Come on. Try it."

As Gilbey was trying to get the hang of making the big front wheel turn in the correct direction I caught a sound from behind me and whirled, expecting an attack from some desperado ratman who'd been knocked down earlier or who'd gone into hiding when the tide had turned. What I found was a weak, cross-eyed Playmate trying to get up from where he'd been laid low by a blow to the head.

I gave him a hand up, which wasn't the best thing to do for him in his condition. I supported him till he could get his backside planted on a bale of hay and his spine pressed against a post. "How bad does it look, Garrett?" I was checking the top of his head.

"You're going to need a real surgeon. You've got a piece of scalp peeled back. The wound needs cleaning. You need a bunch of stitches. You're going to be enjoying headaches for days. What did they want?"

"They never told me but they meant to haul off everything Kip ever made."

"Didn't I warn you?"

"Yes. You did. How's Winger?"

"I don't know. I haven't seen her. She supposed to be here? I'll look around. Manvil, would you keep an eye on my friend, here? You remember how to deal with a head injury? Don't let him go to sleep."

I found no sign of Winger anywhere. I went back to Playmate. "You sure Winger was still here?"

"I still have fresh blisters on my ears from the language she used when this started, Garrett. She was busting up ratmen like she was killing snakes or something. They won't be good to her if they took her away."

"You Garrett?"

I jumped. I hadn't heard this guy come in. He was way shorter than me but plenty wide and all muscle. He had big, brushy eyebrows that met in the middle over mean-looking little blue eyes that, surely, concealed a bright mind. He was clad in businesslike apparel that managed to look shoddy even though it was relatively new. I knew what he was before I asked, "Who wants to know?"

"I do. Lucius Browling. Extraordinary Guard Services. Reporting straight to the director." Lucius Browling didn't offer to shake. Neither was he rude or confrontational.

"The director? What director?"

"Director Relway. Of the Emergency Committee for Royal Security."

Good old Relway. Count on him to paint the outside of his house of righteous thugs with colorful, high-sounding monikers. Monikers that would change as fast as people figured out that each was a hollow mask for something more sinister, probably.

"In that case, Garrett just left. If you hurry you can catch him.

He's a little weasely-faced guy with a skinny black mustache . . . You know, all of you guys would get along with the world a lot better if you could just figure out what it means to have a sense of humor."

"Quite possibly you have a point. The director occasionally mentions how much he values your opinion. Perhaps you can raise the matter personally once we get to the al-Khar." He raised a hand to forestall my next question. "Colonel Block and the director both want to consult you concerning recent events. I'm just a messenger. Just one of a dozen EGS men in the field, hoping to run into you at one of your known haunts."

Implications, implications. They knew I wasn't at home. . . .

There was no point fighting it. "I'll be with you in a minute, then. Let me wrap up here." I stepped over to Gilbey. Manvil had been smart enough to get off the three-wheel before any outsider could get a good idea of what he was doing. Right now he was just a civilian who happened to be hanging around. "Tell Max. Let me know what you guys think." I turned. "Playmate. I want you to go see Drak Shevesh about your head. I've used him. He's the best there is. And it won't bother him that you're human."

I told Lucius Browling I was ready. He didn't cheer. He didn't say much, either. Which was just as well. I was a little preoccupied trying to spot the Goddamn Parrot and being worried about Winger.

I did tell Browling, "If your people have any real interest in what happened here you should round up a bounty hunter named Bic Gonlit. He had something to do with it somehow."

I was getting piqued with Bic. He was as stubborn about sticking to his job as I could be.

# 59

Colonel Block was in a formal mood when Browling led me into the biggest chamber I'd yet seen inside the city prison. It appeared to be several cells converted into a meeting room. There was a large table of mediocre quality, some uncomfortable chairs, no windows, and not nearly enough light. You could hide werewolves and vampires in the shadowy corners. Today those only held Deal Relway, playing ghost. Lucius Browling vanished as soon as I'd been delivered.

Three other, silent men were present. Nobody introduced anybody.

I didn't push. Those three likely told Block what to do and when to do it, and whether or not to smile while he did it. They had that Hill look.

Block said, "We've gotten back our first reports from the country, Garrett."

"Wow. You guys move fast when you want to. I take it something didn't go the way you wanted."

"Our people found physical evidence and local witnesses to corroborate your report. But your silver elves were gone."

So. The girl who got away must've come back to rescue the others. Elven enemies possibly having more in common than silver elves and people do. Or maybe it had to do with wanting a ride home.

Block continued, "The disk-shaped flying engine was gone, as well. The pear-shaped flying engines had been destroyed. Melted down in a heat so fierce they'd sunk right down into the earth. A search of the area produced nothing but these." He showed me several of the gray fetish things, similar but not identical to one another.

Without invitation I suggested, "If they were that thorough about cleaning up after themselves you'd better consider the possibility that those things there were meant to be found."

A small stir. The observers exchanged uneasy glances.

"You been holding anything back on us, Garrett?" Relway asked from his shadow.

"Deal," Block cautioned. "Garrett? It's a pertinent question, despite Deal's tone."

I wondered if Relway ever got to be the nice guy. "And the answer is, probably. Without meaning to. Remember, I brought this stuff to you guys. I don't have any idea what you need to know, let alone anything at all about the much vaster category of 'want to know.'"

"We don't need to get into any pissing contests, Garrett. I have a job. All I want to do is to get it done."

"And I'm not up for any macho headbutting, either. Where we have trouble is, you don't want me to know *why* you want to know what you want to know. You even probably don't want me to know *what* you want to know. Which'll really make it impossible to answer your questions intelligently. But you'll still put the blame on me when you don't hear what you want to hear. Chances are good you'll even accuse me of lying or holding out."

One of the observers made a gesture. Block cocked his head slightly. Although I wasn't included in I understood that there was some communicating going on in much the same fashion as when I conversed with the Dead Man. A very small handful of the most powerful of our wizardly overlords have been able to develop that talent.

I *was* able to read the emotional overtones.

A man entered the room. His interruption earned him frowns from everyone but me. I didn't care. He whispered to Relway briefly. Relway studied me as though he'd just suffered a mild surprise.

That did nothing to make me more comfortable.

Colonel Block admitted, "Your argument has considerable merit, Garrett."

In private I would've accused him of being a poetaster or some other artsy critter equally heinous. In front of people, where I might embarrass him, I said only, "My thinking is that we're all on the same side despite maybe having different goals. . . ."

There was a sign from another of the observers. I shut up because I could sense that this particular guy had taken a negative
shine to me and wasn't likely to invest a great deal of patience in me.

Block said, "These silver elves seem to control a lot of powerful sorcery, the flight thing being only the most obvious. We'd
very much like to explore some of those secrets. And right now
you're the closest thing to an expert on them as exists."

"And I've given you everything. . . . Wait a minute. There's
Casey. Though you should know about Casey on your own."

"Casey?"

"The only silver elf I've actually talked to. His name is something really weird. He prefers Casey. He claims to be a cop. He
says he was sent out to arrest two elves nobody's seen except
maybe one crazy teenage boy. A boy who, after I grilled him mer-
cilessly, turned out to have no clue how to find *any* elves. A boy
who couldn't even find his own way home without help. Casey
wasn't sure what crimes the fugitives had committed. And he
didn't care. That was for his judges to worry about. He had an
apartment . . ." I gave the directions and details and recommended
extreme caution on the parts of any investigators. Questions arose.
I answered as many as I could.

Relway had another visit from the whisperer. He took an opportunity to do some whispering of his own, to Colonel Block, before he left the room in a hurry. To put together a raid on Casey's
place, I assumed.

Once he was gone, Block said, "There're people here looking
for you, Garrett. Legal type people. Did Browling do something
wrong? Did he manhandle you or insult you or in any way demonstrate a lack of courtesy?"

I paused, definitely puzzled, but then observed, "Either you're
really naive or you just don't understand what you and Relway
have created. There isn't any need for Lucius Browling to be anything but Lucius Browling for alarms to sound and people to get
upset."

He didn't get it. We didn't lapse into a philosophical pissing
contest in front of the wizards. For such they surely were, in
mufti.

"You aren't a prisoner, Garrett. You aren't under arrest. You're
an expert we called in to help us with a particular problem. And I
wish you'd tell those people that. Evidently they're making life
very difficult for the staff up front."

"They won't go away just because you trot me out. What kind

of legal beagle is going to take the word of a man who's in the hands of—"

"Thank you, Mr. Garrett. I suspect that I've just learned a valuable lesson. And that I'll be happy that Relway wasn't here to pick it up as easily. Might I request your presence and assistance for as long as it takes Relway to investigate that elf's hideout. I'll provide a small honorarium."

"I'll go tell the folks in the waiting room. But if they're the kind of people I think they are, they won't leave until I do."

Block glowered.

And I was right about the lawyers.

# 60

The Casey raid was a disaster for the secret police. Almost everything had been removed from the place except for an extensive array of booby traps, most of them so cunning there was no way to detect them before they did their evil work.

"There were two corpses in the place when we got there," Relway told us. "According to people in the building both were tenants who sprang traps while they were looting the place. They'd been there a while. They were getting ripe. The same people told us the elf came back this morning, beat-up and dirty. He did whatever he did in his apartment, then went through the building reclaiming his stolen stuff, which he loaded into a waiting wagon. He did leave a few things behind because he didn't have time to recover everything. He was still there, at it, just ten minutes before we arrived. But, somehow, he knew we were coming. At ten minutes he dropped everything and took off."

I offered a suggestion. "Look for a livery stable in the neighborhood. A place that has donkeys stabled. Possibly for rent. And don't count on being able to recognize this guy if you run into him. He loves disguises. And he has sorceries that help him look like other people. And some of the other elves have demonstrated the ability to make themselves invisible."

"What was that about a donkey?"

I rehashed my first encounter with Casey, disguised as Bic Gonlit. And then explained that the real Bic Gonlit seemed to be making his living working for ratman crime bosses these days. And that I suspected that the raid on Playmate's stable had been incited by the false Bic.

Block wanted to explore the whole Bic Gonlit question more closely. There seemed to be one long coincidence right in the middle of things, that being that both Bic Gonlits would cross my path on unrelated matters.

"It probably wasn't total coincidence," I mused. "But I'm confident that there's no grand plot. In order to pretend to be Bic Gonlit, Casey would've had to get close to the real Bic to study him. So Bic's probably had an unexpected friend during recent months. You might see what he has to say about that."

Colonel Block gave me a hard look. I'd just set poor Bic up for some difficult times. But Block said, "Suppose there isn't a coincidence? Is it possible that this Casey wanted to pull you in? Maybe so he'd have somebody who really knows TunFaire looking for the two elves he wants to find?"

I considered the almost compulsive need I had, at times, for finding Lastyr and Noodiss. "It could be. I think it could be." So did that make it the grand plot that I was confident didn't exist?

I don't think so. I have a feeling there was a lot of opportunism and seizing the day going on around me, particularly by Casey and Bic Gonlit.

None by me, of course. I'm too damned dumb. And then some.

"It's been another long day, Colonel," I said. "And I don't see how I can possibly be any more help, no matter how much I might want to be. Other than to get those people up front out of your hair." I was curious about that. I didn't know anybody in the legal profession. Not well, anyway. Lawyerdom is a small community with very little official standing outside the realm of commercial relations. "And you do know where to find me if you need me."

Block seemed distracted as he said, "All right. You're right. You might as well go home."

As I rose, I said, "Here's an idea. Everything that used to belong to the elves. Whatever you've managed to gather up. Isolate it somewhere. Try not to talk out loud around it. And if you try to figure out how something's magic works, make sure you don't give away any of your own. I really believe they can spy on us through those little gray blocks, somehow."

Colonel Block got up and walked me out himself. Once we were well away from that meeting room and the heart of his little empire, he asked, "You do know who those people were, don't you?"

"Not specifically who. I know what."

"All right. Listen to this. You've crossed paths with two of those three before. As I understand it. One of them doesn't like you even a little bit. I don't know what you did to inconvenience him, when or where, but he's definitely not big on forgive and forget. If we convene one of these brainstorming sessions again, consider the remote possibility that you might do yourself the most good by not volunteering any information. Or suggestions. They don't trust anything they don't have to work to get. They're cynical at a level that makes your cynicism look like playacting."

I didn't argue. I didn't see any point. I wasn't quite sure I got the point he was trying to make, either. He was sort of doing that sidewise friend thing where he thought he didn't dare be direct. I guess he was telling me to watch my back where spooky people off the Hill were involved.

To me that didn't seem like a lesson that needed to be taught to anyone over the age of seven.

# 61

The legal talent had been laid on first by the Weider brewing consortium. Manvil Gilbey being quick on the draw. Later, a gentleman had arrived who, allegedly, was associated with a rather more sinister enterprise.

Harvester Temisk has been the legal point man for Chodo Contague for ages. He continues to handle some things in Chodo's name, even though Belinda is in charge now, secretly. Which likely is no secret to him.

I couldn't imagine how Harvester Temisk could've gotten involved with my problems. And he wasn't the least bit forthcoming when I asked. All he had to say was, "I want you to come see me as soon as your current calendar clears."

Inasmuch as his presence might've led to my elevation from detainee to paid consultant, I told him I'd look him up as soon as I could.

I was profuse in my gratitude to the Weider man, too, a skinny little critter with a balding head, a huge brush of a mustache, and the oddball name Congo Greeve.

Neither lawyer could've done a lot for me, legally speaking, because the Guard were pretty much making things up as they went. What the lawyers' appearance did was put the Guard on notice that influential people were concerned about my welfare. And influence, nepotism, cronyism, and bribery are how the system works, Deal Relway's mad notions of universal justice and meritocracy notwithstanding. And the actual producers and the gangsters have far more influence than our masters on the Hill see as reasonable.

* * *

I first spotted the Goddamn Parrot when I was only a block from home. That animated feather duster was getting too clever about going unnoticed.

And just after I spotted the bird I realized that I hadn't been entirely forthright during my interview. I'd forgotten to mention my elven house guests.

In fact, I'd forgotten them completely.

*Take care, Garrett. There are unfriendly ratmen in the neigh-borhood.*

That seemed hard to credit after so many had gone down at Playmate's stable. Still, Old Bones isn't in the habit of being excitable.

It turned out there were only two unfriendly ratmen. And one of those had a limp so profound he was no threat to anyone but himself. The uncrippled individual approached me in a manner so bold that people on the street turned to marvel. "Mr. Garrett?"

"Guilty." This close to the Dead Man I didn't feel any special risk. "What do you need?"

"I bring a message from John Stretch. He has the woman Winger."

This ratman was no Pular Singe. I could barely understand him.

*As a point of information, Garrett, this fellow is John Stretch. He has only a handful of followers left, most of them injured. He fears they will desert him if he demonstrates any hesitance or lack of resolve.*

"Couldn't happen to a more deserving guy. I hope they enjoy a long and prosperous marriage."

The ratman appeared nonplussed. "John Stretch says he will trade the woman Winger for the female Pular Singe."

"Hell, so would I. You're kidding, right? One of my friends put you up to pulling my leg. Right? Who was it? You can help me get him back."

The ratman was confused. This wasn't going anything like he planned. "John Stretch says he will harm the woman Winger—"

"John Stretch isn't likely to live long enough to harm anybody or to make deals with anybody. Rather than making more enemies John Stretch ought to be trying to find himself some new friends."

*Bic Gonlit.*

Yes, indeed. "I *might* do business if Bic Gonlit was available for trade."

The ratman had been difficult to understand when he was delivering a rehearsed message. Now I had to rely on a relay from the Dead Man in order to grasp what he was trying to say.

"You do not want the woman Winger?"

"What would I do with her? Nope. She's all yours. And she's going to take some feeding, I'll tell you. But I am strongly interested in getting my hands on Bic Gonlit. Bic Gonlit has messed me around a couple of times lately. I'm ready to settle up."

"Perhaps that could be arranged." The ratman looked thoughtful.

"Actually, there're two Bic Gonlits. The real Bic is short for a human male. He wears white boots covered with fake gemstones. The second Bic is a pretender. He's a little taller and never wears boots. This false Bic Gonlit has created a lot of mischief. I believe he was responsible for the bad advice that led to the disaster at the stable today."

The ratman had questions, suddenly. He had big trouble asking them without revealing that he was, himself, John Stretch. He was no genius but he did understand that he wasn't going to come out on top if we got into a scuffle.

I told him, "The false Bic is really a wicked elf who has disguised himself so the real Bic will get blamed for the evil he does. I still haven't figured out why he wants to cause strife and unhappiness. I guess he just does. Maybe it's fun."

I didn't believe that but it sounded like the sort of behavior and motivation that would make sense to a John Stretch.

John Stretch was a record-setter of a ratman. He had berries the size of coconuts—but limited smarts to go with them. Though a lack of brains never has been a huge handicap in TunFaire's underworld. Guts and daring get you ahead faster.

"I want them both. But the false Bic more than the other."

The ratman twitched, mad as hell. But he maintained his self-control. "I will inform John Stretch. What should I tell him about the woman Winger?"

"I don't know. She's his problem. You could let him know she's involved with The Call. And that one of her lovers is Deal Relway. Of the Guard. He might find that information useful when he decides how to dispose of her."

The Call is a virulently racist veterans' organization, armed and organized as a private, political army. It shares a good many goals with Deal Relway. I wouldn't want to be a ratman who came to The Call's attention because I'd done harm to a human woman.

And Deal Relway is Deal Relway, increasingly the bogeyman to all those who practice wickedness in TunFaire.

I stopped to visit with some of the pixies. From brief encounters I knew two of the youngsters by sight, a daring boy who called himself Shakespear and a young lady named Melondie Kadare, who was so sweet and pretty I wished I could whack her with a transmogrification stick and grow her up to my size.

Melondie was the pixie who had followed me into the alley out back on the occasion of my first encounter with a silver elf in a Bic Gonlit disguise. Back then she'd been a precocious, curious adolescent. Now she was a serious, refined young woman. More or less. When the old folks were looking.

Pixie lives race away far faster than our own. I think that may be why we're uncomfortable around the little people. They're so much like us, in miniature. Their swiftly lived lives remind us, piquantly, that our own more numerous hours are still painfully and perfectly numbered.

# 62

Singe let me into the house moments after the Goddamn Parrot, evidently under the illusion that he was some kind of eagle, slammed down onto my right shoulder and tried to carry me off to his aerie.

He couldn't work up quite enough lift. So he gave up.

I feared Singe was going to climb all over me exactly the way I'd wished about a thousand young women of passing acquaintance would've done in days of yore. And she might've done so if the sexier silver elf hadn't come out of the Dead Man's room to see what was happening. She wore a tattered old shirt probably taken from Dean's ragbag. It might've served as a child's nightshirt before it acquired all those holes. It was barely sufficient to cover the subject. Most of the time.

That was distracting. Even on her. Because there was nothing but her underneath the tatters.

Maybe it was some sort of experiment by His Nibs.

Singe settled for clinging to my arm. "So what great adventures did you get to enjoy out there today, while the rest of us were locked up here, dying of boredom?"

I detached the Goddamn Parrot from my shoulder. "I traded you to John Stretch for two Bic Gonlits and a sugar-cured ham." I tossed the jungle chicken in the general direction of his perch, in the small front room.

"What?" Singe shrieked.

"John Stretch really wants you. You really turned his head."

*Garrett, do not be a fool. Miss Pular is about to fly into a panic. What you are saying means more to her than it should.*

"I'm sorry, Singe. I'm sorry. I didn't mean that like it sounded. I was teasing you. Yes, I did tell John Stretch that I'd trade you for two Bics. But his chances of . . ."

*Garrett!*

"All right! Singe, no matter what I told John Stretch, I'm not letting you go. Nobody is going to take you away. So relax. Take some time, again, to see if you can't figure out when you're being teased. And I'll try to rein it in. If I can. Humans seldom speak straightforwardly and direct. I find that frustrating myself, sometimes." Like almost every time I spend more than a few minutes in the company of most human women. "Anyway, even if I was that big a villain, how likely is it that John Stretch would keep his word?"

"Because he's nothing but a slimy little rat, you mean, and we all know that ratpeople are nothing but stupid, lazy, lying, thieving, smelly animals?"

While Singe shouted the Dead Man passed along one or two points of interest. *Well, well. The ratman who calls himself John Stretch was born Pound Humility, of the same female one litter before Miss Pular Singe. It may be that his interest in her is less political than personal. Miss Pular suspects an unwanted brother's concern for his sister's welfare. From the viewpoint of a ratman she would be making a huge mistake by getting involved with you.*

"Whoa! Whoa! Singe! I'm sorry! I apologize! That isn't what I meant at all." I felt a variant of Winger's question kicking in. If the woman who heard it wasn't human was the man still wrong? Apparently so. I'd tripped a triggerwire and I wasn't going to talk my way out of this one.

*Good to see that you are not going to deny that she is involved with you, even if you do not feel that you are involved with her.*

The Dead Man rescued me. This once. Because this wasn't a hole I'd dug for myself without help and because Singe was creeping up on the edge of true hysteria. And if there's anything the Dead Man dislikes more than females in general, or as a class, it's hysterical females.

There was one plus side to the whole emotional circus. Although ratgirls do get upset, they don't shed tears.

The silver elf woman just kept standing there, gaunt as Famine Himself in that old shirt, taking the scene in with those huge, strange eyes. She didn't seem frightened anymore. I wondered how much she was picking up from the Dead Man.

# 63

Dean brought food and drink to the Dead Man's room. He seemed to have adjusted to the extended presence of guests. He and Singe, in particular, seemed to have achieved a sound accommodation.

After relating my extensive adventures I asked the Dead Man, "Have you been able to learn anything from our elven guests?"

*A great deal. Beginning with the obvious fact that they are not actually elves, nor are they members of any similar or familiar species. Nor are they a mixture of familiar species. Nothing that I have learned, by the way, was provided to me voluntarily. They suspect, but do not yet know, that they have revealed a great deal about themselves and their kind. This one knows herself as Evas, which is the diminutive for something even I cannot fathom. The other is Fasfir and was the captain of their party of three. They have much more complex interior lives than human beings, yet seem to envy your emotional freedoms. Fasfir, curiously, seems to have a rudimentary sense of humor.*

"All right. Your talents are mighty and your cleverness surpasses anything the world has ever seen. What do we know now that we didn't know yesterday?"

*We now know that Casey is what he claims to be, an officer of their law sent here a year ago to arrest Lastyr and Noodiss. Insofar as I can decipher the images in Evas' mind, which is much easier to penetrate than is Fasfir's, those two are religious missionaries originally sent out by an outlaw cult known as the Brotherhood of Light. Proselytization is a major crime under the laws of these people. Casey is supposed to arrest them, simply for their intent to proselytize.*

*They stole the skyship they used to come here. They were not skilled in its operation. They crashed it into the river. Their motives for teaching Kip to invent things have to do with wanting him to create things that have to exist before they can begin to make the tools that they will need to fix their ship.*

*Which takes them into another entire realm of crime entirely, apparently. That of revealing the secrets of state sorcery. Another department sent out Evas and her companions to seize Lastyr and Noodiss for betraying sorcerous secrets, the fact of those crimes having been included in Casey's reports, which somehow leaked over to the competing bureau.*

"If they needed a ship why didn't they just go down to the waterfront and hire one?"

*Evidently the journey is too long to make in a normal sailing ship, which supposedly cannot travel fast enough to make it to their country in even a Loghyr's lifetime.*

"Wow." What else could I say? I've always known that the world is bigger than what I've experienced in my thirty years, but distances on that scale are beyond my comprehension. "And what about the elves from the flying disk? Who are they? Still more cops?"

*They appear to be something resembling a sorcerer who, though he spends his whole lifetime studying magic and discovering new things about it, never does anything more practical with his discoveries than just write the information down. They are members of a fraternity where the search for knowledge is an end in itself. The excitement about Lastyr and Noodiss alerted them to the existence of Karenta and TunFaire, so they assembled an expedition to come study us. Apparently they wanted to grab Kip Prose because their ship is suffering its own problems and they thought that if they could open communications with Lastyr and Noodiss, working together they could produce one working vessel from the two cripples.*

I do stumble into the weird stuff. And you can't get much weirder than this.

*These last four may also have been doing commercial surveys of some sort, as a condition of gaining financial support for their research. At least one of them may be a ringer who really works for a law enforcement bureau that somehow oversees commerce.*

*Fasfir holds all four in complete contempt. At the same time she is convinced that they are her crew's only chance of ever getting home. If their aerial ship can be made capable of completing one more long voyage, Fasfir sees two ways of accomplishing that. One calls for an improbable amount of good luck making repairs to the one aerial ship you saw up close in the wine country. The other requires that she and her friends find Lastyr and Noodiss so that their wrecked flying ship can be cannibalized to make repairs to the other. Fasfir is much more knowledgeable than is Evas, who seems to be the junior member of the mission.*

*The creature Casey will have a ship of his own hidden somewhere, of course. There is a general consensus that he will rescue no one but himself. He feels no responsibility for the others. But he will take Lastyr and Noodiss back as prisoners. And Fasfir is afraid that those two might be ready to surrender. They came here to save Karentine souls and teach Karentines forbidden magics that would make their lives easier but after a year of exposure to our savage ways, she fears, even those two have to have become convinced that we deserve our damnation.*

"Not exactly original thinking there." A quick visit to the Chancery steps will expose you to all the outrage against the moral destitution of our times that you can possibly stand. Most of us are so poverty-stricken morally that we don't realize that we're missing something. According to the rant-and-ravers.

*It was unoriginal when I was a stripling. It is a long slide indeed that never reaches bottom.*

"You ever find any way to communicate with them directly?"

*I have not yet given the matter much consideration. However, and despite any pretense to the contrary, this one understands spoken Karentine perfectly. They have a sorcery which allows them to learn very quickly.*

Meaning she was tracking my part of the conversation.

*Exactly.*

"Ouch. But is there any solid reason for us to hide?"

Evas stood motionless, regarding me with those huge, unblinking eyes, possibly trying to see inside me, to the place where I was listening to the Dead Man. I wondered if she was having any success. I conjured a vivid erotic vision of the two of us rather energetically being boys and girls together. The Dead Man made his disgust known immediately. The silver elf did not, though by happenstance there was a huge crash in the kitchen.

I did get a somewhat puzzled look from Singe, which confirmed my suspicion that she might be slightly sensitive herself.

*Very slightly. For which be grateful. Had she viewed that image we might be dealing with hysteria all over again.*

"You know, I still ache all over anytime I sit still for very long. I don't want to be a detective anymore today. And when I get up tomorrow I just want to be an accountant trying to figure out how to make sure we get paid for all of this. Can they read and write?"

*I do not know. And now I can no longer see inside Evas' head without hammering my way in. For some reason she has begun to suspect that someone here might be able to read her mind. You would not have any notion why she might suspect that, would you?*

I shrugged. It didn't seem likely, did it?

I'm not usually much concerned about money—as long as I've got some. I was growing concerned because of this mess, though. We were spending and spending and spending to hire help and buy food and there seemed to be an ever smaller likelihood of us managing any return on investment. Kip was back home with his family. The silver elves seemed to have lost interest in him. After the country confrontation, they all knew that he couldn't finger Lastyr and Noodiss.

But Old Bones was having him one hell of a good time, I could tell. This thing was the most fun he'd had in years. It was something *new*. These two weird women, Evas and Fasfir, were, to him, as exciting and alluring as was my friend Katie to me.

I said, "This's the least violent, least traditional thing we've ever been into. I'm not comfortable with it at all. The stakes are trivial and these silver elves are too alien for me to find very interesting."

*Perhaps you will feel differently in the morning. Try considering the stakes from a viewpoint not your own. I will be doing that myself now that I have the mind time free. One obvious avenue of exploration is the possible dangers the Lords of the Hill fear.*

"Those old paranoids are only scared because they think the whole world is infested with people as cruel and wicked and mean-spirited as they are."

*True. But that does not render them automatically wrong in every instance. They can be afraid in a huge way because it is possible for them to have huge enemies to make life terrible, not just for them but for us all. Just one of these silver elves needs to be wicked and willing to use their weird but powerful sorcery against us.*

He was right about that. Those people controlled some very strange powers.

He was right about me feeling differently in the morning, too—for reasons entirely unrelated to any remotely within his consideration at the time.

## 64

I wakened suddenly, thinking those pixies had to go. But they were quiet. Instead, there was a weak light burning and I wasn't alone in my bed. When I turned to tell Singe, yet again, that this couldn't happen, a spidery gray finger fell upon my lips. Another spidery finger touched a large eye, then tapped my temple.

Oh, boy. What was this? The silver elf woman, Evas, knelt on the edge of my bed. She'd seen that naughty image after all. And she'd brought a sheaf of papers with her. I recognized them. They'd all been in my office, on my desk, before I'd come upstairs.

Evas could read and write Karentine. And she'd been a busy little scribbler.

She placed the papers in my hands. The top sheet said, simply, *Teach me.*

She removed that raggedy, short shirt. And again placed a finger on my lips when I started to tell her to go away.

That petite form definitely did have its appeal, suddenly. I couldn't resist wondering about its possibilities.

Later I would wonder if there was any chance my thoughts had been guided from outside.

Evas moved the top sheet of paper to the bottom of the stack.

Followed a story of an extremely ancient people who, ages ago, had decided to set aside the insidious and constant distortions of the intellect that are caused by the stormy demands of sexual reproduction.

I could relate to that. Some would claim that I'm intellectually distorted most of the time. I confess freely that I'd be much more respectable and much less emotionally vagrant if the gods hadn't seen fit to bless and curse the rest of us with women.

Evas declared herself a despicable throwback who suffered wicked urges and curiosities all the time. She'd fought those successfully until now only because she'd always been surrounded by people who wouldn't let her get into situations where she might embarrass herself.

Here, tonight, she had an opportunity to pursue the curiosities that were driving her mad. And her people would never be the wiser.

Chances were excellent that such an opportunity would never come to her again.

She knew the mechanics. She'd taken advantage of her ability to move around unseen to indulge her curiosity intellectually. They all had. She was the only one who hadn't been repelled.

Back to sheet one and *Teach me.*

Hers was a whole new, entirely intellectual approach to the art of seduction. Backed up by what my rude senses could gather of her mental state. Evas wasn't kidding. And in that weak light she looked far more exotic and desirable than weird.

I had fallen into every red-blooded boy's favorite daydream.

At some point Evas took time out to use a thin fingertip to trace letters on my skin to pass me the message, "I will not break." She wanted me to know that she wasn't nearly as fragile as she looked.

# 65

"Good morning, Sunshine," Dean told me, nudging me to let me know he'd brought my tea. I was half-asleep at the breakfast table, unable to stop grinning.

I grunted.

"Odd. You're smiling. And you got to bed at a reasonable hour for once. But you're as crabby as a mountain boozelt."

"Them damned pixies. They never shut up. All night long."

He didn't challenge me. That could only mean that he didn't know any better.

Singe appeared, obviously having been up since the crack of dawn. She was chipper, though possibly more conspiratorial than ever. She was pleasant to me. Nor was I getting any grief from the Dead Man.

When Evas turned up she was coolly indifferent to everything but some tea heavily sweetened with honey. She was exactly as she had been yesterday except, possibly, for projecting a somewhat more resigned attitude toward her captivity. Her sidekick Fasfir, though equally cool, presented a puzzle. She kept looking at me the way you might regard a twenty-foot python you found coiled atop the kitchen table: repelled, wary, awed, maybe a little intrigued and excited.

Still nothing from the Dead Man.

That must've been one hell of a dream I'd had. Especially since it'd reawakened all my aches and pains and had added a few that were new.

Evas might be willing to let me think it had been all a dream spawned by my wicked imagination but I noted, with some satisfaction, that she moved very carefully and did so mainly when she thought no one was paying attention. Fasfir noticed, though.

So. She knew.

My grin spread a little wider.

"What evil thought just burst into your mind?" Singe demanded. There was an actual teasing edge to her voice.

"Nothing special. Just a warm memory."

Once I finished eating, and began to feel a little more awake, I moved to my office. I was feeling positive and eager to get things done. But before I could start I had to go round up a pile of missing paperwork.

During the course of the morning, various people came by the house. Most wanted money. Playmate was effusive with gratitude but didn't bring one copper sceat to defray the costs of my efforts to salvage his madonna's useless infant. I responded to two written requests for clarification or additional information from the good people at the al-Khar. I received a note from Manvil Gilbey telling me that Max Weider wanted in financially. The same messenger brought a sealed note from Max's daughter Alyx, who complained that she was dying of loneliness and that that was all my fault and when was I going to do something about it?

There were other notes in time, including one from Kayne Prose, inscribed for her by a professional letter writer. That was meant to impress me. And it did, a little. Then there was a discreet letter from Uncle Willard Tate, who invited me to the Tate compound for dinner because he'd just enjoyed an intriguing visit from a certain Manvil Gilbey, associated with the Weider brewing empire. The paper on which the letter was written had a light lilac scent. The hand in which it had been inscribed was familiar and almost mocking.

It reminded me which redheaded, green-eyed beauty managed the Tate correspondence and accounts.

I'd have to gird my mental and emotional loins for that visit. Tinnie was sure to play me like a cheap kazoo if I was bold enough to venture onto her home ground.

The afternoon saw the arrival of a formal, engraved invitation to participate in the celebration of Chodo Contague's sixtieth birthday party, two weeks down the road. And a "Just wanted to say hi" note from solicitor Harvester Temisk, implying that he'd really like to visit before Chodo's birthday celebration.

Dean began to grouse about having to answer the door constantly—when he wasn't hard at work pursuing his custom of charming whatever woman happened to be staying in the house. It was he who took Evas far enough along to lure forth a spoken word of gratitude. She didn't pronounce the word right and she had difficulty saying it but she did demonstrate that at least one silver elf besides Casey came equipped with a capacity for speech. Yet one more talent unsuspected by us primitives until she betrayed herself. Possibly she was a throwback in more ways than the one.

Fasfir didn't seem pleased.

I had begun to develop an idea of the personalities of our reluctant guests. Evas was cool and brilliant and collected and always in control. In her own mind. But in real life she'd be her own worst enemy. A sort of foreign Kayne Prose with a mind. With her self-destructive urges skewed at a different angle. Fasfir would *be* cool and collected and always in control but, like the best officers and sergeants, would be skilled at failing to see those transgressions which did not threaten the world with an immediate descent into chaos and anarchy.

Singe invited herself into my office to preen and gossip. There wasn't a lot to gossip about, though, unless she wanted to discuss the recipes Dean had begun sharing with her.

I asked, "How close are you to your brother?" I didn't think family was important among ratpeople, but had only prejudice and hearsay to go by.

"I do not have a brother. What does this one say?" She had started leafing through my papers.

"Which side?"

With unerring accuracy she had chosen the side which said, *Teach me.*

I told her.

"What does that mean?"

"I don't know. This isn't a royal style business. I don't have a few million people I can gouge for taxes anytime the urge takes me so I have to make do with whatever bits and pieces of paper come my way. My stuff is on the other side."

I hoped Singe hadn't done any poking around in here. There were almost two dozen identical sheets of paper inside my desk drawer, with both faces still virgin to the pen.

I stuck to my subject. "What do you mean, you don't have a brother? What's John Stretch, then?"

"Oh. Well. We do not see some things the same way you do. Humility belongs to the litter before mine. He would have a different father." Ratpeople follow social and mating customs much closer to those of rodents than they do those of civilized beings such as myself. Chances were excellent that few of Singe's littermates shared the same father.

"Humility?"

Singe responded with one of her rehearsed shrugs.

"So his real name is Pular Humility?"

"No. It is Pound Humility." That's right. The Dead Man did tell me that. "His sire is believed to have been Hurlock Pound. Chances are good. My mother managed to retain some choice and self-control even during the peak of her season. I hope I will have the strength to do the same. Though I am less likely to go into season as long as I remain in exile."

The name Hurlock Pound meant nothing to me. "Never mind. I'm too groggy to keep up with all that. Let's stick with John Stretch. Why did you get upset yesterday when—"

"Because I have spent too much time around you people. I suppose. And because Humility was always good to me when I was little."

"But now he wants to use you as a counter in his effort to make himself king of the ratmen."

"Just do not go hunting him. All right? That way I cannot blame myself for whatever he gets himself into."

"I guess. Whatever." The child was strange. I was convinced that *she* didn't know what she wanted most of the time. Unlike her doomed brother, she didn't know where she wanted to go.

Then again, I'm sometimes wrong.

"I have been wondering, Garrett. Do you think it would be possible for me to learn to read and write?"

So that was where she'd been going when she'd chosen that sheet of paper. I gave it some thought because, honestly, "I've never thought about it. That's probably because of the prejudices all us humans are brought up with. Do you know any ratpeople who can read or write?"

"No. Reliance is the only one I know who needs to. So he has a couple of slaves to keep his books and write his letters. The same goes for the other ratman gangs."

I kept a straight face. "Have you ever heard of anyone who tried to learn?"

"I've met some who wanted to learn. Wanted to *try* to learn. But who would teach them?"

Who indeed? Nobody in TunFaire, of whatever race, wanted

ratpeople getting notions, taking on airs, thinking above their station.

"All right. Karentine is the main language in TunFaire so it's what you'll know best." I recovered the sheet carrying the request, *Teach me*. Ironic. "Do you know any of these letters by name?"

She didn't then but half an hour later she knew them all and had a solid grasp on the concept of how characters and groups of characters represent the sounds that make up spoken words. That was because she'd paid attention most of her life. To everything going on around her.

I sorted out every paper I had that had anything on it in Evas' handwriting—which was, actually, laborious, tiny printing—and got that all put away. "We humans might ought to have you strangled right now, Singe. I swear, you're going to take over the world in a few more years."

For once she grasped the compliment. She was learning in every direction.

I hoped she was as good in her heart as she seemed. Otherwise, I'd be helping to create a monster.

# 66

I did hear the pixies get excited but missed the knock on the door. I'd fallen deep into contemplation of Eleanor, who seemed to be contemplating me right back. She didn't approve of the way I'd been running my life lately. When Eleanor disapproves I know it's time to do some serious reassessment. I thought I had a handle on it, too.

Dean stuck his head into the office. "There're some very nervous ratmen on the stoop."

*John Stretch.*

"John Stretch?"

"One gave me that name."

"I'm on my way."

*Bring them to my room.*

I swung the door open. "Get in here, guys. They're watching the place most of the time these days. Bic, bitty buddy. How're you doing? Not too good, I guess. And Casey," as a second Bic shuffled forward. "I know that must be you in that disguise. Screwed up, eh? Damn, John Stretch, you got them both. I didn't think you could do it." I made sure the door was solidly locked, just to retard any attempt at a hurried exit. "Go into the room behind the door on the right, please. Dean! These guys look like they're starved. Singe! Where are you? We've got company. Give Dean a hand."

In my heart I was wondering if, perhaps, Singe wasn't the only genius pup produced by her mother. And this other pup did want to be in charge.

John Stretch and his friends didn't know what to make of the

Dead Man. It's hard to do, him sitting there like an idol that gives off just a hint of bad aroma. Chances were excellent that they'd never run into a Loghyr before. It could be, in fact, that they'd never heard of the Loghyr race.

They didn't know what to make of Fasfir when she invited herself in, either. She drew plenty of attention from Casey, though. Casey seemed amazed to find her alive and more amazed to find her clad in ragged native garb. But he kept his opinions to himself. The Dead Man assured me that Casey had closed his mind with a determination that was stunning. For the time being he was locked up tighter than Fasfir was.

*He must suspect something.*

Either that or he was a natural-born paranoid.

I took my seat. "Damn again, John Stretch. How in the world did you manage to round up these two?"

*Interesting. He has a talent of his own. He can use his normal rat cousins to scout and spy for him, much as I employ Mr. Big. Though his reach is very much shorter than mine.*

"It couldn't be any other way." I continued, "You put me in a nasty position, John Stretch. My reputation for keeping my word is my most important asset."

Last time we met, I thought John Stretch must be dim. He wasn't. Not even a little. He understood that I wanted to weasel out. "You agreed to a deal. *We* have fulfilled our undertaking." His Karentine remained hard to follow but was adequately understandable. His courage was beyond question. Ratmen don't talk back to humans, let alone imply threats.

"The problem is, long before I made the deal with you I swore a solemn oath to Singe that I wouldn't let any of you people drag her away from here."

"And he knows that if he does not keep his word to me he will soon wish he was enjoying the torments of one of his human hells instead of basking in my displeasure." Singe staggered under the weight of a tray of hastily assembled sandwiches. She set that on the little table, began to help herself. John Stretch and his ratmen waited only long enough to get a nod from me before they assaulted the pile.

Singe brought her muzzle within inches of John Stretch's. With her mouth full and crumbs in her whiskers, she demanded, "What the hell do you think you are doing, Pound Humility? I am not a pawn in your game. I will not be a pawn in your game. I will not be a quiet, obedient little ratgirl who lets herself be passed around like a weed pipe." John Stretch and his henchmen glared daggers at me. This was all my fault, this ratgirl getting uppity. "If Garrett will not whip up on you and throw you out of here I will kick your mangy tail up between your hind legs myself. Then I will go to work on your idiot friends."

John Stretch could not find words for a while. Finally, he asked, "You are not a prisoner here?"

"What? A prisoner? You are an idiot. I live here. This is where I want to live."

Gah! I had a feeling that the cunning ratgirl had just jobbed me. A strong hint of Loghyr amusement supported that hypothesis. That damned Singe could think on her feet.

*It is quite true that John Stretch believed Miss Pular was in need of rescuing. In addition to being a clever and competent criminal he appears to be an unabashed romantic and as vulnerable as you might want to hope from that quarter—as was, if you will believe it, Reliance, in his time.*

He was going to get bashed if he tried anything here. "John Stretch, let's you and me step over to my private office for a minute and talk, man to man. Go ahead, grab another sandwich. Before Singe consumes the whole pile."

I started in while John Stretch was still reeling from his first look at Eleanor. "What'll your guys do if they find out everything they've been through was just to rescue a ratgirl who refuses to be saved? There've been people killed. A bunch have been dragged off to the al-Khar. You know their prospects are going to be dim there."

"Those will not be much worse than out on the streets. The war is over. There is no more work. Humans have no more motive to treat us with respect. For those imprisoned the misery just will not last as long. The stable disaster was bad luck. Bad timing added to the fact that we were not told just how much material we were expected to remove."

"Maybe you didn't know the temper of the neighborhood very well, either."

"Of course we did not. No ratpeople live there. But the promised payoff seemed worth the risk."

"It always does. Until the pain starts."

"Possession of Pular Singe is more than a personal matter. All ratkind is watching. Yes, I would have rescued her. Even having heard the words from her own mouth, in Karentine rather than cant, I find it hard to believe that she prefers to live among humans."

"I'll tell you why. You know the saying, 'Lower than a rat-man's dog'?"

"I know it. I understand it."

"I'll tell you what's lower than a ratman's dog. A ratwoman. Think about it."

He got it. A point in his favor. Most ratmen wouldn't have if you'd drawn them a picture. "That may be another reason why Reliance considers her an important symbol. She is living proof that things can be done in ways other than the ways they have always been done."

"Reliance has been advised by a higher power. He's renounced his interest in Singe. In return the Syndicate will let him live. But he's just stupid enough to think he's clever enough to sneak around the Outfit, somehow. So I'm going to invest in some rough insurance as soon as we're done here."

"You mean that?"

"Singe is my friend, Pound Humility. She's one of the most remarkable people I've ever met, of any species. I want to see her become everything she can. I want to see what she can become if she's given the chance. Despite the customs and politics of ratpeople. Despite the prejudices of everybody else. You understand?"

"No. But I can accept. If Singe is safe from Reliance."

"Answer my question. What'll your friends do if they find out what you were doing?"

"If we do not have possession of Singe? They might be angry enough to kill me."

"Thought so. You ratfolk aren't subtle people. So maybe you'll want a running start. . . . No. Wait a minute. Wait just a minute. I might have an angle. Hang on here for a second."

I zipped across the hallway. "Singe, come out here. Yes, bring the sandwich." I shut the door behind her. "Singe, my sweet, whatever happened to that now-you-see-me, now-you-don't fetish we took off Casey out in the country?" I knew we hadn't turned it over to the Guard. Mainly because I'd forgotten all about it.

Singe's whiskers folded back. Way back.

The significance of which I intuited instantly. "Oh, no. You didn't. You wicked girl." Not only did she know about Evas, she'd been there to watch. "You figured out how to work the box." Now she was a sorceress, too. And she hadn't said a thing. "Old Bones. Are you listening?"

*I am here.*

"Then show Singe what I want her to do." There were too many untrustworthy ears in the place tonight.

And now the Dead Man knew about Evas, too. He hadn't before, though three people in the house did know. Evas must have some considerable skill at sealing memory blocks, including those in minds not her own.

*But I did know, Garrett. Because the pixies knew. However, it was none of my business.* He had nothing to say about his failure to be a direct witness himself.

But the pixies, too. Who didn't know?

*Dean. So far.*

Even Fasfir?

*Even Fasfir.*

Grrr! He was right before. This was personal stuff. But when had that ever kept him from butting in with his opinion? And why hadn't the senior elf woman blown up like a bad batch of beer?

Now wasn't the time to worry. We needed to get on with business. "Keep Singe posted on what I'm saying." I returned to John Stretch. "Here's what we'll do. Singe will go with you, all docile and bashful, for your sake. Because we think it'll be good to have you for a friend. Let all ratkind marvel at your coup. But I want to warn you. Singe is going to vanish. Like a candle being snuffed. I want you to lie low for a few days after that. Things will be going on with Reliance and his like. Pay attention. Try not to repeat their mistakes after your luck turns."

John Stretch had no idea what I was talking about but he listened.

He'd know the whole story soon enough.

"Have another sandwich while Singe gets ready."

Stretch and his henchrats dug in, eating with an amazing devotion. I told Stretch how he could pick up a little extra pocket change by hunting elves.

I continued to have this strong desire to meet Lastyr and Noodiss.

I heard Singe's distinctive step descending the stair. I met her at its foot. I told her, "I want you to be careful. Don't let anybody get close enough to get a good hold on you. Disappear first time they're all looking at something else. Once you figure they can't blame it on John Stretch. Don't leave a trail they can sniff out."

"You care."

"Of course I care. You're my friend. I worry about you."

"Good. It is all right, you know. You and Evas. Or you and Kayne Prose. Or you and her daughter. That sort of thing does not trouble ratfolk like it does your people. I was curious. Evas suspected I was there after a while but by then she did not care."

If I'd had whiskers they would've been back far enough to tie behind my head. The more I saw of Singe the less well I seemed to know her. Maybe I needed to stop using her as a mirror.

"Please be careful."

"I will be careful, Garrett. Because I mean to have my turn. Someday."

Help!

# 67

"What have we got with these two?" I asked the Dead Man, after I'd seen the ratpeople into the street and after I'd turned the Goddamn Parrot loose to keep track of them.

Singe *needed* watching. Reliance couldn't be blamed if he attacked his enemies and, lo! Pular Singe happened to be tromping around with them. That wouldn't violate the letter of any agreement with higher powers.

"Other than a big-ass grudge, of course."

*Very little that is new or interesting. Mr. Bic Gonlit did persist in trying to sell Miss Pular after you asked him to behave. For which effort his reward has been to end up here, traded for her.*

Bic winced badly. He was getting the benefit of the Dead Man's wisdom.

The thoughts must have been particularly strong. Fasfir stirred back there in the darkness, where she sat cross-legged atop a stool. She would've been an elegant sight had there been enough light to reveal her. None of the silver elves seemed to be acquainted with the concept of underwear. Or of modesty, either.

*Officer Casey did hire those ratboys who just left. A great many of them, going well beyond John Stretch's gang. They were supposed to steal everything from Cypres Prose's workshop, without exception, evidently because Casey's superiors had ordered him to see that it was all destroyed.*

I didn't speak aloud, just articulated my questions softly in the back of my throat. "He can do that? He has the sorcery to be able to talk to people in another country?"

*Evidently.*

No wonder the Hill crowd wanted to lay hands on these people. I had trouble imagining the full power of the weapon that would be instantaneous communication. There would be no defeating armies with that capacity.

*Indeed. It is extremely difficult to dig information out of Casey. But it can be done, slowly, if one approaches the task with considerable patience. He does not appear to be as adept at concealing himself as Fasfir is, when worked over time.*

"So maybe she can get him to cooperate. You have any idea where his ship is? It's the only working one left. If we knew where it was the rest of the silver elves would turn into our best friends."

*Quite likely. And I do know where the ship is. Approximately.*

"Approximately? And? Or is it a but?" It would be something.

*Severe sorceries protect it. And actually finding it might be difficult. Our visitors do not envision spatial relationships the way you do. They see different colors, hear different sounds, sense things you do not sense at all.*

"Oh, well. Will Casey just do more mischief if we cut him loose?"

*He will try. He is what he is. He shares many of your character traits. He will try to do the job he has agreed to do. He has, just recently, received those orders concerning the eradication of inappropriate knowledge. Whatever that may mean. I suspect that that means there is now an actual physical threat to Cypres Prose, simply because he has so many wonderful ideas. Ideas he received from his elusive friends.*

"Then we'll just have to keep him around here." If he got too rambunctious, I could always send him off for a wondrous vacation in the al-Khar.

In a conversational sort of voice, I said, "Bic, we're going to give you one more chance to get out of our way with your ass still strapped onto the rest of you. All it'll take is for you to carry a letter from me to Colonel Block at the al-Khar. Because I don't have time to handle it myself. Can you manage that without getting distracted? Knowing that the letter means enough to me that I'll hunt you down and feed you your magic boots, one from each end, if my message doesn't get through within the hour?"

"Garrett, how come you're so damned determined to make my life miserable?"

"Maybe you'd better look at the facts, Bic. Who did what to who first? I think your beef is with Casey. This critter right here, dressed up like you. He had you jumping through hoops by pre-

tending to be Kayne Prose in heat. While he was working Kayne,
pretending to be you." I'm so clever. Sometimes I can spot a pot-
hole only minutes after I've stumbled into it. "And you and Kayne
both ended up screeching because you couldn't get all the way
lucky. Old Case couldn't pretend that part."

Bic growled. Bic didn't want to listen to any damned theories.
"Look at him, man. He looks like you in a funhouse mirror." A
mirror that skinnied him down and talled him up.

"Never mind. I'm not going to argue till you're convinced."

"So just give me your damned letter and let me out of here."

"And don't forget to remember me in your will. Because I've
treated you better than anybody else in town would've done." I
found myself lusting after a beer. Or something with a better kick.
I hadn't had a drop since our country picnic. But I couldn't take
time out now. I had business to attend to, outside the home. "Bic,
I'd kiss you good-bye but then you'd just come back for more."

I shut the door behind the little man at last, leaned against it. "I
sincerely hope that that's the last time I ever see Bic Gonlit." The
man was like a mosquito. Not a major problem but one persistent
annoyance if you didn't kill him. "Can he possibly have any other
reason to buzz around my ear, now?"

*Suppose the Guard arrest and question him.*

"I didn't think of that." I hadn't, which seemed real dim of me
the second the subject came up. "But he will. And he's clever
enough not to let that happen. I wish the bird was here to send out
to watch him."

*You might send a pixie. They have not yet done much to earn
their keep.*

"That seems a little dangerous. For the pixies. Let's just trust
Bic to do what he said he'd do. I'm going to clean up and change
now. I'm heading up to the Tate compound. To see Willard Tate."

Old Chuckles failed to seize the opportunity, though I'm sure
he noted my unnecessary explanation of why I had to put myself
in close proximity to a certain ferocious redhead who couldn't
quite seem to decide how big a part of my life she wanted to be.

## 68

"I think we're in business," I told the Dead Man when I returned in the wee hours, a little light-headed. Willard Tate enjoys his brandies and loves to share his pleasures with people he likes. He likes me right now.

The rest of the Tates are wine people, every one with a favorite vintage. I'm not much on the spoiled grape juice myself. I prefer that Weider barley soup with plenty of hops. But I couldn't be impolite when a taste was offered.

And it was hard to keep track of how much sipping I did when I was a little distracted, off and on, by Tinnie and her wicked cousin Rose.

I said, "I'll have a sitdown with all the principals as soon as I arrange for Morley to make space available."

I would take Morley on a nostalgic voyage into his past, returning The Palms to the days when it was The Joy House and neutral ground for meetings just like the one I planned. He was a good friend. He deserved to get the business.

*Excellent. And though I do begrudge admitting it, I believe you have suffered one of your better ideas this time.*

"Did Singe get back yet?"

*More than an hour ago. All went well. She ate and drank like a lumberjack, then went to bed. That child has an amazing capacity for beer.*

"If she's going to keep sucking it down here, she'd better start showing an amazing capacity for bringing in cash. What about the jungle chicken?"

*Still out there. Watching the al-Khar now. To see how the Guard responds to your message.*

"There's only one response possible. Don't tell me they haven't done anything."

*Nothing dramatic. There have been comings and goings but, not being familiar with the routine around the jail, I do not know if they are unusual. And it would behoove us to recall that we live in a political world. What Colonel Block should do and what he is allowed to do might not be identical—if someone important up-Hill happens to be an investor in Reliance's undertakings.*

"I know. I know. It's a blackhearted world. I'm going to go put away some beer myself. Then I'm going to sleep till noon."

A man's fondest dreams and dearest ideals often become storm-tossed wrack upon reefs of reality.

I wakened to find myself already deeply involved in some extremely heavy petting.

Evas had decided school was in again. Only . . . It took a few moments of exploration to determine that tonight's pupil wasn't Evas. Perhaps Fasfir had pulled rank.

Fasfir was a dedicated student, give her that. Her focus matched Evas'. It seemed she wanted to practice till she got it right. She didn't go away until people started stirring around the house.

Good thing I'd announced that I meant to sleep in.

# 69

Dean didn't get the word. Or didn't care. He wakened me. His stern look of disapproval was the one he reserved for my sloth, brought out on occasions when he felt he couldn't state his opinion aloud. He would've employed an entirely different and much uglier scowl had he known about Evas or Fasfir.

He told me, "You need to get up. There are messages awaiting your attention. And Miss Winger is in the street outside, apprising the world of all your shortcomings."

"I doubt that. She hasn't had a chance to catalog them. Unless you've signed on as her adviser."

He plowed ahead. "And the workmen have arrived." He said that last quickly and softly, as though it was a minor, mooshy afterthought of no consequence whatsoever.

I didn't think about it. Which was the point.

John Stretch had cut Winger loose. Good for him. Good for her. Maybe not as good for me if she was going to roam the streets accusing me of being in cahoots with those ugly fraternal twins, Mal and Mis Feasance. Although I certainly had trouble imagining why she might do that, considering she slept in their bed herself, most nights.

"None of that sounds all that pressing to me," I grumbled, knowing he was going to be disgruntled simply because I was in bed when it was light outside already.

Dean shrugged. His usual, aggressive morning attitude seemed to have abandoned him. He was intrigued by something on the floor. Something he might possibly have last seen hanging off Fasfir. He frowned deeply as he tried to get a mental grasp on the facts.

I saw the change when he decided he was imagining things.

I said, "I'll be down in a few minutes."

On instructions from the Dead Man, Dean let Winger into the house. She stormed from the front door directly into the kitchen, where I was working on breakfast while surrounded by my harem. "Have a cup of tea, Winger." Then I said, "If you insist on being abusive I'll just chuck you right back out in the street. Where you can keep on entertaining the secret police spies who watch this place every minute."

Winger was wound up. She blistered the air with her extemporaneous remarks. However, mention of Relway's gang got her stuttering fast. Unfortunately for her immortality, I wasn't paying enough attention to recall her exact words for posterity. Which was probably just as well. She hadn't been doing a whole lot of nun-style talking.

"You're running around loose, aren't you?" I wedged the question in while pouring tea for myself and Evas, who seemed astounded that something like Winger existed. "Imagine that. And you didn't get one single precious little hair on your pretty head harmed, either. Amazing." I wasn't responsible but she didn't need to know that.

Winger thought some. The implications made her stumble some more. She decided to sit down and enjoy an eating contest with Singe—at least until she'd worked herself up for a fresh round of accusations.

Once she had her mouth full, I asked, "How did those ratmen manage to capture you? I expected something to happen. Morley was supposed to send some men to back you up. Didn't they show?"

"Those pussies?" I think that's what she said. Her mouth was still full of dribbling crumbs. "Those assholes ran out on me."

I sighed. That wasn't that hard to translate. It meant she'd been such a bitch that Morley's guys had decided that the job wasn't worth it, that Winger deserved whatever she got. Morley would back them up. And would demand that they be paid for their suffering. And he'd have the moral right of it, probably.

Winger remains her own worst enemy.

Maybe she ought to try a little adult education with Sarge.

Some crashing and banging started up front. "What the hell?

Sounds like somebody's beating on the side of the house with a sledgehammer." For a moment I envisioned Doris doing to my house what he'd refused to do to Casey's place.

Nobody told me anything. But Dean's attitude suddenly seemed evasive.

I recalled his having said something about workmen.

I drained my teacup and headed for the front door, noting that I wasn't hurting much of anywhere this morning. Which was wonderful. And surprising. I ought to have some cramps, or something, considering the rigors of my instructional duties.

The racket got the Goddamn Parrot going. "Help! Help! Oh, Mister, please don't. . . ." I leaned in to tell him, "Aw, shut yer ugly beak, ya little pervert," before I went on to the door. "Ain't nobody here who ain't heard it all before."

*Wait.*

"Huh?"

*I believe we are about to have a caller.*

"But somebody's trying to wreck the outside of the house."

*Masons are removing a couple of bricks to permit the pixies access to the hollows in the middle course of the wall.*

The outer walls of my place are three-course brick masonry, a very dark, blackish rough red brick. Typically, the center course of that sort of construction includes a lot of voids.

So some genius had gotten the notion that those voids could be turned into pixie apartments. Gah! Now I'd have them squabbling inside my walls, day and night.

I supposed chances were excellent the guilty genius spent most of his life making and unmaking messes in my kitchen.

As the Dead Man had predicted, someone knocked on the front door. The knock had that peremptory character I associated with the secret police, that combination of confidence and impatience.

Nor was my guess in error, though my visitor was no one I recognized. And had been chosen, no doubt, because of that fact. If they had to deal with me directly, they would show me too many faces to remember. "Yes?"

"Courier. I have a message for you from Colonel Block." A written message at that. He slapped a small, scroll-style document into my hand, then turned and took off, stepping like he was marching to a drumbeat pitched too high for human ears. He headed straight up the street to Mrs. Cardonlos' rooming house, probably to collect the daily reports. Which meant they'd given up bothering to pretend.

*Well?*

Reading, I closed the door with shoulder and elbow. "A report on what they've been doing about Reliance and some other rat gangsters using human slaves to manage their bookkeeping."

*Generous of the colonel.*

"Yes, indeed. And I'll tell you this. I wouldn't want to be a known ratman criminal right now." What Block was willing to commit to paper would be just the tip of the iceberg. And what he'd been willing to set down was so vicious and wicked that I felt belated reservations about having unleashed the whirlwind.

"Here's an interesting 'Did you know?' Did you know that rat-people, alone of all the intelligent peoples of TunFaire, have no legal standing whatsoever? Less, even, than an ox or a draft horse? That anyone can do just about any damned thing they want to them with complete legal impunity? Just the same as if they were regular rats?"

*Easy to understand why, then, they would be bitter.*

"Better believe." Not one in a hundred of my fellow royal subjects had a conscience sufficiently well developed to understand why I found that situation troubling, too.

*Do not bruit that about. Few people know. Were that common knowledge, someone would soon be killing them for their fur or their teeth or their toenails, or something such.*

And people capable of that were out there, strangers to conscience, remorse, and pity, who were constitutionally incapable of encompassing those concepts however often they were explained.

"I've unchained a beast."

*This once may be for the best. Mr. Relway may know no limits but those he imposes from within. Which may make him appear infinitely ferocious even while those internal limits do exist. He will exterminate ratmen with wild enthusiasm but everyone who perishes will have been a true villain.*

"Or if they weren't they wouldn't have gotten themselves dead. Right? I know that game of old."

*Mr. Relway will dwindle away to that point someday, no doubt. But it won't be today. Today he still recalls that he's just a man. An overly idealistic sort of man.*

"Shall I tell Singe?"

*She will learn of it anyway.*

"Tell Singe what?" Singe demanded, having entered the Dead Man's room soundly equipped to avoid starvation for at least a generation.

"That the Guard have attacked Reliance and several other

leading ratmen. With the sort of acutely accurate intelligence you'd expect of Deal Relway. The Guard did it because Reliance has been keeping human slaves." Though the slaves' humanness shouldn't have mattered. Slavery at its most blatant and obvious has been outlawed for generations, no matter the race of the slave.

Today we have indenture and apprenticeship and several forms of involuntary servitude involving debtors and convicted criminals but nobody owns another intelligent being outright. In law. Sometimes reality can be pretty ugly.

Acute and accurate intelligence? Then how come they hadn't known about the slavery? Or had they?

My cynical side quickly had me wondering if the raids weren't just image-building stunts launched at this point only because somebody with a big mouth and an overly moralistic attitude now knew what the ratmen were doing.

I told Singe, "The attacks have been remarkably vicious and violent." Because the Guard wanted to make an unmistakable point. A major new power player had entered the lists.

There would be truly big trouble if Relway ever got so overconfident that he went after the Outfit. Because there are a whole lot more of their bad guys than there are of his good guys. And those bad guys have far greater resources.

"And this would be the insurance you were taking on my behalf?"

There was no ducking the truth. "No Reliance, no threat from Reliance."

Singe did not get upset with me. What distress she did betray she directed at herself. She might not have willed disaster to devour Reliance but a disaster had occurred on her account. "You are right, Garrett. You are completely right. Life is a bitch."

"And then you die."

"Will Humility be all right?"

"I don't know. I tried to warn him. I hope he listened. I think he's someone I could get along with. And what I do, it's all connections."

"What *we* do, Garrett."

I started to speak.

*Might I suggest a level of caution usually reserved for speech in the presence of Miss Tate?*

He might. But that didn't mean I had a whole lot of use for it.

Singe continued, "I am part of this team, now. And I am not really asking for a salary, or anything."

"Nobody draws a salary here. But the more people there are

around here, the more work has to be done to keep everybody in clothing and food. And the way you keep putting it away . . . You aren't pregnant, are you?" All I needed was a horde of rat pups underfoot, atop the rest of the zoo.

*Not a smart suggestion, Garrett. Not a smart suggestion.*

He was right. I'd managed to offend Singe at last. And her main complaint was a sound one: I'd tossed off a remark like that without ever having bothered to learn enough about ratpeople to know that she couldn't get pregnant unless she was in season. Unlike human women. And she hadn't yet gone into season, except once, her first time, under rigorously controlled conditions, with her mother and some older sisters there to make sure nothing untoward happened.

"After the first time any ratgirl with half a brain can manage her schedule. I go to the same apothecaries human women do. And the same hedge wizards." Singe rolled up her left sleeve, showed me a fancy yarn amulet not unlike those worn by every human female I knew who'd passed the age of nine. This is a cruel, wicked, unpredictable, and exciting world. Bad things happen to good girls. Good things happen to bad girls. Nobody with any sense risks having her life shattered by chance joy or evil.

Which isn't to say that there aren't scores of accidents happening out there every day. Common sense isn't.

"It is really easy. But a lot of males do not want females controlling their fertility. And very few ratgirls are as courageous as I am. It takes a lot of nerve to sneak away and get fitted for an amulet. Even though everyone knows where to get one."

"What happens if you get caught using one of those things?"

"Basically, they get really unhappy with you but, mostly, they just take it away. Then they crowd you till your season comes on you. They believe that once a female has enjoyed a vigorous season of mating she won't want to delay another one ever again."

"Is that male arrogance? Or is it true?"

"I cannot tell you of my own certain knowledge. I have seen females little older than myself swilling an herb tea they believe will bring them into season sooner. At the same time taking other concoctions supposed to prevent pregnancy or to terminate one if it starts."

Sounded to me like love amongst the ratfolk could be as mad as it is amongst human folk.

"It is a good thing to be a girl who thinks ahead," Singe said. "So my older sisters tell me. They say a girl can futter herself blind for weeks on end if she makes the proper preparations and takes the right precautions."

I was beginning to get uncomfortable.

Singe fluttered her eyelashes. "Weeks."

My luck was mixed. That didn't go anywhere because Winger burst in. She started barking at the Dead Man and me. "You guys aren't gonna stiff me, Garrett."

"A straight line I cannot resist—"

"Don't give me no shit, Garrett."

"Winger, why do you have to be a pain in the ass every day of your life?" She wasn't, really. Most of the time she was good people. My directness startled her silent long enough for me to add, "I ought to hire the Rose brothers to follow you around with a couple of huge mirrors so every time you start in on somebody they can shove one in front of you so you can see what's happening."

Winger got a big, goofy look on her face. She isn't deep at all. She'll take that sort of remark literally, often as not. This time she cocked her head and thought about it for a few seconds before she decided it was just, somehow, some more of Garrett's candy-ass, goody two-shoes, crapola, pussy philosophy. A category which included anything I ever said that she didn't agree with or didn't understand. She gave her hair a violent toss. "You guys ain't gonna get outta giving me what I got coming."

"Oh, you're going to get what you've got coming. One of these days."

Her blind, fool, drunk good luck has got to run out someday.

Upon repeated advice from the Dead Man, in the face of my own deeply held principles, I sent Winger off with a little money in her pocket. She was happy to get it. She knew perfectly well that she didn't deserve it.

Now she'd go do some drinking, get into a fight with somebody who reminded her of her husband, maybe bed him if he survived the action. Then, while she was still drunk but already beginning to feel the bite of a hangover, she'd drag Saucerhead Tharpe out of bed and try to con him into helping her manage some criminal enterprise noteworthy for its complete boneheadedness. Like the time she got poor Grimmy Weeks drunk, bopped what little brains he had out, then talked him into helping her pilfer the Singing Sword of Holme Prudeald.

That damned sword has no value whatsoever. It's not fit for fighting and its only magical property is its ability to sing. Badly.

The damned blade never shut up after they pinched it. Everywhere Grimmy and Winger went, it boomed out off-key operatic arias about henpecked top gods, brothers who plooked their sisters in order to create psychopathic, dwarf-murdering heroes who tended to forget that they were married to defrocked, doomed, and not very bright Choosers of the Slain. Which might not have been too bad if Winger hadn't gotten a wild hair and tried to sell herself as the nimrod Chooser.

They say it made great street entertainment.

Winger panicked when she figured the sword's owner would get word. She did a runner when Grimmy had his back turned, leaving the poor befuddled dope holding the scabbard, so to speak.

I'm probably the only guy in town who bought Grimmy's sad story about the big blonde who'd led him to his despair.

If Grimmy survives four years of forced labor in the silver mines he'll return to the street having learned a valuable lesson about getting to know your partners in crime *before* you begin to work together.

She hadn't even given him her real name.

"Hey, Chuckles," I said, popping into the Dead Man's room. "What're we going to do with Casey and the girls?" The male silver elf was too much trouble to keep under control. But if we turned him loose he would become dangerous. And he didn't deserve to be turned over to the Guard. And I didn't want to kill him.

*I have been giving that matter some thought. It is not simple. I have been unable to find a satisfactory answer yet. I will continue to reflect. Possibly Casey himself will present us with an idea.*

That didn't seem likely.

I was in my office. After our recent power spending our financial picture was no longer rosy. I scowled. That might mean having to take on more work.

Evas eased into the room, cold and aloof and remote. Today she wore an unflattering tattered dress that had been handed down by one of Dean's much heftier nieces. The dress wouldn't have been flattering when it was new and on the form it fit. The weavers had strung a lot of ugly thread into the woof.

Evas closed the door. Then she began to change into the very friendly Evas. "I . . . cannot . . . wait." I got the sense that she was mildly ashamed of herself because she couldn't control herself.

After a while I managed to get away. The first tentacles of a marvelous idea had begun to stir in the darkened rooms at the back of my mind.

Damned if it didn't seem like Eleanor winked at me.

Had to be a good idea.

If I could survive the next few days. . . .

"How well do you know my parrot?" I asked. "Come on. You should get to know him."

# 70

I made sure my crew were the first to arrive at The Palms. Even Dean came along, mainly to make sure Morley's barbarians did things right. If there was much surprise at the appearances of Singe and Evas, Morley's people hid it well. I'd left Fasfir behind. Fasfir seemed to have learned everything she'd wanted to know during her one protracted lesson.

Quite possibly nothing could surprise them.

One quick glance around and I asked Sarge, "What's going on? I paid you guys good money. You were supposed to set the place up for—"

"You jus' go on up da stairs dere, Garrett. Puddle's up top. He'll take care a you."

Puddle could make that climb and survive?

"Smart-ass," Sarge said, reading my mind. "Dey's gonna come a time when yer gonna have some slick pup mockin' you fer havin' stayed alive so long."

"Maybe so. I hope so." If my luck shaped up.

My manners were less than impeccable.

I scurried up to see what was what, leaving Singe and Evas under Dean's protection. Puddle pointed when I reached the top.

I've been in and out of Morley's place for as long as we've been friends. I'd been upstairs a hundred times. Morley has his office and living quarters up there. I hadn't thought much more about that floor. Now I discovered a narrow hallway beside his office that, on previous occasions, must have been covered with a panel that looked like part of the wall. The hallway opened into a banquet room, complete with dumbwaiter to the kitchen.

I suppose I should've suspected. The existence of the place seemed entirely reasonable once I saw it. There was a lot of room up there. It might be a major adjunct to Morley's business.

I wondered what went on there when he wasn't renting it out to me.

Morley materialized. In his most ingratiating, oily manner, he asked, "Is it satisfactory, sir?" He'd noted the fact that I was non-plussed. He loved it. "Is there anything else I can do?"

A double-width table array had been set up with seats for twenty people, eight along each side and two at each end. The settings were basic but correct as far as they went. Dean didn't register any objection when he arrived, which eventuality occurred while Morley and I were talking.

There was something else Morley could do but we'd get to that later. "No. This's fine. Except you've got extra places set."

"Don't give me that dark look. I'm not inviting anybody in. We've just found that setting extra places saves embarrassment when the invited guests decide to bring along someone you didn't plan to have attend. People do that. Even though it's terribly bad manners."

"I understand." All too well. Dean had brought in a covered birdcage containing one guest I hadn't wanted to invite. This one wouldn't be getting his own chair. And, if I could avoid it, the cover wouldn't be coming off his cage, either. He could be the Dead Man's proxy without participating in anything.

I remarked, "Your guys ran out on Winger at the stable the other day."

"And should've left an hour before they did. The woman is insufferable. And she keeps getting worse."

"She's got a problem with you that she was taking out on them?"

He didn't want to talk about it. So I asked, "You totally trust all your guys downstairs?"

"Of course."

I tilted my head toward Evas. "Colonel Block has some high-level friends who'd love to sink their talons into her. We took a coach over here so nobody would see her on the street."

"If you need to keep her secret, why risk having someone see her?"

"Her presence is an important ingredient for the success of my evening."

"She is a she, isn't she?"

"You'd better believe. Not extravagantly so, just to look at, but between us guys, don't let that fool you. Her public attitude, either. The ice does melt. In fact, it goes straight to steam. A touch of wine helps. So she has an excuse for making Katie seem repressed and distracted."

"You didn't. You know Tinnie will come with her uncle. She'll figure that out before she's all the way into the room."

The possibility had occurred to me. But the potential of the evening seemed worth risking Tinnie's wrath. I mean, that would come down on me sooner or later, anyway. It's like weather. Some days we're going to have some.

"She'll notice Kayne Prose and Cassie Doap long before she notices Evas."

"You didn't. You rogue."

"Rake's the word, I think. But don't go playing pot to my kettle, pal. It took a lot of arranging to get everybody here tonight. And I had to get away from the house for a while. At least none of them are married."

In general, Morley prefers women encumbered with husbands. Rich husbands are especially good. Their wives are much less likely to make demands he'd rather not meet. They have too much to lose. Besides, he's a married elf himself. So he claims. I've never met his wife. He hasn't seen her himself since he was a kid, supposedly. Or maybe she wasn't a wife, just a fiancée.

Arranged marriage. It's an elven thing. And an everybody else thing, sometimes. When substantial estates are involved.

I added, "The rules of our relationship, laid down explicitly by Tinnie herself, clearly state that neither of us has any right to demand anything of the other as long as the relationship remains informal. Which's the way she wants it kept."

"Garrett, you're thirty years old. Do you still believe in the tooth fairy, too?"

"I'd say there's a better chance of me running into the tooth fairy than there is of Tinnie actually living up to the letter of that."

"I hope you know what you're doing."

Morley left us in Puddle's care. He said he wanted to head downstairs so he could make sure my guests went the right direction when they arrived. Which probably meant he didn't want those lowlifes mixing with his class clientele.

I resisted the temptation to let the Goddamn Parrot get away.

Dean assumed his post, the seat to the left of what would be mine at the table head. He laid out paper, pens, and ink, and a cou-

ple of Kip's writing sticks. He'd try to record what got said accu-
rately enough that there could be no arguments later. I was confident that others would do the same. I was just as confident that
there'd be arguments over who said what and when later on.
There's always somebody who insists the records are wrong.

Evas and Singe lurked behind the old man, both of them trying to read his notes as he made them. I wondered how much success they actually had.

It was scary how fast Singe was picking up the art. Writing
was giving her trouble, though. Her body wasn't built to provide
the necessary fine motor skills. I suspected she'd never manage
anything but tedious block printing.

Even that would make her unique.

I separated Evas from Singe. "The man I was talking to was
the one I told you about."

She showed an interest immediately. She'd reached the point
where she was having trouble sustaining her public frost. She was
obsessed. Which had been cute for a while but which had become
disturbing once I found myself ambushed whenever I was alone.

I thanked the stars or fates that Fasfir had needed to try her
wings just the one time. It had been sweet enough work keeping
up with Evas.

I reminded her, "He'd be a better teacher than I am. Much better. Elves are known for their endurance." If you could believe a
quarter of what this particular half-elf said about himself. "He's
not bad looking, either. By our standards."

Near as I could read a silver elf's face, Evas seemed thoughtful.

I settled beside Dean. "All set?" He was studying one of Kip's
writing sticks, looking dubious.

"I'm not sure I can do this anymore."

"If you can't get it word for word make sure you get the high
points. Ah. Playmate's here."

As I moved that way, Singe sidled up. "What are you trying to
do with Evas?"

"Nothing."

"Garrett."

"Just trying to help my best pal get a chance to experience an
amazing phenomenon."

"I think you are up to something."

"Really? Look, I need to talk to Playmate." Playmate had Kip
in tow but not Kip's mother or sister. Or Rhafi. Mustn't ever forget
poor, invisible Rhafi.

Playmate looked exhausted. "It's getting to me, Garrett. Having the Guard watching the place all the time. Having them come around asking questions at all hours."

Even Kip seemed subdued. He hardly fidgeted. He made no effort to wander away from Playmate. He didn't insult anyone.

I asked, "Where are the rest of them?"

"I don't know if they're coming. Kayne said she was but I expected her to get here before we did."

"She has to come. We'll be on real thin legal ice if we put together a company where one of the partners isn't even old enough to draft. We need his mother here."

"I understand that. But you need to realize that Kayne's custodial status won't stand up if somebody big really challenges it. She's a woman. So she's pretty much handicapped when it comes to making contracts herself. If this turns into something involving really big money, you know the jackals are going to start gathering."

Playmate was right. Women who make a name and place for themselves have to do so against the ancient tide of the law. Kayne had the legal advantage of being a widow, had no living father, and neither son had reached his majority. Still, as Playmate said, add money to the mix and somebody would take legal action to become Kayne's legal guardian.

Playmate mused, "I'm worried that the father will turn up and stake a claim."

"I thought he was dead."

"No. He disappeared. He's presumed dead. Even if he is dead, somebody could claim to be him. It would be his word against Kayne's. A woman. Of questionable morals. The sorting out would give somebody plenty of time to do some mischief."

"People can't do much mischief if their legs are broken."

"It wouldn't be that simple."

"I hate people sometimes, Play. In times like these I have trouble convincing myself that Relway doesn't have the right idea about how to handle humanity's scum."

"Might not be your best simile, Garrett. The scum is what rises to the top. Well, somebody is here."

Somebody proved to be Max Weider and his beautiful daughter Alyx. Alyx was coifed and dressed to kill. Alyx loved every second of the attention she attracted. Manvil Gilbey and our first uninvited guest, Congo Greeve, straggled in behind, the bad and the ugly. Congo looked like he had broken out the special, formal occasions cranial wax. His eight-inch part glistened.

Wicked, wicked Alyx headed straight for me, blue eyes sparkling like a bucket of diamonds. She showed me a wicked, wicked smile and leaned forward to offer me a world-class glimpse of a wicked, wicked decolletage.

"Bad girl," I told her. "Daddy's going to spank."

"Promise?"

"You're hopeless."

"I've got plenty of hope. I know you can't resist forever. I see you took the trouble to dress up." She grabbed my right arm, did a little wriggle-and-spin move before I realized what she was doing.

Her daddy was not amused.

"I . . . What're you doing?"

"Tinnie was right behind us."

The devil herself stepped into the room. Red hair, green eyes, freckles, a shape to make men sit up nights cursing the sun and the moon and the stars because there was only one of her to go around. She wore green velvet. She eyed Alyx, checked the goofy look on my clock, shook her head and allowed Puddle to guide her to the side of the table where the Tates would be stationed. Like most everyone else I know who passes as more than a remote acquaintance, Puddle treats Tinnie like an empress.

Alyx said, "Damn. That didn't get a rise out of *her.* How 'bout you?"

"Well, you did get your dad all steamed up. You'll hear from him later." Max and I might be friends but there was no way he was going to let me get involved with his baby. Not that he's a snob. He just don't think my prospects are any better than those of highwaymen or pirates, professions notorious for their high rate of turnover.

Alyx went over and dropped inelegantly into a chair beside Tinnie. They fell into conversation instantly, probably beating up on me. They were close friends, despite Alyx's relentless campaign to slide her shoes under the end of my bed.

Morley reappeared. He had changed clothing. He wore a lady-killing costume now. I kept a straight face. He cast covert glances into the dark corner where Singe and Evas lurked, trying to avoid notice. Evas was busy playing peekaboo with the Goddamn Parrot but didn't miss Morley's return.

Kip had discovered Evas, too. He was scared to death. I said, "Play, tell Kip it's all right. She's on our side."

Well, I was hoping she was. Things might change suddenly if she found out she had a ride home.

"Are you ready to begin serving?" Morley asked. "The kitchen is ready for you."

"Not yet. I'm waiting for the boy's family to show."

He stared at Evas and the jungle chicken, which Evas had just uncovered. "There's something about that creature . . ."

Something she was projecting herself. I'd felt it back at the house more than once. "Yes, there is. Would you like me to introduce you?"

"I'm talking about Mr. Big, Garrett," he lied.

"That's one of the better straight lines you've ever handed me but I'm going to let you off. You were distracted. Let me mingle with my guests. You want something to do, a wine course might be appropriate right now." A suggestion that Dean had offered on the way over, as a way of dealing with time that had to be filled.

There was an extra Tate as well as the Weider lawyer. His name was Lister. He was a cousin in his thirties. Outsiders occasionally confused him with Tinnie's deceased pop, Lester. Lister passed as the family legal expert. He was a square-jawed, dark-haired, immaculately clothed and groomed, painfully handsome character who had a hint of the weasel gleaming from the corners of his eyes. For some reason I think of him as the Lawyer of Times to Come.

I know of no one in the Tate clan who likes cousin Lister. He's tolerated because he's kin and because he's good at what he does.

Cousin Lister has no clue how his relatives really feel about him.

Like every human family in TunFaire, great or small, the Tates have menfolk buried in the Cantard. Full-length frog fur coats are more common than grown men who avoided military service in the war zone.

Lister Tate, without halfway trying, wangled himself an army assignment that kept him right here in TunFaire, as the armed forces' liaison with their biggest suppliers of boots and leather accoutrements. He didn't even move out of the family compound. Nevertheless, he promoted himself an out-of-barracks housing allowance that exceeded the pay rates of men like myself, at my highest rank, even including the combat bonus I got while I was in the islands.

I worked my way around to Tinnie. "My good fortune never ceases to amaze me. I was daydreaming about meeting a beautiful redhead. Look what walked through the door."

"I saw what you were daydreaming about. A slutty blonde young enough to be your baby sister."

Alyx snickered and bounced over a seat so I could settle between her and the redhead. She made some crude remark about the chair's warmth, that would've had her father looking for a switch had he heard it. I gave her a wink. "You could come be my baby-sitter."

Tinnie told me, "You ever call her bluff for real, big boy, you'd better have your running shoes on."

Alyx said, "If he does, he won't be able to do anything but crawl."

"You're going to put it all on me when she's talking like that?" I winked at Alyx again. She stuck her tongue out at Tinnie and started to hop into my lap. Then she noticed her father, Gilbey, and Congo Greeve all glaring at her. She needed to learn that some teasing wasn't acceptable in public.

"Yes. Because I expect you to know how to say no."

That seemed a tad unrealistic but I didn't insist. Instead, I said, "Uh-oh," with very little regard for Tinnie's opinion.

Kayne Prose had arrived. Making a grand entrance, just ahead of Cassie Doap, who seemed to have adopted a flamboyantly flirtatious personality for the evening. Tinnie stomped a foot. She wasn't used to this level of competition.

In fact, she was rather exceeded.

Mother and daughter wore newly made gowns. Their creation must've required the needles of all Kayne's cooperative sisters. Both gowns flattered outrageously what begged for very little flattery in the first place.

Slack-jaw disease raged among the menfolk in Morley's private dining room.

Even Dean's imagination seemed to come to life.

Rhafi came in behind his mother and sister, rendered almost invisible by their glory.

As happenstance had it, Lister Tate was the only married man in the room. The bachelors and widowers all looked ready to revel in their status.

When time and doom catch up with me and I have to slough off this mortal realm, I mean to thank the gods for having blessed me with the chances I've had to get to know so many comely women. I expect to start working on my speech about ten thousand years from now.

Manvil Gilbey caught my eye, projected the unspoken question: Was this something I'd laid on for Max? Max could not seem to stop staring at Cassie Doap.

I shook my head, mouthed, "But if it'll help . . ."

Puddle showed the newcomers to their seats, near Playmate and Kip. Even he was having trouble breathing. There were far too many beautiful women in that room, each of them trying to one-up the others.

Tinnie let me have an elbow, putting plenty of force behind it. "That's for what you're thinking."

"I apologize. I'll never think of you as an object again. From now on it's nothing but business. From now on you'll be Mr. Tate in my every act and thought."

That earned me a repeat stroke of the elbow. "I'd better not be." The fickle woman.

Alyx said, "Look at Dad! I think the old bull's in rut."

Tinnie muttered, "Alyx, sometimes you're *too* juvenile even to amuse me."

I moved up to my place beside Dean, which was my signal that the evening was about to become serious. Those who weren't in their official seats found them. Once everyone sat down there was very little room to spare. Morley had another place setting on each long side but it would've taken a shoehorn to get anybody in. I introduced everyone, including Morley as host, then Evas and Singe as they took their seats to the left of Dean and to the right of me, without explaining their presence. I thought they ought to stay mysterious. They drew stares but not even Lister Tate was gauche enough to demand information about them.

I let Morley know that we were ready to be served.

Kayne and Cassie both managed admirably during dinner. Tinnie was not amused by the regard they received. She was used to being the center of attention. But all the men at this banquet were related to her or had known her since she was a pup. Except for me and Dean and Kayne's drooling baby boys. And she already had Dean on a leash and me wrapped around her finger.

Alyx was amused. She liked seeing Tinnie have to take second chair. Just to rub it in she kept right on flirting with me. Her father wasn't worried about her anymore.

# 71

I tried not to cry when I thought about how much this evening was costing me. I tried to forget the fact that, if it didn't work out, I might end up spending several years working fourteen-hour days just to get back to the point where I could afford to save money buying beer by the keg.

As a business convocation the sequestered evening at Morley's place had to be some sort of precedent. The gang of us came out of there having created a company dedicated to the creation, production, and marketing of the fruits of the imagination of Cypres Prose, ingenious boy inventor. The Weider brewing empire would provide financing. The Tate family would handle the actual production. Kayne Prose and all her offspring would move into the Tate compound, where they would live much better than ever they had before, with no requirement that they do anything but be Kip's support and inspiration. I myself would be the genius who held it all together. Having been the genius who had gotten it all together.

I had a feeling Kayne Prose wouldn't have much attention to spare for industry. Not for a few months, at least.

When Kayne Prose met Manvil Gilbey it was lust at first sight both ways. All the rest of us had to be grateful that they didn't jump on one another right there in the banquet room.

Kayne's behavior wasn't exactly a surprise. I had a feeling she seldom met a man she didn't like. But Manvil Gilbey is as reserved as a wine butt normally.

The absolute absurdity of the universe is declared, in a bellow, once again, by the fact that Max Weider, age sixty, became infatuated with Cassie Doap, a completely ridiculous eventuation not unilateral in nature. Nor did either of those two seem conscious of the fact that Cassie was three years younger than Alyx Weider. And Alyx was the baby of Max's five children.

Max told me, "Of course it's stupid. But she's a dead ringer for Hannah when I first met her." And he was willing to play delusional games with himself in order to defy his pain.

More or less. Nobody cons Max Weider for long. Not even Max himself.

Cassie's positive response, wholly genuine, was a good deal more puzzling. We knew already that neither Cassie nor her mother were out for the easy ride, bought with their looks and bodies.

There're times when people do, honestly, connect on something besides the physical level.

That became one of the fine evenings of my life. One of those times when everything works out even better than you'd dared hope.

Sometime during the socializing, following the creation of the Articles of Agreement encompassing the founders of the new company, my good pal Morley Dotes and the silver elf Evas disappeared.

I suspect that couples who do that tell one another no one will notice but, secretly, don't give a rat's ass if anybody does because their minds are fogged by anticipation.

The capper came when Lister Tate proved he wasn't a complete waste of flesh by, belatedly, providing a device for getting around the legal age problem, as well as the potential problem of a fatherly return. "Willard Tate can adopt the boy. The device goes all the way back to imperial times, when the emperors wanted to handpick their successors. It's not much used anymore, except on the Hill, but the tool is there. Mrs. Prose can allow it. If nobody challenges right away only a Royal proclamation can reverse it. And we could argue against that that only an imperial edict is valid since the adoption went forward under a preKarantine law. I believe there are precedents."

I told Tinnie, "Promise me you'll keep Kip away from Rose."

"I plan to keep him for myself. He has good prospects."

"He'll be your cousin."

"Spice is nice but incest is best. Ouch! You meanie. I'll bet he's got stamina, too."

"My prospects are looking up, too. I won't need a business excuse to get my foot in the door at the Weider place anymore. Ouch! Alyx. She's hurting me."

# 72

*Do you feel like a captain of industry?* the Dead Man asked.

I waved a hand in a dismissive gesture he couldn't possibly see. "What I feel like is a guy dancing six inches above the ground because I have completely, thoroughly, irrevocably nailed Morley's mangy hide to the wall. I have hoisted him on his own petard. I've spent months and months and months trying to map out some absurdly complicated revenge scam to get even with him for the Goddamn Parrot. And in the end a better answer just dropped her bottom into my lap. I just had to introduce Morley to Evas, let Morley be Morley, let Evas be Evas, and let Deal Relway be his own suspicious self."

The Dead Man wasn't pleased. Once I'd decided to point Evas at my pal Morley, I'd launched a companion scheme which resulted in her wanting to keep the feathered clown with her.

Evas couldn't leave The Palms, now. There were too many watchers outside who reported to the Emergency Committee for Royal Security. It may be a long time before they tire of observing comings and goings at Morley's place.

Oh, me! Oh, my! I love it!

I wonder how long it'll take Morley to realize that he's reaped the whirlwind?

No more Mr. Big, trying to get me stoned on the streets, following me everywhere, keeping track, nagging me. No more . . . "Gah!"

A ferocious squabble had broken out inside the front wall.

Soundless, almost gloating laughter seemed to fill the atmosphere.

Well, hell! He might not miss a step.

Still, I could cherish thoughts of Morley's delicious plight.

Although Fasfir didn't approve.

She had managed to establish communications with the Dead Man. She found it painful to be completely alone. When Old Bones didn't make her feel better she joined me in my office. By means of notes, a few words spoken with difficulty, and my small ability to sense moods, she made it known how cruelly terrifying being alone and lonely was for her kind.

I told her, "Casey's here."

But Fasfir found Casey nearly as alien as she did me, and he was a lot less fun after dark. I could scramble her brains and push the fear away for a while.

"Huh? You worked hard enough but I never felt like you got much out of it."

She informed me that she was much more diverted when I was with Evas and she was in Evas' mind. Evas' flesh responded more readily, thoroughly, and willingly than did her own. Though her problem probably existed entirely within her own mind.

Odd. Though she believed she had mental hang-ups she admitted to being every bit as enthusiastic as Evas. Only she enjoyed it best at second hand.

Life gets stranger by the hour.

This is TunFaire. That would be the taproot iron law. Things get weirder.

Ask the Dead Man what it was like in the old days, when he was young and callow. He'll let you know that everything was normal and straightforward, way back then.

The written record, however, doesn't support him. There may be cycles of less and more but weird is with us always.

*Company is coming. Another Visitor.* He had concluded that our silver elves were identical to the strange people who had been called Visitors when he was a child. He'd found fragments in Casey's head to confirm his speculation. So from now on we were going to call them Visitors.

Fasfir whipped past me as I eased into the hallway. She hurried to the front door, then stood there baffled by all the mechanisms. I nudged her aside, looked through the peephole.

A very small, scruffy, nervous brunette was on the stoop. Homely enough to be related to Dean, she was poised to knock but wasn't sure she was ready to commit. She looked around to see who might be watching.

She flickered.

I lifted Fasfir up so she could look. "Is that your other friend?" Fasfir nodded.

I opened the door, which startled the Visitor because she hadn't yet announced herself.

Fasfir revealed herself, slithering around me as lithely as a cat, before the ill-favored little woman could run away.

I shut the door and left the ladies to their reunion.

I went to the Dead Man's room. "You been eavesdropping?"

I got the equivalent of a mental grunt in response. I noted that Casey, who seldom strayed from the Dead Man's room, was lapsing into sleep. Again. By the time he left my place Casey was going to be years ahead on his sleep.

"Finding anything interesting? Like why this one is running around loose when she ought to be a captive of the Masker contingent?"

*Given fewer distractions I might exploit the present moment of emotional vulnerability to unearth those and further significant answers.*

I pinched my lips closed.

*We can call this woman Woderact. She seems to be what we would call a sorceress. She would be the most socially reserved of the female crew. She is not an adventuress. Yet there is about her that same intense suppressed hunger that characterized Evas.* Some not so suppressed amusement. *The Maskers kicked her out because she was of no use to them. She would not cooperate. Also, the Maskers may have thought she could lead them to Fasfir and Evas, either of whom might know something that would help them repair their ship.*

*These Maskers seem to be more hardened than are the other Visitors.*

"Except for Casey."

*Except for Casey. I do believe that it is just marginally possible that Casey could do direct, willful physical harm to another being. None of the other Visitors seem able to entertain the thought.*

*Ah! The excitement of the reunion has begun to ebb. Fasfir's thoughts are no longer accessible. And there goes the new mind. Ha!*

A vast miasma of amusement wrapped itself around me. *My metaphysical side seems to be asserting itself. I have suffered a psychic episode. You are going to have to teach night school at least one more time.*

"I can lock my door."

*But you will not.*

No. Being an empathetic kind of guy, I probably wouldn't. Not for a night or two.

*Please move the women out of the hallway, now. We are about to suffer another caller. It would be best that the Visitors are not seen.*

# 73

I looked out the peephole as someone knocked. I saw a lean bean-pole of a man all dressed in black. He had a black beard and wore a wide-brimmed black hat. I didn't recognize him.

Dean came into the hallway, started to go back when he saw that I'd reached the door first. I beckoned him forward, to answer while I eavesdropped and covered him from the small front room. The stillness and emptiness in there were sweet. With luck the parrot smell would fade away eventually.

Dean followed instructions but didn't fail to stomp and employ his full arsenal of disgusted expressions.

The man on the stoop asked, "Is this the home of the confidential operative known as Garrett?"

Sounded to me like he knew the answer already.

Dean thought so, too. "Yes. Why?"

"I have a message from Miss Contague." Sounded like he was talking about a living goddess, the way he said that. "For Mr. Garrett." Making sure.

He went away without saying anything more.

"That was strange," Dean told me, handing me a vellum document folded and sealed with a red wax seal as ornate as any used by the nobility. "That man had a voice like an embalmer."

"She chooses her henchmen to ornament her own epic. Which she rewrites as she goes along."

"It's a crying shame. Such a lovely young woman to be so twisted. I blame her father."

"So do I. But however cruel Chodo was, he never put a knife to her throat and forced her to do evil. She made the choices." When first we'd met Belinda had been trying to kill herself by slutting it up down in the Tenderloin. At the time that had been fashionable amongst unhappy young women from wealthy families.

Even now Belinda seemed determined to bring about her own destruction. Except that these days she wanted to go out in a flashy orgy of violence. So her pain could be seen and shared by everyone.

The Dead Man once told me that monsters aren't born, they're made. That they are memorials which take years of cruelty to sculpt. And that while we should weep for the tortured child who served as raw material, we should permit no sentiment to impede us while we rid the world of the terror strewn by the finished work. It took me a while to figure out what he meant but I do understand him now.

You just need one intimate look at what a fully mature monster can do to achieve enlightenment.

He may have been the most wonderful pup you've ever known but you don't hesitate to strike the dog if he goes rabid.

*What is it?*

"Belinda found the flying ship that got away out in the wine country."

Dean said, "It took that much paper just to tell you that?" No wondering on his part about why she'd even been looking.

"There's some cry-on-the-shoulder stuff, too." Almost like a confession. Which made me wonder if I shouldn't be more pessimistic about my personal longevity. I might be scheduled to share her funeral pyre. "And her people have found the stable where Casey keeps his donkey." That for the Dead Man's benefit, not Dean's. Dean didn't care. "Things he told the people there led Belinda's agents to another apartment. It doesn't sound as fancy as Casey's Bic Gonlit place but the stuff she says they found there makes me wonder if half of TunFaire's population isn't our pal Casey in disguise."

*Excellent. Will you want to relay any of this to Colonel Block?*

"Not today. Because he'd pass it on." And the people he'd pass it to don't really need more power than they already have. "You think we can use this as leverage to work on Casey?" I wished we'd find something. I was way tired of having the Visitor underfoot. "Can we make him think we have him over a barrel, now?" He'd been around too long just to hand over to the Guard, now. Block and Relway would want to know why I hadn't bothered to mention him earlier.

*Probably. And the point to doing that would be what?*

"Oh. Yeah. He's on a mission."

*I will discuss it with him. Meanwhile, it is time you stopped lollygagging and went back to work.*

I'd begun to loathe the captain of industry gig.

All right. Yes. Everybody did warn me. But . . . I guess it's mostly because my partners don't have any patience with my relaxed attitude toward work. They're worse than a tribe of dwarves trained by Dean.

There is supposed to be a lot of humorless, from under the roots of mountains, all work and no play, dwarfish blood up one of the branches of the Tate family tree. I can't provide any arguments against the allegation, of my own knowledge. Tinnie definitely finds it hard to step away from work for any extended length of time.

I was the only key member of the new company not having great fun with our venture. Kip haunted his vast new workshop twenty hours a day, and usually fell asleep there. Fawning Tate nephews and cousins rushed hither and yon, making sure Kip's genius remained unencumbered by scutwork. Experts from the discontinued military leather goods operations now stayed busy trying to determine the most efficient means of three-wheel production.

My own three-wheel, the only pay I'd yet received for any of my trouble, had been spirited in from Playmate's stable. It now resided in the Tate compound inner courtyard, where there were always folks lined up to take a short ride. The managers didn't want *their* several completed prototypes defiled by the unwashed. Even brother, sister, and cousin unwashed.

Though two-thirds of the shoe factory floor had been turned over to new manufacture, the Tates weren't abandoning their traditional business base. They were just scaling back to the peacetime levels known by their great-grandfathers.

Shoes become a luxury when you have to pay for them yourself.

The Tates would remain the leading producers of fashionable women's footwear. They'd held that distinction since imperial times.

Though I was a rabid fan of the three-wheel and wasn't interested in much else, less than half the reassigned production space was intended for the manufacture of my vehicle. My associates were equally taken with several other Kip Prose inventions. His writing sticks were in production already, in three different colors. And orders were piling up.

The Guard and the Hill folk hadn't taken notice, perhaps because writing sticks don't fly.

Kip was having the time of his life. He was the center of everything. Everyone else was having a great time, meeting the challenges. Everyone but poor Garrett. There wasn't that much for him to do.

I'd used up my ration of genius.

There were no crooks here, trying to steal from the boss. I didn't have any other assets to kick in, except for knowing a lot of different people I can bring to bear on a difficulty. But the only bringing together I was getting done these days took place back at the house, nights. Woderact was proving to be a researcher every bit as dedicated as Evas had been. A tad more shy, initially, but Fasfir kept egging her on. And climbed right in there with us when the adventure called her.

TunFaire gets weirder by the hour. And my life marches in the van.

There wasn't much I could do but all my business associates seemed determined to have me right there at the factory not doing it.

I'm an old hand at skating out of the boring stuff. I acquired that skill in the harsh realm of war. I ducked out of the Tate compound. I recouped my spirit and recovered from my difficult nights by undertaking the promised visits to the troubled Weider satellite breweries.

That killed three days but didn't demand much genius. Like so many TunFairen villains, the various crooks were completely inept. They betrayed themselves immediately. My report named several managerial types who had to go when the thieves went because bad guys as incompetent as the ones I'd caught couldn't possibly have operated without their superiors turning a blind eye while extending a palm for a share of the proceeds.

# 74

Fasfir decided she had to try her luck in person, one more time. No man could've faulted her enthusiasm. But something was missing from her makeup. She just wasn't a Katie. Inevitably, direct participation left her disappointed. But she didn't have problems enjoying what Evas or Woderact shared with her, mind to mind.

Weirder by the minute.

This latest time Fasfir had a different motive for joining me.

Of late we had been refining our communication skills until, using gestures, grunts, a few spoken words, some writing, and what I could pull out of thin air, she could get ideas across. She had a big something on her mind this time.

"You want to get your whole crew back together?" I tried to appear distraught, though that very notion had been worming around in my head for two days. As things stood, my having sicced Evas on Morley hadn't changed anything for me. Except that I didn't have to listen to the Goddamn Parrot anymore. "Could I count on you three to stay out of mischief?"

*Absolutely.*

That came through almost as clearly as one of the Dead Man's messages. I didn't swallow it whole. The ladies hadn't lost their interest in going home.

"I'll see what I can do."

Fasfir became quite excited and grateful.

Moments later an equally excited and grateful Woderact joined us.

Weirder and weirder.

\* \* \*

I hired a coach, grumbled about the expense the whole time, put the lady Visitors inside it. I let them reclaim some of the fetishes Woderact had brought along to the house. They would appear to be human if they were seen on the street.

Casey got aggravated because he wasn't allowed to come along. Neither of the ladies believed him when he told them that he'd help them get home.

"Lookit dis," Puddle enthused as I pushed inside The Palms. "Somebody done fergot ta lock da goddamn door again." Puddle wasn't doing anything but loafing in a chair. His was the only body in sight. I'd timed my visit perfectly.

"Morley around?"

"What was dat?"

"Huh?"

"T'ought I heard somet'in'." A huge grin drove suspicion off his face. "We ain't seen much a Morley da past few days, Garrett. What wit' him spendin' so much time takin' care a dat bird."

Sarge shoved out of the kitchen, clearly having been eavesdropping. "Poor boy is gettin' kinda pale, Garrett. I'm t'inkin' he mought oughta get out in the sunshine more. What da hell was dat?"

"What was what?" I asked, as innocent as the dawn itself.

"I t'ought I heared da stair creak." Sarge scratched his drought-stricken, failing crop of hair. He and Puddle both eyed me suspiciously.

"What?" I inquired.

Puddle demanded, "Whatcha up to, Garrett?"

"Actually, I just wanted to drop in to see if I had any good reason to gloat."

Both men nodded and smiled. They could understand that. Sarge told me, "I don' know where ya found dat little gel, Garrett, but I sure do wish dey was one or two like her aroun' back when I was 'bout sixteen."

Puddle nodded enthusiastic agreement. "Gloat yer heart out."

"I will," I said. "Well, if the man can't come down, then things are going just wonderfully. If you do see Morley, tell him I stopped by. And that I'm thinking of him. But don't let him know I'm having a hard time keeping a straight face when I do."

A feeble groan limped, stumbling, downstairs.

Everybody snickered.

*Before* Sarge and Puddle discovered my latest maneuver

seemed like a good time to move myself along somewhere else. "Later, guys."

Both henchmen observed my retreat with abiding suspicion.

I set course for home, making plans for indulging in some serious rest and brew tasting. I kept breaking out in giggles, which inclined the streets to clear away around me.

# 75

My opinion of the legal profession seldom soars above ankle height. I believe that most troubles would settle out faster without lawyers stirring the pot. So it irks me to have to admit that Lister Tate and Congo Greve really did turn out to be useful.

Tate was a good idea man. Greve seemed to know everybody who was anybody. Well, he did know the legal beagles that everyone who was anyone paid to put words in their mouths. And he knew how to work them when they were just hanging around.

Tate told the rest of us, "We'll create a demand for three-wheels by having them seen underneath the most important people."

I didn't get it. I protested, "You're talking about giving them away! You don't make money giving things away."

"You have to consider promotion as a part of the investment process, Mr. Garrett. It's an investment in public exposure paralleling our investments in tools and materials. We'll only comp ten units, total. And those will be prototype and pilot units we put together while we're figuring out the most efficient way to build the three-wheels."

Congo Greve said, "I've placed all ten already, too. *Two* with the royal household! One with the Metropolitan. Thousands of the best people will see that old goof and his two acres of beard pedaling around the Dream Quarter. Every Orthodox heretic in town will want one to ride to church. Plus I got one placed in Westenrache House, with the imperial family. How about that? Just those four units should give us exposure enough to generate thousands of orders."

I never got a protest in because I couldn't get my jaw moving.

Greve knew people inside Westenrache House? The remnants of the imperial family, with hangers-on, had been forted up, or under household arrest, there, for centuries. Ever since the ineptitude of generations of ancestors let the empire crumble into kingdoms and principalities and tiny quasi states, each of which paid lip service to the imperial crown while ignoring its wishes completely.

The sole function of the empire these days, insofar as Karenta is concerned, is to furnish somebody who can crown the king whenever a new monarch ascends Karenta's throne. Which occurs with some frequency, though we haven't had a coronation recently. Our present monarch is particularly adept at sidestepping assassins. With Deal Relway covering his back he'll probably live forever.

I croaked, "I think I understand." If the King's daughters happened to be seen larking around on our three-wheels, every young woman of substance would demand she be provided one of her own. And the herd instincts of their fathers would ensure that the girls remained indistinguishable from the princesses.

"Good, Mr. Garrett," Mr. Greve said. "Once we establish a list, and the social primacy of our product to the exclusion of all imitators, we'll have written ourselves a letter of marque allowing us to plunder the aristocracy."

I gave brother Greve the fish-eye. That sounded a whole lot like the true lawyer coming through.

Greve sighed, explained, "We *must* ensure that our three-wheel is the only three-wheel the elite find acceptable once the fad gets started. Imitations are certain to appear as soon as someone capable of building them lays hands on one he can tear apart. We have to make sure that anybody who actually buys a competing three-wheel is considered a second-rater. Or worse." His expression suggested that he had begun to rank me with the dimmer of the dimwit Tate cousins.

Lister said, "It's possible that I can work my royal household connections to wangle a decree of patent."

If the Crown so ordered, nobody would be allowed to build three-wheels but us. Until somebody able to offer a big enough bribe got the King to change his mind. Or got the people who made up the King's mind for him to do so. Likely, the King himself would never know about the decree of patent.

"I'm glad you guys are on our side." I thought I could see how Weider beers had become the choice of beer drinkers, now. Snob appeal, backed by suggestions that any tavern brewing its own beverages on premises was an outdated second-stringer, its product likely fit only for the meanest classes.

Which is true. In many cases. The uniformity and consistent quality of Weider brews exceeds anything produced by corner taverns. And I can claim a certain expertise in judging the quality of beers.

Greve continued to pontificate. "Obviously, our ability to produce three-wheels will be limited. Demand will exceed supply for as long as the fad runs. We want to sustain and exploit that situation. First, we'll set a publicly announced fixed unit price—exorbitant, of course—then we'll place our buyers' names on a list. Then Lister and I, being cheesy lawyers, will let those who want to do so bribe us to move their names up the list."

"Excellent thinking!" Lister Tate declared. He actually rubbed his hands together in washing motions and chuckled wickedly till he realized some of us were staring. He grinned, told us, "Sorry I don't have mustache ends to twirl. Here. Let's do this while we're at it. Publish the list by posting it outside the compound entrance. Update it daily. So the buyers will know where they stand. In case they feel an urgent need to move on up."

"Oh, yes! Excellent idea! Here's another idea. We'll put serial numbers on the three-wheels. The lower the serial number, the more exalted the status of the three-wheel."

I said, "I can see people falsifying serial numbers. . . ." Oh.

Both men gave me looks that said they wondered how a grown man could be so naive and still be here among the living.

More than one three-wheel would go out the door with the same low serial number.

Pure, raging, unbridled capitalism. Now, if they could just find ways to steal our raw materials, evade taxation, and not pay our workers their wages, our profit margin might begin to approach what those guys would consider minimally acceptable.

I was becoming increasingly certain that the best thing I could do for the company I had invented would be to stay away. I should just let them haul my share of the profits over to the house aboard a beer wagon.

My mind just wouldn't fall into a businesslike groove.

If I was building a business I'd do it as if everybody involved was a partner. Kind of the way I had things already.

Enough of that.

I saw Kip's family whenever I visited the Tate compound. Kayne was bored. Prosperity was all right with her but she wanted something to do. She was used to working, long and hard. I told her, "There's plenty of work around here. I'll pass the word. Cassie? Rhafi? How about you guys?"

Cassie was extremely adept at doing nothing useful and planned to keep right on doing what she did best. Rhafi was content to polish his loafing and consuming skills as well.

"So be it."

I was in the Tate compound when the workers completed our first presentation three-wheel, half of the pair of gaily painted monsters meant for the King's daughters. We drew lots to see who would pedal it away. I didn't win.

# 76

Sleepily, the Dead Man again asked, *How does it feel to be a captain of industry?* His inquiry had an amused, sharp, mocking edge to it. The sort of edge his thoughts take on when things go exactly according to his prognostications.

"I feel like a man wasting his life. Like the proverbial square peg."

*Indeed? But if you were not working there you would be here either sleeping off hangovers or indulging yourself in some rakish indulgence.*

"Yeah. That'd be great. Indulging in some indulgence."

He was feeling generous. He didn't mention the several Visitor women I'd finagled out of the house not that long ago.

Singe invited herself into the Dead Man's room, then into the conversation. Evidently the Dead Man had kept her posted. She took a sandwich out of her mouth long enough to ask, "Are you having problems with the red-haired woman again? I hope?"

"Absolutely. Always. That goes without saying. But not as many as usual." Mainly because Tinnie was too busy working. And I stayed out of her way.

"I am sorry."

"No, you're not. You've been polishing up your sarky, haven't you?"

"When you are lower than a ratman's dog you do have to try harder. John Stretch was here not long ago. He wanted us to know that he knows where the other Visitors are hiding. The ones we ran into out in the country." Singe still shivered when she recalled that

adventure, though it made her the awe of all ratpeople who heard
the tale. "They are here in the city, now. Their skyship is hidden
inside a large, abandoned structure on the Embankment, a little
ways north of the Landing."

Way up there in strange territory.

*Coincidentally within a few hundred yards of the site where
the ship belonging to Lastyr and Noodiss is suspected to have
gone beneath the water.*

I frowned, trying to picture such a fantasm as an abandoned
building in TunFaire. I'd expect to bump snoots with a unicorn
first. This city is awash in refugees from the former war zone.
Nothing that remotely resembles shelter isn't infested with desperate, dangerous people.

Singe anticipated my question. "People lived there until ten
days ago. Something scared them into moving out." Meaning
maybe somebody more dangerous had moved in.

"What do you think, Old Bones? Worth a look? Or are we out
of the thing since Kip doesn't seem to be in trouble anymore?"
Though how could we be out while we still had Casey underfoot?
I wished there was some way I could give him to Morley, too.

The Dead Man's response was the mental equivalent of a distracted grunt.

"Don't you dare go to sleep on me! Who'll keep Casey under
control?"

The question elicited only a mental snort and the equivalent of
"I was just resting my eyes."

"You don't keep him managed, Chuckles, I won't have any
choice but to turn him over to the Guard. I can't handle him.
We've already seen that."

Mental grumbles. Old Bones was getting testy, a sure sign he
was headed for a long nap. He's predictable. Kind of like the
weather is predictable. You look out the window and tell everybody a storm is on its way. No way you're ever wrong, given sufficient time.

*What is your attitude toward unearthing Lastyr and Noodiss?*

"Not quite obsessed but definitely still interested. Despite all
logic. They planted that one deep, whoever did it."

He didn't tell me what I wanted to know.

"That was supposed to be a hint, Old Bones. Who messed with
the inside of my head?"

*I am inclined to suspect Casey but I do not know. I have not read direct responsibility in any Visitor mind yet. But the Visitors have been exceedingly adept at concealing specific items. Witness Evas and her sisters. Witness Casey himself. He has not yielded up a tenth of his secrets even though he has been in direct mental contact with me for ages now.*

*Also, it might be wise to consider the possibility that your urge is not of Visitor origin.*

"What?"

*We might do well to recollect, occasionally, Colonel Block's several subtle cautions about the intense interest in the Visitors being shown, behind the scenes, by several Hill personages. You have been rendered unconscious with some frequency of late. We might review your memories of those episodes with an eye toward the possibility that some of our own folk might have created an opportunity to implant a compulsion.*

"Maybe who really isn't as important as what. Who wants the secrets of the Visitors' magic isn't truly critical to us. Who won't have much direct impact on our lives."

*Perhaps. If you discount the moral dimension.*

"Naturally."

*And when the talking is over, you do want to meet the mysterious Lastyr and Noodiss yourself.*

"I sure do. I know I'll be disappointed. I always am. But I'd definitely like to see who got the cauldron bubbling."

*Then cease investing your time in the three-wheel business. There is nothing you can contribute there except exasperation for your associates.*

I'd had the feeling that even Willard Tate was considering changing the locks on the compound doors. It isn't just that I ask too many questions, I ask questions that make people uncomfortable.

Even the bloodiest villains have to work hard at conscience management sometimes. Until they get their full arsenal of justifications filed, sanded, and polished to fit their shadowy needs.

*Indeed you do. Also, you must stop juggling the women in your life. I understand that you are trying to live every young man's dream and are managing a twisted approximation. But there come moments when each of us must step away from the dreamtime.*

Sometimes somebody besides me flops something uncomfortable onto the table.

*Find Lastyr and Noodiss. Before they perish from old age.*

I didn't contradict him. But Evas had told me that Visitors

never grow old, nor do they die of old age. They live on until Fate finds a way to squash them with a falling boulder or until they do something really stupid, like going into a horse stall all alone, without a witness around anywhere.

Which sounds like some of those old, false legends about Morley's people.

"Singe, it ought to be safe out there now. You ready for another adventure?"

"Whither thou goest."

"Oh, that's rude. All right. First thing in the morning. Bright and early. For real. But for now, let's just hit the kitchen and tip a few mugs of Weider Select."

I *am* getting old. I thought about heading out to Grubb Gruber's to enjoy a few with the old jarheads. I thought about wandering over to serenade Katie, whom I hadn't seen in so long she might've forgotten her favorite little honey bunny. I thought about several other ways to fritter my evening. And, in the end, I just stayed in, sipping the dark and exchanging brew-born wisdom with my pal Singe. I hit the sack early, never suffering a thought about the feuding pixies.

# 77

Singe and I set out about a week before my normal getup time. We headed for the Casey digs Belinda's connections had discovered. We didn't learn a thing there except that the Guard had the place under surveillance—a fact that would interest Miss Contague a great deal. We also learned that thugs I assumed to be Relway's were keeping watch on us loyal subjects, by means of some very clever operatives and tactics.

The shiftiest operatives alive have trouble keeping up when the folks they're watching can step around a corner and vanish. Which Singe and I did a few times. Then I decided it wouldn't be smart to give away the fact that we really could slide around a corner and disappear.

That invisibility fetish was a wonderful device. I didn't want it taken away by some Bubba Dreadlock.

The pursuit did a hell of a job of hanging on. I'd have to congratulate Block and Relway. Someday.

I told Singe, "We can't shake them. Every time we give them the slip they get right back on track after a while." I hadn't been too obvious about trying to lose them yet, however. I was just pretending to take normal precautions. I didn't want them to know that we knew we were the object of a massive tail.

Singe stopped being talkative as the morning wore on. Her shoulders hunched. She seemed to shrink. Maybe I did a little, too. We had reached the Embankment, which is an ancient docking and warehousing district along the riverbank north of the Landing. It's rough country and I don't know my way around there. Nor do I know a soul amongst its denizens, which isn't true of the waterfront on the south side. The Embankment seemed a bleaker, harsher, less colorful district than its more familiar cousin.

The Embankment is the jumping-off point and home base for all trade along the navigable waterways, some of which reach a thousand miles beyond Karenta's borders, a thousand miles into the heart of the continent. The southside waterfront is the jumping-off point for what seems to me far more exotic destinations along the ocean coasts and overseas.

"What is that smell?" Singe asked.

"The sweet aroma of uncured animal hides." I was able to answer that one because of my intermittent association with the family Tate. "You won't believe this but there are men crazy enough to hunt thunder lizards and mammoths and saber-tithed toogers in the plains and mountains and forests back in places so far away they don't even have dwarves or elves there yet. Flatboats bring hides and teeth and horns and bones and ivory and fur and, sometimes, even meat down to TunFaire. And sometimes gold or silver or gemstones, or lumber or untaxed whiskey. It all gets unloaded right here on the Embankment." Where several of the bigger warehouses belong to the Contague family and store none of the mentioned goods except whiskey.

A broad range of herbs and spices grows wild in the interior, too.

But hunting is the thing.

A bold enough hunter, responding to the appropriate commercial demand, can set himself up for life by making a handful of the right kills. I expect a lot of bold veterans will toss the dice out there before long. And have enough success that the market for animal by-products will get shaky.

Perhaps the Crown ought to encourage homesteading. That would bleed off a lot of extra people.

Generally speaking, the quickest way to get dwarves to give up their silver and gold is to take it away, over their dead bodies. But if you can bring them the head of the right kind of thunder lizard—which they won't hunt themselves, no matter what— they'll throw gold dust at you like the bags are filled with sand. But that head has to come off an adult specimen of one of the major carnivores. Or off a three-horn or the rarer five-horn, because an infusion of powdered horn will scare impotence into the next continent.

I've never heard why dwarves covet the teeth of the great meat eaters, but who better than a lady dwarf to know, intimately, the meaning of rock hard?

Singe told me, "We must pass through this place that smells of old death."

"Huh?'

"The area where they make leather from those uncured animal hides."

"The tannery district." There were places which processed tallow and bone, too, though little of that would be imported. None of those places lacked their enthusiastic odors. "Why?"

"Someone is using ratman trackers to follow us. There can be no other explanation for their success. Yet few of my people have the courage to visit the fastnesses of death. Even if they forget that not many generations have passed since our own kind were killed and flayed to provide fashionable trousers for young dandies, the stench will overwhelm anything as subtle as traces left by you and me. Without leaving it obvious that we were trying to distort our backtrail."

"Ah, my friend, you continue to amaze me."

"A year from now you will be working for me."

There was a thought to rattle me.

Singe jumped up and down and clapped her paws. "I did it! I did it! You should see the look on your face."

"I believe I've created a monster."

Ratpeople aren't built to laugh but Singe sure did try. And she kept her mind on business while she was having fun. She led the way along a path a ratman tracker ought not to find suspicious, yet one that would overload any tracker's nose.

Singe was too naive to understand that anything not going his way would be suspicious to Director Relway.

I may have remained a little naive myself.

Not till after we had begun taking advantage of the district's natural odiferous cover did it occur to me that having Relway's fanatics on my backtrail might be a lesser evil.

# 78

Singe and I were on a holiday stroll, giddy because we had shaken free. Singe more so than I because she had a better appreciation of what she had accomplished—and of its cost. Her own olfactory abilities had been dampened hugely.

A sudden whir. The pixie Shakespear materialized above my right shoulder. He told me, "You must hide quickly. They will be here in a minute."

Another whirr as Shakespear went away. I glimpsed a second pixie, hovering, pointing in the direction of the threat. I heard the wings of several more.

Singe pulled me toward the nearest doorway. It was open. Beyond lay the noisome vats of a small tannery. I wondered how the flies stood the smell. I whispered, "Did you know that the wee folk were with us?"

"You did not know? You missed the sound of their wings?"

"You have better ears than I do. And you're starting to make me feel old. I should've been more aware of what was happening around me." Maybe my friends are right. Maybe I am getting too tied up inside my own head.

There wasn't anything in the tannery. There was no tanning going on, thought the place was still in business. It gave the impression that the entire workforce had slipped out just minutes before we arrived. Curious. It wasn't a major holy day that I knew of, though possibly the place employed only members of some lesser cult.

Still, there ought to be somebody around to keep opportunists from finders-keeping all those squirrel hides.

"Here."

Singe had located a low opening in the outer wall, placed so air could waft in and rise to roof vents, so the tannery could share its chief wonder with the city. The opening lay behind a heap of pelts from small animals. The majority had come off rodents but some were scaly. The odor off the pile guaranteed that no ratman tracker would find us here.

Singe had both paws clamped to her muzzle.

Gagging, I whispered, "Could you pick me out of this?"

Singe shook her head slightly, took a paw away from her muzzle long enough to tap her ear, reminding me that her people also had exceptional hearing. Then she dropped down so she could watch the street between bars that kept dogs, cats, and other sizable vermin from getting to the delicacies. They would have to stroll all the way down to the unlocked and open door if they wanted to compete with the bugs.

Singe beckoned me. I went for the fresh air.

I got down on the dirt floor, amongst the crud and the hair and the fleas off the pelts, and observed. And learned.

The first few hunters weren't unusual. They were just thugs. But they were extremely nervous, very alert thugs. They were thugs whose main task was to protect a brace of extremely unhappy ratmen. The trackers kept glancing over their shoulders. I didn't recognize anybody but wasn't surprised. I didn't know many members of the Guard. And Relway was enlisting fellow fanatics like harvesting dragons' teeth.

Then I saw white boots. With platform soles and cracked, fake jewels. Bic Gonlit was up on top of them. The real Bic Gonlit. And Bic wasn't alone. Nor was he in charge. His companion wore black as tattered as Bic's white but was a lot more intimidating. He looked like he was about nine feet tall. He wore a mask. Arcane symbols in gold and silver spattered something like a monk's hooded robe. An extremely threadbare robe. This particular stormwarden wasn't enjoying a great deal of prosperity.

That would make him especially dangerous.

Singe was even more careful than I was about not attracting attention by breathing. Her people have nurtured that skill since their creation.

I didn't recognize anybody but Bic.

My first inclination was to drop everything and head for home. Let Bic and the big boy play the game. Which is exactly what most people do and what all the big boys expect us to do. They count on that, up there on the Hill. They don't know how to react when ordinary folks refuse to fold and fade.

Usually that's followed by a lot of sound and fury and people getting hurt. Which explains the prevalent cowardly attitude.

Once they passed by, I whispered, "I've got Bic Gonlit figured out, now." He'd taken Casey's money. He'd underwritten his taste for high living by collecting books for Casey, but once things got real interesting the little pudgeball had made a fast connection up the Hill.

That being the case, why hadn't any Hill-type visitors come to the house?

Maybe Brother Bic hadn't made himself a deal so good that he felt like giving up everything he had, informationwise. Or, more likely, the Dead Man had revised his recollections before letting him leave the house.

You've got to keep an eye on the dead guy. He's sneaky.

Old Bones has been getting slicker every day for a long time. He doesn't keep me adequately informed, though, I thought. I must have an unrecognized tendency to blab all over town.

Another pack of intense bruno types came along, following Bic and his buddy in black. They were alert. They were all armed, too, though that was against the law.

Once again, neither Singe nor I breathed.

I'd love to see Relway attempt to impose his idealistic, no exceptions, rule of law outlook on the lords of the Hill. Or even on their minions.

The resulting fireworks would make for great popular entertainment.

Bic's stride faltered. He stopped. He seemed uncertain. He bent to caress his ragged magic boots. Frowning, he looked straight at me, though without seeing me. He frowned, shook his head, said nothing to the ragged wizard. The stormwarden beckoned two ratman trackers. A conference ensued.

The whole crew had become confused.

Nobody had the track now, by scent or by sorcery.

Singe pinched me.

# 79

I breathed, "This isn't the time," because she'd snuggled up like she wanted to get really friendly. It hadn't ever gotten this complicated when I was running with Morley. Then Singe proved that I had misjudged her again.

She pointed back past the heap of possum and muskrat hides.

Several Visitors were up to something back there. Singe had pressed against me to make sure the invisibility spell concealed us both.

I whispered, "What the hell are they doing? They're not supposed to be here." One of the Visitors had his arm in a sling. Another seemed to have a broken leg. Evidently the Maskers hadn't been able to work any medical magic.

Every Visitor carried at least one gray fetish and studied it intently.

I whispered, "There're too many of them." There were more here than the Masker four. I couldn't get them all in sight at once but I definitely counted at least five Visitors. Though it was hard to tell one from another, even when the Visitor hailed from Evas' crew. Unless you charmed them out of their silver suits.

I whispered, "We're still blocks away from where John Stretch said they're hiding."

Singe murmured, "Quit whispering so much," then added a thought I'd had already and didn't want to be true. "Maybe they were warned about us coming. Maybe they are here because they expected us to go to the place where we were told that they would be hiding."

Maybe. Because in TunFaire nothing ought to surprise you.

The possible will happen. The impossible takes only a few minutes longer.

In this case the probabilities were apparent. Certain overly friendly Visitor ladies, desperate to get a ride home, had conned simple old Garrett into returning some Visitor fetishes they said they'd need in order to sneak in and join Evas in her adventures with Morley Dotes at The Palms. Taking advantage of simple old Garrett's understandable and righteous desire to rectify a near-cosmic injustice.

If they got away I hoped the girls were dim enough to take the Goddamn Parrot with them.

Smirk. I'd have to remember to call the place The Joy House next time I dropped in at Morley's. Smirk.

The extra Visitors lurking here had to be Lastyr and Noodiss, erstwhile missionaries. Just had to be. Because no Visitor would be going home if they couldn't all work together, and the Maskers would have been gone already if they'd gotten reinforcements from the old country. The women in particular had to be extremely cooperative with the others. They were at everyone's mercy.

Disdaining Singe's advice, I whispered. "You watch them. I'll keep an eye on the street." The confusion out there had begun to commence to begin to get ready to head on out somewhere else.

Bic and his pal resumed moving, though confusion didn't cease being their guiding spirit. They faded away.

I expected them back. You cast around a bit but you always return to the point where your track evaporated, to hunt for the one thing you missed the last time you looked.

Minutes later Singe murmured a grand understatement. "We should leave. Sooner or later they will stumble over us in spite of this invisibility amulet."

"Or they might have some way to tell if an invisibility spell is being used anywhere nearby." If I invented an invisibility-maker I'd sure try to come up with a way to tell if somebody else was using something like it around me.

"Or they might hear you whispering."

That, too.

We'd come to the Embankment to find Visitors. Although this wasn't quite the situation I'd hoped for. This wasn't good. This didn't fit in with my half-assed plans at all.

Singe was spot on about whispering. But she was a tad off when it came to who would do the eavesdropping.

Yikes! Here came Bic Gonlit and his threadbare stormwarden buddy, hustling like they were being driven by one of the wizard's spooky winds. Their trackers and henchmen scampered along behind them, confused and alert and able to keep up only because Bic had those stubby little pins.

The flotilla's course ran straight toward me.

I poked Singe, indicated that she should peek through the airhole. Once she'd done so we got up on our hind feet and, chest to chest, in careful lockstep, began to ease along the brick wall, toward the cover of another mound of hides. We found it necessary to freeze every few steps because the Visitors had become extremely nervous, suddenly. They were inclined to jump at the slightest sound.

They had to suspect that they had trouble in their hip pocket.

Several Visitors, fetishes extended before them, suddenly rushed the hide pile Singe and I had abandoned. Bic and his cohorts were causing a disturbance outside. And Singe and I hadn't gotten but a dozen feet away. So we froze. And shivered. And held our breaths. And hoped nobody stumbled into us.

The Visitor with his arm in a sling missed running into me by scant inches.

Tension mounted amongst the Visitors. The advent of danger reawakened the bad feelings between the Maskers and Kip's pals. I could sense just enough to tell that the Maskers blamed Lastyr and Noodiss for everything. Kip's friends blamed the Maskers for zipping all over the sky, thereby alerting the savages to their presence.

Lastyr and Noodiss had abandoned the altruism that had brought them to TunFaire. In fact, prolonged exposure to our fair flower of a city had turned them bitter and cynical.

Imagine that.

Singe and I continued to move, teensy baby steps, then with more vigor once we realized that the people outside intended to come inside.

Visitors began flying all over the place. Two quite literally. I didn't see any ropes or wires. "Keep moving," I told Singe, in what I thought would be an inaudible whisper.

Visitors froze.

Something had changed. The Visitors were alert in a whole different way.

The Visitors then unfroze, every man jack getting busy with fetish boxes.

Those guys needed bandoliers to carry all the fetishes they

had. Evidently every task imaginable could be managed with the right gray box.

Two Visitors headed our way, weaving slow, serpentine courses, zeroing in.

Bic's gang poured through the open door.

Big surprises happened. For everybody.

The confusion attained an epic level.

At first it looked like it would be a walk for the startled Visitors. Thugs went down left and right, exactly as easily as I had in my first several encounters with Masker magic.

Then Bic came through the doorway.

The Visitor sorcery didn't affect Little Bitty Big Boy.

Bic selected a paddle meant for stirring the contents of a curing vat. He took a swing at the nearest silver figure, which happened to belong to the Masker with the broken leg.

The Visitor rewarded Bic with a beaten-sheep sort of bleat.

The shabby stormwarden stepped inside. And instantly called down some of that old-fashioned thunder and lightning, the ability to control which gave stormwardens their name.

Weather magic is the flashiest and most obviously destructive power possessed by our lords of the Hill—and the most common.

Hides flew. Vats exploded. People shrieked. Bic Gonlit rose ten feet into the air, spinning faster and faster as he did so. The stormwarden followed, spinning himself. But he threw off spells like the sparks coming off one of those pinwheel fireworks.

I told Singe, "We *really* need to take ourselves somewhere else."

The game looked like it was just starting to get serious.

"I thought you wanted to find the Visitors. . . ."

"We found them. Now let's take advantage of the fact that nobody here has us at the head of their to-do list right now."

# 80

Pixies flitted around us, giggling and squabbling, more annoying than a flock of starving mosquitoes. Not a single one had anything useful to say. Their presence didn't help anything. Singe and I weren't invisible anymore. There was no need.

Nobody was interested in us. But the squawking bugs threatened to attract attention.

For the gawkers, trying to figure out what was happening in the slowly collapsing tannery, a guy hanging out with a ratwoman bold enough to walk the streets by daylight was a secondary spectacle.

Threads of blue light as thin as spider silk crawled over the ruins. The entire heap of rubble hurled itself skyward. Everything inside went up with the building itself. People and debris alike floated on the surface of an expanding, invisible bubble.

More time seemed to pass than actually did.

The bubble popped. And collapsed.

A raindrop smacked me in the cheek. I noted that a cold breeze had begun blowing. The change in weather wasn't unseasonable or unlikely, it was just a surprise because I hadn't been paying attention.

Vigorous lightning pranced over the remains of the tannery. One bolt struck something explosive, probably chemicals used for treating leather. The explosion scattered brick and broken timbers for a hundred yards around. A spinning sliver sixteen inches long flew between Singe and me, narrowly missing us both.

Singe said, "We have found them. Do we really need to stay so close, now?"

"I don't know. You may have a point." I spied a dirty white behind wagging as somebody struggled to back his way out of the mess. When the pile finally finished birthing Bic it developed that he had hold of his employer by the ankle. He strove to drag the wizard out by main strength.

I said, "I think we might move a little farther away."

Lightning bolts, like swift left and right jabs, rained down on the ruins, starting small fires, flinging debris around. Despite his discomfiture and the inelegance of his situation the stormwarden was still in there punching.

Other things were happening at the same time. They were less intensely visual. I credited them to the Visitors because Bic's gang were the people being inconvenienced.

Damn! We'd dropped the invisibility spell and were trying to fade into the onlookers but Bic spotted us almost immediately. But he didn't get the chance to report us. A Visitor floated up out of the ruins, jabbed one of those gray fetishes in his direction. And he fell down, sound asleep. I wasn't feeling real charitable. I hoped he woke up with a headache as ferocious as the worst I'd enjoyed back when they were knocking me out all day long.

I told Singe, "It'll be a week before they get their stuff together back there. Let's use the time."

We did. To no avail whatsoever. Not only were the Maskers not hiding where John Stretch said, there was no sign of their skyship. I'd hoped it would be right there where I could sabotage it. Or whatever seemed appropriate at the moment of discovery.

Why would I want to keep them from going away? The longer they hung around the more likely they would fall into the hands of somebody off the Hill. Which would make times just that much more interesting for those of us who couldn't fly away.

"Singe? You smell anything that might be the Masker skyship?"

She strained valiantly. And told me, "I can tell nothing. What happened back there has blinded my nose."

Poor baby. "Follow me." It was time to get the hell away from the Embankment.

Our line of retreat took us back past the ruined tannery.

Raindrops continued to strike randomly, scattered but getting fatter all the time. And colder. One smacked me squarely atop the bean. It contained a core of ice. It stung. I regretted my prejudice against hats.

"Look," Singe said. We were slinking through the crowd of

onlookers, which had swollen to scores, most of them tickled to see a stormwarden looking like he had a firm grip on the dirty end of the stick.

A groggy Bic was back up on one knee, a black-clad ankle still in hand, glaring at the mob, not a man of whom offered a hand. He spied somebody he thought he recognized, that somebody being Mama Garrett's favorite boy. He croaked out, "Garrett!"

Garrett kept on rolling. Maybe a little faster. Garrett's sidekick puffed and hustled to keep up.

Bic yelled as loud as he could. His excitement didn't do him any good at all. The one response he did get was a growing hum that sounded like a swarm of bumblebees moving in for the kill. It came from within the rubble. Masker sorcery. Bic slapped another hand onto his boss' ankle and went back to pulling.

"Look!" Singe gasped again.

The rubble had begun shifting and sliding as though restless giants were awakening underneath.

The bubble was coming up again. And now the bumblebees were singing their little bug hearts out.

The bubble got a lot bigger this time. Bricks and broken boards, ratmen and squealing henchmen all slid off. Bic forgot about me and Singe. He forgot his manners entirely. He yanked the mask off the stormwarden, slapped his face. I caught a glimpse of pallor disfigured by indigo tattoos. A real heartbreaker of a face. It must drive the hookers wild.

Something began rising up inside the bubble. Something shiny, like freshly polished sword steel.

The bumblebees lost the thread of their hearty marching song and began to whine. The bubble began to shrink and the steel to sink. But the bees picked up the beat after a few false notes.

The Masker skyship emerged from the ruins.

The addled stormwarden popped it with his best lightning bolt.

The skyship popped him back. Enthusiastically. He flew twenty yards, ricocheted off a brick wall, barely twitched once before an incoming Bic Gonlit, tumbling ass over appetite, crash-landed on top of him.

The Masker vessel lumbered into the sky and headed south, the bumblebees occasionally stumbling, the ship itself wobbling.

"A little faster with the feet, I think," Singe said when I slowed to watch. "I am developing a strong need to find myself somewhere far away from here." The crowd seemed to agree with her. Everybody thought it was time to be somewhere else.

"Yes, indeed, girl. Yes, indeed. Before old Bic wakes up and decides to blame us for everything."

We did go somewhere else. But we weren't much happier there than we'd been on the Embankment.

## 81

"I've got a bad feeling about this, Singe," I said, puffing as I headed south, the knees beginning to ache. "I'm willing to bet I know exactly where that thing was headed."

No dummy she, Singe opined, "Mr. Dotes' establishment."

"Yeah."

Yeah.

The skyship was long gone by the time we reached The Palms but people were still hanging around in the street, telling each other about it. There'd been enough excitement for the visitation to become a neighborhood forty-day wonder. I noted a couple of familiar faces among the gossipers, guys asking only occasional questions and doing a lot of listening.

Some snooty galoot got his heart broken when I didn't even slow down going past him at the door—with a rat in tow, for the gods' sake! For a moment I thought I'd finally get me a chance to witness a genuine sputtering fit of apoplexy.

Snooty galoot disappointed me.

People so often do.

"I smells, wit' my little smeller, somet'in' what a man ought not ta got ta smell," Puddle announced from the shadows at the other end of the room.

Sarge hollered from the kitchen, "Dat mean dat Garrett's here?"

"Dat it does indeed."

"Ha! So pay up! I told ya da man don't got a ounce a shame an' he'd turn up before da dust settled."

"Sounds like we guessed right," I told Singe. "They did come here."

"Hey, Greenwall," Puddle yelled. "Ya need more help talkin' people outa comin' in da door?"

The snooty character gobbled some air. It was obvious that Morley had hired him for his upthrust honker, not for his ability to intimidate hard men.

I said, "Don't be too rough on the guy, Puddle." I intended to explain how he naturally went spineless when he saw Singe and me bearing down, but Puddle interrupted.

"Yer right, Garrett. It's his secont day on da job. Ain't every day ya look out da door an' dere's one a dem flyin' disk kinda t'in's landin' in da street out front, wit' goofy-lookin' silvery elf guys jumpin' down an' whippin' up on everybody."

I took a second glance at Greenwall. He did look like a man nursing a ferocious headache. So did Puddle, for that matter. "So the girls all got away."

Puddle stared at me with narrowed eye for several seconds. "Yeah. Dey went. But one a dem had ta be dragged kickin' and da udder two cried all da way 'cause dey didn't want ta go."

"Wow! Your boss is quite the man. He'll be heartbroken, I'm sure."

"Morley's gonna be singin' hosannas, soon as he gets enough strengt' back." Puddle's grin slid away. His face turned serious. "I hate ta be da one what gives ya da bad news, Garrett, but dem sluts, dey stole Mr. Big when dey went."

"Oh, that is awful." What an actor. I know what racket I ought to be in, now. Not involved in inventing and manufacture. I ought to be on the stage. I managed to be convincing in my loss. "O Cruel Asp of Fortune, thou wicked serpent, how painful thy sting . . ."

"Gods, Garrett, you aren't just a ham, you're the whole stinking pig." Morley had managed to get most of the way downstairs. He looked like a guy fighting a big headache, too.

Once again I brought my acting skills to bear and concealed my amusement. "You look like death warmed over. You been playing with the vampires?"

"Of a sort. Right now I don't think I ever want to see another woman."

"Oh, I suspect you'll change your mind. After you recover from the fantasy come true." Given a few days I'd found myself thinking of Katie and Tinnie in a nonplatonic fashion again. But I am a very resilient fellow.

"They stole Mr. Big, Garrett."

"You sound like that bothers you."

Morley's eyes narrowed suspiciously. Like why wouldn't that bother the gods themselves?

"It's no secret that I wasn't fond of the ugly moth. But if you miss obnoxiousness fluttering around you I'll send over some of the swarm of pixies that're living in my walls, now."

"No need. Mr. Big will be back," Morley predicted. He sounded so confident I wondered if I ought to be worried.

"You sound sure. And glum at the same time."

"Evas and her friends are going to come back with him."

"Heh-heh-heh." I pulled my most evil laugh out of my bag of attitudes for special occasions. "You sure they won't just wring his neck when they get tired of him?"

"You'll be laughing out the other side of your mouth when they get here, Garrett."

"I'll move. I'll go into hiding."

"You're marked, buddy. You're special. You started something and now you're marked for their special attention."

"I started nothing. It was all Evas' idea."

"You gave her the idea for her new idea, Mr. Entrepreneur. She's going to get hold of a bigger skyship and start bringing silver elf women to TunFaire for very special vacation getaways. And she sees you as a whole lot better partner in her enterprise than she sees me. She told me so." A bit of wickedness lurked in the corners of his eyes. He just might have had something to do with the lady Visitor's attitude.

Telling stories on me again, probably. I have to break him of that habit.

"Their government will never let them do that." Stopping adventurers was Casey's business. His whole purpose in life was to prevent contacts between his people and ours.

"You really think? It's beyond corruption?"

"Glad to see you're all right," I said. "Get plenty of rest. And get some meat in your diet. You'll need to beef up if you want to make it in the gigolo racket." I began to sidle toward the door.

"I plan to maintain my amateur status. But you being a businessman now, you might want to exploit the opportunity."

Maybe I could recruit Kip and Rhafi and a dozen of their

friends. What they lacked in experience they could make up in enthusiasm.

I sidled some more, noting that Singe was enjoying my discomfiture entirely too much.

"What's your rush, Garrett?" my old pal asked.

"I've got to see a Dead Man about a horse."

Morley took his turn chuckling. Chances were he had a fair notion what was going on in my head. But he said only, "You be careful on the street. There are some ratfolk out there who resent what the Guard did to Reliance. And they think you and Singe might have had something to do with that. Your friend John Stretch is having trouble setting himself up as Reliance's replacement."

"My friend John Stretch is going to get some grief from me, too." I'd concluded that John Stretch had given me completely bum information about where to find the Maskers. That Singe and I had stumbled into the right place at the wrong time almost entirely by chance. That we never would have found the Visitors if Bic and his sorcerer friend hadn't been dogging us.

Dotes got in a final gouge as we stepped into the street. "See you at Chodo's birthday bash. I think you could sell your gigolo franchise to the Outfit."

Chodo's birthday party. That bucket of ice water put everything else into a more favorable perspective. The return of the insatiable Visitor girls sounded positively attractive by comparison.

## 82

"What the hell do you mean, he got away?" I yelled at Dean. "Between you and Old Bones in there you couldn't manage one guy four feet tall and only about fifty pounds soaking wet?"

"You exaggerate, Mr. Garrett," Dean replied with cold dignity. "That creature has Powers. And the thing in the other room went to sleep." He jabbed a thumb in the direction of the Dead Man. "If you insist on pillorying someone for dereliction, I suggest your candidate be the thing actually capable of having exercised control over the foreigner."

"But he's asleep. I can't vent my frustrations by yelling at him."

Dean shrugged. My need to yell was a matter of indifference to him. Unless I showed the slack-witted judgment to zero in on him personally. "I expect you're starved, Mr. Garrett. What do you say to stuffed peppers?"

That was blackmail in its rawest form.

Dean's smile was wicked, even demonic. He'd do it. He'd really make the whole house reek of that foul fruit.

"You watch out I don't change the locks next time you go out of the house."

Dean smiled. It's his firmly held conviction that I can't get along without him.

The man is mad.

"I'm going to go into my office. I'm going to put on my thinking cap. Singe, how about you grab us a pitcher and a couple of mugs?" I really wanted to go pummel the Dead Man but knew I'd just end up driving myself crazy. If he was soundly enough asleep to let Casey get away there'd be no waking him up anytime soon.

Because beer was involved Singe overlooked my treating her more like an employee than a partner, which is what she figured she was.

I didn't give Eleanor more than a passing glance because I knew what I'd find if I bothered to consult the woman in the painting. No help at all and a whole lot of amusement at my predicament.

Singe materialized with the beer. Not one pitcher but two, one in each paw, with mugs. We went to work sipping, nobody saying much. After a while she returned to the kitchen for refills. We sipped some more. I began to relax. Then Dean stuck his head in to tell me that Colonel Block was at the door and wanted to see me.

I hadn't heard him pounding.

Singe hadn't either, apparently. She said, "Just when I was about to seduce you."

"Life's a bitch. There's always a Westman Block ready to jump in and ruin the moment. Colonel! How good to see you. To what do we owe the pleasure?" Singe moved her special chair aside so Block could plant himself in the guest seat.

Block nodded his head sagely. "All right, Garrett. You got me fooled. You're thrilled to see me. I just wanted to share some news. We caught one of those silver elves that have been terrorizing the city."

"Terrorizing?" Being the superb actor I am, I kept a straight face and said, "Really? Congratulations."

"Don't waste the effort."

"Huh?"

"I know what's been going on, Garrett. Lucky for you, most of the time I buy into Deal's concept of the rule of law."

"I'm glad to hear it."

"Your attitude, however, frequently makes it hard to cut you any slack."

"So my best friends keep telling me. I had a rough childhood. My daddy got killed in the war."

Which wasn't the smartest choice of wiseass comments. But the good colonel set me straight.

"Don't be a dickhead, Garrett. Everybody's daddy got killed in the war. That's the way they did it in those days. They waited till a guy created a family before they conscripted him. That way they could be sure there'd be more soldiers coming up."

"Easy. Sorry." This was an aspect of Wes Block I hadn't seen before. "So let's be serious. You've caught one of the silver elves."

"And he isn't talking. We're not entirely sure that he can. The people who've examined him say it might not be possible to make him talk because we don't have the technical expertise."

Clever, clever Casey. He was selling his strangeness. "And?"

"And there have been suggestions, from some quarters, that your partner might be able to fill the communications gap."

Ah. Now we came to the reason for the friendly visit. "There's an idea that hasn't found its time. Assuming there was any way at all he could be talked into underwriting the delinquencies of the people you're fronting, there's still one problem. He's sound asleep. Based on grim experience, I'd say there's a cruel chance he'll stay that way for a long time. Because he's had to stay awake a lot, lately."

"I'm trying to save you some grief, Garrett."

"And I appreciate it. But no amount of good intentions on your part, or of anybody else's wishful thinking, can change the facts. Come on. I'll show you." Like there's anything visibly different about how the Dead Man looks when he's sleeping. "Stick a pin in him if you want. He wouldn't feel it anyway but if he was awake he'd respond to the insult. Or you could say something revolting but true about the Loghyr."

"I'll take your word for it." But his tone wasn't that reassuring. "The trouble is, I have people pressing me who don't really care about such problems."

"You have people pressing you who're stupid enough to risk offending a dead Loghyr?"

"In a word, yes. There really are people who don't know any better."

"People that survived the Cantard?"

"We have a crop of apprentices coming up who didn't get a chance to experience the worst the war had to offer before the Ve-nageti collapse. They don't know they're not invulnerable. They have no grasp whatsoever on their true limitations. And they're in a hurry now."

"You don't say. And you don't know any older, cooler heads who might rein them in?"

Block shrugged. He looked grim. He shuddered. I asked, "What?"

"I never expected it would be easy. But I did hope."

"Which means?"

"Which means that I'm going to have to find a hole and pull it in after me because Relway's gotten a big head lately, too. He insists that if any of those spook-chaser pups do step very far outside the law, he'll nail them the same as if they were muggers on the street."

"Oh, boy. That'll bring their daddies out." I took a huge breath, let it go in a grand sigh. "I didn't think he'd move this soon."

"That little man is crazy, Garrett. But crazy like the proverbial fox. I'd bet he's a lot more ready for a showdown than you or I think he could be. If he does go down he'll make sure it's in a conflagration so dramatic that not just TunFaire but all Karenta will be changed forever."

I sighed me another one of those huge sighs. "All right. I don't want to do this. I hate to get noticed by those people. But there's a slim chance I can get through to your guy. If he's the one we called Casey. I assume he is because all the rest of them seem to have gone aboard the skyship that was terrorizing the city earlier today."

Block gave me one of his squinty looks. He knew that skyship had made an up close and personal appearance at the digs of my friend Morley Dotes. But he didn't press the matter.

I offered him a brief, thoroughly edited version of events on the Embankment, claiming I'd been there in the interest of my client Kip Prose, who still felt threatened. "The point is, I'm still finding myself up to my ankles in Bic Gonlit. Nothing I do gets that guy to go away. He's started to make me wonder if it isn't personal after all."

"Bic Gonlit. With a stormwarden, eh?"

"A thoroughly shabby stormwarden. You'd figure him for a fake, just looking at him. Nobody off the Hill ought to be that scruffy. But he sure brewed up the lightning when the time came to show his stuff."

"I haven't gotten the reports on that incident yet. I'll look into it when I get back." He asked several questions evidently meant to give him clues to the sorcerer's identity. I don't think I helped.

Singe decided to go refill our pitchers.

Block said, "That's creepy, Garrett."

"What is?"

"That rat running around here just like she was people."

"Oh." I didn't start an argument. "You get used to it. You are holding the silver elf at the al-Khar, aren't you?"

"Yes."

Good. It would've been bad—for me—if they'd decided to

question Casey in the cellar of one of those ugly stone piles on the Hill. "Well, let me tie up a few loose ends here, then I'll wander over there with you and take a shot at seeing what I can do with your guy."

Colonel Black was suspicious, right away and right down to the bone. And he was right to be. "What're you up to, Garrett?"

"I'm trying to keep my life from getting infested with parasitic wizards. I've had run-ins with Casey before. If it's him you've got and not some other elf none of us knows about, I might be able to communicate with him. I managed once before. But he's stubborn. And he isn't afraid of anything."

Block's suspicions were allayed only slightly. I don't know why. I'm a trustworthy kind of guy.

"I'm going to go help Singe. If Dean's not there to do it for her she gets beer all over drawing it out of the cold well." I went to the kitchen. "Singe, I need the invisibility fetish."

Somebody trusted me. She handed the thing over without a question.

"You know if we have any more of these things squirreled away anywhere?"

She shook her head. "You gave all the rest back to the women or to that man in there. He's afraid of me, isn't he?"

"In a way. Yes. He'll get over it. Say a prayer for me to the gods of the ratfolk."

"Or maybe I will not. Our gods are all cruel and treacherous. Reflecting the world itself. We just try to trick them into looking the other way."

A philosophy I could embrace wholeheartedly.

# 83

My interview with Casey took place in the same big room where I'd gotten interviewed earlier. The same main players seemed to be on hand. Block was there. Three quiet wizards were there, none in costume, and none of them the one who ran with Bic Gonlit. I'm confident that Director Relway was there as well, back in the shadows, though I never actually heard or saw him.

Casey was there, seated in a hard chair at a bare table when I arrived. They hadn't bothered to restrain him. He was no physical threat. As I settled opposite him one of Colonel Block's men dumped a sack of nine fetish devices in front of me. I said, "Casey, old buddy, we're in the really deep shit here, now. You've been around TunFaire long enough to have a pretty good idea of the kind of people who have hold of you. You have a pretty good idea what they want. And you know they're not real good at taking no for an answer. You have to understand that some things are inevitable and that all you can do is make it easier on all of us." Lines of a sort everyone in that room, probably including Casey himself, would have used numerous times. I took out the fetish I'd brought from home, added it to the pile while staring straight into Casey's strange eyes.

Could he read me at all?

"What's that?" Block demanded.

"One of those amulet boxes of theirs. Singe found it today. When things were blowing up on the Embankment. Figured I ought to bring it over. Casey. Do you understand anything I've said? Do you know what these people want?"

After a long, long pause Casey nodded.

Of course he knew. It was his mission to make sure they didn't get it, from him or the Maskers or, especially, the Brotherhood of Light. I hoped he would keep his mission in mind. Because I was counting on him to get us all out of this mess.

"All right. Look here, Colonel. We're getting somewhere already. Told you I could get through to him. Whoa there, Casey. Slowly and carefully. We aren't sure which ones of those things are weapons."

Casey took such offense that his indignation was plain to everyone. "We do not . . . make weapons!"

That caused a stir, more because he'd spoken than because of what he'd said.

"Is that true? But I've been knocked unconscious over and over again by something that left me with the worst headaches of my life."

I believe Casey would have laughed if Visitors had the capacity for laughter. "What you experienced . . . was an effect . . . of a device used . . . for the removal of . . . the parasites common to . . . the bodies of most . . . of your animals . . . and races. Lice and . . . fleas in particular. With the device set . . . at its strongest . . . power. We do not . . . make weapons."

"I'll take your word for that. Which one of these doohickeys is a flea getter ridder ofer?"

Casey extended one spider leg finger slowly.

"Good. Sergeant, you want to take that one away?"

Excellent. Now I knew that Casey could tell these devices apart. Hopefully. Which would mean that he should know what kind of fetish I had placed on the table.

Maybe he was smart enough to understand what needed doing.

"So. Let's go over the rest of these, one by one. Tell me what they're supposed to do. Start with this one here."

Casey did that. And after we'd reviewed a couple of fetishes I realized that he couldn't really make me understand what he was talking about. I didn't have the vocabulary. Then his voice gave out.

I asked Block, "Can we get him some water in here? He's obviously not used to talking."

Block said something. One of his men moved. I glanced over. And when I looked back Casey wasn't there anymore. Neither were any of the fetishes. An instant later, as the shouting began, the hammer of darkness fell. Again.

# 84

"What happened?" I mumbled. I was the last one to wake up. The delouser's effects were cumulative for sure.

"How about you tell me," Block growled, dragging me into a seated position with my back against a wall.

"I've got a notion I don't have a lot of fleas anymore. Gods, my head is killing me! Hit me and put me out again." I meant it at the moment.

"No. I want you to get up. I want you hurting while you explain what just happened. You won't be able to concentrate enough to bullshit me."

"I don't know what just happened. You were here. You were paying attention. You probably got a better look than I did."

"Maybe I did. Maybe I didn't. I can't shake the feeling that there wasn't a pea under any of the shells."

Nausea overcame me as I tried to stand. Beer and my last meal beat me to the floor.

"Godsdammit! That just tops my whole day off, Garrett!"

I tried to climb the nearest chair. It was occupied. I gasped, "Get me some water. Wasn't somebody supposed to go after water?" And, "What happened to him?"

The man in the chair was one of the sorcerers. His eyes were open but nobody seemed to be at home behind them.

The look was worse than the thousand-yard stare. With that you knew your guy would probably come back someday. Seeing this, you knew he wouldn't, ever.

"I don't know, Garrett. He seems to have turned into a vegetable. They all have. But nobody else was hurt." He stepped carefully, avoiding my mess.

Wow. Casey must've done that deliberately. He wasn't a nice guy after all. Unless he hadn't been aware what they were and this was a by-product of them owning their talent in the wrong place at the wrong time.

Block declared, "I think their intelligence was deliberately and systematically destroyed."

"That would make our Casey a vindictive little bastard, wouldn't it? Completely without a sense of humor about being misused. Why do you suppose he let you and me and the rest of these guys slide? Because we're like him, just battling the darkness the best we know how?"

"Gift horses, eh? You could be right." He didn't say anything for a while. I seized the opportunity to concentrate on feeling sorry for myself. I wondered if Lastyr and Noodiss had gotten away before they gave Kip an idea for a miracle headache cure. I'd better check. Then Block told me, "I'd better have you taken home. I want you to stay inside your house until I get this sorted out. There'll be questions. Some of you men want to get this mess cleaned up? Can't anybody around here do something without waiting to be told?"

It didn't seem likely. Not when everybody was preoccupied with a killer headache.

"This is bad shit, Garrett," Block whined. "This's real bad shit. I'll be lucky to get out of this just losing my job."

"Aren't you being a little too pessimistic?" I clamped down and pushed the pain back. But not very far. "Man, you let yourself get way too impressed by people off the Hill. Did Hill people give you your job? I thought Prince Rupert did that. And what were these guys trying to pull, anyway? They were trying to cut the rest of those witch doctors up there out of the jackpot. You watch. The rest of their kind will take one quick look at the facts and figure they had it coming."

"You do have a knack for looking on the bright side, Garrett. I sure hope it's as easy as all that."

First I'd heard of me being a brightside kind of guy. But what the hell, eh? If I played to that maybe Block would forget to nag me about Casey's getaway.

I reminded the good colonel of his obligations. "I thought you were going to take me home."

# 85

Colonel Block's coach was still a block from my house when it bogged down in traffic. Macunado Street was clogged with bodies, most of them human and only remotely acquainted with personal hygiene, but with plenty of odds and ends and mixtures in the crowd, too. Everybody wanted to see the glowing blob in the sky that seemed so interested in our neighborhood.

This blob wasn't a flying disk. Nor was it like those things that Evas and her friends had flown. This was more of a cylinder with gently tapered ends, with nothing protruding outside. To hear the crowd tell it, the cylinder had descended to ground level several times but was now just hovering, like it was confused. Or just waiting.

I told Block, "I'm telling you right now, flying around up in the air isn't one-tenth as much fun as you might think."

"And you'd know what you're talking about?"

"Hasn't been that long since I took a few rides on a pegasus."

"Garrett, you ought to write all your adventures down. Being mindful not to leave out any of the bullshit you're always laying on people you know."

"I'd do that if there was any way to make a few coppers out of it. But even I have trouble believing some of the stuff that's happened to me."

"You're right. You'd have a credibility problem. I don't believe some of it—and I was there when it happened."

The crowd oohed and aahed as the skyship suddenly dropped down almost to touching level, just about where the Garrett home-

stead stood. It hovered there only briefly. Colonel Block was looking out the other side of the coach at the time. He might not have
noticed.

He did say, "All these weird things going on in the sky lately
have had their positive side effects."

"For instance?" I wasn't paying close attention. I was worrying about Casey's stubborn streak. Was he going to get after Kip
again, now?

"Such as the political shenanigans have quieted down for a
while. We haven't had anybody march for days. And it's been at
least a week since there was a significant race riot."

"People get tired of the same old entertainment."

Casey's skyship rose up against the backdrop of the night,
dwindled till it was a point lost among the stars. I wondered just
how strange his home country could really be. Presumably those
of his people that I'd met were amongst the most bizarre speci-
mens. The normal people would stay home, content to do normal
things.

Colonel Block dropped me in front of the house, the street
having emptied quickly once the show came to an end. "Hang on,
Garrett." He made me wait. "What do you intend to do about Bic
Gonlit?"

I hadn't given that much thought. It didn't need much. "Ignore
him and hope he goes away, I suppose. He's just been doing his
job. He can go on doing it. I don't see how that could involve me
anymore."

Block grunted, said, "I do want to know which stormwarden
he's running with, if you happen to stumble across that bit of information."

"You got it." I started up the steps to the house.

A moment later I was surrounded by a cloud of pixies, every
one of them squeaking, all of them determined to have me adjudi-
cate countless disputes and quarrels. I was rude to them all,
whether or not I knew them.

Singe opened the front door. She held a big, cold mug of beer.
Ah, the little woman, welcoming me home.

As I started to extend my drinking hand Singe tossed back
half the mug. Then she told me, "The Dead Man said you were
coming."

"He's awake again?"

"That Casey woke him up. He said."

"Damn! That's a trick I wish he'd taught me before he went away."

*Garrett.*

"All present and accounted for, near as I can tell. Headache and everything. What's up, Big Guy? What'd the Visitor have to say?"

*Just no hard feelings and farewell and thank you and do not be too concerned about reactions to his report. He does not believe that his superiors will insist upon any follow-up. The damage done by the Brotherhood of Light was slight and should damp itself out within a generation. Apparently it did the same last time around.*

"That's good to know. Whatever it means. I'm going to go sleep off this headache." After I drank some beer and chased it with headache powders.

# 86

Deal Relway himself came to the house. He never made it quite clear why. The little man has trouble articulating sometimes. He did hint that he was convinced that I'd collaborated in the escape of a particular royal prisoner and that I had been an accessory to the total moronification of three already-subhuman subjects of the Karentine Crown. Not that that was necessarily a bad thing in the case of those particular subjects.

As far as he was concerned, justice had been served.

"What was that all about?" I asked the Dead Man after the director took his leave.

The only response I got was the psychic equivalent of a snore. I wanted to scream. I'd counted on the Dead Man to pluck Relway's psychic bones.

# 87

Karenta's current monarch has been so deft at survival that most of his subjects have had the opportunity to learn his birth date. They have begun taking advantage of the fact that the King's Birthday is, traditionally, a Karentine holiday.

This year the people of substance had chosen to collect in the reservoir park. There they would show off their new seasonal outfits and their participation in the latest fad, the wonderful world of inventions called three-wheels.

Any family that showed up without being able to claim at least one three-wheel on order might as well resign itself to being the butt of condescending gossip for at least as long as it took for us to develop a grander, bigger, more expensive model.

I had to attend with my business partners, who brought most of their families. Which meant there were beautiful women in every direction I looked, be they Tate, Weider, or Prose. I didn't get much chance to exercise my eyes, though. Tinnie had decided I was back on her A list. Which, apparently, awarded her complete custody of where I directed my vision.

Alyx Weider was too busy scooting around, showing off her own custom three-wheel, to afford her usual distraction.

I steered myself toward Tinnie's Uncle Willard. "This is an amazing show, sir." Every damned three-wheel we'd built was here somewhere. So it seemed. "When are we supposed to do the judging?" A huge part of the festivities was a contest to see which young lady could dress up her three-wheel the prettiest.

Our end users, so far, were almost all girls and young women of extremely considerable substance. A demographic I'd have found particularly interesting if I hadn't been claimed. For the moment.

"Ha!" I told the redhead. "I *am* supposed to be looking." Then, "Why aren't you out there outshining Alyx and Rose?"

Pout. "One of my wheels broke when we were leaving. They wouldn't let me get it fixed. That would make us late."

Two painfully homely young women, paced by four fierce-looking, thoroughly well armed characters on foot, passed us, leisurely following the bridle path. "Ugh!" I said.

Willard Tate cautioned me. "Those are the royal daughters, Garrett."

"Guaranteed to be winners in the contest," Tinnie added, because I would be too obtuse and democratic to figure that out for myself.

I tried to remember how to do the tug at the forelock thing. I was out of practice. I asked, "How are we doing, businesswise?"

"Overall? We couldn't be plundering the rich more effectively if we were a barbarian horde. And we're doing it without any bloodshed. You hit this one square on the nose. You're a wealthy young man, now. Or you will be before much longer. Have you been giving any thought to your future?"

Beyond maybe getting a bigger cold well installed so we could keep up with Singe's added demands on the beer supply, no.

I said, "Uh-oh."

"What?"

"Sounds like I'm about to be offered an investment opportunity."

Willard laughed, something he didn't do very often. Normally, he was as sour and serious as an accountant. "You might say that, Garrett. Deal of a lifetime. What I'm wondering about is, what are you and Tinnie thinking about?"

"Uncle Willard!"

Uncle Willard ignored Tinnie completely. "You've been playing cat and mouse with each other for several years, now. You're both getting a little long in the tooth to keep it up."

"I'm thinking you might want to address your questions to the cat. The mouse don't get much say." Which observation earned me an enthusiastic dig in the ribs.

"You planning to go on the way you've always done?"

I checked Tate's expression for a clue to how he meant that. I thought I got it. "It's what I do. I find things. I find things out. I try to help people who are in trouble. It's what I'm good at. I'm not good at managing a big manufacturing thing. Hell, I have trouble managing the everyday business side of what I do now. Dean does most of that. So if you need me to fill in as the son you no longer have, well, I can try to play the role, but I don't think you'd be happy with the results." Deciding maybe I wasn't quite as great an actor as had seemed the case the other day.

"I understand that. Come. It's time for the formal judging. I hope you brought enough prize ribbons, Tinnie. Because everybody who's anybody has to get some kind of award."

"I brought one for every unit we've sold, plus a few extras."

"Isn't having been born into the aristocracy wonderful?" Tate asked. "You don't *really* have to compete. You're a winner automatically."

I agreed. "Beats hard work and study all to hell."

"You know what they say. Work like a dog and what do you get? Dog tired."

Tinnie hurried off to one of the Tate family carriages, of which there were several present. She came back with a sheaf of ribbons. I let her slide back in under my right arm, thinking it *was*, maybe, time to start putting the boy's life behind. If *she* maybe thought so, too. The only other candidate I'd ever honestly considered was a young woman named Maya, who hadn't been patient enough to wait for me. And Eleanor, of course, but that would've been a little too ethereal a relationship for me.

Just then a half dozen shimmering objects streaked across the northern sky in a tight formation, low, in the far distance. Three seemed sizable, sausage-shaped vehicles. The rest were exactly like the odd little skyships that Evas and her henchwomen preferred. The Masker ship must have flown home very fast indeed. And Evas' secret hunger must be one she shared with a lot of Visitor women—if this was what Morley had predicted and not some kind of raid.

Dotes might've made the whole thing up.

Still, maybe I ought to get into the entrepreneurial spirit and . . .

Tinnie made herself at home under my right wing again. I was still on her A list. After all these minutes. Despite Uncle Willard. She asked, "Aren't you done with those people?"

"I guess. As long as they're done with Kip." I did worry about the Goddamn Parrot, though. But I wouldn't tell anybody.

I shook the unsettling notion that those larger vessels might be troopships. They were hovering over the Embankment now. Up to something.

Within minutes they headed back the way they had come. With an extra, disklike vehicle floating amongst them.

I tried to concentrate on the three-wheel festival. And spied Harvester Temisk immediately. Riding a three-wheel of his very own. He was headed my way. Looking altogether too serious for my time of life.

Chodo's party was drawing close.

For us heroes party time is never done.

# Whispering Nickel Idols

*This one is for my mom,
who was a rock in a
turbulent stream.*

*With thanks to Jim K.
and Ellen W.*

# 1

There I was, galumphing downstairs, six feet three of the handsomest, ever-loving blue-eyed ex-Marine you'd ever want to meet. Whistling. But it takes me a big, big bucket to carry a tune. And my bucket had a hole in it.

Something was wrong. I needed my head examined. I'd gone to bed early, all by my own self. And hadn't had a dram to drink before I did. Yet this morning I was ready to break into a song and dance routine.

I felt so good that I forgot to be suspicious.

I can't forget, ever, that the gods have chosen me, sweet baby Garrett, to be their special holy fool and point man in their lunatic entertainments.

I froze on the brink of my traditional morning right turn to the kitchen.

There was a boy in the hallway that runs from my front door back to my kitchen. He was raggedy with reddish ginger hair all tangled, a kid who was his own barber. And his barber was half blind and used a dull butcher knife. There were smudges on the boy's cheeks. He stood just over five feet tall. I made him about twelve, or maybe a puny thirteen. His tailor was a walleyed ragpicker. I assumed he had a pungent personal aura, but wasn't close enough to experience it.

Was he deaf? He'd missed the racket I'd made coming down. Of course, he had his nose stuck in the Dead Man's room. That view can be overwhelming, first time. My partner is a quarter ton of dead gray flesh resembling the illegitimate offspring of a human father and pachydermous mother, vaguely. In the nightmare of some opium-bemused, drunken artist.

"Makes you want to jump in his lap and snuggle up, don't he?"

The kid squeaked and backed toward the front door, bent over so he sort of probed his way with his behind.

"And you would be?" I asked, more interested than I could explain just by my finding a stranger marooned in my hallway.

The kitchen door squeaked. "Mr. Garrett. You're up early."

"Yeah. It ain't even the crack of noon. Clue me in, here."

The party exiting the kitchen was Dean, my live-in cook and housekeeper. He's old enough to be my grandfather but acts like my mom. His turning up explained the kid. He was lugging something wrapped in dirty old paper.

Dean collects strays, be they kittens or kids.

"What?"

"You're up to something. Else you wouldn't call me Mr. Garrett."

Dean's wrinkles pruned into a sour face. "The sun always sets when there is fear of saber-tooth tigers."

That means you see what you're afraid to see. My mother said it a lot, in her time.

"This house is safe from tigers." I stared at the boy, intrigued. He had a million freckles. His eyes sparkled with challenge and curiosity and fright. "Who's this? How come he's poking around my house?" I kept on staring. There was something appealing about that kid.

What the hell was wrong with me?

I expected psychic mirth from my deceased associate. I got nothing.

Old Bones was sound asleep.

There's good and bad in everything.

I focused on Dean. I had a scowl on. A ferocious one, not my "just for business" scowl. "I'm not whistling now, Dean. Talk to me." Grease stained the packet the old boy carried. Once again, at second hand, I would be feeding a stray.

"Uh . . . this is Penny Dreadful. He runs messages for people."

Dreadful? What kind of name was that? "There's a message for me, then?" I gave the urchin the benefit of my best scowl. He wasn't impressed. Likely nothing troubled him as long as he stayed out of grabbing range.

I saw nothing suggesting aristocratic antecedents, though

Dreadful is the sort of name favored by the sorcerers and spook chasers on the Hill, our not so subtle, secret masters.

"Yes. There is. In the kitchen," Dean blurted. He pushed past. "I'll get it in a minute. Here, Penny. Mr. Garrett will let you out. Won't you, Mr. Garrett?"

"Sure, I will. I'm one of the good guys, aren't I?" I stood against the wall as Dean pushed past again, headed the other way.

The kid clutched the packet and retreated. Odd. My internal reaction wasn't overpowering, but it was of a strength usually reserved for those darlings who make priests regret their career choices.

I opened the door. The ragamuffin slid out and scurried away, hunched like he expected to get hit. He didn't slow down till he reached the intersection of Macunado Street with Wizard's Reach.

He looked back while he was eating, saw me watching. Startled, he zipped around the corner.

*Buzz! Buzz!* Tinkling, musical laughter. Something tugged my hair. A tiny voice piped, "Garrett's got a girlfriend."

"Hello, Marienne." Marienne was an adolescent pixie of the female variety. A squabbling nest of the wee folk live in the voids inside the exterior walls of my house. Marienne loved to give me a hard time.

"Looked a little young to me," a second voice observed. My hair suffered again. "Too tender for a butcher whose forest is getting a little thin in back."

"Hollybell. You horrid little bug. I knew you'd never let Marienne out of your sight." Hollybell and Marienne are inseparable. Before the leaves finish falling, though, they'll discover boys who aren't all smell and dirt and stupid. Soon the slightest sigh would have universe-shuddering importance.

"Mr. Garrett?"

Dean wanted me. He always horns in when I want to play with little girls.

# 2

Dean had fetched the message packet. "Go in your office. Figure out what this is. I'll bring tea and biscuits, then get breakfast started. I was thinking those little sausages and soft-boiled eggs."

"A real treat." I gave the old boy the fisheye. "What are you up to?"

"What do you mean?"

"What I said. You're up to something. It might include that kid—who the pixies say is really a girl." The red-blooded Karentine boy inside me had sensed the truth. "If you turn polite and start acting like a real housekeeper, you're up to some villainy. There's no need for a show of wounded dignity, either."

The old-timer needed to polish his act. He was as predictable as me.

I settled behind my desk, in the glamorized janitor's closet I use for an office. I turned sideways, blew a kiss at Eleanor. She's the woman in the painting hanging behind my chair. She's fleeing a brooding mansion on a really stormy night. A light burns in one window only. She's terrified. But she was in a good mood at the moment. She winked.

I opened the message wallet. A sheaf of documents fell out.

They were from Harvester Temisk. A lawyer. The kind who is at home in lawyer jokes. But with a perpetually dumbfounded look on his clock.

Harvester Temisk has just one client. Chodo Contague, erstwhile emperor of TunFaire's multiple kingdoms of crime. The king of kings of the underworld. The head crook.

These days Chodo snoozes along in a coma while his beautiful, criminally insane daughter runs the family business. Belinda pretends she gets instructions from the emperor's own lips.

Dean brought orange tea and sugar cookies. "The sausages are cooking. And there'll be stewed apples instead of eggs. Singe wants stewed apples."

More proof Dean was up to no good, serving specialty tea and sweets. "She'd live on stewed apples if she could." Pular Singe has weaseled herself into an apprenticeship and is angling for junior partner. She's good people and good company. She keeps me from turning into a disgusting old bachelor.

Dean scurried away. Yet more proof. He didn't want to be questioned.

I started reading.

Harvester Temisk reminded me that I'd promised to visit him once I wrapped the case I was working last time we met. I never got back to him. "Dean!"

"I'm cooking as fast as I can."

"I can't find my notes about Chodo's birthday party. When did I say it was supposed to be?"

"It's tonight. At The Palms. Miss Contague reserved the whole club. How could you forget?"

"Maybe I didn't want to remember." You don't want to socialize with the Contagues. Well . . . Belinda . . . when she isn't totally psychotic . . .

Belinda Contague is the perfect beautiful woman without mercy. The grim, unforgiving world of organized crime quickly grew deadlier after her advent. Only a few people know she's the true brains of the Outfit. The fact that her father is comatose is a closely held secret. Maybe five people know. One of those is Chodo.

I worry about being one of the other four. I have no trouble seeing the logic of reducing four to a more manageable three. Or even two.

The Outfit may collapse into civil war when the underbosses find out that their orders come from a woman. Though Belinda has worked hard to restructure the organization, advancing people she finds more congenial.

I didn't want to attend Chodo's party. Too many people connect me with the Contagues already. My being there would only convince the secret police that I'm more significant than I am.

Beyond the accusatory note, the packet contained documents signed by Chodo. Before the incident that resulted in his coma, presumably. Maybe Chodo saw it coming.

Harvester Temisk held the opinion that his employer conspired against the future as a matter of course. He had given Temisk a power of attorney, picked some fool named Garrett to handle his mouthpiece's legwork.

All through his dark career Chodo had guessed right. He'd been in the right place at the right time. The exception—perhaps—having been that one time when it had become possible for his daughter to live a nightmare, keeping the man she hated most where she could torment him daily.

The Contagues aren't your ideal, warm and loving, fuzzy family. They never were. Chodo murdered Belinda's mother when he found out she was cheating on him. Belinda is still working on forgiving him. She hasn't had much luck.

Dean arrived with breakfast.

Temisk didn't say what he wanted me to do. Mostly, he was worried about whether or not I would keep my word.

I thought and ate and couldn't conjure one workable way to weasel out of the obligation.

I owed Chodo. Multiple ways. He'd helped me frequently, without being asked. He'd known me well enough to understand that I'd trudge through life oppressed by the imbalance.

As well as always being in the right place at the right time, Chodo understood what made people work. Except Belinda. The mad daughter was his blind spot. Otherwise, he wouldn't be in a wheelchair drooling on himself.

Dean brought more tea. "Do we have a new case?"

He was up to something for sure.

"No. I'm about to pay the vig on an old debt."

He grunted, underwhelmed.

# 3

Pular Singe wandered in later. She didn't fit well, on account of
her tail. She lugged a big, steaming bowl of stewed apples. "Want
some?" She was addicted to stewed apples, a food you don't usually associate with rats.

"No, thank you."

TunFaire is infested with rats, including two species of the
regular vermin and several kinds of ratpeople. Ratpeople are intelligent, smaller than human critters, with ancestors who came to
life in the laboratories of mad sorcerers early last century. As ratpeople go, Singe is a genius. The smartest I've ever met, the
bravest, and the best tracker ever.

"What'll you do after you've gobbled this year's whole apple
crop?"

She eyed me speculatively, sorting potential meanings. Ratpeople have no natural sense of humor. Singe does have one, but
it's learned and can take a bizarre turn.

She knows that when I ask a question with no obvious connection to daily reality, I'm usually teasing. She even manages the occasional comeback.

This wasn't one of those times. "Is there a new case?" She
hisses, dealing with her sibilants. Those old-time sorcerers hadn't
done much to make it easy for rats to talk.

"Nothing I'm going to get paid for." I told her about Chodo
Contague and my old days.

Singe got hold of her tail, wrapped it around her, and hun-
kered into a squat. We have only one chair that suits the way she's

built. That's in the Dead Man's room. Her usual dress is drab, durable work clothing tailored to her odd dimensions.

Though they walk on their hind legs like people, ratfolk have short legs and long bodies. Not to mention funny arms. And tails that drag.

"So you blame yourself for what happened to that man."

Clever rodent.

"Even though it was unavoidable."

Time to change the subject. "Got any idea what Dean is up to?"

Singe still isn't used to how human thought zigs and zags. Her genius is relative. She's a phenom for a rat. As a human she'd be on the slow side of average—though that fades as she gets a better handle on how things work.

"I did not notice anything unusual. Except the bucket of kittens under the stove." Her nose wrinkled. Her whiskers wiggled. No cat smaller than a saber-tooth was likely to trouble her, but she had the instincts of her ancestors.

"I knew it. Kittens, eh? He hasn't tried that for a while."

"Don't be angry. His heart is in the right place."

"His heart may be. But he does this stuff at my expense."

"You can afford it."

"I could if I didn't waste wages on a do-nothing housekeeper."

"Do not yell at him."

That would take half the fun out of having Dean around. "I won't yell. I'll just get him a pail of water. Or maybe a gunnysack with a brick in it."

"You are awful." Then she observed, "You have a lot to do if you are going to be ready for the birthday party."

True. Besides the business of getting cleaned up and dressed up, I needed to visit Harvester Temisk.

"I just had a great idea. I can take those baby cats along tonight and give them away as party favors."

"You are so bad. Go see them before you decide their fates."

"Cute don't work on me."

"Unless it comes in girl form."

"You got me there."

"Come see the kittens. Before Dean finds a better place to hide them." She rose, collected her empty bowl and my tray. We were getting domestic.

"How do you hide a bucket of kittens? They'd be everywhere."

"These are well-behaved kittens."

That sounded like an oxymoron. "I'll just look in on the old bone bag, then be right with you."

# 4

One weak candle burned in the Dead Man's room. As always. It's not there to provide illumination. It gives off smoke that most bugs find repugnant.

Old Bones has been dead a long time. But his species, the Loghyr, get in no hurry to leave their flesh. When they're awake they do a fair job of discouraging vermin. But my partner has a tendency toward sloth, as well as championship procrastination. He's getting raggedy.

The candles work pretty good on people, too. They don't smell much sweeter than the northernmost extremity of a south-bound polecat.

I try to keep the Dead Man's door closed. But kids keep wandering in. They never leave anything the way they find it.

I entered the kitchen saying, "His Nibs is really asleep. I dumped my trick bag. Nothing worked."

Dean looked worried. Singe sort of collapsed in on herself.

"It ain't a big deal. He's taking a nap. We always get through his off-seasons." Dean didn't want to be reminded, though. I never do things the way he wants them done.

I said, "So, Dean, I hear tell a tribe of baby cats has infiltrated my kitchen."

"They aren't ordinary kittens, Mr. Garrett. They're part of an ancient prophecy."

"A modern prophecy has them taking a trip down the river in a gunnysack with a couple broken bricks as companions on the voyage. What're you babbling about?"

"Penny isn't just another street urchin. She's a priestess."

I poured some tea, eyed the bucket of cats. They looked like gray tabby babies. Though there was something strange about them. "A priestess. Right." No surprise in TunFaire, the most god-plagued city that ever was.

"She's the last priestess of A-Lat. From Ymber. She ran off to TunFaire after her mother was murdered by zealots from the cult of A-Laf. Who're in TunFaire now, looking for the kittens."

Somebody had gotten somebody to invest heavily in off-river wetlands. Similar scams are out there every day. People turn blind stupid if you say there's a god involved.

Even Singe looked skeptical. She said, "They are cats, Dean." Coolly.

"Ymber, eh?" I had only vague knowledge of that little city. It's up the river several days' journey. It has problems with thunder lizards. It's supposedly a party town, ruled by a very loose goddess of love, peace, and whatnot. Ymber ships grain, fruit, sheep, cattle, and timber to TunFaire. And lately, thunder lizard hides. It's not known for exporting religious refugees. Or zealots.

One of TunFaire's own main products is flimflam folk. Though I did not, immediately, see how the girl could sting Dean with a bucket of cats.

The religious angle was suggestive, though.

I said, "I'm listening. I haven't heard how the cats tie in."

"They're the Luck of A-Lat."

I tried to get more than that. He clammed. Probably because that's all he knew.

"I'll have to bring the big guy in on it, then."

The whole front of the house shuddered. I growled like a hungry dire wolf. I've had it with people trying to break down my door.

# 5

My current front door was next best to a castle gate. I had it installed on account of the last one got busted regularly by large,
usually hairy, always uncouth, violent fellows. The character I
spied through the spy hole, rubbing his shoulder and looking
dimly bewildered, fit all those categories. Especially hairy. Except
the top of his head. Its peak glistened.

He wore clothes but looked like Bigfoot's country cousin. With
worse fashion sense. Definitely a mixed breed. Maybe including
some troll, some giant, gorilla, or bear. All his ancestors must've
enjoyed the double uglies. He hadn't just gotten whipped with an
ugly stick—a whole damned tree fell on him, then took root.

"Wow!" I said. "You guys got to see this. He's wearing green
plaid pants."

Nobody answered. Dean was fumbling with a crossbow. Singe
had disappeared. Nothing could be felt from the great blob of sagging meat who was supposed to apply ferocious mental powers at
times like this.

The door took another mighty hit. Plaster dust shook loose
everywhere. I used the peephole again.

Yeti man wasn't alone. Two more just like him, also in baggy
green plaid, polluted my steps. Behind them lurked a guy who
might've been their trainer. He wore an anxious expression *and* a
hideous pair of pants.

A crowd began to gather.

Most of the adult pixies from my colony were out. Some
buzzed around like huge, colorful bumblebees. Some perched in
nooks and crannies, poised for action. And, of all people to reveal

a hitherto unsuspected talent for timing, I spied my pal Saucer-head Tharpe half a block down the street.

I glimpsed Penny Dreadful, too.

I strolled back to my office, flirted with Eleanor, dug through the clutter, ferreted out my lead-weighted oaken knobknocker. The stick is a useful conversational ploy if I get to chatting with overly excitable gentlemen like the hair ball out front.

Said gentleman continued exercising his shoulder. My door remained stubbornly unmoved by the brute side of the force. "You ready yet, Dean? Just point the business end between his eyes when he stops rolling."

I stepped up to the peephole. Big Hairy was rubbing his other shoulder. He looked down at the man in the street. That guy nodded. One more try.

Saucerhead stood around awaiting events.

Big Hairy charged.

I opened the door. He barked as he plunged inside, somehow tripping on my foot.

My toy made a satisfying *thwock!* on the back of his skull.

The other two hairy boys started to charge, too, but became distracted as their pelts started to crawl with tiny people armed with tiny weapons. Really, really sharp little weapons. All crusty brown with poison.

Singe leaned down from the porch roof, poking around with a rapier. Its tip was all crusty, too. She'd picked up Morley's wicked habit.

Saucerhead grabbed the guy in the street, slapped him till he stopped wiggling, tucked the guy under one arm, then asked, "What're you into now?"

"I don't got a clue," I said. "You didn't break that guy, did you?"

"He's breathing. He'll wake up. Might wish that he didn't, though, when he does. You want to go clubbing tonight?"

"Can't. I've got a command performance. Chodo's birthday party."

"Yeah? Hey! Is that *tonight*? Damn! I forgot. I'm supposed to work security." Tharpe started walking away.

"Hey!"

"Oh. Yeah. What do you want me to do with this guy?"

"Put him down and head on out. Relway's Runners are coming."

An urban police force sounds like a good idea. And it is. If it don't go getting in your way. Which it's likely to do if you spend time tiptoeing around the edge of the law.

Three Watchmen materialized. Two were regular patrolmen. The third was a Relway Runner. Scithe.

He recognized me, too. "You just draw trouble, Garrett." He eyed my house nervously. The Runners are the visible face of the secret police, known by their red flop caps and military weaponry. They have a lot of power but don't like getting inside reading range of mind-peekers like the Dead Man.

I said, "He's asleep."

Nothing lies more convincingly than the truth. My reassuring Scithe assured him only that the Dead Man was pawing through every dark recess of his empty skull.

He stuck to his job, though. "What were these guys up to, Garrett?"

"Trying to kick my door in." He had to ask. I know. I have to ask a lot of dumb stuff, too. Because you have to have the answers to build toward more significant stuff.

"Why?"

"You'll have to ask them. I've never seen them before. I'd remember. Look at those pants." While we chatted, the patrolmen bound the hairy boys' wrists. "There's another one of those inside, guys. My man's got the drop on him." I moved toward the character that Saucerhead dropped. I wanted to ask questions before they dragged him off to an Al-Khar cell.

A patrolman called from the house, "This asshole won't cooperate, Scithe."

"Keep hitting him. His attitude will improve." Scithe blew his whistle.

Seconds after, whistles answered from all directions.

I stirred the unconscious man with my foot. "These guys have a foreign look."

Scithe grunted. "I can tell right off you're a trained detective. You realized no local tailor would ruin his reputation that way. People! Gather round. What happened here?" He was talking to onlookers who'd come out to be entertained.

Amazing changes are going on. Astonishing changes. Several Karentines admitted having witnessed something. *And* they were willing to talk about it. The more traditional response, after the law caught and hog-tied a potential witness, would be protestations of blindness brought on by congenital deafness having spread to the eyes. In times past actual witnesses often could not speak Karentine despite having been born in the kingdom.

Relway was having way too much success selling civic responsibility.

My pixies were old-school, though.

Witnesses agreed that the Ugly Pants Gang just came up and started trying to break in, ignoring onlookers like they expected to do whatever they wanted, fearing no comebacks.

I tickled the down character with my toe, near his groin, in case he was playing possum.

"Garrett." Scithe wagged a finger. "No, no."

"The victim of the crime should be able to get a vague notion why somebody wants to bust up his place."

"We'll let you know what you need to know."

"That's comforting." I didn't have to decide for myself. The secret police would take the worry off my shoulders. They'd figure it all out for me. I just had to lie back and enjoy it.

I didn't argue. The name Garrett is far too high on Relway's curiosity list already.

Stuff happens around me. I don't know why. Maybe because I'm so handsome and Fortune hates a good-looking man.

I told the pixie sentries that I appreciated their nest's help. "Dean's got some baby cats inside. Tell him I said to roast them up for you."

# 6

Saucerhead fell into step beside me. I said, "I thought you might not get far."

"Smells like a job opportunity."

"I don't really have anything. . . . Wait. There is one thing. A street kid who calls himself Penny Dreadful. Runs errands. Carries messages. You know the type. There's a thousand of him out there. Looks to be about twelve. Might actually be a girl a little older. And might be connected to what just happened."

"Want me to catch her?"

"No. Just find out what you can. Especially where to find her. She's not real high on my list, though. I'm worrying about Chodo's birthday party."

Saucerhead grunted.

Tharpe is huge. For a human being. And he's strong. And he's not real bright. But he's a damned good friend. And I owe him, so a made-up job when I can manage one is never out of line. Especially when he might turn up something actually interesting.

I couldn't conceive of any connection with what had just happened. Nor could I conceive of another explanation. But TunFaire is overrun with people trying to find a new angle.

Still, there's hardly a bad boy around who doesn't know what happens if they get too close to the Dead Man.

That screwball fable about foreign gods had some *oomph!*

"I'm all over it," Saucerhead promised.

I gave him what little I could, including a description so feeble that all Penny Dreadful had to do to disguise himself would be change his shoes. "Promise me you'll stay away from Winger. My

life has been nice lately. I'd rather go right on not having her underfoot." Winger is a mutual friend. Sort of. Being mainly a disaster on the hoof.

She's the most amoral person I've ever met, with the social
conscience of a rock. And all of a rock's obsession with making
the world a better place.

Winger is completely unaware that there are real, hurting people in this world who aren't Winger.

"I don't figure she's likely to be a problem, Garrett."

"She's always a problem."

"She's in a relationship."

"Winger? She's in love? With somebody besides herself?"

"I don't know about love. There's this little winky who's so
gaga about her that she don't get much chance to get into mischief. He follows her all around. Everything she does, he writes it
down. Creating her epic cycle."

"All right." As long as Winger didn't pop up, trying to profit
from whatever was happening. Which is her usual way of doing
business.

"Where're you headed, anyway?" Saucerhead wanted to know.

"To see Chodo's mouthpiece. He's been bugging me to come
by. Something to do with the old boy's will, I guess."

"See you tonight, then."

"Sure. Just don't let all that neutrality go to your head. Old
buddy."

# 7

I never visited Harvester Temisk before. I'd had little to do with him even when his client was active. Puzzle as I might, I couldn't imagine what he wanted.

He didn't put up much of a front. His little shop was less cushy than the hole-in-the-wall I used before I partnered up with the Dead Man, then scored big enough to buy us a house. I slept, cooked, lived, loved, and worked in that tight little space, back then.

Harvester Temisk didn't look like a lawyer. Not how I thought a lawyer ought to look, anyway, so we know them when we see them. There wasn't an ounce of slime or oil on him. He looked short because he was wide. Once upon a time he might've been more thug than mouthpiece.

Chodo being Chodo, that might've been protective coloration.

The mouthpiece's prosperity had suffered. His haircut wasn't nearly as nice as it used to be. And he still wore the same clothing.

"Thanks for coming." A note of criticism crept into his voice. He noted me cataloging the evidence of his newfound indigence. "You don't work much when your only client is in a coma. He set up a trust that keeps me from starving, but didn't make good investments. Did you review the stuff I sent you?"

"I did. And couldn't make sense of it. Nor did I figure out what you want."

"I needed to see you face-to-face. Has anybody from the Outfit been interested in me? Or Chodo's condition?"

"I don't think anybody inside, except for Belinda, knows you're still around."

"That should hurt. But I'm glad. I hope they forget me completely."

He was worried. He couldn't keep still. That didn't suit the image projected by a square head, silver hair, square body, and squinty brown eyes.

"So, basically, you want to remind me that I owe Chodo. And you're ready to call the marker."

"Yes."

He didn't want to talk about it. Once he did, he couldn't ever take it back.

"You'd better get to it. Especially if you want to get something done before the party. Belinda won't reschedule."

Belinda. There was a diversion he could snap up.

"I'm worried about what might happen tonight."

It would be a wonderful opportunity to eliminate a lot of people Belinda didn't like if that was the way she wanted to work it.

Only somebody who knew the truth about Chodo's condition would be suspicious. Though a lot who didn't know still thought that it wasn't natural for the Boss to run things through his daughter. Not for so long.

The rats smelled a rat.

A lot of wise guys would turn up just so they could give the Boss a good glim. His health, or the decline thereof, might suggest a potential for personal advancement.

I mused, "What's she going to pull? How's she going to pull it?"

"Can't figure that out, either."

Something didn't add up. It took me a second to figure out what. "Wait a minute. You got in touch before Belinda announced the party. Did you have inside info?"

"I wish. No. I have almost no contacts inside now. This isn't about the party. It's about . . . I think it's time to rescue him, Garrett. The party just complicates things."

"Mind if I sit?" His best furniture was his client's chair. "Time to rescue Chodo? You mean like round up a couple squadrons of dragoons and go raid the Contague estate? That isn't going to happen."

"Not rescue physically. Mentally. If we shatter the chains imprisoning his mind, the physical side will take care of itself."

"You've lost me completely. I know coma victims have come back. But not very often. Never, if everybody else thinks you being in a coma is so exquisitely useful that it's the next best thing to you being dead."

"You ever know anybody who came out of a long coma?"

"No."

"Ever know anybody who was even in a coma? Besides Chodo?"

"During the war. Usually somebody who got hit in the head."

"Up close, for very long?"

"No. You headed somewhere?"

"Toward the hypothesis that Chodo isn't in a coma, only a post-stroke state resembling a coma, induced chemically or by sorcery. I don't think he's unconscious. I think he just can't communicate."

Giant hairy spiders with cold claws crept all over my back. That presented a gaggle of unpleasant possibilities. "Suppose you're right. Chodo had willpower like nobody I ever met. He'd get around it, somehow."

"Absolutely. He would."

"And you're somehow part of that?"

"That would mean he saw it coming. He was clever, Garrett. He read people like nobody else, but he wasn't a seer."

"But?"

"Yes. But. He was an obsessive contingency planner. We spent hours every week brainstorming contingencies."

"Uhm?" I understood that. We'd done a lot of it when I was still a handsome young Marine making sure the wicked Venagetan hordes didn't come suck the life and spirit and soul out of the king's favorite subjects. Most of whom weren't sure who the king was that week.

"He thought well of you."

"And I'm sure I'm not glad to hear that." We were back to my obligation to Chodo Contague because he'd been so good to me. Whether or not I wanted it.

"His contingencies usually ended up with him or me calling you in to restore the balance."

"Restore the balance?"

"His words. Not mine."

"Have you seen him lately?" I hadn't.

"No. And it was an accident, last time I did. I went out to the estate and just walked in. Like I always did. The guards didn't stop me. I'd done it for years and Belinda hadn't said to keep me out. She wasn't happy, but she was polite. And uncooperative. I didn't actually get to see Chodo up close. I got to watch Belinda pretend to ask him if he felt up to talking business. She told me she was sorry I'd wasted the trip. Her daddy felt too sick to work today. Could I come back some other time? Better yet, how about he came to my place next time he was in the city?"

"And he's never showed up."

"You *are* good."

"I'm a trained detective. Where does that leave us?"

"Here's the thing."

Gods, I hate it when people say that. It guarantees that everything to come will be weasel words. "Umh?"

"Belinda is in and out of town all the time. When she does come in she doesn't leave Chodo behind. Somebody might see him without her standing in between. I found out by spying. By lying in wait, hoping to get to him while she was away."

"Dangerous business."

"Yes."

"The woman isn't stupid."

"Crazy, yes. Stupid, no. She brings him in and stashes him."

"That could be handled by having somebody see when she comes in and find out where she drops him."

Temisk chewed his lower lip.

"You've tried that."

"Yes. And lost the man I hired. I'm lucky he didn't know who I was, anymore. I might've lost me, too."

I tried to recollect someone in my racket turning up dead or missing recently. There aren't many of us. On the other hand, ours isn't a well-known and respected profession like palm reader or potion maker. "Anyone I'd know?"

"No. He was an old soak named Billy Mul Tima who used to run numbers on the north side. I gave him little jobs when I could. He worked hard for Chodo before he got into the sauce too far."

So there I was, snoot to snoot with a crisis, getting a face full of Fortune's bad breath. A cusp. A turning point. An instant when I had to make a moral choice.

I resisted the easy one. And said not one word about a lawyer with a heart, and, more remarkably, a conscience. "Tell me about it."

"There isn't much to tell. I gave Billy Mul what I could and sent him off. I assume he bought all the cheap wine he could carry, then got to work."

"Wino would be a good cover. They're everywhere. And nobody pays attention. Go on."

"They found him in a room on the north side a few days later, after he started to stink. He'd burned to death."

I frowned. For a year there have been reports of people burning up without benefit of a fire, always in some slum on the north side.

"Garrett, he burned to death without setting fire to the place where he died. Which was about as awful a tenement as you can imagine."

I can imagine some pretty awful places. I've visited a lot of them. Especially back when my clientele wasn't quite so genteel. "Somebody brought him there."

"No. I went up there myself. I talked to people. Even the Watch. He burned right where they found him. Cooked down like a chunk of burned fat. Without getting hot enough to start a bigger fire."

That jibed with stories I'd heard about other burning deaths. "How could that happen? Sorcery?"

"That would be everybody's first guess, wouldn't it?"

"Always is when an explanation isn't obvious. We're conditioned by long, direct, dire exposure to those idiots on the Hill."

Sorcery, great or small, isn't part of daily life. But the threat of sorcery is. The potential for sorcery is. Particularly dark sorcery. Because our true rulers are the wizards who infest the mansions on the Hill.

I said, "You don't think sorcery is the answer."

"Those kind of people don't show up in that part of town."

A self-taught rogue set on becoming a one-man crime wave might, though. But how would he profit from burning winos?

"It's not a part of town where humans show up much, is it? Isn't that Elf Town?"

"No. But right on its edge. It's mainly nonhuman immigrant housing now. Here's the thing, though. The building belonged to Chodo."

I nodded and waited.

"When I went up I thought it looked familiar. I dug into the records when I got back. We bought the place four years ago. I handled the legal stuff."

"Chodo wasn't there."

"Not when the body was found. But he might have been. People remembered a man in a wheelchair."

"Uhm?"

"I didn't take it any further. I didn't want to attract attention."

"Probably the smart thing." It's unhealthy to ask questions

near an Outfit operation. You might develop black-and-blue lumps. At the least.

Temisk asked, "Any brilliant theories?"

"Just the obvious one. Billy Mul tried to get to Chodo. Somebody made him dead for his trouble."

"How would they do that?"

"That would be the question, wouldn't it?"

"And why do it that way? Those things are done simple. Unless somebody wants to send a message."

"A burn-up wouldn't be a message anyone could read. They'd just wrinkle their noses and ask, what the hell?"

There wasn't any sense to it. Pieces of the puzzle were missing. Even its general shape wasn't apparent.

Temisk said, "One of the things Chodo paid me to do was bail him out if he got caught up in something weird. This qualifies. And he expected you to help."

"I got that part. I don't like it, but I got it. He knew me better than I know me. What're you thinking about doing?"

"I did it when I got hold of you. You're the expert."

Me. The expert. Cute.

"Then let's set some priorities. What's the most important thing to do?"

"Make sure Chodo is still alive tomorrow morning."

"Back to the birthday party?"

"Back to the party."

# 8

From Harvester Temisk's digs I ambled over to The Palms, an up-scale eatery and club operated by the dark elf Morley Dotes. My number one good buddy. I approached warily. There might be trouble with Belinda's troops if they were setting up already.

"Holy shit! Will ya look at dis? It ain't even been a week an' here it comes agin!"

It's remotely possible that not all of Morley's associates welcome me all the time. "I was passing by. Thought I'd drop in and see how you're all doing. How're you doing, Sarge?"

Sarge is fat and balding and tattooed and nastier than a bushel of scorpions when he's in a good mood. He didn't seem particularly cheerful today.

Another one enough like Sarge to be his ugly big brother, with extra scorpions, shuffled out of the kitchen. "Hey, Puddle. How's it going, man?"

Puddle brandished a commercial-weight rolling pin.

This didn't look encouraging.

Morley emerged behind Puddle. Amazing. Dotes seldom has much to do with the daily grind of his place. "What do you want, Garrett?"

"Damn, Morley. Get a sense of humor. I know a guy on the Landing. . . ."

"What do you want, Garrett?"

"Right now I'd like to know why it's hilarious when you stick me with a foul-beaked fowl like the Goddamn Parrot, but it's haul out the meat cleavers when I get you back with a nympho nymph."

Two more staffers materialized. Lugging industrial-grade

butcher's equipment. In a vegetarian establishment. "Them new-generation eggplants must be fierce." Everybody seemed intensely interested in managing a wily envelopment of their good buddy Garrett.

Not promising at all.

Dotes made a slight gesture. "One more chance, Garrett."

"I wanted to check on how things are coming, setting up for tonight. And to say hi."

"And why are you interested?"

"Because I have to be here, cabbage breath boy. I can't weasel out. And I don't feel good about the setup."

Morley glared at me. Slim and dark, handsome and always impeccably bedecked in the latest fashion, he radiates a sensuality that sets them swooning even when he strolls through a nun shop.

"You got smudge under your nose." He'd begun sporting a thin little mustache.

Morley didn't grin. "Sit down, Garrett."

I picked a chair. The one closest to the door.

Morley sat across from me. He stared. Eventually, he said, "Word's out that you're on Belinda's payroll now."

"That's a crock. Who said that?"

"Belinda. Last time she was here messing the arrangements around."

"It ain't true. You know me better. I wouldn't work for her even if I needed work. And I don't. I've got me a nice little piece of the hottest manufactory in TunFaire. You're just trolling for an excuse to get your bile up."

"She was convincing." Dotes studied me some more. Something big was bothering him and all his boys. Nobody wanted Mama Garrett's favorite boy for a friend.

"Spit it out, Morley. What's going on?"

"This party is bound to go bad. And here you come, supposedly Belinda's full-time top stud, ambling in ten minutes after your honey sends word the party won't happen here after all. The Palms will just cater. The party will happen in Whitefield Hall. Because my place isn't big enough. Too many people in the life want to pay their respects to the kingpin."

"I don't know anything about any Whitefield Hall. Is that the Veterans' Memorial hall that commemorates the War of Coady Byrne's Broken Tooth?"

Karenta had a lot of little wars over a lot of little provocations in Imperial times. Then we changed up, became a kingdom, and

jumped into one big war that lasted over a hundred years. The one
I was in. Along with every human male I know, including my
brother and father and grandfather, and Grandpa's father and
grandfather and all their brothers and cousins and bastard kids.

The killing is over now. So far, the peace has been worse than
the war.

"I don't know anything about your wars," Dotes replied. Being
half dark elf, he enjoys treaty exemption from some human laws.
Like the one establishing conscription. And he doesn't give a
feather about history. He doesn't care about last week—unless last
week might sneak up and whack him on the back of the head. "But
it is some kind of soldiers' memorial."

Morley is shallow. Morley is pretty. Morley is the nightmare
that wakes fathers screaming in the night. He's the daydream their
daughters take to bed, fantasizing. He's the bad boy the girls all
want, thinking they can tame him, before they settle for some
dullard who'll just work for a living and treat them like they're
people.

I'm so jealous.

"I can't picture it. What's special about it? Why would she
move there?"

"I told you. Because she can get more people in. Because it
isn't operated by people she doesn't trust."

"Belinda doesn't trust you?"

"Are you that naive? Of course she doesn't. Not to be what she
wants me to be."

"What would that be?"

"Her tool, fool."

"Don't start with the vegetarian poetry. It don't make sense on
a day when the sun *is* shining."

Dotes shook his pretty head. He didn't want to play. "Belinda
wouldn't trust me if I swore ten thousand ironbound oaths. That's
part of her insanity. She can't trust anybody. Except you. Probably for the same sick reason Chodo trusted you. From where I sit,
that would be because you're too damned dim to be anything but
honest."

Morley's morals and ethics are situation dependent. Which
doesn't stop him being a nice guy. Most of the time. When it's
convenient.

"Your expression of confidence warms the cockles of my
heart, Mr. Dotes."

"What does that mean? I've always wondered. What are cockles?"

"Seafood? I don't know. But it sounds good."

"I'm tempted to change my mind again."

Even so, looking sour, Sarge, Puddle, and the rest went back to work.

"This will be the event of the decade for the Outfit."

"Isn't that special?"

"You know Harvester Temisk?"

"Chodo's legal beagle? I'd recognize him if I tripped over him. That's it."

"He's still Chodo's mouthpiece. Know anything about him?"

"He played straight. For a lawyer. He was Chodo's friend since they were kids. Why?"

Sometimes the best way to handle Morley is to tell the truth. Or something approximating truth, truth being so precious you don't just give it away. Something close enough to get him to do what you want, that's the thing. "He came at me when we were putting the three-wheel company together."

"Where they give you extra profit points to stay away. I've heard about what a pain in the ass you are with your moralizing and ethics jabber."

I refused the bait. "I've got a case."

Morley loves to argue. It makes him the center of attention. "Come tell me all about it when you're done, Garrett."

"You got any idea what she plans to pull tonight?"

"No. But I'll be very careful. Very alert. Very stay in the kitchen. You might do the same. If you really must attend."

"Oh, I must. I must. Maybe I'll wear my iron underwear. You ever hear of Chodo doing anything with sorcery?"

"No. He didn't like it. Though he'd hire a hedge wizard sometimes. That's all. He resented wizards for having more direct power than he did."

"I mean himself. Personally."

"His gifts ran to murder, mayhem, and management. As a wizard he had all the talent of a tombstone."

"That's what I thought." Admitting what I was thinking. Twice. Being right up-front with my pal.

"What have you got going?"

"Temisk says strange things keep happening since Chodo's accident. I want to get a handle."

"That your case?"

"That's not what it's about. It's just something I need to understand."

"Is Temisk working you by claiming you owe Chodo?"

"Some. I need to work that out, too."

"Walk away. Stop being you. Save yourself the pain and grief."

"You know anything about these people who've been catching on fire?"

"No. That part of your case, too?"

"I don't think so. I just wondered. Never hurts to ask you something. You're full up on weird and wonderful. And sometimes, you tell me what you know."

"Weird and wonderful, he says. And he's the one shacking up with a dead thing and a talking rat."

"And Dean. And a bucket of baby cats. I think I'll bring those with me tonight. Give them away."

"There's an original idea. Giving away kittens at a mob summit. The one guy who takes one will feed it to his pet anaconda."

"An idea whose time has come. Feed all the cats to the snakes. Singe would go along."

"Then what do you do with the snakes? They like rats more than cats."

"Know anything about a street kid, calls himself Penny Dreadful?"

"I know he needs to find another name if he doesn't like being smacked around. Otherwise, no. Why?"

"He's really a girl pretending to be a boy. And Dean's source for the bucket of kittens. He has a majorly strange story about the kid."

"Strange stories about people in your life? Fie! Balderdash!"

"Sarcasm doesn't become you, sir. Considering you're one of the main people in my life. And definitely one of the strangest."

"I'm the standard against which everyone else is measured."

"You hang in there. I'll go for help." I eyed the front door, inches away. My chances of making it looked better than they had. "How's your love life?" I cackled evilly, then fled.

*Why* is another story, already told.

# 9

"Hey!"

A rock whizzed past my ear. It hit Morley's door so hard it bashed a hole in a panel.

Dotes bounced out beside me, looking ferocious. "What happened?" he asked.

"Somebody took a whack at me with a sling." I assumed. How else throw a rock that hard?

"Primitive."

"But effective if you aren't ready for it."

"Who was it? Where did he go?"

"I'm pretty sure it was that chunky guy over there. Wearing the stupid green pants. The one so busy looking nonchalant." This one looked like the runt of the Ugly Pants litter. He was hard at work pretending to be interested in the gaps between buildings and the shadows under stoops.

"Stay here. He might want you to follow him. I'll round up a crowd. He owes me a door." Dotes went back inside.

I collected the stone that, but for an instant of luck, might have knocked another hole in my noggin. You need a couple extra to get into my racket, but I wasn't prospecting for more.

The stone had a slight egg shape, being an inch and a quarter in one dimension and just under an inch in the other. It was heavy. It was green, like serpentine or low-grade jade. And it was polished. It didn't look like something a guy would pick up strolling down a creek bed.

Morley returned with some of his troops. I said, "This might be a trick to get you away from The Palms."

"I warned Sarge and Puddle. Where did he go?"

"Turned south into Ironstar Lane."

"Let's go spring the trap," Morley said. Very direct, my friend.

"You're too eager. You make me nervous when you're eager."

"I ever mention that you worry too much?"

"Only on those occasions when I'm close enough to hear you talk."

We jogged off with half a dozen guys who pretend to be servers at Morley's place, none the sort who wait tables because they love the work.

Dotes insists that he's out of the life now, yet persists in surrounding himself with men like these.

I worry, what with the dedication shown by the secret police lately. Deal Relway doesn't worry about due process. In his own mind, he *is* the law. Too often, those left behind will agree that you had it coming.

Nevertheless, the underworld goes on. As strong and committed and obsessed as Relway is, he isn't able to do much but nibble at the Outfit's peripheries.

We turned into Ironstar Lane. And came to a many-legged, confused halt.

The character who'd tried to trepan me with a stone wasn't a block ahead. He ambled along, searching shadows, like he had no idea somebody might chase him down.

"What's the game here, Garrett? That moron is toddling along like he doesn't have a care."

"You can't hold me responsible because somebody else is an idiot."

"It's arguable. Sins of the blood and all that stuff." He came close to using bad language.

I asked, "Instead of standing around debating, why don't we take advantage?"

Morley signaled his boys. We moved out.

Traffic was light, but that's normal in Ironstar Lane. There aren't any shops.

We surrounded the squat man before he realized someone was after him. His response was bewilderment. For an instant I thought I'd fingered the wrong guy. Like all of a sudden everybody in TunFaire had taken to wearing hideous green pants, and bad fashion sense wasn't a sure sign of innate villainy.

Then he charged, went right through one of Morley's boys.

"Wow!" I said.

"Yes. Be careful."

The squat man didn't run. He did make it unpleasant to get too close. At intimate range he was quicker than Morley, who, till now, had held the record. In my experience. And he was strong. He flung me thirty feet, easy.

We took turns bopping him from behind. Which was kind of like bull baiting, only this bull never made a sound. He didn't answer questions. He just fought on, emphasizing doing damage to Ma Garrett's only surviving son.

We outnumbered him only eight to one so it was our great good fortune that police whistles began squealing in nearby streets. We broke it up immediately. Nobody wanted to visit the Al-Khar. Not today.

As though there's any good day now.

"That was exhilarating," Morley said as we inventoried limbs, combed cobblestones out of our hair, and figured out who got bragging rights for suffering the biggest bruises. "If I'm alive in the morning, I'm going to give that guy another look. With Doris and Marsha doing the heavy lifting."

Doris and Marsha Roze are relatives of his. Somehow. They're part giant, part troll, part other stuff. They stand twelve feet tall and can bring down small buildings with a single pound. Too bad they weren't along a few minutes ago.

"Why not? There must be another ten thousand streets that could use a good dusting." It's rare as frog fangs to see Morley Dotes all dirty and spiffed up in rags. "I wish I could preserve this vision for posterity."

"I'll put on old clothes next time. Get back to me on this."

He was upset. I wasn't sure why. You can't win them all.

"I'll do that. Good luck tonight."

# 10

"What happened?" Dean demanded as he let me into the house.

"Somebody tried to kill me."

He grunted, unimpressed.

"You should see the other guy."

He grunted again. He has no respect for my way of life, though it keeps him full of bread and beans.

"Not a scratch on him. Even though I had Morley and six of his guys there lending a hand. We would've turned it around, though, if the Watch hadn't shown up."

That was for Singe's benefit. She'd come to the kitchen to find out what was up. She had a kitten in her paws, petting it. The baby cat didn't mind the incongruity.

I asked, "Think you could pick up a day-old trail using this?" I tossed her the green egg.

"Gak! Underwater. What was it? A bear or an ogre?"

Singe has a talent.

Ratpeople are blessed with an exceptional sense of smell. Some can embarrass a bloodhound. Singe stands out of that crowd.

As noted, she's a genius. For a ratwoman. And has more courage than ten other ratpeople put together. Excluding only her brother.

Even the most daring and wicked ratfolk get scared around humans. The sorcerers who created them saw no need to take that timidity out.

"He was human. From one of the far fringes of the species."

"What did he do?"

"He tried to kill me. With an old-fashioned sling. Using that egg for ammunition."

"Bathing would not appear to be one of his human vices."

I told Dean, "That tongue gets more wicked every day."

Dean scowled. He can't shed all his prejudices. Singe bounced, though, pleased by the compliment. She has one great character flaw. She tries hard to be human.

She's smart enough to know they'll never let her be.

"Why a day-old trail?"

"I don't have time today. I have Chodo's birthday party to do."

"Who are you taking? Tinnie?"

"Nobody."

"Can I go?"

"No. I'm not taking anybody. It could get ugly fast. I don't want anybody getting hurt." Not to mention that she wouldn't be welcome. Virulent prejudice can be ignored only at great peril. Particularly by persons of goodwill.

Singe knows that on the practical and emotional levels. She doesn't let on when she gets her feelings hurt. She thinks that by revealing her feelings, she'd belittle my effort to save her some pain.

I know. But it works for us.

I asked, "Anything stirring on the undead front?"

If the Dead Man hates any one thing enough to almost let it get his blood pumping, it's being lumped with the undead. Vampires, zombies, and whatnot are all predators. He insists that he isn't.

"Not a sign," Dean said. "Looks like he's down for a while this time."

That wasn't good news. I could use some advice. Like maybe the top ten ways of surviving Chodo's shindig, barring the obvious: Don't show up.

When you have no choice about hiking the valley of the shadow, you need to brainstorm ways to cover your ass. I got busy.

I had options. I had connections. Some might even be useful.

Singe's brother, for example.

I recalled a conversation with Morley about the truth of what I mean to Belinda Contague. Not the business meaning. Not the former-lover meaning, nor the outright-fear meaning. The symbolic or fetishist meaning to the secret, frightened little girl hidden way down deep inside Miss Belinda. The little girl who, Morley believed, wanted me for the daddy she hadn't had when she was coming up because her real daddy was Chodo Contague, hardly a paragon as a parent.

I've rescued the woman, one way or another, from the deepest shit several times. Morley says she's chosen me as the bellwether of her personal fortunes because of that. That she'll never let me be hurt because the little girl needs Daddy Garrett out there in case another terror closes in.

"Singe. I've got an idea. Maybe a dumb one. Come in the office and help me brainstorm."

"What's up?" she asked, hissing like a sack of rattlers as she forced the contraction.

"You think your brother might help us with something? If we offer him an appropriate fee? I know! I know! But you had the same mother. Humans figure that makes him your brother."

John Stretch—real name, Pound Humility—is the boss of the ratpeople in my part of TunFaire. He's top rat partly thanks to me. He's Singe's half brother from an earlier litter. They have a stronger relationship than most related ratfolk. He tried to rescue her from my clutches one time. She spanked him verbally and told him to go the hell away—she was happy right where she was.

"I do not know. He suspects that you took advantage of him last time."

"I understand a pride problem. You know better than me if we can do business."

"What do you want him to do?"

"This party tonight. He could help me with it. If he really talks to regular rats."

Singe considered. We both knew John Stretch could get inside the minds of regular rats and use them as spies. He had admitted it in front of us.

"You want him to go over to the place where Chodo Contague's birthday party is going to happen."

"Yes." But now my idea was growing up. "If we could hide him close by, he could stay on the job right through the party and warn me so there wouldn't be any ugly surprises."

"You might not be able to meet his price."

"I'm not hurting for cash."

"He will not ask for cash."

I groaned. "A favor for a favor."

"What use can you be to a ratman gangster?"

A human agent could be very useful to a rat king who knew what he wanted.

"You want me to find him? You do not have a lot of time."

In fact, it was too late. Almost certainly. Nevertheless, "See what you can do."

Singe was ready to go in minutes. I told her, "Leave the kitten. It won't be welcome where you're headed."

She returned the critter to the bucket. "They grow on you."

"So do lice. Don't get too attached. They aren't staying."

I let Singe out right into a major pixie squabble. Those bugs are worse than sparrows. But they're so constant about it that I don't much notice anymore.

I told them, "I want to talk to Shakespear and Melondie Kadare, please." Polite helps a little. Sometimes. Unpredictably. About as often as it does with big people.

If I couldn't get ratpeople help, I might enlist some pixies. Which would be cheaper, anyway, since helping me is how they're supposed to pay their rent.

Melondie Kadare came out, a gorgeous specimen of pixie womanhood. Sadly, pixies live fast. Melondie will hit middle age in about six months. She was a typically obnoxious adolescent when I met her, a month ago. Now she was a woman of standing in her nest.

She piped, "Shakespear isn't here anymore, Garrett. He married a Daletripses. He decided to join her nest."

Pixie clusters are strongly matrilineal. Most times the boys follow the girls.

"Congratulations. I guess. That's an important connection." My pixies are newcomers to TunFaire. Refugees. The Daletripses cluster is an old line, as local pixie tribes go. A marital alliance would serve my tenants well. "Though I thought that you and he . . ."

"Let's not talk about that. I have a husband of my own now. And he don't like hearing about the good old days."

"I'm sorry. If that's the appropriate sentiment."

"Not to worry. He's a little stupid, a lot lazy, and way too jealous, but I'll whip him into shape."

Marriage doesn't take the same form with pixies. Passion is unimportant. Forging alliances and preserving estates are. Passion gets indulged on the side. In some clusters a girl isn't marriage material unless she's demonstrated her fertility with several merrybegots.

"I want to know if I can get some help with a case."

"Hey! We've got to pay the rent, don't we?"

"It might be dangerous."

"Talk to me, Garrett."

I told my story.

"So you have a history with the Contagues."

"More than one."

"Better tell me about that, then. It could have an impact on how decisions are made at the head table."

Belinda wouldn't let sentiment hamstring business decisions. She was harder than her father. And Chodo seldom let emotion get in the way.

"This hall, Garrett. Where this will happen. Is it far out of our territory?"

"You know where the Bledsoe is? The charity hospital? That whole area was all government buildings in olden times. When the Empire was in charge. The hall is over there. It was something else before they turned it into a war memorial. They were more frugal in the old days."

"Are there any pixies around there? Or anybody else who might think we're trespassing?"

TunFaire is a hundred cities piled onto the same hapless patch of dirt, a different one for every race. Some peoples are so different, their TunFaires scarcely intersect. More often, they do, and only us big, numerous types don't need to invest in getting along. We can be as awful as we want to be. And usually are.

"I don't know. I only just found out that the shindig is moving there from Morley's place. I haven't been in that part of town since somebody got me committed to the crazy ward at the Bledsoe."

"That must've been an adventure. How'd you lie your way out? Convince them you were sane?"

"I convinced them I was so crazy they didn't want me there."

"There isn't much time. You'll have to take us with you when you go. Keeping us out of sight."

That wouldn't work. I couldn't walk for miles lugging a carpetbag full of squabbling pixies.

Melondie read my mind. So to speak. "Don't be such a cheapass, Garrett. Hire a coach. We can get there unseen. And you can show up without looking like a refugee yourself."

Everybody nags me about the way I dress.

Nobody believes me if I poor-mouth. They all think I'm rich. Just because I have those points in the three-wheel factory.

Melondie's idea was sound. "Can somebody fly a note to Playmate's stable?" My friend Playmate doesn't have a coach of his own, but he can come up with one at a moment's notice, usually. And I like to give my business to friends. Plus, as a bonus, Playmate is about nine feet tall and handy to have around when a debate turns physical.

"I suppose." She wasn't enthusiastic. Long-distance flights are risky for pixies. Too many things out there think they look like food.

"Excellent. I'll write one up and we can get the circus moving."

I spied Singe returning. A couple human kids were giving her a hard time. I didn't go chase them. She wouldn't like that. She wants to fight her own battles.

Melondie had none of my problems. She whistled into the gap her tribe uses to get in and out of my walls. A half dozen adolescent bugs zipped out and hummed down the street. They got behind the human kids' heads and started tormenting them.

Singe arrived. "John Stretch says he will be thrilled to help the great Garrett with a case. He insists that he bring his own rats instead of relying on those that will be in place already, though."

"Fine. I'm sending a note to Playmate to bring a coach."

"You changed your mind!"

"Don't go getting all excited. You'll stay inside it. You'll help John Stretch run his game."

# 11

Playmate brought a huge mahogany coach. It had to belong to somebody from way up the food chain. "This isn't going to be missed, is it?"

"Not unless we don't let it get back before the end of the week." Playmate jumped down to help load. "I'm more worried about getting blood all over it. Or leaving a corpse inside."

"That wasn't my fault. You need to take a more positive attitude."

"Familiarity with the Garrett experience suggests that guarded pessimism is the safer approach."

Playmate is a huge black man who looms even huger than he is.

He's bigger than me, stronger than me, and almost as handsome. His big shortcoming is that he's a wannabe preacher who isn't as mean as he looks. Who isn't *really* nine feet tall. But seven feet wouldn't be out of the question.

"You're sure?" I could see where a crest had been removed from the coach door. "I don't want some stormwarden stomping me because his coach isn't there when he decides to go for a ride."

"Want me to take it back?"

"That's all right. I was just checking. What's this?"

A goat cart stopped behind the coach. No goat was employed in its locomotion, though. A ratman had put himself into the traces.

Singe's brother. With a load of wooden cages filled with large, brown, unhappy rats. "Am here," John Stretch said. His Karentine wasn't as polished as his sister's.

"Let's get those critters into the coach, then."

"Where is Singe?"

"Taking her good sweet time getting ready. You sure you can manage this?"

"Will have Singe to help. And them. Yes?" Pixies swarmed into the coach like Melondie meant to bring all her friends and relations.

Playmate remarked, "You're looking pretty good there, Garrett. Did you hire a consultant to dress you up?"

I spread my arms to the sky. "You see the torments I suffer? Take me home now."

Singe came fluttering out of the house, a young woman running late. Though how you get behind when your wardrobe is as limited as hers, I don't know. But what I know about women, even limiting the sample to my own tribe, would fit in a thimble with room left over for a brigade of dancing angels.

Singe brought the kittens with her. She piled into the coach.

"We're ready," I told Playmate. I glanced at the goat cart. "John Stretch, you'll lose your cart if you just leave it there."

"No problem. Is not my cart."

Great. So now the Watch would find a stolen goat cart in front of my house. Because, with my luck, the damned thing would sit there undisturbed for six months if it took that long to embarrass me.

I clambered aboard the coach.

Total silence reigned inside.

The pixies warily split their attention between the baby cats and the rat cages. The baby cats peeked out of their bucket, intrigued by the bug people and the rats. The rats glared at everybody.

What should have become chaos on the hoof declined into inexplicable relaxation.

"Well," I said, relaxed myself, despite what lay ahead. "How about that?"

The pixies found perches. They gossiped. They didn't squabble and they didn't bother the rats. Normally, given half a chance, they would've swarmed any rodent. A plump rat could provide the main course for a huge feast.

Singe couldn't control the kittens, though. Several got away and began investigating everything. Without bothering the rats or bugs. They were remarkably well-mannered, for cats.

As we turned into Wizard's Reach I glimpsed a familiar face

outside. It belonged to the man Morley and I had had the misfortune to catch earlier. He was watching my house. From a bruised visage.

His presence made me nervous. If he got obnoxious and kicked my door in, the Dead Man would be no help at all.

I couldn't turn back. I'd have to trust the process. A notion I find dubious in the best of times.

My neighbor Mrs. Cardonlos is a police spy. And, possibly, a friend of Mr. Deal Relway, director of what, this week, is called something like the Unpublished Committee for Royal Security. Mrs. Cardonlos' great pleasure in life is spying on me and imagining my life being more exciting than it is. Relway pays her a small stipend.

She'd keep an eye out while I was gone. The most interesting stuff happens at my place when I'm not home. That's when the stupid shines. That's when the unprepared find out that they should've done more research.

The Dead Man has fun with stupid thugs.

My partner can be as cruel as a cat with an unbreakable mouse.

But, oh, woe! He was on a sleeping holiday today.

"What kind of kittens are those?" I wondered out loud. They looked like basic gray stripy alley lurkers, but not quite. They were odd. However, all I know about cats is that I like them better than dogs, except maybe beagle and sausage dog puppies.

Oh, wondrous day! Singe and John Stretch both actually understood that I didn't expect an answer. Both looked like they expected praise for being that clever.

I nodded and smiled my approval.

Speaking of pixies, which I wasn't, "Melondie. Did you guys get into some poison, or something? I've never heard you all so quiet."

Miss Kadare fluttered over a tad drunkenly. She assumed a widespread stance on my left palm, hands on hips, wobbling, not in time to the coach's rocking.

"You been drinking?" Pixies love alcohol.

"Not a drop." She staggered, plopped down on her tiny but gorgeous behind.

"You *are* drunk!" I accused.

"No way!" she snapped. Then she giggled. "I don't know what's happened. I was fine when we flew in here."

The other pixies were drunk, too. Most more so than Melondie Kadare.

I nudged a curious kitten away from a male pixie who had fallen to the coach floor and lay there on his back, buzzing occasionally, like a downed locust.

It was weird. But I had trouble giving a rat's ass. I was mellow, at peace. Without personal ambition whatsoever.

Some acquaintances would insist that was nothing new.

Singe and John Stretch seemed vaguely puzzled and sleepy. Ditto, the rats.

I never heard of a drunk spell, but that didn't mean one couldn't exist. It only meant that I'd never been hit by one before.

The pixies passed out. I started suffering urges to sing the Marine Corps hymn or something similarly patriotic. Which don't hit me when I get snockered the hard way. Not often.

The coach suddenly bucked, jolted to a halt. What the hell? Traffic couldn't be that bad. Could it?

I was two heartbeats away from falling asleep when Playmate yanked the door open. "We're here. Huh? What's the matter with you all?"

I extended a hand. He helped me descend as elegantly as a duchess. Good man he, he did the same with John Stretch and Pular Singe while deftly keeping the kittens from getting away.

He closed the door on the pixies and baby cats. "What I'm going to do now is, I'm going to stay right here. I'll come in and pull you out if something bad happens."

That said a ton about Playmate.

"That's white of you, Play. I'll be more relaxed in there, knowing you'll rescue me if I need it."

Playmate had nothing more to say. His eyes had begun to wobble. Meantime, I was recovering. Fast.

I was way early in arriving. Even so, several coaches were lined up beside the hall already, each cared for by somebody big and dumb and covered with scars. And with tattoo collections for seasoning. They stared at my companions and their cages filled with rats.

"Round up those kittens, Singe." The drunk was gone. Just that fast.

"You want to take them inside?"

"Oh, hell yeah. They're going to be all over in there."

These kittens did not behave like cats. They weren't contrary. They let themselves be caught and tucked into their bucket, with the cloth folded over them, theoretically to keep them in. Only a couple had to be caught and tucked a second time.

"How many of these monsters are there?" I asked Singe. I couldn't get a hard count. Hasty estimates during the day had ranged from four to nine. Since even a dead cat can create havoc in two places at once, I suspected the true number was closer to four.

Singe said, "Five or six. It's hard to tell because their markings are so alike."

It didn't matter. As long as I had the majority with me when I went in.

As I approached the goons checking invitations, I tried to work out why I thought I should go armed with baby cats.

I guess because I hoped nobody would stay belligerent with a gang of them underfoot.

One of the goons asked, "The hell you luggin' a pail a pussy for, slick?"

"Somebody might want a kitten. I got some to adopt out." I saluted him with my pussy pail and strolled on into Whitefield Hall.

# 12

Belinda had a second goon squad set up behind an inverted L of tables inside the front entrance. Clever girl, she'd made sure these guys weren't beholden to her. They were freelancers. Saucerhead Tharpe was one. I recognized two of his three companions, Orion Comstock and June Nicolist. Both had reputations much like Tharpe's. Absolutely neutral.

"Garrett."

"Mr. Tharpe." I've known him for years, but his real first name escaped me. No matter. He prefers Saucerhead.

"Anything to declare?"

"Eh?"

"Weapons. Of any sort. You got 'em, you got to declare 'em. You don't got to surrender 'em, though we'd rather you did. You do, June gives you one of them beautiful scarves. You collect your tools when you leave." June held up a bright green kerchief. He had a pile handy, and a grin that betrayed teeth of the same shade. Saucerhead said, "That'll mark you safe."

"All right. Give me a hankie. This's all I've got. One bucket of cats." One bucket of remarkable cats. There was something wrong with them. Any other litter would have staged several jailbreaks by now.

Saucerhead eyed the kittens. He looked at me. "You're serious."

"As a dose of typhoid." I needed to move on. I had to fix up some way for Melondie Kadare to sneak inside.

Tharpe asked, "You didn't even bring your knobknocker?"

"Nope. Nothing but my own bare hands."

Saucerhead sighed. "You may be sorry."

"I'm a trained Royal Marine."

"You used to be. Here." He handed me a yellow kerchief instead of letting June give me a green one.

"Yellow, huh?"

"It don't mean nothing. Green and yellow was what was the cheapest."

"What keeps a guy from just stuffing the hankie in his pocket?"

"Nothing. Except that you should be wearing it."

He waved me past. I proceeded to hunt for a window to crack. Behind me, Saucerhead's pals expressed doubts about me being the famous Garrett.

I was still looking for a window when I spied a plump brown rat. The critter took time out to stop and wink.

Once I jiggered a window, Melondie and her swarm wobbled inside and fluttered around, finding places to hide. Nobody noticed. Everybody focused on a screeching knock-down-drag-out about table setups. I shut the window, grabbed my bucket, went looking for the hostess and guest of honor.

I heard scurryings in the walls and floors and the hum of little wings overhead.

I glanced back. Somebody I didn't know was suffering through Saucerhead's checkpoint.

Maybe Tharpe did do me a favor. He never patted me down like that. Though if I wanted to sneak something in, I would've hidden it under a stack of docile baby cats.

Whitefield Hall had been slapped together with nothing but function in mind. It was mainly an open floor where you could dance, hold a banquet, have a grand meeting, put on a play, do anything you wanted to do without having to endure a lot of weather. Nowadays plays were the big thing.

Plays are a big thing around town, period. Drama is the latest fad.

The memorial commission also rented the hall for private functions. Like wedding receptions. Or birthday parties for underclass personalities who loom large in city life.

The floor had enjoyed loving care forever but remembered generations of feet shod in working-class shoes. The ceiling was twenty feet high. There were tilt windows up there so you could let the heat out in summer—or whenever there were too many bodies jammed into the hall. There was a stage at the end opposite the main entrance, facing it from a hundred feet away, three feet higher than the floor. Bickering workmen dragged tables in through a door to the left of the stage.

The two directing setup might have been chosen for their devotion to stereotype. Their wrists were limper than a dead octopus's arms. They bullied one another like a pair of harebrained girls. Still, there's hardly an adult male human today who isn't tough. Anybody over twenty-four had what it took to get through five years of wartime service with his ass still attached. Including this squawking brace of fancies.

The guys doing the actual work were the sort you don't offend gratuitously. They didn't have half a neck between them. If their shirts got ripped off by a freak wind, they'd show more body hair than cave bears. They probably had trouble recognizing their own names in print even if you gave them two weeks' head start.

Our hostess made her appearance through the doorway to the right of the stage, from the kitchen area. She wasn't dressed for the occasion. Yet.

"Garrett. You sweet man. You came early."

Strange. My eyes didn't roll up inside my head. I didn't drool. No gush of nonsense syllables erupted from my mouth. I didn't forget she was deadly and dangerous. Maybe I was immune. Finally.

Belinda Contague is a tall, slim woman in her mid-twenties, as beautiful as you can imagine a woman to be. Her hair, as ever, was absolute black, with sheen. Her skin she'd whitened whiter than ivory, I hoped with makeup rather than arsenic. Her eyes were so blue I suspected cosmetic sorcery. Her lips were the color of arterial blood. She has serious emotional problems.

And all this before she put herself together for the evening.

"I had to be early. I heard there'll be some unsavory characters showing up. Have you lost weight?"

"You noticed. You are a good man. Yes. A few pounds."

Too many pounds, I thought. She was gaunt. Another indication of internal problems?

She was in a positive mood. That's always good.

She said, "I need to get Keron and Arnot focused on their work. They shouldn't bring personal problems with them." She gave me a peck on the cheek. It was one of her specials. It told me she'd gladly put it somewhere else. "Then I'll have the technical staff try to turn me into something presentable."

"You're a step or two beyond that already."

"Hardly. Wait till you see. You won't be able to resist."

"Go. Do what you need to do. And don't blame yourself if you find out that I've turned into an old man."

"Why do you have a pail of kittens? Are they dead? I guess not. One just winked at me."

"You know Dean. He took in a litter. I brought them because I had this crazy notion somebody might want one." A mad idea, indeed. Most people looking for free cats are furriers, violin makers, or those guys who turn up at the edge of crowds, selling pigs in a blanket and other theoretically meat-based products of mysterious provenance.

Belinda shrugged, then set sail toward the two men trying to set up according to two different plans.

The squabbling ceased instantly, and was heard no more. The two clowns turned almost as pale as Belinda herself.

You could look her in the eye and know, absolutely, that you were nose to nose with swift, remorseless death. There would be no appeals, no continuances, no stays, no reprieves, no commutations, no mercy. This death no more cared for your soul or emotions than it did for those of a roach.

Chodo had had that knack, too. But he'd indulged in random acts of commutation. All of which had worked out in the long run.

Where *was* the old man?

Melondie Kadare dropped onto my shoulder. "You're a real bright candle, aren't you?"

"What did I do now?"

"You shut the window after you let us in. We need to come and go. Unless you're figuring on getting reports from the rat king through divine inspiration."

"Oh. Yeah." I hadn't thought that part through. But I'm not used to deploying a special-needs entourage. "I'll fix it. Have you seen an old man in a fancy wheelchair, looks like he might be dead?"

"No. The rats might have. They're all over. Ask John Stretch."

"I can take a hint."

"Really? Amaze me."

Is that a female thing? A youth thing? Or am I just a lightning rod for cynicism and sarcasm?

I cracked the same window a few inches, then roamed around trying to spot villainy before it happened. And looked for Chodo. I wanted to see what Belinda planned to roll out.

Melondie Kadare buzzed up behind my right ear. "When are you going to open that window, ace?"

"I just did, bug. You were there. You saw me."

"Oh. Yeah. I did, didn't I? Well, it ain't open no more, stud. And Aliki Nadkarni wants in."

She was right. Some moron had closed the window. I opened it, then headed for the kitchen.

I didn't get there. Melondie brought her henchwoman's report about what John Stretch had heard from his rats. Wouldn't it be grand to leave out the middlepixies and middleratfolk? Where could I get a fast lesson in conversational rat?

The information was good, considering. It gave me a fair idea of the layout, including more than I wanted to know about odors in the basements and under the building where there were no basements.

I learned where Chodo was stashed. A dark pie pantry, halfway underground. Like an idiot cousin who had to be kept out of sight so he wouldn't embarrass the family.

Nobody paid attention to anyone who was inside already. You must be all right. You'd been checked out. I could go anywhere I wanted.

Melondie Kadare caught up as I headed for Chodo's hiding place. "That window is closed again, Big Boy. You want to do something about that? Like jamming it in its frame?"

I set my pail of cats down. "You guys wait here." Like I thought they'd stay put. Just because their behavior had been exemplary. From the human point of view.

Hello, Garrett. The relationship between cats and people has just one dimension: the value to the cat, at a given moment, of a handy set of opposable thumbs.

I opened the window, stood back, waited. Pixies zipped in and out. Rats slunk along the base of the wall. Or rattled around inside it. No one else noticed.

One of the setup queens came by, spotted the window. "Darn it! Who keeps opening this thing?"

"I do. And I'm not in a charitable mood. Next time I find it closed I'll throw somebody through it. You get the picture?"

The young man looked willing to fight. Briefly. "It's too darned cold. . . ." His belligerence faded. I'd been about to recommend a place he could go if he wanted to warm up. But the window suddenly wasn't worth a fight.

A kitten mewed and started climbing my pants.

Even when they're little their claws are sharp. "What're you doing? Hell. I guess the honeymoon is over."

My bucket had sprung a leak. Baby cats were everywhere. Thirty or forty of them, it looked like. I steeled myself for a blowup.

It didn't come. Nobody seemed upset. They *were* weird cats. They never made anybody jump or stumble.

The skinny gink with the window fetish went back to his tables. Still without feuding with his partner.

# 13

I went back to hunting the man whose birthday was the excuse for the gathering.

I stole a candle, lit it, slipped into the pie pantry. There he was, slumped in a wheelchair, looking two decades older. "These aren't the best circumstances," I told him. There was barely room for all of us and the wheelchair. "But I promised Harvester Temisk that I'd do what I could. That guy is your best friend." Near as I could tell. A few years in my racket will leave a saint cynical about the motives of nuns. Too many people don't have a pimple of conscience to slow them down.

Chodo did not move, twitch, or demonstrate any awareness of my presence.

A kitten did meow nearby. I took that to be a good omen. But there was a scurry as a rat took an opposing view.

"I wish there was a way to tell if your mind is alive in there. But I can't get you away someplace where we could work on it."

Speaking of out, there my candle went.

I headed over where there was enough light to see while I relit the candle. Somebody hustled past, duck waddling with a huge pot.

"Smells good," I told him.

He clomped onward, dead silent. I don't think he agreed.

There was a lot of new racket as the catering crew arrived. I wouldn't have much more time with Chodo.

I ducked back into the pie pantry. "You didn't sneak away when you had the chance." Chodo hadn't done anything but breathe. Which was good. Real good. Because, all of a sudden, I had an awful spooky feeling.

Something wasn't right. And I didn't know how to make sense of it. Or figure out what it was.

I dropped to my knees so I could look Chodo in the eyes. They were open. They blinked. But they weren't seeing anything. They weren't blinking out messages. I told him to blink once for yes and twice for no, then asked questions. He blinked yes at random.

Was his brain alive at all? Temisk thought so, but I saw no evidence here. If I had him stashed somewhere safe, I could study and experiment on him. Or I could take him home and put him in with the Dead Man. Old Bones would wake up someday.

Yelling broke out not far off. Time to get back on the job. One last experiment, though. To see if he felt anything. "Nothing personal here, Chief." I touched the candle flame to the outside of his left wrist.

The pie pantry filled up with burned-hair smell.

Chodo did nothing. I could've roasted him whole if I wanted.

Voices were almost close enough to be understood.

The candle went out. *Snap!* That sudden, without a breath of air in motion.

A shriek came from the kitchen.

"Got to go, Boss."

Burned-hair and burned-meat smells hit me. In the scullery I found people standing around a smoldering rat. But the screaming came from the kitchen proper. Voices yelled the sort of things people do in an emergency where nobody knows what should be done, but everybody wants somebody to do something.

The burned-flesh smell was stronger there. I heard a crackle like bacon frying.

Water flew through the air. A slim tide washed my toes, then receded. The crackle of bacon lost its zeal.

People made unhappy noises. I recognized some as part-time kitchen help of Morley's. "Out of the way!" I barked. "If you're not doing something useful, change your luck by getting the hell out of the way."

I got through. Somebody calmer than most had rolled a heavy woman in wet tablecloths. A couple guys kept dousing her with water. She kept screaming. She was on fire under those wraps, somehow. The bacon sizzle was all her. Buckets of water rapidly slowed that down.

Morley appeared. "What's happening?"

I shook my head and shrugged, then nudged a couple men

who were supposed to be setting tables. "Hoist her into the tub where the beer kegs are cooling. After the kegs are out."

That bacon crackle was coming back.

The woman never stopped screaming.

She went into the ice bath as Belinda Contague arrived. The woman went silent as the fire finally died. She would hurt for a long time, though, if she was burned as badly as I suspected.

Belinda eased close. "What happened?"

"I don't know. It started before I got here. Looks like she caught on fire somehow." I raised my voice. "Anybody see how this started?"

"People don't catch on fire, Garrett." She didn't sound convinced, though.

"Check her out. Tell me I'm wrong." They lifted the woman out of the ice bath. She was unconscious. The crackling didn't start up again.

A short man in an apron, with nervous hands, told us, "I was here first. Because she started yelling. She was beating on herself. I thought she'd caught her clothes on fire. I wrapped the wet table-cloths around her."

Naturally. No witnesses to how it started. The stoves? It was a kitchen setting up to serve a banquet. "Belinda, you got a healer laid on? She'll need a shitload of help."

The Contagues' underworld reign is characterized by care for its foot soldiers. Those who keep faith find the Boss looking out for them in the crunch. Chodo understood two-way loyalty instinctively. He took care of his people and they took care of him. Belinda stuck to the precedent.

She told me, "I'll have her cared for. What was that?"

"What was what?"

"I thought I saw a rat."

"You're in the city now. They haven't caused any trouble."

Belinda kept toward the pie pantry. She wanted to check on her father, but she didn't want to be seen doing it.

She eased away. I paid no attention. The burned woman was being stripped. A challenge. Bits of clothing had become embedded in her flesh. The burned fabric seemed to have acted as wicks for burning off body fat.

Weird. Creepy. Yet the physical evidence couldn't be denied.

A couple kittens seemed extremely interested in the burned woman. They kept darting out to sniff her and touch her with their paws.

Belinda was back. "What do you want to happen here?" I asked. She looked mad enough to chew rocks.

"Get her over to the Bledsoe? Find out her family situation? I don't know. Why do I have to worry about this stuff?"

"Because it's your party. Because you're in charge. Because you're the one who's going to get blamed."

Belinda indulged in a bout of creative linguistics, then demanded, "Why doesn't somebody do something about the rats?"

# 14

I went back to the main hall. Progress had been made. A couple dozen thugs had accumulated on the safe side of Saucerhead Tharpe. The little fellows had them help set tables.

My window remained cracked. I went to it. In moments I had a pixie woman ornamenting my shoulder. "What news, Melondie?"

"There's something going on, for sure. Your vampire woman may not be the worst schemer."

"Oh?"

"That's from Singe. She heard it from John Stretch. Who got it from his rats. That's a long chain full of feeble links."

"You're getting contemplative."

"I'm getting worried. Everybody thinks some people might not survive the celebration."

"Really?"

"Would I make this stuff up?"

"When Belinda's father took charge he held a do so the differences between neighborhood bosses could be settled. They were. He got rid of underbosses who might cause trouble later. By bashing their heads in with a centaur tribal mace."

A minor numbers man called Squint Vrolet approached me. "Who you talking to, Garrett?" He wore the perpetually suspicious expression of a man too dim to grasp the whole picture— though he did manage the numbers on his patch honestly and well. He had the territory from his cousin Green Bean Ractic. Green Bean killed two birds with one rockhead. He found a relative a job and he put the patch in the hands of a guy who didn't have imagination enough to skim.

Squint Vrolet didn't even have imagination enough to take advantage of the fact that he was a known gangster.

"I talk to myself, Squint. Because I know somebody who cares is listening."

Squint squinted. It was his signature move. "That's right. You don't got that frickin' parrot no more? Them elves done conned you out of him."

"Somebody ran a con on somebody, Squint. So what's your take on tonight? Is it true, Chodo's gonna retire and leave everything to his kid?"

Squint gawked. "I never heard that. Hey! Great to see you, G. But I got to go see a man about a dog." He headed straight for his cousin Green Bean instead of the garderobes, though.

Melondie Kadare told me, "That was mean, Garrett."

"When he comes to double-check if he heard right, I'll twist it around."

"Why torment him?"

"I'm not. I'm messing with Green Bean. He'll be sure Squint heard something important but got it twisted between his ears and his mouth."

"That's still cruel."

"Don't you do that to me?"

"No."

"You sure?"

"Sure, I'm sure. I can think of more amusing ways to mess with you. One of your sweeties drops by. Say, Tinnie Tate. I slide in and whisper some other honey's name in the redhead's ear at just the right time. . . ."

"That don't sound like fun."

"Not for you. I'd laugh till I puked and my wings fell off. Tinnie's too good for you, anyway. . . . Whoa! Peace! Just teasing. You'd better mingle. So that something unexpected doesn't happen."

"You might think about getting in the psychic racket."

Belinda turned. She'd changed clothes again, to something more businesslike. "I sent that woman to the Bledsoe. Under my name. Would you check on her tomorrow? Make sure they're really treating her?"

"Sure." So she expected me to have a tomorrow. Good to know.

"What do you think happened?" she asked.

"I don't. I've never seen anything like it."

"You think there's something strange going on?"

"Is that a trick question?"

"Garrett, don't do that. I'm not in the mood. I feel this getting out of hand before it even starts."

"All right, yes. There's something strange going on. I just figured you were behind it."

"There're rats everywhere. There weren't any when I looked at the place. And there's your kittens. Cute and friendly buggers, but still cats. You shouldn't have brought them. And, I swear, I even saw pixies from the corner of my eye. Only they weren't there when I looked."

That was the essence of pixie. Delivering more annoyance than a gaggle of mosquitoes.

"Watch my back, Garrett."

"I always do."

"Why?"

"Because it's a lovely back."

"You're full of shit. But I like it. I think."

Moments later, Melondie Kadare sneered, "It's such a lovely back? Could you be any more lame?"

"I wasn't at my best. I was distracted. I had a big-ass bug buzzing in my ear. And a lovely back to contemplate."

Miss Kadare bit me on the aforementioned ear. "You're lucky I'm not your size."

# 15

The celebration got started. It rolled along just fine. Night fell. Morley's waitstaff fired the floating wicks of globular little oil lamps at each place at table. They poured wine, TunFaire Gold, the best rotted grape juice in the world. The bad guys settled themselves and sucked it down. They got happier by the minute. The majority seemed amazed to find themselves having a good time. But whenever somebody cracked a dirty punch line the astonishment went away for a minute.

I was surprised by the number of guests. Not only the underbosses and their lieutenants had shown, but so had Squint Vrolet, Spider Webb, and dozens of other foot soldiers of little consequence.

No matter. Everyone seemed pleased to honor their empress. The fun grew more exuberant without growing rowdier. Louder without getting physical. Food came. More wine flowed. And a whole orchestra of alarm horns hooted and tooted in the paranoid cellars of my mind.

Of the gathering I was alone in not swilling wine. I have no taste for spoiled grape. I'm a beer, ale, mead, and stout man. Though the stout brewers tend to shovel in too much mud.

A baffled Morley Dotes observed from the door of the passage to the kitchen. More drink than food was coming out now.

Would tonight turn out like evenings in the old-time valhalls, where the thane's men drank themselves unconscious and collapsed on the straw-strewn floors? In their own puke. Among the household livestock and table waste.

No straw here. Darn.

Up front, Saucerhead and his crew had scorned the demon grape, too.

My rat and pixie friends did not immediately fall under the influence, either, though not for lack of trying. I heard Melondie Kadare bitching because the biggies were tracking every ounce of TunFaire Gold. The cheap-ass bastards.

I left my table and drifted over to Morley. "What do you think, old buddy?"

Dotes murmured, "If you know anything, you're two legs up on me. It's like one of those temples where they smoke and drink to get closer to God."

"Yeah. They'll bring out the accordions any minute. Meantime, what the hell is happening?"

"All I know is, I had to send out for more wine. Look at them. They're completely messed up."

"So the bloodshed we imagined don't look like it's going to happen. How are we fixed for Relway alerts?"

This gathering would be a wet dream come true for Relway's crowd. So how come they weren't all over outside?

"Don't worry about them," Morley said. "Worry about what Belinda still has in her trick sack. All this happy might be part of her scheme."

Our hostess was being kittenishly cheerful with the top goombahs—with a kitten in her lap. But . . . "She hasn't been drinking." I nudged a cat away from my foot. "That's a new shoe, hair ball." Then, "Think she put something in the wine?"

"No. I bought it. From vendors she wouldn't know. It isn't the wine. If it was that, they'd be cutting each other's throats."

Right. No one was immune, drinking or not. "It's in the air. The wine just makes it worse."

"Picture the possibilities if dancing girls came in."

"Put the old emperors to shame. Look. Even Belinda isn't immune."

Miss Contague loosed a blast of cackling laughter. She slapped Rory Sculdyte on the back. Rory bellowed his own hilarity.

Rory Sculdyte was the man most likely to treat Belinda to a dip in the river wearing iron swimwear. Rory knew in his secret heart that he had been cheated of his birthright when Chodo took over.

I told Morley, "You better get back to work.'Cause here she comes." Morley did. And Belinda did. I told her, "You need to laugh more, woman. You're more attractive when you laugh."

"And when I don't?"

"You're still attractive, he admitted reluctantly because it blunted his point."

"Tell me something, old friend. Why am I having fun?"

"If I knew, I'd get my business partners to come bottle it."

"Seriously, Garrett."

"Seriously, Contague. Maybe somebody put wormwood in the wine casks. You saying it's not your fault? Not part of your evil master plan?"

"I'll take credit. But I didn't plan it. No. You know I expected tonight to turn darker. But I can't go through with it now."

"Then get on with the business with your father. Save the bad-girl stuff for when I'm on the other side of town. Work some magic here so you don't have to do the bad-girl stuff."

"What have you been smoking?"

"I don't do that. I can dream, can't I?"

"Not now. Now I need you wide-awake and alert. I'm going to bring Dad out."

# 16

Melondie Kadare plopped onto my shoulder. Her aerial navigation was erratic. "You been nipping the Gold, Bug?"

"Just a little. They're watching too close. I thought this was supposed to turn into a big brawl."

"Everybody did. What's up?"

"There's a situation shaping up outside. Those ugly men who tried to break into our house are prowling around, looking for trouble."

"They're here?" Too many puzzles for one night.

"Yup."

"Why would they want to get into it with this bunch?"

"Garrett, none of them look smart enough to put on a hat when it rains. They don't know what's going on here. They don't care. They might not care if they did know." Then she confided, "I think they're after that girlie boy. That Penny. She was skulking around out there, too. Maybe they followed her."

"Did they?"

"We maybe haven't been paying enough attention. Blair and Russ figured out how to get some wine."

"The rats aren't drinking, too, are they?"

"I don't know about the little ones. The big ones got a taste or two."

I wanted to bark and howl and go spank Singe. Instead, I said, "Melondie, slide back out there and keep an eye out. I'll send help if I can."

She needed three tries to line up the window well enough to buzz through the gap.

Tharpe and his cohorts were now enjoying their own little party within the party. I went to visit. "Saucerhead."

"Man, Garrett, here you come in one of your moods. What's up?"

"There're some guys in green pants outside, looking for trouble. The drivers might not be able to handle it themselves."

"You lank-shank sack a camel snot . . ."

I left too soon to appreciate Tharpe's full list of my horrible shortcomings. I know what they are, anyway. Tinnie keeps me posted.

I got back to my table just as the guest of honor came out.

Belinda had gotten Chodo looking presentable. He appeared to be asleep in his chair, not incapacitated.

That impression lasted only briefly.

Silence filled Whitefield Hall. Although there had been rumors, they'd been disregarded because the Outfit retained its Contague edge. But here was proof that Chodo Contague wasn't the Boss anymore. Clearly, he hadn't been in charge for a long time.

A neatly arranged blanket covered his lap and legs. His bony talons lay in his lap, right on left. His bare forearms were purplish. His chin rested on his chest. He drooled.

Hard men there were appalled and repelled.

Belinda said, "The guest of honor. My father. Chodo Contague. Celebrating his sixtieth birthday. Let's toast the man responsible for our prosperity."

The shock waned under the weight of wine and good cheer. Some shill burst into song. Others picked it up. A few wondered what this meant to the overall organization.

I caught snippets. Some saw this as a chance to improve themselves. But they couldn't concentrate, even though they kept talking about trying.

I was ten feet away when Chodo came to life, though only just barely. He raised his chin three inches, the effort herculean. His whole body shook. His gaze found me momentarily.

A kitten leaped desperately toward his lap.

The hall slammed into darkness. Then fire exploded as the decorative lamps shattered and spewed burning oil. People pounded their clothing, to kill the flames there. The air began to heat up.

So did panic.

The latter included Belinda, who ran blindly.

This definitely wasn't on her program.

I caught her, gripped her arm with one hand, and spun Chodo's chair with the other, headed them toward the kitchen. Everybody else rushed the front door.

Morley quickly sent his troops to fight the fires. He keeps a cool head however filthy the scat storm gets. When even queens of the underworld are losing control, Morley stands short, proud and calm.

A swarm of cats streamed past. Rats were in motion, too. Pixies zoomed around overhead.

The confusion eased in the kitchen. "You stay here," I told Belinda. "Where are your bodyguards?"

"Good question. I mean to ask."

"I'll find them." It was a puzzle, them vanishing. They should've surrounded Belinda the instant the excitement started.

The baby cats headed back into the big hall.

Belinda seized my arm, for one moment a scared little girl. Which is one way she manipulates me. Then the woman who ran the Outfit reemerged. She snagged a butcher knife. "Be careful."

"Watch out. Don't leave unless you have to. There's some kind of excitement going on outside." I followed my kitties.

Fires still pranced and murmured in a dozen places. Only the little blazes had been slain. The excitement up front had ended. A few bold fellows had turned back to help, though the effort looked hopeless. The remaining fires weren't going to let mere mortals push them around.

I found Belinda's bodyguards. They'd gone down where they were posted. They hadn't bailed on her at all. Two were smoldering and dead. One was just plain dead. Two more were smoldering but alive, unconscious, in desperate need of help.

I discovered several more goombahs in like condition, alive but unconscious. "Morley! Over here! Problems bigger than those fires." The goombahs were burning like that woman had. "How do we get them out?"

Dotes barked, "Theodore! Take Beans up front. See if you can't get some help in here." He bounced over beside me. "This is ugly, Garrett. Really ugly. Smells like sorcery." Thugs crackled and popped.

"I don't know. Grab his legs." We huffed and puffed and dragged a man out to the ice bath. I reminded Morley about my meeting with Harvester Temisk.

"It had something to do with all this?"

"Maybe. But I don't know where he'd fit. Cause or effect? Symptom or disease? On three. One. Two. Three."

Ice water splashed. A kitten protested getting its feet wet. It strutted off indignantly, shaking each paw as it came off the floor.

The cat led us back into the main hall, where it bounded into the pail I'd used to bring the litter aboard. That pail was full of cats already, all with paws on the rim, watching anxiously. I shouted, "Just find somebody who's breathing and get him out of here!"

Morley told me, "Grab your cats and go, Garrett. I'll get these guys out. Hell! This one is gone now. Sharps! Give me a hand with this."

Melondie Kadare appeared, wobbling worse than ever. "Help," she whimpered. "I'm too ripped. . . ."

"What're you doing back inside?"

She squeaked. "I need to get my people out."

"How many are in here? It's going up."

"What was I going to tell you? Shit. It's hard to think straight when you're fucked-up. Oh. Yeah. You need to get away from here. The Watch are coming. Because of the fighting."

"What fighting?"

"Outside . . . it went all to shit. I need to get out of here. But I'm ripped."

"Hang on to me, then."

Morley and his guys got out, carrying the last surviving body-guard to the ice bath. I warned him, "Get going. Relway is coming."

Where had Relway been? Belinda would've arranged a diversion. Something blatantly political. Deal Relway loves racialists less than gangsters.

Me and my pail roared through the back door. It was every-man-for-himself time. The coaches were gone. The parking area retained nothing but a dusting of large, ugly men who were either unconscious or dead. They had no friends to help them get away.

Morley faded into the night with his men, disappointed because their efforts had been wasted. Both bodyguards had died in the ice bath.

I made like the good shepherd myself, wondering about a batch of baby cats who would get together so their staff could lug them out of danger more easily.

Melondie Kadare started snoring. Brutally. I tucked her into a chest pocket.

# 17

It didn't take long to realize that somebody was following me. Somebody either very good or blessed with a little magical assistance. I couldn't shake him, nor did I manage to ambush him.

Melondie Kadare kept on snoring.

The kittens didn't like delays. They got antsy when I tried to lie in wait. Then noisy when I fooled around too long.

"You guys getting hungry?"

It was quiet tonight, the weather good despite the season. A big old moon up top silhouetted bats zipping around above the rooftops. There was a nip in the air. Scatters of cottony cloud tumbled across the sky. I didn't think the bats would find many bugs. Winter wasn't far away.

Melondie groaned and whimpered. "It's your own fault, Bug." In the distance, Whitefield Hall cast a cheery glow. The pixie crawled out of my pocket. She tried her wings. I caught her before she crashed, tried to put her away again. She wasn't interested. She clung to my shoulder instead. But when I stopped to listen for footsteps she slithered inside my shirt. When you're small you lose body heat fast.

"Don't bounce around so much, Biggie. And keep them cats away."

The streets remained deserted, which was unusual. TunFaire goes round the clock. But I was content. It's nice when no sense of dark imminence hangs in the air.

"Hey, Bug. We're almost home. And I've got an idea. How about you help me catch this spook that's dogging us."

"My head!" She groaned. "What you mean, us, Big'un?"

"All right. You. Because who the hell would be after me for a bucket of cats?"

"Smart-ass. All right. I'm listening. But keep your voice down. What's the plan?"

The plan was, I plunked my little friend on a ledge, out of sight, then headed on along. I took a right at the next cross street, took another right and then another, and soldiered on until there I was, plucking my shivering sidekick off her ledge.

"Did you have to stop for a beer?"

"Whiner. I would have, if I'd seen a place. It's past my time to start sipping. So, Bug. What's the evil word? What wicked dark lord off the Hill is dogging me through the alleys of the night?"

"You're so full of shit, Garrett. A blivit. Hell, the world's first hyperblivit. Forty pounds of shit jammed into a ten-pound sack instead of just twenty."

"But I'm so pretty. All the girls want to love me."

"If they're some kind of weird, like sky elves. Or ratgirls. Or troll jiggles so ugly they can't find themselves a guy who's rock hard."

"Unfair." No troll girl ever chased me. "You're upset because you're too teeny to enjoy the special Garrett charm." I wondered how trolls tell the girls from the boys.

"Sure you're not imagining things, Garrett? Because that's not what I hear."

"Ooh! How sharper than a frog's tooth. Come on, Mel. Who am I dragging along behind me? Before I need to scope out how to turn my last two hairs into the perfect comb-over."

"You're no fun anymore. All right. It was that little girl-boy. Or boy-girl. The one who brought the cats."

"Penny Dreadful? That kid can bang around behind me, keeping up, and I can't catch her? That's hard to believe."

"I can believe that. You being you, with your appreciation of you. Face it. You don't have the mojo this time, Big Guy."

"I'm thinking about showing you some genuine Garrett mojo, Bug. I know some things. I know some people. I could have you bigasized."

"You couldn't handle it. You'd have a stroke or a heart attack."

And so it went. We headed south on Wizard's Reach, turned west on Macunado. And there we were, home again, home again, ziggity-zig. In time to get behind the door ahead of a band of do-gooder city employees who missed seeing us by half a minute.

They pounded on my door. I used the peephole but didn't open up. Melondie Kadare snickered and giggled. She was having a good time.

"Why don't you check on your people? I've got cats to feed."

She couldn't do that from inside. I'd been clever enough to make sure the pixies couldn't bring their special culture into my castle.

My bucket leaked cats fast. They bounded off toward the kitchen. I followed.

Singe and her brother were there, each with a beer in paw. The platter between could serve a party of forty. Singe asked, "Where have you been?"

"I had to work tonight. Then I had to walk home because my ride disappeared. Leaving me lugging a bucket of ungrateful me-ows while listening to the world's worst bitching pixie complain because she's too small to be my girlfriend."

Even John Stretch looked me askance then. Melondie produced a resounding raspberry and started wobbling around in search of something small enough to use as a beer mug.

Singe shook her head, too damned human. "You hungry?"

"Just like a rat. Everything comes down to food. I could use a sandwich. I didn't get a chance to eat at Chodo's party."

What a dumb failure. Nobody ought to be so focused on business that he forgets to eat free food.

The platter had a dozen fried cakes aboard. Dean delivered four more, still crackling from the hot oil. "The square ones are sweet. The round ones have sausage inside."

"Uhm?"

"An experiment. Looking for something different."

Pigs in a blanket weren't new at my house. But this wasn't a biscuit dough production.

Melondie gave up looking for a mug. She went to work on a square cake half as big as she was. The wee folk eat more than we do. Because of all that flying.

I tried a sausage cake. "Good," I said with my wet mouth full.

Dean scowled, not flattered, as he brought me a cold lager. He put down more food for the cats.

I asked, "Singe, you got any thoughts about tonight?"

"Not unless you want to hear your species belittled."

"Belittle away. If you have any useful observations."

"Useful, how? John Stretch and I went along and tried to help, but we do not understand what you hoped to accomplish. That may be because you were not clear on that yourself."

I need new people around me. My old crew knows me too well. "Dean. Any sign of life from His Nibs?" I could run what I had through the bone bag's multiple minds.

I'm not as dumb as I let on. Hard to be, some might say. There were at least two different things going on. Maybe three. All getting tangled up because of a common denominator named me.

Dean was not encouraging. "The thing remains inert. Sadly, it's still too early to dispose of the remains."

"Way too soon," Melondie Kadare piped. "There're a dozen sparks still burning inside that blubber pile."

"You can tell?" I asked. "You can read that sack of rotting meat?"

"I need a drink. And it better be something more substantial than this off-color lager. Something with a little kick."

"I'll give you a kick, Bug. Answer the question."

"Nope."

"Nope? Nope, what?"

"Nope, I can't read him, Biggie. Not the way you want. All I can do is tell he ain't gone. He might be thinking about going, though."

"Huh?" I dumped another mug down the hatch. Having started late, I had to hurry to catch up.

Another frosty mug settled in front of me. A dream come true. It was hailing beers. Dean earned himself a suspicious glare. There's always reason for caution when Dean caters.

He was up to something, hoping that getting me tanked would distract me from something or make me agreeable to something. Again.

John Stretch shipped an admirable quantity of beer in one big gulp. "It was an interesting evening."

Singe told me, "Find out what he found out right now, Garrett. He does not handle alcohol well."

So I focused on the big rat in the rodent underground and listened to what he had to say. Which didn't make much sense, since, evidently, regular rats mostly understand their surroundings in terms of sounds and odors.

Interesting.

Melondie had little to report. Except that she hadn't gotten much from her cohorts. Yet. She promised, over and over, to deliver the best from the rest after she sobered up.

Dean filled our mugs. He was smug. Things were going his way. We all were concentrating on getting outside as much beer as possible. The four-legged, furry crew focused on filling feline bellies. Nobody asked him uncomfortable questions.

Full of sausage, bread, and milk, the kittens piled into their bucket and fell asleep in one warm, purring pile.

We talked till we could no longer understand one another. Dean excepted. Killjoy boy hit the sack as soon as he was done cooking.

# 18

The second morning was nothing like the first. I wakened in a foul temper, head pounding. Dean and I needed to share a word. Cutting costs is all very well, but not by buying cheap brew. Just so he could pocket a few extra coppers that, no doubt, he'd waste on food for cripples and orphans.

I was first downstairs. Except for Dean, of course. But Dean was out shopping. Or something. Because he'd left food on the table, around the suffering remnants of Melondie Kadare.

The John Stretch leftovers would be around the house somewhere, too.

The rain-on-your-parade boys from the city were on the job. They pounded the oak occasionally. It stubbornly refused to open. Eventually, they gave up.

The rules are odd. And Relway sticks to them like a limpet—if he suspects that you might be one of the good guys.

Those associated with the dark side increasingly show an alarming tendency to disappear. Alarming to the bad boys, that is.

People applaud that, saying nobody with a clear conscience needs to worry. Till Relway's troops show up because they've done something that, in their reasoned opinion, wasn't really a crime. Never mind what the law says.

Let's review:

1. Absolute power corrupts absolutely.
2. The road to Hell is paved with good intentions.
3. No good deed goes unpunished.

All applicable where Deal Relway is concerned.

Brother Relway has only the best interest of the people at heart.

I have trouble faulting the man. Sometimes. "He needed killing" is a valid argument before the bench. Director Relway seems able to meet the burden of proof when challenged.

I ate. Biscuits with honey. Biscuits with damson preserves. Leftover sausage from the previous night that the cats hadn't gotten.

The sweet buns with sausage inside aren't good cold.

Finished eating, I scooped Melondie and headed up front to hand her over to her own people.

Through abiding and ancient habit, I used the peephole.

There were people out there. Big, ugly, hairy people. Only one wore green pants. The rest were incognito. Every man jack came equipped with bandages. One had an arm in a sling. Another had a leg in splints. He and a third were getting around on multiple crutches. None of them seemed to have concluded that bothering me was not a good idea.

Penny Dreadful's friends. What had become of her? She'd faded like a wisp of steam once Melondie identified her.

The Ugly Pants Gang had to be in an even bleaker mood than I was. Considering the state they'd been in when last seen, I assumed they would be grumpy.

Trust sweet old Garrett to get stricken paranoid. Why would this crew be on my doorstep?

I shrugged. Not a worry. I had a ton of food laid in. I had a backup keg of beer. Dean had a platoon of homely nieces he could stay with during a siege. If he was smart enough to spot the watchers and stay away.

Meantime, I could do some speculating. Why was I involved in this? And I could figure out some way to waken the Dead Man.

I went back to the kitchen, made tea, took a mug into my office. Eleanor wore a sneer of disdain. "So you're in a mood this morning, too." Which only squeezed more juice out of the lemon.

Somebody pounded on my door. I didn't go see who. I was comfortable with my brooding and Eleanor's dreary mood.

I shunted from puzzle to puzzle, free-associating. The medicine I'd added to the tea quieted the worst pounding inside my head. What really happened at Whitefield Hall?

"Meow."

A cat climbed my leg. A second bounced into the client's chair. Two or three more chased each other around the room, then back into the hall. I scratched and petted the one in my lap, then hoisted him and gave him the full eyeball bath.

He was just a baby cat. Though chunkier than most. Maybe his daddy was a bobcat.

"What's so special about you, little guy? How come the world's ugliest fashion retards are out to get you?" But were they? That deserved reflection, too.

He didn't answer. Flat refused to solve any puzzles for me. The people—and critters—you have to deal with in this racket. Ugh.

"Eleanor. What do you think? Is it all about the cats? Or the bucket they came in?"

Eleanor didn't say. I felt her worrying about me being slow to grasp the obvious.

The drill instructors and senior sergeants figured me out quick in the Corps. They'd already seen every get-around and get-out-of-it scam ever invented a long time before I turned up making like I was dumber than a bushel of rocks. But I can work that on most people here in TunFaire. People in this burg see what they want to see.

I strive to remain underestimated.

Or so I tell myself.

"This feels good," I told Eleanor. "I could just lean back with a lapful of cats and nap the afternoon away." Then I'd go out tonight because I couldn't sleep. Somebody would tell Tinnie Tate, who thinks she has a claim on me. And does. And *vice versa*. But I've got the worst case of Retarded Commitment Capacity Syndrome west of Morley Dotes. Morley being of international-competitor status.

Eleanor's disapproval pattered down like an iron rain. I needed to do three things. See Harvester Temisk. Visit the Bledsoe. And catch Penny Dreadful. While dodging Relway thugs and large men in hideous pants.

It sounded like the sappers had brought up a battering ram. The door remained stubborn.

I might be betting to an inside straight, but I couldn't see Relway not responding if the Ugly Pants Gang stuck around long.

His top men would be out there keeping an eye on my place.

"I'm going to try to get Old Bones to bestir himself. Again."

Eleanor's attitude was suitably discouraging.

"If I have to, I'll fill his room up with cranky old women."

The Dead Man doesn't have much use for the obstinate sex. And he's never been pleased that my attitude is the opposite.

He's been dead for four hundred years. He's forgotten all the good stuff.

Old Bones did exactly what I expected. A whole lot of nothing.

The assault on my front door faded briefly, resumed as a new villain laid on.

My pixies ran out of tolerance. A flurry of anger heralded a whir of little wings. It sounded like a full cluster launch.

I sighed, lit a new bug candle, proceeded to commence to begin out there on my front stoop.

Muttering like one of those scramble brains who bustle through the streets on grave, unimaginable missions, debating it all with themselves, I went to the peephole. Outside, chaos celebrated the spontaneous self-creation of the deities of disorder of the thousand pantheons that afflict TunFaire.

Pixies, pixies everywhere, pestering biggies without prejudice. Relway's Runners and their fellow travelers had arrived but were waiting to see what developed.

I offered no evidence that my place was anything but deserted. The Watch knew better, but wouldn't press the issue.

Only the Green Pants Gang were dim enough to keep on keeping on. They *had* to be clueless about the Dead Man.

I snickered at the prancing big guys as the pixies pestered them. Like a dance number in a musical play about an army field hospital.

I spotted Dean. The old boy did have sense enough to stand back.

I spied Penny Dreadful, too, across the street, to the left of and behind Dean. She couldn't be seen by the big guys unless the one at my door turned and looked for her. She did well at being just another gawker.

The pixies pricked the big guys enough with their poisoned blades. They began slowing down. They just couldn't get a handle on the fact that people might keep them from doing whatever they wanted. Ymber must be a strange town.

Whistles shrieked.

The Watch moved in.

They couldn't wait anymore. My neighbors were getting restless. The Watch couldn't let the situation deteriorate till witnesses began damaging city property. The property in question being the street itself.

When a TunFairen crowd gets rowdy it rips up cobblestones for ammunition. A grand brawl can strip an entire neighborhood of its pavements.

Relway's boys didn't have much trouble with the groggy bad guys.

The villains seemed less numerous when they were laid out like logs ready to be floated off to the mill. There were just four of them.

Some must have gotten away.

# 19

The next man to hammer on my door was an old acquaintance. And no surprise. Whenever anything interesting happens in my life, Colonel Westman Block turns up drooling official remarks.

I opened up. "You're half vulture, aren't you?" The door wouldn't swing all the way back. I scowled grimly at its mutilated face.

Block surprised me. "Bring out your dead."

"So what the hell is it now?" I grumbled. "Why'd Relway let those oversize morons go and sic them on me?"

"You're a pip, Garrett," the good colonel assured me. "But you won't be selling me a bucket of your bullshit this time."

"But it's the good stuff. The only kind I've got. If you want a better grade of poo . . ."

"Can it. You've been mostly straight with me. Meaning I still haven't caught you in a bald-faced lie. I will, someday. Meantime, I'll remain confident that you suffer a congenital inability to tell the whole truth."

"You want the truth? You can't—"

"Save your breath. Let's go in your office. I've been on my feet all day. While you're walking, make up a good story about why those thugs were trying to bust into your place."

"I don't know. This stuff just happens. It's like weather to me anymore."

"But have a notion or two, because you're never as dumb as you make out."

"I'm thinking maybe it's time I moved on. To somewhere

where everybody don't think they know what's going on inside my head."

"Here's a thought, old friend. Take a barge upriver and set up shop in Ymber."

"I don't get it."

"Sure, you do. Those guys are all from Ymber."

Being the villain he thought I was, I volunteered nothing. "Uhm?"

"There are ten of the big, ugly, stupid creeps in green pants, plus two normal-looking management types who run things. We think. We now have nine thugs and one normal clown in custody. It could take time for Deal's specialists to make them explain themselves, though."

So. Relway hadn't turned anybody loose. He'd staked out my place so he could collect some more ugly pants.

Colonel Block's nondescript face presented an expectant expression.

I saw no reason not to be forthright with the one man able to control Deal Relway. "I'm not real clear on this mess. It's all Dean's fault. He brought home this bunch of kittens and the kid who had the cats. I didn't get a good look at him before he made tracks. Dean has a whole song and dance about priestesses and prophecies. You can squeeze the snot out of him when he turns up, if you want."

Block grunted.

We have that kind of relationship. Half inarticulate noise.

"You really don't have any idea? You've had part of the herd since yesterday."

"They haven't said much. Yet. They're too stupid to connect their silence with the pain they're exposed to."

"You've got one of the managers. Officer types don't usually stand up . . . oops."

Block glowered. Being an officer type.

"Oops again," I said. "I get so comfortable with you I forget you aren't one of my pals from down in the islands."

"Move to the country, Garrett. You could fertilize a whole county."

I shrugged. "It's the times we live in."

He wasn't buying what I was selling, even though I was giving it away.

"I don't get you, Colonel. I've always been straight with you.

Ever since Prince Rupert made you the top guy at the Al-Khar. But you never believe me."

"Because you never tell the whole truth, only what you think I'll work out for myself."

"So where do we stand?" I asked. "You aren't half as dumb as you let on, either. You've got something on your mind."

"Of course I do. But it doesn't have much to do with those lunatics."

"I love how you work to make me glad I was born when I was, in this time and place, when life was never better."

"You might fertilize more than one county."

"Even so."

"Even so, I admit to a passing curiosity about what happened at Whitefield Hall last night."

"You and me both, brother. Somebody tried to burn the place down with me inside." I gave him a mildly edited story. Certain he knew the basics already. I left out unimportant details like pixies, ratpeople, Chodo's health, and people catching fire. "You can ask all the questions you want. I don't know what it means. I don't know what was supposed to happen. I can't explain what did happen. Despite what you may have heard, I was there only in a professional capacity."

"Save the snow, Garrett. I'm just interested in what you picked up about the kingpin."

Dirty trick. For sure the man wasn't as dumb as he looked.

"I saw him one time, right before the fires started. He was in a wheelchair. He didn't look healthy. I didn't hear him say anything. Then the situation went all to hell. Bam! Lamps exploded. Burning oil flew everywhere. I ran like hell."

Block wasn't happy but had no grounds to challenge me. He would've been all over me if he had anything. "Was the fire an attempt to get Chodo?"

"I never thought of that. Let me think about it. Man, it'd have to be somebody who wouldn't care if he wiped out the whole Combine."

Westman Block will grab any angle to nab an advantage. He never reveals all he knows despite deploring the identical attitude on my part. He won't bore in hard. Giving you the benefit of the doubt. Meaning you can't ever forget that he's always handing you yards and yards of just enough rope.

"No. Chodo wasn't the target. Not even Relway would

wholesale it that way. I do think the fires were started by sorcery. Or something."

"There's no obvious evidence. Experts checked." Block glared at Eleanor. "There any way I can buy that off you?"

"Eleanor? No. Why?"

"It's haunted. It gives me the creeps. I know a fireplace I'd like it to meet."

"Sir, you're disparaging my first love." Maybe he didn't know that story.

"Where is Chodo now?"

"I don't know. Wherever Belinda is, I imagine."

"Maybe. And maybe she lost track of him, too."

"What?" That couldn't be. That wouldn't be good. Especially not for Belinda.

But she wouldn't have rolled Chodo out if she hadn't been sure she had everything under control. Would she?

"You know where she might be?"

"At home?"

"She flew there if she is. She didn't leave town through the gates."

My subversive side urged me to keep him talking. He was letting slip facets of the Watch's capabilities, both to collect information and to move it. Meaning that Block and Relway had more manpower than was suspected. Which implied that . . .

Well, every implication suggests something else. This time the indicators pointed to a possible serious outbreak of law and order.

Which would stumble once it inconvenienced our more substantial royal subjects. Privilege means private law.

"You know everything I know, Colonel. Really. I don't have any interest to protect. Other than my poor front door."

"There are rumors about you and Belinda Contague."

"I've heard. She started them. They aren't true." I cocked my head, listening to a voice only I could hear. Like the Dead Man was giving me the razz without including Block. "Yeah. Good point. I've got stuff I need to do. Now that I can get out without being eaten by dragons. Dean! Good. You're home."

The old boy had come to the office door. He looked grumpy.

I said, "You need to get hold of the door guy. Those morons bent the hinges."

Dean scowled at Colonel Block, dragged his haul on toward the kitchen. He doesn't approve of Westman Block. Simply because Block exists in his peculiar professional niche he guarantees that there's mischief afoot. Dean would prefer a world where the law and order were fixed in place before he arrived.

Block said, "You're not going to help me."

"I gave you everything I've got. Including the news that I don't have any reason to hold out on you. What more do you want?"

"I hope that's true." He headed for the front door. I followed. He said, "You're a likable guy, Garrett. I don't want you to get in so deep we can't save your ass when the big changes come."

"Say what?"

"The wild era is about over, Garrett. We've worked hard to do what Prince Rupert wants done. The rule of law is about to dawn."

I had no idea what that was about. It sounded scary.

I'm a law-and-order guy myself. But I don't want the people involved interfering in *my* life.

I did say, "You're too optimistic. How bleak a season would it be if your hard-liner secret backers get everything they want?"

Block beamed. "Wouldn't that be marvelous?"

He didn't get it. And never would. People like him make life inconvenient for the rest of us.

"You'll let me know what you find out from those guys, won't you?"

"You don't make me want to do you a lot of favors."

"My heart is breaking. Here's something I really do want to know. How come those idiots wear those stupid green pants?"

Block chuckled as he slipped outside.

I closed. The door shut easily enough. Fortress Garrett remained sound and inviolate.

# 20

I checked Dead Man. He wasn't stirring. I told Dean, "I'm going out. I've got stuff to do." I mapped a route in my head. Morley's place, Temisk's office, then the Bledsoe to check on the burned woman.

"You have your stick?"

"What?" His asking startled me.

"Shouldn't you be ready for the worst? Considering recent events?"

I gawked. That was out of character. But he was right. And didn't know the half. A lot of bad guys saw me at Whitefield Hall. Some would believe I was hooked up with Belinda.

I loaded up on self-defense devices, a few enthusiastically disapproved by the city Watch.

The boys at The Palms weren't pleased to see me, but they didn't haul out any cleavers. For a wonder, though, I caught Morley working for the second day in a row.

"What's going on?" I asked Puddle. "What's his problem?"

Puddle's face exploded in a big old ugly, broken-tooth grin. "He's down here getting in da way. He don't got to be upstairs."

I raised an eyebrow.

"One a dem silver-elf womens is here."

I chuckled an evil chuckle. "It took me a long time. . . . Hey, buddy! I came to see what you think about last night."

Morley pulled up a chair. "Sit. Puddle, tell Skif we want a pot of tea. The real stuff. My friend doesn't like weed leaves."

"You don't really drink herb tea, do you?"

"I serve it. You give the marks what they want. I've heard a rumor, says you've already had some excitement today."

"A double dose. Some Green Pants guys tried to break in. Then Block showed up, wanting to know all about everybody's business."

"And you told him?"

"The truth, the whole truth, and nothing but the truth. I don't know nothing about nothing. He mostly wanted to know what happened to Belinda and Chodo after the party. He didn't care about the fires, the riot, or the dead men."

"Belinda better take care of Chodo. We're picking up storm warnings. Some of the underbosses are getting ambitious."

"Rory Sculdyte?"

"Teacher White, too."

That wasn't good. Though they do tend to kill only each other. Which Relway would encourage wherever he could. "Figures. They got out alive."

"You said the Green Pants Gang hit your place again?"

"Yes." Stupid me, I'd been too excited about being able to get out. I hadn't gotten the promised reports from John Stretch and Melondie Kadare. "Block's gang has them. He claims he has all but two locked up now. One of those two is following me right now."

"We can take care of that."

"You might want to be better prepared than yesterday."

"Same guy?"

"I think so."

"Not to worry. Help is on its way. About last night. What happened?"

"You were there."

"I was kitchen help, Garrett. I didn't see anything."

"You saw as much as I did. Probably more. You had a whole crew in there and none of them were blind."

"I'm sure it was your fault everything turned weird. Weird things happen when you're around."

"Only because of my unfortunate taste in friends."

"You're a misfortune for anyone who gets close to you. What's the thing with Block and Chodo?"

I explained.

He said, "There was a lot of confusion. Somebody might've grabbed Chodo. But you would've heard about that from Belinda. She'd want Daddy Garrett to save her again."

"Maybe."

"Want some advice, Garrett? Stay away from Belinda. No telling how hairy it might get, but she isn't likely to be the winner."

I drank the tea Skif brought. "They'll be that knee-jerk?"

Of course they would. The Outfit includes the most old-fashioned people alive. They don't want a girl running the show.

I mused, "I wonder, though. Last night fell apart on Belinda, but it didn't go the way anybody else expected, either. She's no dummy. And she's got a big head start."

"She remains, still, just a woman."

"I'm telling you, don't underestimate her. Especially if you suddenly notice yourself between her and somebody giving her a hard time."

He nodded. I doubt that he meant it. He asked, "Where are you headed from here?"

"Harvester Temisk's place. Then the Bledsoe."

"You can stand that place?"

"I don't hold any grudges."

"I mean, it's the antechamber of one of your most pedestrian human hells. I get the wet-spine creeps just thinking about it. Let alone getting close enough to smell it."

I held my tongue. TunFaire's poor depend entirely on that nightmare establishment for what little medical attention they receive.

"I know what you're thinking, Garrett. And I don't care. You know perfectly well where the road paved with good intentions leads."

# 21

I was being followed. As I'd reported. But now I had an entourage. The guy in the green pants was only the closest and most obvious tagalong. And the least skilled or most naive. He seemed to think I wouldn't notice him. He didn't notice the parade behind him. Which, at first, I thought was Morley's crew.

Using a few tricks meant to look like accidents, I decided I was wrong. One was a man who worked for Relway. And Spider Webb, an enforcer for Teacher White, who was a small-time renaissance crook Chodo never liked but who'd always avoided giving offense enough to get his run canceled.

Why would Webb and Teacher be interested in me? White wasn't big enough to try for Chodo's spot.

Were my fans aware of one another?

They all knew about Ugly Pants. Webb didn't seem to notice Relway's people, maybe because half a dozen were taking turns.

I decided to forget Harvester Temisk. I angled off toward the Bledsoe. I took a stroll through a tight neighborhood, turned a few corners quickly, ducked into a church. I scampered up into its bell tower. That gave me a view of the developing confusion.

Morley did have men out, including himself. They laid way back, observing. Morley eyed the belfry as soon as he knew that I'd disappeared.

The Watch had a less relaxed attitude. Their immediate response was to arrest Spider Webb and Ugly Pants. Spider surrendered meekly. He knew you don't mess with Relway's Runners.

When I left the church there were six people dead or crippled. Ugly Pants had developed a bad case of being the former. I was glad I didn't like green. The secret police was about to make green pants a lethal stylistic faux pas. Meantime, Spider would be back on the street before dark. He'd helped them drop the moron in the ugly trousers.

I'd just hove in sight of the Bledsoe when Morley fell into step beside me. "Any theories?" he asked.

"Other than that Ymber breeds them strong but stupid?"

"That was a dirty trick, back there."

"I·learned from a master."

"Conscience not bothering you?"

I looked inward. "You know, it isn't."

"You sound surprised."

"I am."

"You've turned into one of the boss class since you got involved in that manufactory business."

"What're you talking about?"

"Some other time. I have a new venture, too. It'll be a place where crackpots can spout whatever nonsense infests their pointy heads."

"We have a place for that. The Chancellery steps."

"Not anymore. Relway is moving them out. Nobody was making any money off it, apparently."

"Sure, there was. The sausage guys. The rat-on-a-stick guys. The tempura tarantula guy."

"Who bought those?"

"I don't know. Somebody. Or he wouldn't be out there every day. Yuck!"

That wasn't a comment on deep-fried spider. We were close enough to the Bledsoe to hear and smell the place.

It's a hell in brick. Those who deliver themselves to the hospital's mercy are, generally, thoroughly desperate. Meaning parts may be falling off already. The stenches of disease, rotting flesh, and deep despair lie heavy on the whole area. The neighbors pray for foul weather to wash and blow the stink away.

The sound was the choir of madness singing in the insane wards—lair of the Bledsoe's deepest and most abiding horrors.

Those wards do help finance the hospital. For a few coppers you can tour them. For an extra copper you can rent a stick to torment the mad folk. You can even rent the most dramatic loons for home entertainment.

Money. That's why.

Money and the complete indifference of ninety percent of the population. That's why.

The Bledsoe is a charity hospital. Its main support comes from the family that provided emperors to the Empire before the kings of Karenta replaced them. The Empire survives in the imaginations of that one family, so there are still emperors around. But nobody cares. Other than the directors of the Bledsoe, who depend on the imperial family for the donations they steal.

The Bledsoe is the most corrupt institution in TunFaire. We'll see truly interesting, entertaining times if Director Relway ever goes after the parasites there.

"What the hell is going on?" I asked, stopping to stare once I got a clear look at the hospital. Its face was covered by scaffolding. Masons, hod carriers, and other workmen bustled around cleaning and restoring the facade. Though there weren't many of them.

"You know, I don't know," Morley said. "This is new to me, too."

Repairs were decades overdue. How come the money for this hadn't gotten stolen? I had no trouble imagining somebody donating enough to renovate the place. But I couldn't believe that its directors would use the money for its intended purpose. "We need to look into this."

"Why?"

"Uh . . ." He had a point. This wasn't a battle that needed Garrett galloping in in rusty, secondhand armor. Garrett was here to look dark and dangerous and make sure a client of Belinda's got the sort of treatment the Bledsoe can provide when its staff wants to bother. "You're right. One thing at a time. I'll do what I came to do. Relway will get to this place someday."

"I'll just stroll along with you. I'm curious about the construction."

He did sound curious. Like a gangster wondering how anybody would be doing something without getting his permission first.

A large man without a hair on his head had a notion not to let us in. I'd never run into guards before. Morley asked, "You're kidding, right? You don't really want to be the next patient here, do you?"

My guess is, the bald guy recognized Morley. He got out of the way.

Next obstacle, an admissions clerk. Who was no challenge at all.

The clerk was a volunteer. Of the female persuasion. Ellie Jacques. Meaning it took Morley about thirty-seven seconds to have her ready to jump her counter and devour him. She gave up the whereabouts of the burned woman immediately. The patient was Buy Claxton. She *was* getting the *best* care the Bledsoe could deliver. With Morley making eyes Ellie admitted Mrs. Claxton was getting the best because the doctors knew the Contague name.

The Contagues and the Relways tend to get results.

I asked the clerk, "What's going on outside?" Which earned me a look of disdain. How dare I intrude on her romantic interlude?

Morley offered a whispered apology. I was good of heart. And the question intrigued him, too.

Homely and middle-aged, Ellie was desperate to please. "A charitable trust came in. They wanted to fix the place up. But they wouldn't hand over the money. I guess they're not stupid, even if they are bumpkins. They insisted on doing the work themselves. The directors resisted till they came up with the notion of going after matching funds."

Morley batted his eyes and made implied promises. Ellie implied a willingness to play any game Morley wanted.

Bumpkins? Yes. A consortium of civic-minded, successful businessmen from Ymber. Yada yada yada. The "give something back" yammer nobody with smarts enough to get in out of the rain ever buys. Give it back? What did you get in the first place? From whom?

Morley suggested, "Why don't you visit Mrs. Claxton?" Reminding me that I had a mission. He swung the charm beam back to the volunteer. Who admitted she was a Mrs., too, but wasn't fanatic about it.

"Right," I said. "Why don't I go check on her while you hang around here?"

"Absolutely perfect, my friend."

Enjoying the therapeutic aroma of the Bledsoe, I climbed two flights of stairs to one of the hospital's celebrity suites. The crooks in charge are clever enough to keep a few available in case somebody with lots of money stumbles in, bleeding. Belinda's father had used one occasionally when he was younger and got into those sorts of situations.

Buy Claxton's physicians had betrayed their normally hidden competence by making her pain go away, then followed up by doing mysterious, wonderful things to reduce the damage caused her by burns. Their respect for the Contague name led them to bring in a wizard with a strong healing talent.

I don't doubt that they found gentle, unobtrusive ways to pad their fees.

Buy was awake. "I remember you. You tried to help."

"Yes, I did. Miss Contague asked me to make sure they're taking care of you. And to see if you need anything."

"They're treating me like a princess. Because they're scared shitless of what'll happen if they don't."

"Are you unhappy about that?"

"Shit, no. I'm thinking maybe I'll just camp out here from now on. I got no fuckin' desire for my ass to be some kind a symbol to them what thinks the ruling class . . ." They must have drugged her as soon as I showed up downstairs. Just in case. She mumbled through most of that, then faded completely.

"Belinda put the fear of God in them," I told Morley as we left. "And how was your day?"

"The things I suffer for friendship."

"Bet you she cooks you a nice two-pound steak. . . . What do you suppose these clowns are really doing?" We'd stopped to watch the men working on the Bledsoe's sad face.

"Looks like they're taking bad bricks out and putting in new ones."

"No. They aren't. I worked as a bricklayer's apprentice for about six months one week, back before I went in the Marines."

"You left an honest career for life as a tick on society's underbelly?"

"I got fired. I couldn't make them understand that the workday shouldn't start before noon."

"All right. You're an authority on bricklaying. What do you see that I don't?"

"They're fixing things that aren't broken. This place is still sound. It just needs the rotten mortar scraped out and new mortar tucked in. But they're making holes in the wall." I could see several places where bricks had been removed to create hollows.

"All right. I see that."

"Didn't your friend say most of the workmen didn't show up today?"

"She said the financing came from Ymber. I recall that."

"Why don't you pop back in and find out if those philanthropists had bad taste in trousers. I'll talk to these guys here."

Dotes looked sour, but he went. He had his own beef with the Ugly Pants Gang.

I strolled over to a hod carrier of fifteen summers who seemed to share my youthful lack of enthusiasm for clambering up ladders lugging mass quantities of bricks or mortar. "I'm trying to figure out what they're doing up there."

I got the right note of naive bewilderment into that. After an instant to decide whether the old guy deserved some attitude, the kid grunted. "They're just tuck-pointing and replacing bad bricks." TunFaire is built almost entirely of brick. Everybody knows something about the upkeep of brick buildings.

"I get that. I did your job when I was your age, a couple hundred years ago. I never saw nobody pull good bricks out."

"Oh. That. They're making these niches. Usually, there's a lot more guys working. They put these metal things inside, then brick them up. Over there you can see where they've already done that about ten times."

"So you're, like, getting in on a slow day, eh?"

He chuckled. "This is the best day I've had since this job started. Aw, crap! I had to open my yap. Now my old man wants me to bring up some mortar."

The boy stirred the mortar in a nearby mixing boat, splatted twenty pounds into a mortar hod, then went up the ladders and scaffolding like a monkey. I wasted ten seconds hating him for being that young, then drifted over to where the boy had pointed out some finished Ymber craftsmanship.

They weren't bricklayers by trade. Not even apprentice bricklayers.

Morley said, "You're psychic," from behind me.

"I've been accused of everything else. Why not that?"

"The philanthropists from Ymber brought a crew of volunteer workmen. Every single one wore filthy green plaid pants."

My new young friend spidered to the ground as Morley made his remarks. He overheard. I asked, "Would those be the guys who didn't show up today?"

"Yeah. And I ain't missing them, neither. I never seen such a bunch of useless assholes."

I tried to find out more, but somebody up top kept hollering nonsense about lollygagging and slacking. I told Morley, "Sounds just like the guy who fired *me* fifteen years ago."

The kid said, "That's my old man. Don't worry about him. He's all hot air." But he got busy working the mortar boat. You don't, the mortar sets up.

# 22

Morley seemed preoccupied.

I was preoccupied myself. Just what was going on at the Bledsoe?

Here it was, direct as a smack in the chops with an iron fist. The Green Pants Gang was underwriting renovations in order to install metal somethings inside the Bledsoe's outside walls. Dean was sure the gang was in town to catch Penny Dreadful and her kittens.

What would Penny say, if pressed? "We need to catch that kid who dumped the kittens on Dean."

"*We* do? Believe it or not, I do have a life outside my career as your sidekick. Considering Belinda Contague is involved, you might look into doing your own lifting and carrying."

"Ouch!"

"My point being, I don't need to catch something that's looking for you."

"Man. You're a pal, all of a sudden. Like Puddle or Sarge in a bleak mood."

"Could be. Life isn't fair. You going to try Harvester Temisk now?"

"Yes."

"Good luck. I'm headed home. Before one of those idiots burns the place down."

What suddenly made him want to get away fast?

Harvester Temisk hadn't resurfaced. He had, however, begun to interest somebody besides me. A minor, dim thug named Welby Dell was asleep across the street from Temisk's, in a spot well suited for lurking and watching. Dell was another associate of Teacher White's.

Being a thoughtful kind of guy, I toddled on without disturbing Welby's nap.

I picked up a tail. He wasn't anybody I knew. He didn't care if I knew he was there. Meaning he was a Relway Runner.

I changed course, headed for the Al-Khar, where I asked to see Colonel Block. Naturally, the ground level of the bureaucracy made that impossible. So I asked for Director Relway. With identical results.

I trudged on home. Smug. Block couldn't accuse me of evading my civic duty. Dean was in the throes of creating chicken and dumplings. He can be a killer in the kitchen when he wants.

Melondie Kadare was on the table, still hungover, in a foul temper. Singe sulked because I'd taken off without getting John Stretch's report. Her brother had gone and come and gone again in my absence.

Dean was in a good mood. "Mr. Mulclar will be here to fix the door tomorrow."

"Good." I settled down to eat. A kitten climbed my leg and set up shop in my lap. Others prowled the kitchen. Singe held one. It wore the smug look of master instead of pet.

"Dean, talk to me about Penny Dreadful and these cats."

He started to hem and haw.

"Dean, this is serious. People are getting busted up. They're getting dead. The guys who keep trying to break our door down got into fights with Belinda's people, Morley's guys, and Relway's gang. More than once. And when they aren't picking fights they're doing exterior renovations on the Bledsoe. What's the connection there?"

Dean grimly said, "You'd better tell me the whole thing. I may have been too trusting."

"You think so? That's never happened before, has it?"

Singe said, "You do not have to be nasty, Garrett."

I resisted a temptation to insist that I had the right. I related the highlights. "I don't think the Watch has the whole gang. Colonel Block says there were ten guys in green and two more who were in charge. At the Bledsoe, though, I got the impression that there were more than that."

Dean sucked in a gallon of air, set it free. "All I know is, those men serve A-Laf, some kind of masculine devil god. His cult has taken over in Ymber. It's really aggressive and intolerant. The feminine cult of A-Lat was its big competitor. I told you what Penny had to say already."

"And because she big-eye-orphaned you, you swallowed her story whole."

"Admitted. Which doesn't mean she was lying."

"Don't mean she was telling the truth, either. How do we get hold of her?"

Dean shrugged. "That's up to her. I don't think she'll come back here. Not since she saw the Dead Man. That rattled her."

"I'll bet." Hardly anybody wants to be around the Dead Man when he's awake. If they know what he is. I have reservations myself. I continued. "Give me a guess about the connection with the Bledsoe. The Ugly Pants Gang is putting out a ton of money so they can put metal statues in the walls."

Dean looked bewildered. "I don't have any idea. This is the first I've heard."

Singe brought me a cold mug of beer, reminding me that we had business of our own to attend.

She made sure surly little Melondie got a tiny cup to nurse, too. Always thoughtful, my pal Pular Singe.

"So, darling junior junior partner. What do I need to know that nobody's bothered to tell me yet?"

Melondie Kadare piped, "You need to know that your goddamn superior friggin' attitude needs a major adjustment, Biggie."

"Ouch!"

Singe said, "She is giving you attitude because her tribe was most incompetent at gathering useful information. They were too busy stealing food, wine, beer, and small valuables to accomplish anything."

That started Melondie on a classic rant. She sputtered and raved for eight or ten minutes. Her big problem was Singe's being right. Her tribe had demonstrated a decided lack of discipline.

"Do you have any idea how the fires started?"

"No. I was outside." She produced a fair picture of the encounter between the Ugly Pants crew and Playmate, Saucerhead Tharpe, and the drivers of sundry carriages. The good guys won by weight of numbers. Though Melondie thought the outlanders were sluggish, confused, and weak.

For no clear reason, and to his own astonishment, Dean announced, "It was dark, wasn't it? 'A-Lat' means 'Queen of the Night.' "

"Uh . . ." I mused. "I guess that's handy to know."

Not to be outdone, Singe promised, "John Stretch will have a better report once he gets his rats together."

"That's good," I said. Not believing for an instant. The rats from Whitefield Hall couldn't possibly remember details this long after having their brains scrambled by terror.

"It's been a hard day," I grumbled. "And it's getting dangerous out there. I'd better not go drinking. So here's my strategy. I'll do my drinking and thinking here, after you all go to bed."

Singe filled my mug. She refilled her own. Melondie tapped the rim of hers, an ivory thimble that came down to me from my mom.

# 23

Dean said, "It's Colonel Block again."

"Uhn?"

"At the door? You just told me to answer it? Remember?"

"Sir, I have no recollection of those events." Making mock of a statement heard frequently in the High Court lately, as the Crown reluctantly prosecutes the most egregious disturbers of the peace involved in recent human rights rioting and minority persecution. The Crown Advocate's usual attitude toward minorities is that they should expect to be treated like minorities. If they don't like it, they shouldn't come here in the first place.

Dean brought the Colonel to my office. I'd already settled in to sweet-talk Eleanor in fluent Drunkenese. I asked, "Don't you ever take time off?"

Block isn't married. He isn't engaged. He isn't the other kind, either. He has just one love. And she's blind.

He romances her continuously, hoping she stays blind.

He'll be sorry someday.

"Uh . . ." It never occurred to him to step away and relax.

"Go fishing."

"I tried that once. I didn't like it. But if you want to come along? . . ."

I flashed a yard of my most charming smile. "Point taken." To go fishing you need to go out into the country. Where the wild bugs are, and the hungry critters, some of them as big as houses. I don't go there, given a choice.

I did my time with the bloodsuckers and carnivores in the Corps. "You wanted to share something with me?"

"I was more hoping that you'd open up to me."

"Naturally. You're hoping I did Relway's job for him and now, because I'm a civic-minded kind of guy, I'll fill you in on anything that's puzzling you. Like Relway don't have a couple brigades of thugs to do his hoof work for him."

"Good point, Garrett. But Deal isn't on the inside. Deal somehow managed not to have even one friendly eye in the neighborhood when Belinda Contague held her summit at Whitefield Hall."

I flashed another yard of charm. "I was you, I'd think about that. How could she flimflam the whole damned Watch? What did you do, all go roaring off to the far south side after a bunch of human rights nuts? Were there even any nuts down there?"

"An orchard full. They haven't gone away. There was a bureaucratic screwup. The right hand didn't keep the left posted. The people responsible have been reassigned to Bustee patrol."

"And next time I visit the Al-Khar their identical twins will be sitting in their old seats."

Block nodded, shrugged. "What can you do about human nature? We still have Watchmen willing to supplement their salaries by selling inside info or by doing favors." He slumped like a jilted lover.

"That's good. You can face the truth."

"There's a lot of wishful thinking at my shop. You're right. But changes are coming."

"I hope you're right. Your guests in green say anything interesting yet?"

"Yeah. They're gonna save the world from the Queen of Darkness."

"Oh, goody! What's that mean to us who aren't religious wacks?"

"I don't know. We're looking for an expert on Ymberian cults. I want to know what's really going on."

That was why I admired Block. He understands that when people are involved, not much is what it seems at first glimpse. Though you never go wrong by suspecting the worst and working back.

Feeling generous, I talked about my thwarted visit to the Al-Khar.

"They're putting statues in the walls of the Bledsoe?"

"Not anymore. You've got most of them locked up."

"Why would they do that?"

"I hope you're just asking you. Because I have no idea." I

doubted the Green Pants guys really felt compelled to do charitable deeds. Old cynic, I.

"I'm fishing. One must when dealing with you."

"Here's a notion. Assuming the Green Pants boys are religious gangsters, maybe the Bledsoe business has to do with their religion."

Captain Block gaped. My leap of intuition stunned him. "I'll be damned, Garrett. I take back everything I ever said about you. I bet you *can* find your toes without the Dead Man and Morley Dotes to show the way. You might even be able to count them without having to borrow an extra hand."

"Oh! How sharper than a serpent's tooth the cruel envy of a civil servant. Dean! We need a pot of tea."

"Don't bother. I'll be going. I found out what I needed to know."

That had a sinister edge. "Uhm?"

He didn't explain. Which left my nerves with split ends. Which was his whole point.

"Here's a thought, Garrett. Or two. Find Harvester Temisk before anyone else does. Then keep him away from the Combine."

"Uhm?" You can count on Detective Garrett to spout argot and attitude and sparkling repartee.

"Deal has friends in low places. There's a new trend in goombah thinking. They're all asking, 'Where's Harvester Temisk?' Even underbosses who aren't sure who Temisk is are looking. They don't want to get left behind. They haven't done much yet because they're all still nursing totally hairy hangovers."

"They did party like it was their last shot before the Trumps of Doom." I levered myself out of my chair, to take up guide duties so Block didn't get lost on his way back to the door. He's been known to do that. "Did you notice anyone watching the place when you got here? Besides Mrs. Cardonlos and the Watch goon squad operating out of her place?"

"Goon squad? You wound me, sir. The Watch employs only the cream of the cream of TunFaire's most civic-minded subjects." Denying nothing. "Tell you the truth, Garrett, I didn't pay attention. That's a luxury we're starting to enjoy more."

"What's that?"

"Not having to give a damn who's watching. Or why. Comes from knowing you're doing such a good job your credit with the people who could fire you is inexhaustible."

"Oh." That was a message.

Somebody somewhere liked what the Watch was doing just fine.

"I'll have the boys poke around under the stoops and in the breezeways."

I gave him a look at my raised eyebrow.

"All part of the service, Garrett. We maintain order and protect the public." Out he went into the chaos of Macunado Street.

What had he come to find out? More disturbingly, what were the people behind him up to now that the war was over?

Soon after Block disappeared a stir passed through the neighborhood like an unexpected gust through a poplar grove. A dozen clean-cut men rousted out another dozen who looked much less obviously official.

Spider Webb was the only one I recognized.

I went back to my desk still wondering what Block had found out.

During my absence my teacup had been refilled. It must've been magic. I never heard a sound.

I picked up the egg-shaped stone one prime sample of rustic elegance had striven to sling through my skull. It didn't feel as slick or greasy today. It felt warm, alive. Just holding it, fiddling with it, relaxed me. I slipped off into a nap.

# 24

When I wakened I ambled back into the kitchen in search of fuel.

Dean was darning socks and slow cooking a sauce involving tomatoes, spices, garlic, and shredded onions. He had an admirably large mug of wine in front of him, which was out of character. He splashed some into the sauce. Oh.

Singe had swilled enough beer to get silly. Time to order in a new backup keg. Melondie Kadare was in a state where she wasn't much more than a sack of jelly, venting noises vaguely reminiscent of primitive language.

I said, "We need to lock Mel in a box until she dries out."

Singe snickered. A sight to behold and a unique, gurgly sound to hear. She was feeling less pain than I'd first thought.

There were kittens all over. I couldn't keep track.

Dean said, "Get the front door. I'm too busy."

His ears were sharper than mine. This guy must have mislaid his sledgehammer.

I was the only hind-legger able to navigate, so I snagged my mug and headed south. After a weary trek, o'er dale and under mountain, I positioned myself at my peephole.

One gorgeous, thoroughly frazzled, blue-eyed brunette had taken station on my stoop. I was surprised. I was more surprised to see that it was dark out. And still more surprised that she'd shown up without bodyguards or her ugly black coach. She wasn't wearing her usual vampire wannabe look, either. She wasn't stylish at all. She had gone lower-class, raggedy, housewifey instead of whorish.

I opened up. Eyeballing the darkness behind her, I observed, "A lot of work go into the new look?"

"Yes. You want to move so I can get in before somebody figures it out?"

I moved. Belinda got inside.

"You by yourself?" I was used to seeing her motate around with several shadows who resembled woolly mammoths operating on their hind legs.

"All by my lonesome. I don't want anybody guessing I'm me. Not to mention that I lost my whole crew in the fire."

"Uhm?" My vocabulary word of the day.

"You know how many people are watching your place?"

"I have a notion. What I'm not sure of is why. I thought they'd go away after they swept up the last bunch of vandals who tried to wreck my door."

"I have no idea what you're babbling about. From a business point of view it would make sense to look over your shoulder twenty-five hours a day, eight days a week."

"Uhm?" There I went again.

"Shit happens around you, Garrett. Weird shit. *Really* weird shit. You draw it like horse apples draw flies."

"And here you are, buzzing around my hall." A gurgling peal of pixie laughter reminded me. "We're having a party in the kitchen. Come on back."

Belinda scowled.

She'd lost something. Emotionally, she was back where she'd been when I'd met her. Scared, beautiful, crazy, in a shitload of trouble. She wasn't as scattered as she'd been back then, but she wasn't the ferocious Contague crime queen anymore, either.

I said, "Come on. You need to relax."

Not the best strategy, possibly. Belinda wasn't beloved by anyone in my kitchen—though Dean probably thinks her worst flaw is her willingness to be seen with me.

Singe gave me bitter looks Belinda didn't recognize because she doesn't know ratpeople. Melondie Kadare didn't contribute. She was on her way to becoming extinct. The kittens *were* pleased to see Belinda. Fifteen or twenty of them piled on as soon as she sat down.

I scooped Melondie off the tabletop. "I'll take Mel home. Before one of these critters forgets his manners." The pixie buzzed feebly. I got a grip so she wouldn't flutter off and smash her head against a wall or ceiling she couldn't see.

I checked the peephole, saw nothing but bats zipping through the moonlight. I opened up, whistled softly. There would be a sentry. He might need waking up, though. Pixies greatly prefer the daytime.

They found Melondie's husband. He and her family took over. She was snoring like a six-inch-long, horizontal lumberjack. They bound her wings so she wouldn't do anything lethal in her sleep.

I went back inside.

Belinda was at the door to my office. She had a pitcher of beer, a pot of tea, a small oil lamp, and appropriate auxiliaries on a tray.

"What's up?"

"I didn't feel welcome in there. And I don't want them listening."

"Let me get the lamp going. Damn!" I missed stomping a kitten by a cat's whisker. I dumped another cat out of the client's chair. It bounced onto my desktop, where it puffed up and hissed at the stone that had come another whisker short of braining me.

Belinda filled me a mug and poured herself a cup of tea, added cream and a hunk of sugar the size of a flagstone. She stroked the kitten that laid claim to her lap.

I asked, "So what's up?"

She stalled. She wasn't sure she wanted to talk after all. She forced it. "Do you know where my father is?"

What? "No. Last I saw him, you were getting him out of the hall."

"Oh."

"Why? What happened? Did you mislay him?"

"Sort of. I got him out, got him into the coach, started to look for you. The coach took off and hasn't been seen since."

"Wow." I found myself playing with the stone egg—in preference to the unhappy cat in my lap. In a leap of intuition I understood why folks were interested in Temisk. "Any chance one of the district captains grabbed him?"

"No. I'd feel my arm being twisted already. Instead, they're running in circles trying to figure out what's going on."

"Maybe he decided to make a run for it."

"What?"

"Maybe he'd had enough and made a run for it."

"He was in a coma, Garrett."

"You think? You're sure? One hundred percent? He wasn't just paralyzed?"

"You know better than that."

"No, I don't," I lied. "You never let anybody get close enough to tell."

She didn't bother to argue.

I recalled Morley's hypothesis that some guy named Garrett was the moral anchor and emotional touchstone of the spider woman. I didn't want the job. Everybody knows what girl spiders do when boys get too close.

Maybe it was one of those deals where, you save a life, it's your responsibility forever after.

You put the knightly armor on, and sometimes they don't let you take it off.

"What're you thinking?"

"I'm thinking you're a dangerous woman to be around. And I'm around you a lot."

"Tinnie knows you pretty well, then."

"Unfortunately. But my personal life isn't what I meant."

"You're afraid of me?"

"There's that. You've got a temper. But the real problem is, you swim with sharks. I expect jaws to clamp on me any minute."

"With all your guardian angels?"

"Angels? Name two."

"Morley Dotes. Deal Relway. Westman Block. Playmate. Saucerhead Tharpe. Not to mention your business partners. Max Weider is no angel. Neither is Lester Tate. And then there's me."

Made me feel humble. For maybe ten seconds. Then my natural cynicism got its second wind. Someday I should fake my own death and see how things shake out.

"So you lost track of your dad. Let's slink on down to the bottom line. How come you're in a state where you sneak off? . . . You aren't just looking to hide out, are you?"

"No. I walk back out of here in the morning and be who I've been since the first time we met."

"In the morning?"

"I don't have anywhere to go tonight."

I began to fiddle with that slingshot stone a whole lot more seriously.

"It isn't like you don't have other friends stay over."

"You want to know the truth?"

"Maybe not, the way you're looking at me."

"None of those friends are as scary as you."

Belinda went on petting that kitten, scowling because she'd

heard something she didn't like. She stared at my hands. "What the hell is that thing? What're you doing?"

I explained. "I left it here before I went to the party. I don't know. It relaxes me when I handle it."

Belinda extended a hand. I let her have the stone. "You're right."

Dean stuck his head in. "You need anything before I go to bed?" He was lugging a brat cat of his own.

"I can't think of anything."

He scowled at Belinda but couldn't get his heart into it. He sighed and went away.

Singe didn't bother to check us out. Which meant she was sulking but didn't have ambition enough to make anybody miserable.

Belinda poured herself a beer once she finished her tea. We played with kittens and let our hair down, talked like teenagers deep into the night, giggling at stupid jokes. I found out that she'd never had any girlfriends when she was younger. Never had the chance. Her role models were all the sort polite folk don't invite to holiday dinners.

We drank a lot of beer.

# 25

Singe wakened me at some godsforsaken hour, chivied in by Dean, who couldn't face direct evidence confirming or disclaiming the prurient imaginings slithering round the interior of his hard black skull. The fact that his imaginings were exactly that, and only that, meant nothing.

By the time we'd retired neither Belinda nor I was sober enough for anything more energetic than sleep.

Singe's attitude was sour enough.

"What?" I snarled. The morning light at play on my curtains shrieked that it wasn't anywhere near noon. In fact, it had to be closer to dawn, a time when only mad dogs and madmen got after the early worm.

"A messenger brought a letter from Colonel Block."

A kitten crabbed out of the covers, stretched, hopped down, and stalked proudly out of the room. Belinda made "Leave me alone!" growls and burrowed deeper into the covers. "Do I need to sign or something?"

"No. It was just a letter."

Then why was she waking me up now? "Then why are you waking me up now?"

"I thought you'd want to know."

"Sure, you did."

Feelings bruised, Singe left. I didn't care. There is no courtesy and no compassion before noon.

I didn't care, but I couldn't get back to sleep.

When Belinda started snarling about the tossing and turning

and threatened me with an amateur sex reassignment, I surrendered to my conscience and dragged on out.

I sipped black tea thick with honey. No help. I kept seeing two of everything. If I hadn't spent five unforgettable years as a Royal Marine, I might've suspected double vision to be nature's revenge on fools who believe rational behavior includes hauling out at sunrise in less than apocalyptic circumstances.

Singe bustled around, doing chores, so Dean could do even less real work to earn his board and bread. She was fanatically perky and cheerful. And her coconspirator had put the butcher knives out of reach.

"You are awful in the morning," Singe declared.

Exercising maximum restraint, I chirped, "Yep."

"Is that the best you can do?"

"I could say, 'Eat mud and die!' But you'd get your feelings hurt. I have more consideration for you than that. So how about we get together with this critical communiqué?"

Dean and Singe installed me in my office with hot black tea, biscuits, and honey. I got started. More or less. Weighted heavily toward the less.

"What does the note say?" She'd tried to read the message but Colonel Block's clerk had inscribed it in cursive. She can't read that yet.

She's a fast learner, though she'll never teach Karentine literature. Which consists mainly of sagas and epics inhabited by thoroughly despicable people being praised by the poets for their bad behavior. Or passion plays, which are hot today, but which are moronic if you read them instead of watching them.

"It says the priest at the temple of Eis and Igory, in the Dream Quarter, is from Ymber. It says the Watch wouldn't be disappointed in their old pal Garrett if his curiosity caused him to visit this Bittegurn Brittigarn, whose thoughts about guys in green pants might be of mutual interest."

"Meaning they do not think the priest will talk to them and they have no convincing excuse to pull him in."

"Basically."

"Garrett, what would the world be like if everyone was as caring as Dean?"

"It would be knee-deep in hypocrisy, standing on its head."

"Which still makes him better than most everyone else."

"Glory be, girl. Don't *you* go turning into a street preacher."

"The more I become a person, the more I get upset by how people treat each other for being different."

"I don't want to get into a debate."

"Too early in the morning?"

"No. Because I'd have to play devil's advocate and argue that stranger means danger. Which nobody can say is wrong. We've all got those harsh moments somewhere in our lives."

"Very good, Mr. Garrett," Dean said from the office doorway. "Indeed, flawless."

"We can't afford it."

"Sir?"

"Whatever you're buttering me up for. Hey, I don't want either one of you outside today." I heard Belinda beginning to stir upstairs.

Dean and Singe looked puzzled.

"The Dead Man." I told them, "We've had several visitors the last couple days. The kind that pay attention. They've probably picked up on the fact that he isn't doing much singing or dancing right now. Folks tend to get bold when they think he's snoozing."

Dean looked numb. This was his nightmare. He loathes the Dead Man. But we need the Loghyr's protection. People carry grudges.

"It would help if you two took a real shot at waking him up while I'm out there, one lonely man, a flawed white knight holding the fragile barricade between honor and the chaotic abyss."

Belinda appeared behind Dean. "Gorm, Garrett. You couldn't be more full of shit if they pounded it in with a hammer."

Dean headed for the kitchen. He came right back with everything Belinda needed to tame a hangover and get set herself for another glorious day of crime and corruption.

She announced, "Whatever Garrett claims, it's a lie. He was snoring before I got my shoes off."

Dean was pleased. Though he'd heard it before, from me. But that was different. My version didn't signify. He preferred not to believe me if that could be avoided.

I asked, "What am I supposed to do with you? Besides get you out of here before Tinnie hears rumors?"

She hadn't considered that. But really didn't care.

"Take care of it, Dean," I said. "Try to avoid making a millennial-celebration kind of production moving her out."

The old man gave me a look. It said I had the advantage of him, this once. And he didn't like it. "I'll handle it, Mr. Garrett."

I might ought to put on my chain mail underpants.

# 26

I didn't wander alone. A secret-police tail fell in behind me half a block from the house. He made no effort to be discreet.

Spider Webb was intimidated. But he didn't give up. He just dropped back. He vanished later, when I wasn't looking. So did several others whose fashion sense suggested a connection with the world of untaxed adult entertainment. But my main man just shuffled along with me, so close I had to listen to him hum.

He never stopped. But he had more trouble lugging a tune than my favorite antisinger, me. I never could tell what he was laying down.

The Dream Quarter gets its name because humanity's spiritual imagination runs riot there. And because the war in the Cantard produced generations of veterans so cynical that belief in anything traditionally religious could only be a bad joke that nobody got. In the Cantard nobody prayed for help cleaving to the path of righteousness. It was all, "Dear Lord, won't you please save my scruffy butt?"

Heavenly responses were random and erratic. Some of the sorriest clowns in the Cantard were guys who got what they asked for. Life with an ass but no arms or legs ain't all it's cracked up to be.

The Dream Quarter is one long street that runs from the river's edge deep into one of TunFaire's wealthiest enclaves. Location on the street defines the status of the deities established there. In a complex dance that remains mysterious even after my several encounters, the gods and goddesses of the Dream Quarter move sedately up and down the street, from temple to temple, according to how many worshippers they claim. And, more significantly, according to how rich their congregations are.

One rich, backsliding hypocrite of a parishioner is worth a gaggle of destitute mendicants, however devoted. A god can make the eye of a needle big enough to pass the whole damned herd of camels. And try to find a goddess who doesn't have six or eight hands out for contributions.

Bizarrely, the temples change to accommodate the look expected of their particular gods, goddesses, or pantheons.

I've heard that the gods reflect us instead of the reverse. Well, a smart god would have better sense than to create worshippers in his own image. Given a choice.

My instincts told me to start at the bottom end, down where a couple temples teeter over the chunky russet flood. The first person I asked indicated wreckage two steps short of the worst on the street. I'd visited the place once before, a while back, on another case. New management hadn't made any improvements.

Eis and Igory were doing better than other cults. Which meant the river would have to go a yard over flood instead of a foot to sweep their cathedral away.

Mind like a steel trap, I realized that this Ymber cult was faring better locally than the two visiting the miseries on me. A-Laf and A-Lat had no temples at all.

Even after having lived with me for thirty years I was reluctant to approach the hovel. It boasted one open room capable of holding thirty people—if they were small and didn't mind finding their noses in each other's armpits.

The priest wasn't what I expected. Which should have been no surprise since religion and I have so little in common. He could've passed as a fat apprentice friar from one of the regular churches at the successful end of the street. He even wore similar black robes. But his had eluded soap and water for so long that, at this late date, congress would be fatal for the cloth.

It was still some unholy hour before noon when I stepped inside. Brother Bittegurn Brittigarn got his tongue tied trying to introduce himself in turn. He'd already had a couple or nine pick-me-ups to start his day. By the time he pulled himself together he'd forgotten my name. "Who the hell are you? What the hell do you want?"

"I hear you're the top expert on the religions of Ymber. I've got problems with people from Ymber. I'm knee-deep in cats and plagued by big guys too stupid to know that you ought to grin and suffer frostbitten buns before you wear plaid green pants."

"Huh?" Brittigarn took a pull of wine. He was my kind of guy. He had his priorities set. He wouldn't fake anything to please anybody.

The Dead Man encourages me to cope with the unexpected by drawing on experience and common sense. Meaning, basically, don't run blindfold sprints in an active cemetery. Experience suggested that Bittegurn Brittigarn was dimmer than a bushel of rocks.

Bittegurn had a round, apple-cheeked face notable for a huge white drooping mustache. The hair had migrated there from the top of his head. He growled, "Well, is it a secret?" He took another swig of wine. I could smell the vinegar from ten feet away. "Smooth." He sneered, wiped his mouth on his sleeve.

I explained again. "I'm Garrett. I find things out. I look for people. I ask questions. I'm here to ask questions about religion in Ymber."

"Ain't no religion in Ymber."

"What?"

"It's all here in TunFaire now. Which one are you doing now?"

"Asking questions so I can figure things out."

He waited. Probably hoping I'd offer a bribe. I waited. He asked, "You going to start?"

"All right. To review. You're from Ymber. Supposed to be an expert on its religions. I'm having trouble with religious people from Ymber. My house is overrun by cats dumped on me by a street urchin who's supposedly a religious princess. Who's disappeared. Now my neighborhood is infested with thugs wearing hideous green pants. They supposedly work for a god named Aleph. When they're not destroying private property they do volunteer maintenance and rehab at the Bledsoe. Where they're putting metal animal statues in the walls."

"A-Laf."

"Huh?"

"The god's name is A-Laf. Not Aleph."

"I stand corrected. Is that important?"

"I doubt it. Damn. That dead soldier was the last of his regiment."

Subtle.

"I'll see if I can't scare up some recruits. As soon as we finish." Part of being a crack investigator is finding a thread to tug. I'd grabbed hold of a rope.

"What's that?"

"What?"

"That thing you're fiddling with."

"A rock. Somebody tried to kill me with it. Tell me about A-Lat."

He didn't correct my pronunciation. "A-Lat is the Queen of the Night. The Mother of Darkness. Love and death wrapped up in one ugly bundle. Her cult used to be big on temple prostitution. It doesn't exist anymore. Can I see the stone? It don't look natural."

"How long ago did you leave Ymber? If the cult is extinct, how come I'm up to my ears in its enemies?"

"I've been here two years. My faith fled when the A-Laf cultists began murdering unbelievers. Especially A-Lat's women. They tortured the last high priestess to death. They sacrificed the goddess's sacred feline avatar to the idiot idol in A-Laf's temple."

Ah. Finally. Actual information.

The Dead Man is right. Patience wins.

Notions fell into place. There was a pattern and rhythm here. TunFaire would be the secondary impact zone. In Ymber there'd be prophecies and rumors of secret heirs to unknown obligations. There'd be brave fighters continuing the struggle even though all hope seemed lost. One-eyed men and left-handed men missing a finger from their right hand. The stuff of high heroic tales. On a farm community scale, of course. Where most of the king's subjects don't give a rat's ass about any of that. They have thunder lizards to skin and crops to get in.

"Let me see that thing."

I handed BB the stone despite an instant of irrational reluctance.

He grunted. He stared. He grew pale as he moved deeper into the light flung off by a phalanx of votive candles. He squeaked, fumbled the stone, regained control, shoved the rock back at me. "Keep that away from fire. Any kind of fire. No matter what else you do."

"Huh?"

"You let a flame touch it, you'll be sorry the rest of your life. Which will last maybe as long as another minute. If you're friggin' beloved of the gods."

I didn't like the sound of that. "What the hell?"

"You don't got no idea what you got there, do you?"

"I have a green rock. Somebody tried to brain me with it. I started carrying it around because I tend to slow down, relax, and think clearer thoughts when I'm fiddling with it."

"Your hands are warm. It likes that. So it makes you feel good."

Warm hands? Tell that to Tinnie. "How about a little hint?"

"It's egg shaped. Right? That's on account of it's an egg."

"Huh?" Old Garrett is quick as a glacier sometimes.

"Friend, you've laid hands on a roc's egg. I don't know why anybody would try to brain you with it, but—"

"Great pun, Slick. Egg-shaped rock. Rock's egg. Where baby boulders come from."

"Roc. Bird of fire. Burn your house down around you in half a minute if the egg touches flame and it hatches, roc."

"Bird of fire? I thought that was a phoenix."

"Same difference. I was you, I'd jump outside and see how far I could fling it out in the river. It'd stay plenty cold down in the mud."

"Rocs are huge. They carry off mammoths."

"An exaggeration. There are four species around Ymber. The biggest might be able to take a lamb or a small dog. People remember them big because they're so busy getting under cover they don't have time to look close. The littlest roc ain't much bigger than a sparrow. Zips around like a hummingbird. That egg you got, that's from what they call the bird of paradise phoenix. Looks kind of like a pheasant in a clown suit."

"Like a parrot?"

"Gaudier. Tenderloin gaudy. On account of which, they've pretty much been hunted out for their feathers."

"How do you hunt a roc down and take his feathers?"

"Like the joke says. Carefully."

I gave him the fisheye. He'd distracted me from comparative-religion research. "My mother used to call things 'rare as roc's eggs.' When she wasn't on about frog fur or hen's teeth."

"More roc's eggs around than frog fur coats. But they ain't common. Especially the big ones. It takes a rare combination of guts and inspired stupidity to raid a phoenix's nest."

"I know some guys who'd fit."

"Indeed. A-Laf's sextons are chock-full of stupid and brave. But the deacons, the dicks who tell them what to do, wouldn't waste them that way. You got a sweet mystery there, my friend. No telling how one a them got hold of an egg. Maybe from when they took A-Lat's temple. She had them all." BB paused to irrigate his pipes by chugging half a pint of wine.

"Thought that dead soldier was the last of his tribe."

"You didn't run out and volunteer to . . . you didn't volunteer to run out and . . . hell. We got a new regiment coming into the line. Aged in the cask since last Sedonaday."

"Which?"

"Sedonaday. Holy day of obligation for Ymnamics. Day before yesterday. Man, I'm telling you, if that was my egg, I'd prance outside and see how far out I could throw it. Get it way out there, down deep in the cold, cold mud."

I ignored BB's chatter, which was one hundred percent pure bull specks. But he had gotten me thinking. "Suppose I wanted to kill somebody by setting them on fire?"

BB's face got redder. "I ain't getting rich here, Slick, but I ain't the kind that—"

"I don't want to kill anybody. I want to figure out why they're dying. It's something else I'm looking at. People catching on fire." I explained a little, naming no names.

"I can see where you might think rocs' eggs, not having heard about them before. But your target would have to cooperate. The big question is, why even try? There're easier ways to kill people. It does sound like a sorcery problem, though. Look for a fire kind of wizard with rabid bats in his belfry. Or some stray pyro talent who hasn't been spotted by the horrors on the Hill yet. A refugee, maybe."

BB's latest bottle, come out of nowhere, seemed particularly potent. He developed difficulties enunciating. Before long he would shift to a language no one but Bittegurn Brittigarn understood.

"Maybe somebody who came to his abilities late and thought he could keep them hidden? Somebody with a deep streak of darkness?"

"There you go, Chief. You keep on keeping on, there you'll be."

This was starting to head for one-hand-clapping country.

"Give me a little help before you get all the way gone, Pastor. I need to know about the A-Lat cult. You say it's dead. But I know a girl who says she's the high priestess of A-Lat."

Bittegurn Brittigarn focused on those skills needed to lift a wine container to his lips with no wastage.

I asked, "How does a roc's egg turn into a projectile meant to brain me?" If that really was an egg, how come it was hard as a rock?

"I don' know, man. Go ask the sexton what flung it."

That was on my list. If Block and Relway would indulge me.

BB was sliding fast. "The A-Laf crowd. Why would they rehab the Bledsoe?"

He wasn't native born. He had to have the charity hospital explained. Then, "For fifty years nobody but the imperial pretenders have put one copper into the Bledsoe." Gross exaggeration. The Bledsoe is *the* big charity for TunFaire's well-to-do. But that didn't matter now. "I really want to know why they're putting those metal animals in the wall."

Bittegurn Brittigarn took him a long, long pull of wine. "For the pain."

"What does that mean?"

The priest's eyes closed. When they opened again they held a strong "You still here?" quality. He didn't say anything. Probably couldn't. But I had some interesting angles to pursue now. "I appreciate you taking time out of your busy day. I have to go. My mom is probably in a panic."

He didn't respond, other than to drool. In half an hour he'd gone from sober, friendly, and evasive to slobbering waste.

He did mutter, "The pain," over and over. "They feed on the pain."

He settled on the floor with his back to a wall. Making sure he had a fresh bottle in hand and several more in easy reach. He began to mutter a song in dialect, either liturgical or that dread tongue known only to those who drink sufficiently deep.

*Wham!*

The impact flung me against the wall. I turned as I bounced, wobbled toward a wide little woman swinging the business end of a broom in from the other side of town.

*Wham!*

"Hey! What the—?"

"So you're the bastard who's lured Bitte into the Realm of Sin!" *Wham!* She got all her weight into her swing.

"Lady, I never saw this guy before half an hour ago."

"You maggot! You bottom-feeding pustule of sin! You . . ." There was more unjust defamation. A lot. By dint of longer limbs and skills honed in combat, I maneuvered around the stout little harridan and escaped.

She didn't chase me.

I stood beside the doorway, out of sight, and eavesdropped as she turned her fury on a shiftless, lying, no-good, wine-soaked bastard Bittegurn Brittigarn.

I headed home convinced that I knew why Brittigarn had developed a love affair with the spoiled grape.

# 27

Armed with marvelous new knowledge, I ambled toward my own part of town. I didn't pay attention. It took me a while to realize my secret-police angel was gone and Spider Webb was back.

Spidey just wanted to know where I went and who I saw. Chuckle, chuckle. I led him to the Al-Khar, then wandered on after being refused access to Block and Relway. Relway's very existence having been denied despite his being publicly proclaimed chief of the Unpublished Committee for Royal Security. I detoured past Harvester Temisk's digs. He wasn't there. I circled The Palms without disturbing Morley Dotes or any cranky henchmen. By then I was running cross-eyed. It don't pay to get up early.

I ran into Saucerhead Tharpe four blocks from home. He wasn't alone. I didn't duck in time.

"Hey, Butthead Boy," Winger bellowed. "I seen you. Don't you be trying to hide." The woman has a tendency toward loud. Tharpe seemed embarrassed to be caught in her company.

Winger is a good-looking woman. Blond, with the right stuff in all the right places, and the gods were generous when they built the best parts. But there are detractions from those natural attractions. Her size and her attitude.

Winger is as tall as me. And argumentative on her best day. Lucky me, I manage to avoid her a lot nowadays.

Saucerhead tried to look apologetic without saying anything that would get him an ass kicking. "I done some checking on that thing you wanted me to find. I know where it's hid."

"Do you? You know where it is now?" Because I could see

Penny Dreadful down the block, conspicuously inconspicuous as she lurked and loitered. She was tailing Tharpe and his convoy. No doubt trying to find out who was sneaking around her and why.

A squeak of a voice caught my ear. "Are you really Garrett? *The* Garrett? The man who—?"

"Yeah," Winger said. "That's him. Definitely the man who."

Set beside Winger this guy was almost invisible. He was ten inches shorter, bone skinny, bone pale, twitchy as a whore in church. "Jon Salvation, Mr. Garrett. It's a *huge* honor to meet you. I've heard *so* much about you."

"His name is Pilsuds Vilchik," Winger barked. "I call him the Remora."

Jon Salvation broke out a big, nervous smile.

Saucerhead said, "He's the boy I told you about. Follows Winger around and writes up everything she does."

Jon Salvation smiled again and bobbed his head.

I asked, "How come?"

Winger said, "On account of I'm a heroic figure and I'm so busy being heroic I don't have time to write my own saga down."

"Not to mention that you're illiterate, eh?"

Saucerhead chuckled. "The real story is, she let the boy have a little one time when she was plotzed. He liked it so much she ain't been able to shake him since."

Winger snarled, "That ain't what happened. Not quite."

I glanced at Jon Salvation. Seemed he didn't mind being talked about like he wasn't there. The story of his life, probably. Some people are like that. Naturally invisible. There are years when I envy them.

Salvation produced a little board with sheets of cheap paper fastened to it by rivets at the top. He scribbled furiously using the writing stick we make in the manufactory where I'm a minor shareholder.

Feel sorry for them if you like. Jon Salvations create themselves.

"Pleased to meet you," I said. "Don't write down anything the Watch can use for evidence." I wondered what he'd done in the war. Obviously, he'd survived.

Winger sneered.

I told her, "You're always on the edge, sweetie." That's her nature. The way she wants it. Fine by me. As long as she don't drag me in. "Saucerhead. One more time. Where's the item of interest right now?"

"On the shelf, I reckon. Worried about getting out and about."

"Actually, she's right over there, skulking around in front of Scuttleman's coal yard. Watching you."

Nobody looked. Not even the Remora. Tharpe muttered, "Damn sharp for a kid."

"I don't know." Plenty of kids Penny's age are resourceful enough to survive. Saucerhead was one himself once upon a time. "This one may have more talents and resources than most."

Saucerhead eyed me expectantly.

I told him, "I'm headed home. If somebody turned up at my door with a special prize, I might turn up holding a fat bonus."

"Gotcha."

Winger tried to horn in, hoping she could carve off a slice. I ignored her, which isn't always wise. She's liable to knock you down just to get your attention. "Good job, Saucerhead. Thing you could do next is, find Harvester Temisk."

"The shyster?"

"Him. Don't be obvious. Especially not if you find him. Teacher White wants him, too. And not to give him a birthday present."

"Gotcha."

"Later, then. Winger. How about you stun the gods above and the gods below speechless?"

"What?"

"Stay out of trouble."

"You're a complete horse's ass, Garrett."

"But snuggly warm and lovable."

"Like one a them giant porkypine thunder lizard things."

She *is* a woman. She *will* have the last word. Since they live longer, there was no point me trying to win out of stubborn. I made my getaway.

Jon Salvation wrote it all down.

# 28

There was a subtle difference about home when I got there. And it wasn't all the loiterers from the Watch and Teacher White's gang. Welby Dell and a sidekick. Welby's partner was a six-foot-five albino so emaciated a little girl once called him Skelington. It stuck. They seemed unaware of the presence of the law. The law, on the other hand, was well aware of them.

There were Relway Runners all over. Mrs. Cardonlos' place was busier than a termite mound.

I knocked. The door man obviously hadn't come round yet. My key would be useless.

Pular Singe let me in. "Did you learn anything?"

"I'm more popular than I thought I could ever be. Fans by the legion are following me around. None getting in my way, though."

Singe hissed. She saw something behind me. I turned, too late. "What?"

"One of those men with the obscene trousers."

"So Relway hasn't caught them all. What's going on?"

"Unh?"

"Something feels funny."

"John Stretch is in the kitchen."

"And he wants something."

"He wants to give you his report. Why don't you come in so I can shut the door?"

Not a bad idea with a Green Pants goon around. He might own a sling and have a pocket full of rocs' eggs.

On cue something whizzed past my right ear. Not a sniper's effort, though. It was Melondie Kadare. She hovered momentarily, then headed for the kitchen, doubtless after hair of the mad dog. Where she got into it with Dean. Dean had no sympathy for her. The man has an attitude problem. He's determined to call a hangover a self-inflicted wound.

Being a trained observer, I observed, "He's in a foul mood."

Singe said, "Things have not gone his way today."

I sensed a story. She didn't give it up.

John Stretch followed his nose from the kitchen to my office. I said, "I never noticed how long his snoot is before."

John Stretch scowled. As much as a ratperson can.

"Just messing with Singe," I said. I helped myself to a seat behind my desk. My lap had a cat on board almost instantly. Melondie Kadare whirred in a moment later. "He didn't use a flyswatter on you. Puts you ahead of the game. So don't go whining to me."

John Stretch started telling me what his rats had seen at Whitefield Hall. I stopped him. "Hang on. I need to write stuff down." He had much more than I'd expected. He had quotes from Belinda's underbosses, some quite revealing of their thinking.

Before he finished I had an idea where every major player stood. I just hoped he wasn't making stuff up because he thought I wanted to hear it.

"You're a gold mine, John Stretch." These nuggets would set Director Relway to singing and dancing. Plainly, Chodo's appearance at Whitefield Hall had changed the underworld dramatically.

Unfortunately, none of it was of any use to me.

"Hang on," I told the lord of the rats, figuring John Stretch so styled himself in his own heart. "Melondie, girl of my fantasies, I see you bubbling. You remembered something you haven't told me already?"

Not really, it turned out.

"So, did anybody figure out how the fires started?"

No. All those eyes hadn't seen a thing I'd missed.

"Was it some kind of sorcery?" Fire just doesn't materialize out of nowhere. Does it?

Neither Melondie nor John Stretch had detected any obvious sorcery.

"Any speculations? The first victim was a rat. Then Buy Claxton. How did they catch fire? Nothing else in that kitchen was harmed."

They had nothing.

It made no sense. Though it did look like Chodo Contague was the common denominator in a lot of incidents.

Damn! I wished I hadn't sent Saucerhead to catch Penny Dreadful. He could go up north to do all the miserable but necessary legwork.

"I'd tell you if I could. If I knew!" Melondie Kadare snapped. "You're special to me."

I glanced over my shoulder. Eleanor seemed amused. Which convinced me immediately that things were about to get worse.

It began as I pulled the notion together.

Dean appeared with refreshments. His clock radiated the kind of smug, wicked look he gets when he knows that I'm inescapably in for a life experience involving a whole hell of a lot of work. Not because we need money but because, in his lame view, it's good for my soul.

Somebody started pounding on the door.

Dean's smirk deserted him.

He couldn't avoid answering. The rest of us were busy. Plus, it's his job.

Muttering, he headed up front. I poured tea. Singe and John Stretch hit the muffins, fattening up for the winter.

Dean returned, his sneer restored. "Mr. Tharpe is here, sir."

Saucerhead filled the office doorway. He looked scared, an eventuality rare as rocs' eggs. "You got a back way out, Garrett?"

"What's up? What did you do?"

"I didn't do nothin' but what you told me. Which you owe me for. It's all your fault."

"Whoa, big guy. Put some blinders on that mule. And back the cart up to where it started."

"You told me to go catch that Penny Dreadful kid. So I did. No sooner do I lay hands on her, though, than she starts yelping rape an' sodomy an' incest an' all that shit." Which didn't bother him nearly as much as the fact that, "An' people *listened*! You hear me talking, Garrett? People *listened.* An' not only that, some a them come an' tried to help her! An' not only *that,* they chased me when I guve it up as a bad job an' decided to go away."

"That what the crowd noise out front is all about?"

"I don't know. They's probably getting all rowdy an' shit because they want you to come out an' teach them to dance the dublarfared. You being a famous dancer."

I shook my head. I took a deep breath, sighed. I shook my head again. What was the world coming to? When did TunFairens start caring what happened to one of the city's countless feral brats?

Saucerhead blubbered, "This is all your fault, Garrett! Ever since you got in this investigation racket you been doing the meek-are-gonna-inherit polka. An' now half the burg is buying into your do-gooder crap."

"It won't last," I promised, despairing of his ever grasping the do-gooder point. "Too much social inertia. Too many people too vested in the old ways. Especially up on the Hill. Just take it easy. They'll get bored and go away. Dean. Did you get Belinda off all right?"

He admitted that he had. And that she hadn't attracted any attention. Meaning the watchers outside figured her for one of my sleepover friends. Meaning, further, that I'd have some explaining to do once Tinnie got word.

She always does.

"Long as you're all here and don't have anything better to do. Listen to this." I told the tale of my visit to Brother Bittegurn Brittigarn's temple of Eis and Igory.

I hadn't gotten BB pinned down about his own religious attitudes. Dean pointed that out. Smugly.

Singe wanted to see the roc's egg.

They all did. I let them pass it around.

John Stretch said, "That priest pulled your leg, Garrett. This rock came out of a creek bed. You can get a thousand just like it at the arms bazaar."

Singe said, "Our ancestors collected slingers' shot for the army."

The sling was never an official weapon in any Karentine formation, but both sides employed native auxiliaries in the Cantard, some so backward they considered the sling a technological marvel of such murderous capacity that the gods themselves would rail against its use.

There was universal agreement. My roc's egg was a rock and BB would still be snickering.

There was a racket at the front door. Saucerhead jumped. He developed a haunted look. Scowling about the injustice, Dean headed for the bows of the Garrett barge.

He came right back to announce, "Just neighborhood rabble. Did you want to talk to them?"

"No. If you took in dogs instead of cats, we could set those on them."

The monster in my lap stirred, but only to wriggle into a more comfortable position.

John Stretch asked, "Does it look like a long siege? I need to get back. My people have a knack for mischief."

Dean shrugged. "I don't know. But Mr. Garrett is right. Eventually, they'll get bored and go away."

Once my pals in the Watch started rumors that would make the idiots decide that home-cooked food was more interesting than hanging around shouting obscenities about a fake complaint.

Oops. Suppose Relway's Runners snatched the girl?

"Hey, Saucerhead," I said. "What happened to Winger and her pet?"

Tharpe sneered. "Closed chapter, buddy. Winger is all after a fisa . . . fiso . . . something collalogistical of some kind who wants to shove things up our . . ."

I shuddered, absent the remotest notion. If I understood him at all, Winger was right and we needed to hunt down somebody who found that stuff exciting. Whatever it was.

I said, "That's interesting." Like I meant it. "This has been one of the longer days of my life. Thanks to these two villains." I pointed an indicting finger at Singe and Dean. "They started on me before the worms came out looking for the early birds. I'm so tired now that I probably won't go over to the factory tonight."

Singe said, "Tinnie is not finished being mad at you. You should stay away till she's ready to accept your apology."

"And when she hears about Belinda?" Life gets complicated if you get too engaged with it.

Dean sneered.

Saucerhead asked, "How was you figuring on getting out? On account of I still need to get out of here myself."

"Just wait till they get bored."

"There's still plenty of racket out there."

I shrugged. Tired was wearing me down. Also, that hint of the weird closing in that I'd begun to feel as soon as I came home.

*Crash!* Thunder shook the house. Stuff fell off my desk. Eleanor's portrait wobbled and ended up at a steep tilt. Dean dashed off to the kitchen. My ears rang. I hadn't heard anything fall out there but probably only because I couldn't hear.

Singe's eyes went wide with terror. John Stretch's, too. The primal rat took over. They didn't run only because there was nowhere to go.

Melondie Kadare was out cold.

"That was a close one," I said. My voice sounded weird to me.

I felt rather than heard the thunder rumble off into the distance. "That must have hit down here in the neighborhood."

Saucerhead grunted feebly.

I've never been bothered by thunder and lightning. I find a good lightning show enjoyable. But I'd seldom had the hobnailed boot of a god slam down quite so close. "That ought to break up the mob out front, Saucerhead."

He couldn't hear me, but the idea occurred to him on its own. He got moving toward the front door.

Dean returned, half of his favorite teapot dangling from his right forefinger. There were tears in his eyes.

A second peal of thunder started way off to the east and stumbled toward us, roared overhead, hugely loud, then ambled on westward, diminuendo. Soon afterward a lightning symphony opened to a vast audience.

Then some antic vandal of a boy god knocked open the sluice gates of heaven. The rain came. Torrents hammered the house.

Kittens poked their noses out of hiding places. Well. The world was still here.

Saucerhead came back. "That broke them up. Man, you got to see the hailstones coming down." He was more awed than frightened now.

I went to look.

Tharpe was right. It was an awesome show, the lightning flailing around, thunder's hammers pounding the anvil of the sky, hail coming in a downpour heavier than any I'd ever seen.

People always exaggerate the size of hailstones. That's human nature. So I'll say only that there were tons of them, they were big, and on the ricochet they knocked over carts and wagons. Then daring, enterprising, dim-witted youths hit the street with buckets and baskets, harvesting the ice while it still hammered down.

A flash almost blinded me. Thunder's roar came a heartbeat later, so strong I felt it right through my body. Had gangs of stormwardens decided to rumble? My ex-army pals claim they saw a lot of this sort of thing in the main war theater.

There were material as well as social advantages to being a Marine. Marines on swampy islands in the Gulf didn't have to worry about getting caught between dueling sorcerers. Sorcerers, on both sides, didn't mind cruel and deadly warfare, but they refused to become physically uncomfortable while they were fighting.

Saucerhead pushed past behind me. "I might freeze or drown, but I'm getting while I can get."

I had a couple of kittens underfoot, trying to figure out what hailstones were. They weren't impressed.

I asked, "You want a cat?"

Tharpe gave me a look colder than a bushel of hailstones.

"They're cute."

He left me with a one-finger salute.

# 29

Once again I got up earlier than was rational. Since I'd gone to bed early, though, I missed no sleep. I just didn't regain what I'd lost the day before.

Everybody else was up before me. Of course. Go figure. And they were all in good moods, despite wet and windy weather. Dean had a warm fire going. I settled in and observed professionally while he continued to deal with the storm damage. "How much do we need to replace?"

"I'm making a list. Not a lot. We had too much to begin with, since we never entertain." He produced tea in a cracked beaker. I drank.

"What's Singe up to?"

"She and her brother are in talking to the thing."

"The thing? Old Jolly woke up? Why didn't you say so?"

"It may be old age confusing me. I thought I just did. The fury of the storm woke him up."

I didn't buy that. Now I knew why I'd felt weird after I got home yesterday. Old Bones was awake and lying back in the weeds.

"Give me a refill, here, and I'll be off."

He muttered something about my not needing any tea to get there.

Singe had half the lamps in the house in the Dead Man's room. He makes her nervous. Though I don't know many people who are comfortable around corpses. Particularly around corpses still inhabited by the original occupants, like a ghost that can't get up and walk.

Asking what kind of mood he was in would waste time. Ill-tempered usually covered it. Instead, I asked, "Where are the cats?"

"Hiding," Singe said. "They are terrified."

"Makes sense. In his time His Nibs was known as Terror of Kittens."

John Stretch eyed me like he wasn't sure I was joking. He was rattled. If he were human, he'd have been a bloodless white.

"You sure he's awake?" I asked. "I've been in here a whole minute and he hasn't contradicted me yet."

*There are matters of greater weight to consider, Garrett. A dozen minds in the street outside need examination. Employing a pickpocket's touch inasmuch as they believe that I am no longer viable.*

"Ah. Were you ever?"

*And still the man wonders why I prefer sleep to suffering his company.*

He was employing one of his lesser minds to communicate. He didn't have his heart behind his snaps. He was distracted. Which was a good sign. He'd found this new world exciting enough to engage his intellect.

*Here is what you must do. Beginning immediately. Have Mr. Tharpe and Ms. Winger come see me. Employing your considerable talent for fabrication, get each of the following to visit, as well. Colonel Block and Deal Relway. Miss Contague. The child, Penny Dreadful. Any of the men who wear green pants. Or their handlers. The priest you visited. Teacher White or one of his henchmen.*

*Once I have interviewed a few of them it should become possible to develop strategies. Finding Mr. Contague and Mr. Temisk will be critical. Those two will be able to clarify the developing shakeout in organized crime.*

That's the Dead Man. He goes on and on. And on. The bottom line is legwork for me.

*Where is the bird? I do not sense the parrot.*

"Gone," I said. I tried to sound thrilled, but the truth is, I do miss the foulmouthed chicken. Just a little. In rare, maudlin moments.

*Ah. An interesting turn of events. Most of which I am thankful to have missed.*

"You didn't miss much."

*Do you honestly believe you can mislead me?*

"I don't remember who, but somebody said that where there's life, there's hope."

*My cousin Duphel said it first.*

"What?"

He responded with the mental equivalent of a shrug. He had wasted time enough. *Here is your schedule.*

My partner. Already in there bullying me to collect the bits he needed to make sense of the senseless. He makes connections quicker than I do.

*Should you prove able to approach Mr. Dotes in such fashion that his subsequent actions appear to be independent of your visit, ask him to stop by. Then go to the Bledsoe. See what more the outlanders have done.*

Didn't seem like they could've gotten much done. Most of them were in jail.

*There is a witch you know.*

"I know several."

*Exclude your stable of floozies.*

"Ouch! I was."

*Retain one and ask her to come here.*

"One who doesn't know about you?"

*That would be preferable.*

"I'm starting to wonder why I'm always determined to wake you up. Life is simpler when you're asleep."

*But it goes nowhere.*

"Wrong, Butterbutt. It goes the best places of all."

He started rummaging around inside my head, evidently under the delusion that he'd been invited. In seconds he was appalled in a big way.

*Where is the parrot?*

"Mr. Big? Pursuing a higher calling." The Goddamn Parrot belongs to days gone by and other stories. If there's any mercy in heaven, he'll never be more than another dyspeptic memory.

Chuckles tromped around inside my skull like twenty drug-crazed home invaders wearing sensible shoes. Being Himself, he dropped the question of the pestiferous, overdressed chicken like a maggoty dead mouse. He plowed on as though Mr. Big never existed.

"Speaking of critters. Tell me about the cats infesting the house. They don't seem normal."

*It is impossible to slip anything past you.*

"Answer the question."

*They are not normal cats. As you have surmised. They do demonstrate points of character we associate with domestic cats. I am unable, yet, to see into their minds. They are afraid of me.*

"Sounds like a healthy attitude. Everybody ought to be."

*You might adopt it yourself.*

"But I know what a big old cuddle bear you really are."

*Be careful when you leave. The kittens may attempt to escape.*

I was being dismissed. Told to get on with my chores. Sometimes he forgets who the senior partner is.

I returned to my office, found me a scrap of paper with a little clean on one side, made myself a list.

# 30

I leaned into the Dead Man's room. "You awake enough to reach somebody a block away?"

*Be more specific.*

"I just took a look out front. If you can reach a block, you can nab a character called Skelington, who works for Teacher White."

*Where?*

I described the spot.

*It may be that I am* not *sufficiently awake. If that bird was here, I could send him out and ride along.*

"Gotcha." He wanted me to go out there. "Don't be surprised if Skelington runs when he sees me coming, though."

*At this point in your career you should be capable of making an unthreatening approach.*

No point debating. "I'm on my way." I hitched my pants, patted myself down. I had an adequate low-intensity arsenal on board.

I was ready.

The weather drama was over, but a drizzle continued. Not a day when I'd work if Himself weren't back there with a sharp stick, poking.

Skelington was less thrilled to be out than I. Huddled in misery, he failed to see me coming till it was too late.

I told myself, "That went well," as Skelington entered my house. Maybe drizzly weather wasn't all bad, after all.

\* \* \*

Nobody was at home at Saucerhead's place. He hadn't been seen since yesterday. So he hadn't gone home from my place. I left a message mentioning the possibility of paid work.

Winger wasn't in her usual haunts. I couldn't run her down at home because I didn't know where she lived. I left word that Garrett had cash for her if she came to my house.

I couldn't think of a scheme to lure Block or Relway.

I strolled past Morley's place. Sarge was out front doing some wet-weather sweeping, pushing litter and horse apples over in front of a neighbor's dump. He showed me a scowl so black I waved and kept rolling. Just passing through. Didn't have no notion to drop in.

At Harvester Temisk's place two no-neck types muttered to one another about the chances of snow. I didn't recognize them. I did spot a familiar Relway Runner keeping an eye on the two brunos.

Not once during my icy-drizzle-down-the-back-of-my-neck wanderings did I spot Penny Dreadful. Which goes to show that even a fourteen-year-old girl has better sense.

Belinda I disregarded. I had no idea where to look for her nor any notion where to leave a message.

I wandered over to Playmate's stable, just to get in out of the miseries.

"Garrett, you look like that thing they talk about the cat dragging in." Playmate was banging hot iron in the smithy of his stable. Building horseshoes. Weather got in because he hadn't repaired all the damage done during some excitement we were involved in not long ago. He grumbled about not having the money.

Money couldn't be the problem. He had points in the same manufactory I did.

"Us honest folk got to work no matter what the weather is like."

Play whopped a hot horseshoe. "You make me regret that I've heard a calling, Garrett. Sometimes I want to cut loose and tell you how full of the stinky you are. This is one of those times."

"How come everybody does me that way, Play?"

"Everybody knows you."

I grumbled but didn't remind him that I was always there when any of them needed something.

"So to what do I owe the honor of your presence? What favor do you want now?"

"Nothing. Except to get in out of the rain. I'm headed somewhere else."

"Why aren't you home resting up for an evening of debauchery?"

"The Dead Man is awake."

"Oh. Thanks."

"You see? You're forewarned. The only guy in this cesspool of a city who is. So don't pass it along."

"I said thank you. Want some tea? There's water." He never lacks for heat in the smithy.

"Sure. Hey. You have any idea what happened to Antik Oder, used to have a storefront down the street?"

"Aha! So now we get to it."

"To what? The Dead Man wants a witch. Elderberry Whine kicked off when I wasn't looking."

Playmate made tea, his grin ivory in a mahogany sea. "Antik is still there. She isn't what you're looking for, though."

"Why not?"

"She's a fraud."

I grunted, sipped tea. "There's something in this."

"I dribbled in a dollop of vanilla rum."

I'm not big on hard liquor, but this was *good*. I rendered myself incapable of competent behavior in minutes.

It seemed like a good idea at the time.

Playmate isn't the kind who lets friendship get in the way of business. Much. "Rain's slowing down, Garrett. Time to move on."

I'd told him most of what was happening, hoping he'd have a suggestion. I'd wasted my breath. He asked, "Where are you headed from here?"

"I don't know. I'm thinking about crawling into the hayloft and grabbing forty winks."

Playmate frowned. He thought I was scamming, but couldn't figure my angle. "I guess it can't hurt. But shouldn't you show more ambition?"

"Ambition? About what?"

"Your job."

"Why? There ain't nobody paying me."

He doesn't stint the critters. The hay in the loft was first-rate.

It retained enough sweet clover smell to remind me of idylls in country pastures.

He was wrong. The drizzle hadn't slowed. It had grown into a steady rain. The rattle on the shingles overhead was a powerful soporific. Or maybe that was the rum.

I was gone in half a minute.

# 31

First I thought it was the change in the patter of the rain. Then I thought it was the cold. But the war taught me to wake up carefully and not to trust first impressions. I lay still, controlled my breathing, listened.

Playmate had company. That company wasn't looking for a place to stash horses.

I moved glacially till I could see.

Teacher White was down there, safely distant from Playmate, not coming across half as fierce as he wanted. He looked more like a pretend bad guy.

Assisting Teacher were two wide-load no-necks who looked like they were from out of town. Plausible, given that Teacher had only a half dozen soldiers of his own, none heftier than Spider Webb or Skelington.

Teacher cautioned the wide bodies, "Careful. There's more to the man than meets the eye." Though I can't imagine anybody underestimating Playmate.

Teacher told him, "There ain't no need for nobody to get hurt, Play. All you—"

"There is, you come in here pushing me around."

I steeled myself to jump in, though I suspected Playmate would be all right. The shoe might be on the other hoof. The bad guys might need help before the straw settled.

Playmate is all religious. He preaches turn the other cheek. But he takes an eye-for-an-eye attitude when it comes to professional scum.

Teacher asked, "Where's Garrett?"

Playmate didn't answer.

The wide loads moved in. Playmate met one with an invisibly fast straight jab to the schnoz that rocked the man's head back like it was about to pop off its stump. He plopped down on his back of beyond with a stunned, goofy look.

The second thug took a punch to the chest. Pure amazement filled his face. This didn't happen when you educated civilians.

Playmate collected a hammer. He showed it to Teacher White. Teacher took note. "Time to move along, boys."

Good thing, too, because I was just about to jump down and make life really harsh for Teacher.

Then I saw what I would've jumped into.

Spider Webb and guys named Original Dick and Vernor Choke showed up to help the wide loads leave. They hadn't made a sound there under the hayloft.

Vernor Choke had been born to his name. I didn't know the story on Original Dick. I wouldn't hang the moniker on anybody, but that didn't mean his mother hadn't.

I climbed down half a minute after Spider Webb exited, the last of the crew to leave.

Playmate observed, "Once again there's proof that just knowing you is a bad idea."

"What was that all about?"

"They're looking for some guy named Garrett. Said they followed him here. They didn't say why. They seemed pretty determined, though."

I put on my best baffled face. Without faking. "I don't get it. They've been following me around long enough to see that I can't tell them what they want to know."

"And what would that be, Garrett?"

"Huh? What would what be?"

"What do they want to know?"

"Well, hell!" I had no real idea. "Maybe just a closer look at my pretty face."

They *did* know that I couldn't find Chodo or Harvester. Didn't they?

"Oh, sure. That's got to be it, Garrett. How did that get past me?"

# 32

I gave Teacher and his crew fifteen minutes to hurry off to some far place where they could get out of the wet and forget harassing a handsome but ignorant investigator. Playmate supported my tactical view.

"I couldn't figure out what they *really* wanted," he admitted. "They changed stories three times. The bottom line, though, was that they really, really, *really* wanted to lay hands on a guy named Garrett."

"Thanks for not giving me up."

"Gratitude noted in the Book of for Whatever That's Worth."

"I am a handsome young man."

"Duly noted in the Book of Natural Fertilizers. Why don't you get out of here so I can get some work done?"

Some folks are obsessed with being productive.

"I can take a hint." I left messages for Saucerhead and Winger, in case he saw them before they got the word somewhere else.

The rain wasn't heavy, but it was steady. It wasn't one to please the farmers. They want their soakers in the springtime.

A voice husked, "Garrett."

I was a block from Playmate's. I was hunched over, wishing I had a poncho. The ones we'd used in the islands hadn't kept us dry, but they did keep us from being wounded by the larger raindrops.

"Spider." I hit Webb alongside the head with my stick, then spun and got Original Dick in his namesake. I wove easily past a wide-eyed Vernor Choke, smacked Teacher White between the eyes, and slid behind him while he wobbled. My stick lay across his throat. I lifted him a little.

Spider leaned against a wall, trying not to get dragged under by a concussion. Original lay curled up on the cobblestones in a smear of his own puke, fighting for air. Choke put on a show of dancing around looking for an opening. Teacher complained, "You broke my nose! I got blood all over my new jacket!"

They hadn't expected me to explode.

I hadn't brought enough explosives. I whispered, "Teacher, how about you tell me why you guys keep dogging me?" Then the big boys responded to all the whining.

I popped Teacher again, from behind, with immense enthusiasm, then faked right and ran left, headed for Playmate's place.

One of the brunos grabbed Vernor Choke and flung him like a bola. And Choke did the job, what with all those legs and arms trying to latch on to something as he flew by. I took several solid thumps before I got untangled. Seeing double, I had legs too watery to run.

Where was the Watch when a little interference might be useful?

Following Welby Dell, who was disguised as a handsome investigator by a cute illusion you can pick up for next to nothing on the black market.

I was too busy hurting to care. I got in a good whack at a kneecap. The other wide body kicked me in the ribs. Then somebody hit me from behind with that bucket of rocks than which he was dumber.

# 33

"Hey, Teach, I fink da asshole's comin' round," a voice said. It turned out to be Vernor Choke's.

I was tied into an ancient wooden armchair. The setting was the sort of hideout gang guys run to when there's a war on. There were pallets scattered around. Spider Webb and Original Dick occupied two. Both were in worse shape than me.

Choke got behind me. He lifted my chin, showed me Teacher White slumped in a chair close by, still leaking a little red.

Welby Dell appeared with a bowl of water, some cloth pieces, and a dirty hunk of sponge. He went to work on Teacher's face.

White mumbled something.

Dell relayed. "Where's Chodo?"

I shrugged. "I don't know. At home, I reckon. He don't get out much."

White mumbled. Dell asked, "Where's Harvester Temisk?"

"He don't keep me posted." I tried to turn my head. I wanted a fix on the wide bodies. Choke wouldn't let me. "Aren't you a little low on the food chain for this kind of crap?"

Welby Dell grimaced. Exactly what he thought. All this was going to make life tough later. Teacher was betting their asses on one pass of the dice.

So Teacher hadn't polled the troops before hiring outsiders and dumping everybody in the kettle. Nor had he leveled with them yet. They'd have a grand scramble, saving their butts.

Teacher mumbled, "I believe you, Garrett. I was pretty sure you wouldn't know. But you're a whiz at finding things. So you're going to find Harvester and Chodo for me."

I tried to work my muscles so they'd be loose when I jumped up out of the chair.

Teacher grumbled, "Where the fuck is Skelington? I got Original and Spider down. . . . That asshole was supposed to be . . . he bail on me?" White's eyes narrowed. He'd had a thought. That was so unusual that he took a while to get used to it before he asked, "You know where Skelington is, Garrett?"

I shook my head. That hurt. "Ask Director Relway." Maybe I wouldn't do much flying around. I had cracked ribs to go with my dented head.

Something was nuts. Teacher White wasn't stupid enough to come at me like this. He had to have an angle.

"Fucking Skelington! Fucking moron Skelington! He chickened out! He bailed. We gotta get the fuck outta here. Goddamn Skelington."

White's intelligibility began to fade.

"Brett. Bart. About time, you assholes. You find Kolda? You get the stuff from him? Give it to Garrett. Now. We got to get the fuck out of here."

A ham of a hand grabbed my hair and yanked. Another got hold of my chin and forced my mouth open. Another one packed my mouth with shredded weed that had enjoyed a generation as skunk bedding before it got into the herbal-supplement racket. Yet another hand turned up with a lumpy old unfired mug full of water, most of which ended up on my outside.

The several hands forced my mouth shut, then covered my nose so I couldn't breathe. The ancient trick for making a critter take its medicine.

"Swallow, Garrett," Teacher told me.

I fought, but there was no winning. The lump went down like a clump of raw chaw, blazing all the way.

Teacher told me, "You'll nap for a while, Garrett. You just swallowed a drug that will see to that while Kolda's weeds have time to work." Teacher strained to hold it together long enough to give me all the bad news. "When you wake up you'll notice that it's getting hard to breathe. After a while, if you don't think about it, you'll stop. If you stop, you'll die."

I felt something spreading from my belly already. It wasn't the happy warmth of a Weider Select lager.

"Here's the deal. You stay awake and pay attention, you'll be all right. You fall asleep, you'll die. You can't remember to breathe

if you're asleep. Bring me Chodo or Harvester before you croak—
I'll give you the antidote. You know my word is solid."

That was Teacher's reputation. Though it did rest exclusively
on the testimony of people who were still alive. Those he'd done
real dirt to weren't around to bear witness.

"Nighty-night, Garrett. Don't waste no fucking time when you
wake back up." White snarled, "The rest of you get this mess
cleaned up. We got to get away from here."

The man was an idiot. He'd jumped on what looked like a
good idea without thinking it through. His biggest failing was
right on the tip of my tongue when the sleepy drug dragged me off
into the dark.

The question was, how did I find him when I was ready to
hand Chodo over? Assuming I found Chodo.

Overall, Teacher White qualified as a smart crook. The proof?
He was still alive. He'd reached middle management. He'd stayed
alive by being careful never to show any imagination.

His actions now constituted rock-hard evidence that he didn't
have what it took to be a schemer.

He was going to get killed.

There was a damned good chance he'd take me with him.

# 34

Damn, my head hurt.

That wasn't a hangover. This was real pain caused by real blows to the head. Accompanied by pains everywhere else.

I was in the same chair. I wasn't tied down anymore. It was raining. Still. Moist air gusted in through a door that banged in the wind. It was the middle of the night. The rain was no heavier, but the wind was colder and more fierce. Occasional barks of thunder rattled the walls.

I got up. The change in elevation made my head swirl. My temples throbbed. My ribs screamed in protest. I might have made a sound or two myself.

There was no light. I wasted no time looking for a lamp. I headed for the doorway, landmarked by the lightning. I had to get out. I had to get moving. I couldn't get caught here.

I was at street level but didn't recognize where. I tried to get my thoughts wrapped around memories of Teacher White's territory. That didn't help.

It was cold and wet out. I wasn't dressed for it.

Not only had Teacher's guys disarmed me, but they had taken my jacket. They'd taken my roc's egg and my belt. I was going to be cold and wet and miserable before I got home. Assuming I figured out which way to go.

I clung to the doorframe, feeling too sick to move. Chunks of hardened rain took the occasional nick out of my face. I looked back at what I needed to leave behind, fast.

There were dead bodies in there. Original Dick and Spider Webb. I didn't know why. Or how. I wasn't going to check. Original was still curled up where he'd been all along, clinging to his midnight specials.

I staggered into the weather and hiked. I reached an intersection. It told me nothing. I clung to my assumption that I was inside Teacher's patch. I turned left because that would take me uphill. A higher vantage might reveal a familiar landmark next time the lightning flashed.

I shivered a lot.

I figured out where I was after two more blocks. Headed the wrong direction. Four blocks down that way . . . stumble. Stumble. And there I was, in a lane I knew, that led me to a street everyone knows. Two blocks east I hit a thoroughfare that would take me home.

But my head wasn't clearing up. I had a serious concussion. And huge trouble breathing.

# 35

Somebody too close to me had breath that should've drawn flies. Then I realized that stinky mouth had kept me breathing with the kiss of life.

Then I was home. Installed in a chair in the Dead Man's room. With no clue how I'd gotten there.

In a chair. Again. Barely rational. Among many chairs, some occupied by people maybe worse off than me.

The Dead Man had them under control. I felt his grip on me, which I resented immensely till I worked out that I was still alive because old Smiley was working my lungs for me.

The Dead Man's company included Skelington, looking more cadaverous than ever, John Stretch in his sister's chair, Saucerhead, Winger, and the Remora. Jon Salvation glowed because he was mind to mind with the famous Dead Man. Oh, and there were three guys who worked for Block or Relway, tossed in a corner.

*Relax, Garrett. I have to examine your memories directly.*

I was focused on breathing so didn't argue. Ah. Here came hot soup and a toddy. Here came Singe and a baby cat that wanted nothing to do with the Dead Man's room. She set it in my lap. The arch went out of its back. Its fur lay down. It started purring. And I became both calm and optimistic.

Winger and Jon Salvation got up and left, obviously on a mission. Saucerhead left soon afterward. Then Dean appeared. He said the rain had eased up enough for pixies to fly. If any flying had to be done.

He went away and returned shortly with a toddy for my other hand.

I began to feel more upbeat. My tummy was full, the toddies were warming me, and Singe was tending my dents and dings. "Careful with the ribs." The concussion seemed to have faded.

Old Bones had turned off all my pain. Singe is no light-fingered nightingale. She poked, prodded, dug, gouged. "Nothing broken. This time. I need your shirt off to see how bad you are bruised."

Several of Morley's men were on hand, looking nervous and inclined to be elsewhere. One snickered. Puddle's hulking shape made a sharp gesture. The others kept it to themselves after that.

I focused a thought, wondering what they were doing here.

*It will be done as soon as possible. I must install memories in the one named Puddle that will permit him to carry information to Mr. Dotes without his recalling having had contact with me.*

"What happened to me?"

My mind filled with outside recollections.

One of Morley's boys had found me on his way to work. He'd been late. A woman was responsible. Married. To somebody who wasn't him. He wouldn't have noticed me if I hadn't been pointed out by some street kid.

He told Morley that his friend Garrett was in the gutter down the street, bleeding in the rain.

So I'd tried to reach The Palms after realizing that I couldn't make it home.

A rescue team went out and scraped me up.

*There.*

Puddle and the boys departed, zombielike. Dean made sure they all left the premises.

I recalled the terrible bad breath. And decided never to mention the kiss of life.

Puddle has trouble with his breath.

*I find myself in a quandary.*

"Yeah? That anywhere near Ymber? Dean. How about another toddy?" I'd apologize to Max Weider someday. Rare though they be, in some moments beer isn't the best choice.

Dean looked to the Dead Man momentarily before stating, "You get one more. Then there'll be no more drink."

"The quandary?"

*I must see Colonel Block or Deal Relway. I will need them to help me get into the minds of the servants of A-Laf.*

"Then you turned Puddle loose too soon. Him and his crew could spread the word about how they brought me home and it don't look like I'll make it and you won't wake up to help. Or send that stack o'Watch in the corner."

The front wall reverberated to a major pixie launch.

*I will correct that oversight. Dean. Take a few coins to the front door to express our gratitude to Mr. Dotes' men.*

*Let Miss Pular put you to bed now, Garrett. You need not worry. As you surmised, Teacher White blundered badly.*

"Makes you wonder if *anybody* could be that dumb, don't it?"

*Never underestimate the reserves of stupid lying within this city. Nevertheless, an amble through Mr. White's mind might prove interesting.*

I wanted to ask what Skelington had revealed, but Singe didn't give me time.

*I know where to find you. Dean, see to the door, please.*

# 36

I slept like a baby, thanks to my partner. One of his lesser minds managed my breathing. The samsom weed caused a sleep almost as deep as a coma. I had visitors during the night and was unaware of it. They included the herbalist who named what I'd been given but who knew of no antidote except good luck, time, and lots of water. He was amazed that I was still alive, so the luck did seem to be in.

Skelington knew Teacher White got the sleepy weed from a character named Kolda. Skelington believed there was an antidote and he thought Kolda had it.

Also in were a witch and a healer of the laying-on-of-hands variety. Neither did me any immediate good. Both agreed that I should drink water by the gallon. And Old Bones got to visit with a witch even though I'd been unable to deliver. He never explained why.

Others came in response to rumors of my ill health but waited till sunrise. Except for Tinnie Tate. She found a way to put the contrary aside when life got down to its sharp edges.

I woke up long enough to say, "Sometimes dreams do come true."

Tinnie Tate is one incredible redhead. All the superlatives apply. She's the light of my life—when she's not its despair. In some ways she's the gold standard of women, in some the source of all confusion and frustration. The trouble with Tinnie is, she doesn't know what she wants any better than I do. But she won't admit it.

She was there. And that was enough for now. She looked thoroughly distressed—until she realized that I was awake. Then her demeanor turned severe.

"When you do that, the freckles just stand out."

"You're a bastard even on your deathbed."

"I'm not gonna die, woman. 'Cept maybe from lack of Tate."

"And crude to your last breath."

"Cold. It's so cold. If I just had some way to keep warm . . ."

She was a step ahead.

Only one weak candle provided light. It was enough. For the hundredth time I was stunned and awed that this woman was part of my life.

How can I rail against the gods when once in a while they back off and let wonders like this happen?

Nothing happened. The Dead Man was right there in my head, disdaining discretion.

# 37

It don't matter who spends the night, snuggled up or otherwise. Pular Singe will drop in before the birds start chirping. And blame it on Dean. Or the Dead Man. Which was the case this time.

"You are needed downstairs."

I doubted it. His Nibs could have summoned me without troubling Singe. I grumbled, growled, muttered, disparaged some folks' ancestry. But by the time I arrived in what Old Bones had turned into an operations center, I knew all he wanted was my managing my own breathing so he could free up the secondary mind keeping me huffing and puffing.

There was a vast, ugly conspiracy afoot, designed to confine me to the house. So I wouldn't get involved in anything strenuous, like, say, discouraging somebody who wanted to twist little bits off of me.

I sat. I watched folks come and go. I breathed. Smiley didn't fill me in. This was how he worked. He gathered information. He looked for unexpected connections. Usually, though, I'm the main data capture device.

Dean brought food and tea. I ate. And sat some more while people came and went. I wondered who was paying them. Being a natural-born, ever-loving blue-eyed investigator, I intuited the answer. And felt the wealth sucking right out of me. My associates have no concept of money management.

I wondered who all my guests were. Some were complete strangers. Not Relway Runners, Combine players, Green Pants thugs, nor even part of the Morley Dotes menagerie.

"What are we doing?"

The Dead Man didn't answer me. *You believe Teacher White's men took your roc's egg?*

"I had it before I turned unconscious. I didn't have it when I woke up."

*Exactly.*

"Excuse me?"

*I sent Mr. Tharpe to the place where you were held, immediately after I determined where it was. His examination of the site and the corpses suggests third-party involvement.*

"Huh?"

*When drugged you were supposed to remain able to do Teacher White's dirty work. The you who staggered away from there may not have been intended to wake up at all. You have contusions and abrasions unaccounted for in your memories. There are indications that someone attempted to strangle you.*

"How do you figure all that?"

*Circumstantial evidence. Your condition. The fact that Spider Webb was strangled with your belt. It was still around his neck when Mr. Tharpe arrived. The other man was strangled, too. There were bruises on his throat. Similar bruises are on your throat.*

*More suggestive is the fact that the bodies and other evidence were gone when Miss Winger went up there this morning.*

"Teacher is in deep gravy and don't even know it? Who?"

*That would be the question.*

"A question, certainly."

*We may be able to ask Mr. White himself soon. His associate Mr. Brix has told us where to find him.*

"Who's Mr. Brix?"

*The man you know as Skelington. His name is Emmaus P. Brix. With the middle initial standing for nothing. Ah. Mr. Tharpe has achieved another success.*

Two minutes later Saucerhead's associates from Whitefield Hall, Orion Comstock and June Nicolist, stumbled in, struggling with a wooden box obviously heavy for its size. Dean appeared immediately, armed with a specialized pry tool. Another product of my manufactory.

Singe paid Nicolist and Comtock, painstakingly recording the transaction. Neither seemed troubled by the Dead Man. They thought he was still hibernating. Despite the crowd, all of whom seemed part of the Dead Man's club.

*These gentlemen have not been here before. They may not come here again.*

"Oh."

Orion Comstock took the pry bar from Dean.

Nails shrieked as they came loose.

Kittens screamed all over the house. I heard them run, in confusion, upstairs, then back down into the kitchen.

*Ah. As I suspected.*

"What?"

*To whom do you suppose they will think you are speaking?*

I covered by heading for the hallway. Dean said, "I'll go. You need to be here." He sounded upset.

Singe, too, seemed troubled. Her exposed fur had risen. That doesn't happen often.

There was even an undercurrent of revulsion in my connection with the Dead Man. Then I started to hear new voices. Inside my head.

I edged nearer Comstock and Nicolist.

The wooden box was lined with sheets of lead. Inside sat a matched pair of shiny metal sitting dogs, each nine inches tall.

*Jackals,* Old Bones opined. *Almost certainly carrion eaters.*

"You guys get these from the Bledsoe?"

Comstock eyed me suspiciously. "That was the contract, wasn't it, slick? You saying—"

"Just startled. Saucerhead trusts you—I trust you. The ones I saw weren't sitting."

Comstock shrugged. "We seen some that was standing and some that was lying down. One was suckling pups. But Saucerhead said you wanted ones that was sealed up already. These are them."

"That's true. You did fine." I started to shove my mitts into the box.

*Stop!* Disappointed whispers echoed afterward.

"Careful there, slick. You don't want to touch them things with your bare skin."

I stopped. Cold rolled off the statues.

Nicolist showed me the outside edge of his left little finger. "That was just an accidental swipe."

A piece of skin was missing, a quarter inch wide and three quarters long. Cruel bruising surrounded the wound.

"Aches a bit," I supposed aloud.

"A bit. We need to get out of here, Orion. Runners are bound to turn up."

A concern that hadn't occurred to me, though it was inherent in the situation. "I'll let you out. And thanks, guys. You really helped out. We'll come to you first next time we have a tough job."

Orion and June exchanged looks, shrugs, and headshakes.

I used the peephole. I didn't see anything remarkable. Except that my door-fixer-upping technician, Junker Mulclar, had pulled his cart up behind one that must have brought the metal dogs. I told Comstock and Nicolist, "Nobody there but the people who always are. Move out cool and nobody will notice."

They went to the street. Mr. Mulclar hoisted his toolbox to his shoulder. He was wide, short, dark, craggy, an ugly man who counted a dwarf among his ancestors somewhere. He owned one of those faces that need shaving three times a day just to look dirty.

Junker is overly fond of cabbage, in both kraut and unpickled form. Whenever he stays in one place long that becomes overwhelmingly evident.

"Good morning, Mr. Mulclar. It seems to be the hinges this time."

"Call me Junk, Mr. Garrett. Everybody does. What happened?" He rumbled enthusiastically at the nether end. He didn't apologize. All part of the natural cycle.

"Same as always. These bad guys were bigger than usual, though."

"No! That can't be." He punctuated with a minor poot. "That door I put in last time ought to stand up to—"

"It isn't the door, Mr. Mulclar. It's the hinges. And if you saw those guys, you'd preen like a peacock for ten years because your work stood up so well."

Mulclar indulged in a rumbling chuckle, proud. Then rumbled in the opposite direction. The air was getting thick. Junk didn't notice. "You got some spare room in your basement? Space you ain't using? On account of I'm over here a whole lot anyway and my wife is throwing me out. . . ." He cut a competition class ripper. "Not sure why. Maybe she found a new heartthrob. Anyways, then I'd be right here whenever it was time to service my mainest account."

"That don't sound like such a bad idea, Junk." Hard to converse when you don't want to inhale. "But I already have more people living here than I can manage. And, nothing personal, but I owe them all more than I owe you."

"So it goes. I'll stay with my cousin Sepp. Or my sister." *Rip!* "It'll all work out. Though I'm going to have to diversify. With all this law and order going on they ain't so many doors getting broke down."

Junker Mulclar is a genius with hands and tools. There aren't enough like him in the Brave New TunFaire of postwar Karenta.

I gulped in some fresh air as a whiff breezed past. "Junk, I'm going to do you a favor. If you swear on your mother's grave you'll fix my doors forever."

*Rumble!* "Sure, Mr. Garrett. I thought we had that deal already."

"You know where the three-wheel manufactory is in Stepcross Pool?"

"Sure."

"You go find the green door, tell the man there I said you should see Mr. Dale Pickle. Take your tools. They'll give you all the work you can handle, and then some. And a place to stay, if that's what you need."

My business associates, all of whom possess percentages bigger than mine, agree that we should take care of our workers. Max Weider built his brewing empire by valuing and rewarding the people who made it happen for him.

Weider brewing employees are happy and ferociously loyal.

The manufactory could use a man of Mr. Mulclar's skills. And if he lived in, he'd soon become less aromatic. They wouldn't let him do his own cooking.

Mulclar did me an immense favor. "If you'll move out of the way, I can get those hinges fixed. It'll take maybe an hour."

Good luck with that, I thought.

I noted that Comstock and Nicolist hadn't taken their cart. If stolen carts kept turning up out front, there were bound to be questions.

I went in to warn everybody that we wouldn't have a door for a while.

# 38

It was quiet in the Dead Man's room. Singe and Dean had grown scarce to the point of invisibility. Several guests remained fixed in place. So did the metal statues in their lead-lined coffin.

"Those two had a point, Chuckles. It can't be long before we have a visit from the Watch." I heard whispers again. Saying evil things.

*Excellent.*

"You want them to?"

*I hope Colonel Block comes himself.*

"There's a chance. If he thinks you're snoozing. We'll never see Relway again, though. He's too clever and too paranoid to take a chance."

*No doubt.*

"You seem distracted."

*I am trying to locate the creature Penny Dreadful. I feel her close by, but she is extremely elusive. Even the pixies could not pinpoint her when I sent them out last night. If the parrot were available . . .*

"He's gone to a better place, far, far away. Tell me about these statues." I could make out no words, but the whispers continued.

*In a moment. I want to examine an idea I found cowering in the back of your mind.*

It must have been skulking around *way* back there. I couldn't recall having any that didn't involve heading back upstairs to Tinnie.

*Yes. I do have sufficient capacity. Think about your breathing. You will have to manage for yourself for a while.*

"Huh?"

I felt a distinct difference when he let go. I thought he had already.

Minutes later one of our guests got up and sleepwalked out of the house. Focusing on my work, I breathed steadily as I watched him ease past Mr. Mulclar. He didn't notice the miasma, which had taken over the hallway. He didn't hear the voices. He was operating on another plane.

Old Bones retained control all the way down to Wizard's Reach, well away from Mrs. Cardonlos' place.

So. Now I knew what had been plucked from my brain. A wisp about filling empty heads with conflicting false memories so we could get these people out from underfoot. So we didn't have to feed them and take them potty and otherwise be weighted down with them.

A second man rose and went away. I didn't see him off. I didn't need another exposure to Mr. Mulclar. "Is this premature? Letting them go before we get somebody in to ask about the metal dogs?"

*Jackals.*

"Whatever. You see my point? Them being missing for a while, then turning up all confused and not knowing anything?"

*I see your point. However, you fail to credit me with sufficient ability to confuse the issue.*

"I'd never do that."

*Do you recall past instances of dereliction by members of the Watch?*

"Sure. There's probably a lot, but less than before Block and Relway took over."

The rest of our guests, excepting Skelington, left us eventually.

"So. About these dogs—all right! I know. Jackals. We've got them. What about them? What are they? Why have them stolen?" Getting rid of them would suit me fine. Especially if doing so would get rid of the voices in my head.

*I have not heard of this cult of A-Laf, but there are suggestive similarities with others, particularly in the matter of the metal animals. If they are nickel, or some alloy that is mainly nickel, their function will be much like that of the nickel figurines that graced the altars of Taintai the Gift some centuries ago.*

I'd never heard of Taintai the Gift. But there must be brigades of gods, goddesses, and their supporting casts who haven't sailed across my bows. Deities come and go. Their cycles are just longer than human ones.

"Interesting stuff, Chuckles. It'd be even more interesting if you'd drop a hint or two about what's going on."

I felt his amusement as he sent, *That will have to wait. We are about to have official company. Deal with it in your office instead of here.*

Vaguely, I caught the edge of a thought directed at Melondie Kadare. My pixie tribe were paying their rent now.

I scooted across to my office. I couldn't hear the incessant dark whispering over there.

Dean passed me in the hallway, headed for the front doorway. Where, after an hour, Mr. Mulclar did not yet have the bent hinges repaired or replaced.

I wondered if he heard the dark mutterings.

# 39

There was some racket in the hallway. Dean making offended noises. Somebody had gotten past Mr. Mulclar. More clever than I thought he could be, Dean fought a valiant retrograde action that lured the invader past the Dead Man's room to the open door of my office.

The man who burst into my office looked like he had been slapped together from parts taken from other people. On the south end he had spindly little legs and almost no butt. On top he had the chest and shoulders of a Saucerhead or Playmate. Then a head that went with his antipodes. All wrapped up in a badly fitted blue uniform.

He came in with mouth a-running. "What do you think you're doing, stealing religious relics?" Followed by fulminations that grew louder when I failed to acknowledge his presence.

Gently, calmly, conversationally, I asked, "Are you right-handed?"

"Huh? What the hell?"

"Which hand do you use to abuse yourself? That's the arm I'll break first." I ignored his associates. One wore a blue uniform jacket but not the matching trousers. His were brown. Maybe he couldn't afford the full outfit.

The fact that I remained more interested in paperwork than a raving home invader took the blusterer aback. Clearly, I rated him barely a nuisance.

I pretended to sign something, then looked up. "You didn't answer me. Nor have you introduced yourself. Are you married?"

"Married?"

"You keep on being an asshole, I'll need to know where to send the pieces."

I was playing a dumb, macho game. I could afford to. I had the Dead Man behind me.

Said sidekick let me know, *This nimrod is named Ramey List. He is a political appointee assigned to the Watch over the objections of Prince Rupert, who seems to have had little choice. His rank is captain. He is, nominally, a staff officer. The motive for putting him into the Watch seems to have been both political and to position him where he can get himself killed.*

"So that's what the new staff uniforms look like."

Captain Ramey List gaped.

His sort aren't uncommon. He was an incompetent aristocrat who suspected his own shortcomings and compensated by being obnoxious to social inferiors.

"Now that we're civil, what can I do for you, Captain List?" The Dead Man hadn't explained what he'd sent me. I assumed he'd raided the heads of List's companions for perspective. "Have a seat."

Captain List sat. Chuckles would be sedating him some.

List's companions remained at the doorway. The one with a uniform jacket offered a slight nod of approval.

"What can I do for my friends in the Watch?"

Captain List was confused. "Uh . . . Colonel Block wants to know why you defaced the Bledsoe and stole certain metal ornaments."

"I didn't. If that happened, I had nothing to do with it." Which was true.

List believed me, a remarkable eventuation for an officer of the law.

Dean brought refreshments, identical little trays for List and his companions.

In minutes List relaxed and, puzzled, was trying to swap jokes. He butchered every attempt. A born diplomat, I tossed in the occasional charitable chuckle. I said, "It's still early, but if anybody wants a beer? . . ."

Something stirred behind List's eyes. Bingo! I knew his vice without Old Bones clueing me in. A problem with drink combined with a vile personality is a recipe for unpleasant excitement.

Captain List won that fall with his demon. It was early in the day. The devil wasn't wide-awake and thirsty yet.

Then Dean appeared with a tray of frosty mugs. Nobody shunned the opportunity.

Dean said, "I'll need to go out today, Mr. Garrett. Unless you choose to stop entertaining. We're down to the bottom of the backup keg."

"Ouch."

"There's wine in the cellar. But it's probably gone off."

"We'll arrange something. Later."

*One beer should leave the man marked by aroma enough to make him suspect.*

"I suppose."

Captain List frowned. "You suppose?"

"I suppose it's time to get back to work. Dean, do you have your shopping list? Where did he go?"

The Watchman in the blue jacket told me, "He went back to your kitchen."

I got up. List did the same. We shook hands, me thanking him for coming by.

*Keep him moving. Do not give him time to think.*

Which I did. And during his flustered exit he did what might be the only socially useful deed he'd ever perform. "Dagon's balls, man!" he snarled at Mr. Mulclar. "Did a skunk crawl up your ass and die? Do something! You could gag a maggot."

The Watchman not in uniform hung back. "I don't know what you just did, buddy, but if you figure out how to bottle it, I want some. I've got to babysit that asshole six days a week."

"Some time when there's just you and him in a bad part of town, get behind him with a board and whack him in the back of the head."

The man grinned. "I like the way you think. Shit. There he goes, starting to whine."

I turned to head back inside to visit the Dead Man. Mr. Mulclar asked, "Do I have a problem, Mr. Garrett?"

"Sir?"

"That fellow that just left said . . ."

"Yes, Junk, you're eating too much kraut. That's something you can change, though. He'll never stop being a dickhead." I hurried on into the Dead Man's room. "Was there a point to any of that?"

*That man is, in effect, Colonel Block's second-in-command. He is convinced that he will replace the Colonel before the end of the year. He has been assured that that will be the case.*

"There's a plot to get rid of Block?" I was surprised but not amazed. "Is List more competent than he lets on?"

*Less. Under his supervision the Watch will collapse back to its corrupt old days. At best. At worst he will become a puppet of conspirators no more competent than he. They discount Deal Relway because he is not of their social stratum.*

"Then they're in for a nasty surprise."

*Indeed. The nastiest. There is no practical brake on Mr. Relway but Westman Block. Who removes the Colonel sows the whirlwind.*

"Did we find out anything else useful?"

*If you are interested in making a chain-of-command chart for the Watch, we now have all the names. Or if you're interested in the identities of informants and undercover operatives who work for Colonel Block, we have that. The list includes one Sofgienec Cardonlos. Never legally married.*

"Aha! I was sure she belonged to Relway."

*That is not impossible.*

Of course. "Anything about the Green Pants Gang?"

*He is not allowed near them. But he hears rumors.*

We went back and forth until I knew what he wanted me to know. I asked, "So how about we get back to the dog statues?"

*Jackals! Are you stupid?*

"No. Why is the distinction a big deal?"

*Words are important, Garrett. Especially when they are names. The same is true of symbols. Religious symbols in particular. The jackal is important in many religions. None more so than those with a dark view of earthly existence. The cult of A-Laf appears to hold one of the darkest.*

He'd clue me in about the jackals in his own sweet time. If he had any real notion. He isn't above claiming knowledge he doesn't actually have. He doesn't just have multiple minds—he has multiple egos.

"You reached that conclusion based on what?"

*Their behavior. The all-round implication that the cult is blacker than its feminine counterpart, which seems grim itself. Combined with recollections of historical precedents.*

"You mentioned past cults before. Without explaining."

*Past cults, yes. None quite like this. These people are not creating the pain and despair they harvest on behalf of their god. They collect it where . . . oh.*

"What?"

*We are about to have company. Again. Get them inside as quickly as you can.*

"You keeping an eye on Mulclar? He's seeing a lot of coming and going."

*He is oblivious. His entire being is focused on his work and his unfortunate flatulence. The possibility that his gassy nature is responsible for his outcast status never occurred to him before. Get those people inside.*

So he wasn't going to explain the jackals now, either.

Did he have any real idea?

# 40

"Those people" arrived aboard a big black coach driven by Morley's man Sarge. The guy I knew only as Theodore rode beside Sarge. They were alert.

The coach door facing the house opened. Puddle popped out. He cursed when he banged into the cart abandoned by Comstock and Nicolist, looked around like he expected to see Venageti skirmishers. I saw no weapons but suspected an arsenal was available.

Puddle beckoned. A man descended from the coach, pushed. He had his hands bound behind him. He was blindfolded. Welby Dell. Ah. Interesting. Puddle made him run.

Theodore jumped down and helped Puddle extract a reluctant Teacher White. Teacher had no idea where he was headed, but he meant to fight all the way. It took Puddle and Theodore both to get him in the house.

There were two more passengers. A Combine third-stringer named Trash Blaser and my very good pal Mr. Morley Dotes. I wasn't entirely surprised to see him. Nor was I stunned when neither of Teacher's imported thugs tumbled out of the coach. Which headed on up the street as soon as Sarge saw his boss slide past Mr. Mulclar.

There was a roar that could only be the tradesman losing control of something he'd been holding far too long. Morley gasped, "Oh, gods of the Rime!"

I delayed a half minute, hoping the breeze would disperse the miasma. While waiting, I noted that my pixies were as busy as bees, to sling an old chestnut.

My wait was pointless. Mr. Mulclar repeated himself with a true cathedral clearer just as I got there.

"I'm sorry, Mr. Garrett. I can't help it."

"I know that, Junk. None of us can. But we can watch what we eat. How much longer are you going to be?"

"It shouldn't be long. What the problem is, the screws—"

"I'm not concerned. It's your craft. One thing you can do for me, though, is keep an eye out for anybody who looks like they're interested in my place. The kind who try to break doors down might try to get in while this one is off its hinges."

"Oh. Yeah." *Rumble!* "I never even thought about that. I'll keep a eye out for sure."

"Excellent. You're a good man, Junk." I beat a hasty retreat. Teacher might have done me a favor, fixing it so I didn't have to breathe.

The new arrivals gathered in the Dead Man's room. None of them were happy. Morley less than most, probably. He sensed the truth immediately. The Dead Man wasn't napping anymore.

I confirmed his suspicion. "You and your guys want to get on out of here, go. If you'd be more comfortable."

They would. The whole bunch tramped back out, Morley leaving me with a dark look and an invitation. "Come by the club when you get a chance."

"Sure."

He followed his guys.

The ghost of a chuckle filled the psychic atmosphere.

"They didn't get out fast enough, did they?"

*No.* More psychic mirth. *They never do.*

He was having a good time, glad, now, that he'd wakened.

Singe came in, halfway slinking. She still isn't comfortable with the Dead Man, either.

His Nibs gave us our instructions.

Singe removed Teacher's blindfold and gag, but left his hands tied behind him. He found me seated facing him.

"So. Teacher. Things change. You got anything to say?"

Teacher wasn't happy. Not even a little. But he couldn't see the Dead Man from where he sat. He didn't yet know true despair.

He didn't respond. He wasn't a complete mental lightweight. He wanted to scope out his situation before he did anything.

"Here's how it is. Your poison didn't take. Not completely. So I'm not going to hold a grudge." I raised an eyebrow, then winked.

He wasn't naturally as pale as Skelington, but he came close. He couldn't see the Dead Man. Skelington was in plain sight.

*His mind is well shielded. I am making headway. While moving carefully enough not to make him suspicious. Distract him.*

"Teacher, didn't you do your homework? Why didn't you know that you couldn't pull something like you tried and get away with it?"

Teacher had nothing to say.

"Seemed like a good idea at the time, though, eh?" I gave him a few seconds. "Somebody put you up to it? Dean, I'm getting dry. Can you bring me some water?"

*The supporting staff know little of any value. Although, between them, they have developed an extended list of places that Mr. Contague and Mr. Temisk cannot be.*

"And might there be a pattern? A hole somewhere?"

*Your continued queries have alerted Mr. White to the possibility that I may not be fully expired.*

I didn't need Chuckles to tell me when Teacher grasped the truth. He turned paler than he had been already.

I asked, "What did you do with my stuff you took? In your wallet? Good. So. Who killed Spider and Original? No? You can't tell me? You didn't know? You left them there with me."

"They was supposed to look out for you. To make sure you didn't croak or nothing before you woke up."

*He believes that to be true.*

"What happened to Brett and Bart?"

"I didn't need them no more. I paid them off. Cut them loose."

Dean arrived with water. And a shopping list. Which looked all right. And made clear just how expensive all the entertaining was getting. "We're completely out of tea?"

"We are."

Grumble. "What's Singe up to? She get the kittens settled down?"

"They aren't happy. They're all huddled in their bucket. But they're not in a panic anymore."

The voice in my head told me, *The gentlemen from out of town were subcontracted through one Squint Vrolet.*

A ladder of wickedness popped into mind. Squint worked for Green Bean Ractic. Neither ran a patch where they'd have need of Bretts and Barts. But Green Bean reported to Tizzy Baggs. Tizzy's sister was married to Merry Sculdyte, Rory Sculdyte's stupid but enthusiastically homicidal brother.

Rory's psychotic little sibling managed a stable of violence specialists.

"Teacher, any chance you've been doing legwork for somebody without knowing? Merry S., maybe?"

*He thinks so now.*

Teacher had nothing to say, though.

*Our reluctant guest is extremely angry, Garrett.*

"I would be, too. Teacher. What about my antidote?"

White looked at me like he wondered if I was hopelessly naive. He asked, "Am I going to get out of here?"

"You got a good chance. What shape you'll be in remains to be determined. Think we could get Squint and Green Bean in for a sit-down?"

He understood me perfectly. "There *is* an antidote."

"I know that. But I don't trust you enough to send you after it. Not until we fix you up with an unpleasant situation of your own."

*Easily done.*

"Huh?"

*This man has a strong natural wall around his thoughts. But he cannot protect them consciously.*

"Where are you going?"

*He has friends inside the Watch. Inside the Al-Khar. Properly pushed, he might help us lay hands on one of those Green Pants fellows.*

"Interesting. But why waste the knowledge? Block himself might bring them over."

*You could be right,* he admitted. Reluctantly.

"Here's your situation," I told Teacher. "My friend just planted a Loghyr mindworm in your brain. It'll make you go crazy. Slowly. Like those guys you see walking around arguing with themselves. Only it'll keep getting worse. Until a Loghyr pulls it back out. And there's only one Loghyr around these days."

I didn't highlight any ironies. I didn't say anything about who did what to whom. At the Dead Man's urging, I told White, "Get any of these people over for a chat—your life will get a whole lot easier."

The Dead Man sent him a roster that included the heaviest heavyweights of TunFairen crime. Teacher promised to get someone into the Dead Man's clutches somehow, but it might not happen fast enough to suit us.

*It will,* the Dead Man predicted, including Teacher in his sending. *Or it will not happen at all.* Moments later, White was loose. The Dead Man surrounded him with confusion so he could get a head start.

# 41

"Was that mindworm business for real?"

*He will think so. That will be sufficient.*

"I hope. Those people don't like to be bullied."

*They tolerate it from one another. Did you recover the egg?*

"I've got it right here." He doesn't miss much.

*Bring it here.*

I did so. That put me in position to see the doorway. Several kittens were watching from the hall. Singe slid past them. "Mr. Mulclar has finished." She made an entry in the ledger, took money to pay Mulclar. Finally.

The miasma had reached the Dead Man's room.

I asked, "Are Saucerhead or Winger likely to be around soon?"

*I do not expect them.*

"I was hoping one of them could go shopping with Dean. We need groceries. And he's a little old to be out there alone in times like these."

*I see. Are you certain this is the egg that was thrown at you?*

I looked closer. "The light ain't so good, but . . . it looks a little different."

*This is a stone. And nothing but a stone. Either Bittegurn Brittigarn spun you a tall tale or you no longer have the original.*

"I'll take it out into a better light."

I went to the front door, intending to go out into the daylight. I peeked past Singe, saw Mr. Mulclar just getting his cart moving. And . . . a couple of pedestrian women stared at Mr. Mulclar in awe. Then began gasping and waving their hands in a vain attempt to make it go away. "Hey, Chuckles. That Penny Dreadful is right across the street."

*Where?*

"In front of Elmer Stick's apartment building."

*I sense nothing. Be as precise as possible.*

"On the steps. Second step up, left side, leaning against the railing." I eased on outside, to get a better view.

*Ah!*

Penny Dreadful leaped like somebody had just branded her bottom. She ran, bumping off pedestrians who flung curses after her. She had trouble controlling her limbs, but she never fell down.

The farther she ran, the more control she gained.

I studied my rock in the better light.

It wasn't the same stone. There were tiny red veins in its surface. It wasn't as smooth. And it didn't produce that warm, relaxed feel when I fiddled with it.

I stepped back inside. "She too slippery for you?"

*Exactly. She presents an incredibly small target. And an elusive one. One that senses my interest the instant it touches her.*

"This isn't the same rock."

*I did not think so. It is time we examined your memories concerning that rock.*

"Why?"

*It must be important. Certainly, important enough to be switched.*

"Teacher White—"

*Do not get ahead of yourself. Things do happen without the connivance or awareness of Mr. White. Sit down. Relax. Consider how useful it would be to have that parrot available for situations like the one with the Dreadful urchin.*

"I do wish you wouldn't keep harping on that."

*A good partner nags. To The Palms. To your first encounter with the stone.*

I felt his mental tentacles slide into my brain, down deep into my memories of those brief moments.

I'm used to this—though I don't like it—so I focus on something else while he relives my life, rooting out details I failed to note consciously. I concentrated on breathing.

*Done.*

"And?"

*You made some incorrect assumptions.*

"That would be a first. Bring them on."

*It starts when you walked out the door of The Palms. You did not, in fact, see the Green Pants Gang member sling the stone at you. The stone whizzed past you; you ducked; then you spotted the Green Pants thug. You put three and three together and came up with five. Green Pants did not do the dirty deed. His presence may have been happenstance.*

"He ran away."

*Did he?*

"That's the way I remember it."

*He did not. You do recall that he was amazed when you and Mr. Dotes set upon him.*

"Yeah." Green Pants *had* acted like he was completely boggled. "I get a feeling we'll never find out the whole truth there because that guy got himself dead.

"If he didn't do it, who did? And why?"

*Excellent questions, both. You did not see anything, even at the unconscious level, at the time, that sheds any light.* And, with wicked glee, he nailed me. *So you may have been right in the first place, but for all the wrong reasons.*

"What the hell are you blathering about?"

*The Green Pants goon may have slung the stone at you after all.*

"Is this where I jump up and run in circles, shrieking and yanking out my hair?"

*The point is, you may have come to the truth back then, but if you did, you did not do so based on the evidence. You harkened to your own prejudice and the fact that you saw no one else in the street.*

"I'm thinking about setting fire to this place and walking away. So I don't have to suffer these convolutions again."

*I am exposing you to the sort of thought processes that unravel. . . .*

What could've turned into a fun squabble over not much went on hiatus when a frazzled Tinnie slipped in and demanded, "Why didn't you wake me up?"

"I tried. You said you'd chop my ears off if I didn't leave you the hell alone. That you were up all night and you needed some sleep." Tinnie hasn't been much of a morning person lately. Either.

The other thing we have in common, from a redheaded point of view, is that I'm always wrong. "Guess I should've been a little more firm, eh?"

She used to snap up that kind of straight line. Maybe we've gotten too comfortable. Her language wasn't ladylike. "I was supposed to be in the office four hours ago."

"Sorry I disappointed you by surviving, love. I'll time it more conveniently for you next time."

She glared but kept quiet.

I said, "Since you're late, and since everybody in your family will assume that a woman your age who was out all night in a situation involving somebody named Garrett was up to no good . . ."

Usually that sort of stuff winds Tinnie up. This time she was in no mood. She just kept scowling.

"Since you're going to be late anyway, how about you take Dean to the market?" Tinnie is a recognizable personality. People would stand back, not because she's my girl but because she's Willard Tate's niece. Willard Tate is one of those New Wave industrialists whose genius has begun to make him a huge power in postwar TunFaire.

Tinnie's expression was priceless. Too bad there's no way to record all those freckles in motion. "You want *me* to bodyguard Dean? Why? So you can lay around with your beer and any bimbo who drops in?"

Her eyes glazed over. For half a minute she was the perfect girlfriend. Drop-dead gorgeous. And quiet.

The Dead Man was talking to her.

Tinnie clicked back. "I'm sorry," she said, moving in and bringing the heat. "I forgot what that villain did with his drugs."

I suffered her consolations for as long as it took Old Bones to become impatient.

"All right!" she snapped, pulling away.

I'd reconsidered. "You just go on home, sweets. You don't have the skills to protect Dean from the kind of people who're bothering us."

Tinnie is the contrariest person I know. Excepting my partner. I expected a big ration. Being contrary, she fooled me for the thousandth time. She didn't argue at all.

Maybe she was learning to listen.

It could happen. Even with a redhead. Sometimes the dice do come up snake eyes.

I suffered an inspiration as I walked Tinnie to the door, where a peek revealed nothing untoward. As we exchanged sweet sorrows, I suggested, "Go over to the Cardonlos place. There'll be police types all over. See if you can't get a couple of them to walk you home."

Right. A wiggle, a jiggle, and a giggle and the herd would take off carrying her on their shoulders.

"That might be a good idea. While I'm at it, why don't I borrow a couple to babysit Dean?"

Truth be told, I'd thought of that before I thought of looking out for her. But a certain minimal cunning has infected me lately. "Why didn't I think of that? I guess you distracted me."

"I'll distract you permanently if I find out you've got something going with Belinda Contague that isn't just business."

How do you spank a rat? The tail gets in the way.

*Not Miss Pular's fault, Garrett. All mine, I am afraid.*

Ah. Just as well, probably. Tinnie wouldn't listen to anybody else. Especially not some clown named Garrett.

After a final bout of nuzzling, the professional redhead moved out. And could she move. She passed through the crowd oblivious to the drooling, staring, and stumbling.

She's never been conscious of how strikingly attractive she is. If I say anything, she figures that's just me being me.

I watched her sail boldly into the Cardonlos harbor, where she disconcerted the crowd. And was on her way again in five minutes with a big, brave, alert policeman on either hand. While another headed my way.

"Scithe."

"Garrett."

"What can I do for you?"

"Miss Tate suggested that you might be able to get my wife's name bumped up the waiting list for three-wheelers."

"She did, did she? But she put it on me when she has a bigger piece of the pie than I do?"

"She said to remind you that she isn't the one who needs the favor."

"She would, too. All right. I can get her moved, but not all the way to the top. I don't have that much juice."

This stuff started the minute our three-wheels became the hot novelty everybody had to have, demand dramatically exceeding supply. The waiting list is two thousand names long. My ethically challenged associates pad corporate income by taking bribes to move names up the list. They'll harvest every loose copper in the kingdom if they can.

"Here's what I'm thinking," I told Scithe. And wove an elabo-
rate scheme that used Dean for bad-guy bait. "All I'm interested in
is having my man get his shopping done safely. If somebody
messes with him, the credit, the collar, and any info bonus is all
yours. Unless it has to do with me. Then I'm majorly interested, of
course."

"Of course."

We exchanged a few more pleasantries, then I went inside and
told Dean he could go marketing now. "And be sure not to forget
the new keg."

Then back into the Dead Man's room. "How long before I get
enough poison out of me so I can go outside?"

*You have just begun detoxification. And you are not taking
your fluids.*

Sullenly, I reported, "Penny Dreadful is watching us again."

*Let her. It means nothing. Except that she is worried about her
kittens. We need to get Bittegurn Brittigarn in here. By whatever
means necessary. He was the one who took your roc's egg. While
spinning a tale meant to get you to fling the substitute into the
river. Which would eliminate any suspicion.*

"You really think he's a villain?"

*He may be. Given the chance to interview him, I could deliver
a definitive answer. He may just be weak.*

"And what I get for my troubles is sarcasm."

# 42

Saucerhead dropped in. "They done forgot me already out there, Garrett. Nobody yelled nothing about there goes the guy what tried to rape the little boy the other night. Speaking of which, that nasty little critter is sitting on Elmer Stick's steps, bold as brass, eyeballing your place. Was I a betting kind of guy, I'd put money on she's trying to figure out how to bust in here, then make a getaway. The big guy still awake?"

"Once he wakes up he tends not to go down again till he drives the rest of us buggers. Unless him going to sleep will inconvenience somebody in some really huge way."

"I need to see him. See if Dean's got—"

"Dean's out shopping. On account of we're out of everything, especially tea and beer."

"Damn! I need something liquid."

The Dead Man let an implied sneer ride along on my shoulder as I headed for the kitchen. *Drink some water. Water is your only reliable antidote.* There wasn't an ounce of beer in the house.

I grumbled and mumbled but did as I was told. He was right.

I handed Saucerhead his water. Muttering about Bittegurn Brittigarn.

*Excellent. Though you have to grant the priest his due. His sleight of hand was so fine I cannot pinpoint the instant when he made the exchange.*

The more I reflected, the more I wanted to spank BB till he gave up something useful. The roc's-egg story was a bushel of salamander dust. But the stone must have some bizarre, rare quality. And value.

*He must be lured here somehow. Although unlikely to be part of the puzzle, he may hold the key.*

I considered Saucerhead. Tharpe was babbling a report that was a waste of breath. The Dead Man was sucking info straight from his head.

Old Bones was impatient.

Saucerhead had been out getting the skinny on human combustions, the when, where, and who. The latter being the most difficult because the victims hadn't been anybody anyone missed. Too bad we don't have connections on the Hill anymore. One of the heavyweights up there might be able to save me tons of work.

*Good work, as always, Mr. Tharpe. Miss Pular will pay you. If you wish further employment, there is a man in the Dream Quarter I want to see. Chances are, however, that he will not come here voluntarily. Explain, Garrett.*

I told Tharpe about Bittegurn Brittigarn.

"Drinks a bit, eh?"

"Like a school of fish."

"Then he won't be that hard. He passes out down there. He wakes up here."

"He does have a guardian harpy," I explained.

"Maybe you could get Morley to go with me."

"I doubt that we'll see Morley for a while. Too much excitement in the underworld. He'll want to stay out of the way."

"Best thing, till it settles. I reckon. Guess I'll have to sweet-talk her myself."

I said nothing. That wasn't easy. For Saucerhead sweet talk means hitting things with a smaller hammer.

Singe paid Tharpe and recorded the outlay. Saucerhead cooled his bunions for a while, grumbling about his love life. It was the usual story. He had him a woman who treated him bad.

"Pity there's nobody in our circle who's musical. We could set your life to music and create us a tragical passion play."

"It ain't funny, Garrett."

"So you keep telling me. Then you go pick the same kind of woman and make the same dumb mistake all over again."

"Yeah. Only I never see it out until it's too late. I'm on my way. Do I got any expense latitude?"

*Just bring the man here.*

"Hey!" I protested. "That's my money you're throwing away."

*Cost it out in your Keep On Breathing account.*

"This puzzle really grabs you, eh?"

*Your cases always wander the tombs of chaos. This time more than most. Good luck, Mr. Tharpe. Help us create order out of incoherence.*

I said, "It only looks chaotic because there's a bunch of different things going on at the same time."

*True. But those things keep banging into and tripping over one another because they have you in common.*

A couple of kittens grew bold enough to enter the Dead Man's room. Tentatively, though. "That's kind of scary."

*It is, indeed.*

# 43

I snoozed. My partner kept me breathing. Next thing I knew, Singe was shaking me. "Dean needs help bringing stuff in."

I grumbled but dragged the loose parts together and headed for the front door. This was TunFaire. Somebody had to watch the goods while somebody else lugged stuff inside.

Dean probably planned to deploy his skills as watcher, yielding to me as a journeyman lugger.

He fooled me. "You stand by the cart and look ferocious. Mr. Sanderin and I will get the kegs installed. Singe, will you help? Or are you just going to stand there looking pretty?"

Singe scooted down and loaded up.

I spied Scithe and a pal across the street, headed for the Cardonlos place. Scithe waved.

Dean had conned a beer delivery guy into going out of his way. A Weider brewery guy. They're hard to distract, normally. But this Mr. Sanderin had let Dean pile on a bit of everything we needed around the house, including a sack of potatoes and a bushel of apples, which wouldn't last long once Singe got to stewing.

Sanderin had a case of nerves, probably because I'm the guy who checks up on Weider brewery employees. "Relax, Sanderin. I didn't even see you today."

When Dean came back after moving the first keg inside, I said, "Your pal Penny is hanging out across the street again."

"She's worried about her kittens. But she's afraid to come across and find out how they are."

"So you told her, eh?"

"I told her they were all right. They're getting enough to eat. Nobody is hurting them."

"Which would be why she suckered you into taking them aboard in the first place. Right?"

"She wanted to take advantage of the Dead Man's reputation. Without having to deal with Himself. But he woke up."

"Pity."

"No need to be sarcastic, Mr. Garrett."

"Maybe not. But it sure feels good. She's welcome any time. We don't bite. Well, I might. But I promise not to leave scars."

"You need to see the situation from her viewpoint."

"Dean, don't bullshit me. You don't *get* to bullshit me. That's no child. She's not twelve years old."

Dean sighed. "You're right. She's just small for her age. And she's been on her own since she was twelve. She's sharp as a knife about some things and stone naive about others. And I want it to stay that way."

I got the message. "I should feel hurt by your underlying assumptions. How about you tote a barge or two? Lift a bale? Singe is on her third load."

Dean got Mr. Sanderin to help him. Once they couldn't see, I blew Penny Dreadful a kiss.

Relway's boys noticed. Maybe they'd give the kid a hard time and she'd come looking for shelter.

Singe caught me. "You are a black-hearted villain, Garrett."

I grinned. "Ain't life fun?"

She just said, "Looks like more rain."

Yes. It did, actually.

# 44

The rain started in the afternoon. It began gently, but cold. After a round of thunder, it turned to freezing rain. Lucky me, I didn't have to hazard streets gone foul and treacherous.

I was in with the Dead Man, halfway napping, feeling restless. Like I never would have if I'd been free to go out. The Dead Man was having fun needling me about my sudden surge of ambition.

Somebody came to the door.

Dean clumped on up there. He was tired of playing with kittens and trying to manage an intelligent conversation with Singe. He can't ignore what she is for long.

Voices rattled but got lost in the clatter of the rain. Which fell with great enthusiasm, coating everything with ice. Morley came in looking as bedraggled as ever I've seen. He had ice on his head and shoulders. I said, "I'm speechless."

"If only that were true."

"What's a dog like you doing out on a night like this?"

"It wasn't bad when I started. I was two-thirds of the way here when it turned awful. I huddled in a doorway with refugees until it was obvious it wasn't just weather god whimsy. Here was closer than home, so I came ahead. I fell several times. I may have sprained my wrist."

I chuckled, picturing him huddled up with a bunch of street folk. "I suppose I ought to sit on my mirth until you tell us what you're up to."

Morley told the Dead Man, "Your little boy is finally beginning to develop social skills."

*Enough contusions and abrasions eventually wear the corners off even the roughest blockheads, given time.*

"I can't argue with that," I confessed. I started to lever myself out of my chair.

*Never mind. Dean and Singe are coming. They are eager for something to do that does not require them to be good company to one another.*

Dean arrived carrying a chair. Singe was equipped to dry Morley out and wrap him in a comforter. Dean said, "We'll get something warm inside you as soon as can be."

"I'll be fine," Morley said. "I just hope those idiots at The Palms don't burn it down while I'm gone."

Morley is a micromanager. He isn't comfortable giving his people an assignment and letting them run. I said, "You went off to the Cantard with me one time and it was still there when we got back."

"That was in the old days. You couldn't hurt the place when it was the Joy House."

He went on, but I listened with only half an ear. I was marveling at the Dead Man. He'd dropped "Miss Pular" in favor of the informal "Singe." He had accepted her into the family.

Such as it is. Strange as it is.

Maybe I ought to recruit a dwarf now.

I asked, "What's become of all the dwarfs?"

Which question garnered bewildered looks.

I said, "It just hit me. I don't see dwarfs anymore. Come to think, there aren't many trolls around anymore, either. Even elves aren't as common as they used to be."

"Members of the Other Races are leaving TunFaire," Morley said.

I gulped me some water. I couldn't  tell if it was all in my head, but I seemed thirstier all the time. "You saying all that human rights racialist stuff is working?"

"It is. Though not quite the way you're thinking."

"Eh?"

"You don't really think a bunch of drunken yahoos with ax handles would intimidate a troll, so you?"

I had to admit it. That didn't seem likley. "We're getting old."

"Speak for yourself. What brought that on?"

"We're sitting around a fire talking instead of being out in the weather having adventures."

"And I'm just as happy. If I'm careful, I'll last for centuries."

"Then how come you're out when even the mad dogs have crawled under the porch?"

"I didn't plan it."

"I got that much. Thanks, Singe. Pull up a chair. Listen to the master tell tall tales."

"I wish," Dotes said. "What did you do to Teacher White?"

"Nothing. Just chatted him up. What you'd expect. Why?"

"He's gone insane. He hit Merry Sculdyte. You don't mess with Merry—unless you catch him with his pants down. Which is what Teacher must have done. Rory will have smoke coming out his ears."

"So Teacher did something stupid. Is that a major departure? You got any more details?"

"No."

I noted the Dead Man's absence from the conversation.

"What got into Teacher?" I mused rhetorically. "He was pissed off because two heavies he borrowed from Merry croaked Spider Webb and Original Dick on him. But he didn't seem suicidal when he left."

The Dead Man said nothing. I'm sure he wasn't feeling guilty, though.

I admitted, "We did ask him to get a couple people to come by. I didn't think he'd go start a war."

Dotes mistook me. "Your name isn't in. Yet."

"Not entirely reassuring. But good to know."

Dean seldom takes an interest. But he had no work and it was too early for bed. He brought a chair in and nurtured the fire while he listened. He kept quiet.

I told Morley, "Interesting stuff, but why come out in this?"

"I was concerned that Rory might think you had something to do with his brother's misfortune." Friendship and the showmanship involved in being a manly man leads us through dumb contortions, sometimes.

"What do you think, Old Bones?"

Nothing.

"Come on. I know you're not asleep."

*Indeed not. I am monitoring the approach of the grand villain Teacher White and his merry men. Including a man named Merry, whose appellation seems singularly inappropriate.*

"Headed here?"

*Five minutes. Teacher White knows the truth, but Merry Sculdyte will come in blind.*

I felt him get busy telling everybody else what to do.

He's a take-charge kind of guy.

# 45

Though Morley was bedraggled, he was his old svelte self compared to Teacher White, his crew, and their prisoners. That whole gaggle was on the far marches of the drowned-rat category. Though Singe would have bristled at the cliché.

Teacher told me, "Here you go, asshole. Green Bean, Squint, Brett Batt, and Merry Sculdyte. This'll probably get me killed. And here's what Kolda told me was your friggin' antidote when I bought the samsom weed. Now have your monster get this nightmare outta my head."

I stood around gaping like a yokel while Teacher's henchmen piled bodies in the hallway, and halfway wished my monster would get the whispering nightmares out of mine. The black murmurs just wouldn't go away. Dean sputtered about the water being tracked in. The captives were bound. They were all bloody. Some were still leaking. That did nothing to make Dean happy, either. I couldn't imagine what White's bunch must have done to pull this off. I had more difficulty imagining what the Dead Man could've done to Teacher to get him so motivated.

*Excellent. Most excellent. You have performed prodigies, Mr. White. I am sure that, at this point, you would like to disappear for a while.*

"No shit."

*Go quickly, then. The watchers are paying no attention because of the weather. Go quietly.*

"What about the mindworm thing?"

*I have removed it already.*

"That fast?"

*That fast. That easily. You will begin to feel much better soon. Go. Watch your footing. Move that coach away from here, even if it is stolen.*

Just what we needed. Another stolen vehicle abandoned in front of the house.

The White crew went away, fast.

"Did you get anything new from them before they left?"

*Nothing useful. Though Mr. White certainly had himself an adventure. It will become an underworld saga if he survives.*

"Interesting." I checked the pile of twitching, battered bodies delivered by my once and future enemy. "What about this lot?"

*Where to start?*

I gave Brett Batt a huge kick in the ribs. "Right here. Put in two of those mindworms."

*Garrett.*

"All right. I'll be civilized."

Morley opined, "I was beginning to wonder."

"Meaning?"

"I was beginning to wonder if you hadn't developed sense enough to bust a moose like that up when the chance was there instead of waiting till it's fair."

*Move Mr. Vrolet out into the weather. Leave him under someone's stoop. He knows nothing.*

There was an edge to his thought that left me mildly suspicious. "It's freezing out there."

*The chill will wake him up.*

"Everything's covered with ice."

*Then you will have to make sure of your footing. No one will see you. Those tasked with watching us have chosen to do so in warm, dry places.*

I muttered and grumbled. The crowd of Dean and Morley eyed me like they thought I was being a big baby. And I was. It was nasty out there. But I latched on to Squint. Dean worked the door. I hauled the villain off into the night. The front steps didn't improve his complexion.

"How many times did you fall down?" Morley asked when I stumbled back into the Dead Man's room.

"I lost count. Dean. Can you make hot cocoa?"

It arrived immediately. A cup all around, except for the bad guys. Maybe smelling it cooking was why I asked.

*Mr. Ractic can be removed now, Garrett. Once you finish your cocoa.*

"Is that the way it's going to be with all of these goons?"

*You have a better plan?*

"Any plan that doesn't take me out into the weather."

*That would result in our guests' waking up here in the house. And, possibly, remembering it later. An insalubrious eventuation.*

"Easy for you to say." I considered kicking Brett another time or two. "How am I supposed to move this ox?"

*I am confident that something will occur to you.* Deeply amused.

He was having fun with me. And I didn't know what it was all about.

I sighed and got to work dragging Green Bean. I didn't damage him much getting down the front steps. I planned to dump him somewhere on Wizard's Reach, but when I got to the stoop where I'd left Squint, Vrolet was gone. I replaced him with Green Bean.

The rain continued to fall. Most of it found a way to get under my collar in back. I needed a hood or a big hat.

Gloves wouldn't hurt, either.

*Garrett!*

I jumped, startled. "What?" I was still ten yards from my stoop, clinging to an abandoned, stolen goat cart, halfway unconscious, trying to keep from sliding back downhill.

*Remember to breathe. You are lucky to be close enough to be assisted.*

Yeah? I had a feeling that I'd just been manipulated somehow, so I'd learn a lesson.

I went in and attacked some more cocoa. Then hot tea, then cold water. I crowded the fire. I asked, "Are we learning anything? Has any of this been worth my trouble?"

*You will be pleased to learn that Mr. Rory Sculdyte considers you one of the most dangerous men in TunFaire. Worth murdering preemptively.*

"Oh, my. I'm a made man now. Are we headed for another anticlimax, with these guys all being marginal?"

*Not quite. You were a target of opportunity for the Batt brothers, not the point of the exercise. Merry Sculdyte had instructions to put you to sleep if the opportunity arose. Perhaps the stone egg was slung at you by an opportunist Sculdyte soldier. You are on the list not only because you are a general nuisance but because you might find Chodo before the Sculdyte crew. You have an astonish-*

*ing reputation among these thugs. Clearly, they do not know you at all well.*

"What're my chances of digging them out?"

*Getting better by the minute. Every thug able to get up on his hind legs has been looking. We know a very great deal about where Mr. Contague is not.*

"Is he with Belinda? Or does Harvester Temisk have him?"

*The consensus is that Miss Contague is hunting her father with more vigor than anyone else. And your idea did occur to me. I have asked John Stretch to put word out in the ratman community, offering a substantial reward.*

Clever. Ratfolk go everywhere. Nobody pays attention, except to yell. I glanced at Singe. She seemed quite pleased. And tired.

It was getting late. I realized, with some surprise, that we hadn't yet tapped the new keg.

How long could that last?

*This Brett Batt is ready to go. You cannot imagine what a banal personality the man has. Though knowledgeable. Certainly knowledgeable.*

"You got something useful?"

*A few points of interest did lurk in the corners of his mind.*

"Such as?"

*I will see that you know what you need to know if a situation should arise where you need to know it.*

All right. We were going to play games. More games. He'd fished something tasty out of Brett's head. He didn't want me to know. Or maybe to obsess about it.

*More or less. It has little to do with anything we are investigating now. Take him out of here.*

Grumbling, I laid a two-hand grip on Brett's collar and started hauling. The only help I got was Singe's volunteering to work the front door.

Brett was one lucky bruno. His good buddy Garrett had hold of him at the head end instead of by the feet. Because of this his good buddy Garrett one-manned him down the ice-rimed front steps without banging his skull on even one.

"What'cha doin'?" Saucerhead Tharpe asked. He had collected coagulated precipitation till he looked like the abominable iceman. He wasn't alone. A wobbling companion, clinging to his arm, also looked like a perambulating ice creature.

"I'm dragging this butthead over to that cart." I'd suffered the inspiration of a fanatic slacker. If I could just get Brett aboard that thing . . .

Tharpe and his pal grabbed hold and helped me hoist Brett into the cart. Then Tharpe said, "Me an' Bitte are gonna get on in outta the weather. All right?"

"Go ahead on. There's hot cocoa. And we got a new keg in. I'll be there in a minute." I eased in between the double trees, got a good hold on those poles. When I broke their ends loose from the ice, the cart began to roll.

It worked like a rickshaw in reverse. Me behind. Trying to keep up.

Macunado Street slopes gently down for a third of a mile. Long before that I turned loose. The cart rolled. It went on. I flailed around, slipping and sliding, never quite falling down. I couldn't keep up and didn't try.

Brett's ride managed not to smash into anything for longer than it took me to lose sight of it in the dark. I heard it glance off something, continue on, ricochet off something else, then participate in a huge crash. I imagined Brett flying through the night, then spinning on up the glassy street on his prodigious pecs.

His problem. I headed on home wondering why I hadn't broken some of his bones before I let him roll.

I found Singe waiting to let me in. She was amused. "How many times did you fall this time?"

"Not even once."

She was disappointed.

Saucerhead and his drinking buddy wandered on into the Dead Man's room, where Old Bones continued to entertain Merry Sculdyte. *Garrett, I need you to transcribe what I am recovering from this villain. It is not my custom to meddle in civil affairs. However, my rudimentary sense of social obligation compels me to provide this information to Colonel Block and Director Relway. This man is intimate with the darkest and most secret machinery of the underworld. Much more so than Mr. Dotes. Or even Miss Contague. This man knows where the bodies are buried because he buried most of them. He knows which officials are corrupt. He has a good notion which people on his own side could be suborned by Director Relway. In a mundane manner of describing it, Mr. Merry Sculdyte is the pot at the end of the information rainbow.*

"Excellent. We're in the money. Have you noticed Saucerhead's guest?"

Brother Brittigarn wasn't so wasted that he failed to notice that

I wasn't talking to Morley. He wasn't so wasted that he failed to recognize me in the light. "Oh, shit. Man.'Head, you jobbed me."

*I am aware. I will start on him once you begin writing.*

Brittigarn decided to make a break for it. He managed a step and a half before he froze. Then he turned and walked to my usual chair. Mechanically. He sat, rested his palms on his thighs, stared at infinity. And dripped.

Dean peeked in. "Is there anything more you need from me? It's past my bedtime."

"Some rags for this clown to drip on. Where'd Singe get to?"

"She's in the kitchen trying to tap the new keg."

"That should be amusing."

I went over to my office, where I could be comfortable while I wrote.

It was around sixteen o'clock. My hand was an aching claw. I couldn't go on.

*Get some sleep. We will continue later.*

"How much more is there?"

*The man is a bottomless well of wicked memoirs.*

What I'd already recorded would be invaluable to Colonel Block and Belinda both. And any number of Combine second-stringers like Teacher White scheduled for involuntary retirement after Rory Sculdyte helped himself to his patrimony.

"How're you doing with BB?"

*The man has an intriguing mind. Get some sleep.*

I pried myself out of my office chair, joints creaking and popping. I need more exercise. My body is beginning to show wear and tear.

I stuck my head into the Dead Man's room. People were all over, sleeping. Singe was nowhere to be seen.

# 46

This time the old slug thug himself dragged me out at a criminal hour. He was eager to go on. Excited, even. He borrowed a colloquialism when I protested the absurdity of the hour. *Paybacks are a bitch.*

I didn't get it until I was halfway through my second mug of black tea. When he started nagging me about dragging my feet.

He was getting even for all the times I'd dragged him out of his little naps, just so he could earn his keep.

"Life's a bitch."

*How is your breathing?*

I hadn't paid attention. It was working. What did I care?

He withdrew. It wasn't me making it work. I wasn't back on automatic yet.

"I still have to think about it. Maybe the stuff Teacher brought isn't the real antidote."

*Possibly not. He was not deeply concerned about an antidote when he purchased the samsom weed.*

"Typical of the breed."

I let Dean serve me breakfast. Singe came in. She'd been outside. I felt the cold roll off her fur. She said, "You need to take a look out there before it all goes away."

I finished my mug, went and looked.

The world was glass. Or crystal. Actually, all coated with ice. So much ice that the weight had broken limbs off trees and pulled gutters off buildings. A kitten thought about going out with me but changed up as soon as he laid paws on ice. He jumped back, shook each paw in turn, indignant. "Don't blame me. You're the one who wanted out."

I surveyed my neighborhood. Nothing moved but a family of mountain dwarfs trudging up Macunado like this was just a brisk morning in the hills back home. It had been an age since I'd seen TunFaire this quiet.

I retreated from the cold. "You're right, Singe. It's fairy-tale beautiful. And now it's starting to snow." Which would make the ice even more treacherous by masking its wicked face.

Dean met me at the door to the Dead Man's room. He'd brought more tea. "You'll need this."

I accepted and went inside.

The faces in the crowd remained the same. Saucerhead was sprawled on his back, taking up a vast amount of floor space, snoring. Brittigarn and Merry Sculdyte were in chairs, limp, under mental sedation. Morley was awake. But he's the sort of pervert who doesn't mind being in that state when the sun comes up.

"You still here?"

"You brought a blast of cold air in with you. Meaning you just looked outside."

"It's pretty out there."

"Pretty isn't a problem for you. You're already home."

I raised an eyebrow.

"I'm nimble. But not nimble enough to make it to The Palms without breaking something."

"I saw a family of dwarfs out front. They were managing."

"This is skinny-dipping weather where they come from. And you said there aren't any dwarfs around anymore."

"I said you don't see many. I just caught the not many on the move."

"You may have to give up beer."

"That's a zig when I expected you to zag. What brought that on?"

"Singe."

"Oh." It would be a problem if she became too dedicated to barley soup. "You don't suppose all that smoke out there is because Sarge and Puddle burned your place down?"

"I have an abiding suspicion that people are firing up their fireplaces."

"It isn't winter yet." The sharp, softly bitter smell of woodsmoke is a sure sign of winter. More than snow is. People fire up their fireplaces only when they're sure that the cold has arrived for real.

Fuel is dear. Most of it is barged in from way upriver.

I noted the presence of several kittens. One had homesteaded Saucerhead's chest. Another had set up housekeeping in Merry Sculdyte's lap.

The Dead Man didn't intimidate them anymore.

They avoided BB, though. Despite his snoring.

Morley observed, "It won't be Sarge and Puddle who do me in. Neither one of them is smart enough to start a fire. The ones who worry me are the ones who *think* they're smart enough."

The Dead Man didn't acknowledge my arrival until then. *How is your hand this morning? Are you ready to resume?*

I noted that I was favoring my left. "It's stiff. I won't be able to do much."

*Find a trustworthy professional letter writer.*

"Have you paid any attention to me and Morley?"

*I try not to indulge in frivolity.*

"The weather situation isn't frivolous."

*Oh, my.*

He did seem surprised.

*The season sneaked up on me.*

I felt him recalculating how long he'd been asleep. "It's unseasonable. But severe."

*It is snowing heavily now. Once several inches accumulate, the footing will become less of a problem.*

"Hell, there's an old pair of skates down in the basement somewhere. I could dig them out. I could fix them up, sharpen them up, refurbish them up, put them on Morley. . . ."

Morley said, "Morley don't skate."

"Oh?"

"I tried it once. See this scar? In my eyebrow? That's what hit the ice first. Split me right open. Why are you grinning?"

"Nothing, really." I was just delighted to discover that I could do something he couldn't, well and with style.

*We will make do until the footing improves.*

I noted a twinkle from under BB's brows. He was awake but pretending not to be.

Old Bones noticed, too. *Our friend from Ymber is producing some interesting information.*

"So give me all the gory details. Unless all that needs to be written down, too."

*Some will have to be, eventually. The man is a charlatan. A successful charlatan, to be sure, but a charlatan nonetheless. He was not born in Ymber. He migrated there before the religious squabbles turned bloody. One of his recent ancestors was not human. He has a touch of what he sells as psychic power. His religion he cobbled together himself. It went over well in Ymber because many people were tired of the feud between A-Lat and A-Laf.*

"I thought open warfare was something recent."

*Yes. It would be instructive to compare Penny Dreadful's recollections with those of Mr. Brittigarn. His are entirely self-serving.*

Old Bones fed me the tale of a con man whose scam had worked well until it caught the attention of A-Laf's deacons and sextons after a fundamentalist, activist faction seized control of A-Laf's cult. They sharpened their teeth on BB's followers. The survivors fled to TunFaire, where they failed to support their pastor in the style to which he wanted to be accustomed. The sin pots of the big city picked them off. Now that the battle between A-Lat and A-Laf had immigrated, it didn't seem likely that Brother Brittigarn would enjoy the Dream Quarter much longer.

"How about my roc's egg?"

*He did not bring that with him. Mr. Tharpe received no instructions concerning it. So the stone is still in the temple of Eis and Igory.*

"But he did switch it out and then not fling it in the river?"

*The stone is much too precious to be thrown away.*

"No!"

*Sarcasm does not become you.*

"No. But I do tend to get sarcastic when you say something that obvious."

*He is reconsidering making a run for it.*

"Then stop him. How hard is that to figure?"

*It may not be that simple if he realizes what natural tools he possesses.*

"Use your standard tactic. Baffle him with bullshit. Why does he want the stone?"

Proof that Old Bones hadn't lavished much attention on BB then surfaced. He didn't yet know why. He had to go pearl diving in a mind naturally indisposed to surrender its treasures.

*This will take a while. He appears to have been of several minds concerning the stone. Though each of those focused on wringing the biggest profit possible from the windfall.*

Classic crook-think. Calling a theft a windfall. "Why?"

I felt a little prickle in my mind. He was checking to see what I meant. Instead of asking.

"You're awfully impatient this time, Old Bones."

*There is so much going on. And I am so excited.*

"You've become sarcasm incarnate. How is the egg important? Why is it valuable?"

*Because he may have told the truth about how dangerous the rock is. Even though it might not have been stolen from the nest of a fabulous bird. He wants to auction the egg on the Hill for enough to get out of the priest racket. The stone does rate description as "rare as rocs' eggs."*

"I'm confused."

*I am surprised that you would notice.*

He has a bite like a saber-toothed toad.

"Have Singe do your transcription. She needs the practice. And it'll keep her out of the beer."

He offered the mental equivalent of a harrumph.

"So. About the stone?"

*It can be used to start fires.*

"Is that so?" I sensed that he didn't know anything else, in any concrete way, but was chock-full of speculation.

*I have Miss Winger working an angle that may tell us something useful.*

Which he wouldn't share right now, of course, because he doesn't like to speculate or brainstorm—except among his own minds. He doesn't like being wrong. But I could guess what he was thinking. I'd considered it myself and decided the idea was too far-fetched. *You should have mentioned the stone to Mr. Tharpe.*

Saucerhead groaned. He sat up, clapped his hands to his temples, swore, and lied, "I'll never do that again."

"What is that?"

He realized he hadn't taken on his career as a cat mattress by indulging in too many adult beverages. "What happened?"

Morley told him, "It was too nasty for you to go home last night."

"What time is it? Oh, gods! I shoulda been over to . . . she's gonna kill me!" He tugged at his clothes, retied his shoes, hoisted himself to his feet, and headed for the front door. I tagged along so his misery would have company once he looked outside.

Saucerhead took his look. "Holy shit! What did you do?"

"Man, you can't blame the weather on me."

"Sure, I can. No law says I got to be logical." He showed me his biggest shit-eating grin. He stuck his head back outside, retreated again. "I blame it on the peace."

"What? You blame what on the peace?"

"The weather, man. When we had us a war going we never had no weather like this. Not this early."

"What the hell are you babbling about?"

He grinned again. "Just yanking your chain, brother. I keep hearing that kind of crap out there in the taverns."

"Oh."

"You don't get out there no more. You don't know the latest lunatic theories."

Saucerhead Tharpe lecturing me about lunacy. It's a strange old world. "You going to jump on out there or not?"

"I think I'll hang out here. That's just plain too ugly."

It was a good thing Dean got a chance to lay in supplies.

I did what I could to loosen my writing hand, went back to work transcribing Merry Sculdyte's memoirs. Singe and Morley spelled me. There wasn't much else to do but try to play chess.

I found one more area where I could feel superior to my favorite pretty-boy dark-elf breed buddy. Though he insisted I was getting secret help from my sidekick.

And his handwriting is barely legible.

# 47

One by one my guests slipped away.

Morley left first, after waiting almost all day. An hour later Saucerhead plunged into the snowfall, which had passed its peak. It now consisted of glistening little flakes that looked artificial. There was a foot on the ground. And not much wind, which helped ease the misery.

With Tharpe gone, I asked, "What do we do with these other two? BB has a wife."

*The woman at the temple is his sister. He lets her believe she is the brains behind his confidence games.*

Singe was writing, tongue hanging out the left side of her mouth. She concentrated ferociously, head tilted way over. She wasn't quite ready for illuminated manuscripts.

"Singe. You think other ratfolk could learn to copy stuff?"

"What?"

"Do they have a high tolerance for boredom and repetition? If they could learn how, we could start a copy business."

I turned back to the Dead Man and BB. "Is she? The mind behind?"

*He does not believe it. He may be incorrect. You will have to feed him. Soon.*

"Have to? Can't I just cut him loose, chock-full of confusion?"

*There is more to be had from him. Something he does not know he knows. Something that has his unrealized talent fully wrapped around it, protecting it.*

"Is it critical?"

*I will not know till I chip it out. It could be the final clue to the meaning of life. Or his mother's recipe for buttered parsnips.*

Taking into account my standing as fool to the gods, a quick calculation suggested that Brother B. would be partial to parsnips.

The Dead Man suggested I take over for Singe. He was impatient with her striving for perfection. I refused.

"We aren't going anywhere in any hurry. How about Merry? Is he mined out?"

*There is nothing left to be learned from Mr. Sculdyte. But his release into the wild must be handled carefully—after long delay.*

*His absence will leave his brother indecisive. It will cause competing underworld factions to act with restraint. They will all be nervous and his disappearance from the criminal scene will work to Miss Contague's advantage. Merry Sculdyte is the one enemy who was able to penetrate the Contague household.*

"What?" This was news to me.

*Perhaps he was exaggerating to make himself look better. Read the manuscript and find out.*

"But—"

*Read the manuscript. That will keep you out of trouble.*

Dean brought supper for everyone. After supper Singe and I moved over to the office to read each other's transcripts.

When I went up to bed I was aswirl with emotions. Once the Unpublished Committee for Royal Security reviewed Merry Sculdyte's memoirs, organized crime would suffer hugely.

The nagging question, as I fell asleep, remained, where were Chodo and Harvester? Were they together? Was all this something they planned way back when? Had Temisk pulled a dramatic rescue? Or was he working some huge scam?

I shivered down under my winter comforter. It seemed my bed would never warm up. I checked my breathing.

Despite having downed a well full of water and most of Teacher White's antidote, I still needed help.

I kept on shivering.

# 48

Dean made soft-boiled eggs for breakfast, an expensive treat this time of year.

The whole crew was determined to spend me into the poorhouse.

"Stop whining," Singe told me. "You are not poor."

"I'm going to be, though. I'm working for nothing. You're all eating like princes and throwing money down . . . the storm sewers." I'd been about to mention rat holes.

Dean grumbled about quails' eggs and giving me something to bitch about if I really wanted to bitch.

Singe said, "He is this way because it is morning."

She had a point. It was way early. And I couldn't blame my situation on anybody but me. Nobody dragged me out this time. I did it to myself.

I shivered. I hadn't shaken that yet. And I heard the whispering of the damned, in relaxed moments, from far, far off in my mind.

After I ate I checked the weather.

There wasn't a cloud in the sky. It was blinding bright out. Pedestrians slogged through half a foot of slush, carefully. The ice hadn't gone away. Scavengers were gathering fallen branches for firewood.

I retreated to the Dead Man's room. The contrast in light levels left me blind.

*How is your breathing?*

Startled, I realized I was breathing on my own.

*Be cautious. You are but a third of the way recovered. You have no wind. It will be days yet before you dare strain your self.*

"No running or fighting?" Maybe the samsom weed was why I couldn't stop shivering.

*Nor anything else you indulge in that causes an increased heart rate.*

"Oh."

Psychic snicker.

"Then you'd better scare the redhead off if she comes around. Because I don't have a surplus of self-discipline where she's concerned. Hey! Where's my pal Bittegurn?"

*I sent him back to his temple to recover the firestone.*

That didn't sound like the smartest move. "Think he'll bother to come back?"

*He will return. He is convinced that he has found a way to make the big score that has been the secret goal of his life.*

"I feel you wanting to crow. What did you do? Crack that last shell inside his head?"

*Exactly.*

"So how much stroking will I need to do to get you to tell me about it?" I shuddered, the worst fit of shivering yet. "Did you do that?"

*Did I do what?*

"I've been shivering since last night. But this was worse. A completely creepy feeling for a second. That feeling people get when they say somebody walked over their grave. It wasn't the first time, either. And I hear things. Whispers. That are just a hair too far off to make out. So. What did you get from BB?"

*The connection. No. A connection.*

"With what?"

*Between the excitement in the underworld and the Ymberian question.*

"Huh? No. There isn't any connection. There can't be."

*Historically, there is. However, you are correct in thinking that there is not one now. Not directly. None of those ambitious felons out there, eager to take possession of Chodo Contague, are aware that while he was establishing himself, he rented muscle from the cult of A-Laf. They did great violence that could not be traced back to him. For his part, he later provided similar services to the aggressive faction now controlling the cult. You will remember Mr. Crask and Mr. Sadler.*

"You got all that out of Brother Brittigarn?" I shivered, just remembering Crask and Sadler. Being glad that those two were among the angels now. Because, in their time, they'd been much worse than Merry Sculdyte. Much more in my face, far more often.

*I did. That is, he knew the secret history of the A-Laf cult well enough to let me fill the gaps. He did not know the name of the TunFairen criminal captain whose blood money financed the growth of the cult. But what he knew made it obvious that Chodo Contague must be that hidden ally. I expect Mr. Contague would be considerably nonplussed to discover what his assistance has made possible.*

"No shit."

*Excellent thinking.*

"What?"

*You were thinking that it might be useful to see Mrs. Claxton again and interview her from a new perspective.*

"Yeah? Yeah! I'm so clever." I shuddered again, again stricken by that totally creepy feeling that made the chills worse than ever. The whispers were almost intelligible. I had a notion that it would not be good to really understand.

*Got that this time. Ugh. I should have seen it.*

"You going to fade into one of your mystery moods while I figure it out for myself?"

*Not this time. It would be too dangerous to wait that long. The mood you feel, the whispers you hear, are caused by the nickel jackal idols. They came here fully charged with pain and misery and madness. All that has begun to boil off. Someone did not re-seal the box properly.*

"Begun? This has been going on since they dragged those things in here. I just didn't make the connection." I began to have trouble breathing. But none whatsoever shivering.

*No need to get upset.*

You can't breathe, maybe you do need to fuss.

I stared at that damned box. The lid was closed. But it hadn't been nailed down tight.

A baby cat trotted in, headed my way, bounced, landed in my lap. It made itself at home. But it stared at that box, too. With an intensity suggesting that it saw things invisible to me.

*Much better.*

"What?"

*You are calmer now. Once you are comfortable with it, nail that box shut.*

"Sure. I'm a rock." But he was right. The panic was gone. The whispers had receded. My hands weren't trembling. "How much longer is this going to last?"

*That cannot be predicted. It may become necessary to catch this Kolda and make him tell us about samsom weed. I do not want to deal with flashbacks and seizures indefinitely.*

"Yeah? Consider my point of view."

*Ah.*

"Ah? Ah, what?"

*The rumor of your imminent demise may be about to pay dividends.*

"I am on my way," Singe said, heading for the front door. A moment later I heard Scithe talking, though I couldn't make out individual words. Singe came back to report. "That was a Watchman. He wanted to know if it was true about you. I said yes. On inspiration, I told him you had been forced to take a poison Teacher White got from somebody named Kolda."

*I did not cue her,* Chuckles informed me. *She thought of that herself.*

"Good going, Singe. They'll round them all up."

Singe puffed up with pride.

*No time for patting one another on the back. Garrett, you need to be in bed, dying.*

"Block is at the Cardonlos place, eh?"

*It seems logical. I believe he is. Mr. Scithe suspects he is, though he has not seen the Colonel. He was sent here because of his ignorance. But he is brighter than they suspect. He believed his real task was to find out if I am awake. He will report that he found nothing suspicious.*

Block being Block, *that* would be suspicious. "They'll think you messed with his head, then."

*Not amusing. Go be sick.*

# 49

The being sick part didn't require much acting. I still had aches in my pains and bruises on my bruises and those were turning colorful. I hadn't gotten near a razor in modern times. I kept hoping Tinnie would come back and give me a sponge bath. I shivered and shook.

I fell asleep. Which I needed to do. I'd wasted altogether too much time not sleeping.

Tinnie woke me up.

"Oh, hell!"

"Thank you so very much. I'll just go back home."

"I wasn't being . . . you're here because you heard I was dying. Somebody from the Watch told you, right?"

"Yes. How did you know?"

They knew she'd been here before. They'd walked her home. They'd visited her before doing anything else.

"And you told them I'd be all right because the Dead Man keeps me breathing."

"Oh-oh. I goofed."

"Yep. We wanted to fish Block into coming over here. The Colonel was too clever for us this time." Did Block know something he was eager to keep to himself? Probably not. He just had a dislike for having his secret mind exposed.

My breathing seemed almost natural. But thinking about Tinnie and sponge baths alerted me that I wouldn't be living the fantasy anytime soon. "Life is a raging bitch."

"Dean said you'd be in a bad mood. You haven't been drinking as much as you should. Water, I mean."

My, my. She could be right. I was thirsty right then.

I climbed out of bed, rocked dizzily. "Oh."

"You all right?"

"Dizzy."

"You're shaking, too. Is the Dead Man starting to rub off?"

"He's been contagious lately." I sat back down. She was right about the shakes. My dizziness didn't improve. "Maybe you'd better get Dean or Singe to bring some water."

The dizziness not only did not relent. It got worse. Likewise, the shakes. I felt the Dead Man touch me, concerned. Dean brought water. I sucked a pint down without taking a breath.

*You are not supposed to become genuinely sick.*

"I guarantee you, it wasn't in my master plan."

Tinnie said, "You're running a fever."

I collapsed back onto the bed. "This may need to run its course."

Dean invited himself in. He seemed disappointed not to have caught us in midfrolic. "I brought a pitcher of beer. A rapid pass-through might do some good."

I gave him the most potent fisheye I could muster while teetering at the brink of unconsciousness.

I drank all the barley soup I could hold. It was prescribed. I did pass out then, shivering, outraged because this had happened to *me, now*.

Vaguely, I heard Dean opine that I must've caught it that night I was out in the weather. Less vaguely, I tried to get the Dead Man's attention because it might be those damned metal dogs again.

*Jackals.*

I wakened with a mild headache and a solid, coughing cold well started in my left lung. Tinnie materialized before I got all the way upright. I grumbled, "Aren't we getting domestic?"

She had thoughts on the matter. She didn't share. "Drink this." She'd brought a steaming hot mug of something more fetid than aged swamp water.

"Are there wiggly things in here?"

"Dean forgot to add them. I'll go get some. Start on this in the meantime."

I took the mug, held my breath, downed a long draft. Fighting a cough as I did. I don't get sick often. If I do, Dean usually conjures some effective remedy.

Tinnie didn't leave. She made like a stern mother forcing her recalcitrant scion to polish off his rutabaga pie.

"Guess the poison and the exposure did me in."

Tinnie smirked. "Once you're strong enough, go downstairs. Dean has a steam thing set up."

A steam thing. I hadn't been steamed and herbalized since I was a kid. Somebody thought I was on the brink of pneumonia.

"What the hell? This morning I was—"

Miss Tate silenced me with a scowl. "This morning was a different world. You got sick. Fast. In a big way."

I didn't collapse when I got up. But my world whirled on its axis. I was in trouble.

The kind of trouble you're in when a gorgeous redhead gets under your arm and up against you, pretending she's helping you when she's actually torturing you with no shred of shame.

I didn't have much trouble breathing while Tinnie was helping me. Just the opposite.

*It looks like the worst may have passed. Which means you will be back to your usual uncouth self before the rest of us adjust.*

"I'm hoping, Old Bones. Before this one gets away."

That earned me an elbow in the ribs. The sore ribs.

"Easy, woman. What've you got against compliments?"

"Their artificiality? Their lack of sincerity?"

"I'm a little lame in the brain right now. How does that saying go about sharper than a frog's fang?"

"Serpent's tooth. Which you know. Because you haul it out every time somebody disagrees with you."

"Who could possibly disagree with me? I'm so cute." I had to sit back down, then lie back down. I'd used me all up.

"Drink some water."

"You're awful cranky."

"I haven't been getting enough sleep."

Sense was setting in. I thought before I spoke. "How long have you been here?"

"Fifteen hours."

Wow! That explained some things. "I must've been a long way gone."

"You're lucky the Dead Man is awake. And not just because of the breathing."

"Huh?"

"You made me so mad I almost killed you last night. You tried to die on me."

"Uh . . . all right." This sounded like one of those times when anything I said would be the wrong thing. Even silence wouldn't cut it. But silence would bring on the fewest lumps and bruises.

"You probably shouldn't get up. But we need to get you bathed and get your bed changed."

"Sickness is a bitch. Has to happen right in the middle of everything." We'd lost what, two days already?

*Nothing has been lost by your suffering. Nothing has happened.*

Tinnie got that, too. She told me, "It's snowing again. It's weird. We've had half a winter's worth and it really shouldn't have started yet."

More water arrived. Dean didn't carp about anything. That meant I'd definitely had a close call. I drank some, then said, "I'm starving. But I feel nothing better than chicken soup coming on."

"And be thankful for that."

"Old Bones. Was it the samsom weed? Or something else?"

*You have Mr. White to thank for your situation. If not the person called Kolda. The supposed antidote appears to be another poison.*

Teacher. The kind of guy who went to the trouble he'd gone to to get even for Spider Webb and Original Dick might've wanted to get even with me.

"Hey! Why didn't you warn me? Wouldn't you have seen it in Teacher's head if he was trying to poison me?"

*White appeared to have no conscious villainy in progress.*

Dean brought the anticipated chicken soup. Only it was nothing but broth. All the good stuff had been strained out.

It was warm and thick and I was starving. I sucked it down till I couldn't hold any more.

Minutes later I declared, "I'm starting to feel human." Pause. "Well? Somebody going to jump on the straight line?"

"Nobody's in the mood, Garrett. The last fifteen hours were misery curdled. Ready downstairs, Dean?"

"Steamer's going. Water's hot. The tub is out. I'll get something to dry him off and we'll be set."

Tinnie snapped, "Off your butt, big boy. It's bath time."

I stood. With help. The world hadn't gone stable, but it didn't have that awful wobble where I tripped and stumbled into a nightmare dreamland.

I felt stronger by the time we hit the kitchen. Where the air was thick with steam, the herb stench watered my eyes, and the heat was overpowering.

Dean had dragged the big copper laundry tub up from the cellar. Two smaller tubs were heating on the stove. I said, "This ought to cook a few demons out of me."

"If only," Tinnie and Dean sneered at the same instant.

*If only. You should be beyond crisis, Garrett. But we must make sure. You are doing most of your own breathing. Secondarily, Dean and Miss Tate wish to render your personal aroma somewhat less piquant.*

I didn't have energy enough to get my feelings bruised.

Tinnie grumbled, "Arms over your head. Off with those filthy duds."

In the steam and heat I caught whiffs of what everybody else had been suffering all along.

No wonder Singe and her miracle nose were elsewhere.

That weed sweat was pretty awful.

# 50

They steamed me for the rest of the century. They were generous with water and beer, but still I sweated a good ten pungent pounds. And was too weak afterward to make it back to bed on my own.

My bedding had been changed. Somebody had opened the window briefly, despite the weather. A charcoal burner was warming the room now. Herbs had been added, meant to mask bad smells.

I collapsed. My last recollection was Tinnie cursing like a Marine as she levered loose extremities into bed.

I regained consciousness with a furious hangover—again—and a worse attitude. How many times would I go round this circle of misery? Hell. Maybe I could get my karma all polished up in one lifetime.

I had no strength. I was a big glob of pancake goo, just splattered there. If I'd been able to feel sorry for anybody else, I would've reflected on how awful life must be for Chodo. But from the surface of the griddle the horizon is close. Only a strong caution from the Dead Man and a residual dollop of survival instinct kept me from taking it out on Tinnie.

*It is not her fault. It is not her fault.* He is handy, sometimes.

"The Dead Man says you're cured." Damn her eyes, she was chipper. Perky, even. Which made it harder to hold back. "There's some work you can do today. Notice, you're breathing on your own now." Tinnie fed me watery porridge and honeyed tea. "You more inclined to concentrate on the manufactory full-time now?"

Here came some potholes in the high road to romance.

"I thought you all wanted me to stay away." On account of I mutter and sputter and carry on like the group conscience. Particularly when they're trying to expand the corporate profit margin.

"You could keep your mouth shut. You can contribute without making everybody want to smack you with a shaping mallet. Security is getting to be a challenge. We've had parts go missing. We think somebody is trying to build a three-wheel at home."

Singe arrived with a tray. But no food. "This tea has willow bark in it. Dean thought you might have a hangover."

I did, but I was getting better. "Thanks. How come nothing else?"

Singe eyed Tinnie's tray. "Your gut can't handle anything heavier."

I was ready to tie into a mammoth steak. "Not even soup?"

"Soup for lunch. Maybe. Maybe something solid for supper. If you keep the soup down."

I was cranky enough to chew rocks. But some damnable shred of decency wouldn't let me snarl and bitch when people were babying me. Probably supplemented by a suspicion that the babying would stop.

I drank tea. I drank water. By the time I finished dressing and got downstairs I was thirsty again.

Dean gave me apple juice. The flavor hit my mouth like an unexpected explosion. After an almost painful moment I understood that I had my sense of taste back, never having realized that it was gone.

*How is your writing hand? Recovered, I trust?*

I muttered. I grumbled. I made noises like I might not only go to work at the manufactory full-time. I might move there with all my treasures and none of my burdens.

I got a big mental sneer in reply. And a confession that, *The transcription is complete. Merry Sculdyte has departed, in a state of vast confusion. He has memories he knows are not his own. But he cannot sort those out from others that are. He is afflicted with suspicions of his brother and benevolent feelings toward Teacher White. Who, he vaguely recollects, saved his life and nursed him back to health after somebody tried to assassinate him.*

"You seem to have lost some scruples."

*They are not lost. They are in abeyance.*

I was so amazed I forgot to feel sorry for Ma Garrett's baby boy for nearly a minute. "Oh? Explain a little more."

*The Sculdyte family has a plan. An extreme plan. Not advanta-*

*geous for TunFaire. Much better if Miss Contague continues to wrangle the underworld. Her victims are her own kind. And deserving.*

I understood once I skimmed notes from those Merry memories not recorded in my own fair hand.

Rory did have a plan. It involved destroying the Watch. He expected backing from the Hill once the killing started. But Merry had known no names. It sounded more like raw wish fulfillment than solid scheme, but Sculdyte was convinced that a reckoning with the Watch was imminent. Upon removal of Chodo and his wicked daughter.

The Contague name still had conjure power.

# 51

I napped while Colonel Block read. The trudge over to the Cardonlos place had worn me out. Even with Tinnie along to pick me up if I got lost in a snowdrift.

My honey shook me when it was time. The poor girl was ragged.

Block was done. And hot enough to boil water. He glared at me. "How dare they? How *dare* they?" Then, less rhetorically, "Did you really have a close call?"

"You're going to worry about me? That makes me nervous." But I sketched my age of suffering.

"I don't need to hear about every twitch and burp, Garrett." Then, "That doesn't allay my natural cynicism. I can't help wondering, if you're willing to turn this over, how much more interesting is the stuff you're holding back?"

"It's hard, going through life misunderstood."

"I doubt that anyone misunderstands you even a little, Garrett. Eh, Miss Tate? Nevertheless, we're in your debt."

"Really? We could use a visit from some Green Pants guys."

"That might serve our purposes." Without hesitation or argument.

"Send a clerk, too. Somebody without imagination enough to be scared of the Dead Man. I can't write anymore." I showed him a hand shriveled into a claw.

"It isn't that I don't believe you're literate, Garrett. I've witnessed incidents. What I can't envision is you doing that much work."

I shrugged. I'd surprised him before.

His heart wasn't in his banter. It was broken. Somebody out there was so indisposed to the rule of law that he meant to make war on it. "Where is Merry now?"

I shrugged again. I was getting a heavy workout. "I was asleep. They put him out in the snow. In a state of confusion, apparently."

"Assuming your story has a nodding acquaintance with the truth, then, Rory may guess that his baby brother ran into the only Loghyr left in TunFaire."

Not all of TunFaire's crooks are terminally stupid. Only most of them.

I asked, "Any idea where Belinda Contague is?"

"No. She's as elusive as her father. Why?"

"Curiosity."

Block grunted. He was antsy. He wanted me to go away so he could go talk this over with his unsocial sidekick. His claw within the shadows.

Sighing, Tinnie hoisted me to my feet. I groaned. It would be a long, cold trek home. I told Block, "We wouldn't mind seeing one of the foreman type Ymberians, in addition to the standard wide load with the bad fashion sense."

The good Colonel nodded, distracted. He wasn't exactly caught up in the moment.

# 52

The wind was no longer as wicked. It was behind us now. And I was too wiped out to be distracted by externals. I couldn't focus on much but hunger and wanting to get back to bed.

Nevertheless, that old Marine training persisted. "See the waif beside the steps down there?"

"Yes. That the kitten girl with the mighty name?"

"The very one."

"She don't look like a princess."

"How do I convince her she doesn't have to be afraid?"

"Get the eunuch operation?"

"Come on, Tinnie."

"I love you, buddy. But love doesn't have to be blind. She's female. She's old enough to stand on her own hind legs. Which means she'd better not get close enough for you to do your helpless little-boy routine."

Story of my life. They want to mother me instead of let me treat them badly, Morley Dotes style.

"You're too young and beautiful to be so cynical."

"You might wonder who made me that way."

"I will. When I find out who she is, I'll give her a piece of my mind."

"Sure you can spare it?"

We were home. She whacked on the castle gate. I puffed and panted. The long climb left me without wind to argue.

I swear, there were still echoing whiffs of Mulclar swirling round the stoop.

Singe opened up. Tinnie handed me over. "Give him lots of

water, some broth, and let him nap. I'll be back." She returned to the street. Singe didn't give me time to thank her.

The Dead Man demanded, *Do you have something to report?*

"Save time. Do it the easy way." I settled into my chair, half-heartedly trying to remember when we'd shed all our guests.

I felt him stir the sludge inside my head. I went to sleep. After what didn't seem like thirty winks, I woke up to a meal set up on a small table beside me. Singe ambled in from up front, where she had admitted a snow-encrusted redhead.

I said, "I thought you went home."

Tinnie frowned. Then, "No. I went to talk to the princess." She didn't sound like she was awash in sympathy for Penny. "She's as stubborn as a rock. She won't come over and get warm."

I asked, "She sat still? She talked to you?"

"She didn't feel threatened."

"What's her problem?"

"She's the last one standing, Garrett. She's still a kid. But she saw her mother, her aunts, and her grandmother murdered. By men."

"Men in green pants, not harmless little fuzz balls like me."

"Men. That's the point. The A-Laf cult. Which, the way she tells it, is a lot nastier than we imagined. They think women are evil. That they're fit only to be breeding slaves."

I sensed faint but constrained mirth. "Careful, Old Bones. She's wound up. And your attitude is pretty bad."

"It isn't his attitude I had in mind, big boy."

Time for a change of subject. "Dean! Where are you? Bring something for Miss Tate. Singe, how about you help her with those wet things?"

Tinnie glared. I was being thoughtful.

The air of amusement grew. *As I have observed previously, when you get hit hard enough for long enough, you do begin to learn.*

Tinnie glowered.

*Your visit with the girl was more productive than you think, Miss Tate.*

He left it at that. Until Tinnie had eaten and warmed up and grown less cranky. Then he told us that Tinnie had distracted Penny enough for him to slip a couple of suggestions into her divine head. *I could not browse. The girl has been trained to recognize and resist a probe. Therefore, I fed what was there. Fear. Despair. Loneliness. And physical misery.*

He didn't share the latter with Tinnie, who was likely to turn all outraged.

She was still eating. And listening to Singe talk about chances for a bath followed by a long nap. Singe suddenly shut up, stood upright, and stared at the Dead Man with glazed eyes. Then she headed for the front door.

*This should be interesting.* He didn't explain. Back to Penny Dreadful. *The impulses insinuated should heighten the child's entire range of emotion. We can expect her to look for emotional support.*

*It would behoove you to make sure that Dean does not leave the house before she cracks.*

# 53

Butterbutt sent Dean to the door. Dean did try to sneak out. Chuckles didn't let him. The old boy got all foamy-mouthed about supposed shortages in our stores.

The rest of us got excited about the three bipeds delivered by Scithe and several Relway Runners. Scithe told me, "Ask and ye shall receive. Sign this receipt, Garrett."

I signed, checked his catch. "The bruno seems a bit dull."

"That would be his natural state. Though they did drug him up. It was the only way to keep him docile. This other one, you smack him some and he gets cooperative."

"The long, skinny one the clerk?"

The third man was tall and vague. He slouched with hands in pockets. Defeated. The part in his hair was four inches wide and ran back to his crown.

"Yeah. He's a twofer. A bonus baby. He'll do your transcription. Call it public service, to work off bad behavior. The Director gets a kick out of that kind of thing."

"What'd he do?"

"He poisoned one of our more exotic Karentine subjects."

I didn't get it. I was in slow mode.

"Kolda, Garrett. Your herbalist. They ran him down this morning."

"Relway has a twisted sense of humor."

"We enjoy it. Got to go. Always more bad boys to catch."

Dean saw the strongarms of the law to the door. He attempted another escape. Old Bones shut him down. Singe took him back to the kitchen.

I stared at Kolda. Stared and stared. The man almost killed me. Though not deliberately. Teacher White asked for a tool. Kolda delivered. He would've sold the same drug to me if I'd asked, with silver in hand.

*He does not know who you are.*

"Too bad. Suppose we put him to work." I'd get even later.

Before he started on the Green Pants crew, the Dead Man rifled Kolda's head. He didn't find much. *You have brought women home who have more between the ears.*

"Hey! Tinnie resents that!" Knowing he wouldn't have included her in his last.

*He is a power within his own field, however. He could write a major grimoire on medicinal herbs. He is not a social creature. Though he does have a wife and three children.*

"Marvelous. Good for him. I can barely keep my eyes open. Before I fall asleep I'd like to know if you mined any nuggets out of these fools."

Kolda and the Ymberian foreman became suspicious. Kolda turned scared. The Dead Man calmed him down, set him up to record what he dug out of the other two.

*Ah. Here is an interesting tidbit. Our once-upon-a-time friends Mr. Crask and Mr. Sadler began their careers as sextons in the A-Laf cult. Chodo Contague suborned them. Not that they were especially devout. Being sextons allowed them to indulge their needs to hurt people.*

That sounded like those boys. And my old pal Chodo.

The Dead Man made the equivalent of a girlish squeal of dismay.

"What?" I couldn't keep my eyes open.

Tinnie had gone up to bed already. But she'd had a hard few days.

*The smaller one has hidden defenses. Nasty ones. He is pulling them together now. He has only just realized the truth of his situation.*

"A little slow, is he?" Not surprising, though. A lot of line boss types amble around with their heads stuck in dark and smelly places.

*Our friends in the Unpublished Committee treated him with a preparatory drug, too. Therefore, he is slower than he might be.*

*Ouch!*

"What?"

*There are mousetraps in there. I got a finger nipped. This* will

*be challenging.* He was excited. *And dangerous. He has some minor training in the use of sorcery.*

Oh, hell. What did I get myself into now?

I'd worry about it after another nap. If Butterbutt didn't provoke the Ymberian into imploding the house.

# 54

Three hours was time enough to restore me to a functional level.

There'd been changes. Saucerhead had turned up. He nursed a mug of something warm. John Stretch was in Singe's personal chair, hard at work on a big bowl of stewed apples. My mouth watered. Melondie Kadare was absent. I hadn't seen her for a while. The weather must have caught up with her tribe.

Singe brought me a bowl. Summoned by Chuckles, no doubt. It was gruel.

"I see the place is still standing." Both the Ugly Pants foot soldier and Ugly Pants manager appeared to be sleeping.

*The most powerful wizard who ever lived cannot work his wickedness if he cannot focus. The key to sorcery is will and concentration.*

What might the Dead Man be doing inside the deacon's skull? He had me confused and boggled without even trying.

"Good to know. To what do we owe the honor of foul-weather visits from Saucerhead Tharpe and John Stretch?"

*Ask them. I am occupied. As you proceed, however, go through the pockets of the sexton.*

Singe brought John Stretch another bowl of apples and a mug of beer. Saucerhead had a beer himself. Singe is a generous girl when it isn't her purse that's being drained.

Saucerhead seemed less likely to be distracted. "So what's the word?"

"I got your rock back. Bitte put up a fight, but . . . actually, I brung that back when you was still sick. It's on your curio shelf."

We have a set of shelves where we keep memorabilia. Some are good for a chuckle. Now that the pain has gone away.

"Thanks. And?"

"I been going on tracking down all those times where somebody caught on fire and died."

That must've been exciting. Maybe the gods did me a big favor, letting me get poisoned. "So?"

"So I started with forty-one cases where human combustion was supposed to be involved. That was bullshit, mostly."

Huh? "All right. Go on."

"Well, right away I found six times when what it was, it was kitchen accidents. Grease fires. And with the other cases, almost every time they was a ordinary explanation. What're you doing to that guy?"

"Rolling him. Chuckles thinks he has something in his pocket."

Singe, pandering to our freeloaders, asked, "How is the new girlfriend?"

Color appeared in Tharpe's cheeks.

I said, "Huh?"

Far be it from me to discourage a man, however hopeless. I did not pursue it now, though I did wonder how Saucerhead had found time to get involved with another woman. "So most of the supposed . . . what did you call them? Human combustions?"

"Yeah. Spontaneous human combustion. It's sorcerer talk."

Really? We'd look at that later. "So most weren't what rumors make them out to be."

"Nope. They was some that there wasn't no explanation for, though. I got the feeling some more could be explained if somebody can work themselves up to admit that they done something really stupid. But, even so, some has got to be them spontaneous human combustions."

"Including Buy Claxton?"

"Who?"

"The woman who caught fire during Chodo's birthday party."

"I don't know nothin' about her. I didn't look at her. But she was in a kitchen when it happened, wasn't she? What did you find?"

I'd found a little green egg in Big Boy's pocket. A dead ringer for the one on my curio shelf. Interesting. Some secret mutual identification charm for members of A-Laf's gang?

My partner could root that out.

"How many cases?"

"Seven that need a closer look on account of they all involved Chodo."

"Ah. Ah?"

"Chodo owned the places where the fires happened. Some of the other ones, too, but in these ones Chodo was there."

"You're shitting me."

"Not hardly. You're my favorite turd."

"Saucerhead. We're in mixed company here."

"As mixed as it gets, I'd say."

"Talk to me about Chodo's part."

"He was there. Every time. Hang on. I might be misspeaking. Somebody in a wheeled chair was there before the fires happened. But not when the bodies was found."

At this point Saucerhead's marvelous legwork petered out. Meaning there might yet be legwork reserved for me.

I went through the other Ymberian's pockets. He didn't have his own roc's egg. He did come equipped with a little teak box. Inside: "One of them metal dogs." Frost formed on it. Despair hit like a kick in the gilhoolies. Whispers of darkness filled my head. I just managed to shut the box. "Whoa! That was ugly."

Saucerhead and John Stretch were glassy-eyed, with Tharpe smitten harder than the ratman. Cutlery hit the floor in the kitchen. A-Laf's boys didn't react. Because the Dead Man had frozen up. Those he controlled had followed his lead.

Old Bones had taken the psychic equivalent of a punch to the breadbasket. He huffed and puffed, on the mental side, getting his balance back.

"That was some bad shit," Saucerhead rumbled, shivering. "How about you don't open that friggin' box no more?"

"You got a deal, buddy."

# 55

The situation improved once those of us who weren't guests of the Crown surrounded a few beers. I told John Stretch, "You've been quiet."

"As a mouse." A joke? "My mouth has been full."

"You got a point. It's not full now, though. What's up?"

"We have located your lawyer."

"What?" I chomped down on Harvester Temisk's name in a moment of paranoia. "Why didn't you say so?"

"I just did. And your partner has known since my arrival." John Stretch no longer seemed intimidated. "There is no need for haste."

It was night out and winter out and the Dead Man wasn't excited about getting something done right away. Maybe it *could* wait.

Saucerhead reminded me, "Chodo don't move so fast and light no more, Garrett. I figure, wherever the mouthpiece has got him stashed, that's where he'll stay till he gets flushed out."

"That's the common wisdom now? That Temisk kidnapped him at Whitefield Hall?"

"Ain't no better theory ever come up. Some folks even wonder if the Green Pants guys wasn't just a diversion for to cover his getaway."

Interesting theory. "And, flushes him?" What? I felt an idea trying to be born. Kolda. Yeah. And my late bout with herbal poisoning. "Hey. Old Bones. What're the chances Belinda's been poisoning her old man? Temisk might be trying to get him straight."

*If so, the woman is more clever than we credit. She has been*

*here many times, betraying only her ongoing complicity in profit-*
*ing from her father's misfortune. In the financial and emotional*
*senses alike.*

*There may be substance to your speculation, however. If other*
*parties had regular access.*

"Didn't Merry say Rory has somebody inside?"

*Interesting. Yes. Let me reflect on the possibilities.*

"It would explain some stuff. You sure I shouldn't hit the
bricks right now?"

*You are not yet recovered.*

John Stretch said, "My people will keep watch."

That wasn't reassuring. Ratfolk are notorious for cashing in
on anything salable. The whereabouts of the kingpin might be the
most marketable commodity in TunFaire today.

John Stretch tried to reassure me. "My watchers do not know
who they have staked out. They believe we are watching a bur-
glary ring whose plunder hoard we intend to convert to our own
advantage. They know only that they are to inform me who goes
in and out."

This ratguy was a natural. Dangerously bright. "Can you track
somebody to their next hideout in this weather?"

"Singe can."

I was skeptical.

*Your anxiety is understandable, Garrett. And not misplaced.*
*But you* must *regain strength. You are not yet capable of an ex-*
*tended journey, let alone physical excitement.*

"If John Stretch can find them, so can Rory or Teacher."
Chodo had had friends on the Hill. No doubt Rory Sculdyte did,
too. Those people and Syndicate bosses are sides of the same
coin, down in their bloody, greedy black hearts.

And there are countless low-talent, self-taught storefront and
street-corner magicians. Not all of them are charlatans.

"Good work, all," I said. "What do I owe you, Saucerhead?
After deductions for food and beer?"

"What? You got no sense of hospitality. I wouldn't never try to
charge you if you was a guest at my place."

"How do I know that? I don't even know where you live."

Saucerhead showed me one of his professional hard-guy
looks. It didn't take. After a pause, he said, "Singe paid me."

"If I go get in line now, a place might open up in the work-
house before I'm completely destitute."

"I wisht I was half as bad off as you're always poor-mouthing. I'd have to go live on the street."

I could see how. Saucerhead comes equipped with low expectations and a knack for showing up at suppertime.

John Stretch told me, "The stewed apples and Weider's Select are compensation enough for me." He had to work at "compensation."

I nodded but thought, "Not good." What insanity would the rat king drag me into if I stumbled into his favor-for-a-favor universe? That kind of nightmare had me chasing Chodo now.

The Dead Man suggested, *You all should turn in for the night. Garrett, I will generate a distraction that will allow you to leave unnoticed in the morning. Mr. Tharpe. We have further need of your services.*

Evidently I was expected to improve dramatically during the night.

So I went upstairs and slept some more. I had to move Tinnie with a crowbar. If she'd been any more asleep, we would've needed an undertaker.

## 56

Singe woke me.

"Don't you ever sleep, girl? Where's Tinnie?" I was alone.

"She went home. Saucerhead took her. She was not feeling well. She was afraid she caught what you had. She wanted to be where she could get a real physician to visit."

"Crap!" Something to worry about on top of everything else.

"She said don't worry on her account. She will be with her family."

"Double crap. You know what that means."

"In my limited experience, I would say it means you had damned well better find room in your busy day to go hold Tinnie's quivering hand. You can rest after you are dead."

She'd read Tinnie pretty good. "Nothing I can do about that right now. So why wake me up?" There was no light from outside.

"The Dead Man says it will be time to get moving when Saucerhead gets back. Also, Mr. Dotes just returned. I thought that might be important."

I glanced at the window. It had better be real important. It was flat dark out there.

Singe told me, "Dean is grumbling like a volcano god, but he is cooking and fussing about going back to bed later. When you dress, remember that it is raining again. And looks likely to turn to ice or snow."

"Sounds exciting." I swung my feet onto the floor, stood. I didn't know how bad I'd felt before until I realized how good I felt now. "Wow! I think I'm cured."

"Yes. And your bed buddy left a little too soon." She nodded toward half-mast.

I glanced down. And flushed. "We're getting too casual and comfortable with each other around here."

Singe resisted further comment. "I should consult the poisoner. I'm due for a season. None of us need that distraction."

She was right. Ratgirls in heat distract everybody. They have no more control than a cat in heat.

"Where are our kittens? I haven't seen them for a while."

"Hiding from A-Laf's wicked men."

"I see." Interesting.

We all breakfasted while Morley explained his appearance at such an ugly hour.

"My place caught on fire."

"With you there? Your boys are more clever than I thought."

"Yes, with me there. And it wasn't their fault. To my surprise. Though, shall we say, not so much a surprise after all, considering. I hear you got your rock back from the guy who switched it out. May I see it?"

"Huh? On the curio thing. Top shelf." I looked at Old Bones. He wasn't inclined to explain.

"There are two here, Garrett. Which one?"

"The one with the scratches is the one that got flung at me."

"I don't see any scratches."

"You can feel them. And there's a chip out of the pointy end. Do you see that?"

"A little black spot?"

"Yeah. What's up?"

"The fire started in the dent where this hit my door. I don't know how. Or why. Or why now. It was like a charcoal fire. About this big when we found it." He made a circle with his forefingers and thumbs. "It wouldn't go out. We ended up taking the door down. We piled ice and snow on, but it kept burning till the wood was all gone."

"I know a good door and hinge man."

"Well, you'd have to. Wouldn't you?"

"Ha! And ha again. Old Bones. What do you think?"

*Consider the possibility that you were not the target of that stone. The intent may have been to burn Mr. Dotes' business.*

"That's a long jump."

*Not too long considering what I prized out of the Brittigarn person. And hints I find in these minds. Though one is a wasteland and the other remains mostly locked.*

"What motive could these lunatics have?" Morley asked. "I hadn't heard of them then."

*Possibly they wished to distract you from Garrett's situation. No. That is too great a stretch. We do not have sufficient information. You have eaten. Garrett, I suggest you get started. Mr. Tharpe is about to arrive.*

"Am I up to this?"

*Yes. Though you will not be alone.*

"What's up?" Morley asked as Singe appeared, ready for the weather.

"Got a couple of things to check out. Buy Claxton first."

"Oh. I'll tag along on that."

I didn't argue with him or with Singe. The Dead Man told me, *Singe knows where you are going. Do you?*

Not unless he told me. Because John Stretch hadn't chosen to trouble me with that little detail.

# 57

First thing I noticed—after I stopped whining about the cold—was that Penny Dreadful was no longer across the street. "I hope she found someplace that's warm."

"She'll be all right," Saucerhead told me.

"You in this with Dean now?"

"Tinnie took her home. On account of she was half frozen. She was killing herself."

We went on over past The Palms, where Morley's troops lurked behind a down comforter hung in place of the door. He showed me the seared hardware. "Not much to see, is there?"

"There is a stench of all evil unleashed," Singe said. She breathed in little puffs, the way I would do around a badly blown carcass. When Puddle came out I told him how to get hold of Mr. Mulclar. "He'll cut you a discount if you tell him I referred you."

"That's exciting," Morley said. "Why am I suspicious of your generosity? Why do I think you're straining to keep a straight face?"

"I don't know. Why?"

If Mr. Mulclar hadn't changed his diet . . . heh, heh, heh.

Morley stayed with us. It was a short half mile on to the Bledsoe. It was getting light. The scaffolding outside the hospital was clotted with ice and snow. An incessant drizzle had no luck washing them away. The scaffolding seemed abandoned. The mortar boats were gone. Any bricks that hadn't been set had walked away. I was surprised the scaffolding hadn't disappeared.

"Armed guards," Saucerhead said. I didn't see any. He told me, "You want to, grab on to something that ain't yours."

"I take it you know who's on the job."

"They're Watch guys picking up a little extra on their own time. I would've done it myself if I wasn't already helping you."

"Who's paying them?"

Tharpe shrugged. He didn't know. And probably didn't care.

We entered the hospital unchallenged. Morley said, "I'll see what I can find out." One weak lamp burned ahead. Its light was enough to show us an unfamiliar woman at the reception desk. She was delighted to see Morley. His earlier conquest must've talked.

"I cannot come in here!" Singe told me suddenly, after not having spoken since we left home, except to whine about her tail dragging in the slush.

"Nobody will give you any crap."

"That is not the problem. The problem is the air. It is thick with madness. I cannot endure it."

"I'm sorry. I should've thought of that. Mr. Tharpe. Would you stay with Singe? In case some moron gets obnoxious?"

Tharpe grunted. He and Singe went back outside. Morley turned on the charm spigot. I headed for Buy Claxton's suite. And got there without seeing another human being.

I wasn't surprised. This was the Bledsoe, warehouse for the sickest of the poorest of the poor and craziest of the crazies. Their dying place.

Some crazies were venting madness right now.

Buy Claxton was awake. She was knitting by candlelight. A dead flower in a clay pot stood on a stand with the candle. She remembered me. She didn't seem surprised to see me. "See what the lady sent me?" She indicated the flower, uncommon for the season.

"The lady?"

"Miss Contague. She's quite thoughtful for a woman of her position."

"She has her moments."

"Did she send you to see how I'm doing?"

A small fib wouldn't be entirely misplaced. "And to see if we can't find out what happened, now that you're feeling better."

Mrs. Claxton put her knitting aside, teary-eyed. She controlled herself. "I'm no widow, you know. And I have two sons and three daughters. My Ethan died in the Cantard. He'd be your age. He's the only one with a good reason for not visiting."

"I'm sorry to hear that. Some people are thoughtless. Especially family."

"I'll bet you're good to your mother."

"My mother is gone. I did try when she was still with us." But I've been a louse since then. I haven't visited her grave in years. "But let's not be sadder than we need to be. Not here."

"That would be sound thinking, young man. How can I help?"

"It's the fire. I'm supposed to find out what happened."

"I don't know. It just happened. It hurt! Bad." She smiled weakly.

"I can tell you this, Mrs. Claxton. . . ."

"Call me Buy."

"Yes, ma'am. You might not have noticed because you weren't looking for it, but that didn't just happen. There must've been something leading up. So I want to go over the whole evening with you. Why were you there in the first place? You didn't work for the caterer."

"No. For Mr. Hartwell."

"Is that the Mr. Hartwell who manages the Contague estate?" A man I'd never trusted. A slimy type. But I couldn't imagine him stealing from the Contagues.

"His son. Armondy. He asked me to help set up, do kitchen work, and clean up afterward."

"So it wasn't odd that you were there?"

"No. I don't think."

"Interesting. When did you get there? Did anything unusual happen when you did?"

"A little after noon. There wasn't anything to do then. The unusual thing was that I caught on fire and almost burned to death." She ranted about her husband and children. I let her vent the anger.

"Who did you report to when you arrived?"

"When they finally showed up, them fancy boys. I just hung out till they got there."

"I met them. They were in charge?"

"They wanted to think. They were decorators. They were there to arrange the tables and chairs. I only paid attention if what they said made sense. No. I took my orders from Mr. Temisk. I knew him from years back."

"Harvester Temisk?"

"That's the one."

"So Mr. Temisk was there. Early. In the back." I hadn't known that. Nobody had mentioned seeing Temisk.

"Where I first run into him was in the pantries. I don't know why he was back there. Looking for lamp oil, he said. Since I seen some in the kitchen, brung by the fancy boys, I showed him where I seen it."

"What about Miss Contague? When did she show?"

Mrs. Claxton confirmed my suspicions. "She was already there when I got there. With her bodyguards. Checking for trouble, I guess."

"Mr. Temisk wanted lamp oil? Why?"

"Well, he took out this little wood box and shook this green, flaky stuff in the oil and shook the jars. He said it was incense. He had me fill the lamps to go on the tables."

This didn't look good for Harvester Temisk. "Then what?"

"I don't know. Then he went away. I didn't see him again. I worked around the kitchen. Oh. And Mr. Temisk gave me this little jade pin. For being so helpful, he said."

Didn't look good for Temisk at all. "This flake stuff. Did any get spilled? Or miss getting into the lamp oil?" If it was what I suspected, it got tracked around by an unwitting rat.

Mrs. Claxton considered. "Come to think, he did fumble the lid of the box when he started to spice up the first oil jar. He cussed something awful. Because the spice was so expensive, he said."

Yes. No doubt. We talked a while, mainly about her sad family. I didn't learn anything useful. "Did anyone else see Mr. Temisk?"

"I don't know. I never seen no one else around."

"Did you see the lady's father? Chodo Contague?"

"Well, no. But he musta been there somewhere, eh?"

Temisk's timing had been amazing if he'd been missed by my pixies and rats. Although there hadn't been any reason for them to watch for him and no reason for them to recognize him if they did see him. A guy named Garrett was the only one who needed to miss him. Plus Chodo's beloved only child and a few underbosses, the latter of whom had no reason to visit the kitchens.

This was beginning to look like a huge, ugly Harvester Temisk murder scheme piggybacked onto whatever plot Belinda was running. Which meant that Temisk used me from the start.

Everybody's schemes disintegrated in the chaos inside Whitefield Hall.

I'd have some hard questions for lawyer boy when I caught him.

"Thank you, Mrs. Claxton. Do you want me to check on your family?"

"Thank you, young man, but no. I'll handle them myself. I *will* get out of here someday."

"I hope so. You keep that attitude, it won't be long."

# 58

Morley was reluctant to leave. His new friend was loath to let him go. But other people were arriving for work. Being people, they were nosy, noisy, and demanding.

"You learn anything?" I asked as we slipped outside. And, "Where the hell did those two go?"

Singe and Saucerhead were nowhere to be seen.

"A trust fund pays for the guards. There's Tharpe."

Saucerhead beckoned from a gap between buildings where overhangs provided some protection from the drizzle.

"Is it worth chasing the money trail?"

"Why bother? Unless you've got something going that I don't know about. Block and Relway might give it a look, though."

"I've got a feeling they've lost interest in the Ugly Pants Gang. For now. What're you guys doing over here?"

"Trying not to be noticed by Plenty Hart and Bobo Negry," Saucerhead said.

"Who?"

"A couple of Rory's men," Morley told me. "Middle level. Dangerous. What would they be doing here?"

"Maybe Merry is inside," I speculated. "He was in ragged shape when the Dead Man was done with him."

"Maybe." Tharpe doubted it, though. "They was looking for somebody."

"Us? Did Big Boy not do a good job of getting us away?"

Tharpe shrugged.

"Singe?"

"Do not ask me. I am a tracker. I can help you find an answer only by tracking those men back. If they came here on our trail, that would be obvious in a short time. Do you wish to try that?"

"Would it take long to make sure?"

"Ten minutes," Singe promised.

"Saucerhead, stick with her. Soon as she makes up her mind, head for . . . where, Singe?"

"The Tersize Granary."

"Sniff Morley and me out, Singe."

"Or Garrett and I," Dotes said. Then, once they took off, "You planning on rushing into this?"

"You have a suggestion?"

"Same old, same old as always. Be ready for trouble."

He meant weaponry. Armaments, in fact. He'd lug a siege ballista if he could get one into a pocket. And use it at the least excuse. And feel no remorse afterward.

"I have my stick."

Morley was not overawed.

"If I need something nastier, I'll take it away from somebody."

"You're not as young and quick as you think you are."

"Is anybody? Ever?"

"So stipulated. Without excusing your silly refusal to look out for yourself."

"Oh-oh. I get the feeling my weapons habits are about to take second place to my dietary habits."

"Since you bring it up . . ."

And so it went. Thirty minutes later we sighted the Tersize Granary. Which, till recently, had been the Royal Karentine Military Granary, whence vast tonnages of feed grains, flours, and finished baked goods (read rock-hard hardtack in hundredweight barrels) barged down a canal to the river and thence to the war zone. The operating Tersize family acquired it from the Ministry of War, cheap after the killing stopped.

I said, "The Tersizes are related to the Contagues somehow, aren't they?"

"Chodo's stepsister Cloris married Misias Tersize. But they weren't in bed with the Outfit. That I've heard. The place isn't what it used to be," Morley said of the sprawl of redbrick milling and storage facilities.

Much of it appeared to have gone derelict. "You know this area?" I didn't. "I don't see any sign of squatters." TunFaire is inundated with refugees from a war zone that no longer exists.

"No. The place used to be a fort. The millers and bakers

couldn't get in or out without a military pass. You want to wait for Saucerhead and Singe?"

Recalling times when I'd just charged in, "I think so."

"Developing a taste for caution? At this late date?"

"I have responsibilities now. Dean. The Dead Man. Seven kittens. And a girlfriend who'll hunt me down in Hell if I get myself killed before I can visit her in her sickbed."

"Why don't we just slip into the lee of one of these buildings while we wait, then? Because I've just figured out why there aren't any squatters."

I caught what his sharper elfish eyes had spied already.

Three sizable men ambled along the street beside the westernmost wall of the granary. One checked the doors that existed at regular intervals, formerly for loading and unloading. The streetside walls of the granary were the outer faces of the various structures included in the complex, connected by the outer faces of single-story sheds. Tinnie's family lived in a similar complex. It included family housing, worker housing, warehousing, and manufacturing workshops. The Tate compound, though, had a smaller footprint and was less imposing vertically.

"You know, brunos look pretty much the same wherever you find them. But I have a definite feeling that these three wouldn't be embarrassed if their mothers dressed them in green plaid pants." Had Block cut them loose? Or were there more of them than suspected, now avoiding the Bledsoe project and public attention?

The door checker of the three performed his function again, using a stick much like the one I carried. The others were better armed. Or worse, if you have a tendency to acknowledge the law. One carried a set of swords, long and short. The other lugged a siege engine of a crossbow, drawn and loaded. They were looking for trouble.

"You have a nasty way of thinking, my friend. But you're right. Go talk to them. See if they have a country accent. If they are Green Pants people, we'll know why there's always more of them than we expect to see."

"You go. Beauty defers to age."

"Speaking of beauty and beast. Tharpe and Singe should have been here by now. I'm getting a chill."

"If we have to walk all the way around the place, you'll warm up. . . . Uh-oh!"

The stick man had found a door that swung inward. That it shouldn't have done was obvious instantly.

Blades came out. The crossbowman backed off a few steps. The stick man moved in, with no caution whatsoever.

Ratmen boiled past him. Preceded by a swarm of missiles that might have been tavern darts. That was so remarkable that stick man and sword man alike failed to do anything but duck. Crossbowman managed only to take the striped stocking cap off the head of an especially long, gaunt ratman. The pack was too chaotic for an accurate count. They disappeared before the security men pulled themselves together.

The three looked around, realized there was nothing they could do about the ratmen, went inside to see what the ratmen had been doing.

Ratmen materialized. I recognized John Stretch. They slammed the door shut and nailed it in place. Then the rat king headed our way while his minions congratulated one another.

"He knew we were here," I said.

"Yes." Morley examined our surroundings thoughtfully.

I checked for normal rats myself till John Stretch was close enough to hear me ask, "What was all that?"

"We wanted the patrol out of our fur. They will not be missed for a while. But we have no time to spare."

"You timed all that for our arrival?"

The ratman seemed concerned about my intelligence. "No."

"But you did know that we were lurking around out here."

"Yes. Where is Singe? I expected her to bring you here."

"She's coming." I explained the delay.

And here she came. Trudging through the snow, holding her cold tail, looking miserable. Saucerhead limped along behind.

A flurry of activity commenced at what would've been the next door checked by the trapped patrol. A flood of ratpeople went in. Then the stream became bidirectional. Those exiting were loaded down. Singe took one look, dropped her tail, and tied into her brother. "Are you mad?"

"Easy, girl," I told her.

"This is insane! The humans will forget the Other Races! The Watch will help the racialists persecute our folk."

"Easy, Singe. Did you think about that, John?" While he considered his reply, I asked Singe, "What's the word? Were we being followed?"

"No. They just took the same route for a long time." Then, sort of vaguely, "But they might have been looking for us even if they did not know they were following us."

I shook my head. She was starting to think like the Dead Man. "What's your story?" I asked Saucerhead. He was hanging on to a wall, favoring his left hip.

"I fell. On some ice. It was under some fresh snow. It's snowing back there, just a couple blocks."

"Really?"

John Stretch said, "There will be no complaints to the Watch."

"Oh?"

"Thieves do not complain to the law when other thieves take what they have stolen."

He'd never swapped war stories with veterans of the Watch, I guess. But I got his point. "There's illegal stuff going on over there, eh?"

"All this part in back. Behind the smokestacks. It is all shut down and sealed off from the rest. Not used anymore. Except by criminals."

"I see. Saucerhead. How are you going to babysit me if you keep falling on your ass yourself?"

He muttered something about how dumb do you have to be to let Teacher White ambush you and make you eat noxious weeds?

I sneered, asked the ratman, "These bad boys look like the ones who caused a fuss in our neighborhood. Are they foreigners?"

"Out-of-towners. Yes."

"Definitely explains why there's always another one around after the Watch thinks they've got them all."

Morley observed, "We didn't come out here for a committee meeting."

"Good point. John Stretch. Where is my friend the mouthpiece?"

The ratman sighed. "Follow me."

Our path led past the door the ratmen had nailed shut. Tremendous impacts hit it from the other side. Dust and splinters flew.

I said, "That convinces me. They're just not wearing the pants. I've never seen anybody that stubborn."

John Stretch showed concern. "They will be in a bloody mind when they do get out."

"Likely. They're not used to not getting their own way. Your guys threw darts. Weren't they poisoned?"

"No. I did not know where to acquire that sort of drug."

Too bad. But I wasn't inclined to clue him in now.

Singe offered no suggestions, either.

# 59

We used the doorway the plundering ratpeople were running in and out of. Who stole all that in the first place? The crew from Ymber wouldn't waste the time.

John Stretch led us up a dusty, rickety stair slick with bat droppings. The bat smell was potent. He led on through a maze of ups and downs. The granary had been built in stages, over generations. The army had wanted everything connected. The ratman said, "I am sorry. I have not yet seen this myself. There must be a more direct route. I believe we are close now. Be silent."

Silence it was. We're good at silence. All of our lives have depended on silence at some point. And we're all still here.

We got around by light that leaked through gaps in roofs and walls. There were plenty of those. Unfortunately, they also let in critters and the weather. Eventually, Singe smelled smoke. Flickering light appeared ahead and below. "Looks like firelight."

We entered the loft of what once had been a vast stable. Moldy hay still lay here and there, inhabited by Singe's unimproved cousins.

The flickering light came from an indoor campfire. We advanced carefully. Everybody wanted to see. And what we saw was half a dozen people trying to keep warm around a fire being fed wood torn from nearby horse stalls. There were tents around the fire, four of them, facing the warmth.

The camp had been there awhile. There wasn't much lumber left. There was trash. Laundry hung on lines. That included green plaid pants. Which I noted only in passing. I concentrated on Harvester Temisk and the old man in a wheelchair. Who looked more lively than a man in a coma ought.

I got down on my belly, at the edge of the loft. Morley dropped beside me. Chodo wasn't talking, nor was he moving. Still, he was farther into our world than when last I'd seen him.

John Stretch settled to my right. Ordinary brown rats collected around him, worshipful.

Were Temisk and Chodo prisoners? Guests? Or in charge?

The unrelated things were converging, suggesting potential cause and effect relationships.

Chodo had an arrangement with the A-Laf cult. It went back a long time. A-Laf's thugs came to town to charge their nickel dogs with misery. Before Temisk got in touch with me. Before Penny Dreadful turned up with her spooky kittens.

The appearance of the Green Pants Gang must have emboldened Harvester Temisk. He decided to rescue his boss. Powerful old allies had arrived. And they owed Chodo.

But that left plenty of questions. How had Temisk meant to use me? Surely, Teacher White, Rory Sculdyte, and others hadn't been factored in fully. They hadn't been expected to survive the Whitefield Hall fire. Then there was Penny Dreadful. Her kittens had been a jinx on everybody.

Was Penny the straight goods? Was she getting up all our noses for a reason? Was most of what she'd told Dean true?

Her presence certainly excited the Green Pants Gang. My front door was proof.

And the human combustions? I had only hints.

And now a new question arose. How the Tersize family fit. Warehousing stolen goods and housing out-of-town religious gangsters wouldn't happen without them noticing. Hell, they were using A-Laf's Ugly Pants sextons for security.

And why had that stone been slung my way? I couldn't make that fit. It had gem-plus value because of its dark capabilities.

Had Colonel Block and Director Relway taken stones off the Ymberians they'd arrested? Would they guess what they had?

Something to think about.

# 60

A tall, thin old man with wild white hair and exaggerated facial features rushed into the camp. He moved fast for his age but had a major stiffness in his hips. He walked goofy. I couldn't hear what he said, but it had to be about ratman raiders. Everybody but Temisk and his buddy moved out fast, armed.

"Showtime," I whispered. Morley nodded.

I didn't sneak now. I went to a ladder and climbed down. Those two weren't going to run.

As I descended I noted a coach hidden in a shadowy corner. No doubt the vehicle used to spirit Chodo away from Whitefield Hall. There was no sign of a team.

My advent startled Temisk. He pulled himself together quickly, though. "How did you find us?"

"That's what I do." Chodo, I noted, seemed fully alert.

"The trouble outside is a diversion?"

"No. But I'm taking advantage."

"So you found us. Now what?"

"Now you tell me what's going on."

He thought about that. Then he leaned aside and stared, eyes widening in fright.

I'd been joined by several hefty rats. They perched on their haunches like squirrels, studying Temisk.

Temisk gaped. More rats arrived. He gasped, "You . . . you have the power to control rats?"

"We have a working arrangement."

Temisk shuddered. Squeaking, he took a swipe at a big bull clambering into Chodo's lap.

"Don't do that." How did John Stretch know Temisk had a problem with rodents? "There're more of them than there are of you."

"There were rats in the kitchen at Whitefield Hall. The rats told you how to find us."

"Rats go everywhere. They see everything. They hear everything."

Temisk had the full-blown heebie-jeebies now, but his brain hadn't shut down. "You got this connection because of the rat-girl, eh?"

"Talk about what you've up to, solicitor. Not about rats. I know all I need to know about rats." No horses for the coach. I wouldn't get Chodo and Temisk out the easy way. "I'm not happy with you."

"I just wanted to get Chodo away from those people. All right?"

"You tried to kill people. A lot of them. Deliberately. Including me. With fire. But none of us died."

He put on a show of confusion.

"You tried to set me up, Temisk. But it fell apart. Before it came together. Same for your friends from Ymber."

I kept an eye on Chodo. He was intensely interested.

I waved at the air. Morley and Saucerhead materialized. Singe took longer. She climbs ladders faster than she comes down them.

John Stretch remained unseen.

I said, "We need to move these two out before those thugs come back. Singe. You recall that evil stone?"

"Yes."

"Sniff around. See if you can find another one. Or anything else interesting. Morley. Peek out that street door. Check for witnesses."

"You aren't thinking about just rolling them out of here, are you?"

I had been. But I saw the problem before he pointed it out.

"You really think you can wheel Chodo around in public and no one will notice?"

"Let me think about that."

Morley reported, "We don't want to leave this way. There's a mob out there grabbing stuff the ratpeople didn't get before they took off."

"We'll go back the way we came. Me and Saucerhead will take turns lugging Chodo." Tharpe put on an expression of pained disbelief. "You and Temisk handle the chair. Singe. You find anything?"

"I just started. You should stop talking and start doing."

Temisk was terrified now. He had a notion what the future held. He didn't want to go there. Chodo wasn't thrilled, either.

Saucerhead hoisted Chodo as though he were weightless. And there wouldn't be as much of him as once there had been. I told Temisk, "Grab that chair and start climbing, solicitor." I heard voices approaching. "Singe, hurry up."

She beat me into the loft. "I will lead the way." There was no sign of John Stretch.

He would be watching, though.

# 61

Morley peeled off near The Palms. He needed to clean up for the evening trade.

I was squeezed up inside a borrowed covered goat cart with Chodo and his wheelchair. Saucerhead and Harvester Temisk pulled. Renewed weakness had overcome me soon after we escaped unnoticed from the Tersize Granary, with a battle between Green Pants guys and wannabe looters warming up around the corner.

So now another stolen cart would turn up outside my place.

Singe hurried ahead to alert the Dead Man. Complaining about her cold, wet tail as she faded into the distance.

Occasionally, I suspect Saucerhead of being less dim than he pretends.

My nap ended when he backed the cart up suddenly—bang—into the corner of a building. The cart's tongue rose slowly, putting me at increasing risk of getting dumped into an icy mess in the mouth of a dark and fetid alley.

A voice said, "How about you grab back onto that cart, Tharpe? Otherwise, you could get hurt." I didn't recognize the voice.

Saucerhead let me know. "You kidding, Fish? I'm on a job. I ain't gonna let you mess it up."

Fish? That would be Fish Bass, then. One of Rory Sculdyte's less daunting associates. A manager, not a serious physical threat.

"Plenty, get Temisk. Bobo, Brett, spank Tharpe if he interferes. And see what's in the cart. Chodo Contague his own self, I'll bet. Because where would Chodo be if he wasn't with his lawyer pal? Rory wants to talk to you, Temisk. Damn it, Tharpe—" A meaty thump interrupted. "Shit!"

Harvester Temisk squealed. Suggesting Saucerhead had laid a good one on Plenty Hart.

Saucerhead said, "You try to run, lawyer, you wake up wishing you was dead."

Meanwhile, I dribbled out the back of the cart, counted arms and legs to make sure I hadn't left any behind, then unlimbered my head knocker and iron knuckles.

I heard grunts and thuds as Tharpe exchanged love taps with Rory Sculdyte's infantry. There was some chatter farther off as people gathered to be entertained. The cavalry didn't arrive.

I checked the situation from ground level. Saucerhead had gone into action on the side of the cart where it butted against a wall. So, although he was cornered, nobody could get behind him. And I had room to go to work.

I sucked in a bushel of air, bounced into the contest. I smacked a startled Fish Bass between the eyes, whacked Harvester one that put him down and discouraged him from taking a powder, then popped Fish again so he wouldn't interfere.

I approached Saucerhead's dancing partners from behind. "Can I cut in?" Bobo Negry was no problem. Saucerhead had hold of him with his left hand, using him as a crutch. Iron knuckles to the back of his head shut him down.

Which left Brett Batt. Brother Batt had a big mouse over one eye, a bloody nose, and several split lips. And was having the time of his life hammering on Saucerhead. Tharpe was going to lose this one. He was too exhausted to fight much longer.

My first mighty swing missed Brett. My second was a glancer that did little but get his attention. I didn't have much go left myself.

Brett flailed behind him, knocked me down, resumed demolishing Saucerhead.

I put everything into a whack at Batt's right knee.

Good enough. Brett yelped. His leg folded. Saucerhead launched a roundhouse kick he'd saved for the right time, connected with Batt's left temple.

Two more kicks and a few more love taps from my stick and the wide load went to sleep. Finally. He would enjoy aches, pains, bruises, a headache, and a bad limp for days to come.

I got my feet under me. "We've got to get out of here." I checked the others.

Fish Bass had him one thick skull. He was a hundred feet

down the street and gaining speed, though unable to navigate a straight course. Harvester Temisk was inclined to make an exit of his own, but his world was spinning so briskly he couldn't keep his feet under him. I tossed him in with Chodo, then asked Tharpe, "You all right, man? You look like shit."

"Just shut up and get me to your place."

"But—"

"He got me in the goolies, all right? Go! We got to disappear." Yeah. Word was spreading. I hadn't heard any whistles, but Watchmen would be closing in. Let them find nothing but broken Sculdyte henchmen. And better hope none of the gawkers were civic-minded enough to follow us.

We ran into Singe on Wizard's Reach, tail in paw, coming back to meet us, a block from where the Dead Man would be able to offer some protection. A swarm of shivering pixies accompanied her. Saucerhead and I had kept one another going while making sure Harvester didn't escape. And he did try.

"What happened?" Singe asked. Melondie Kadare hovered behind her, trying to keep warm.

"Ran into some bad guys. His Nibs ready to bring us in?"

"Yes. But—"

It hurt to talk. Still, "We got to hurry. Then this cart needs to go away. Fast. People will be looking for it."

"So move if you need to move. Mr. Tharpe should get somewhere. . . ."

"I think it's going to snow again." We resumed trudging.

"What? What the hell do you mean, Garrett?"

"I mean you ought to calm down and—"

"Look out!"

I was supposed to look out for Teacher White, leaping out of cover with wild eyes, wilder hair, and no obvious awareness of the misty drizzle. He looked like he had been living on the street. But he did come equipped with a fully loaded, cocked, safe-catch-off war surplus crossbow. It looked huge from my downhill end. A wild grin full of bad teeth shone behind the weapon and a seedling beard. "You ruined me, you son of a bitch! But I got your freakin' ass now!"

A man ought not to get so worked up he forgets what he wants to do. I know. I overthink all the time.

I never broke stride. Teacher swung his aim to track me. Melondie Kadare darted into his face, stabbed him in the tip of the nose. His eyes crossed. Melondie's companions buzzed his ears.

Teacher let go the crossbow with his left hand. I placed a long jab on the back of the hand he'd raised to his nose. He yelped. Tears blinded him.

He dropped the crossbow. It discharged. The bolt whizzed away, ricocheting off brick walls.

I said, "Go home, Teacher. Better still, go somewhere where Rory won't look for you. Lay low. The Sculdytes won't last out the week."

"You broke my nose!"

A good pop in the snot locker has a way of clearing the mind behind. "You're right. And if you don't want it getting uglier, disappear."

Anger and humiliation hadn't abandoned Teacher, but his nerve had. He limped away, holding his nose, glowering.

Saucerhead hadn't said a word or done a thing. He glowered back. He was not in a good mood. He'd have bloodied somebody if he'd had the strength to do anything but keep on putting one foot in front of the other.

Teacher kept moving. Melondie and her friends buzzed him, kept him going. Singe collected the crossbow. "Damn! This thing is heavy."

"Dump it in the cart. It's illegal. We don't want to attract any attention."

A sense of foreboding came over me as we approached the house. But I didn't see even one obvious watcher.

# 62

The Dead Man's glee was almost malicious. He couldn't believe I'd enjoyed such complete success. But, boy, was he eager to capitalize.

Singe and I got our captives, our cargo, and Tharpe inside as fast as we could. Dean even lent a hand. Then he grabbed the cart's tongue and took off downhill. I gawked.

*I sent him. He was doing nothing useful. Come inside, please.*

Uh-oh. He was being polite. That's never a good sign.

*You will find yourself dealing with the Watch if you do not cease dallying immediately.*

Now he was seriously impatient.

With cause. We were about to be visited by Captain Ramey List and his shadows. Both henchmen now wore complete new uniforms.

I got in and closed the door. Old Bones told me, *Something big is happening. Captain List is the only body the Watch can spare for a stakeout.*

"There'll be a big dance with the Outfit. Going on already, I think. Because of the material we provided." I had to get a copy to Belinda still. I'd been too sick or too busy to figure out how. "Did you pry anything useful out of our guests?"

*Absolutely. I understand much of it now. It all ties together through the people involved. None of whom are pulling in the same traces. But I see that residual weakness is about to bring on a collapse. Take a nap.*

"I can last awhile. With your help."

*I do not have the attention to spare. Mr. Tharpe is injured. We will not be able to get a physician past the Watch anytime soon.*

I let it drop. You can't win with Butterbutt. And fatigue was about to overwhelm me.

Captain List hammered on the front door. He bellowed nonsense that would amuse the neighbors. His best effort was embarrassingly feeble compared with those of the Green Pants guys.

"I'll just park it in my chair. You need to know what I got from Buy Claxton. Poke around when you get time."

Vaguely, as I drifted off, I heard Saucerhead groan.

The Dead Man couldn't read my mind and control Tharpe's pain, both. He must have been using all his mind power to control the Ymberians and deal with Captain List. List's essential nature would make him try to win himself a name.

I slept.

# 63

I wakened. There was something in the air. Cooking smells. And a girlie fragrance suggesting something tastier.

Something tastier arrived with a steaming tray.

Clearly, Captain List had gone away.

*An agent from the Unpublished Committee came. Captain List was needed for a secret assignment that could be handled only by one of the top members of the Watch. Director Relway and Colonel Block were tangled up in obligations they could not shed. It was critical that this assignment be handled immediately.*

I chuckled. "And he took the bait. Along with the hook, the line, and the pole."

*He did.*

"I love it." I felt good despite my fresh collection of bruises. "It's got to be something that will end up with Ramey List embarrassed in a big way."

*The possibility bubbled in the back of Mr. Scithe's mind.*

I gave Tinnie a peck on the cheek and a suggestive leer a foot to the south, then prepared to pile into an equally beautiful omelet. "I thought you had what I had, darling."

"I do some. But mostly I was just tired."

*But I think it more likely that Captain List will die an heroic death.*

"Really? Do they hate him that much?"

*Mr. Scithe came on behalf of Director Relway, not Colonel Block. Mr. Relway, you may have noted, has simple, direct ways of handling personnel problems. This time because he sees an opportunity to end a threat to the Watch.*

"Morley and Relway ought to be pals. They think a lot alike."

*One would murder the other within hours. That sort of personality does not tolerate itself well in others.*

He was right, of course. "What do we know now that we didn't know yesterday?" I gave Harvester Temisk the fisheye. He remained terrified. Chodo appeared to be napping. Even guys in wheelchairs need to sleep.

*We know the Bledsoe drew the Ymberians to TunFaire. The Bledsoe is the mother lode of despair. Their nickel idols accumulate despair. The idols they installed in the Bledsoe walls are connected by sorcery to smaller companion pieces in their headquarters. Which always has been that place where you found Mr. Temisk and Mr. Contague. They plan to scatter the charged idols in areas where they intend to proselytize. You found one of the smaller sort on our guest deacon. The intent is to broadcast oppressive despair—which the priests of A-Laf will dispel, inside their temples.*

"I see. And those wouldn't be located where the prospects don't come equipped with plenty of money."

*Truly, you are possessed of a deep, humming streak of cynicism.*

"Am I right?"

*Probably more so than you think. When the cult of A-Laf fell into the hands of fundamentalists—aided by Mr. Contague, remember—the brains in charge were not motivated entirely by spiritual fervor. Mr. Contague worked hard to install his allies. Nevertheless, they did not join forces with Mr. Contague—though, as we know now, they helped advance his career by eliminating human obstacles.*

*Eventually, the Ymberian end forgot its connection with the TunFaire underworld, except at the most shy level.*

"Until they came to town, eh?" A baby cat bounced into my lap.

The kitten put its paws on the little table by my tray. He sniffed. And eased his nose ever closer to my plate. Never glancing back like he might actually need permission. Like, "I am the cat. The cat rules. All else exists to attend the cat."

The little tyrant hadn't gained an ounce since his arrival.

*The kits have realized that the scary men are harmless. For the moment. They are incurable optimists. They cannot remain frightened long. The optimism of A-Lat is a major contributing cause of its conflict with A-Laf. Which might seem unusual, A-Lat being the Queen of the Night. But that does not make her a dark goddess in all her aspects.*

*Her principal aspect is the feminine.*

*Be that as it may, it is not our concern. We must concentrate on those problems that have caught us in their web.*

"Go," I said. I pushed the cat aside. He paid no attention. He went right back to sticking his nose in my plate.

*Some weeks ago Mr. Temisk became aware of the arrival of the A-Laf cultists. They, of course, were unaware of Mr. Contague's state. Knowing the balance of obligation tilted toward Mr. Contague, Mr. Temisk contacted Ymberians. He invoked their obligation, as he did yours. The cultists knew him as the interlocutor for Mr. Contague, so he continued in that role.*

"How did he kill all those people? And why?"

*Ah. Now it becomes convolute.*

"Uh-oh. That's what you hear when somebody is fixing to make an excuse for somebody." I couldn't imagine him doing that for anybody but himself, though.

*We are not amused.*

"Leave that alone." I flicked the kitten's nose.

"Don't do that." Tinnie snapped. She'd come to check my tea. Carrying a tray. I was buying breakfast for my guests.

"We've got to figure a way to make money out of this, Old Bones. I'm feeding half the city."

*We will profit. Though perhaps not in cash money.*

"No chickens. No moldy bread. No spoiled sausage. No skunky beer. I don't take payment in kind anymore." As I raised my teacup, I spied a glint in Chodo's eye. He was awake. "Where were we?"

*I was about to inform you that circumstances surrounding the deaths of those who burned are more complicated than it would appear. Mr. Temisk is, indeed, responsible. But was not, at first, aware that he was responsible. However, once he understood that there was a connection between the fires and his visits to Mr. Contague, he remained willing to send personalities like Mr. Billy Mul Tima to their ends.*

I'd had my suspicions about Temisk but hadn't had information enough to work it all out. Maybe if I hadn't been sick all that time.

*We would not have discovered the truth without bringing Mr. Temisk here. There is no evidence outside his mind. He has been clever about leaving no traces. Miss Winger has been on Mr. Temisk's story for days and has yet to find anything even circumstantial. Mrs. Claxton was his sole loose end. Which he has had no opportunity to tie up. He felt he did not dare leave Mr. Contague alone with the Ymberians.*

"He's a lawyer. They're naturally crooks."

The Dead Man was not amused. Maybe he was a lawyer in another time and place.

"So Brother Temisk was behind the burning deaths? And he did it for his pal?"

*In essence. But it is a bigger story. Mr. Temisk, despite protests to the contrary, has solid contacts inside the Contague household. Which could be true for Mr. Sculdyte as well. Mr. Temisk suspects that Mr. Rory Sculdyte knew the truth but was abiding an opportunity to make best use of the information.*

"I'm guessing Chodo's been drugged. Systematically and continuously. I'm thinking he would've recovered by now otherwise."

*True. He has been drugged regularly. But he would not be in command now if he had not been fed those drugs.*

I grunted. Tinnie had her back to me. She was bending over the subject of our conversation, spoon in hand. I couldn't concentrate.

Mental sneer. *Mr. Contague's interior is scrambled. He is mad in a deeply sinister way. Ultimately, he is more responsible for the combustion deaths.*

"Can you get to your point?"

*No.* More amusement.

I dragged my attention away from Miss Tate long enough to pull the kitten off my plate. There were several of those in the room now, all over everybody. Including the scary people. One perched on the Ymberian deacon's shoulder, washing a paw. The deacon knew. He was apoplectic.

The Dead Man noted my interest and was amused yet again. *That should crack the final barriers in his mind. If his heart does not explode first.*

"The combustion deaths, partner?"

*Mr. Temisk's agents in the Contague household told him they thought Miss Contague might be poisoning him.*

"Might?"

*There is some ambiguity. Someone else might be guilty.*

"Doesn't Chodo know?"

*He was drugged.*

"Gah!"

*Wait! There is madness there, as noted. Extreme and dark. Worsened by the drug. Mr. Temisk's contacts identified the poison. Mr. Temisk searched for an antidote.*

"Which he found. And which has something to do with people catching on fire." I was making intuitive leaps left and right. Maybe the fever left me psychic.

*Yes. Be still. Mr. Temisk's contacts informed him that Miss Contague came to town once or twice a month, and more frequently in times of crisis. Her father accompanied her. Always. She would not trust his care to anyone at home.*

"With good reason, obviously."

*Obviously. When she did come to town Miss Contague secreted her father in a tenement her family owns on the north side, on the edge of Elf Town. Mr. Temisk knew the building because he handled its acquisition and management. Mr. Contague operated his early business out of there. Once he knew Miss Contague's routine, Mr. Temisk acted.*

*To conceal his role, he hired alcoholics to sneak in and medicate the man in the wheelchair with the antidote. These men received one-quarter payment beforehand and the balance afterward.*

Sounded risky. The drunk would brag about his score. "But the drunk turned into a human torch. Right?"

*Not the first few times. Not until Mr. Contague began to shake the influence of the poison. Once he was able to understand his situation, frustration at his helplessness drove him mad.*

"Temisk turned Chodo into a mass murderer by trying to help him?"

*Essentially.*

"I'll bite. How?"

*The antidote is a crushed form of the stone hurled at you at Mr. Dotes'—*

"That causes fires!"

# 64

Harvester provided his cat's-paws with a flaked form of the stone, which resisted powdering. He acquired it from the A-Laf cult, at an extreme price. The cult obtained a hoard of the stones when it took over the temple of A-Lat. Numerous stones went astray before being inventoried. A-Laf's sextons were not as devout as their superiors desired.

Bittegurn Brittigarn wasn't wrong when he connected the stones with rocs. The Dead Man said they originated in rocs' gizzards. The phoenix legend came about because roc chicks, like kids, will swallow anything. Which sometimes makes the stones ignite. That chick goes up in flame while its nest mates bail out, possibly giving a distant observer the impression that he's watching a rebirth.

The stones were priceless because they could start fires. Anywhere, anytime, in most any material, from a distance, if you knew how to trigger them. Using sorcery. Or a mental nudge after the manner of the Dead Man.

Chodo discovered that he could spark residual firestone flakes on the hands and clothing of Harvester Temisk's alkies. Not being suicidally mad, he eliminated them only after they left him.

Harvester Temisk's crime was that he kept hiring disposable people after Chodo began killing them.

"He tried to burn Whitefield Hall down with everybody inside?"

*He did. Doctoring the oil in the lamps. Mrs. Claxton was targeted specifically. She received a pin because she had seen Mr. Temisk at work. It ignited much earlier than Temisk planned. Mr. Contague was in a rage. It was chance that the doctored lamps were out of his range by then.*

"So the mystery of the human combustions is solved."

*More or less. There have been incidents that cannot be traced back to Mr. Contague and Mr. Temisk. But we are not interested in those.*

"I've got a lot of questions, Smiley. Who slung a rock at me? Why? How come it took so long for Morley's door to catch fire? What about Rory Sculdyte? And Belinda? These damned cats and Penny Dreadful? And what do we do about Temisk and Chodo?"

I owed Chodo. I had to discharge that debt. Which clunked me right into a bubbling pot of moral quandary.

The Dead Man knocked the Ymberian deacon out so he could free up enough brainpower to show me the nightmare inhabiting Chodo's head. A nightmare as bad as that of a claustrophobe trapped in a coffin and unable, ever, to die. It was just a glimpse. Just a little teasy peek, secondhand, of a seething black hell haunted by genius. Supreme ugliness under only the most primitive, selfish control.

The madman was imprisoned in an herbal cage. Though the cage had created the madman, the madman now belonged there.

The kittens seemed fond of him, though.

"What do I do, Old Bones? We can't turn that loose."

*Worry about something else. Concentrate on Mr. Temisk, whose own madness is gaining momentum. His conscience is withering. He is no longer troubled about what he might be unleashing. Though he is not blind to the possibility that he might be its immediate victim.*

"He's like me, then. Obligated to good old Chodo. Wanting to believe that this is the same old Chodo. He just can't walk or talk."

*Worry about something else.*

So I watched Tinnie feed the Ymberians. Beauty and the beasts.

Singe leaned through the doorway. "Do we have a plan for dealing with the people out front?"

"Who is it?" Pounding had occurred, off and on, for hours. The Dead Man seemed uninterested. I'd taken my cue from him.

"That List person."

"He's still alive?"

"He must be lucky."

"Is the door holding up?"

"Mr. Mulclar's pride is in no danger."

"Any idea what he wants?"

"Maybe somebody saw us bring those two in and recognized them."

I didn't think so. We would've drawn somebody more important than Captain Ramey List. "Hey! Smiley! We done with Big Bruno yet? How about I fling his ass out like I did Merry and his crew?"

The Dead Man did not respond. For one panicky instant I thought he'd fallen asleep. But he was just too busy to be bothered.

The racket up front stopped. Ramey List went away again.

I decided to indulge in another nap. I dragged my disease-ravaged carcass upstairs and dumped it into bed.

# 65

Tinnie was there when I woke up, but she wasn't feeling playful. I avoided irritating questions till after breakfast. Then I asked about the weather.

"Am I supposed to know? You were there. Did I suddenly pop outside?"

I sighed.

Singe cursed. Dean cursed. A drunken Melondie Kadare cursed like a platoon of Marine storm troopers. Incoherently. She'd been in the kitchen sucking it down when we'd brought Chodo and Harvester in. We needed to put her in a cage. Those cats couldn't ignore their own nature forever.

"So the weather hasn't gotten any better."

Tinnie growled and grumbled like it was all my fault she couldn't go home and get to work.

Being a rational, reasonable man, I noted, "If you can't get to work, neither can anybody else. So there wouldn't be any reason for you to try."

"You are so full of crap. . . ." And so forth.

The patient sort, I waited for the black tea to kick in.

*Garrett.*

I jumped and ran. Pure horror reeked off the Dead Man's summons.

"What the hell?"

*Do not speak. Not one more word.*

I'm a quick study. I sealed my yap. It had to be hugely important.

*We are on the brink of a holocaust.*

I'm so good I just stood there and said a whole lot of nothing.

*Being careful not to let Mr. Contague or Mr. Temisk see you, pocket those firestones and get them out of the house. I believe you can fathom why.* Several seconds later, he added, *We should have recognized that danger earlier. I should have seen it.*

Somebody should have. It was right there in front of us. The end of us all. Maybe the gods do love fools, drunks, and their favorite toy. Or they've got something uglier planned for later.

This once I was in such a hurry I forgot to look out the peephole first. I opened up and got smacked between the eyes with the wonder of snow gone wild. I told Singe, "I was six last time I saw it like this."

There was a fresh foot on top of the old mess. More pounded down in hunks so big each flake should've made the earth shake. I couldn't see the other side of the street. Meaning a watcher over there couldn't see me slide out.

I trudged over to Playmate's place. That took an hour. I wasn't in good shape when I got there. It was going to be a long time before I got my old vigor back. And I didn't like this feeble new me, even temporarily.

I needed to get into a conditioning routine. Right after . . . whatever I thought up as needed doing first.

I'd give procrastination a bad name—if I ever got around to it.

Playmate asked, "So what's this I hear about you trying to die on us?"

"It wasn't quite that bad." I gave him the full story.

"Your luck amazes me. The Dead Man was awake and Tinnie put aside her grudges."

There was no arguing that. I explained our current best theories. And added, "I need to know what to do with these firestones."

"You brought them with you?" That made him nervous.

"They don't blow up. They need a psychic nudge to set them off."

"Tell me about them."

I did. It didn't take long.

"I wish I could experiment. Since I can't, let's put them in a lead-lined iron casket and bury them under the stable floor. If they go off and melt through the box they'll just sink down into the earth."

"Ingenious." I got the stones out. I'd also brought the little box we'd taken off the deacon. "Put this in there, too. No! Don't open it." I explained about the nickel idols. "They turn into pure, concentrated despair when they're charged up. You're close to them when they cut loose, you hear ghosts telling you to kill yourself." Maybe you took sick, too.

What a weapon for someone into dirty politics.

Playmate considered, then asked, "You poked around inside the Bledsoe?"

"I visited the woman Temisk tried to kill. That's all."

"I'm wondering if there isn't an upside to this villainy. A chance that, with evil intentions, they might be managing something good."

Playmate might be the only guy in TunFaire able to worry about the pavements of the road *from* hell. I asked, "How so, Swami?"

"If the nickel idols suck despair out of the Bledsoe, then the inmates might be getting better."

"The statues might drive wack jobs sane?"

"Seems logical. Though despair isn't the only reason people go mad."

I began to see possibilities. I began to get excited. "The right arms get twisted, the Bledsoe could actually do some good."

"You'd need the Ymberians. They know how the system works. I doubt they're interested in curing anyone, though. But yes, think about it. Just suck the pain right out. Smash it into the idols and . . . uh-oh."

"Yeah. The charged idols would be dangerous. And men who'd use them for their own purposes outnumber you and me. This'll take some thinking. We've got to get it right."

"We?"

"What?" He never shirked a chance to do a good deed.

"I do see it, Garrett. But I'm only one man. Who'd have to fly into a frenzy of ambition. Which I don't have much of anymore."

"I see." I saw. "It wouldn't be a one-man mission, Play. If it's workable. We can worry about that later. I'll see what Max Weider thinks. I just had to get this stuff out of the house. We'd be in deep brown if Chodo had one of his psychic spasms."

"Is there anything else?" Playmate hadn't offered the customary hospitality. I could've used a drink. He must've had a woman stashed. Or wanted to get back to work. Or something less flattering to my ego.

I thought I'd stop by The Palms, take a break. After half an hour of slogging through snow up to my knees, into the wind. Uphill. Barefoot. . . . But the place was boarded up and showing no light.

# 66

The Dead Man heard my thinking about the Bledsoe and whispering nickel idols. *Creative. Consider deep-sea disposal. With the charged jackals sealed into slow-rusting containers. The idols would discharge their darkness very slowly, down in the darkest deep.*

That was supposed to be a joke.

*We could call that part of the ocean the Depths of Despond.*

"I got it. We'd have a lot of depressed fish. Not to mention the big uglies that live down there. Picture a school of really cranky krakens."

*An interesting fabulation. But I have another concern. One we can discuss with Colonel Block once our present troubles clear.*

"Yeah?"

*Two things concern me.*

"Is this an auction?"

*Three things. But your attitude, like the disposal of the nickel jackals, can abide a less stressful moment.*

I figured staying quiet would cause him to get to the point.

It worked. He felt impelled to fill the vacuum. *First, the child, Penny Dreadful, has not responded to the seeds I planted in her mind. Second, we have had no contact with Miss Winger for several days.*

"You gave her work?"

*I did. As mentioned. I have her examining Mr. Temisk's back trail.*

"You paid her up front?"

*A percentage.*

"Big mistake. She won't turn up till she thinks you're asleep. Then she'll try to con me about something you supposedly promised her."

*You are* too *cynical. But we will table that, too. Singe's brother approaches. His thoughts are veiled, but he is troubled.*

I opened the door. The snow hadn't let up. John Stretch looked as miserable as a ratman can get.

"In, brother," I told him. "That's incredible."

"It is like nothing my folk remember. Some wonder if stormwardens are not feuding."

Singe met us at the door to the Dead Man's room. She had hot cocoa for her brother.

"How about it, Old Bones? Is this weather natural? Is there any precedent?"

*There is no obvious storm sorcery. Yes, there have been worse snowfalls. But Mr. Pound did not come here for small talk about snowfalls. Mr. Pound?*

John Stretch shook like a dog drying off.

"Creepy, ain't he?"

"Some. But he is correct. I came to report that there is war in the streets."

I considered a crack about a chance to get rich selling snowshoes to the combatants. *Hush. This will be important.*

"Who's fighting?"

"The Syndicate. The part that belongs to Rory Sculdyte. And the Unpublished Committee for Royal Security. They hit the Sculdytes hard, everywhere, at the same time."

I was surprised Relway had started so soon. Though, surely, he'd had plans roughed in ahead. He thought that way.

"I expected something. But not so soon."

"They have killed most of the Sculdyte crew. Rory and Merry and a few others have escaped, so far."

The Palms was boarded up. Had Morley gone underground?

*You are correct. We must be on guard. The Sculdytes could make a connection between us and their parlous circumstance. And you were seen entering with Mr. Temisk and Mr. Contague. If they were recognized, we will draw a great deal of interest.*

"Count on Mr. Mulclar. Dean. How are we fixed for supplies? Honestly."

It seemed we were good as long as we could survive without stewed apples and beer.

We couldn't hold out forever, though. And forever wouldn't be long enough if Block and Relway wanted to root us out. Assuming they survived their current adventure.

Aloud, I wondered, "Do you suppose they went now because they'd have a better chance of getting away with it in this weather?"

*Given the devotion of Mr. Relway's department, the weather should prove an advantage. News will be slower to reach those inclined to interfere. People who are loath to get their feet cold or wet. Colonel Block and Director Relway are bright enough to recognize a window of opportunity. But that is their crusade. Ours is . . . I am no longer certain what ours is. The adventure has been exciting but anticlimactic.*

I was no longer sure, myself. I'd done my bit for Chodo but didn't feel I'd discharged my debt. I hadn't rescued him. Harvester Temisk had enjoyed more success, though not yet as much as he'd wanted.

I hadn't done well with the Green Pants Gang, either. Though any threat they'd posed had been negated. The Watch knew them now.

*They came to TunFaire in quest of converts and wealth. They will not create a bigger Ymber now. Inadvertently, they may cause considerable good. All because Dean was a pushover for a girl with sad eyes and a sadder story.*

"We still need to talk to that kid. She might be a villain herself."

*An interview should prove instructive. Particularly if she approached Dean in hopes of provoking exactly what has happened. She could be using us to fight A-Lat's war with A-Laf.*

That would mean Penny Dreadful carefully figuring us out before she conned Dean into taking care of a bucket of kittens. You hate to think a kid that young could be so calculating.

"Having any luck working the kinks out of Chodo's mind?" I knew he'd planned to try.

*There has been little opportunity. The deacon is a multiple-mind project himself. He possesses secrets, still. For example, why a firestone would have been slung at you or The Palms. Neither of our guests sees the sense, but both believe the deed must have been done by one of their own. No one else had access to the stones. They are kept in the heart of A-Laf's temple.*

"Yet our boy here had one in his pocket. And Temisk bought flake as a pharmaceutical and a murder weapon."

*Even among true believers there is corruption.*

"And the sky is blue on a sunny day."

*More cynicism.*

"Always. Rooted deeply in everyday observation." I chuckled. The Ymberian deacon had become a gathering point for kittens. He wasn't pleased. But the more furious he became, the more cats arrived.

*He may suffer a stroke.*

"Good old apoplexy. That would save some trouble."

*You need something to occupy you.*

Oh-oh. Smelled like a job assignment creeping up. "I was thinking about going over to check on Tinnie."

*And I was thinking you might prepare a report on the Tersize Granary for Mr. Relway and Colonel Block.*

"Redhead trumps. Have Singe do it." Those guys were busy, anyway.

He didn't like my idea. Singe was too slow.

Singe didn't like it, either. It would get in the way of her quest to get rid of the beer supply.

"Too bad pixies can't write."

*Pshaw!*

The wee folk were in semihibernation because of the weather. Even Melondie Kadare, now, despite her determination to support Singe in her mighty quest, had been put away at the insistence of her family.

# 67

I was exhausted—again—by the time I got to the Tate compound. The snowfall continued, light but persistent. A teenage cousin whose name I couldn't remember let me in. He pretended he was pleased to see me. I pretended I didn't know every male Tate and all their forebears nurtured an abiding desire to see me suffer some debilitating misfortune. Or that Tinnie would come to her senses.

The boy made chitchat. He seemed terribly young and inanely naive. I couldn't help reflecting that if these were the war years, he'd already be engaged in part-time basic training in anticipation of his call to the colors.

"It was a bad day," I told Tinnie. "Mostly a bad day. You weren't in it. How did yours go?"

She tried giving me the grand glower with rheumy eyes. I was on her list for barging in when she was at less than her ravishing best.

"Don't start that. You were there when I was dying. Now I'm here."

"I just have a bad cold."

Sounded like it, too.

"Tell me about it," she suggested. Once I had, she said, "We should've suspected the Tersize people. There had to be a reason they bought a business that has no market for its product."

"They still do some legitimate baking and milling. You know them?"

She shrugged. "I never liked them much."

There would be more to the story. Maybe some history.

She grabbed my hand. "Don't mind me. I'm glad you're here. You must be exhausted."

I nodded but didn't go on about it.

"My father wanted me to marry one of the Tersize boys when I was fifteen. He wanted the business alliance. He didn't have his heart set on it. I got around him."

I couldn't imagine her not manipulating any men before she was out of diapers.

She mumbled, "I know some of the answers to the questions you still have."

"Great! How about the meaning of life?"

"Life's a bitch. And then you die." A moment later, she started snoring.

So I held her hand and fell asleep myself.

A teenage niece popped in. Food and drink were her excuse. Tinnie's people are busybodies, too. Only there're more of them. This was a fifteen-year-old edition of the professional redhead. Sizzling. And knowing it. And stoked up with all the attitude I would've expected of Tinnie at that age. She was disappointed in us old folks. Antiques, just holding hands. And snoring. Not doing anything embarrassing.

Tinnie rips a mean log. Naturally, she'll never admit an accomplishment so unladylike.

We ate. I said, "You were going to give me the answers to all my questions. After which I'll launch the cult of Saint Tinnie the Delectable."

She said, "Kyra, invite yourself out. Please." "Please" as an afterthought, in the command form.

Showing a pout that guaranteed she'd lurk in the woodwork, eavesdropping, the apprentice redhead departed.

"Don't be such a chicken, Garrett. Grab hold of my hands again."

"But then you'll kick me."

"I might." She smiled. But she didn't mean it.

Time to be a little less me. "Sorry."

"You can't help it. Your mouth takes over when you're nervous."

"I'm not nervous."

"Of course you are. You're scared shitless that I've gotten up enough nerve to decide what I want from you and me."

Good point. I'm always afraid that will happen and I'll respond by shoving both feet a yard down my own throat. But I was afraid we'd never work it out, too. "Some," I confessed. "Because chances are, someday you'll have an attack of good sense and make me go away."

"That, probably, would be best. Half the time I just slow you down. But I'm spoiled. I grew up overindulged. I can't picture my life without you in it."

Gah! This was gonna get deep. "I know what you mean. I can't, either."

"But that isn't what I want to talk about. That just came out."

Sure. The woman has no self-control whatsoever.

"I wanted to talk about Penny."

"Oh?" I squeaked. She saw the relief flood me. She managed a credible scowl. The effect of which was lost when she had to blow her nose.

"All right. What about Penny?"

"She isn't really a priestess."

"No! The surprises never stop."

"Knock it off, smart-ass. She isn't a priestess because she wasn't ever invested. She was too young. She's still too young. She's only thirteen. Though you'd never believe it if you saw her undressed. Which damned well better never happen, even after she does turn fourteen."

"I'm missing a detail or three to pull all that together."

"She turns fourteen—she's officially an adult. In her cult, that means it's time to be a holy semipro. Putting it out to honor the goddess—and add a little cash to the temple pot—until she finds a husband."

"Ymber must have been interesting, back in the day."

"You would've loved it. You would've been in church every damned day instead of just for weddings and funerals."

Could be. If the religious catch wasn't too big. "I could surprise you."

"You could, but I doubt it. You'll never be anything but sixteen when it comes to that. You can't see beyond the moment."

She wasn't entirely incorrect. But we were getting personal again.

She said, "That's not what we need to talk about. I shouldn't fuss about that. She won't let you get near her, anyway. She's scared to death of you."

"Huh? But I'm just a big old huggy bear. Why be scared of me?"

"Because—"

"Tinnie." Theses words were scarcely louder than a whisper.

Penny Dreadful, pale as the weather outside, peeked round the frame of Tinnie's open bedroom door. She did look scared as hell.

"Are you sure?"

"I have to do it sometime."

# 68

I retreated toward the dormer window on my side of Tinnie's four-poster. That put the bed between me and the immigrant urchin priestess princess.

She oozed around the doorframe by degrees. Somebody had run her down, stolen her rags, scrubbed and rubbed her, washed, combed, trimmed, buffed, and polished her, then stuffed her into something old of Kyra's. Yep. She'd worked wonders disguising herself as a boy.

"I've seen you before," I said. As a girl Penny Dreadful looked familiar.

Tinnie slapped my hand. "Stop drooling, big boy. She's still a baby."

"You're wrong this time, sweetness." Then, "Where do I know you from?"

The girl shivered, turned pale again. Which made her look like the ghost of Belinda Contague's past.

That was it. She resembled Belinda, though her hair, clean, was auburn with a hint of natural curl.

My ancient talent for leaping to conclusions coalesced. "Chodo Contague was your father."

Tinnie gasped, choked on some phlegm. "You're insane, Garrett," she hacked.

"Probably. But—"

"You're right," Penny said in her tiny, frightened voice. "My mother said . . . how did you guess?"

"In this light, dressed like a girl, you look a lot like your sister."

"Belinda. . . . she wouldn't . . . she . . ."

"You talked to her?" Belinda hadn't ever mentioned Penny or a half sister. Or any visit from somebody running a lost-relative scam.

"She wouldn't see me." Penny grabbed the bedpost kitty-corner from me, her knuckles whitening. "When our temple was besieged my mother told me about my father. Which is against the rules. We're not supposed to know.

"I tried to see him, too. They wouldn't let me, though."

Prodding gently, I got Penny to tell her life story. "This man came to see my mother twice a year. And me. He always brought presents. I didn't know who he was till my mother told me. At the end. But he stopped coming after he got important here. I never saw him after I was ten. A-Laf's priests started going wild after he stopped coming. First they took over the city offices. After a while there wasn't any difference between the town elders and their council of deacons. Then they started on the other religions."

Unsubtly. Bullying adherents and committing arson. The weak of faith converted. The stronger fled or died. In time, only A-Lat remained, and her empire consisted entirely of the mother temple. "Then they came for us."

"And you got away."

"My mother sent me away. She made me bring the Luck to TunFaire. In disguise. She told me to find my father. So I came. And I can't get to him."

Penny didn't appear to have witnessed her mother's murder. I gave that no weight. Witnesses do have trouble keeping time straight. When she was told to run and when she took flight could've been weeks apart.

A skilled cynic keeps his mind open to all the darker possibilities, though.

Penny teared up. "I thought it would be easy. I'd just find my father and he'd make everything right again. He's an important man."

"You really want to see Chodo?"

Frightened little-girl nod.

"Does he know who you are? Would he recognize you?"

Another nod, but not entirely confident.

A scheme began to stir in the shadowed rat's nest of my mind. "I can take you there."

She seemed honestly excited—till she realized that I must want to take her home. Her pallor returned. She looked ready to bolt.

How carefully had she studied us before she swooped down on Dean?

"When did you come to the city?" I asked.

"Uh . . . months and months ago. Right after the war was over."

She was a kid. Kids don't pay attention to anything that don't have them at its center. Which I say based on personal experience. I used to be a kid. "So A-Laf's people arrived after you did. They came looking for you?"

"No. They didn't know about me. They thought the Luck had been destroyed. They wouldn't have found out, either, if I didn't get caught spying on them."

"Is it me you're afraid of? Or my partner?" I asked after she began to relax, thinking she'd changed the subject.

Tinnie, I noted, was quite interested in the answer.

Her suspicions abide in a realm distinct from mine. She thinks any female within stone's throw will fall under my spell.

Yeah. Right.

I hear tell a rich fantasy life is a good thing.

Again, yeah, right. "Tinnie will always be right there, ready to jump in between us."

That earned me an evil glare from my honeycomb.

"It's not you. I learned how to handle men in the temple."

"That's good to hear." Tinnie didn't relax a bit. "So why be worried about my associate? Did Dean hand you one of his tall tales? Old Bones is harmless. Like a big old stuffed bear."

Tinnie managed a straight face. But Penny wasn't buying. "I know what he is."

I considered telling her the Dead Man wouldn't get into her head uninvited. But he'd tried already. "What secrets can a girl your age have that would embarrass a four-hundred-fifty-year-old Loghyr? What do you have to lose? If it has to do with those weird cats, he already knows." If he did, though, he hadn't told me.

"Uh . . . no. It's just too personal. It'd be like rape."

I've never felt that way. Most people don't. Still, some might. "Your father is at my house. It isn't likely he'll leave soon."

You could see her emotions warring. Cynical old Garrett wondered if she was acting. Cynical old Garrett suspected that Penny no longer needed to connect with Chodo. Her problems with A-Laf had been resolved, at least locally.

Block and Relway wouldn't let the cultists resume their wicked ways—particularly now they were known to be part of a criminal enterprise.

I told Tinnie, "Talk to her. She won't trust anything I say."

"About?"

"Having a chat with my sidekick. Colonel Block and Director Relway will need all the ammunition they can get when friends of the Tersizes intercede for them and their immigrant pals."

The Tersizes had high connections, forged during generations of war. As did the Tates. But the Tates found legal new ways to make money. Some of which float my boat a little higher.

Tinnie said, "Leave us alone. We'll talk."

"Don't tell her too many lies about me." I eased round the bed. I could raid the kitchen during my exile.

Tinnie read my mind, in her own special way. "You stay right there in the hall. I don't want you around Rose or Kyra."

Rose would be Tinnie's evil cousin. The black ewe of the family. I hadn't seen her for a while. I hadn't missed her, either.

I slid into the hallway, commenced to amuse myself working heavy math problems. Two times two is four. Four times four is . . . uh . . . sixteen! Sixteen times sixteen is . . . uh . . . well, enough of that stuff.

Later, hovering at the brink of some huge intellectual breakthrough, I got porlocked. Tinnie yelled, "Garrett! Get your homely tail back in here." I got. Too much thinking is scary. "We have a deal. Let me get dressed. Then we'll head for your place."

"You sure? You up to it?"

"Yes."

"Oh, boy. Let me get my fingers loosened up and I'll help."

"Back in the hall, daydreamer. Penny can help. We're still talking."

I went back out. I tried to remember what my great breakthrough would've been, worried about Tinnie's health some, then wondered how she'd gotten to the kid.

# 69

I went in first, delivered Tinnie's message. Which was that she wanted to come have a sit-down about the need to leave Penny's head alone if she came to see us.

The Dead Man agreed. He granted every wish. Even before Tinnie finished laying out the terms. Suspicious. I know my fairy tales.

Chodo had supplanted the deacon as favored loafing place for the cat population. He had about two dozen splashed all over him. And seemed pleased. Unlike the deacon, he smiled. Sort of. His eyes tracked. His mind was active. He managed enough expression to approve my choice in women when Tinnie stalked in. He didn't seem able to move anything else.

"Made any headway?" I asked the Dead Man.

*Some. But a saber-tooth never stops being a tiger.*

"The deacon seems subdued."

*He is in an induced coma. He is strong and stubborn. He refuses to accept defeat. He fights on despite no longer having anything to protect.*

"So what great secrets did you ferret out?"

Chodo watched me move around. He watched Tinnie, too. Hungrily. Creepily. She shuddered.

*Little of direct use. His compatriots mean to conquer the world, purportedly for the greater glory of their god, but in reality because they like being rulers instead of the ruled. He was a dastard and a crook before he converted. He remains a dastard and a crook. He was, in fact, one of Mr. Contague's significant associates inside A-Laf's cult. Today, either would happily sell the other's soul to get out of this house.*

"And you wonder why the Goddamn Parrot made his getaway."

*I am fully cognizant of the facts in that matter, Garrett. I note that Miss Tate accomplished what you considered impossible.*

Miss Tate had that look people get when the Dead Man starts rooting around inside their heads. It's a cross between pants-wetting terror and severe constipation.

"Penny has issues with men. But she's desperate to see Chodo."

*Excellent. We can accommodate her. He is ready.*

"Are you?" I checked Chodo. He seemed close to human, buried in kittens. Almost the Chodo of old.

*I offer my most sincere bond. I will not enter the girl's mind unless she asks me in.*

I asked Tinnie, "Can you make her believe that?"

"Is is true?"

"His word's always been good, far as I know."

"A ringing endorsement for sure."

Singe came in with a bunch of paper. "Do we have any more paper? I don't have enough to finish this report."

"Huh?"

"What we have for the Colonel. From our guests."

"Hmm." Interesting. "We?"

"That poisoner. Kolda. He is in the small front room, recording what the Dead Man wants put into writing." Facing the Dead Man, she added, "He needs rest. His penmanship is becoming unreadable."

"Kolda's been here all the time?" I wasn't sure why I thought he'd left while I was out. Maybe my frugal side was hoping I'd shed a hungry mouth.

Tinnie interjected, "Don't we have something more pressing to deal with?"

"So go get her, my treasure. Work your wiles on somebody who don't wear pants." I turned to the Dead Man. "You have Kolda jot down anything from Mr. Temisk or his best pal?" I was thinking maybe we now had us a record of where the other bodies were buried. That could be handier than a wagonful of spades.

Tinnie left. After giving me a poisonous look. Singe let her out.

"You have something up your sleeve, Smiley. Be careful. Tinnie is steamed already."

He seemed mildly amused.

Dean came in complaining about shortages.

"We aren't under siege right now. Jump on out there. Get what you need. Keeping in mind that we will end up besieged again if anybody finds out who we've got here."

The Dead Man volunteered, *No one is watching at the moment.*

Excepting Mrs. Cardonlos, of course. But she didn't count for much, anymore. Even the other biddies don't have much use for a known informant.

Funny how everybody favors law and order in the abstract, but don't want to get into the kitchen and help cook.

Dean was ready to go. Singe let him out. He was gone before I realized that I'd just given him the chance he'd been laying for. "Damn! I wanted to keep him away from the girl."

*Not to worry. He is focused on marketing.*

I became distracted myself. How much of the true tale had we gotten out of Chodo? Could we use that to restrain the man?

Probably not. Chodo was clever enough to weasel his way out of almost anything. Usually at somebody else's expense.

# 70

Penny Dreadful came in shy as a mouse, ready to bolt at the least excuse. Nobody said a thing. Chodo was the last person she eyed, excepting for the deacon, whose presence disturbed her.

Her presence bothered him, too. Despite his supposed unconsciousness. His nose pointed her way. His nostrils flared, then squeezed shut against an offensive odor.

"Friend of yours?" I asked.

She spit on the deacon, then plopped into my empty chair. Cats came from everywhere, swarmed all over her.

"Somebody's glad to see you," Tinnie observed.

Penny scowled at Chodo.

He recognized her. Even I could feel the emotion.

There was a human bone in the kingpin's body. A paternal bone.

I'd seen it before, of course. He'd been uncommonly indulgent with Belinda. Who'd loathed him all the more for it.

*Find a way to lure Miss Tate out of the room.*

What was he up to? "Sweetums, let's see if Dean left the kettle on."

Lame. It earned me a dose of maximum-potency fisheye. She smelled something. She didn't catch on, though.

While we got the kettle on, my fat old weasel partner sold Penny the notion that the only way she could communicate with Chodo would be through him. Which, at the moment, was true. But the process didn't have to include unfettered access to the inside of her head.

It was that old chestnut about age and treachery trumping youth and talent. She let emotion override reason.

Which was why he wanted Tinnie out of the room. She might warn Penny.

He fed me a trickle of news so I'd know to keep Tinnie occupied while he facilitated the exchange between Penny and her pappy. That smidgen was interesting in the extreme. *The stone is explained.*

"Huh?"

Tinnie's gaze popped up from loading the tea ball. "You get more primitive by the minute, don't you?"

"Ungawa! See fire hair woman! Yum. Me grab'um."

"You want hot water down your pants leg, keep it up."

"Make up your mind, woman."

Meantime, Old Bones continued. *The girl slung that stone at you. That is the main secret she wants to protect. The presence of the sexton there was not accidental. He was looking for her. He had been following her.*

He anticipated my question. *She wanted you out of the way. You were making it too difficult for Dean to help her.*

"She's just a kid." But Chodo's kid. Of course.

Tinnie gave me the fisheye. Again.

*The level of malice was not high. It did not occur to her that she might kill you. She wanted you injured so you would be out of her way while she got to her father and won him over.*

*She was sure he would help her turn the table on A-Laf. Being unaware that Mr. Contague helped midwife the modern cult.*

*She does not, by the by, appear to be aware that the phoenix stones start fires, nor even that the priestess of her temple considered them particularly valuable. Along with the kittens, her mother gave her sacred jewelry, holy books, and a sackful of rocks. Without explaining the importance of the jewelry or rocks. Were I as cynical as you I would suspect that most of the stones confiscated by A-Laf's partisans were really creek pebbles.*

Tinnie caught on. She swatted my hands away, snatched at the kettle. "You're a total swine, aren't you? What's he doing to her?"

"She tried to kill me."

"Bull. She didn't, either. She just—"

"You knew?"

"We talked a lot. She's lonely without her kittens."

"And you didn't—?"

"It was private, Garrett. You didn't get hurt, did you?"

I rolled my eyes in appeal to the sky. Even my best girl now?

Before I could protest further, she said, "Somebody's at the door."

It couldn't be critical. Old Bones wasn't spouting warnings. Dean couldn't be back already, could he? The redhead wasn't *that* distracting.

Singe appeared. "Saucerhead is here. With that woman."

"Which woman?"

"Winger." Her tone left no doubt about her esteem for my friend.

Tinnie looked relieved.

"Saved by the cavalry, eh?"

She stuck out her tongue.

"You'll pay, woman. Mark my words, you'll pay."

She just sneered.

Winger was more wasted than Melondie Kadare ever managed. "Garrett!" she burbled, blurry-eyed, using both walls to stay upright. "Yer a sum um a bitch, even if yer one a the good guys." She leaned against one wall. "Jes need a minute. I'm fucked-up."

"What's this?" I asked Saucerhead.

"A very drunk woman."

"That part didn't get past me. I've got skills. I was thinking more along the lines of, why? And why here? She might make a mess."

"I think she's done all of that she can. Less'n she can get her socks up."

"Even so. Singe, stand by the door. We'll toss her out if—"

Tinnie interrupted, "It'll take all of you to do it."

Winger started snoring. She sank toward the floor.

Tharpe told me, "The Dead Man said bring her in. He wants to know what she found out."

"She found out there's a limit to how much she can drink."

"She's upset. She's misplaced Jon Salvation. She don't remember where. Or how. She's scared she might've killed him. Or something."

"Great! Well, let's see if we can't drag her—"

*There is no need to bring her in. I have examined her memories. They support what we have learned from these other sources while including little of additional interest.*

Winger's snores turned into what sounded like a desperate fight for air. Her eyes popped open. She climbed the wall. "I know what I done wit' 'im. I t'ink. Damn fool." She stumbled toward the front door.

"Winger, you ain't in no shape to go out there," Tharpe told her. "You'll freeze your ass. Tell me where he's at. I'll go scoop him up."

"Head, yer a sum um a bitch, even if yer a one a the good guys."

"So you keep telling me. Why don't you just relax? I'll find Jon."

"The Remora? You know where 'e's at?"

"You were going to tell me."

"You been holding out on me, Head. You never did like him." Winger began to sag. "That place that's like a ship. Grimes' Cove. I 'member he was wit' me there."

Tharpe turned toward the door. The Dead Man filled us in on what Winger knew without knowing she knew. I said, "You don't want to go back out without warming up, do you? Tinnie and I were making tea."

"A snack wouldn't hurt, neither." Tharpe shook his head, looking at Winger. "The things we do for folks just on account of they're friends."

I avoided any comment.


Saucerhead was working on a stale roll when Singe yelled. We burst out of the kitchen. Singe indicated Winger. Winger was making weird noises. She had her guts behind them.

"Come on!" I swore some. "Get that damned door open!"

Tharpe and I each grabbed an arm. Tinnie sort of nipped around the booted end, like a puppy trying to help without knowing how. Singe flung the door wide. Cold air blasted us. It woke Winger as we heaved her out against the rail on the stoop.

Her socks came up.

"Hey!"

Dean was back. With a cart. Which I hoped wasn't stolen. Winger's rude greeting missed him by inches.

Dean wasn't alone. Seemed he always found somebody to help with the cart. Whoa! Hell. That bundle of rags was the lone member of the Contague tribe not already installed in the Dead Man's room.

"You. Get inside before somebody recognizes you." Potential watchers should all still be gone to war, but why take chances?

Draped over the rail, Winger gasped, "Blindar, yer a bitch even if yer a one a the good gals." She cackled. "An' yer sure as hell ain't." She tried to laugh, but her stomach revolted.

I said, "Inside. Wait in the hall with Tinnie. I'll help Dean." Singe came out, too, while Tinnie took charge of Belinda. With little of her customary empathy. "Did you clean out the whole damned market?"

Saucerhead concentrated on Winger. Winger was trying to aspirate her own puke.

"You told me to get ready for a siege," Dean said.

"I did, didn't I? Where did Belinda come from?"

"I ran into her in the market. She was pretending to be a refugee. I told her to come get warm."

I grunted under the weight of a sack of apples.

"I thought that would be better than maybe having her go back into the Tenderloin."

"Yeah." Damn! Those apples were heavy. "But why is she here? She should be back home waiting out the storm. She has to know there's a war on."

"I think she's afraid there're traitors there."

"What does she know about the situation here?"

"She knows it's warm. And safe."

I started to growl. Exhaustion was closing in again. I was getting cranky.

"I told her nothing. Her problems come from her disaffection with her father. It might be useful if she confronts him."

"Good thinking." Maybe. I didn't like his deciding what was best for somebody else. He tried too much of that with me.

Singe went by. "Once again the ratgirl does the work while the human folk stand around jawing."

Belinda wasn't in the hallway when I went inside. "Uh-oh."

*It is under control. Join us once you deliver your cargo.*

Leave the rest for Dean? Fine with me.

# 71

Belinda took three steps into the Dead Man's room. She froze, gaped at her father.

Chodo sensed the new presence but could not see who it was.

*Take the deacon out when you go. Put him into the cart. Get rid of him.*

Dean gave me a hand. For reasons probably having to do with externally applied inhibitions, I didn't wonder what Colonel Block would think about us turning his prisoner loose. Nor did I wonder why Old Bones wanted him running free. With my experience I should've been more suspicious.

After a long adventure through nasty streets, Dean and I abandoned cart and deacon not far from the Al-Khar. We trudged home exchanging lies about who was more tired. I got there to find the seating arrangements in the Dead Man's room revised. There seemed to be plenty enough kittens to provide several for every Contague. The big boy from Ymber was snoring. Harvester Temisk looked like he was dead. But he kept on breathing. Poor Harvester. His only role now was to take up space.

I asked, "What happened to Saucerhead and Winger?"

"Winger is in your office," Singe told me. "Saucerhead went looking for her friend and to find someone the Dead Man wants to consult."

"Who? Why?"

"I was not invited into the planning."

The way things usually work around here. "Winger is in my office? Gods! I hope she's empty."

"She is now."

Dean muttered something about the ever-expanding population of the house and disappeared. I thought he was off to whip up something to eat. Instead, he dragged his sorry ass off to bed.

I settled in the Dead Man's room, leaning against the wall. There were no seats available. Nor would be soon, I suspected. I was ready to collapse from exhaustion. Yet again. But I didn't want to miss anything.

The Dead Man was working some Loghyr mojo on our dysfunctional family guests. Assisted by a gaggle of cats.

Chodo was more alive than ever. I stared. I wasn't frightened. I felt creepiness instead. In times gone by there'd always been terror when I was near the kingpin.

"Am I over that?" Seemed like a good time to find out if my sidekick was paying attention.

*Unlikely. Changes are going on inside Mr. Contague. The impact of the kittens is much greater in the company of their high priestess. Which the girl has become by default, as sole survivor of her temple. A-Lat herself is hidden inside the child. And inside the Luck. Too scattered to have much power. Which is our great good fortune. We would not stand up to her otherwise. Nevertheless, the effect here will not be one hundred percent. And there is little chance of permanence.*

I made grunting sounds. Deities make me nervous. There are a zillion of them, all real, all at cross-purposes, all unpleasant. Ninety-nine out of a hundred have no interest whatsoever in the well-being of mortals. Particularly if the mortal is named Garrett. And there was little evidence that this encounter would turn out positive—despite A-Lat's salutary impact on Chodo's madness at the moment.

"Can I note that more than one heart is in agony here?"

*Careful what you wish for. Some may not enjoy being cured.*

Not till later did I realize he was painting *me* with that brush.

I told anybody who cared, "I'm going to bed. We can wrap this up tomorrow." I had some thinking to do, too. I do that best without distractions.

# 72

Singe wakened me. She'd brought tea. "Don't you ever let up?" I was accepting no peace offerings today.

Somebody kicked me in the back of the legs. "Shaddup!"

"So that's it, huh? Trying to catch us up to something again."

"No. The Dead Man wants you."

I got kicked again. "This don't seem like a hot sell, Miss Tate," I grumbled at the bushwhacker. "If this is what I've got to look forward to." Which got me kicked again. In my own bed. I suffered the slings and arrows, rewarded my long-suffering with a hot cup of tea.

Ten minutes later, biscuit and mug in my left hand, half a foot of sausage in my right, I trudged into the Dead Man's room. Dripping grease. I was groggy but no longer cross-eyed with exhaustion. I was looking forward to the day I had my old self back.

"Looks like I'm the first man on the job." Sleeping folks were strewed everywhere.

*Excepting Singe, Dean, and I. And the Luck.*

Yeah. Several dozen cats were on the bounce.

"Weather any better? Can we move these parasites out?"

*Probably not. Not comfortably. Unless you move fast.*

"Huh?"

*An associate of Mr. Dotes brought a message while you were loafing.* There was an overwhelming implication of paybacks for all the times I'd complained about him snoozing when I had a strong desire for a little genius backup.

"What's on your mind?"

*I wish to propose that you have fulfilled your abiding obligation to Mr. Contague.*

"What? He's just . . . he's still . . ."

*He remains confined to his wheelchair. It is unlikely that he will ever leave it. Only a Loghyr mind surgeon can repair damage done by a stroke. Loghyr mind surgeons were rare as roc eggs even when our tribe was bountiful. But Mr. Contague is possessed of a powerful will. I would not bet heavily against him accomplishing anything—if he can stay out of the hands of those who wish him ill.*

"Meaning family?" Family was snoring a yard from my feet. Belinda and Singe had quaffed a few quarts after I went upstairs.

*Family, yes. But Miss Contague was not the worst of his tormentors. He possesses recollections of being force-fed by persons other than his daughter. Persons most likely associated with Merry Sculdyte. Who was not always forthright with his brother.*

"Merry was working against Rory?"

*At cross-purposes, certainly. Mr. Contague recalls incidents that distinctly suggest an enduring hatred by Merry toward his brother. There are deep shadows in Sculdyte's mind. He is twisted and torn because he loves Rory, as well. You will find the details in the written history. That is not important at the moment. Decisions about what to do with Mr. Contague and Mr. Temisk are.*

"Huh?"

*Have you not been considering what to do next?*

"Sure." Though not very hard. Chodo and his pal couldn't hang out here forever. And I couldn't see Chodo going back home. That would put him back where he started. But my conscience wouldn't turn him loose on the world again, either. Nor would it allow me to tell Old Bones that I was satisfied that I no longer owed Chodo.

*I anticipated as much.*

Uh-oh. He was up to something. And was way ahead of me in whatever his scheme was.

"You say he's more or less sane now?"

*As much as can be. To roughly the baseline that existed at the time of his stroke. More than that is beyond even the Luck of A-Lat. And that will persist only so long as he remains within the influence of the child and the kittens.*

"So what do we do with him?"

*Exactly.*

"Well?"

*Waiting on you, Garrett. I owe him nothing. I would hand him off to Colonel Block. Along with his memoirs.* Then he issued one of his cryptic, one-hand-clapping pronouncements. *There is a*

*workable answer implicit within the existing situation, though it is
as complicated as the situation itself.*

All right. He's a little windy for a perfect master.

Passing everything and everyone off to the law was, no doubt,
a rational final solution. And one I wish I was hard enough to in-
voke. But I'm me. Garrett. The old softy. "What about his family?"

*Also as healed as can be. But wounds leave scars. And scars
never go away.*

"Hey! What about that message from Morley?"

*Mr. Dotes says the Sculdytes and their associates are dead or
in custody. He suggests we wrap up anything we don't want examined closely because we may find ourselves the focus of the Watch
as soon as Colonel Block and Director Relway have rested.*

"You should've told me that first."

*The matters are related. Mr. Contague, Miss Contague, and
most of these others need to be out of here when the law invites itself in. Make no mistake—if they make a hard decision to get us,
they can.*

"I have no interest in a game of macho with the Watch."

*We may not have many more unencumbered hours. I have set
certain processes in motion, but no good will come of them in time.*

Of course. They'd start out just watching. But well-rested men
would rotate in behind the first wave, two or three for one, and so
forth, till they stood shoulder to shoulder. If Block and Relway
felt the need. They were planners. They didn't move without being
prepared. For all the speed they've shown trying to establish the
rule of law.

Crushing the Sculdytes wouldn't mean an end to organized
crime. Nobody is dim enough to think that's possible, or even entirely desirable. But the Outfit's power to corrupt would be re-
duced dramatically. Its power to play favor for a favor would be
pruned way back. Meaning those villains on the Hill wouldn't
have so many dirty hands on call. Let alone the occasional beakful
of found money.

"Singe. Get Tinnie down here. Dump a bucket of slush on her
if you need to."

"I will defer to the grand master on that."

"Huh?"

"Do your own dumping. Tinnie dislikes me enough already."

## 73

Colonel Block came himself. He'd believed Constable Scithe, who'd believed me when I told him Chuckles was snoozing. Or, as seems more likely, he didn't care. He thought he didn't need to hide anymore.

He came in looking tired, ragged, and suspicious. His gaze darted around like he expected trouble. He must've been right out there on the sharp end of the spear.

"You seem awful twitchy."

"It was a close-run thing. Thank heaven I've got committed people. And had bad weather. That kept my friends off my good back. They couldn't help me with negative advice. But they'll catch up yet. I may be looking for work soon."

Dean showed up with refreshments. Then Singe brought Kolda's voluminous scribblings. I told Block, "You'd have time to read all this then."

He paid no attention. Just held the papers in his lap. "Where are they?"

"Where are what?"

"The people you were hiding here."

"Kolda is in the small front room, sleeping off a bad case of writer's cramp. The big bruno from Ymber is in with the Dead Man. His boss we dragged back over to your shop on account of he was too strong and stubborn for Chuckles to manage and keep up with everything else he wanted to get done before he drifted off."

"Same old Garrett. I don't give a rat's ass about those people."

"And Tinnie's upstairs, in bed. Sick."

"A higher power than I has decided the A-Laf cult is too dangerous to tolerate. I want to know where Harvester Temisk, Chodo Contague, and Belinda Contague went."

I put on my dumb look. Like all my sergeants during basic, he didn't buy it. Coldly, he reported chapter and verse of comings and goings at my place for the past several days. Every one. From a very specific point in time.

The Dead Man was more flabbergasted than me. He thought so much of himself. When he'd said nobody was watching he'd done so in absolute confidence.

"Captain Ramey List," I said. "He wasn't what he seemed."

*Captain List was exactly what he seemed. He brought something in without knowing it. Almost certainly aboard one of his spear carriers, who* would *have been more than he seemed. Now that I am aware of its existence I will not be long locating it.*

"Now that it's too late and doesn't matter."

Colonel Block allowed himself a thin smile.

*He is not aware of details. Director Relway was behind the plant. Which appears only to have betrayed comings and goings, not anything that was done or said.*

"Then we're in good shape."

"Where are they, Garrett? We could put paid to the whole underworld right now."

"You can't possibly believe that. It's part of the social fabric. All you've done is make life easier for Belinda. You got rid of the people most likely to have eliminated her. Made for a smoother transition of power."

"Stipulated. But the baddies won't be the old bunch. Well?"

"Well, what?"

"You refusing to tell me what I want to know?"

*Colonel Block's recent activities left him more exhausted intellectually than he is aware. He is not thinking clearly. Consequently, he is dramatically overconfident. It is not necessary to be stubborn. He will not remember anything he hears.*

"Not at all. Not at all." Probably wouldn't hurt to tell him everything, even if he did remember. Old Bones wasn't clueing me in about much these days.

Several kittens chose that moment to set up housekeeping in the Colonel's lap. Block petted them but paid no attention otherwise.

Chuckles and the Luck made a dangerous team.

"Tell you the complete truth, I have no idea where they went or what happened to them. The way it was explained to me, what I don't know I can't blab to some nosy Watchman."

I wouldn't overdo the truth stuff in any case. The Dead Man isn't infallible. Block's confidence might be justified. He might've had a metal plate installed in his head to block out Loghyr thoughts.

I wasn't untruthful. I *didn't* know where the crowd had gone. I couldn't think of anywhere to stash them that the Watch wouldn't look right away.

I wasn't confident that Saucerhead, Winger, John Stretch, and Jon Salvation could manage that crowd, either. However much Penny Dreadful seemed inclined to cooperate now.

Being a natural-born, ever-loving, blue-eyed cynic, I didn't buy that kid being satisfied with a father who wasn't the avenger with flaming sword she'd come to find.

Block kept trying to get steamed up. But another kitten arrived every time the red began to show in his cheeks.

I changed the subject. "You heard anything to explain this strange weather? I don't like it. People can't get out and show off their three-wheels. The fad might go away before I get rich."

"You'll never be rich, Garrett. You don't have what it takes to hang on to wealth and make it grow."

"I'll buy that. I should get rid of these freeloaders. Thanks, Singe." She'd brought beer.

He was distracted. He'd begun to look confused. Like I do when I walk into a room, then stand around trying to remember why.

The Dead Man had Block, subtly enough that the Colonel didn't realize it. But then, we'd lied to him about Old Bones being asleep.

We had a few beers, relaxed, solved most of the problems of TunFaire. On Block's side, that reflected Deal Relway's conviction that to set the world right we need to kill the people who get in the way. Every little bit, he'd realize he was out of character and get upset. A cat or two would pile on long enough to distract him. After Tinnie joined us the cats were unnecessary.

The man would offer some competition if he could.

*You can release him back into the wild, Garrett. The worst is past. He is not likely to be concerned about us for several days now.*

# 74

I shook hands with Block. He frowned, unable to shake the suspicion that he'd missed something critical. He went down to the street hugging his bundle of papers, stopped, shook his head, went on. He had trouble steering a straight line.

I shook hands with a groggy and thoroughly confused Kolda, too. The poisoner winced. He couldn't close his fingers into a fist. It wasn't much, but it was some payback. He headed out, dispirited. He passed a bent old man coming uphill slowly, leaning heavily on an ugly, polished teak cane.

I just had time to notice him, then had to get out of the way as the Green Pants wide load shuffled out of the house. A-Laf's sexton had less grasp on the world than did Kolda. And smelled bad besides.

Watchmen moved in on him, grinning. The big guy went along docilely.

Penny Dreadful observed from her usual perch. How did she shake loose?

The little old man reached my steps. He stopped. He wore a huge brown overcoat, far too large for him. He pushed hard on his cane, forcing his body upright. He looked at me. He didn't seem impressed. "You Garrett?"

"Garrett! You going to hold that door open until we all freeze?" Tinnie was not in a good humor.

"Yes." Meant for the old man but heard by the redhead. And taken to heart.

*Bring him to me.*

"Who?"

*Silverman.*

"I am Silverman," the old man announced. As though that explained creation itself.

"How marvelous for you." What the hell was this? "Come on in."

"I'll need help. These steps look treacherous."

The air was warm. The snow was melting, making the footing dangerous. There'd be flooding in the low parts of town.

On cue, in a roar of tiny wings, pixies exploded from my wall. The swarm streaked out into the weather. Except Melondie Kadare. Mel tried to flit into the house. Tinnie slammed the door before she got there.

I went down to help Silverman, baffled. "I suppose you're expected."

He gave me an odd look. "Stay close. Catch me if I slip." After a three-step climb he paused to catch his wind.

"Wouldn't be a big cabbage eater, would you?"

"Eh?"

"Never mind. Who are you? What are you?"

Melondie perched on my right shoulder.

"Silverman. You don't know why you sent for me?"

I'd overlooked it when I became a dual personality. The one in charge now didn't have a clue. "I don't think so." If you were two people in one slab of meat, would you know it? Werewolves usually do.

"Your man came. He seduced me away from my work. He said you can get my daughter moved up the priority list. . . ."

"But— Stop that, Bug!" Melondie was messing with my ear.

*I sent for him, Garrett. Will you cease dawdling? Bring the man here.* I caught a hint of unease. Something wasn't going quite the way he wanted. I didn't think he was fussed about the pestiferous pixie, though.

Nothing for it but to ride the tiger now.

The door was locked.

"Lookit here, Mel. I got time to deal with you." I faked a swat. She buzzed and pouted. Her husband and family materialized. A typical pixie debate commenced. The subject, Melondie's drinking, got lost in the general uproar.

Tinnie opened up, sheepish and defiant. I grumbled, "I hope we aren't headed there." I jerked a thumb at the wee folk. "It isn't sport to me."

Shaking his head, Silverman eased past Tinnie. He didn't fail to note her fine points. As usual, she did fail to note his appreciation.

We met Dean and Singe in the hall. They carried an array of refreshments. Silverman's good opinion was important to my resident stiff.

Silverman wasn't intimidated by the Loghyr. Maybe, like the Dead Man, he had roots so deep in time nothing bothered him anymore. He settled into my chair. His eyes widened when Old Bones made contact. He didn't react otherwise. He built a complicated cup of tea, sipped, relaxed, asked, "Now, sir, why did you lure me away from my art?"

Old Bones meant to have fun with it. Whatever it was. He didn't include me in the conversation. I soothed my bruised feelings by easing over to Tinnie, where I got some exercise getting my hands slapped.

Chuckles stopped that. *Silverman is a jeweler, Garrett. A custom designer of uniquely powerful pieces. Shall I have him create something special for you two?*

Panic.

Amusement from the realm of the dead.

Sigh of relief from me once I understood that Tinnie hadn't caught any of that.

*But I could include her.*

"I'll be good."

More amusement.

I have to get over this, somehow.

Silverman didn't say much. The Dead Man answered his questions before he articulated them.

Singe got the expense ledger and cashbox. I caught the twinkle of noble metal as she put money into Silverman's wrinkled pale hand. Under instruction, of course. Then, not under instruction, she sidled over to show me the inside of the cashbox.

It contained a handful of gritty green copper and two cracked, blackened silver pieces of indeterminate but exaggerated age. The kings could no longer be recognized.

"I knew it! What have I been telling you all? You people have finally done it!"

*Quiet. You will recover your investment. In time. Ah. At long last.* I had no trouble sensing his relief. Plainly, he'd been worried about something. *Stand by to answer the door.*

"And make sure Melondie doesn't get in. I can't afford to support her bad habit."

*You go, Garrett. Take your stick.*

"She gonna be that much problem?"

*Do not be contrary. It does not become you. The stick is a precaution, unlikely to be needed.*

That wasn't reassuring, even so.

I was going to be a whole lot contrary for a big long time. They really were spending me into the poorhouse.

I did as he suggested. The situation, of course, wasn't as bad as my instructions implied. Dean didn't show up trying to figure out how to work his crossbow.

# 75

I was speechless. A state apparently desirable, if some can be credited.

Tap-tap-tapping was the A-Laf deacon Old Bones had cut loose. Looking determined but bewildered. Like someone naturally slow on the uptake valiantly pressing forward in life. With him was a matched pair of bruisers, mortified by having to appear publicly in disguise. Twins, distraught because they couldn't wear their signature ugly pants.

There'd been guys like that in the Corps. The uniform helped them define who they were. Without it they became rudderless.

*Will you cease dallying? Time is critical. Colonel Block's minions have noted their arrival. Someone may want to investigate.*

"Wouldn't mind finding out what—"

*Move it!*

Whoa! Somebody was getting cranky.

I moved it, not without sulking.

The Ugly Pants crew entered without pleasantries. With a "My feelings are bruised just by being here" kind of attitude.

I grumbled, "I might be a little better motivated if I knew what the hell you were up to."

*I am trying to wrap this neatly, with maximum benefit to all. Before the advent of the new millennium. Bring them here. Today.*

Sometimes you've just got to go along and see what happens.

I herded the daft deacon and his water buffalo into the presence. "Anything else you need? Dancing girls? Tinnie might come stumble around. Or can we get to the point?"

*I wonder if that samsom weed might not be coming back on you again.*

That was a thought. I did my best to ignore it. But there could've been something to it.

The A-Laf deacon went straight to Silverman. One of the big boys placed a box in the old man's lap. Silverman produced a loupe. He opened the box.

I jumped.

The casket contained a nickel dog. A pup. All right! A jackal. This one wasn't charged, though. It was just a hunk of metal.

Silverman studied the critter. Then he stared at the Dead Man. Then he studied the statue again. "It will be difficult. But I enjoy a challenge. Especially work in unusual metals. This won't be enough material, though."

Voice barely audible, the deacon said, "More is available." He was cooperating only because he wasn't strong enough to fight the Dead Man.

"I need ten more pounds," Silverman said. "Preferably in small pieces." Responding to a query from the Dead Man, who hadn't included me. He was amusing himself. Getting back. All that juvenile—

*Garrett!*

I responded with a scowl. But I paid attention.

*Accompany Deacon Osgood and his associates. Make certain they move the necessary materials to Silverman's workshop. Stick with Deacon Osgood until he has executed his commitment in full.*

"Hey, all right." I confess to a certain sarcasm. "You gonna bother telling me how I'll know when he has? There's always a chance—remote as the moon, naturally, but statistically possible— that I won't figure it out for myself."

*Deacon Osgood is going to surrender A-Laf's despair confiscation system. Mr. Silverman will make modifications. Deacon Osgood and his henchmen are not pleased, but have spent enough time in our forward-looking city to appreciate the enthusiasm of the Watch.*

He was smug. Proud of himself. And likely twisting everything to make a certain defunct Loghyr look like an ingenious trouble tamer.

*I have planted strong mindworms in all three servants of A-Laf. Deep fears and compulsions will carry them through the wrap-up.*

*Even so, arm yourself. The deacon has a strong mind. The proximity of active jackals may attenuate the mindworm's efficacy.*

"I see." I didn't comment on the fact that mindworms weren't imaginary anymore. Though I'd suspected hanky-panky with the facts when he'd sold the goods to Teacher White.

*Relax now. I have to fill the vacuum inside your skull with what you need to carry this stage through to its best conclusion.*

# 76

A-Laf's minions hadn't done badly, making connections round
TunFaire, building on foundations provided by Harvester Temisk
and Chodo Contague. Their associations with the Bledsoe and the
Tersize family had been useful. Best of all, from their viewpoint,
was an alliance on the Hill, with the Spellsinger Dire Cabochon,
birth name Dracott Radomira, cadet of the royal family, a compar-
ative unknown whose name never came up in any review of the
ruling class's crimes and misdemeanors. Cabochon was particularly useful because she was defunct, in fact though not yet
legally. Unlike my resident cadaver, the old witch just sat in a corner mummifying. Her pals from out of town hadn't reported that
the air had gone out of her.

The out-of-towners didn't note the unnatural postdemise good
health of the remains, either.

The old witch must have sung spells around herself before she
surrendered to the unavoidable. The right people might be able to
bring her back. If they were of a mind.

Not my problem. I wasn't of a mind.

Tinnie made noises indicating repugnance. I comforted her
not at all. She'd insisted on tagging along. Let her enjoy *all* of it.

I was still wasting mind time looking for an argument pointed
enough to penetrate redheaded stubbornness and make Tinnie understand that there were parts of my life she shouldn't share.

I said, "It don't smell bad for somebody being a long time
dead."

Deacon Osgood's crew wasted no time. They collected metal
dogs, metal scraps, and metalworking tools from a sitting room

converted into a workshop. If I was a cynic, I'd have thought they wanted to hustle me out of there.

They piled everything into old vegetable sacks. Osgood was as happy as a guy working with a migraine. He feared the Watch would find out about this shanty now. But he couldn't not help me.

This would have been the administrative headquarters for A-Laf's TunFaire mission. The base in the Tersize establishment had been living quarters.

I checked the dead woman. It wasn't immediately obvious whether her demise had been natural or assisted. Colonel Block could work that out.

There was a crackly sense about her that said, "Don't touch!" I didn't. That might be all it took to reanimate her.

Old Bones must have known. He hadn't informed the Watch. He didn't want his scheme hip deep in law and order.

"You. Garrett." Deacon Osgood seldom spoke. When he did he sounded worn-out. "Carry this sack. You. Trollop—"

Tinnie popped him between the eyes with a handy pewter doo-dad. Those eyes crossed. He staggered. His troops gawked. This was beyond their imagining. Still, I was glad Chuckles had taken time to stifle their natural tendencies to break people whenever something happened that they didn't understand.

"Ease off," I told Tinnie. She was winding up for the coup de graêce. "We need him."

She shed her weapon, but her look said hostilities would resume the instant the next chunk of sexual bigotry plopped out of Osgood's mouth. Sweetly, "You were about to ask me something, Deacon?"

Grunt. Headshake to clear cobwebs. "Sack. There. Carry." He couldn't get all the way to "please." But that was all right. He'd been disadvantaged in his upbringing. By goats.

Shortly, I noted that everything in need of carrying was in the hands of someone who could do the lugging, but the good old deacon wasn't weighted down with anything heavier than his conscience. I asked Tinnie, "Worth making a scene?"

"Let's get what we want out of him first."

I'd seen that look before, mainly when I'd done something to offend. I'd enjoyed an opportunity for regrets every time.

Silverman examined every tool and every piece of metal before saying, "Satisfactory. I can work with this." He asked Osgood. "Are you one of the artisans?"

Osgood shuddered like a dog trying to pass a peach pit. The compulsion remained solid. "No. Those who survived are imprisoned now."

I asked Silverman, "Will that be a problem?"

"No. It will just take longer to fulfill your principal's needs."

Tinnie smirked, reading my mind. Deftly, I managed to disappoint her. "Not yet. Let's get what we want out of him first." Not that I knew what that was. The Dead Man had stuffed my mush with stuff without ever betraying his plan.

Silverman barked. Men and women, young and old, all obviously related, swarmed. They grabbed the stuff we'd brought. I muttered in language forms I hadn't used much since coming home from the war. I'd have my nose to the grinder for years to pay for this.

Silverman told me, "You. Out. I'll send word when it's ready." He told Tinnie, "You can stay."

Instead of popping him, aè la Osgood, she kissed his cheek. He glowed.

The deal with Osgood was that he'd be cut loose now. We parted outside Silverman's workshop. I hoped he and his crew would hop a keelboat back to Ymber, but told Tinnie, "Call me cynical. I'd bet we haven't seen the last of them."

Disgruntled, I headed toward home. Wondering how long the Watch would let Osgood run loose.

Those tailing us decided that keeping tabs on Ymberian rubes was more important than watching me. Which conformed to the Dead Man's prognostications.

I had instructions against the chance that I found myself running free.

## 77

"You know either one of those guys?" Tinnie and I were peeking around the corner of a decrepit redbrick tenement. The men in question had Harvester Temisk's dump staked. There was no foot traffic. They stood out. They weren't happy.

The weather was turning again. And wasn't going to be long getting nasty. The sky was filthy.

"No." Tinnie was shivering. She wanted to go somewhere warm. But she was made of stern enough stuff not to whine after having bullied me into letting her tag along. "I don't. Should I?"

"I hope not. They're the lowliest lowlifes. The tall one works for Deal Relway." I'd seen him with Relway occasionally. But I let her think I'd deduced it, employing special detective powers. "The other one is a gangland operator." Actually, more likely a stringer or wannabe on the pad now because Relway's fervent work ethic had drained the bad-boy manpower pool down to the muck on the bottom. I knew him by affected mannerisms and dress, paramount to him when it would be smarter to be invisible.

Relway's man recognized him, too.

He, however, hadn't made the lawman, despite his being right there in plain sight.

I explained. "So what you do is—"

"You're trying to get rid of me."

"I'm trying to utilize your talents since you're here. Go tell the sloppy one you're lost. Bat your eyes. Get him to help you."

"Why not the tall, handsome one?"

"Because he's tall and handsome? And, probably, not likely to be distracted by a pretty face. Not to mention, if he leaves to help you, the other dimwit won't tag along. He doesn't know that Handsome is there."

She mulled that. "The tall one would follow?"

"I would. I'd figure that you were a messenger. I'd want to see what was up." Because I'd know that the Sculdytes had gotten hammered, so this fool would be working for someone else whose interests paralleled those of the departed faction.

In this neighborhood that meant good old Teacher White.

"Scoot," I told Tinnie. "Vamp the man. Get him out of here." I dug in my pocket. The key was there. Harvester Temisk had managed, somehow, to lose it while he was at my place. I didn't know what the Dead Man had gotten from him, just that he wanted me to toss Temisk's place. Something the Watch and the Outfit had done already, I suppose.

"If he touches me . . ."

"I'll die of envy."

She stuck out her tongue, headed out. Haughtily.

I couldn't have scripted it better. Her victim didn't have one ounce of brain above his beltline. Tinnie set her hook, pulled him in, and led him away in as much time as it takes to tell it. And Relway's man decided he needed to see what was going on.

# 78

It was gloomy inside Temisk's digs. Not much light crept in through the feeble excuses for windows. There wasn't a lot out there to spare. But I didn't fire up a lamp. Its light would slip out and alert the world that somebody was housebreaking.

The first thing I learned was that nobody had had a notion to toss the place. Though it did look like somebody had taken a polite look around.

I did little but walk around at first, getting a sense of the place. The Dead Man wanted me to find something. Unarmed with a single hint.

The building was three stories tall. Temisk had the ground floor, which wasn't all that big. Who lived upstairs? I couldn't recall having ever seen any other tenants.

I checked the street. It was a ghost town out there. Fat flakes had begun to swirl, anticipating the main event. I slipped out. It had gotten colder fast. A nasty wind snapped and snarled between buildings. I crossed, turned, immediately saw where the stair to the upper floors had been. It had had an outside entrance on the right side as I faced the building. The outside steps were gone. A bricklayer had done well matching colors but hadn't disguised the shape of the old entrance.

Upstairs windows had received the same treatment.

Not unusual in a city where everybody is paranoid about invasions and break-ins.

I caught movement from the corner of my eye. A long, lean, slumped figure shuffled toward me, obscured by the snowfall, hunched miserably.

I drifted back into Temisk's place.

Skelington hove to outside.

So. Teacher was still in the game. Without showing much imagination.

I resumed examining Temisk's place. Nothing jumped out. It wouldn't if it wasn't supposed to. But . . . there was a grand fireplace on the wall backing on the stairwell. A fireplace that didn't look like it saw much use. In a location that made no architectural sense.

I'd just discovered the iron rungs in the unnaturally ample chimney when somebody tried the street door. There were voices there. Querulous.

I quickly kicked the fireplace gewgaws back into place, hoisted myself. I'd just gotten the feet out of sight when the newcomers busted in.

"Where did he go?" Teacher demanded. "Quick. Check in back. Maybe there's another way out." Feet tramped around, fast and heavy.

"There ain't no back way," Skelington said. "I watched this place enough to know."

"Good for you. I'm really trusting your good sense and thinking these days."

There were four of them. I was in no shape to handle those odds. Not even Teacher and his clowns. It had been a long day. And the samsom weed still had some effect.

"Ain't no sign of him, Boss." I didn't know that voice.

"Allee allee in free, Garrett," Teacher called. "Come out, come out, wherever you are. Skelington, you sure he came in here?"

"I was right there in the damned street." Skelington didn't have much patience left for his chief. I couldn't imagine why he hadn't defected already.

"All right. All right. And you let the girl get away, Pike?"

"Wasn't no 'let' to it, Boss. I told you. That Tin Whistle was all over me soon as I made my move. She bugged on both of us. I wouldn't of come got you if she didn't. Hell, I'm lucky I got away from the damned Runner. I could be sharing a cell tonight in the Al-Khar."

Teacher grumbled something about maybe that would've learned him something.

None of those boys were happy. Nothing was going their way, they had no use for each other, and the guy in charge had gone totally whiny. They were sticking together out of habit and a slim hope that the worm would turn.

Teacher muttered, "That bastard is here somewheres. Temisk must of told him about his secret places."

"What secret places is that, Boss?"

"I don't know! Shit! Think, Vendy! He's a fuckin' lawyer. That means he steals stuff an' hides people from the Watch. An' shit like that."

Ah. Brother White had been loading up on the artificial courage.

"He never worked for nobody but Chodo, Boss."

"Don't you never believe that, Vendy. Don't you never. He mighta said that. He mighta had Chodo snowed. But he never really worked for nobody but Harvester Temisk. He's a fuckin' lawyer. He had something going on under the table. Where the fuck is that creep? I need to break some bones. Take a look up that damned chimbly."

That was it. I was caught. If I scrambled up, I'd give me away with the racket. But Vendy would spot me if I stayed where I was.

It was one of life's special moments.

A face appeared below. Vendy just looking so Teacher would shut the hell up. His eyes almost popped. I whacked on his bald spot.

He fell to his knees, mumbling. Conscious but incoherent. Teacher growled, "Ya fell outta the goddamn chimbly? You're one useless piece a pork snot."

I climbed while there was moaning and complaining to cover the noise. Only a few feet farther up I stepped out into the stairwell that had been bricked off at street level. Wan light dribbled down from a far skylight too small to admit the skinniest burglar. At high noon in clear summer weather it wouldn't have admitted much light. It served more as a beacon now.

I did not, however, go charging on up.

I explored the new territory foot by foot, looking for an ambush or booby trap.

Below, "You're shitting me. There ain't nobody in here."

Mumble whine mumble.

"Right. Skelington. Climb on up in there."

Graphically, and with a marked lack of respect, Skelington finally resigned his position with Team White. He had other options.

"All right. Pike, you go."

"Right behind you, Boss. I got your back."

The front door rattled and slammed. Teacher's whole crew

electing to seek their fortunes elsewhere. A clever boy, rendered abidingly suspicious by experience, I didn't count on what I heard being what actually happened.

But it did seem to be.

Only Teacher stayed. He cussed and muttered and slammed things around. And slammed things around. And lightened a flask or two that he was lugging. He began to mumble in tongues.

Bottled courage, mixed liberally with stupid and anger, drove him into the chimbly. Muttering steadily, he climbed. He slipped twice before he got into the closed stairwell. "I knew that sumbitch had shit hid. Goddamn lawyers. They're all alike. Bunch a thieves." He climbed the stair one step at a time, a hand on each wall, forgetting that the danger ahead once looked fierce enough to send somebody else up first.

I heard my name mentioned. His opinion hadn't improved.

He was huffing and puffing and didn't put up much of a struggle when I disarmed him. He just whimpered and gave up. I tied him up with whatever was handy. He started snoring.

I lit lamps and commenced a serious examination of Harvester's hideaway. And was amazed. Harvester Temisk definitely had an inflated notion of his own cleverness.

The first lamp came off a trestle table covered with the alchemist's gear Temisk had used to prepare his firestone surprises. Evidence to convict was there. A lot was on paper. Standouts were a map and notes about Whitefield Hall, that neighborhood, and the disposability of one Buy Claxton. The papers lay under a loaf of bread that had not yet sprouted a beard.

Harvester had visited since the birthday party. With the place being watched.

He had a secret way in.

No surprise there. In TunFaire, some neighborhoods have a problem with buildings collapsing because of all the tunneling underneath.

I'd look into that later.

So Temisk had hidden out here. Smirking. Without being as clever as he thought. It hadn't been that hard for me to get in.

Temisk was big on books. And not orderly. They were everywhere on the second floor. Dozens of books. Scores of books. A fortune in books. Only churches and princes can afford real books. I recalled my idea about ratfolk copyists. And wondered where Temisk had stolen those books. He'd never been flush enough to buy any.

The third floor was more orderly. It was furnished but hadn't been used. I concluded immediately that the mouthpiece had created a sanctuary for his friend. Long ago. And never got the chance to use it. When he did get hold of Chodo he hadn't been able to sneak the old boy in.

Back to the second floor, where I discovered that Harvester was a compulsive diarist. The Dead Man must've known. And hadn't bothered to tell me.

Almost every moment and every thought ever experienced by Harvester Temisk seemed to have been recorded, on a profusion of mostly loose papers.

The lamp was almost empty. I'd dozed off twice, though Temisk's memoirs were interesting. Each time I did, Teacher White stopped snoring. His trying to slip his bonds woke me up.

Then the yelling started downstairs.

I stayed quiet.

Teacher had a notion to fuss, then didn't because he recognized voices.

That was Winger bellowing. And Tinnie, slightly more lady-like. And Saucerhead, looking for me. Presumably in a snowstorm. In the middle of the night. All worried. And I didn't want to reveal my discoveries. Not to Winger.

I'd figured out the Dead Man's scheme. I thought.

If I didn't do something, though, they'd start looking for the body. And find everything else.

That damned Winger. Always in the wrong place at the wrong time.

I grabbed pen and ink. The devils in the sky smiled on me. For once. The nib was sharp. The ink was fresh. I wrote a quick note. Now to sneak it down where somebody could find it. I crept past Teacher and down the stairs. As I eased into the chimney I heard Winger cursing and banging things.

Tharpe said, "Control her, Jon Salvation." Laughing. "Garrett ain't under no wooden chair, dead or alive."

His suggestion that somebody could control her set Winger off all over again. She raved and slammed off to the back of the place.

"She drinks a bit," Tharpe explained. "Jon, we better watch her, just so things that don't belong to her don't accidentally fall into her pockets."

My luck stayed in. Sort of.

I fell out of the chimney as I tried to lean down for a peek. That was the bad news. The good news was, nobody saw but Tinnie. Who kept her mouth shut when I held my fingers to my lips. I passed the note. And got back out of sight before Winger lumbered in to investigate.

Tinnie said, "I knocked over these andiron things. Trying to get this down off the shelf. It's a note from Garrett. In case somebody comes looking for him."

"What's it say?" Winger smelled a rat.

Tinnie read it out loud.

"That say what she says, Jon Salvation?"

The little guy reported, "Word for word."

"You'd a thunk that asshole White woulda learned. Whadda we do now?"

Tinnie said, "How about we go back to Garrett's place?"

"Something's rotten here."

Saucerhead observed, "You don't have hardly no flaws, darling Winger, but one teensy little problem you do got is, you think everybody's head is just as twisted as yours."

"What the hell is that supposed to mean?"

"It means most people don't have an angle when they tell you what they think."

"Oh, bullshit! You ain't that naive, are you?"

That was the last I heard. The street door closed behind them. A puff of cold hit me. Air did go up that chimney.

I waited. Winger was the sort who might pop back in, too.

I went down. They'd left lamps burning. I'd thought Tinnie had better sense.

Ah. Of course she did. Including enough to realize I'd need to see what I was doing.

# 79

Despite problems getting a schnockered Teacher down the chimney, I almost caught Tinnie and the others, heading home. And that despite the weather. Which hadn't turned as awful as I'd feared. Yet. Just cold and slick.

I brought White along. He needed some special Dead Man work to get his mind right.

I took Teacher straight to His Nibs.

*Oh, my! We are in a mood, are we not?*

"Yes, we are. It's time to quit fooling around. Hi, sweetie." I gave Tinnie a hug and a peck and ignored everybody else.

*I stipulate that I was remiss where Mr. Temisk was concerned. However, I was preparing Deacon Osgood and had no attention to spare.*

Half a minute later I knew the treasures at the lawyer's weren't part of his scheme. He hadn't been aware of them.

*I expected more of you at Spellsinger Dire Cabochon's home. However, Osgood cleverly hustled you through and so did his own cause no harm.*

I didn't get to pursue that. Somebody started hammering on the front door. With amazing enthusiasm.

*That is Mr. Scithe. On behalf of Colonel Block, who became suspicious of the results of his earlier visit. Allow him to enter. But only him.*

I went to the door. It was late. Dean was asleep. I didn't have him and his crossbow to back me. But Saucerhead and Winger came to watch. They were enough to keep out the unwanted—except for a high-velocity pixie who surprised us all.

No matter. The kitchen door was closed.

I told Scithe, "You ought to demand a raise, the hours you're working."

"My wife agrees. But I do got a job. Plenty don't. You could mention it to the Colonel, though."

"I will. What's his problem now?"

"You visited the Hill today."

I didn't deny it. What was the point? "So?"

"So after you left, a gang of ratpeople stripped the place."

"After I left. Right. No doubt being watched every minute." I glared at the Dead Man. That inanimate hunk of dead flesh managed to radiate false innocence combined with smugness.

"Enough to know you didn't carry anything away personally."

A fib. Everybody but Osgood carried something out of Dire Cabochon's forty-room hovel. "I don't do that sort of thing."

"You hang out with ratfolk."

My resident ratperson had turned invisible during my trek to the door.

The Dead Man seemed more radiant than ever.

"That was the scheme, was it?"

"Excuse me?" Scithe didn't understand that I was snapping at my sidekick.

"His scheme. To try to blame me. He's always doing that. And he never gets me."

"I'm sure it's only a matter of time." Scithe wasn't quite focused. Tinnie Tate was in the room. And she'd smiled. At him. He mumbled, "There was a body in there."

"Sir?"

"Come on. An old woman. Dead. In a chair."

"I saw her," Tinnie volunteered. "I went there with Garrett."

That left Scithe with mixed emotions.

"He's like a four-year-old. Needs constant supervision."

That turned the situation around. Sort of. When the Tinnie weather let up momentarily, Scithe asked, "Where were you all afternoon and tonight?"

"I don't see where you got any need to know, but the fact is, I was trying to get a line on those guys your boss claims I'm hiding. Chodo and his tame lawyer."

He didn't believe me. Oh, wound me to the heart. But he had hopes Tinnie could tell him more about the dead Spellsinger, so he didn't press.

He didn't quite try to make a date. Probably because he remembered mentioning his wife.

Somehow, without getting many questions answered, Scithe became satisfied that he'd learned what he'd come to find out.

I let him out. Where his grumbling henchmen waited in the cold and the falling snow. Tinnie tagged along, smug as she could possibly get.

She'd begun to notice her power.

There was a crash in the kitchen.

"That damned Mel! How the hell did she get in there?"

With Singe, of course. That's where Singe had gone while I was letting Scithe in.

I opened up again. Snow was coming down in big, slow chunks. I told Melondie's tribe to come drag her home.

One of my less inspired ideas.

The brawl made so much racket Dean woke up and came down to restore order in the kitchen.

The mess was worse than after the thunder incident.

I threw up my hands and fled to the Dead Man's room. Singe tagged along, evidently summoned. She retrieved the cashbox and ledger, made entries, then paid Winger and Saucerhead for helping try to find me.

I didn't say a thing till after they left. Along with the pixie swarm, still squabbling, Melondie Kadare not alone in betraying signs of alcohol poisoning.

Sweetly, I asked, "Do we have a magic cashbox now? Always money inside when we open it, however much we spend on made-up jobs for our friends?" I spoke to Singe but eyeballed my sidekick. "Or did we pawn something?"

Chuckles ignored me. Of course. And Singe shrugged, indifferent to another incomprehensible moral outburst. "We had a windfall."

I started to get all righteous. His Nibs cut me off.

*Would you feel more comfortable if the A-Laf cult's resources went to Director Relway? When their bad behavior depleted our resources? That is your alternate option.*

It had been a cruelly long day. And the residual effect of the samsom weed really had kicked in. "I'm going to bed."

# 80

We had an easy ten days. More or less. Morley came by when the weather permitted, mostly to remind me that I faced a reckoning.

The repair and replacement of his front door had been a unique experience. The Palms had been forced to suspend business for days while the place aired out.

"My man Junker Mulclar is your proper modern vegetarian gentleman, ain't he?"

"Grumble rumble rabble bazzfazzle!"

"You muttered something under your breath, sir?"

"Browmschmuzzit!"

John Stretch was in and out. He seemed willing to make himself at home.

Equally frequently, Penny Dreadful, having conquered her terror of the Dead Man, visited the Luck. Without offering to take them away. She meant to open a temple—real soon now—as soon as she found the right place. I had my eye on Bittegurn Brittigarn's dump.

I hung around the Tate homestead plenty. Too much. Tinnie's male relatives made that obvious by their attitudes, though they never failed to be polite.

Business is business.

Deacon Osgood and the surviving lovers of A-Laf escaped custody. Bribery was suspected. They decided to end their mission to this fractious city.

I wished those boys devilspeed on their journey home, and foul weather all the way.

The unseasonable weather seldom let up. Before long it would be seasonal.

Colonel Block's people, and Relway's Runners, never ceased to be underfoot. Block was sure TunFaire would mend its evil ways if only he could catch good old ever-loving blue-eyed Garrett with his hand in the cookie jar.

My friend Linda Lee at the Royal Library knew the whereabouts and provenance of lots of special books. And she knew what books had gone missing from the King's Collection and private libraries over the past dozen years.

Using Winger and Saucerhead, because they couldn't read the messages they carried, I informed certain collectors that a cache of purloined tomes had surfaced during an unrelated investigation. It was possible some of their treasures were part of the hoard.

Harvester Temisk's memoirs, detailed though they were, recorded only the dates when he'd added to his collection. Neither sources nor the name of his specialist provider was mentioned. Nor did I get many opportunities to revisit Temisk's place. Good guys and bad alike kept right on watching it. Teacher and the Sculdytes were gone, but others still had designs on Chodo, his mouthpiece, and his designated heiress.

Finding people and things is what I do. Usually by being hired to, but finding is at the root of the Garrett reputation. After ten days, nineteen of twenty-four bibliophiles had made generous arrangements for recovering their treasures.

The others would come around.

Collectors are that way.

Teacher White stayed with us four days. He left with his mind washed clean and his heart set on a career as a knife sharpener. Playmate accepted him as a part-time apprentice. Play honestly believes there's good in everybody. Excepting maybe me. He'll make a great Godshouter someday. If I don't get him killed.

Old Bones didn't go back to sleep.

His uncharacteristic taste for the real world made me suspicious. Deeply, abidingly suspicious.

# 81

I'd just completed the successful reunion of several books with one Senishaw Cyondreh, the past-her-prime spouse of a grimly named habitué of the Hill. The woman had an eye so hungry I'd nearly run for it, shrieking. Once I'd gotten my hands on the ransom. Reward. Finder's fee. If I ever dealt with her again, I'd drag a squadron of eunuch bodyguards along.

I'd peeked inside before I turned the books over. They were what are called pillow books. Blistering. I blushed when we made the exchange.

There was something different about the old homestead. I sensed it when I spotted the odd coach among the abandoned goat carts. Having suffered a similar dyspepsia on occasion recently, I thought about heading on over to Tinnie's place. But I was carrying the take from the pillow book swap.

There are villains out there who can *smell* noble metals.

I took a glim at the weird coach before I went inside.

It had been fabricated of some silvery metal, then painted wood grain with paint I didn't recognize. "I have a bad feeling about this."

Distraction arose. Silverman, riding a donkey cart and surrounded by younger men afoot, all cast from the same mold, appeared. The youngsters carried cudgels. A Tin Whistle tagged along behind, curious.

"Ah. Garrett," Silverman said, reining in. "I've completed the commission. Executed to a much finer standard than the original specifications. Tough to do even after I determined how the spells were written."

"Why aren't I surprised?"

Silverman straightened his bent back enough to meet my eye. He wasn't accustomed to sarcasm or back talk. He was an artist. And the old man of his clan.

"That forced us a little over on costs."

"Of course it did. So let's you and me just go inside and see what my partner thinks." Old Bones would sort the thief out.

I ended up carrying a heavy sack because two of the young guys were helping Silverman get to the door.

The Dead Man, of course, knew we were coming. Singe opened up as we arrived. "Who's here?" I whispered. In case it was somebody who didn't need to know about Silverman.

"Morley Dotes and a girlfriend."

A shiver hit me. I had no chance to pay attention. Silverman banged into me from behind. I moved on, to the Dead Man's room. Where a shadow of all night falling lay in ambush.

I squeaked in dismay.

A grinning dark elf occupied *my* chair, sipping *my* tea, while one of his sky-elf ladies occupied another and appeared to be in deep communion with the Dead Man. It wasn't the skinny, almost sexless woman that dismayed me, though.

My ancient nemesis, Mr. Big, best known as the Goddamn Parrot, was snoozing on her left shoulder.

*Please pay Silverman another twelve gold florins.*

Rattled, I managed only, "They don't make florins no more. Haven't done since the New Kingdom came in."

Morley saw my horror over the clown bird. He indulged in a grin of delicious enjoyment.

*Then give him the current equivalent.* Exasperation. *They did not change the weights, just the names. Correct?*

"Not exactly. They're called sovereigns. The closest."

*Pay the man.*

"But—"

*The workman is worthy of his hire. Silverman is an artist. He took his commission well beyond what I asked of him. He is an intuitive genius. Pay him.*

I didn't know if I could. Twelve florins translate to thirteen royal sovereigns.

Singe handled the payout. I couldn't bring myself to face my cashbox. Thirteen sovereigns is more than most people earn in a year. More than some of my acquaintances will come by during their entire ambition-challenged lives.

"Will you stop hyperventilating?" she whispered, smacking me between the eyes with the biggest word she'd ever spoken. "We are quite sound financially. Now."

Her assurances were no help. I glanced at the sleeping parrot. That thing might wake up any second. Which possibility drove me straight out to the kitchen. I tossed off two quick mugs of Weider's Select Dark. Less distressed, I went back to confront my terrors.

My best pal kept right on grinning like a shit-eating dog.

Silverman was just leaving. He told me, "I need a little head start. I'll meet you there."

His boys were lugging the same sacks I'd just helped haul in. He had no trouble getting around under the weight of all that gold.

I wanted to demand, "You're not even gonna keep what we paid for? After he robbed us?" But Old Bones leaped into my head before I could.

*Please accompany Mr. Dotes. It is now within our capacity to place a satisfactory capstone on this affair.*

Morley kept right on smirking. Enjoying watching me anticipating the hammer's fall.

I accompanied Mr. Dotes. Leaving the house last, just to make sure the Goddamn Parrot didn't accidentally get left behind.

*Garrett. You are forgetting the cats. Take the cats.*

I wasn't forgetting anything. It hadn't occurred to me that there was any need to drag a herd of critters along. Why would it?

"Hang on," I told everybody. "I got to get something."

I found the Luck all piled into their traveling bucket, bright-eyed and ready to roll.

Creepy little things. They weren't kittens at all. That was just a disguise.

I took them outside. Their bucket went into Silverman's cart once I caught up. He wasn't wasting any time.

At some point Penny Dreadful attached herself to the parade. She was careful not to get inside my grabbing radius. I wondered if Tinnie or Belinda was to blame, or if she was still just that untrusting of the world.

Morley followed along behind, he and his friend in the strange metal coach drawn by the two-horse team that caused snickers all along the way.

No one out there seemed interested in us, otherwise. In particular, we were invisible to the city employees loafing around Macunado Street.

Half an hour later I knew where we were headed. Because we were there.

The scaffolding was gone. The bad boys from Ymber had finished their work, doing good despite themselves. The Bledsoe's masonry hadn't been in such good shape for ages.

I eyeballed the brickwork. Even work that hadn't been done last time was now complete. Had the Dead Man gone so far as to compel Deacon Osgood to finish his charity work before letting him go home?

Evidently.

Scary.

Morley dismounted. He announced, "I'm up."

"What?" Morley was . . . he knew what was going on when I didn't.

Me and my second banana needed to have us one long talk.

By the time I ambled inside, the little shit had his old friend Ellie Jacques, the volunteer, cooing and starry-eyed—right in front of, and without offending, his sky-elf friend.

Silverman knew what was going on, too. He and his boys followed Penny Dreadful into the deep gloom of the hospital, headed for the stairs. Penny, two-handed, bowlegged, hauled the bucket of cats hanging in front of her.

I hustled to catch up.

Chodo and Harvester Temisk occupied a suite. They shared it with Belinda. There were guards outside, Saucerhead's acquaintances Orion and June. I felt my purse being squeezed again. I whimpered softly.

They didn't know who they were protecting. Had they done, the temptation to sell that knowledge would've bitten them good by now. The door was locked from their side with three locks. I could've gotten through those, no problem, given a little time, but not in front of an audience.

Penny Dreadful had a key. So did Mr. June Nicolist. And, to my dismay, Silverman had the third, which he handed to me after he used it.

The system didn't make sense to me.

I was nonplussed about them being hidden practically in plain sight. How did Old Bones and the rest expect this to stay secret?

June Nicolist's key fit the middle lock. That one didn't secure the suite door—it let a small hatch swing open. Communications was possible that way. So how come the prisoners hadn't bribed their guards?

Number one sidekick had him a lot of explaining to do.

Once everyone with a key exercised his or her talent, I said, "June, this would be a good time for you guys to take a break. Mr. Dotes will handle the guard duties while you're away." Mr. Dotes and his harem had caught up. The Goddamn Parrot showed signs of fixing to commence to begin waking up.

Not good.

Comstock and Nicolist had been in their racket awhile. They didn't get miffed by any implied lack of trust. Nicolist said, "We was just changing shifts, anyways. I'll just head on home. Give Orion the key when you leave." Since it had done its job already, I handed it to Comstock now.

The door opened into a tiny foyer. Beyond that lay a sitting room as comfortably appointed as any in Chodo's own mansion. Without windows.

Chodo and Harvester were playing chess. Belinda was nowhere to be seen. The boys looked like they were staging. Like kids interrupted in the middle of mischief suddenly pretending exemplary behavior.

Penny released the Luck. Kittens streaked toward the men, excepting two who peeled off through a doorway to another room.

Silverman didn't seem impressed. Maybe he didn't recognize anybody. He spread out. Tools appeared. His boys started measuring and pounding. They ignored everybody.

Belinda came out. She was unkempt but looked less stressed than I'd ever seen. Penny darted over. They started whispering. Girl talk? Belinda suddenly being the teenager she'd never been, with her little sister?

Morley stuck his head in just long enough to satisfy his curiosity, then made like a sentry.

Chodo was in his wheelchair. He wasn't the breathing corpse Chodo of Whitefield Hall, though. He had strength enough to turn his chair. "Garrett." His voice had no timbre yet. It was a harsh rasp. But he was talking.

"Sir."

"I must thank you."

"Sir?"

"The favors I did you have paid their dividends. I'm not really much less a prisoner now, but my mind has been set free. Thanks to you."

He didn't look at his daughters. They weren't interested in him. Under the current regime, family stress had to be managed through mutual indifference. Enforced company couldn't tear down those walls.

Harvester avoided my eye whenever I glanced his way. I expected a peck of lawyering weasel words. He didn't bother. Probably didn't want his good buddy to hear what I might say back.

Nobody mentioned the outer world.

Chodo husked, "Can I ask what they're doing?"

"Sure. But I can't tell you. I don't know. The Dead Man set it up." Silverman's guys were installing little tiny nickel dogs in niches they made in the walls.

My response didn't please Chodo. But his irritation faded even before the extra kitten arrived. The nickel critters were sucking up the dark emotion already.

Silverman beckoned Belinda. "You. Come here."

Her eyes narrowed. People didn't bark at Belinda Contague. But she did as she was told.

"Left hand."

She extended her hand. Silverman snapped a charm bracelet around her wrist. The charms were all tiny dogs in various doggy poses. All right! Damn it. Jackals. Every one enameled black. Presumably to prevent cold burns.

"Hold still."

Belinda frowned but did as she was told.

Silverman snapped a black choker around her throat. It boasted a half dozen squares of what looked like obsidian, each with a nickel critter inside.

Done, Silverman turned to Chodo.

Chodo would have indulged in a good old-fashioned shit fit if he could have. But Silverman was stronger than he was.

He didn't get a choker. He got bands on both wrists and a neck chain on which an enameled dog pendant hung under his shirt.

Harvester Temisk got one around his right ankle and one on his left wrist. And a pendant to match his best buddy's.

"And that takes care of that," Silverman said. "I have a few extra pendants, any of you others suffer from mood swings."

I volunteered to pass. As did Penny. I did think it could be useful to make tons of this kind of jewelry, though—if it really sucked the crazy out of people.

"As you wish. I wouldn't do that, miss."

Belinda was trying to unfasten her bracelet.

There was a flash and a harsh pop. She yelped.

Silverman said, "You can't take it off. It won't let you."

I saw why the Dead Man thought so well of Silverman.

The old man told me, "Give them a few days to get used to their jewelry. Then you can release them to their regular lives."

I told him, "Thank you, sir. I'll move your daughter as far up the list as I can." A board meeting was coming up. I had some ideas to present, involving both Silverman and the employment of ratpeople to copy books. They'd let me talk as long as I didn't go trying to waken their consciences. I'd just need to talk business first.

"You're a good businessman," Silverman told me, with a smile I didn't figure out till later. "Thanks for everything."

I said, "I think we're done here, then. Belinda, Mr. Contague, I'll be back in a few days."

Penny stayed behind. With her cats.

Morley was patient while I visited Buy Claxton. Who was riding her stay for all it was worth, now that her health was not endangered. Human nature, I suppose. When I came back, I decided, I'd take her upstairs and see if she couldn't get back on with the family. While the shyster panicked.

Silverman's attitude soon explained itself.

My deceased associate had been bitten by the entrepreneurial serpent. Possibly because he was tired of having to wake up and earn his keep a couple times a year.

He'd robbed the A-Laf cultists of everything there was to know about the nickel dogs—all right! Jackals! Then he'd rung in Silverman, who owned the skills needed to exploit that knowledge.

They partnered up to drain the pain from the Bledsoe. With Silverman somehow bleeding off the accumulations and earthing them where they would do the world no harm.

It wasn't many months before the improvements became noticeable.

Morley played the parrot hand for all it was worth, heading back to the house. I suppose that wasn't unjustified, after the yeoman blow delivered by Mr. Mulclar.

He did say, "The underworld should calm down for a while, just to sort itself out."

"Good news, good news. Maybe I can talk Tinnie into going

off to Imperial New City for a couple weeks. We could tour the historic breweries. What the hell is this?"

The street was blocked. Mummers, jugglers, people in period costume, guys on stilts, whatnot, were crossing in front of us.

"One of the playhouses trying to pump up attendance, probably. Like everything else does, the playhouse fad has gone into overkill."

That's my hometown. When one man strikes gold everyone else tries to cash in by imitating his success. Instead of panning new gold.

This looked like a sizable show. It held us up for ten minutes. I concluded, "I saw so much here. Why should I go to their playhouse?"

"Because there you get a story?"

"I don't need a story. My whole life is a story."

Thinking no more about it, I trudged on toward my showdown with a partner who insisted on toying with his associate. And a date with the new keg of Weider Select that Dean was supposed to get in today.

Maybe I'd go see the redhead later, see if she was interested in a brewery tour.